*Berkley Prime Crime titles by Margaret Coel*

*Catherine McLeod Mysteries*

BLOOD MEMORY
THE PERFECT SUSPECT

*Wind River Mysteries*

THE EAGLE CATCHER
THE GHOST WALKER
THE DREAM STALKER
THE STORY TELLER
THE LOST BIRD
THE SPIRIT WOMAN
THE THUNDER KEEPER
THE SHADOW DANCER
KILLING RAVEN
WIFE OF MOON
EYE OF THE WOLF
THE DROWNING MAN
THE GIRL WITH BRAIDED HAIR
THE SILENT SPIRIT
THE SPIDER'S WEB
BUFFALO BILL'S DEAD NOW
KILLING CUSTER
NIGHT OF THE WHITE BUFFALO
THE MAN WHO FELL FROM THE SKY
WINTER'S CHILD

*Anthologies*

WATCHING EAGLES SOAR

WINTER'S
CHILD

# WINTER'S
# CHILD

## Margaret Coel

BERKLEY PRIME CRIME
New York

BERKLEY PRIME CRIME
Published by Berkley
An imprint of Penguin Random House LLC
375 Hudson Street, New York, New York 10014

Copyright © 2016 by Margaret Coel
Penguin Random House supports copyright. Copyright fuels creativity, encourages diverse voices,
promotes free speech, and creates a vibrant culture. Thank you for buying an authorized
edition of this book and for complying with copyright laws by not reproducing, scanning, or
distributing any part of it in any form without permission. You are supporting writers
and allowing Penguin Random House to continue to publish books for every reader.

BERKLEY is a registered trademark and BERKLEY PRIME CRIME and the B colophon
are trademarks of Penguin Random House LLC.

Library of Congress Cataloging-in-Publication Data
Names: Coel, Margaret, 1937–author.
Title: Winter's child / Margaret Coel.
Description: First edition. | New York : Berkley Prime Crime, 2016. | Series:
A Wind River mystery ; 20
Identifiers: LCCN 2016011310 (print) | LCCN 2016017539 (ebook) | ISBN
9780425280324 (hardcover) | ISBN 9780698191297 (ebook)
Subjects: LCSH: Holden, Vicky (Fictitious character)—Fiction. | O'Malley,
John (Fictitious character)—Fiction. | Women lawyers—Fiction. | Arapaho
Indians—Fiction. | Wind River Indian Reservation (Wyo.)—Fiction. |
BISAC: FICTION / Mystery & Detective / Women Sleuths. | FICTION / Mystery
& Detective / General. | GSAFD: Mystery fiction.
Classification: LCC PS3553.O347 W56 2016 (print) | LCC PS3553.O347 (ebook) |
DDC 813/.54—dc23
LC record available at https://lccn.loc.gov/2016011310

First Edition: September 2016

Printed in the United States of America
3   5   7   9   10   8   6   4   2

Cover art by Tony Greco & Associates Inc
Cover design by Lesley Worrell

*For my friend and mentor Virginia Sutter, who,
for many years, has guided me in the Arapaho Way.*

# ACKNOWLEDGMENTS

My heartfelt gratitude to the late Virginia Cole Trenholm, who first told me the story of Elizabeth "Lizzie" Fletcher Brokenhorn, and to Jeff Broome, Ph.D., who generously shared with me his extensive research on Lizzie and her family, as well as his enthusiasm for Lizzie's story.

Many thanks to those who shared their expertise and took the time to advise me on various aspects of this novel, and to those who read parts or all of the manuscript and made superb suggestions that brought the story and characters into sharper focus: Karen Gilleland, Carl Schneider, Virginia Sutter, Jim Sutter, Sheila Carrigan, Bev Carrigan, Veronica Reed and, of course, my husband, George Coel.

*It wasn't what I expected.*
*What a surprise*
*When it came to me.*
*And then I chose it.*

—Margaret Coel

1

SNOW HAD FALLEN all day, dense cotton fluff that cocooned the brick bungalow in a white world and obscured the small sign: Vicky Holden, Attorney at Law. Now the snow dissolved into a white dusk as Vicky drove through the side streets of Lander, tires thumping over ruts and ridges. The heater kicked into gear, and warm air streamed into the frosty cold that gripped the Ford. She hunched over the steering wheel. She was late.

The monthly meeting of the Fremont County Bar Association would probably end early. Always a speaker, followed by a little socializing, catching up, exchanging gossip, which she suspected was the real purpose of the meetings; but with the blizzard, everyone would be eager to head home.

The call with Jim Peters, Fremont County prosecuting attorney, had lasted longer than she'd anticipated. She had almost given up hope of convincing him to allow her to turn over her client, Vince

White Hawk, to the sheriff at a prearranged time tomorrow. Five o'clock, say. Earlier, Peters had said. Vince could take it into his head to disappear. She hadn't argued, just kept insisting. The last thing she wanted was the police at his mother's house, a SWAT team swarming the place. Vince would panic and pull out whatever weapons he had stashed away. Somebody would be shot, probably Vince, and maybe an innocent bystander. And for what? Attempted robbery at an ATM? Granted, the woman Vince had threatened—he had not had a weapon on him, she had pointed out, and Vince claimed he was only panhandling—had been scared, thrown her purse at him, and bolted for her car. Not so scared that she hadn't managed to get Vince's license number as he tore out of the parking lot. Now he faced a felony charge.

"Come on," Vicky had pleaded. "You have my word Vince will turn himself in tomorrow afternoon." In return, Peters would recommend to the court that Vince be released on bond and sent to rehab. Vince White Hawk needed rehab.

Finally, a long, weary sigh had come over the line and the prosecutor had agreed. But—always a warning—if she failed to deliver, every cop in the county and on the reservation would be on Vince's trail. A hollow feeling had invaded her chest as she hung up. She had to find Vince and convince him.

She had called Betty White Hawk, Vince's mother. Yes, he was there, Betty said. Sleeping it off. The woman sounded beaten down, as if the weight of worrying about her son had pushed her into the ground.

"Tell him I've worked out an arrangement for him to turn himself in. He'll be free on bond and sent to rehab. It's his chance." She tried to disguise any hint of her own worry that Vince would run. "I'll pick him up tomorrow afternoon."

\* \* \*

NOW VICKY PULLED a slow turn onto Main Street, wishing she hadn't promised Clint Hopkins she'd attend the meeting when he called this afternoon. Clint had a one-man practice in Riverton devoted to family law, DUIs, and minor assaults, similar to her own practice, but Clint specialized in adoptions. If you had a difficult adoption case in Fremont County, Clint was the attorney. She had consulted with him herself on a couple of cases. It had surprised her that *he* wanted her to join him as cocounsel on a case. A complicated case, he'd said, involving an Arapaho couple on the rez.

"Complicated? Most adoptions on the rez tend to be pretty straightforward," she had told him. It wasn't unusual for grandparents, aunts, or uncles to step in and raise children abandoned by alcoholic or drug-addled parents. His request had caused her to draw in her breath, press the receiver against her ear, and concentrate hard.

"Nothing's straightforward about this case," Clint had said, a tight, anxious note in his voice. He hadn't wanted to discuss it on the phone, and they had made an appointment for ten o'clock in the morning. But he wanted her to have his notes before then. He would bring them to the meeting tonight. She would be there, wouldn't she? The whole conversation, with its sense of urgency and secrecy, had left her unsettled.

The vehicles in the parking lot that bordered the Sagebrush Motel and Restaurant looked as if a giant crane had dropped them at random angles. She circled twice before she slid to a stop and waited for a sedan with red beams of light sweeping over the snow to back out. She turned into the vacated space and, wrapping her scarf about her head and clutching her coat, made her way past the parked vehicles to the sidewalk. A narrow path had been cleared, leaving a sheaf of ice littered with blue deicing crystals that popped under her boots. Through the fogged plate glass window, she saw people milling about with bottles of beer and glasses of wine. Her breath floated ahead in the cold air.

Vicky let herself through the heavy front door into the aroma of beer, coffee, and grilled meat that drifted across the restaurant. People moved from group to group, mired in the buzz of conversation and the crack of laughter. No one looked familiar, and yet everyone looked familiar—faces she had seen in court, chatted with at other meetings, nodded to on the street. Other lawyers practicing in Lander or Riverton or in one of the other small towns flung about the county. But not friends, merely acquaintances moving around the same track she was on. She ducked into the coatroom on the right, hung her coat and scarf among the piles of coats already occupying the hooks, and went back into the reception. Nodding and smiling, she worked her way to the table propped under the window and was about to pour herself a glass of sparkling water.

"Allow me." A tall man materialized beside her and took the bottle. He wore a navy blue blazer over a white shirt opened at the collar and blue jeans. A silver watchband studded with turquoise flashed beneath his cuff as he twisted off the cap and filled the glass almost to the brim.

"You must be the bartender," she said.

"Nowhere near as important, I'm afraid." He was smiling as he handed her the glass. "Rick Masterson. I would remember if I had seen you in the audience."

"My apologies for coming late." She recognized the name. Rick Masterson, this evening's speaker. A lawyer from Cheyenne, known across Wyoming, Montana, Idaho, Utah, and Colorado for teaching other lawyers how to seat the most sympathetic juries for whatever case they were trying. "Rules for Reading Jurors" was the title of the speech on the flyer the bar association had e-mailed about the program. He was holding out his hand, and she slipped her hand into his. "I'm Vicky—"

"Holden, Arapaho lawyer. You practice in Lander."

"You know every lawyer in the state?"

"Pretty much in the Rocky Mountain region. It's my job." He was still smiling. "Hang on a moment," he said, backing away. Then he turned and plunged into the crowd.

Vicky sipped at the water and headed into the crowd herself, searching the faces for Clint Hopkins. A few people brushed past on their way toward the coats. The reception was starting to break up. Finally, she spotted the sandy-haired man with the quarter-sized circle of freckled scalp on the crown of his head seated at a table, bent in conversation with two other men. She veered diagonally in his direction.

Clint glanced around, then jumped to his feet with surprising agility for a man in his fifties with the stiff, bowlegged look of a rodeo rider. He had a slim build with narrow shoulders and a long, sun-blotched neck that stretched out of the collar of his plaid shirt. A bolo tie hung down the front. He looked more like a rancher than a lawyer. The weather lines at the edges of his eyes crinkled as he grasped her hand between both of his. "I had about given up."

She found herself apologizing: A conference call that ran late. His hands were rough and strong.

"You're here now." Clint released her and gave a little wave. The vertical worry line between his eyes set him apart from the other lawyers standing about, drinking beer, tossing their heads back in laughter. He lifted a briefcase from the floor and guided her to a corner near the doorway to the motel reception area. She could feel the slight tremble in the hand he placed on her back.

"We can talk over here." He threw a dismissive glance at the crowded room. "I appreciate your willingness to cocounsel," he said, slipping an envelope from inside the briefcase. He held the envelope close for a moment, as if he were reconsidering, then handed it to her.

"I can't make any promises until I know what the case is about." Vicky let her glance run around the room. "This place is filled with lawyers who have handled adoptions. It makes me wonder why you called me."

"This isn't about family members adopting a child whose parents can't raise her." He leaned in close and lowered his voice. "This is about an Arapaho couple and a white child."

Vicky sank against the wall, aware of the roughened plaster snagging her spine. White people wanting to adopt an Arapaho child from the Wind River Reservation—that she understood. A tribal matter. Only if tribal officials allowed the adoption would it proceed. Lawyers for the white people always portrayed them as good—saintly, even—God-fearing folks who would give the Arapaho child every advantage. One day the child would come to forget she was Arapaho, that she had ever been part of something bigger and richer than all the advantages. Or she would begin to wonder who she was, where she had come from, where she belonged.

Clint looked down at the envelope Vicky held in her hand. "Myra and Eldon Little Shield in Ethete. I assume you know them."

Vicky shook her head. Close to twelve thousand people lived on the reservation, nine thousand of them Arapaho. The rest Shoshone. She couldn't know all of them, but outsiders labored under the belief that every Arapaho knew every other Arapaho in the world.

Names were another matter. Names had history; names came trailing their own stories. Shadowed and contoured by people from the past: the old chiefs, the warriors, the medicine men. People had something to live up to, to aspire to, in names. Something glorious and admirable and never forgotten, passed down in stories of the Old Time. She had heard so many stories while sitting cross-legged around the fire in Grandfather's tipi when she was growing up—the tipi was where stories were passed down, not in the small frame house where her grandparents lived—that the people from the Old Time seemed real to her, as if they still walked the earth and might, at any moment, drop in for a visit. Their names were recognizable. If she had run into a couple named Little Shield in New York City, she would know they were Arapaho.

"Little Shield signed the Treaty of Fort Laramie." She lost him with that. She could tell by the distant look in his eyes, as if a snow cloud had passed between them. She pushed on: "An important treaty that made it possible for the people to come to the Wind River Reservation. He was much admired for his foresight."

"You're saying you don't know Eldon Little Shield or his wife."

Vicky shook her head. The crowd was dissipating. Every now and then a blast of cold air funneled into the room as the front door opened. The men Clint had been talking with at the table had left. She had the sense that they were alone, off in the corner.

Clint shifted his gaze to the envelope. "Read the notes. I'll fill you in on the rest tomorrow. I've been dealing with this case exclusively for a couple of weeks. Nothing about it is routine, and I worry about the consequences of pursuing the adoption." He looked up, eyes shining with the anxiety she had sensed during their phone conversation.

"Consequences?"

"You'll understand." He scanned the room. "Looks like the meeting's over. Come on. I'll walk you to your car."

Vicky slid the envelope into her bag as they crossed to the coatroom, where a few coats still clung to the hooks. Clint helped her with hers, then pulled on a dark, bulky jacket while she searched for her scarf. She found it draped under another coat, and she headed toward the entrance, Clint's boots clacking behind her. Through the window, the night was filled with snow.

She was aware of the pressure of Clint's hand on the small of her back, the briefcase swinging in his other hand. Great billowing flakes floated against the black sky and blanketed the trucks and cars in the parking lot. "I'm parked across the street," Clint said. "Where's your car?"

"Vicky!" A man shouted behind them just as she was about to gesture toward the Ford. They stopped in unison, she and Clint, and looked back. Coming through the front door and slamming it behind him was a man in a dark cowboy hat and a sheepskin jacket with the collar pulled up around his ears. She blinked against the snow that splashed her cheeks and eyes. The man started toward them, and through the glow of light in the window she saw that it was Rick Masterson. He held out a package.

She turned to Clint. "Go ahead. I'll see you tomorrow."

He divided his glance between her and the man hurrying through the snow and nodded. Wiping a gloved hand across his face, he turned, stepped off the curb between the dark hulks of parked vehicles and started across the street.

Vicky looked back at Rick Masterson. The package in his hand was the size of a book. "When I got back to give you this, you'd been whisked off into a corner by a very intent Clint Hopkins. I didn't like to interrupt, but I did want to give you this." He held out the brown package, an offering.

Vicky peeled back the bag far enough to read the top line of the title: *Rules for Reading Jurors.* "Thank you." She dusted off flakes of snow and folded the bag back into place. "I'm sure I'll be able to use it."

"Anytime you'd like to get together and talk about . . ." He stopped, lifted his face into the snow a moment as if a miraculous event were taking place around them. "I'd like to see you again. Dinner, lunch, whatever time you might have. I'm in the area consulting for a few days. How about it? You're not involved with anyone at the moment, are you?"

In the way he said it, the way he tilted his head and stared at her, daring her to disagree, she knew he had done his homework. Check out the background on the juror would be the first rule in the book.

She gave a little laugh, a brittle sound in the cold, like the spark of a match. "You don't leave anything to chance."

"Not if you want to win the case."

An engine roared behind them, like the sound of a diesel locomotive speeding down track. Vicky swung around, clutching the brown package against her chest. A truck was racing down the street, yellow headlights jumping through the haze of snow. In a blink, as if she had snapped a photo, she took in the entire scene: Clint Hopkins halfway across the street, a dark figure in the falling snow, briefcase in one gloved hand, silhouetted against the white night. The truck bore down, headlights jumping.

"Clint! Look out!" She was running into the street, the sound of her own voice enveloping her, cutting through the roar of the truck. "Clint! Clint!"

She was barely aware of Rick Masterson sprinting ahead, shouting around her. "Clint! Look out!" And the truck still coming, Clint frozen in place, stopped in time by the all-enveloping sound and the sheer incomprehensibility of it. Then he was flying over the hood, bouncing sideways, dropping onto the street like a limp bag of trash as the black truck sped past.

Vicky threw herself toward the dark, motionless figure, the bulky jacket pulled halfway off his shoulders, the plaid shirt ripped open. She was barely aware of Rick Masterson kneeling across from her. "Oh my God," she heard herself saying. "Oh my God."

Other people appeared from nowhere. Out of the parking lot and the restaurant. Out of the darkened shops up and down the street. Someone shouted: "Did you see that? Ran him down like a dog."

Vicky was fumbling in her bag for her phone when she realized that Rick had his phone out. He shouted: "Ambulance on the way. Don't move him."

Something had changed, and she realized Rick had taken off his sheepskin coat and laid it over Clint. She set the tips of her fingers against Clint's neck. "I can't find a pulse." She sank back onto her heels. "Oh God. There is no pulse."

# 2

THE POLICE CARS and ambulance screamed in the distance, a wall of sound and a haze of blue and red lights coming through the snow. Clint was staring up at the sky, eyes wide in surprise, and Vicky reached over and closed his eyelids, the way Grandmother had closed the lids of her grandfather lying inert on the narrow bed, a view of the tipi out in the yard framed in the window. Closed his lids, a sign that he had seen enough. There was nothing more to see.

She felt the pressure of Rick's hand on her arm, helping her to her feet, steadying her, and walking her across the street. "Was he a friend of yours?" he asked. When she didn't reply, he filled in the answer. "I'm sorry."

They stood at the curb and watched the vehicles pull up: three or four more police cars, a coroner's van, a couple SUVs. A growing crowd of officers in bulky blue jackets and plastic bags over their caps, others in parkas with knit caps pulled around their faces. Several officers had fanned out among the spectators, asking questions, jotting down notes on small pads they tried to shelter from the snow.

An officer stopped in front of them. "I saw it happen," Vicky told him before he'd asked. "The truck was waiting down the street. As soon as Clint started to cross, it pulled out and sped toward him."

"Did you get the license?"

"The license?" She heard the brittle sound of disbelief in her voice "It happened so fast. Clint was thrown over the cab. I ran toward him."

"You know the victim?"

"Clint Hopkins. A lawyer from Riverton."

"And you are?"

"Vicky Holden. I practice law here in Lander. We were at a meeting of the county bar association."

"You're saying the driver of the truck deliberately struck the victim?"

"It was deliberate."

The officer filled the small page in his notebook, turned to the next page and smoothed away the flakes of snow. He fixed his eyes on Rick. "You?"

Rick gave his name and said he had just come out of the restaurant and stopped to talk to Ms. Holden when the accident occurred.

"So you believe it was an accident?"

Vicky felt as if the world had ground to a stop. But it wasn't the world that had stopped, she realized; it was she who had speeded up, shot forward on adrenaline. Is that what the other witnesses were telling the police? An accident? Had no one else seen what she'd seen? Not even the man who had been standing next to her?

She rounded on him. "Clint was murdered."

"The driver didn't see him in the snow."

"The truck came after him," she insisted. "It must have been waiting for him."

"Let the police figure it out, Vicky."

The officer spent another moment writing in the notebook, then started toward the bystanders a couple yards away.

Vicky felt Rick's arms around her, pulling her against the sheepskin coat that had covered Clint as he died, but the cold had already infiltrated her, turned her to ice. She realized she was crying, the tears like needles pricking her cheeks. Was she the only one who had witnessed a murder?

SHE WASN'T SURE how she had managed to drive home through the whiteout that had descended over Lander, tires bouncing through the snow, the radio blaring: Accident alert! Don't go out if you don't have to. And always moving ahead in the snow, the image of the dark figure in the middle of the street, the truck bearing down.

Inside the apartment, she dropped her bag on the counter that divided the small kitchen from the dining room and headed down the hall to the bedroom. She couldn't stop shivering. She stripped off her clothes and stood in the shower a long time before the shivering finally gave way to an occasional muscle spasm. She closed her eyes and lifted her face into the stream of hot water and tried to think back to the meeting. Clint Hopkins, alive, worried and anxious, caught up in an adoption case. Not a usual case, yet still a normal part of a lawyer's life. Go ahead, she had told him. I will see you tomorrow.

She toweled off, wrapped herself in a heavy robe, and went into the kitchen, steeled against the coldness that threatened to overwhelm her again. The dark figure had imprinted itself in her mind. She wondered if she could ever leave the image behind. Her black bag looked like a cat that had stretched itself over the counter. She could hear Clint's voice: *Read the notes. I'll fill you in on the rest tomorrow.*

She made herself a cup of tea, retrieved the sealed envelope from her bag, and settled into the corner of the window seat in the living room. The front of the envelope was blank. She managed to work it open and unfold two sheets of paper. Photocopies of what looked like pencil and pen jottings made at different times, as if Clint had jotted down thoughts as he'd delved into the case. She lay the pages side by side. A collection of notes was not what she had expected. She wondered why, if Clint wanted her to cocounsel, he hadn't given her a printed summary of the details. Nothing here other than random jottings, ideas that might have come to him at odd moments.

Scrawled across the top of the first page were the words: *Notes Little Shield Adoption.* The handwriting looked consistent, words neatly formed, lines running straight. But on the second page, the handwriting began to deteriorate. Scribbled words, difficult to make out. Lines bolted up and down, running into one another. She searched for the beginning of a sentence, but there were no capital letters, no punctuation marks. Another chill ran through her, and she took a long sip of tea. The random thoughts of a man in a hurry. An anxious man. A frightened man.

She read through the notes, teasing out the facts from the rambling asides and comments:

*I don't know. Doesn't seem possible. Maybe. Look into this. Eldon and Myra Little Shield, Arapahos, Ethete. No appointment. Urgent matter. Agreed to see them. Desire to legally adopt*

*five-year-old daughter, Mary Ann. White. Raised by LS's from
infancy. Foundling. Left on front doorstep. Midwinter. Snow and
cold. Woman ran away and got into truck. Truck sped off.*

*Did not call police. Felt sorry for woman, probably mother.
Believed she would return for baby. Healthy, strong. Had been
cared for. Own child dead at birth a few weeks earlier. Waited
for mother. Never returned. Baby theirs.*

*Mary Ann five years old, starting school. Need legal adop-
tion. Based on desertion? Check with relatives, friends. Newspaper articles. Internet. Police? No police. LS's adamant. Must not
lose child.*

Vicky refolded the notes, slipped them back into the envelope,
and drew her knees to her chin, folding herself together. She stared
out the window at the snow falling over everything like a white
shroud. There was nothing in the notes to indicate the Little Shields
had reported the abandoned baby to the police, which could leave
them in a vulnerable situation. Certainly the police should have
been notified.

ANNIE BOSEY, HER secretary, was already in the office when Vicky arrived. Computer humming and coffee brewing, fluorescent lights
flickering overhead. The office had a warm, welcoming feeling that
reminded her of grandmother's kitchen after she and her cousins
had been building snowmen.

"Are you okay?" Annie, her usual solicitous self, came around
the desk in the reception area. "I heard about Clint Hopkins. What
a lousy night to be out."

"It was a hit-and-run." Vicky took off her coat and draped it over the wooden coat tree. She wrapped her scarf on top. "If it had been an accident, the driver would have stopped. Right?" She'd reached that conclusion somewhere in the night. An innocent driver would have stopped.

Roger Hurst, the other attorney in the two-person firm, emerged from the back office, the same look of solicitation stamped on his face. "Clint was a good man," he said. "He handled the Mountain Man case, remember? Rip and Edith Mountain Man adopted their grandson."

She gave a quick nod. People from the rez often found their way to Clint's office.

"Good lawyer. Thorough," Roger said.

"Too much, you ask me." Annie sank into her chair and swiveled back and forth, tapping a pen against her lips. "From what I heard, he delved into Rip's and Edith's backgrounds until he started finding things. So what if Rip did time in Rawlins when he was twenty-two for getting drunk and assaulting some guy? Who doesn't do stupid things when they're young? He'd lived a responsible life for thirty years. It was like Clint took on both roles, working for the couple and against them. Like his real client was the boy. What was best for the boy? Rip and Edith were afraid the judge would rule against the adoption, then what would have become of the boy?"

Always the dilemma, Vicky was thinking. The choice between the best and the available. They were not always the same thing. Clint had been dogged; Annie was right about that. He threw himself into adoption cases. He never gave up until he believed he knew what was best for the child. She squeezed her eyes shut at the image that had arisen unbidden, unwanted: the dark figure in the yellow headlights.

"What else do you know about Clint?" She looked at Annie.

"Was he married?" For some reason, she believed he was married, but she had never met his wife.

Annie had started tapping the keyboard, looking straight at the screen. The printer on the table whirred into motion, and a sheet of paper popped off the top. "I figured you'd want to pay your condolences. Wife is Lacy. One child, a daughter at the University of Wyoming." She handed Vicky the sheet. "Address and telephone number are at the top."

"Thanks." Annie was good at anticipating her needs, Vicky thought, especially at times like this, when she wasn't sure she could anticipate them herself.

She had started for the beveled doors that closed off her office when Annie said, "There's something else."

Vicky swung back. Something else? She didn't want anything else, not today, not after last night.

"Betty White Hawk called. She said Vince went out last night and hasn't come home."

What had she expected? Betty had told her son he had to turn himself in today, and he had bolted. Vicky felt herself sagging against the glass doors. "Get her on the phone, please."

"You sure you feel like working today?" Roger took a step forward, as if he might catch her should she slump to the floor. "I can handle whatever you have going on."

"I'm fine," she called over her shoulder as she made her way to the desk. "Everything's just fine."

# 3

JAMES TWO HORSES was six feet tall with short black hair slicked back behind his ears, skin the color of cinnamon, thick wrists and knuckles surprisingly knobby for a man in his twenties. He had sown his wild oats, he once told Father John. Sown more than he could remember, since most of the time he had been drunk. Sober now and had been for five years, and for the last two of those years, he had felt the calling. Waking him from a deep sleep in the middle of the night, a quiet voice in the back of his mind: *Come follow Me.*

On two or three mornings each week for the last six months, James had shown up at St. Francis to serve Mass. Weighing the possibility of a vocation to the priesthood, he had explained. Seeking to experience what it might be like.

Father John O'Malley hung his cassock in the closet of the sacristy next to the altar while James arranged the Mass books, the stole, and the chalice in the cabinets. Father John was grateful for the help. For some time now, either he or Bishop Harry had offered the early morning Mass without a server to help set up the altar, bookmark the prayer books for the proper readings, and tidy up afterward. They alternated the weekday Masses, he and the bishop. Today had been his turn.

It was the fourth Tuesday in March, the Moon of Buffalo Dropping Their Calves, according to the Arapaho way of keeping time. A handful of parishioners had scattered themselves about the pews, the Old Faithfuls, he called them. No matter the weather, the blowing snow and icy roads, they propelled their old trucks to St. Francis Mission for early Mass. They were gone now. The silence in the church made its own sound.

He had offered his prayers this morning for the soul of Clint Hopkins, a white man hit by a truck last night in Lander, and for the family the man had left behind. James told him about the accident while Father John was robing for Mass, pulling on the long white alb, the stole, the chasuble. "I hear he was a lawyer," James had gone on. "Adoption cases for the most part. He helped a number of Arapahos and Shoshones adopt kids. Witnesses saw the accident. Hard to see anything in the blizzard last night, you ask me. It's a wonder folks don't have the sense to stay home."

All of which, Father John gathered, James had learned from his sister, the night dispatcher at the Lander Police Department. Somehow, between last evening and seven o'clock this morning, the news had made its way across the moccasin telegraph.

Father John, pretty sure the telegraph hadn't missed any details, had asked if Clint Hopkins left a family. In his near decade at St. Francis Mission, he had come to regard the moccasin telegraph as nothing less than a miracle of technology.

"Wife and daughter," James had told him. "They must be in

shock. The man went off to a meeting he'd probably gone to dozens of times. Everything the same. Sure, the weather was lousy, but he'd lived in the area all his life, so he probably thought he could handle whatever the storm handed out. He never came back."

"We'll pray for his family." So many deaths, and yet each one a shock, a disruption of nature, a realignment of the world.

With everything in its place in the sacristy, Father John followed James back through the small church built by the Arapahos more than a century ago. Faint odors of cold-stiffened leather and tobacco and perspiration hung in the air. He stopped to scoop up a wool scarf from the back pew before exiting through the front door that James held open.

The mission was iridescent in the sunlight that had broken through the clouds and blazed like fire across the snow-covered grounds. Father John squinted into the brightness as he came down the front steps. The redbrick residence across Circle Drive, the old stucco school building that housed the Arapaho Museum, the yellow stucco administration building; all shining in the snow. He had been at St. Francis Mission on the Wind River Reservation nearly a decade, six years as pastor. Longer than Jesuit priests usually stayed in one parish. This was home.

James waited at the driver's door of his blue truck, the only vehicle still parked in Circle Drive. Red lights flickered in the tunnel of cottonwoods as the last parishioner drove toward Seventeen-Mile Road. Father John started to thank the man for helping out this morning, but James put up a black-gloved hand, palm out. "Got time for a sit-down soon?"

He always had time, Father John told him. He could see his breath in the brisk cold. He took his gloves out of his parka, pulled them on, and started down the snowy path across the center field to the residence. He turned back. "Give me a call first. Make sure I'm here." Things had a way of turning up at the mission. Emergencies, unexpected delays. The day was never his own. And this morning, his niece, Shannon O'Malley, the third of his brother Mike's six kids, was arriving. He had to pick her up at the Riverton airport.

Behind him he could hear the engine of James's pickup coughing into life and sputtering around the curve in Circle Drive out to the cottonwood tunnel. Walks-On, his golden retriever, came romping through the snow toward him, tossing snow with his nose and leaping on his three legs as if the snow were a disc he could snatch out of the air. Walks-On fell in beside him, and he patted the dog's head as they walked up the steps to the residence. He had shoveled the steps in the dark this morning before going over to the church, but a sheen of snow clung to the concrete.

He was thinking James would make an excellent pastor at St. Francis. It had always been a Jesuit mission, but there were fewer and fewer Jesuits, and the day could come when diocesan priests might have to take over. James would fit right in, one of the people. But years of seminary lay ahead. He was jumping ahead, he told himself. James was still pondering whether he even had a vocation to the priesthood.

Father John let himself into the front hall, draped his parka over a hook, and tossed his cowboy hat on the bench below. He tried to shake off the thought of another pastor at St. Francis Mission. But every now and then rumors reached him that the Provincial officials were reevaluating their commitments. There were times when he could feel the day when everything would change, closing in on him.

The dog skittered down the hallway, and Father John followed

him into the kitchen. The odor of fresh coffee mingled with an unusual burned smell.

"Help yourself to the oatmeal." Bishop Harry Coughlin—in his
late seventies, round-faced and bald except for a stubborn fringe of
gray hair that wrapped around his pink scalp—sat at the table, the
*Gazette* opened beside his coffee mug. "Elena called. Her grandson's
pickup was dead this morning. She'll be in as soon as they find
someone to give them a jump. I made the coffee and oatmeal. I believe you will find them tasty."

Father John poured dry food into Walks-On's dish and set it on
the floor. He took a bowl from the rack in the sink and ladled in
some oatmeal, trying to avoid the brown, crispy chunks that clung
to the bottom of the pan. The coffee he poured into his mug had the
washed-out look of dirty rainwater. He smiled at the image of
Bishop Coughlin, who had spent thirty years tending to the spiritual
well-being of Catholics in Patna, India, puttering around the kitchen,
preparing oatmeal and making coffee. Father John had never known
Elena not to make it to work. If her grandson's car didn't start, there
was every chance she would stride out cross-country through the
snow. He set the bowl and mug on the table, took his cell out of his
shirt pocket, and called the housekeeper's home. He told the young
woman who answered—probably the wife of Elena's grandson—
that he'd be glad to drive over and pick Elena up. "Oh, they got a
jump and she's on the way, Father," the woman told him. "She was
anxious about you and the bishop not having breakfast."

He slid the cell back into his pocket and sat down across the
corner from the bishop. "Elena's on the way," he said. In her seventies, maybe her eighties, he was thinking, but she would never admit
it. She didn't even admit to her seventies.

"Anything wrong? Bad news was on your face when you came in."

Father John took a bite of the oatmeal. It had the taste of burnt toast. Picking up the coffee mug, he turned toward the bishop. "A lawyer from Riverton was hit by a truck last night in Lander. He didn't make it."

"The blizzard." The old man shook his head and looked away. "We all hang by a very thin thread, I'm afraid."

"Clint Hopkins. He handled some adoptions for people on the rez."

"Another friend lost. Did you know him?"

Father John shook his head. He wondered if it was Hopkins who helped his parishioners Jan and Mike Rivers adopt their niece last year. He made a mental note to give them a call, offer his condolences for the loss of a man they must have trusted.

"On a happier note, I'm looking forward to meeting your niece."

"So am I," Father John said. The last time he had seen Shannon, she was twelve years old. The woman stepping off the plane this morning would be someone else, a twenty-four-year-old doctoral student at the University of Chicago doing a dissertation on two sisters captured by Indians in the nineteenth century. There had been many white captives. Some had been rescued after a brief time, but others spent years with the tribes. Still others, like Cynthia Ann Parker, captured by the Comanches when she was a small child, had grown up with the tribes—become Indian—before being forcibly returned to their families. Those were the saddest cases of all, he thought after he'd read some of the stories. White women who no longer belonged in the white world, forced to live in a culture they didn't remember or understand.

Shannon had called a couple weeks ago. She was researching the lives of Amanda and Elizabeth Fletcher, captured in 1865 in a Cheyenne raid on their family's wagon train. Amanda had been rescued within months, but her two-year-old sister had had been traded to the Arapahos. She had lived out her life as an Arapaho. Lizzie Brokenhorn, as she was known on the reservation. "Think I could talk to one of Lizzie's descendants?" Shannon had wanted to know, and he had told her he would do his best.

He glanced at his watch, got to his feet, and carried his bowl with the half-eaten oatmeal and the mug still nearly full over to the sink. Bills to pay and calls to return, and only a couple hours before he had to leave for the airport. He thanked the bishop for a lovely breakfast.

"My pleasure." The old man was beaming. "I decided this morning to take up cooking. I believe I have a natural talent, and it's so relaxing and rewarding to make a meal for someone else. Yes, I do believe I'll take up cooking."

RIVERTON REGIONAL AIRPORT occupied a high plateau northwest of town. The wide, empty spaces of the reservation stretched into the distances with the Wind River Range rising into the Western sky. The music of *Il Trovatore* blared from the CD player on the center of the seat. A white world this morning, seamless and bright in the mid-morning sun. Father John bumped through the snowy ruts that crisscrossed the parking lot in front of the terminal, parked close to the main entrance, and turned off the CD. In the distance he could hear the low roar of a jet, but the sky remained as clear as newly washed glass.

A few people stood around the polished vinyl floor next to the gate that accommodated the passengers. Father John walked over to the wall of windows that gave out over the runway and the great openness beyond. The plane was coming in low from the south, a metallic twinkling in the blue sky. He watched it glide, until finally it was on the ground, coming down the runway, braking gradually. It stopped outside the windows.

He had been wondering if he would know her; she'd been so young the last time he saw her. A child still, with light, reddish hair and blue eyes, teasing and mischievous. She had liked to play games, and he remembered long stretches at the dining room table playing Monopoly and gin rummy and poker. Shannon O'Malley played deliberately, her freckled forehead wrinkled in concentration, but she jumped to her feet, shouted, and high-fived everyone in the house when she won.

A line of passengers started down the metal steps, but there was Shannon, standing on the landing, looking around. He would have known her anywhere, even on the crowded streets of Manhattan. Tall and slim with masses of curly hair that caught the sunlight in waves. And so like her mother that, for a fleeting moment, Father John felt something grip his heart. Then down the steps she came, hopping, half running, a backpack bouncing on her shoulders. The same exuberance she had shown after bankrupting him in Monopoly.

Dodging around the other passengers, glancing about the airport, she came through the door. "Uncle John!" she called as he made his way toward her. "It's so great to see you." She was in his arms, hugging his neck, kissing his cheek. "You haven't changed at all."

He held her for a moment, then set his hands on her shoulders and took a step back, wanting to take her in. This daughter of Eileen and Mike—part of him, his own family. She was laughing and smiling, pinpricks of light in her blue eyes. She had her mother's creamy complexion and delicate nose. But the way she stood, the deep blue of her eyes, and the frankness in her expression were her father's. "You're beautiful," he said.

She tossed her head, laughed, and waved away the compliment. "I'll bet I'm the only girl you can tell that to."

"Pretty much."

He reached for her backpack, but she shrugged away. "I'm used to it," she said. "It's part of me, like a large hump I carry around."

"Any other luggage?"

She shook her head. "I travel light. You can move faster that way."

# 4

"I'VE FOUND SOMEONE for you to interview," Father John said. They drove off the plateau onto the straightaway that led into town, through the traffic light, a few cars and pickups in the two lanes. "Di tale amor" was playing softly. Snow alongside the road had melted into streams that splashed the windshield. The wipers in the old Toyota pickup operated on a hit-and-miss basis, and he had to lean sideways to see through a cleared space.

"*Il Trovatore*," Shannon said.

"You like opera?" He glanced over at the girl in the passenger seat, one elbow braced on the window frame, the backpack on her lap. She seemed at ease, almost at home, as if she knew the road well and had driven it many times.

"Doesn't everyone?" She gave him a wide smile. "I never doubted you'd find someone for me to interview. You've been on the reservation so long, you must know everybody. One of Lizzie's grandchildren, I hope."

"Wilbur Horn, a great-grandson."

Shannon let out a yelp. "Fantastic. How old is he?" Gloved fingers strummed the straps of the backpack. He could almost smell the excitement emanating from her.

"Probably in his sixties. Hale and hearty."

"The closest I can get, I'm sure. Lizzie had five children who would be centenarians now. Wilbur sounds perfect." When he looked over again, she was smiling. "It's a good place to start. People send you on, you know. Wilbur could remember other family members who might have different stories"

It was true, Father John was thinking. It had taken only a couple phone calls before he found that Wilbur Horn, one of his own parishioners, was descended from Lizzie Brokenhorn. He had gone out to Wilbur's ranch and over a cup of coffee explained that his niece was writing her dissertation on his great-grandmother and her sister. Stories were private, Father John knew; they belonged in families, defined families, gave them understanding, courage, and strength. They weren't for students who could never grasp—feel— the importance. They weren't meant to be scattered to the winds as if they were nothing.

"You say she's your brother's child." Father John had nodded. In the Arapaho Way, his brother's child was also his child. Wilbur had nodded with him, a silent agreement struck.

Now Father John smiled at the exuberance in Shannon's voice and the truth of what she said: "I never know where the road will lead, but I know it will lead to something I couldn't have anticipated or even imagined from reading the old records." She shifted toward him and plucked at the straps of the backpack again as if she were playing a melody on a guitar. "The history books, the old records and archives, only tell part of the story."

Father John met her smile for a moment. Her blue eyes crinkled in the bright sunlight. "And sometimes the records are wrong." How many times since he had been with the Arapahos had he come face-to-face with the way that stories passed down by people who had lived through the massacres and the terror in the Old Time contradicted the official reports accepted by historians? If it was written down, it must be true, historians believed.

"They do tell us a lot, of course," she said. "You can't ignore them."

"Of course not." Not if you want to get your doctorate.

"They give you the outline of what happened. A good starting point. Take the women I'm concentrating on. Amanda Mary Fletcher, Lizzie's sister, in a Cheyenne camp for seven months. Elizabeth Fletcher, never rescued. Lived her life as an Arapaho."

Shannon was still leaning toward him. He could feel the intensity of her concentration. "What I'm looking for, Uncle John, is the outside of history, the details and feelings never written down. What happened to these women? How did they live out their lives? I've interviewed five of Amanda's descendants. What was it like for her when she returned home? Did she continue as if nothing had happened? Just a little blip in her life journey? Questions like that. And what about Lizzie? Changed from being white to Indian in a matter of minutes. What did that mean? How did that determine the woman she became?"

"I'm proud of you," Father John said. She was going after the lost parts of history. Going for the whole, or as much as she could find. Not just the accepted truth. She was doing what he should have done twenty-five years ago, back at Boston College, when he'd been studying to become a history professor. Before his own life took a path he hadn't anticipated. After graduation, he had joined the Jesuits, the Society of Jesus, and eventually taught history in a Jesuit prep school, doing research for a doctorate. All those records and archives to plow through, and the loneliness and the terrible thirst that had taken him over. The crash had come hard.

He turned right and drove south toward the reservation. Setback storefronts and snow-gripped parking lots started to give way to warehouses, liquor package stores, and the edges of trailer camps. A passing semi splashed snow and gray slush over the windshield, blinding him for a moment until the wipers surged into action. It had led him here, all of it, to an Indian reservation in the middle of Wyoming.

Shannon was saying something about starting with the records, and he tried to concentrate. She was so much further ahead than he had been at her age. So much wiser. "Take Elizabeth Fletcher," she said. "The records tell us all about how Jasper and Mary Ann Fletcher set out from Illinois in 1865 for the California gold fields with their five children. They had joined a train of seventy-five wagons on the North Platte River trail through Indian country, all of their belongings piled inside two wagons."

She went silent a moment, gazing out the window as if she could see the family and the wagons. After a moment, she went on: "Jasper made a big mistake. Instead of staying with the large train, he pulled ahead. Northwest of what is now Cheyenne, he stopped the wagons so the kids could wade in the river, cool off, and have a little lunch. That was when a band of Indians led by the Cheyenne chief Sand Hill attacked. Wounded Jasper, left him for dead, and killed Mary Ann. The three young sons ran back for the wagon train. The Indians were busy ransacking the family's wagons, so they let the boys go. But they took Amanda Mary, who was seventeen, and her baby sister, Elizabeth, who was two years old.

Tied their feet and arms, threw them on horses, and rode away before the large train could arrive. For the next thirty-five years, Amanda Mary feared her sister had been killed, but she never stopped looking for her. In the early 1900s she learned that Elizabeth was living on the Wind River Reservation. So that's it, the story outline. I'm here to fill in the blanks."

"How far along are you?" Father John turned right into the reservation. Empty white spaces stretched around them, broken here and there by blocklike houses and ponies nodding in corrals. The melting snow had turned Seventeen-Mile Road into a creek. The sun shimmered on the hood of the Toyota pickup.

Out of the corner of his eye, he saw Shannon shrug. "Two weeks in Michigan and Iowa interviewing Amanda's descendants. A variety of stories, little glimpses of truth in each one, I suspect. The problem is, her story changed over the years. She was a prolific writer, not shy about recounting the horrors of her experience with the Cheyennes. At the time she was rescued by a white trader, she said the Cheyennes had treated her well and that Sand Hill's wife had been good to her. As the years went by, she began filing claims against the government for her family's losses. Anyway, with each filing, the amount of losses grew and so did the horrific sufferings she claimed to have undergone."

"You don't believe the claims."

"You said it: records can be wrong."

"What did her descendants say?"

"They were all over the map. A couple of great-granddaughters recited all the horrible things that had happened to her: beatings, starvation, struggles to keep warm, lack of sleep, being treated like a slave. Pretty terrible, and straight out of the reports Amanda had filed with the government, which made me wonder if the great-granddaughters really had heard any stories at all. Other descendants—further removed, I grant you; great-greats—claimed their parents and grandparents had heard Mary describe her captivity as filled with hard work. But all the Indian women worked, and she had to work alongside them. In times when food was scarce, everybody went hungry. Most of their buffalo-hide tipis had been destroyed at the Sand Creek Massacre the year before, and their canvas tipis barely kept out the cold."

"So you have to make sense out of it." Framed against the blue sky ahead was the large blue and white billboard with the words *St. Francis Mission* splashed across it.

"Our job as historians, right?" She let out a long sigh. "What Amanda wrote makes it harder to zero in on the truth."

"You're saying what she wrote could be unreliable?"

"Historical records." She shrugged again and shook her head.

Father John slowed for the left turn onto the road that ran through a tunnel of cottonwoods. Globules of snow dropped off the branches and splattered the windshield. The rear wheels shimmied on the slush.

"So this is the mission." Shannon sat forward, craning toward the windshield as he drove out of the tunnel and onto Circle Drive. "Let me guess. Your office is over there." She nodded in the direction of the administration building, yellow stucco and two stories high, easily the largest building on the reservation, a ghost from the past. "The church over there, just like your Christmas cards. Seems as if the steeple floats in the sky. The gray stone building must be the old school you turned into the Arapaho Museum."

Father John took a left into the alley that ran between the church and the administration building. Past Eagle Hall, where the social activities took place. Boy Scouts, Girl Scouts, Sunday morning do-nuts and coffee, the women's social committee, the Ladies Altar

Society, the Men's Club, Alcoholics Anonymous, the New Moms group.

Shannon had shifted herself partway around and was staring out the back window. "That redbrick house over there must be where you live. I don't see the baseball diamond."

"Behind the redbrick house," he said. Lost in the snow, he was thinking. A wide-open field of snow.

"And I will be staying in the guesthouse." She was bubbling on, all of it a new adventure. "Your e-mail said you've put up a lot of famous people in the guest house. Name one."

"Everybody who stays there has a claim to fame." He slid to a stop near the front stoop.

"Because they stayed there?"

"Something like that." He got out and started through the wet, melting snow to the passenger side, but Shannon O'Malley was already off her seat. She slammed the door behind her and gripped the backpack to her chest.

"Let me help you." He reached for the backpack again, and this time she let him take it. She spun around. "I feel like I know this place. Every year I confiscated your Christmas card and tacked it up in my room over my desk. It was the first thing I saw every morning. After a while I had five or six, all lined up in a neat row. Each one with a different photo, and all those photos formed a big picture of the mission. I took my collection with me when I left for college, and every Christmas I added the next card. Tacked up in a whole series of dorm rooms and apartments with a lot of roommates and"—she swallowed—"boyfriends wanting to know where those cards came from. Africa? The Serengeti? Some other exotic place? Oh, you'd be surprised by the exotic places they suggested. I guess that's what the Christmas cards meant to me, a grand adventure in an exotic place. You were my hero because you got away. I mean, nobody else I knew when I was a kid ever got away."

Father John pushed the front door open, gestured her inside, and wondered what he had gotten away from. Family? Home? What he had found again, here. He set the backpack down on the worn sofa, which sloped sideways and its pushed-up springs bit into your thighs when you sat down. Better than no sofa at all, he reckoned, and none of the guests ever complained. "This is it," he said. "I've stocked the kitchen with some essentials: coffee, cereal, milk, fruit, sandwich meat and bread, in case you get hungry while you're working."

Shannon brushed past him into the alcove that served as a kitchen. She thumped the top of the old oak table. "Perfect place to set up my laptop. It's sure quiet here." She rolled her head around, as if she expected to detect noise somewhere. "I'm not used to so much quiet."

"You get used to it." It was one of the best things about being here, the infinite quiet. "Bedroom's in back, extra blankets in the closet. Make yourself at home and let me know if you need anything at all."

Father John turned toward the door, then looked back. "Lunch at the residence promptly at noon; dinner promptly at six. I'll drive over and get you."

"No. No. No. I love to walk in the snow."

"See you in a little while."

"Oh, Uncle John," she called as he stepped outside and started to close the door. "Are you always prompt?"

He glanced back. Her eyes were dancing with mischief. How had she figured out that, despite his best intentions and promises to change, he seldom made it to meals on time? Something always intervened. He and Elena had reached what he thought of as a good working arrangement: he promised to be on time, and she pretended to believe him. "I'm afraid I'll have to take the Fifth Amendment," he said, pulling the door shut behind him.

# 5

VICKY MADE HER way through the white faces in the Hopkinses' living room. A comfortable, lived-in room with overstuffed sofa and chairs, small tables piled with magazines, and a bookcase crammed with books. Mullion windows framed broken pictures of the snow-heavy trees in the front yard and the cars passing in the street throwing up fountains of snow and slush. She didn't recognize any of the faces—Clint's colleagues, family, friends. She was an interloper, an intruder on private grief.

"I'm a colleague," she told the woman with the not-unfriendly face and the taut look of someone who spent hours in a gym. She had light hair with dozens of colors in it that brushed the shoulders of her light blue dress.

"Oh, you must be Vicky Holden." She peered at Vicky with wide, blue eyes behind small, wireless glasses that gave her the mock studious look of a seventh grader.

Vicky recognized the high-pitched, childlike voice of Clint's secretary. "Are you Evie?"

At this, the woman—she looked like she was in her mid-twenties—produced a tissue and began dabbing her eyes. The glasses jumped upward, riding along her nose at a precarious angle. She adjusted them and bit into her lower lip. "I've been with Clint since I was seventeen, just out of high school. I needed a job bad, with my dad out of work and Mom sick and my two brothers still in high school. Clint was struggling to get his practice going. 'I don't know if I can pay you,' he told me. 'I don't even know if I'll have any clients.' Well, it was better than nothing, which was what I had. I found out later that Lacy has plenty of money, so money wasn't a problem. Plus Clint was good at what he did." She went back to dabbing the tissue at her eyes, the glasses stuttering about. "Lacy will be glad you came by." She swiped her eyes a last time and adjusted her glasses.

Vicky followed the woman through the gauntlet of white faces. She could feel the laser heat of eyes on her back. Did they all know? How Clint had gone to the meeting in a blizzard to meet her? How he had started across the street alone? She had tossed about all night, half-asleep, half-awake, going over and over those last minutes. If she had crossed with Clint, would the truck have roared out of the snow?

"Lacy, Vicky Holden is here." The secretary leaned over a small woman with sandy hair and red-rimmed eyes who sat, shoulders hunched, on an armchair. "The Arapaho lawyer from Lander," she said, stepping back and beckoning Vicky forward.

A hush dropped over the living room like the quiet fullness of a rodeo stadium when a bronco rider flies into the air, just before he hits the hard-packed earth. There was a faint sound of water running from a faucet somewhere. The coffee smell was so strong,

Vicky could almost taste it. A woman sitting next to Lacy got to her feet and Vicky took the chair. She leaned sideways, but Lacy was staring across the room at something only she could see with a distant look in her expression, as if the people milling about had vanished.

"I came to tell you how sorry I am about Clint," Vicky said.

Lacy did not respond. Still staring off into space, a private movie in her head. A moment passed before a girl who looked about nineteen, with long dark hair and lively eyes, stepped over to the armchair. "I'm Julie," she said, looking at Vicky. "We've had a terrible shock." Her mother's hand lay in her own like a dried leaf as the girl leaned forward. "This is one of Dad's colleagues, Mom."

Something inside Lacy seemed to switch on, and she made a slow, robotic turn toward Vicky. "Thoughtful of you." She spoke in a whisper. "I don't know why Clint went to the meeting last night. Do you? It was a terrible night. No one should have been out."

"I'm afraid he wanted to give me some papers about a case he wanted me to cocounsel. We had arranged to meet this morning . . ." Vicky stopped. This was not a road she had intended to start down. At this very moment, Clint Hopkins should have been seated in her office. They should have been discussing the efforts of a couple named Myra and Eldon Little Shield to adopt their little girl. Instead she was seated in Clint's living room across from his shell-shocked wife.

She hurried on, making a futile effort to cover up what she could see in Lacy's eyes: an acknowledgment of what should have been. "Clint wanted me to read through his notes before we met."

Lacy was shaking her head. "Yes, of course. It was an adoption case. I begged him not to go out, but he said it was important. All the adoptions were important. Every child was Julie looking for a good home. He took every case personally. Carried it around like precious baggage. Brought it home, dropped it in the middle of the living room, carried it to the dinner table, took it to bed. Every case, the most important in the world. Naturally, if he wanted to talk to you about a case, he would go out in a blizzard. He would have gone to hell and back for some kid because that kid was always Julie."

She was sucking in rapid gulps of air, moisture blossoming at the corners of her eyes. "Did you see what happened?"

Vicky nodded. "We had walked out of the restaurant together. Clint started across the street where he had parked his car. I saw the . . ." She hesitated, picking through the minefield of words. "I saw what happened."

"You saw him die?"

"There was nothing anyone could do, it happened so fast. I ran over and knelt beside him." Vicky could feel the tears pressing in her eyes. "I'm so very sorry. I didn't get the license plate number."

"The driver didn't even stop." Julie sat down on the armrest, pulled her mother close, and kissed the top of her head.

Vicky didn't say anything. The driver. A man who had wanted to run down someone. A murderer. "I'm sorry," she said again. "If I can help you in any way . . ." She left the thought hanging between her and the two women huddled together. What a flimsy gesture. What could she ever do to lessen the pain and the horror? She felt light-headed as she got to her feet and started for the door.

The living room was more crowded now. People jammed together in little groups, sipping coffee in Styrofoam cups, glancing over at Lacy and Julie and shaking their heads. "Do you have a minute?" Vicky realized that Evie had fallen in beside her and was guiding her toward a side door.

"We can talk in here," the woman said, depositing her in a small room with the look and feel and smell of a study. A masculine study, where Clint Hopkins had sat at the desk, file folders upright in a metal rack and a laptop computer, open as if Clint had just stepped away.

"Do you really believe it?" Evie closed the door against the hum of conversation and the odor of coffee.

"Believe what?"

"It was an accident."

"I don't know."

The woman turned partway toward the window and looked out, clasping and unclasping her hands. The blue dress clung to the curves of her hips and calves. "It's just that . . ." She faced Vicky again. Her glasses looked smudged and cloudy with moisture. "I've been worried about Clint. He spent the past two weeks working on the Little Shield case. He wanted you to come in with him. I've never seen him so obsessed. Oh, Clint was always obsessed with whatever case he was working on, but this was different. I could see it taking a toll."

"Did he say what was he worried about?"

Evie shook her head. "He was never one to blab about a case, but he talked to various people and did research on the internet. The more information he collected, the more uptight he became. When I heard what happened last night, I got a sickening feeling. What if he'd stumbled onto something he wasn't supposed to know?"

"Have you told the police?"

She dropped her head into both hands for a moment, then looked up. She straightened the little wireless glasses. "All I have is a strange feeling. I guess I'm just looking for a rational explanation, and the truth is, there isn't any. All Clint cared about was getting little Mary Ann legally adopted by the people who loved her. The last thing he would want is for me to start stirring up trouble. If I went to the police with my crazy feeling, they'd open an investigation. I can't do that to the Little Shields." She held out a hand as if she were soliciting alms. "I went into the office this morning to contact a few of his associates. Make sure the file drawers were locked, the computers locked. I canceled his appointments. Tidying up, I guess, because I didn't know what else to do. The phone was ringing off the hook. Eldon called the minute he heard about Clint. I could tell by his voice how upset he was. He trusted Clint. He wanted to know what they should do now, so I told him Clint wanted you to cocounsel the case. I suggested he call you."

Vicky remained quiet a moment. If her instincts were right—if the secretary's instincts were right—she could be stepping into whatever had gotten Clint killed. If he was murdered, he must have been apprehensive about what he'd uncovered. Still, he had gone forward because of a little girl.

"Clint gave me some notes to read over," she said. "There's nothing in them he hadn't mentioned when we spoke."

The secretary drew in her bottom lip again, a habit, Vicky thought. It made her look like a child, except for the pencil lines that formed on her forehead. "I'm afraid he was somewhat paranoid. Kept very sparse notes and put very little on the computer, you know, in case somebody hacked it. He kept everything in his head, and he was very thorough. I hope you can help the Little Shields."

"I can talk to them. I don't know if I can help."

Evie looked startled, as if Vicky had thrown out an idea she hadn't considered. "Clint was sure you would know how to handle the case."

"If I take it on, I'll need his records."

"I told you: he didn't keep records. Everything is in his notes."

"There was nothing helpful in the notes."

"Well, Clint was thorough but concise. I'm sure he would have filled you in on the details when he came to your office." She took a moment before she went on: "I can check his computer, but I don't expect to find anything else."

"Perhaps some other case Clint was working on that might have worried him?"

Evie shook her head. "He spent all of his time recently on the Little Shield case. He interviewed a lot of people."

"And didn't make notes?"

This stopped the woman, as if a brick wall had descended. "Like I said, I can check his computer in case he left something else."

"I'll speak with the Little Shields," Vicky said. "I can't agree to anything until I hear what they have to say."

Evie nodded. "They're good people, and little Mary Ann has a happy home."

Vicky left the woman standing in the small office surrounded by the items that had belonged to Clint, the space permeated by his presence. She made her way across the living room, visitors shifting about, new visitors coming through the front door that closed with a sharp thwack.

She let herself outside and, hurrying down the sidewalk to the Ford parked at the curb, checked her text messages. One message from Annie: "Vince's mother called."

Vicky slid onto the driver's seat and started the engine. Cold air blasted out of the vents. She pulled her coat around her, found Betty White Hawk's number and pressed the call key. Five rings on a cell phone somewhere on the reservation, then a voice said: "Hi, this is Betty."

Vicky was waiting for the familiar *leave a message* when the voice went on: "Vicky? I've been waiting for you to call."

"Have you heard from Vince?" Vicky checked her watch. Still several hours before the time she had promised to deliver Vince to the sheriff.

"Not yet, but I've left messages all over the rez. He's got a lot of no-good friends, but they'll tell him to call me. I have to give them that—they don't want a lot of cops creeping around their places looking for him." The faint sound of hope broke through the weariness in the voice. "Soon's he sobers up, I'm sure he'll call and tell me where he is."

"Call me as soon as you hear anything." Vicky was about to end the call when she said, "If you talk to Vince, it might be best not to mention that I will come by to pick him up wherever he is."

"I got it." The voice was faint with apprehension.

Vicky pulled into the lane, turned onto Federal, and drove south toward Lander. She was coming around the bend past Hudson when the cell rang. Annie again. "You just got a call from Eldon Little Shield. He wants to see you right away. I told him you'd work him in this morning."

Clint Hopkins wasn't dead twenty-four hours yet, and the Little Shields wanted to talk to another lawyer. "That's fine," she told Annie before she hit the end key. It was the way it was. No matter the horror of what had happened, the Little Shields wanted to adopt their little girl, and nothing would prevent them from trying.

# 6

THEY MIGHT HAVE been any family on the reservation. At the powwows, tribal meetings, celebrations at Blue Sky Hall, dozens of get-
togethers. A serious look about them: responsible, involved. Good
people, Vicky would have said if anyone asked, the best of her people. The man in a parka, blue jeans, boots. The woman in a red
flower-print dress, coat hanging off her shoulders. A little girl, about
five years old, with hair the color of sunshine and eyes like blue ice.

"Eldon Little Shield." The man advanced across the office, hand
extended, a warrior leading the way into unknown territory, his wife
and child a couple steps behind. He was tall, a little paunch above
a silver buffalo belt buckle, a cowboy hat clasped against one thigh.
He tossed a backward nod. "This here is my wife, Myra. And this is
our daughter, Mary Ann." He reached over and placed a protective
hand on the child's head.

Vicky came around the desk and shook the man's hand first, the palm roughened and wind-seared. His wife's palm was softer, the grip surprisingly strong and resolute. "Hello, Mary Ann," she said, leaning down toward the pretty little girl, who lifted a hand and gave a little wave.

Vicky gestured toward the chairs in front of her desk, then took her own seat and waited for the family to settle in. Mary Ann had a small bag, beaded and quilled, which she spread on her lap. She removed a pad and pencil and set about drawing something.

"Clint's secretary mentioned you might call," Vicky said. An awkward beginning, an awkward circumstance.

Myra Little Shield pulled a tissue from the woven bag on her lap and began dabbing at the corners of her eyes. She glanced over at the child, who looked up and gave her mother a reassuring smile, then went back to her drawing. The smile seemed to fortify Myra, who straightened herself against the chair and drew in a long breath. Thirtyish, black hair brushing her shoulders, no makeup or lipstick, and a take-me-as-I-am look about her. She was attractive, with traces of the kind of beauty that had propelled a number of young Arapaho women to the Miss Indian America crown. She gave Vicky a weak smile, squeezed the tissue in the fist she dropped on top of her bag, and turned toward her husband. Waiting. It was his place to lead the way.

Eldon took his time. Vicky could almost see the thoughts shadowing his face. Sun splashed the window behind the couple, and a column of sunlight illuminated the dust in the air. Finally Eldon said, "We were shocked when we heard about Clint. Never expected anything like that to happen. Talked to him yesterday, and he said he was going to meet with another lawyer. That lawyer being you, from what Clint's secretary told us. He sounded a little, I don't know . . ." He shrugged. "Serious."

"Did he say why he wanted to bring me in on the case?"

The man gave another shrug, then gripped the armrests hard, knuckles popping white in his brown hands, like a cowboy steadying himself on the fence before the bronco hurtles out the gate onto the rodeo grounds. He glanced down at the little girl, then back at Vicky. "This isn't the time . . ."

Vicky came around the desk and smiled down at the child. "Mary Ann, would you like to keep Annie company in the outer office?"

"Who's Annie?" The little girl made several pencil swipes on the pad before she looked up, blue eyes filled with innocence and wonder in a heart-shaped face. There was a little dimple in her chin. Her fingernails were rosy pink.

"My secretary. You met her when you came in. You could show her your drawings. She would like that very much."

The little girl gave her father, then her mother, a sideways glance. They both nodded, and she jumped up and started for the outer office. Vicky went with her. "Mary Ann has some drawings to show you," she told Annie as the child sidled in next to Annie's chair and opened her pad.

Vicky closed the beveled glass doors behind her and went back to her desk. The Little Shields had angled their chairs toward the doors so they could keep an eye on Mary Ann and—more important, Vicky realized—so Mary Ann could keep an eye on them.

"Clint wasn't one to talk about his business," Eldon said. "Went about doing what he had to do."

"Never wanted to give us reason to get discouraged." Myra's eyes locked on her husband as if they were the same person. His turn to speak, then hers; one story.

"Fact is," Eldon went on, "Clint believed in our case. It was obvious we were Mary Ann's parents. We raised her from the time she was no bigger than a puppy. We been worried sick some nosy social worker could show up on our doorstep and take Mary Ann away, despite the fact we take good care of her. I've got a steady job at the body shop in Riverton going on eight years now, and Myra works part-time at an insurance company. We see that Mary Ann has everything she needs. We talked to Father John at the mission. He's the one said we need legal papers saying she's ours so nobody can take her away. You can bring him in on this, if you want. He knows all about our case."

"Why don't we start at the beginning?" Vicky said. Of course they had gone to Father John O'Malley. He was the man her people turned to for advice and consolation and help. "Tell me how you came to have custody of Mary Ann."

Eldon swallowed several times, his Adam's apple bobbing. "Five years ago last week, March twentieth—what we call Mary Ann's birthday, 'cause that's when she was born to us—there was a knock on the front door. It was pretty late. We were just about to go to bed, and we sure weren't expecting company."

"I remember being scared." Myra squared herself to the desk and kept her eyes on Vicky. "I sensed something wasn't right. It was snowing hard, and nobody should've been out. I told Eldon not to answer." She glanced at her husband. "Thank God he ignored me and opened the door. I was right behind him, and I saw a woman running toward a pickup parked out by the road. Her boots made holes in the snow, like post holes. She had on a black coat that came down to her knees. I remember the way her long, black hair swung from beneath the knit cap pulled low over her ears. Like a black shadow running through the snow. Eldon shouted, 'What do you want?' but she jumped inside and the pickup took off. Bounced down the road, taillights swirling in the snow, like whoever was driving couldn't get away fast enough. I was so busy watching the pickup I didn't notice the box until Eldon said, 'What's this?' I looked down and saw the kind of brown carton you get at the grocery store. Stuffed with a pink blanket and the blanket was moving. We didn't say anything. We stood there like rocks."

Eldon shook his head and smiled off into the distance. "It was like we were dreaming. Something moving inside the blanket? I thought it was a small animal. Maybe a puppy or a kitten. Well, we had a couple dogs and some cats that lived in the barn. We sure didn't need any more."

"But the pink blanket," Myra said. "I knew it was a baby. I lifted the box and took it inside. It was so cold out, and the blanket sparkled with snow. I could barely pull the blanket back, I was shaking so hard. A thousand thoughts went through my mind. How can this be? She was beautiful." Myra stopped and drew in a long, shuddering breath. Her eyes were shiny. She seemed to make an effort to steady herself before going on: "A tiny pink face, just a wisp of hair, little clenched fists. She looked at me with the biggest blue eyes you ever saw, and it was like she knew I was going to be her mother."

Eldon reached over and patted his wife's hand. "It was like a miracle," he said. "Our little girl died at birth only five weeks before, and here was this perfect baby whose mother was giving her away."

He looked sideways at his wife, who nodded, lips clenched. "I picked her up, our precious little baby, and held her close, and it was like . . ." The tears started as she mimicked rocking the baby back and forth. "Our own baby had come back to us. I remember saying her name: Mary Ann. Mary Ann, I said, over and over, and that became her name."

Eldon waited a moment, before he said: "I figured the mother

must be in a terrible situation to leave her baby like that. I told
Myra she was sure to come back. If not right away, she'd come back
for her baby when she got herself into a better situation. I could see
that Myra was"—he patted his wife's hand again—"falling in love,
and after what we had been through, losing our own baby, I didn't
want her to have any more grief. I tried to warn her . . ."

"It didn't do any good." Myra flashed a sideways smile toward
her husband. "I was already in love. All I wanted to do was take
care of her. I felt she was mine, that for some reason the mother
wanted me and Eldon to raise her as our own. She was white, but
that didn't make any difference. We were going to be her parents.
We still had everything ready for our own baby: crib, clothes, dia-
pers, formula, all in her own bedroom. We had closed the door
because I couldn't bear to look at it. All we had to do was open the
door. Eldon had found a rocker at a secondhand store and painted
it red, and I had made a bright, cheery cushion. I took Mary Ann
into the bedroom and cuddled her in the rocker and I . . . I let her
nurse. She had been breast fed, because she knew how to nurse. It
was a miracle the way my milk started to come back. Not right
away. I had to give her formula for a couple of days, but I kept offering my breast, and after a few days, I had enough milk for two
babies."

For an instant, the memories flooded back: her own babies tug-
ging at her breast. Vicky swallowed hard and said, "Did you ever
hear from the mother? Did you try to make contact?"

"Not a word." Eldon gave a quick, dismissive shake of his head.
"She abandoned her child, and that was that. As for trying to make
contact, we had no idea who she might be."

"Indian," Myra said.

"Why do you suppose so? The child is white."

"Half-breed, we decided," Eldon said. "Father was probably white. I figure that's why the mother gave her up, because her daddy didn't want a half-breed kid. I guess the mother wanted him more than she wanted her own baby. It happens."

Oh, yes, it happens, Vicky was thinking. A parade of clients, usually grandparents or aunties and uncles seated in the same chairs the Little Shields occupied, explaining how they had been left with a child, sometimes two or three children, because their daughter or sister or niece or even a close friend had run off with some man she couldn't live without, no matter the price.

"If you think the mother was Indian . . ."

"The way she ran away, the black hair, the pickup truck," Myra said. "Everything about her said Indian."

"You didn't see her face."

The couple shook heads in unison. "We knew," Myra said.

"I'm surprised she didn't leave the child with relatives. Is it possible one of you is a relative?" When neither spoke, she said, "Why didn't you call the police?"

They seemed to be struck dumb by the question, as if it were unfathomable. Finally Eldon said, "The police? We didn't even think about it. We called Myra's cousin over at social services and told her about the baby. She got us papers that said we could keep her while they investigated. The papers were notarized. Said we had temporary custody. We thought everything was okay, and we just took care of our baby."

"She was our baby," Myra said, "come to us out of nowhere. I couldn't bear the thought of losing her. We told folks she was our foster child, and nobody said anything. Then my cousin had a stroke and died, and we never heard any more about an investigation. I guess she knew we needed a baby. Pretty soon it was natural for there to be three of us. Everywhere we went, powwows, Sun Dance, people knew Mary Ann was ours."

"What has changed?" The case had fallen through the cracks. It should have been settled five years ago. From the outer office came the muted sound of the phone ringing. Both Myra and Eldon swiveled toward the beveled glass doors. Mary Ann was still at Annie's side, pushing the pencil over her pad. Annie picked up the phone.

The couple looked back at each other, regathering their thoughts. "We've changed," Eldon said after a moment. "We want the legal papers that say we are her parents and no one can take her away. We have to register her for school. They're going to want her birth certificate."

Myra pulled at the tissue in her hands. "Mary Ann worries. She looks in the mirror and sees she doesn't look like Mommy and Daddy. She wants to know who she is, where she came from, and we're afraid to tell her the truth about being left on our doorstep because there'll be an investigation for sure. We tell her she is our child and we couldn't love her more if I had given birth to her. She needs to know she is legally ours."

"We found Clint on the internet," Eldon said. "His Web site said he had experience with adoption cases."

Vicky nodded. The adoption should have been easy, a clear case of abandonment. Nothing Clint couldn't have handled himself. "Did Clint mention finding anything that might have stopped the case from going forward?"

Myra was shaking her head, but her husband stared into the center of the room, a somber look about him. "When we hired him, he said the fastest way to finalize the adoption was to prove abandonment. It should be easy, given the facts, but the judge would want to make sure we had done everything to find the birth mother.

Clint put two ads in the *Gazette*, asking if anybody knew about an infant abandoned five years ago. We gave him a list of our relatives and friends that knew we'd been caring for Mary Ann. He went out and talked to people. Last time I asked him how things were going, he said he would get back to us. Like I said, he called the day he died. He didn't sound upbeat, like usual. Now he's gone."

Vicky could picture the notes Clint had given her, the tight, hurried handwriting, the tension growing page by page. Newspapers. Interviews. The usual ways to obtain information that would support the clients' claim. "I'll need a copy of the list you gave Clint," she said.

A sheet of paper materialized from the woven bag on Myra's lap. She scooted forward and handed the paper across the desk. "Does this mean you have to start all over? We were hoping to have the adoption finalized by now."

Vicky glanced down the sheet. A number of Little Shields scattered among other familiar names on the rez. No one she knew, but she supposed that, at one time or another, she had crossed paths with most of them. "I'll see if I can find out if Clint ran into any obstacles." She glanced up and tried for a smile of encouragement. "I'll be in touch."

It took a moment before the Little Shields seemed to realize the appointment was over. Myra crunched the woven bag, then swung the strap over one shoulder and got to her feet; Eldon gripped the armrests and propelled himself upward into the sunlit motes of dust. They started toward the beveled glass doors.

Vicky walked them out. She watched Myra bundle Mary Ann into a pink coat, pull a blue hat over her hair, and help her with her mittens. Then the family was out the door into the glare of sunshine and snow, Mary Ann between her parents, holding their hands. A peaceful family picture, yet she could still feel the turmoil and anxiety in Myra and Eldon Little Shield.

She went back to her desk, another image crowding into her mind: the dark figure in the falling snow, the headlights snapping on, the truck roaring down. What is it you learned that you had to die for?

"Vicky?" Annie stood in the doorway. "Are you all right?"

She was not all right; she was thinking, but she tried for a reassuring smile.

"Rick Masterson wants you to call him." Annie walked over and placed the message on the desk.

She had turned back when Vicky said, "See if you can reach Clint Hopkins's secretary and set up a time when we can meet at Clint's office. The sooner, the better."

# 7

SHANNON O'MALLEY WAS like her mother, kicking up white clouds as she came down the alley, the same air of confidence and assurance Father John remembered in Eileen, as if she would soon make the world turn her way. He went to meet her. "You're early," he said, falling in beside her. She was tall beside him, filled with energy, sunlight shimmering in her reddish hair. Elena wouldn't serve lunch for ten minutes. This could be the first time, he realized, that he was on time for a meal. "All settled in?"

"Doesn't take long to unpack a backpack." She glanced up at him. "Can't wait to transcribe my notes and start writing." She tossed her head about. "You didn't tell me about the buffalo herd on the other side of the fence."

Ah, the buffalo. The rancher next to the mission had raised buffalo for decades. Quiet animals, grazing in the pasture in the summer and fall, nibbling on bales of hay the rancher tossed out. If you stood close enough to the fence, you could sometimes hear a buffalo snorting, but most of the time he forgot the herd was there. "What did you think?"

"I landed in the Wild West. Wyatt Earp and Doc Holliday could show up at any minute. Any gunfights lately?"

"Not lately." You never knew. You never knew. "Did you see the church?"

She stopped walking and turned toward the white stucco church across the alley. "Looks interesting."

"Come on, we'll have a look."

"Do we have time?"

"It's a small church." Father John ushered her up the frosty concrete steps that sparkled in the sun. Opening the heavy oak door, he nodded her into the vestibule. It was chilly inside. The furnace he had adjusted this morning and the sun splashing through the stained glass windows were not enough to banish last night's frigid temperatures.

Shannon started down the center aisle, taking in the windows on one side, then the other. "The geometric symbols are Arapaho," he said, staying with her. "Horizontal lines for the roads we must travel. Rectangles for the buffalo that give their lives so the people could live. Tipis for the people and the villages." Dozens of different symbols; he was still learning the meanings.

Shannon nodded and walked over to the small tipi the women had made from tanned deerskins, the finest skins. Geometric symbols painted in red, blue, black, and yellow, decorated the outside. "The tabernacle," he said.

"And that's the altar?" She nodded toward the large drum next to the tabernacle, then twirled about, taking it all in again, before she began walking back down the aisle. "It's beautiful," she said when they were outside. "Like a church in a fairy tale."

"Fairy tale?" He walked her across Circle Drive, over the hardened ridges of tire tracks, and through the snow-mounded field, following the footprints he and the bishop had left that morning.

"Where Cinderella marries Prince Charming. Nice, if you believe in fairy tales."

"And you don't?"

"Come on, Uncle John." She stopped in her tracks and was looking up at him. "No one in my generation believes in fairy tales. *Ever after* just doesn't happen. It never did, really. Your generation was the last to cling to that belief. My generation, we take things as they are. Don't expect the impossible. People change and grow, and they need to move on. What works for a while doesn't work forever."

She was looking away now, out across the mission grounds and the open, snowy plains where the buffalo herd grazed, and he caught the shadow of disappointment in her expression. She covered it up quickly—she was a good actress, like her mother. He had never been certain where he stood with Eileen. Always off balance.

"Anyway, David and I . . ."

"David?"

She took a moment, as if this was a road she wasn't sure she wanted to start down. "I guess you'd call him my boyfriend. We've been together three years now. We live together. We knew it wasn't forever, and that was okay. It's been great, but now it's time to move on. He'll finish his Ph.D. in religious studies this spring and take a position at the University of North Carolina."

They started up the shoveled sidewalk to the residence. "You could write your dissertation anywhere," Father John said.

"Maybe for your generation things were that simple, Uncle John, but we accept that everything has an end."

They took the steps side by side, and he pushed open the front door. No, things were never simple, he wanted to say. Twenty-five years ago, he had come to that same point, where it was time to move on.

"I'm just saying we don't pretend to believe in *happily ever after*. We're okay with the present." She was pulling off her jacket, and he took it from her and hung it on a hook. He set his own jacket on the bench and placed his cowboy hat on top. Maybe that was the real difference in their generations: the ability to move on without regret. With gratitude, even. But in the smile she gave him, he detected the smallest flicker of sadness and disappointment, which disappeared as quickly as it had flared up.

"If you ever want to talk," he said, but Walks-On came clicking down the hallway, and Shannon swung toward him.

"And who might you be?" She leaned over and ran a slender hand over the dog's coat. "My, you're a handsome fellow. What happened to your hind leg?"

"He lost it on Seventeen-Mile Road when he was a puppy." The conversation about fairy tales and going forward without regret— oh, yes, without any regret that this niece of his would ever admit to—was over.

"Let me guess. You found him and brought him home."

"After a trip to the vet's. He pretty much patrols the mission, keeps us in line."

"Of course you would have a dog. I can't imagine you without a dog."

Walks-On had pivoted about. Looking back to make sure his two charges were in line, he headed down the hallway to the kitchen. The air was filled with smells of tomato soup and grilled cheese, the lunch his mother used to make, Father John was thinking, on frosty winter days.

"Shannon." He kept his voice low, a few feet behind her. "If there is anything you would like to talk over . . ."

"There isn't." She glanced back and flashed the same knowing smile he had found so annoying and attractive in her mother.

"Welcome." Bishop Harry, wrapped in a white apron, pushed himself off the edge of the counter and plunged toward Shannon, hand extended. "A pretty Irish lass, I see. I'm the pastor's assistant."

"Bishop Harry Coughlin," Father John said. "I may be the pastor, but he's the bishop. This is Elena, our housekeeper."

Elena stood at the table, holding several plates. She nodded in Shannon's direction and went about placing the plates on the table. The Arapaho Way, Father John knew. She would hold back until she decided what type of character Shannon had, whether her heart was good. There was no sense in giving yourself to a bad heart. As soon as she decided Shannon had a good heart, Elena would take her in and love her like an orphaned child.

"We've prepared a sumptuous lunch in your honor." The bishop waved at the stove, where grilled cheese sandwiches browned in the frying pan. Father John glanced over at Elena, who looked up and rolled her eyes. "I am pleased to say I am learning to prepare new dishes today. Cooking is not hard if one applies himself. Do sit down." The bishop made a courtly gesture of pulling a chair from the table. "Make yourself at home, because this is your home for as long as you like."

Shannon smiled and shrugged and thanked the old man, then settled herself on the chair. Father John took his usual chair across the table. "I hope the cooks will join us," he said.

"Yes, yes. Naturally." The bishop scooped the sandwiches onto a platter, which he set in the middle of the table, while Elena moved over to the stove and began ladling soup into bowls. One by one, the bishop delivered the bowls. Finally he dropped onto the chair next to Shannon. Fingers of steam curled above the thick red soup.

Elena took her usual place across from the bishop. "Eat up," she said, scooting her chair into the table. Since Father John had been on the reservation, Arapahos had been placing food in front of him and telling him to eat up. Just like in the Old Time, he knew, when no one was sent away from an Arapaho village hungry. You never knew, heading onto the plains, when you might find food again.

Shannon had dipped her spoon into the soup when Bishop Harry said, "Let us pray." Father John bowed his head, conscious of a sense of contentment flooding over him. Shannon O'Malley, not much more than a girl, carrying with her a connection to his family, to his own past, and to an essential part of himself that, he realized, he sometimes forgot to remember. He had settled in here, at a remote mission on a remote Indian reservation that many of his classmates in the Jesuit seminary, bound for teaching positions at Georgetown or Marquette or some other university, would have considered the dead-end of a career, where priests like Bishop Harry Coughlin went to recuperate from the frailties of old age.

"We thank you, Lord, for blessing us with the presence of Shannon O'Malley, and for allowing us to share this meal together."

"Amen," Elena said. "Dig in."

Shannon took a sip of soup and told Elena how delicious it was. "I would love to know how to make it."

"One cooking student is all I can manage at the moment." Elena stirred her own soup and stared at the bishop.

"A very fine teacher you are, I may add," the bishop said. "I had no idea toasted cheese sandwiches could require so much effort. Why, you must watch them like a hawk or one may burn."

"Or two." Elena reached over and pushed the plate of sand-

wiches in Shannon's direction. A first step, Father John was thinking, in accepting her.

The bishop helped himself to a sandwich and shoved the plate
toward Father John. "I understand you are researching the lives of
white sisters held captive by the Plains Indians."

"There were a number of captives between 1860 and 1880."
Shannon's voice sparkled with excitement as she moved into familiar territory. "I'm interested in how those who survived viewed their
captivity. In what way did it influence or change their lives? I'm
especially interested in Elizabeth Fletcher, who was never rescued.
She lived here on the reservation."

"Lizzie Brokenhorn." Elena spoke softly, as if the name had trig-
gered a memory.

Shannon gave a smile of acknowledgement, which Elena ignored.
"She lived as an Arapaho. Married an Arapaho man when she was
only fifteen."

"John Brokenhorn," Elena said.

Father John could feel the excitement building in his niece as she
shifted sideways toward the housekeeper. He could almost read the
questions popping in her eyes. He stared so hard at her that finally
she glanced his way, and in her glance he saw that she had some
comprehension of what he was trying to convey. Be patient. Wait.
Elena was still making up her mind about Shannon's heart.

"I wonder if it was hard for her to leave her own family and
culture behind and live in a completely different world. Oh, I know
she was practically a baby when she was captured, but still, a part
of her must have known she was different from the people she
thought of as her family. Like a blood memory that stayed with her,
shadowed her. I can't help but think there were times when it was
hard for her."

This seemed to do it. A young white woman's sympathy for an Arapaho captive. Father John watched the lines in Elena's face soften into a smile. She reached over and touched Shannon's hand. "My grandmother was a friend of hers."

Shannon sat upright, questions jumping in her eyes, and Father John shot her another look. Elena had offered a small gift of information. She would offer more if she wished, and all the questions Shannon might come up with wouldn't pry another piece of information out of the housekeeper if she didn't want to provide it.

"My grandfather's ranch was next to Brokenhorn's," Elena said after a moment. "They had been scouts for General Crook when he was chasing the Sioux around, so they went back a long ways." Elena nodded as if to punctuate the friendship. "Only natural the women were friends, too. Grandmother tended to Lizzie when she gave birth, and Lizzie did the same for her. Giving birth was women's work. The men went down to the river, smoked pipes, and waited. Grandmother and Lizzie raised their kids together. Kids went back and forth from house to house. Felt at home wherever they went. Always a mother to feed them, put them to bed when they were tired, make sure they were doing okay."

Elena lifted her head and stared at the ceiling as though an old black-and-white movie were playing there. "It was a hard time when the people first came to the reservation," she said, still watching the ceiling. "Government had already sent the Shoshones here, and they weren't looking to share the rez with Arapahos. We had no place to live. All our lands gone. The hunting grounds, the villages, all gone. Everywhere we went, the people were hunted down. Soldiers, white posses, ranchers, homesteaders. Open season on Indians back then. Shoshones say Chief Washakie's heart was so big he couldn't turn us away."

Elena lowered her eyes and turned toward Shannon. "Hope you'll get it right when you tell your story."

"I want to very much. I'll do my best."

Elena patted Shannon's hand again. "Remember that Lizzie was Arapaho. She lived Arapaho. Grandmother said Lizzie hated the way she looked. She rubbed dirt on her face and arms to make them dark. She washed her hair in mud to turn it black, but she still had light skin and hair as golden red as wild grass in August. But no one thought of her as anything but Arapaho."

The bishop had finished eating. He stacked his soup bowl on top of the empty sandwich plate. "I'm thinking she must have been a remarkable woman to make the best of what life had dealt her."

"Oh, more than that." Elena shook her head at the obstinacy of the white people at her table. Her table, Father John knew. Her kitchen, her house to keep, and her white priests to marshal about. "Grandmother said Lizzie loved her husband, and he loved her. He got scared the government agents would take her away after it dawned on them she was white, so he found a place in the mountains that was real hard to get to. No roads. You had to go cross-country on horseback. He built a shack. Of course, Indians weren't supposed to go anywhere without the agent's permission. Darn near needed permission to go to the outhouse. But Brokenhorn swore he would do whatever was necessary to protect Lizzie. Sure enough, the agent started snooping around, asking questions, so Brokenhorn took his family to the mountains. Grandfather kept denying Brokenhorn had gone anywhere. Just off helping neighbors round up cattle. After a while, the agent stopped coming around, and grandfather went up in the mountains and told Brokenhorn it was all clear. Before winter set in, Brokenhorn, Lizzie, and the five kids came back. Grandmother said she was sure glad to see Lizzie again. The house next door had seemed lonely without them."

Elena got to her feet and began clearing the table, and Father John understood this was the end of her story. He stood up and took his dishes over to the sink. "Thank you, Elena." He waved a hand to indicate both the lunch and the story, everything that had taken place in the kitchen.

"Yes. Thank you very much." Shannon cleared her dishes and went back for the bishop's.

"A very delicious lunch." The old man lumbered to his feet. The white apron still hung from his neck and was looped about his waist. "A most interesting story and, I must say, a most enlightening cooking lesson. At what time shall we start preparing dinner?"

Elena threw a glance over her shoulder at Father John. There were layers of meaning in her glance. He could write a whole sermon on how we are made holy by the way we claim our place in the world and do our work the best we can. Another glance from Elena, and he decided he would have a talk with the bishop.

He motioned Shannon ahead and followed her down the hall, Walks-On between them. The dog had an uncanny sense for adventure, and he didn't want to miss out. Most days he climbed into the pickup and accompanied Father John on rounds of visits to the elders and the sick and those needing someone to stop by for a chat and a cup of coffee.

But not this afternoon. Father John didn't know if Wilbur Horn would welcome a visit from a dog. He helped Shannon with her jacket and pulled on his own jacket before he leaned down and patted the dog's head. "You have to take care of Elena and the bishop today," he said. Then he opened the door for Shannon, followed her out into the bright, cold air, and set his cowboy hat on his head.

Shannon hurried ahead down the snowy path. "I have to get my laptop," she called over her shoulder

"You won't need it."

"To make notes during the interview." She stopped in the middle of Circle Drive, shadows of impatience on her face. Did she have to explain the obvious?

He placed an arm around her shoulders and steered her along the drive to the passenger side of the old pickup. "You can make notes when you get back."

He closed the door behind her and gave her a smile through the windshield as he walked around to the driver's side. "So that was the look you were shooting at me over the table," she said as he jiggled the key in the ignition and tried to coax the engine into life. "I recognized the O'Malley look. Dad used it on us kids when we asked too many questions. It was his way of saying, 'Stop talking and you might learn something.'"

Father John laughed. The pickup jumped ahead as if it knew the way through the tunnel of cottonwoods, out to Seventeen-Mile Road. In his mind was a flash of memory: his own father shooting the O'Malley look across the table to him and Mike.

"I get the way it works around here," Shannon said. "Ask no questions and pray for answers. Write it down later."

A cottonwood branch scratched at the top of the pickup, and a pile of snow slid down the windshield. He flipped on the wipers and tried to keep the pickup steady through the tunnel. Then he turned left onto Seventeen-Mile Road and glanced over at Shannon. "That's about it," he said.

# 8

WILBUR HORN STOOD at the edge of the driveway, gloved hand waving them forward. Across the barrow ditch and along the two-track that marked the driveway. The old pickup shuddered and jumped over the ice-hardened snow. "Lizzie's great-grandson?" High notes of excitement rang in Shannon's voice.

He glanced over and smiled. For an instant he was back in grad school at Boston College, researching some obscure event in American history, and with a turn of a page or an idle remark, he'd be plunged backward in time, as if the past itself had reached out and grabbed him. He could still feel the excitement.

She gripped the door handle with one hand, bracing herself against the dashboard with the other and nodding, excitement shooting off her like fireworks. He stopped at the end of the driveway in a clear spot Wilbur had waved to. Then the man yanked the door open. He might have been a doorman at a hotel. "Nice to see you, Father." He had a wide grin and black eyes that sparkled with light in the shade of his cowboy hat. His denim jacket was lined with fur that poked out around the collar. "This your niece?"

"Shannon O'Malley," Father John said, but Wilbur was already advancing toward Shannon, who had let herself out on the passenger side.

"Sure a lot prettier than you." Wilbur smiled at Father John while he pumped Shannon's hand. "Well, let's not waste good daylight. Come on inside." He dipped his head in the direction of the rectangular house with yellow siding and a three-step stoop at the front door, like most of the houses on the rez. Inside two bedrooms, bath, living room, kitchen. Larger than the log cabins and tiny shacks that, for nearly a hundred years, the government had considered satisfactory houses for Indians.

Wilbur led the way across the hardened snow and up the steps. He pushed open the door and gestured them inside. The house was warm, suffused with smells of freshly brewed coffee and sizzling oil. "I put on a pot of coffee." Wilbur took a few steps across the living room toward the kitchen. "Belle made fry bread before she went to work this morning. She's going to stop by on her lunch break." He motioned them through the arched doorway, tilting his head in the direction of a round table and four wooden chairs in the corner of the kitchen. Shannon took one of the chairs, and Father John sat next to her. When he had spoken with Belle Horn at a powwow last summer, she told him she had just taken a job as the nursing supervisor at the health clinic.

"Belle's got a bug about all this history stuff." Wilbur was bustling about the counter, pouring mugs of coffee, setting them on the table. "You'd think she was the one descended from Lizzie and

Brokenhorn. She was always telling stories to the kids about their great-great-grandmother, the white captive. You like fry bread?"

Shannon nodded, and Father John caught the flash of curiosity and amusement in her eyes. Indian reservation, fry bread, the descendant of Lizzie Fletcher Brokenhorn. Exactly what she would have imagined. This girl had a big imagination and, he was learning, a big appetite for life.

"Bread's nice and warm." Wilbur lifted a plate stacked with fry bread from the oven and set it in the center of the table. The chunks of bread were rounded and irregular, like biscuits. Then, a stack of small plates, paper napkins, a bottle of honey, and a plate of butter and a knife appeared on the table. "Belle's proud of her fry bread. Used to watch her grandmother make it in a pot of hot oil on the campfire. Help yourselves." Wilbur dropped onto the chair next to the window. "She'll expect a good review." He nodded toward the vacant chair, as if Belle were about to materialize.

"I'm not sure how to do this." Shannon took a chunk of bread, set it on a plate, and studied it as if she might unlock its mystery.

"Butter first." Wilbur pulled a piece of bread apart, lathered on a slab of butter. "Honey next." He held the bottle of honey over his plate and let the golden liquid drizzle over the bread. "Then, good eating."

Shannon had followed along. She took a bite of the honeyed, buttered bread and sat back, a look of contentment flowing over her like water. "Oh my gosh," she said. "Nothing like this in Boston."

Father John helped himself and bit into the warm bread. Fry bread always came with the memory of the first time he'd eaten it: a brush shade at the Sun Dance, temperatures hovering around a hundred degrees, a little breeze stirring the cottonwood branches that covered the ceiling and three walls, the Fast Pony family gathered around, proud of the family's fry bread recipe—no one could make it like Grandmother—waiting for his confirmation. Like Shannon, he had realized how much he had been missing. Odd how such memories crowded him lately. He had an urgent sense that he should capture every experience, keep it safe so that he wouldn't forget.

Then came the whoosh of the front door opening. A stream of cold air shot through the kitchen, and the door clacked shut. Belle Horn, younger than her husband by a few years, clutching a brown bag of groceries, walked into the kitchen, and Father John got to his feet. "Good to see you," he said as the woman set the bag on the counter. She turned and took his hand. A handsome woman, on the stout side with a strong grip, broad shoulders, and shoulder-length black hair streaked with gray.

"No way was I going to miss this." She let go of his hand and turned to Shannon. "I'm Belle, the better half."

Shannon started to get up, but Belle placed a hand on her shoulder. "Don't let me interrupt. Keep on talking about whatever you were discussing."

"I was just about to ask how our guest likes the rez." Wilbur kept his eyes on Shannon, took another bite of bread, and washed it down with coffee. Now would come the polite preliminaries, before the conversation moved to the topic that Shannon, Father John knew, was eager to talk about.

Belle pulled a carton of milk out of the bag and set it in the refrigerator in a slow, relaxed motion. She hadn't missed anything important. Then she hung her coat on the back of the vacant chair, sat down, and helped herself to the fry bread, switching her gaze between her husband and Shannon.

Father John tried to give Shannon another look. He hadn't

warned her about the polite preliminaries, but she was sipping at her coffee, eating her fry bread. Nodding and smiling at Wilbur Horn. She liked the rez fine. Wide spaces that go on forever. She'd never seen so much space and so few people. "Beautiful," she said, and Wilbur and Belle grinned. Oh, this niece of his had an instinct for fitting right in, picking up the reins, and riding along.

Shannon looked over at Belle. "The fry bread is delicious. Thank you for making it."

Belle smiled and shrugged. After all, it was what she did, saw to it that guests were fed, like any other woman on the rez.

After a few minutes on weather, the snow expected tonight, Wilbur said, "I understand you're writing a report on my great-grandparents."

Great-grandparents. Shannon glanced over at Father John, something new in her eyes. They were a pair, weren't they? Part of each other's lives, Lizzie and John Brokenhorn.

"Yes." She turned back to Wilbur and told him she was researching the lives of Lizzie and her sister, Amanda, both captured by the Plains Indians. "I'm looking for the details. Personal stories that make the women human and help us to understand them."

"History books get things wrong," Wilbur said. "They make out how bad things went for captives, like all Indians were barbarians. Sure, some of the white women had it tough, especially when the warriors went on the rampage after that terrible massacre in Colorado."

Silence dropped over the kitchen. Shannon kept her eyes on the last piece of bread on her plate, then looked over at Father John. He had read about the Sand Creek Massacre in 1864, the massacre that drove the Arapahos and Cheyennes from their Colorado homelands. "It was a terrible time," he said.

"I'm not saying the Cheyennes didn't mistreat white captives."

"Plenty of white men mistreated Indian women," Belle said.

Wilbur leaned forward. "History books lump all the tribes together. Arapahos traded for white captives. They returned them or kept them with the people. Those old Arapahos knew it was a good thing to have new people and fresh blood. Good to strengthen the tribe. You see Arapahos with blond hair and blue eyes on the rez today. They come down from whites, some of them captives. Like my family. Blue eyes here." He lifted a hand to his eyes. "I'm proud I came down from Lizzie Brokenhorn. I got cousins with hair the color of pink sand, like hers. We're all proud."

"I'm not sure how Lizzie came to the Arapahos," Shannon said. A comment, not a question. His niece was a quick study.

Wilbur sipped at his coffee. Finally he said, "She wasn't captured by Arapahos, like the history books say. My father did his own research. Talked to some of the elders that went back to the time of Sand Creek. Lizzie was captured the next summer in 1865. There were some Arapaho warriors riding with Cheyennes that day, but it was a Cheyenne attack. After Sand Creek, there was no peace. Cheyennes had been raiding on the North Platte that summer, and Arapahos joined them."

"Lizzie never would have been captured if her father had used common sense." Belle shook her head and pulled apart a piece of bread. "Tell them what your dad found out."

"Jasper Fletcher, Lizzie's father, decided to move his family from Illinois to California so he could find gold and get rich. He and Mary Ann had five kids. Jasper had joined a large wagon train that no Indians with any sense were gonna attack. He should've stayed with the train, but he decided to pull ahead. Stop along the river, have lunch. That's when the Cheyenne Chief Sand Hill and his war-

riors rode down on them. Killed Mary Ann and wounded Jasper.
The boys got away. The Indians took Amanda Mary and Lizzie and
rode off."

"Seven months later"—Belle was shaking her head—"a trader
found Amanda Mary in a Cheyenne camp and ransomed her. But
there was no sign of Lizzie."

"My father told me the old Indians he talked to said that Cut
Nose, another Cheyenne warrior, gave Lizzie to his wife as their new
daughter. She was a real pretty little thing, with blue eyes and light-
colored hair. Cut Nose called her Little Silver Hair. He always
treated her kindly, and his wife kept her dressed in fine clothing. She
grew up speaking Cheyenne."

Shannon sipped at her coffee. Holding the cup in both hands, she
said, "I didn't realize she grew up Cheyenne."

"Cheyenne, until Brokenhorn and some other Arapahos went to
Cut Nose's camp to trade. Great-grandfather always said the minute
he laid eyes on Lizzie, he knew she would be his wife. At first Cut
Nose refused. There weren't enough ponies or robes or glass beads
or tobacco to make Cut Nose give her up." Wilbur shook his head
and smiled to himself, a faraway look in his eyes, as if he could see
the Cheyenne warrior standing firm, refusing to trade his daughter.
"Brokenhorn didn't give up. He kept coming back to Cut Nose's
camp. He trailed a half dozen ponies packed with pots and pans and
food he'd gotten trading with other bands. Everything he owned, he
brought to Cut Nose. It still didn't persuade him."

Belle tilted her head back and laughed at the ceiling as though
she were reliving the bargaining herself. "The one who persuaded
Cut Nose was Lizzie," she said. "Brokenhorn had taken the opportunity to talk to her alone. Followed her to the creek when she went
for water, waited for her in the brush when she went to pick berries.

They fell in love. Finally, Lizzie convinced her father to let her marry Brokenhorn, and Cut Nose himself presided over the wedding. There was a big feast, and afterward, Brokenhorn and Lizzie went to Brokenhorn's village. Her father gave her the ponies Brokenhorn had given him because Cut Nose did not want his daughter to come to the Arapahos as a beggar. She rode into the village as a proud and much-loved Cheyenne woman. She was fifteen when she became Arapaho. After that, she was called Kellsto Time."

"White folks always want to know, were they happy?" Wilbur clasped his hands on the table and leaned forward. "Like that's all that matters. My father told me that great-grandfather always looked after Lizzie. They were traditionals, stayed close to the old ways. In the summers, Brokenhorn pledged the Sun Dance and Lizzie cooked for the dancers. Even after the government outlawed the Sun Dance and threatened people with prison if they took part, Brokenhorn and Lizzie and the other traditionals went into the mountains, where the government agent couldn't find them, and held the Sun Dance anyway. That's the kind of people they were. After she married Great-grandfather, she never spoke another word of Cheyenne. She took pride in being Arapaho."

The coffeepot made a rhythmic blipping noise in the quiet that dropped over the kitchen. Wilbur had told the story he intended to tell; there was nothing else. "Thank you," Father John said.

"Oh yes." Shannon jumped in. "Thank you so much."

Belle shifted sideways toward her husband. "You suppose your relation Daisy might talk to them?"

Wilbur drew in his lips and shrugged. He took a moment before he said, "That old lady makes it her business to keep track of family history. Spends most her time off visiting her grandkids. Not sure you can catch her."

Belle had turned toward Shannon. "Daisy's a granddaughter. She thinks she's an expert on the Old Time. She likes telling stories."

"Self-proclaimed expert." Wilbur started to his feet. "Doesn't think anyone else has a right to poke into family history. I'll give her a call and see if she's around. You might want to see if you can talk to another old granddaughter. Theresa Horn is pretty sharp sometimes, and other times not so much. Give her grandson, Thomas, a call and see if the old lady will talk to you."

Father John stood up and pushed his chair into the table, catching Shannon's eyes as he did so. That was the way research went, just as Shannon had said. You start somewhere and are sent somewhere else. You never know where you might go. He thanked Wilbur and Belle, and Shannon joined in. Praising the delicious fry bread, the generous gift of information, the Arapaho hospitality.

THROUGH THE TUNNEL of cottonwoods shimmering in snow, Father John spotted the dark maroon truck in front of the administration building. He turned onto Circle Drive and pulled up alongside the truck.

"Looks like you have company." Shannon had talked nonstop on the drive back to the mission, recalling everything Wilbur had said, exclaiming over the emptiness of the reservation, the small houses, the abandoned cars and trucks and appliances in the yards, laundry stiff as cement on the lines.

"How did you get used to this place?" she had asked at one point.

He wanted to say it had been easy. It seemed easy now, but ten years ago, fresh out of rehab for the second or third time, frightened that this was his last chance, an Indian reservation nobody had ever heard of—at least no one he knew—in the middle of nowhere. The truth was, it had been hard.

"I like it here," he said. Then he told her that James Two Horses, a parishioner, had stopped by to fix his Wi-Fi.

"A parishioner? I'd like to meet him."

Father John got out and started around the pickup toward the passenger side, but Shannon had already jumped out. She bounced ahead of him up the steps and into the administration building.

# 9

"HEY, FATHER. YOU have Wi-Fi again." James leaned into the corridor from the doorway to the bishop's office. "Just saying my good-byes," he said, walking toward them. "This must be the niece I've heard so much about. You're uncle's pretty proud of you." He took Shannon's hand; a large brown hand enclosing the small whiteness.

"I can't imagine why." Shannon tossed a glance over one shoulder toward Father John. "I mean, he's the historian. I'm just getting started."

"Well, getting started can be the hardest thing to do."

Shannon left her hand in James's, and for an instant Father John felt as if he had stumbled on a live wire with electricity shooting around. Finally, Shannon withdrew her hand. "You fix computers?" She tilted her head back, staring up at the Arapaho.

"Pretty much keep the computers up and running for the school districts in the area." James hadn't taken his eyes from her. Was this the way it happened? Father John had forgotten, or maybe he had decided not to remember. Eileen walking across campus, red hair blowing back in the breeze, and everything about her perfect somehow. He had known before they had spoken a word to each other that she was the woman he wanted to marry.

Some memories were better left forgotten. He had been called elsewhere. In the middle of the night. And he had broken off their engagement and answered the call, and two months later—he was still settling in at the seminary—Eileen had married his brother, Mike. And here was one of their six kids, this beautiful young woman, as close as he would ever come to having a child of his own.

He had many children. He tried to grab on to the idea. A whole reservation full of children. He was a father in a different sense. God help me. Let these memories pass.

James was saying something about installing a different router. No problem. He had a whole closet full of routers the school district had discarded. This one worked just fine.

"I'm in your debt."

"How about dinner one of these days? I hear Elena's a great cook."

"She has a good assistant." Bishop Harry made his way down the corridor. "And her assistant hereby invites you to dinner anytime."

James was still watching Shannon. And this, from a man who believed he had a calling to the priesthood. Odd how the calling to the priesthood went, Father John was thinking. It didn't always encompass everything.

"I was thinking you and I could go out to dinner this evening." James said.

Shannon hadn't stopped smiling. "I think I'd like that a lot."

"Good. I'll look forward to hearing about your research on Lizzie Brokenhorn."

"You've heard of her?"

"Hard to find anybody on the rez who hasn't. White woman with blue-eyed, blond-haired Arapaho descendants."

"I'd love to hear your stories."

"I'm not a descendant." James looked up at the ceiling and laughed. "At least as far as I know. See you later." He edged past them.

"Six o'clock," Shannon said just before the door closed. She was still smiling when she turned back.

"Let me show you where we hang out." Making an effort now to break the spell that had dropped over the corridor, Father John gestured toward the doorway to his office on the right.

"May I issue a formal invitation to visit my abode at the end of the corridor?" The bishop made a little bow and started back toward his office.

Shannon moved past Father John. She took a moment, surveying his office, the desk and chair, the worn visitors' chairs scattered about, as if a strong wind had blown them onto the brown rug with the path worn down the middle, the bookcases along the back wall, crammed with books that stood upright and fell against one another, the CD player on the top shelf, the little metal table with the coffeepot and jars of creamer and sugar.

She turned on her heels. "I assume he isn't married."

"The bishop?"

Shannon rolled her eyes at his attempt at humor, like one of his students in the Jesuit prep school where he had taught American history.

"If you mean James, he's been busy getting an education and starting a career, I suspect." It was on the tip of his tongue, the fact that James Two Horses was considering the priesthood, but he didn't say anything. James would have to tell her.

"There's more to see." He nodded her back into the corridor and around the corner into the side hallway. A small kitchen. Bath. And over there, the mission archives. She was welcome to use them. "Lizzie was a traditional," he said, "but even traditionals sometimes came to the mission. They prayed both ways, the old way and the way the early missionaries taught."

Shannon smiled up at him. Light flickered in her eyes. Another place to do research. The reservation, a treasure trove of the past.

She took a minute, new thoughts flitting through her expression. "He seems very nice." She hesitated, then pushed on. "Centered. Yes, that is how I would describe him. Centered. I mean, he looks like he knows himself and what he wants."

Maybe not, Father John was thinking. James, struggling with what he wanted. It was not an easy struggle.

"Let me show you the rest of it." Father John retraced his steps past the bath and kitchen and headed across the corridor, the tap-tap of Shannon's boots following him. He opened the door into a storage closet—a hoarding place, really—where generations of Jesuits had dropped old, broken equipment, used-up light bulbs, stacks of newspapers and magazines they no doubt intended to read someday, three-legged chairs and cracked tables, and more junk than he had wanted to wade into, but he had waded into it anyway. Now it was a small office. Desk, chair, filing cabinet, and crooked-neck lamp that flooded the room with light.

"You're welcome to work here"—he stood back and ushered Shannon inside—"anytime you'd like to be in the center of things, rather than off by yourself in the guest house."

"Parishioners dropping in all the time? Phone ringing? A buzz of activity?"

"Pretty much."

"I think I'd love it." She stepped back into the corridor and eyed the door. "I'd better start recording my notes while the interview is still fresh."

"First, the bishop's abode."

"Oh yes." She laughed, and her laugh was like music, he thought. It was her mother's laugh. She headed down the hall and disappeared through the last doorway.

Father John followed and poked his head around the door frame. Shannon was examining the laptop, the easy chair, the braided rug the bishop had resurrected from the storage closet, the wall poster of Arapaho dancers whirling about at a powwow, a blur of bright reds, blues, and yellows. A cozy office Bishop Harry had made his own. But then, the bishop could probably make any place his own. Wasn't that part of the calling? To go wherever you were sent, and make the place your own?

"Very comfy," Shannon said with the bishop beaming under her approval. She was used to charming her way, Father John was thinking.

"I look forward to more of your home cooking." She pushed the edge of her coat sleeve back and checked her watch again, and then she was through the doorway, leaning back. "Just not this evening. Sorry."

Bishop Harry let out a bark of laughter. "I'd say she's got the number of a couple of bachelors."

"She's like her mother." Father John perched on the seat of the wooden chair in front of the bishop's desk.

"Oh yes. I believe you've mentioned her. Eileen, wasn't it? She married your brother after you went to the seminary. I assume it has been a happy marriage."

Father John took a moment before he said, "I hope so." He

pushed on, as if the topic were unimportant, a thing of the past not worth considering. "There's something I would like to talk to you about."

The bishop lifted a hand and pulled it toward his chest; he might have been waving the words forward. "About Shannon?"

"James," Father John said. Odd how Bishop Harry had jumped ahead. Perhaps the topic would eventually be about Shannon. "Has he mentioned he believes he might have a calling to the priesthood?"

"I gathered as much." The bishop shifted about, settling himself against the back of his chair. "Serving Mass almost every morning before going off to work. Yes, it makes sense he is grappling with a possible change in his life."

"I believe you could be a great help to him. I'm sure you've counseled many young men thinking about entering the priesthood."

"As have you, John. I can see how the man looks up to you. You're his ideal priest."

"I hope that isn't the case." Father John heard the sound of his own laughter, forced and choked. "You have far more experience and the wisdom that comes with it."

Bishop Harry tipied his fingers under his chin and swiveled toward the window. The sun had disappeared behind a sky as flat and gray as a sheet of metal. The bare cottonwoods looked like streaks of brown painted on the exterior of Eagle Hall.

He swiveled back. "I would have to pull out my notes and read through them, refresh myself about some of the issues James may be grappling with. It has been a long time since I went down that path myself, and the times were different then. There's been a lot of research on how to counsel young men considering the priesthood since my day. I would have to read the most recent literature. Quite a project, I would say." The old man's eyes had come alive. "Of course, if you believe I could be of help, I will be glad to offer James my services."

"Thank you." Father John got to his feet and started toward the corridor.

"By the way, you had a call this afternoon."

He stepped back, took the small piece of paper the bishop handed across the desk and read the message scribbled down the middle: *3 p.m. Father Jameson. Please return call as soon as possible.*

"Father Jameson in the provincial's office?" He looked over at the bishop, waiting for confirmation, snatching at time—a little more time here at St. Francis. "Did he say what it was about?" He knew what it was about; the call that had always been coming, down through the weeks and months and the years at the mission.

The bishop shook his head. "Very businesslike, Father Jameson. Said an important meeting had been scheduled. One of my seminary students thirty years ago when I was teaching theology . . ." He shook his head. "Well, one never knows what the Holy Spirit has in mind."

Father John stuffed the message into the pocket of his jeans and glanced at his watch. "I have to go out again," he said. "Should be back in an hour or so."

"Something else has occurred to me," the bishop said as Father John started into the corridor. He swung back. The old man was rocking in his chair, hands clasped over his chest. "It strikes me this new project of counseling James will take quite a bit of my time. I may have to give up other projects, like my cooking lessons." He gave Father John a wide, knowing smile. "But you knew that, didn't you?"

# 10

HER NAME WAS Dolly. At least that's what Vince told his mother. Dolly was all she knew, Betty said, when Vicky had tried to push for some other identification. Dolly lived in an apartment on the northeast side of Riverton, that two-story building with brown shingles on the outside walls, like they had run out of bricks or cement blocks and just kept putting on shingles.

Vicky knew the building. Friendly to Indians; a number of Arapahos lived there, moving in and out, piling in with friends for a time. Dolly lived on the ground floor, first door on the left, a fact that Betty White Hawk remembered from the time Vince had called and said he was sick and she had picked him up there.

"How do you know he's there?" Vicky had asked. She could still feel the raw irritation she had felt after Vince threw her hard-won deal with the prosecuting attorney out the window and took off.

"Jason Eagle, you know him?" Betty hurried on, not waiting for an answer. "He didn't want to tell me. You know, boozers don't snitch, sort of a code, cover each other's tracks. I convinced him you were the only hope Vince had for staying out of Rawlins. Nobody wants to get sent down there. The county jail looks like a resort compared to prison, so Jason stalled and tried to make me believe he'd call me back. I said, 'Jason, I know too much about you. Tell me where Vince went.' The minute he said, 'Dolly's place,' I thought, geez, I should've figured he'd go running to his ex-girlfriend. I called over there and Dolly picked up. Took ten minutes to get her to admit Vince was sleeping it off in the bedroom."

That had been thirty minutes ago. Vince White Hawk was like a shadow that crossed time zones, disappeared in the blink of an eye. Vicky had thrown on her coat, grabbed her bag, and, on the way out the door, told Annie to have Roger handle her afternoon appointments—there were two: Mo Standing Bull seeking workmen's compensation for injuries at the loading dock where he worked, and Mara Whiteman, facing a third DUI charge. Roger was perfectly capable of explaining options and consequences and suggesting possible steps.

And Vince could already be gone. Vicky tightened her grip on the steering wheel and pressed down on the gas pedal, pushing the Ford as fast as she dared, past the pine trees drooping under pillows of snow, past the bungalows that resembled her own office, to Main Street. She followed the wide curve out of town, through Hudson and north onto Highway 789.

On instinct now. She had a sense of where the brown-shingled apartment building was located, but not the exact address. God, she could be driving up and down side streets for fifteen minutes before she happened across it, and Vince would melt away.

She wondered why she cared. She had done her best to help this twenty-two-year-old, despite the message drummed into her at the law firm in Denver where she had worked after graduating from law school: save your energy and time—the firm's precious, expensive time—for appreciative clients who work with you, not against you. And wasn't that exactly what Adam Lone Eagle had said when they practiced together in Lander? Holden and Lone Eagle, specializing in natural resources law, important matters. Losers don't deserve you, Adam used to say. Which she supposed made logical sense, in Adam's world. But weren't they the reason she had gone to law school? The losers, the people who *couldn't* help themselves? They had gone separate ways: She, back to what Adam always called "little cases," and he, to a large natural-resources law firm in Denver.

Up ahead, on the corner, she spotted the brown-shingled building. The street was unplowed, thick with snow, crust-hardened and slushy at the same time. She steered the Ford alongside the curb, got out, and hurried up the sidewalk to the door. She rapped twice, hard, and leaned in close, listening for footsteps, the scrape of a chair. Nothing. She glanced about. No sign of Vince's tan pickup on either side of the street. She could feel her heart hammering. The friend would have called Dolly, who would have told Vince, and Vince would have taken off.

She removed her glove and knocked again, and this time, the thin wooden door jumped beneath her fist. "Vince," she called. "I know you're here." That was a laugh. There was no reason in the world to believe he was still here. "It's Vicky Holden. Open up."

She heard it then, a slow shushing noise, like wind blowing through a tiny crack. The door slid open the width of a chain lock, and part of a face appeared, a single eye, a Cyclops, blinking at her. "Dolly? I'm Vince's lawyer. I have to talk to him."

The door slammed shut. There was the rattling, disengaging noise of the chain breaking loose, then the door opened wider. Filling up the narrow space was a young woman, slender, bent forward, as fragile-looking as a twig that might snap in two. Blond, with eyes like pewter, flat and opaque. It took Vicky by surprise, the blond hair and white face and arms that hung from a tee shirt with ragged edges where the sleeves had been. She had expected Dolly to be Indian. Arapaho. This was an apartment building where Arapahos lived.

"He's not here." The woman could have been anywhere between eighteen and forty, vacant-looking, with sunken eyes above sharp cheek bones and the sucked-in look of a woman who no longer had back teeth. Meth did that to people.

Vicky could almost taste the defeat rolling off the woman. "Are you Dolly?"

She hunched her shoulders and gave a slow, obsequious nod. Yes, she was Dolly.

"Where is he?" Vicky tried to push past the sadness of it, the loss of a life.

Signs of a struggle worked through Dolly's expression: the desire of an addict to please warring against the desire to protect a man she might love, who might even love her. "I'm trying to help him," Vicky said. God, Vince could be miles away, heading to some obscure house on the rez where no one would think to look for him. He could hide out for days. Sooner or later, it was bound to happen, one of his buddies would give him up and the cops would show up and Vince would fight or run or try to do both, and he could be shot.

"I can't help him if I don't know where he is. Look . . ." Vicky leaned in closer. There was the acrid smell of some half-dead thing about the woman.

The pewter eyes blinked against the moisture welling at the corners. "I promised not to tell anybody."

"If you care about Vince, help me to help him."

That seemed to convince her. The signs of struggle disappeared, the pale face hardened in a new resolve: She would have to help Vince because, yes, he loved her. She was sure he loved her. She said, "You just missed him."

"I need to know where I can find him."

"He left to get some more booze. He needed a drink real bad, and I didn't have nothing left."

"Is he coming back?"

She gave a weak smile and shook her head. "Like I said, I didn't have nothing around. He'll go drink somewhere else 'til he gets enough of it and is sick as a dog, then he'll come back around. He always does."

"Where did he go for the booze?"

She lifted her thin shoulders. "He was pretty thirsty."

The nearest liquor store, Vicky was thinking. She tried to picture where that would be. On Federal, a few blocks away. She thanked Dolly and hurried down the sidewalk, barely aware of the door cracking shut behind her. Vince had a good ten or fifteen minutes on her.

Vicky spotted him as she turned into the parking lot in front of the liquor store. Stooped forward like an old man, wearing a dark sweatshirt, clutching a brown bag to his chest. The door swung shut behind him as he started weaving toward the tan pickup at the curb.

She drove down the rows of parked vehicles and braked in front of Vince, who jumped sideways, surprise and fear stamped on his face. She jumped out, walked around, and stood between him and the driver's side of the pickup. "We had an appointment," she said.

He tossed his head back and forth, as if there might be some-place to run, fright and desperation in his eyes. "I got other things to do."

"We have to talk. Let me buy you a cup of coffee." Vicky set her hand on the man's arm. Pulling him forward, guiding him along the snow-patched sidewalk, past the liquor store, the barber shop, the knitting store to the coffee shop. She could feel the trembling deep inside him. And something else: the hard metal of a gun be-neath his jacket.

"This is no good." He yanked himself free.

"It's important, Vince. You can use a cup of coffee." She held the door open and gestured him inside. The booth next to the door was empty, used napkins and cups with traces of coffee in the bottoms piled in the center. The next booth had been cleared, but it was a good three feet farther into the shop, an extra moment in which he could swing around and run back outside.

She handed him into the red plastic seat and sat down on the other side of the table. "The sheriff is expecting us," she said.

"Well, I changed my mind." Vince was still holding the brown bag close to his chest, leaning over it so that the top of the bag crumpled under his chin. "No way am I going there."

"It's your only chance."

The waitress appeared and scooped the dirty cups and napkins onto a tray, then waited, as if words weren't necessary for the obvious.

Vicky leaned toward Vince. "Do you want something to eat?"

He threw her a dismissive look. Food wasn't what he wanted. She couldn't decide where he was in the cycle of alcoholic addiction: Coming off a bender? Going into a bender? Not yet sick enough to have been drinking for a while, she realized. Vince was still getting started.

"Two coffees." Vicky waited until the waitress had turned on her heel and disappeared into the back of the shop, then she said, "I've worked out the best deal possible." She kept her voice low, confidential. "Now is not the time to walk away."

"I don't want nothing to do with the law."

"You don't have a choice." My God, what was he thinking? The whole legal system would just ignore an attempted robbery charge? "You tried to steal a woman's grocery money at the ATM outside the supermarket. You're all over the video. You were there, you did it, and the prosecuting attorney can't overlook it."

"Jeez, Vicky. You're supposed to be my lawyer. I told you what happened. I just asked if she had any extra change 'cause I was . . ." He bit on his lower lip a moment. "I was bad thirsty. I needed a bottle."

"A good story." Vince White Hawk could charm snakes. He could conjure any scenario he wanted. "The prosecuting attorney has watched the video and so have I. You were aggressive and threatening. The woman threw her purse at you and ran for her life."

Vicky leaned back. The waitress was at the table again, delivering cups of coffee, a metal pitcher of milk, a bowl of sugar packets. She rummaged in the pockets of her apron and pulled out two spoons, which she dropped next to the cups.

"Look . . ." Vicky said, moving forward against the edge of the table when the waitress had left. "You turn yourself in, and Peters will consider lowering the charges from attempted robbery to a misdemeanor." She was thinking she would have to find a way to get the gun before she took him in. "It's your choice whether you do time in Rawlins," she went on, "or in the county jail with a rehab program thrown in. We have to be at the sheriff's office this afternoon, the sooner the better. Not tomorrow after you've finished off the bottles."

He was shaking his head, and Vicky realized he had been shaking his head the whole time, denying, refusing. "I'm telling you, there's no way I'm giving myself up."

"What is it? You were willing to go along with the deal. What's changed?"

"I got plans." Vince tried to lift his coffee cup, then set it down, hands shaking. Brown liquid sloshed over the top and ran in rivulets along the table. She knew what had changed. Vince had been desperate for booze. So desperate last week he had tried to rob a woman at an ATM. There was no money for booze, so he had agreed to the deal. Since then he had somehow come into money to buy the three bottles in the brown bag. And he had a gun.

"I'm laying low on the rez until I can get out of here. So far away the cops'll never find me." He bent his head over the bag and slurped at the coffee.

"Listen to me, Vince. They will find you. They will find you at whatever drinking house you hide out in. One of your buddies will snitch on you to get some kind of a deal for himself. Every cop in the county will be looking for you. You'll never make it out of here." She took a moment, watching for any sign that what she'd said had sunk in. "Where did you get the money?"

Vince slurped at the coffee, his eyes on the table.

"The money for the booze. The money to leave here. Gas. Food. Motels. Booze. Where did you get the money?"

"You're crazy." He had started shaking, as if the trembling she had felt earlier had worked its way to the surface and spread over him like a rash.

"Your mother's worried sick." Vicky tried a different tack. "She wants you to take the deal."

"You don't get it. Everything's different." Vince went back to his coffee. "There's no more deal."

"I can take you to the prosecuting attorney's office and he can explain your options."

Vince pulled himself upright, still shaking. "I got my pickup here," he said, as if that were the most important matter.

"I'll arrange to have your pickup taken to your mother's."

He didn't protest. She had worn him down, she was thinking. He really didn't have any options. She glanced around for the waitress, but there was no one at the counter. The shop was empty. Then the waitress sauntered out from the back, as if she had been summoned, and took up her place behind the cash register.

Vicky dug several bills out of her wallet. "Wait here." She slid out of the booth, walked over to the counter and plopped down the bills. She told the frozen-faced waitress to keep the change, then turned back.

The booth was empty, the door still swinging shut. Through the plate glass window, she watched Vince weave toward the pickup, holding on to the brown bag as if it were a wall that held him upright. She stopped herself from running after him. She couldn't stop him.

She watched him fall into the pickup, then lean out so far to pull the door shut that, for a moment, she expected him to tumble onto the pavement. There was a burst of black exhaust as the pickup backed up, then shot forward toward the street. A cop will stop him, she thought. God, let a cop stop him before he kills somebody.

# 11

STEEL-GRAY CLOUDS MASSED over the mountains and crept across the reservation and into town. Snowflakes dotted the windshield. Vicky fiddled with the temperature controls until the heater whirred into life and warm air burst from the vents. In the short time she and Vince had been in the coffee shop, the temperature had plunged ten degrees. Another storm on the way, with fresh snow piling on the corrugated surfaces of last night's storm.

She reached inside her bag on the passenger seat, found her cell, and ran a finger over Betty White Hawk's number. A phone rang somewhere on the rez, long beeps that melted into Betty's voice: "Hi. Can't take your call right now. Leave a message."

Vicky swiped disconnect. The time at the top of the phone was 3:48. Betty was a custodian at St. Francis Elementary School on the road to the mission, twenty minutes away. She might still be at work. Vicky could swing by the school, give Betty the bad news that her son would probably hole up in a drinking house tonight and drink himself senseless. But there was always the chance he could regain his senses tomorrow and agree to give himself up before the cops called out the SWAT team.

Except that the deal with the prosecuting attorney would be off the table. The deadline was almost an hour away. With any luck, she could talk to Betty and get ahold of Jim Peters before he left for the day. She would have to convince him to extend the deal.

She drove past the warehouses, liquor stores, and trailer parks that led out of town, then took the turn into the reservation. The snow was getting heavier. Always a surprise, how fast the weather could change. Touches of spring one moment, a blizzard the next. All part of life on the plains, and probably the reason her people had become experts at adapting. You had to know how to adapt, change your plans in the space of a heartbeat, hunker down in the storms and make new plans. And wait. Survival required adaptation and patience.

Rising into the gray sky was the blue billboard with white letters that spelled out *St. Francis Mission*. The rear tires skidded on the slippery new snow as she slowed for the turn onto the mission grounds. Familiar, all of it. The cottonwoods, bare and silent with snow tracing the branches, marshaled on either side of the road. She hadn't seen John O'Malley in several months. She laughed at the idea of not remembering the last time she had seen him. Of course she remembered. The exact day, the sun moving west, a red ball of fire gathering energy for the plunge over the mountains and the wind plucking the sleeves of his plaid shirt. She tried to blink back the memory because memories never meant anything, except that she missed their times working together for her people. She would not blink away the memory of those times.

Just before the road bumped into Circle Drive, which wound through the mission grounds, she turned right onto the road to the school. The low brick building with the two-story entrance shaped like a tipi lifted into the sweep of gray clouds overhead. A few pick-ups and cars stood about the parking lot next to the school. She slowed down and scanned the side of the road for the driveway, a narrow spread of gravel and snow that crossed the barrow ditch. She swung right, took a diagonal route across the parking lot to the front of the school, and parked at the sign that read Buses Only.

Inside the entrance, the tipi poles rose high overhead around glass panes that shimmered in the fading light. The school had the shocked, left-behind feeling of a deserted building, the life and energy having moved elsewhere without warning. Faint smells of wet wool and used crayons and mud-caked boots floated down the wide corridor that led to the classrooms. At the mouth of the corridor was a glass-enclosed office under bright ceiling lights. The door in the back opened and a round-faced woman with black, silver-streaked hair walked over to the counter that divided the office from the corridor. She slid back a glass window. "Help you?" she called.

"I'm Vicky Holden. I'd like a brief word with Betty White Hawk."

The woman was shaking her head, silver streaks in her hair catching the ceiling lights. "Betty's on duty. She'll finish her shift soon." She stole a glance at her watch. "You'll have to wait outside."

"I'm her lawyer, and I need to speak to her now."

Lawyer. The word tumbled across the woman's expression. Well, one never knew. A custodian with a lawyer.

"It will only take a moment."

The woman pushed a clipboard across the threshold of the window. "Sign in here. Technically, I shouldn't allow this, but if Betty's in some kind of trouble . . ."

"She isn't." Vicky signed her name and added the time: 4:13. "Where can I find her?"

"She usually finishes up in first grade. Three doors down on the left."

Vicky thanked the woman and started along the green vinyl that gleamed like polished marble. The roar of a motor flooded the corridor. She followed the noise to the third door. Inside, Betty White Hawk hunched over a machine that crawled along the floor, its giant brush reaching under desks and chairs. The noise expanded inside the classroom like wind funneled through a canyon. Vicky maneuvered around a desk and waved. It took a moment before Betty located the switch and turned off the machine. She stood up straight, fingers tightened around the handle as if she were ready to meet bad news head-on with the machine for strength. "Where's Vince?"

"I don't know." Vicky leaned back against the edge of a desk, grateful for the solid support. "I found him at a liquor store in Riverton. For a few minutes I thought he would come with me to turn himself in, but . . ."

Betty waved away the rest of it. "Vince can make you believe anything. He can change the temperature, the time of day, the day itself, all by making you believe it's different. You know what's funny? He can make you think you got the facts all botched up. I swear"—she was shaking her head, half laughing, half crying—"my son should go to Hollywood and get in the movies. He'd be the best. He's handsome enough, don't you think?" She was crying now, shoulders shaking, knuckles turning white on the handle. "Everything going for him, except the booze. He can't lay off the booze. He's gone somewhere to drink, right?"

Vicky waited a moment to allow the reality to claim its own

place, fill up the vacancy in the room. "There's one thing I don't understand."

Betty let out a harrumph. "Only one?" She found a tissue in the pocket of her blue jeans and mopped at the moisture on her cheeks. "Sometimes I think I don't understand anything about my son. I've been thinking he's been two or three different people, depending on what he wants you to believe. Vince was twelve when his daddy died, but he figured out he had to be two people. The boy and the man in the house. He had to take care of things, and I . . ." She was crying again, blotting the corners of her eyes. "I encouraged him. He was like a headstrong pony, and I gave him his way. So there he was, fifteen and already drinking like his daddy. He made me believe he could do anything, even quit drinking if he wanted. I've been praying for him to want that."

"Where did he get the money to go on a bender?"

"What?" Betty's eyes opened in wide circles. She went back to gripping the handle.

"It takes money to drink. He had three bottles in a brown bag when I found him. Last week he tried to rob a woman for money to buy booze. What has he been up to? Did he rob somebody else?" God, it was possible. Staged a robbery, and this time got away with it.

Betty looked as if she had been jolted by a live wire. Then she studied the floor for half a minute before she glanced up, shaking her head. "I gave him money yesterday . . ."

"You gave him money?"

"Five dollars. Not enough . . ." She let her voice trail off. "He was flat broke, and he needed gas money to meet up with some friends. He promised he'd give himself up today, so I figured, what difference did it make if he had a little fun before he went to jail?"

She gripped the handle, knuckles popping out like rocks, then turned sideways and stared at the rows of crayoned stick-figure drawings tacked to the wall.

"What is it?"

Betty stayed quiet a long moment. Finally, she looked back. "It's nothing."

But it was something, Vicky knew. Something different and new had invaded the space between them, like a physical presence she could sense but not see.

"Tell me, Betty. How did he get the money? What are you afraid of?"

The woman's fingers moved toward the switch. "Vince is a good boy," she said. "He didn't do anything. Got drunk sometimes, and tried to panhandle that woman, but that was because he needed another drink real bad. He never would have hurt her. Vince wouldn't hurt anyone."

"Then what are you afraid of?"

"I don't know what you're talking about." An index finger moved up and down on the switch.

"Listen to me. I'm trying to help your son. He has a chance if he turns himself in. If there is anything you can tell me . . ."

"I already told you what I know."

"Who did he go out with last night?"

"What?" A dull, opaque look clouded the woman's eyes.

"What friends? He could be with them now."

Betty bit her lip. "How would I know? Vince has lots of friends."

"You knew who to call this morning. You found out Vince had gone to his old girlfriend's place."

"Yeah. Well, I got lucky." She had bitten her lip so hard that a tiny trickle of blood started down the crease alongside her chin.

"Besides, chances are none of his other friends are snitches. So what does it matter who they are?"

"I can't help Vince if you won't help me." This was becoming her mantra, she thought. Help me to help a client who doesn't want my help.

Betty was shaking her head. She stared at the ceiling and ran her finger over the switch. "He'll be okay. He knows what he's doing. He's always had what you call a sixth sense about what's best for him."

"Don't you understand? The police will come for him with guns. Anything could happen." And would happen, she was thinking. "I need to find your son."

Betty stared into some distant space beyond the desks and the tacked-up papers as if she were considering the possibilities. After a moment, she blinked and brought her eyes back to Vicky. "This is all a mistake. Vince must think he's going to be railroaded into prison 'cause he stopped a white woman and asked for a little help. It's no reason to put a man in prison. He's desperate. He knows what he's got to do."

Vicky took a moment before she said, "There's something else. I think Vince is carrying a gun."

Betty dropped her eyes and studied the vinyl floor, flecked with brush strokes and lines of wax. She gave a little shrug. There was effort in the way she brought her eyes back to Vicky's. "Ridiculous. Why would Vince carry a gun?"

"Does he own one?"

"He never pulled a gun on that woman at the ATM."

"No, but he's carrying a gun now. Level with me, Betty, or I can't help him." Vicky waited, hoping the woman would say something that made sense. Her son was on the run, and he was carrying a gun, which made it all the more dangerous for the cops to try to arrest him. Betty White Hawk was making excuses, denying facts.

The woman flipped on the switch, and the noise rose to a high, whining pitch. The conversation was over.

Vicky took her time. Turning around, walking toward the door, waiting for the noise to stop and Betty White Hawk to call her back. The noise followed her down the corridor and into the tipi. The glass in the high, pointed ceiling had turned dark with the oncoming dusk.

She sat in the Ford several minutes, replaying every conversation with Betty. Two days ago, Betty had come to the office and begged her to help her son. She had seemed to understand the importance of the deal Vicky had struck with the prosecuting attorney. This morning, Betty had called to say that Vince had disappeared. Then, another call: he was at Dolly's. Always cooperative. At what point had her attitude changed?

The money. The truth of it jumped out at her like a rattlesnake. Vince had gotten his hands on some money, maybe a lot of money. Enough to purchase bottles of whiskey. Enough to make him think he didn't need a deal. Enough to take off, light out of here.

That was what had frightened his mother—the thought of what Vince might have done to get the money.

Vicky fished the mobile out of her bag and tapped in the prosecuting attorney's number. It took a moment to get past the secretary to Jim Peters himself. "I'm going to need more time," she told him. "A couple of days."

"Any more fairy tales?" Peters made no effort to conceal the disdain in his voice. "I take it your client skipped."

"Vince is a sick man. He's drinking, and he's incapable of making a rational decision until he sobers up."

The line went quiet for several seconds; nothing but the faint sound of breathing. "You got a one-day extension," Peters said finally. "Then we're coming for him."

The call ended before she could say anything. She stared out the windshield. The day was moving into evening, shadows lengthening. The voice rang in her head: *we're coming for him.*

Finally, she made herself check her messages. One message, from Rick Masterson. "Dinner tonight?"

# 12

THE FALLING SNOW diminished the buildings that crouched against the darkness on Main Street. The sidewalks were empty, snow piled everywhere. An eerie orange glow hovered over the streetlamps. Vicky gripped the steering wheel hard as she drove along the stretch where Clint Hopkins had been struck, forcing herself to focus straight ahead, avoiding the place where she had left Clint and turned back to Rick. The dark figure was still there, looming before her.

She drove onto the next block and parked in front of the restaurant. The dining room on the other side of the foggy plate glass windows was nearly empty, a few customers scattered at the tables, a waitress moving listlessly about. A sheen of ice shimmered on the sidewalk. Warm air wrapped around her like a blanket the instant she stepped inside. A man in a white shirt hurried over. "One?" he said, examining a seating chart on top of the podium.

Vicky started to say she was meeting someone when Rick Masterson materialized out of the dining room. "She's with me," he said.

"Oh yes." The man started to pick up a menu, but Rick waved it away. He helped her out of her coat and hung it on the rack. His hand was firm and confident against her back as he guided her through the dining area to a table next to the window.

"I'm glad you called," he said when they had sat down. "I've been wondering how you're doing. Last night was pretty tough."

Vicky spread a red napkin on her lap and studied the menu. How should she be doing? Was there a protocol, a way of behaving, after witnessing a death?

She glanced up at the man on the other side of the table. "I went to see Clint's wife and daughter this morning." She hesitated. "It made the whole thing real. Until then it was like a nightmare. I'm not sure which is worse. Reality or nightmare."

"Do you care for a drink?"

"No thanks." Is this what alcoholics like Vince were in search of? A place between nightmare and reality?

A waitress had appeared: black hair pulled into a ponytail, orange-red lips, blue-black eyebrows, and a notepad in one palm. They ordered ravioli, lasagna, garden salads. One glass of red house wine.

"How about you?" Vicky asked when the waitress had walked away.

"Trying to stay busy to keep the images out of my mind."

"Clint starting across the street in the snow." Vicky left the rest of it unspoken: headlights and the truck out of nowhere. The words would only bring the image into clearer focus.

Rick was nodding. His eyes were gray, almost silver, and they caught the light the way a piece of metal catches light. He had a broad forehead and a prominent chin with laugh lines carved into the sides of his mouth. Flecks of gray shone in his sandy hair. It struck her that he was handsome.

He started to say something, then sat back and waited while the waitress delivered the plates of food, all of it crowding the tabletop. She added two waters, the glass of red wine. When she left, Rick lifted the wine and said, "To happier times."

He took a sip, set the glass down, and leaned forward. "It's been a hard day. Everywhere I went, people wanted to talk about Clint. It was like a shockwave had hit town, and people were reeling, trying to make sense of it."

Vicky took a bite of the ravioli. Hot and spicy, and she realized how hungry she was. She hadn't stopped to eat all day. She took another bite and thought about how different her day had been. Except for Clint's wife and secretary and the Little Shields, nobody else had mentioned the man's death. Not Vince White Hawk. Not his mother. As if it had happened in another time zone, somewhere far away and unimportant.

"There are a lot of theories about Clint," Rick said. He worked at the lasagna a moment before he sat back again and gazed at her. "He was a damned good lawyer. Every other lawyer I talked to today mentioned how good he was, especially at adoption cases. Nobody wanted to be on the opposing side of Clint Hopkins. He was dogged and thorough. Kept all the details in his head, but no one could cross him up. Interesting way to practice law. Almost as if he feared someone looking over his shoulder."

Vicky nodded. She pushed the plate of ravioli away and started on the salad. "I know he had a good reputation."

"Not in everything."

She looked up. "What are you saying?"

"You know how it is. Someone dies a sudden death, and people start to remember things they had forgotten, or chosen not to remember. A couple of lawyers brought up Clint's secretary, Evie Moran.

Evidently she's a big part of his success. Started working for him when she was still in high school and never left."

The words fell like stones between them. Vicky stared at the man for a couple of seconds. "What are you implying?"

Rick spread both hands on the table. "I'm not implying anything. No one made any outright accusations . . ."

"That there was something more between them than a professional relationship."

Rick shook his head. "I gathered he meant the world to her. He was her life. And he depended on her."

Vicky sat back. She reached for her water and took a couple sips, trying to organize the thoughts tumbling through her mind. "Someone could have had a motive to arrange for Clint's death."

Rick blinked at her, as if she had pulled a rabbit out of a hat and were holding it up for display. "It was an accident. The driver didn't see him in the snow. Clint was like a shadow."

"Why didn't the driver stop?" Vicky felt a surge of annoyance. It was no accident. It was as obvious as the white tablecloth, the half-eaten ravioli and lasagna, the traces of wine in the glass. "If Clint was having personal problems . . ."

"I didn't say that."

"An inappropriate relationship with his secretary that he refused to give up. Maybe his wife found out. Either woman might have been desperate, not thinking straight."

"Listen to me, Vicky. You are not thinking straight. We don't know anything inappropriate was going on. Do you really believe either his wife or his secretary could have . . ." He paused and searched the ceiling for the exact words. "Arranged for his death?"

"It happens." Vicky rolled her napkin and tossed it onto the table.

"The driver didn't see him. It was an accident. A terrible accident. The driver was frightened, so he drove away. He might not have realized he'd hit someone. He could come forward as soon as he gets the nerve, and we'll know the truth."

"You were there, Rick. Walking beside me. We saw the same thing." God, it was so obvious. "The truck waited down the street until Clint came out of the restaurant, carrying a stupid briefcase. Who carries a briefcase to a dinner meeting? The driver spotted him, cranked up the engine, and pulled out into the street. Going for him, the dark, shadowy figure in the snow."

"Don't make it something that it wasn't, Vicky. It's terrible enough."

Vicky got to her feet, barely aware of Rick standing up beside her, the soothing tone of his voice—"Wait. Hold on."—as if he were trying to reason with a balky child. "Don't run off."

She found some bills in her bag and tossed them on the table. "I know what I saw." It was still in front of her, and Rick Masterson wanted her to believe she had seen something else. That she was delusional, imagining things, coming up with plausible explanations, not thinking straight.

"Don't tell me I didn't see what I saw." She threw the comment over her shoulder as she started for the door.

# 13

TEN THIRTY, AND still no sign of Shannon and James. Father John felt like a parent, pacing the floor, listening for an engine on Circle Drive. The mission grounds were shrouded in falling snow, the streetlights shimmering gold against the black sky.

He forced himself back into his chair and stared at his laptop screen. James Two Horses had shown up just before six o'clock, a loud roar that swung into the curb in front of the residence and cut off. Then he was at the front door, knocking softly, as if he could conceal his excitement and determination. Shannon had walked over from the guesthouse and was standing in the entry. She hadn't even removed her coat and scarf. She opened the door and James had burst in.

"Hope I'm on time."

Well, yes, he was. From the kitchen came sounds of dishes and pots and pans clanking together and the noise of running water.

Father John was about to suggest that Shannon and James have dinner here. Elena always made plenty of food, in case someone dropped by. It was the Arapaho Way.

"A good hamburger place has opened up in town," James said, all of his attention focused on Shannon. "Are you up for hamburgers?"

Shannon assured him that she was and began snapping together the fronts of her coat, which she had just unsnapped. He supposed he shouldn't be surprised. He had seen the look that passed between them earlier outside his office. They had gone off, a young woman with things still unsettled with her boyfriend back home and a young man who might have a vocation to the priesthood. One never knew, could never predict. Human beings, always full of contradictions and surprises.

Was that how he had be been almost thirty years ago? Picking up Eileen at her apartment for a bite to eat at the local hamburger joint, or was it that mom-and-pop Italian place they'd liked, where no one spoke English and they had to guess about the menu, which made it fun, exciting. All the time, the voice playing like a melody in the back of his head: *Whom Shall I Send?*

Now he tried to concentrate on the list of Web sites he had pulled up. He had started with Elizabeth Fletcher, which produced an overview of the surprise Indian attack on Jasper Fletcher's wagons on a sunny, blue-sky day in Wyoming. Jasper had come from England, where he and his brothers owned coal mines, which put him in a higher social status, he believed, than the other men on their way to the California gold fields who had nothing except dreams and scrawny women and children. They built fires out of timber scavenged on the plains, roasted hanks of deer, if they were lucky, or rabbit. Content to stay alive.

It was better to pull ahead, distance themselves from the rabble. Until the Indians had ridden out of the sagebrush and the hot dust. When it was over, Jasper lay wounded, his wife dead. Their young sons had made a run for it, and the Indians had let them go, too busy tearing into the wagons for food and clothing and pots and utensils. When they rode off, they took the girls, Amanda Mary and Elizabeth.

Father John skimmed the rest of the site: how Amanda Mary was rescued seven months later, how Elizabeth grew up, became an Arapaho, married John Brokenhorn, and lived on the Wind River Reservation.

Nothing that Shannon called "outside of history," such as how Lizzie had felt about her life. He had closed the site, typed in Lizzie Brokenhorn, and another list materialized. The noise of an engine gearing down came from outside. His senses went on alert, a thousand tiny antennae sprouting on his skin. The noise faded into the distance. A truck out on Seventeen-Mile Road.

Past eleven o'clock now. How long did it take to eat a hamburger? Stop it, he told himself. He trusted James Two Horses. Trusted the man with his niece.

He scanned the Web sites, looking for something different, personal. Halfway down the page he read: Lizzie Brokenhorn on the reservation. He clicked on the link and waited for the text to sort itself onto the page. It was a short newspaper article, a feature story on how a white woman had lived as an Arapaho for almost fifty years. How she had had five children who'd grown to adulthood.

He moved to the second page. Here was something: The photo of a crumbling shack on the plains, the panorama of the foothills in the background and splotches of sunshine on the barren ground. He enlarged the photo and read the caption: "The cabin built by John Brokenhorn for his wife and family."

He sat back, taking it in. He had passed the shack a thousand times, out on Blue Sky Highway, falling down and forgotten, a barbed wire fence running next to the road. So this was where Lizzie and John Brokenhorn had lived. He'd had no idea of the history attached to a shack that resembled nothing more than a pile of logs. But why wouldn't the shack have a story? There were stories all over the reservation; the past was everywhere.

This time the noise of an engine was coming closer, growing louder through the tunnel of cottonwoods. He got up and peered out the window, wondering what Shannon would make of his attempt to stand in for her father, waiting for her to come home. He laughed out loud. She was twenty-four years old, an adult, hardly in need of her father—or, for that matter, her uncle—telling her what to do. He watched the thin stream of headlights bounce through the snow and turn onto Circle Drive.

He went back to the computer, relief washing over him, and pressed the print button. The old printer on the bookshelf whirred into life. He grabbed the photo of the old cabin as soon as the printer spit it out, then checked the window again, expecting to see James's pickup turning into the alley between the church and the administration building.

A sedan, light colored and splotched with snow, was wobbling and slipping around the drive, heading toward the residence. He felt as if an icy hand had clutched his heart. What was this? What bad news at this time of night? What had happened to Shannon?

He watched a woman—slight looking, bundled in an outsized jacket, scarf looped around her neck, a dark hat pulled low over her forehead, head bent against the snow—start up the sidewalk.

Father John opened the door as Betty White Hawk was about to knock, a fist lifted like that of a boxer. Gratitude and something else—worry, despair—crossed her face. "Oh, thank God, you're still up. I didn't know where else to go."

"Come in." He pulled the door back. She lunged inside, bringing with her the frosty cold and pellets of snow that flew around her. He helped her with the jacket, draped it over the hook above the bench, and motioned her into the study.

"What's going on?"

"It's Vince."

He could have guessed as much. A talented athlete, Vince had played shortstop for the St. Francis Eagles. Smart kid, doing well in school, looking at a promising future. Then alcohol and most likely drugs, and a tough crowd, had taken over. He had dropped out of school, out of his life. This wasn't the first time Betty had come to the mission gripped in desperation.

"Can I get you something? Coffee?" He pulled an armchair closer to his desk.

Betty White Hawk sank down and shook her head, the frivolity of sipping coffee absurd, out of the question. He walked around the desk and sat down. "Talk to me," he said.

"He's in trouble, and I don't know where to find him."

"You mean for attempted robbery?" Last week the *Gazette* had reported that Vince White Hawk was wanted for trying to rob a woman at an ATM machine in Riverton. The article said the police were looking for him.

Betty nodded. The despair sat on her thin shoulders like a heavy cape. She was still fairly young, early forties, he guessed. Raising her son on her own, sitting in the bleachers and cheering him on, bringing cupcakes for the team. She had once been pretty. She looked faded and worn now, as if a gauzy veil had fallen over her face.

"Vicky made a deal with the prosecuting attorney," she said.

"She was supposed to bring in Vince today and the charges would have been lowered to a misdemeanor. He was supposed to plead guilty and get sent to rehab. God, he needs to go into rehab. He agreed to everything yesterday."

"What happened?"

"What you expect." She shrugged and drew in a long, noisy breath that she held on to as if it were her last. "He went drinking last night. I guess I can't blame him. The thirst overpowers him; he can't help it. One last drink, that's all he wanted."

Father John was quiet. There was more; he could almost see the words bunching in her throat. He had learned from years of counseling and listening to confessions to wait and allow the words to find their own way.

It took a moment before Betty said, "He got some money, so he thinks he can do what he wants. Nobody telling him what to do. No court sending him into rehab. No white people controlling his life. He took off."

"Where did he get the money?" Another robbery attempt, Father John was thinking, one that was successful. He was aware of the cold draft creeping through the windows.

Betty blinked hard and shook her head. "He went out last night and never came home. I called some of his friends and found out he'd gone to an old girlfriend's place in Riverton, so I called Vicky. She went and found him. She told me he had a wad of money on him. Instead of going to the prosecutor's office with her, he took off. I don't know what he's been up to. I don't know who he's been hanging out with. He could have some new friends I don't know about. All I know is, the cops are coming for him and . . ." She closed her eyes against whatever images had materialized. "Somebody's going to die. I'm afraid Vince is going to die."

There was an ominous tone in the woman's voice, as if she had seen the future. "What else haven't you told me?" he said.

"He's carrying a gun. I knew he got an old revolver in a trade last year. Said it was for target practice. Far as I knew, he kept it in a box in his closet. I checked the box. It was empty. Vicky says he had the gun on him. That's how I know he's made up his mind nobody's going to arrest him. He's making a plan. He's going to leave here and go somewhere else. Denver or Los Angeles. Somewhere nobody knows about an arrest warrant for attempted robbery." She drew in another long breath. "I've been calling everybody I can think of. Nobody's seen him. I'm at my wits' end. I don't know what do."

"Is there anything he might have said about his new friends? Anything that might suggest who they are?"

"No. No. No." Betty curled her hands into fists and rubbed at her eyes, then dropped both fists into her lap and stared at him. "I figure he got the money from them. God knows what they've been up to."

"Where could he have met them?"

She gave a shout of laughter that resembled a sob. "Anywhere. Everywhere. No shortage of lowlifes around, especially when you're hooked on alcohol or drugs."

"At a bar? Did Vince go to bars?"

Her head snapped backward. "A bar, yes. That's where he met them. One of the guys I talked to this morning said the last time he'd seen Vince was a couple weeks ago at a bar. What did he say? The Buffalo something . . ."

"Bar and Lounge."

"Yeah." She reached out with both hands, as if she could grab a lifeline. "Vince never said anything about going to a bar, but . . ."

She dropped her hands, fists curled, back into her lap. "He never told me what he was up to. I didn't ask. I didn't want to know."

She jumped to her feet as if a bolt of electricity had hit her. "Somebody at the bar might know where Vince is."

Father John got to his feet and stole a glance at his watch. Eleven fifteen. The bar would probably be open. "I'll go with you," he said.

HE DROVE THE old Toyota, bumping and slipping over the snow, Betty in the passenger seat, her breath a small cloud on the side window. Something different about her now, some twinge of hope running through her. She had pulled on gloves and she clapped her hands, making a soft, swishy noise. The pickup plunged into the tunnel of cottonwoods, the branches sagging under the new snow.

Yellow headlights turned off Seventeen-Mile Road and came toward them. Father John slowed and moved to the edge of the road to make room for the pickup: James giving a little salute in the driver's seat, Shannon beside him, waving.

Father John felt his muscles relax. Of course she was safe.

# 14

RIVERTON LOOKED DESERTED. A few pickups crawling through the snow, streetlights casting a dim glow over the buildings that huddled in the shadows. Father John slowed on Federal and hunched toward the windshield, searching for the Buffalo Bar and Lounge. "On the corner ahead," Betty said, but when it wasn't there, she told him to try the next block. The woman wasn't any more accustomed to visiting the local bars than he was.

There were a number of bars, you realized, when you started looking for one. Each bar an oasis of light and activity with music thumping into the night past the clapboard and shingled walls, the plate glass windows singed with frost.

*Buffalo Bar and Lounge* pulsated in white letters on a sign ahead. The bar itself was a dark brick affair with traces of light escaping around the front door and shimmering in the window. Father John turned into the lot next to the bar and pulled into a vacant space.

The headlights washed over the words *Owner Parking* printed on the curb.

Betty was already out of the pickup. Stomping toward the front door, head bent in the falling snow. He followed her inside. The heavy wooden door rattled and creaked shut behind them. A warm fug of steam mixed with smells of beer and spicy barbecue filled the place. The wide mirror behind the bar reflected the half circles of light that dangled over the tables. A dozen customers lounged about the tables and hung on to the bar. Country music thumped through a loudspeaker.

Betty stood frozen in place, glancing about, taking it in: this was where Vince found new friends, friends who had helped him get a wad of money and the chance to escape.

"He's not here."

Father John wondered how she could be so sure. It was hard to distinguish one patron from another. The same cowboy hats, long-sleeved shirts, blue jeans, and boots. The wide shoulders, tapered backs, and slim waists of men who worked outdoors. The off-shoulder blouses and swishing skirts and cowboy hats of the few women.

Aware of the heads lifting over mugs of beer, the eyes following them, he took Betty's arm and steered her around the tables to the bar. Cowboys had claimed either end of the bar, but the middle was vacant, and that was where he led her. The bartender was a big man, as big as a bouncer, with an apron tied around his waist and a methodical manner about him as he swished glasses in a sink full of soapy water. He looked over, not breaking the back-and-forth rhythm. "Dining room's closed."

"We'll have something at the bar."

"Yeah?" This seemed to take him by surprise. "Hold on a sec."

Betty turned sideways and stared at him with wide, frightened eyes. "All I want is to find Vince."

"What'll it be?" The bartender had moved toward them. He swiped a wet cloth over the bar.

"Two coffees."

"Make mine a Coke." Betty seemed to have caught on that what they needed was information, and information came at a price.

"Irish coffee? Bourbon and Coke?"

"Just plain," Father John said.

The man shrugged, stepped away, and went about pumping Coke out of a nozzle and into a glass. Then he poured a mug of coffee and set them both down. "Never seen you in here before." He put his hands on his waist, elbows crooked outward, and waited.

"Father O'Malley from the mission." Father John nodded at the jar of creamer on the bar and the bartender slid it toward him. "This is Betty White Hawk. She's looking for her son, Vince."

The man was shaking his head. "Look," he said, as if he'd seen the picture and didn't like it, "customers come here for a little R and R, you know what I mean? Maybe they don't like folks knowing where they are." He turned to Betty. "Sorry, ma'am, but that goes for mothers."

Father John stirred some cream into the coffee and took a sip. "You know Vince?"

"I just said . . ."

"He could be in trouble. There might be somebody here who could help us find him. We know he liked to come here." It might be true, he was thinking. "I hear he has friends here. Any of them around?" He turned and glanced about the tables, as if one of Vince's new friends might step forward and identify himself.

"What kind of trouble?"

"Nothing that involves the bar."

"He tried to rob somebody, I heard."

"His lawyer's taken care of that."

Betty was sipping the Coke. She set the glass down. "He can be a hothead. I'm trying to keep him from getting into trouble."

The bartender studied her for a moment, as if a different picture had started to form. The ATM robbery attempt had been taken care of, there wasn't any new trouble. Just the effort to keep Vince away from trouble.

"Tell you the truth, we never had more than a few words. Another Indian from the rez. They're all the same, pretty much stick to themselves. Have a couple beers, ignore everybody else just like the cowboys ignore them." He shrugged. "I don't need any cowboy-Indian trouble. So Vince comes in once in a while . . ."

"Was he here last night?"

"I don't want any trouble."

Father John gave him a nod of understanding.

"Came in early. Ordered a beer, carried it over to a table and had a powwow with another Indian. Only guy I saw him talking to last night. I seen them having a couple drinks together a few times."

"Who was it?" Hope flared in Betty's voice.

"Ask him yourself." He gestured with his chin toward a table over on the side where a thin, bent Indian sat alone, cowboy hat pushed back, empty beer glasses lined up in front. He was working at another beer.

Father John thanked the man, laid a few bills on the bar, and started after Betty, who was already halfway across the dining room, shoulders back, like a runner at the finish line. She stopped at the table as if she had hit an invisible wall and stared down at the soiled, rain-marked brim of the Indian's cowboy hat.

Father John moved in close, slid out a chair, and motioned Betty to sit down. He took the chair between her and the Indian, who was looking at Betty as if she had sprung, genielike, from an empty bottle.

"Don't recall inviting you."

"Sorry to bother you." Father John set both hands, palms down, on the table. He had no intention of leaving, and neither did Betty, a fact the Indian must have comprehended, because he gave a little nod and went back to looking over Betty, who was trembling, face flushed.

After a moment, the Indian shifted sideways. He had a jagged scar that ran across his cheek. "I seen you at the mission," he said. "Who's this?" He tossed his head in Betty's direction.

"You know me." Betty was leaning forward, fists clenched into small balls on the table. "You can't have my son. Tell me where he is, or I swear . . ." She let the rest of it hang like smoke over the table.

"Vince?" The Indian held a steady gaze. He might have been in a poker game.

"White Hawk." There was something between them, Father John was thinking, something out of the past that nipped at the present. But that was true with a lot of families on the rez. Old animosities and conflicts, sometimes going so far back nobody remembered what they were about.

"Are you a friend of his?"

"Might've had a few beers with him." The Indian lifted and dropped his shoulders, as if he were used to shrugging away uncomfortable moments. And yet there was something forced in the gesture, as if he were hiding a deep nervousness.

"What about last night?" Betty leaned even closer. Her breasts pressed into the edge of the table.

"What about it?"

"We're trying to find him," Father John said. "Any idea of where he might have gone? Friends he might be with?"

"He never ran his social calendar by me." The Indian gave another shrug. "So we had some beers a couple times. Don't make me his keeper."

Father John leaned back. "You used to come to the mission?"

"Long time ago."

"Your people still come? Let's see, that would be the Yellow Horses?" He was guessing. The Indian hadn't given his name. The fastest way to find out which family an Arapaho belonged to was to place him in the wrong family.

The Indian sensed the trap. A wily hunter. "Yellow Horses? Never associated with the likes."

"I remember everything," Betty said, keeping her eyes on the man. She leaned in closer. "Vince is all I've got. For God's sake, tell me where he is or . . ." She clamped her lips over the rest of it.

The Indian drew back, bringing the glass of beer with him. "Or what? You gonna cough up a lot of stuff nobody cares about anymore? Can't help you."

Father John took a moment. Whatever lay between the White Hawks and this man was raw and unsettled. "Anyone else," he said, glancing around, "who might have had a few beers with Vince?"

The Indian gave another shrug, finished the last of his beer, and lifted an arm into the air. "Far as I know, Vince tended to his own business. Good idea, I'd say."

The bartender had sauntered over, an unhurried, end-of-the-night air about him. He wiped his hands down the sides of his apron. "About to close," he said.

The Indian looked up sideways, brown neck muscles stretched

out of the collar of his Western shirt. He had a long, narrow face with a hooked nose, as sharp as a blade. "Another beer."

"Haven't you had enough, Lou?"

Lou. Father John had it now. Lou Bearing. Lou and his wife—what was her name? Debbie—had come to Mass a few times when he had first come to St. Francis more than ten years ago. He hadn't seen them since, as if they had disappeared, taken a different path. It happened. Most of his parishioners retained their traditional Indian beliefs. Attended the Sun Dance every summer, went to the sweat lodges and healing ceremonies. The ancient ceremonies that connected them to the ancestors. They still came to the mission. Mass and confessions, baptism and confirmation, funerals. Arapahos were the most spiritual people he had ever been with. Pray and pray and pray some more, he had heard the elders say. Pray in every way.

It was possible that Lou and Debbie had decided to leave off with the mission and keep to the Arapaho ceremonies. Or leave off with all forms of worship. The moderns, the skeptics, those who didn't need any spiritual help because they didn't believe.

He wondered what it had been.

"Just bring me a beer," Bearing said. "I don't need a lecture."

"What about you?" The bartender glanced around the table, but let his gaze linger on Betty. The flush of hope had dissipated, and the pale, worn-out look had returned, making her seem older, tired out.

She waved away the question, and Father John said, "Nothing for me." They were done here, he was thinking as the bartender walked away. Lou Bearing had told them everything he intended to, which was very little. It was what he left unsaid that counted. He knew Vince White Hawk. He drank with him. They'd been drinking together last evening and on other occasions before Vince had miraculously come into a wad of money and started carrying a gun. He had been the only one Vince had talked to in the bar, which suggested that last evening's meeting had been set up, prearranged.

And there was more. Father John had the sense that the man was covering up something.

Father John stood up. Across the table, Betty pushed herself to her feet. She looked unsteady, holding on to the back of the chair. He took hold of her arm and started to turn toward the door, then stepped back. Out of the corner of his eye, he caught the massive figure of the bartender carrying a mug of beer. He leaned close to Bearing. "Whatever trouble Vince is in might implicate you. If you know anything that could help find him, I suggest you help yourself by telling me."

The Indian watched the mug appear on the table, then brought it to his lips. A foamy white mustache smeared the top of his lip when he set the mug down. "You threatening me?"

Father John rapped his knuckles on the table. "If you decide to help, you know where to find me."

"WHAT IS IT?" They were outside in the pickup, the engine sputtering and trying to catch. "Why do you hate him?"

Betty sat hunched over beside him, her breath raspy. She kept her eyes down. "It happened a long time ago. Like he said: nobody cares." Then she looked up at him with so much alarm and pain in her eyes that he leaned closer.

"Betty," he said, "what is it?"

She was shaking her head. "He's going to kill my son."

# 15

THE DOOR WITH *Clint Hopkins, Esq.* etched in the pebble-glass window was locked. Vicky tried the knob a second time, then knocked. A moment passed before a shadow moved across the glass and the door swung open. Evie leaned into the edge. Behind the small, wireless glasses, she had the flushed red-rimmed eyes of someone who had been crying hard.

"Sorry about locking you out." She didn't look sorry. She looked sad and helpless as she gestured Vicky inside

Vicky walked past, taking in the front office at a glance. Desk swept clean, surface polished to a glow. A pair of upholstered visitor's chairs that looked as if they had been vacuumed. Filing cabinet with drawers closed—probably locked—and a small trophy on top with the figure of a golfer. Bookcases against one wall, books neatly stacked around a plant in a pottery bowl and a large, clear vase. The office of a man who was no longer there.

She turned around and realized the young woman was still leaning against the edge of the door. "Are you all right?" Evie Moran, the beautiful secretary Clint had hired out of high school and never let go. And Evie had not wished to leave. It could be true, the gossip. It always struck Vicky at how secretive and tight-lipped lawyers could be about a case, and how schoolgirl gossipy they were about one another.

"It's been so hard," the young woman said. And she was young, Vicky was thinking. Maybe even younger than she had guessed yesterday, but yesterday the secretary had been in shock, drawn and pale. "I mean, Clint was . . ." She stopped and bit into her lower lip. The word she had been about to utter seemed to float in the air between them. *Everything.*

She hurried on: "Crazy people do crazy things. They get hurt, so they strike out, hurt everybody else."

"What are you trying to tell me?" God, she could have hit on the truth. Last night in the restaurant with Rick, she had jumped to the conclusion that Clint's wife might have had motive to arrange his death. A wild conclusion, plucked out of her own exhaustion and shock.

"You said you didn't think it was an accident." Evie was still clinging to the door. "That means somebody killed him."

"We don't know for sure." Vicky could feel the weight of the truth in Evie's words. "I believe the police think it was an accident. The investigation . . ."

"The hell with the investigation." Evie slammed the door, sending little shock waves through the carpeted floor. "They can miss the truth by a mile."

"What do you think happened?"

"Somebody wanted him dead and hired a killer. It happens, you know."

Vicky waited a moment before she said, "Who would want him dead?"

"I'm not saying." The young woman shrugged and rolled her eyes. "I don't want to be next. I've got to think of myself."

"Are you referring to his law practice or to his personal life?"

Evie had been advancing into the room. She tripped forward, then caught herself. "How would I know about his personal life? I don't care what gossip you've heard. I was his secretary."

Vicky absorbed this for a moment. Evie had heard the gossip. Legal secretaries talk to one another. "Do you think," she said, trying to change direction, "someone believes you know whatever Clint knew?"

Evie gave another shrug and sank into a chair. Vacuum streaks ruffled the gray carpet at her feet. "All I know is, I'm out of here as soon as I can get away. I've been tidying up, putting things in order. It's the last thing I can do for Clint. He and a lawyer in Casper had an arrangement to close up each other's practices, if something . . ." She squeezed her eyes shut against the moisture clouding her glasses. "Shouldn't take long to close down. Adoption cases? Not exactly big ticket. A lot of cases Clint took pro bono. He didn't care about money. He fell for any kid with a hardship story. All he wanted was to get kids into safe, permanent homes."

"I'm not following." Vicky perched on the other chair and swiveled in a half circle to face the woman. "Why are you anxious to get away?"

"Maybe he stumbled onto something he shouldn't know. He was always on the internet. Somebody might think I know what he found." The woman tilted her head back and laughed. "He kept things locked in the vault, the vault being his head. He was paranoid about people breaking in or hacking his records."

Dead end. There was nothing there, Vicky was thinking. No sign that Evie Moran believed Clint's wife was behind his death. She could see herself in the restaurant last night, arguing with Rick Masterson over what they had seen, grasping at the gossip and jumping to the conclusion that Lacy Hopkins could have been responsible.

She blinked back that train of thought. She had seen the black truck smash into Clint, toss him over the hood, and no explanations could change that.

"Did you find anything that might be helpful in the Little Shield case?"

Evie looked at her as if she were trying to place her, recall why she was sitting across the office asking questions. Finally, comprehension spread across her face. She jumped to her feet, walked around the desk, and yanked open a drawer, then thrust a folder toward Vicky.

"Clint's calendar for the last couple weeks," Evie said. "People he interviewed on the Little Shield case. I checked his desk in his study to see if he had brought any work home. Funny, when you think about it. He trusted the doors on his house more than the doors here. I found this folder in the top drawer."

Vicky took the folder. Most likely Clint had intended to bring it to her office. He would have explained the details missing from his notes. Without his explanation, she didn't expect any notations on his calendar to make much sense.

The folder contained two sheets, each representing a week, with the days across the top of each sheet. Monday. Tuesday. Wednesday . . . Lines of tight, black writing filled the space beneath each day, the letters as upright as posts. There were various names, followed by comments and memoranda.

She slipped the sheets back into the folder. "Did you make a copy?"

"That is the copy," Evie said.

"If you come across anything else . . ."

The young woman held up a hand, palm out. "I know Clint." She swallowed hard. "There won't be anything else."

ALL LEGAL NOTES are alike: a collection of terse facts. And the notes Clint had jotted on the calendar were the same, except they were more terse and less informative than Vicky had expected.

She lay the calendar pages on her desk, then began marking the names on each page with a yellow highlighter. A dull splash of daylight filled the window. From the outer office came the muffled sound of tapping, then the sound of the phone ringing. Through the beveled-glass doors, Vicky saw the distorted figure of Annie reaching for the phone.

Vicky took the list of contacts Myra Little Shield had left with her and started comparing the names on the list with the names on the calendar. They lined up chronologically. A methodical man, Clint. He had started with the top and proceeded through the list. The buzzer sounded, and she pressed the button. "Betty White Hawk on line one," Annie said.

Vicky lifted the receiver, her gaze still on the pages. "Have you heard from Vince?"

She understood by the silence that the answer was no. A long moment passed before Betty said, "Last night I ran into a man that knows him. I think he knows where Vince is hiding out."

Vicky waited, and finally the voice went on, low and precise, as controlled and deliberate as the upright letters of Clint Hopkins's handwriting. "I remembered Vince saying something about a bar, so we went to the Buffalo Bar and Lounge. We met up with Lou Bearing."

"We?"

"Father John."

John O'Malley. Vicky gripped the phone while the woman went on talking, the words blurring together with no logic or meaning. It had been a long time since she and John had worked together, a long time since anyone had needed both a priest and a lawyer, the excuse that brought them together. At times she had imagined making up an excuse, inventing a client. What a laugh. He would see through it immediately.

"Do you know him?"

"Father John?" Vicky tried to refocus her attention.

"Lou Bearing."

The name was familiar. Vicky glanced down the names on the calendar. She had just run yellow smudges through the name Lou Bearing, listed three different times. Odd, she realized now. Clint had x-ed out three days between the first two mentions of Bearing's name and the last. Also odd: The name was not on Myra Little Shield's list. "What did he tell you?"

"Nothing. He didn't tell us anything. But the bartender said Vince and Lou had a couple beers together the night before last. And he'd seen them drinking together before that. You ever get that feeling when you know, you just know somebody's lying?"

"Who is Lou Bearing? What did Father John say?"

"I don't know. I don't know anymore." There was an edge of hysteria in her voice. "I keep seeing cops at a crummy house somewhere and Vince going crazy. He won't let them take him." She had started crying, loud sobs that bolted down the line. "He's gonna get himself killed."

"Listen to me," Vicky said. "I'll see if I can locate Lou Bearing. It's not too late. I can still bring Vince in today if I can find him."

"Oh my God. You have to find him, Vicky. Please find him."

Vicky was about to say she couldn't make any promises, she would do her best—a mouthful of platitudes that she realized were unnecessary. The line was dead.

She went back to comparing the Little Shields' list with the calendar entries. Clint had visited each person once, yet he had interviewed Lou Bearing three times. Twice on succeeding days, followed by three days that were x-ed out. The third visit was the day he had died. Next to the name, the spaces were blank.

She read through the calendar again. Alongside all the other names he'd written the same terse words. *Confirm. Will swear. Good parents. Child happy.*

She sat back. What else would these contacts say, except that Eldon and Myra Little Shield had raised Mary Ann since she was an infant, they were good parents, and Mary Ann was happy. They would swear to that in court. They were all related to the Little Shields. Cousins, in-laws, cousins of in-laws: a whole web of relatives.

All the notes missed the main question: how had Eldon and Myra gotten custody of Mary Ann? Another relative, a social services employee, had gotten them some sort of paper that made them think they had custody. The relative had died, and the matter had been forgotten—a small child stuck in limbo. And the Little Shields hadn't called the police, because they didn't think they had to. The relative had taken care of the legalities. For five years, they stuck to the story they had created: Mary Ann had been placed in their custody as a foster child.

Was there no one who could swear to the truth, except for the woman who had left Mary Ann on a doorstep in the middle of a blizzard? Except for her, whoever she was?

She stared at the blank spaces around Lou Bearing's name. Three times Clint had talked to the man, yet he hadn't jotted down any comments.

Who was Lou Bearing?

She started through the Little Shields' list again, comparing it to the names on the calendar. Rosemary Little Shield was the last name on the list. Next to it, Clint had jotted the word *neighbor*. He had interviewed everyone in order. Nothing set him off course. Which meant Rosemary Little Shield had been the last person interviewed before Lou Bearing. And Lou Bearing could be her neighbor.

She stacked the sheets in order and placed them inside the file folder. She would have to follow Clint's trail, but she would start with Rosemary Little Shield.

# 16

SHANNON MARY O'MALLEY was her full name. Irish Catholic to the bone, like all of the family Father John had left behind in Boston. He thought of them often, and he kept them in his prayers, those people from another time, a lifetime ago. Seventeen-Mile Road unspooled ahead, the snow crisscrossed and rutted, soft and fluffy as cotton on the surface and sharp as knives below. He was aware of the girl's soft intakes of breath beside him. "Soli or siamo!" played softly between them.

It was after ten this morning when Shannon had arrived at the administration building, a blast of cold air trailing her down the corridor and into his office. She gripped a coffee mug in one hand. *Any coffee, by chance? Sorry she had missed breakfast, but she hoped Elena wasn't offended. She'd overslept. All she really needed was coffee.*

He remembered smiling. Looking up from the letter of recommendation he was writing for Justin Spearman's application to Creighton, and taking her in. Bundled up in a jacket twice her size, knit cap perched on the red hair that sprang over her shoulders, face flushed from the cold. She was like a breath of fresh air. He'd gotten to his feet and filled her mug with coffee at the little table next to the door. He made fresh coffee every morning for the bishop and himself when he got into the office, and usually by midmorning, he made another pot. This was the second pot.

"Enjoy your evening out?" His voice had come back to him tentative and insecure. He was on shaky ground in this parental role.

"Yeah, it was great." She had held up the envelope-thin laptop she grasped in her other hand. "I'm reworking my notes on our talk with Wilbur Horn. Strange how much more you remember, the more you think about something." She took a sip of coffee, then toasted him with the mug. "You don't know how much I needed that. Off to the office," she said swinging into the corridor.

"Shannon, wait."

She looked back and for a moment he'd thought he glimpsed a flash of resistance in her expression, as if she had expected him to interrogate her about last night. He walked back to his desk and rummaged through the pile of papers he'd brought over from the residence. Dear Lord, being a parent was tough. Shannon was leaning against the door frame, drinking the coffee. He'd found the page he was looking for and carried it over to her.

"Oh, that! I found it on the internet some time ago." She had given a dismissive wave, coupled with a sly half smile, as if she appreciated his efforts, but she was the scholar here.

"I thought you might like to visit it."

That had stopped her. She tilted her head back and stared at him, as if a different uncle had appeared in front of her. "You mean . . ."

"It still stands west of Blue Sky Highway, near the foothills."

"Oh my God. Lizzie's house! Yes. Yes. How soon can we go?"

He'd told her to give him a minute to finish something, and she had clumped down the corridor in her heavy snow boots. He had heard her fiddling with the door to the little office he'd cleared for her. Then the door opened and closed. In ten minutes she was back, refilling the mug. Jacket still on, zippered up, scarf looped and re-looped around her neck, the knit cap pulled lower.

He had finished e-mailing the letter to the Creighton admissions office and closed the laptop. She was heading for the front door as he pulled on his jacket, grabbed his cowboy hat and walked to the back office. He told the bishop that he and Shannon were going out, and the bishop said what he always said. He would hold down the fort.

Shannon was on the front stoop, stomping her boots with impatience. He followed her down the concrete steps glazed with ice, buttoning up his jacket as he went. Her boots left a trail of notches through the snow to the pickup. Inside, he jiggled the ignition and, under his breath, encouraged the old engine to turn over one more time. Finally it sputtered into life, a low growling noise, like that of a man waking after a long sleep.

Now, after that first outburst of excitement, Shannon settled into a dreamy silence in the passenger seat, gloved hands around the coffee mug she lifted to her lips now and then. Houses slipped past, silent in the cold air, lopsided piles of snow on the roofs, frost fringing the windows. Everything stopped in the winter, but Father John knew that wasn't true even as the thought crossed his mind. Pickups and cars bobbed down the frozen road toward him, some with headlights flashing through the grayness. From time to time, depending upon the direction in which the road bent, he glimpsed a trace of sunshine over the mountains.

"In case you're interested, James was a perfect gentleman." Shannon's voice erupted like that of an announcer on a radio program that had been off the air for a while.

"I wouldn't expect anything else."

"After we ate dinner, we went to his house."

His house.

"Used to be one of the ranch buildings behind the house where his mother lives. James insulated it, fixed it up. Put in a wood stove that keeps the place pretty cozy. He's very handy."

"Ah." He was learning more and more about James Two Horses.

"We talked for a couple hours." Four or five. "About everything. Have you ever met anyone you felt you could talk to for the rest of your life and never run out of things to say?" Father John felt her eyes playing over him. "I guess not. But let me tell you, it is a wonderful thing. I felt I could tell him anything. He didn't judge me or tell me how stupid I've been or how I should have made better choices. All that stuff. What do you think?"

He was thinking that James Two Horses had the makings of a good priest. He said, "I hope it was helpful."

She laughed at that. "What I ought to do and what I probably will do are different things for me. Always have been."

"You're talking about your . . ." He hesitated.

"Lover. You might as well call it for what it is. David is leaving. I've always known that. I wouldn't be surprised if he's moved out already."

Father John let the silence ride between them a moment. Then he said, "Are you all right?"

"Yes, of course. James let me talk it all out, all the dysfunctional aspects of David's and my relationship. When you step back and look at it, there was no other way it could end. Or should end." She took a long drink of coffee. When he looked over, he caught the sheen of moisture in her eyes before she turned toward the window.

He braked at the stop sign and waited for three trucks on Blue Sky Highway to pass, then took a right. There would be a cutoff ahead, not much more than an alley that could be obscured in the snow. He took his foot off the gas pedal to let the pickup coast, and he hunched forward, looking for the cutoff.

A truck turned out of the snowy field that ran between the highway and the foothills, brown and traced with snow. Father John tapped the brake and slowed to a crawl. As soon as the truck turned, he swung into the cutoff and maneuvered the pickup into the twin ruts sprinkled with dirt and black splotches of oil that zigzagged ahead. The white fields folded around them.

"Lizzie must have liked it out here," Shannon said, "in the middle of nowhere. Maybe people forgot about her and her white skin and freckles."

Father John smiled to himself. How easily the barriers between the past and the present slipped away when you took a step into the past, into those long-ago lives, and imagined yourself living them. It had happened many times when he was studying American history, researching the life of somebody no one else cared about. But he was caught up, as if he had stepped out of his own skin and into that of a man who had lived a hundred years ago, and he had known—*known*—how that man thought and felt and engaged the world.

And now Shannon was caught up in the life of a woman by the name of Elizabeth Fletcher Brokenhorn.

He came around a wide, lazy curve conscious of the rear tires slipping a little. He'd been thinking he should get new tires for some time now, as soon as the mission finances looked a little better. A perennial hope, he realized. The finances never changed. Random donations from people he'd never heard of. For a moment, he thought about the upcoming meeting in Milwaukee, the discussion on whether St. Francis Mission could continue to operate. He knew he had been putting off returning Father Jameson's call.

There it was, leaning sideways in the snow as he came out of the curve, the Brokenhorn cabin, a century of hand-hewn logs and resolve. Shannon let out a loud gasp beside him. He turned off the CD; "Il balen del suo sorriso" faded into the quiet.

He was thinking he should have tried to reach Thomas Horn for permission to visit the cabin. He had called Wilbur, who told him to call his relation, Thomas, who looked after the old place, but Thomas didn't seem to be around. Father John tapped on the brake, searching the road ahead. No driveway, no cut into the waves of untouched snow. He stopped the pickup in a direct line from the cabin. "Hope you brought your snowshoes," he said.

Shannon was out of the cab, slamming the door behind her, before he had slid out. Still studying the expanse of snow, searching for any hint of an easy way across. Shannon was already striding into the field, snow banking around her boots and crawling up the legs of her jeans. Then she was running, yelling with delight, hands in the air, like a kid playing in the snow. He could feel the charge of excitement as he started after her.

The door hung slightly ajar, the windows gaped open, any glass that might have been in place at one time was gone. Shannon was yanking at the door, which squealed and creaked and held steady, frozen in place. Father John took hold of the edge, tugged upward until he felt the hinges settle into place, then pushed the door inward. He stood back, expecting Shannon to lunge inside, but she laid a hand on the frame and leaned forward, and he understood that she was stepping into the little house in her imagination, like Lizzie a hundred years ago.

He waited, not wanting to break the spell. Finally, she turned toward him and smiled. "Let's see what it's like."

It was freezing inside, as if the cold had burst through the open windows and expanded into something hard and permanent. Snow blanketed the floorboards. He clapped his hands together, conscious of the whoof his gloves made in the cold. Shannon was patrolling the rectangular perimeter, not more than fifteen feet by ten.

She stopped in front of a window that framed a view of the foothills and stared outside for a long moment. "Lizzie stood here," she said. "She saw this same view. Winter, spring, summer, fall—all the changing colors." She walked over to a wall with a round hole cut into the logs. "This is where she cooked. The stove stood here." She pointed at the hole and swiped at the snow with her boots, as if she might uncover evidence of a wood-burning stove. "She cooked everything. Whatever John could bring home. Whatever commodities they received from the government. She made bread from the flour they received. For a few weeks they would have bread, until the flour ran out."

She circled the area in front of the stove. "They slept here, the whole family. Lizzie and John over here." She gestured to the right. "The five kids here." A gesture to the left. "Huddling close for warmth, wrapped in buffalo robes." She glanced up with a start, as if she had just realized she wasn't working things out alone. "Don't you think so?"

"I hope so." Buffalo robes would have been scarce on the reservation. Sold off to traders long before for food, and impossible to replace. The great herds of buffalo were gone. It was likely that Lizzie and her family depended upon the thin, woolen blankets they got from the government, along with the other rations promised in exchange for the Indian lands.

"Lizzie is so close. I can almost feel her presence here, in her home. Can't you?"

He smiled. He supposed she was right. If he let himself move into that realm of imagination—lose himself, as he did back in graduate school—then he supposed he could *feel* Lizzie Brokenhorn's presence. That was a long time ago.

The shot came like thunder that split the air and rumbled beneath the snow-covered floorboards. "Get down!" He took hold of Shannon's shoulder and pushed her to the floor, then, stooping low, he made his way to the nearest window. The field was open and quiet, their footsteps the only trace of activity. He moved to the side window, near the spot where the stove had been, and peered past the edge. He could see a pickup parked behind the Toyota, and a man standing next to it, rifle raised.

Another shot blasted across the field, and Father John dropped to his knees, his heart hammering. "Lie down flat," he said. *Dear Lord, don't let anything happen to her.* "I'm going out."

"You can't do that! Please, don't do that."

Hunching down, he worked his way across the floor and pulled open the door. "It's Father John from the mission!" he shouted into the white abyss. "I'm coming out." God, where was his handkerchief? He dug into the front pockets of his jeans, then the rear pocket, the other rear pocket, and finally pulled it free and, shaking it out into a small white frame, he reached around the door and waved the white handkerchief in the direction of the road.

"It's Father John!" he shouted again. His own name reverberated across the field and over the cabin. He got to his feet, sheltering next to the door frame, still waving the flag.

"No!" Shannon's voice sounded behind him, high-pitched in terror. "Don't leave me."

He stepped outside, holding the flag of truce. Waving. Waving. He could feel the man watching him. "I mean no harm," he shouted. "I was visiting the Brokenhorn cabin." He kept walking.

The man didn't move for a long moment. Then, he lowered the rifle and started stomping through the snow toward him. "Father John?" He came closer. "What in tarnation you doing here?"

Father John felt the tension leak out of his muscles. He recognized the man. Thomas Horn.

"Sorry about the warning shots," Thomas said. "Only way to keep trespassers from vandalizing the place."

"My apologies. We should have asked permission." Father John heard Shannon coming up behind him. Felt her rather than heard her. She approached silently in the snow. "This is my niece, Shannon O'Malley. She's researching the life of Lizzie Brokenhorn."

Thomas Horn gave a quick nod, as if Shannon were in a long line of folks interested in Lizzie. "I got your calls." The man turned and began stomping back toward the road. Father John took hold of Shannon's arm; she was shaking, and color had drained from her face.

"Sometimes grandmother's memory is sharp as ever." Thomas had stopped and looked sideways. Then he started off again, and they fell in beside him. "Other times, she can't remember me. I was waiting for the best time to get back to you. She's been real good the last couple days. I expect she'd like a couple visitors, you want to stop by now."

# 17

SHE WAS AVERAGE height, a little stocky, with rolls of flesh that bulged through a long-sleeved white tee shirt and rolled over the top of her blue jeans. *Full-figured* would be the correct term, Vicky thought. The figure of a middle-aged woman with a full resume of kids, ranch work, and part-time jobs to hold it all together.

"Come on in." Rosemary Little Shield flung the door wide open. She had a way of looking at you out of the corners of her eyes, which reminded Vicky of Rosemary's relative, Eldon. Rosemary was Eldon's mother's cousin, to be precise, which Myra Little Shield had explained when Vicky called to get the woman's address. Not that it mattered. All relatives were the same.

Rosemary lived on a ranch that ran into the foothills west of Fort Washakie, Myra had told her, then adding the rest of the story: Rosemary and her husband, Larry—also Little Shield, another distant cousin of Eldon's—had inherited the ranch from her father. They had hoped one of their kids—they had four—would stay on and help run the place, but the kids had scattered. The way of kids these days—off to college, a job in some city, forget they're Arapaho. Larry ran the ranch. Took on a hired hand when he could afford it.

"Clint said he was going to interview Rosemary," Myra had gone on, "but we never heard what she had to say. Knowing Rosemary, she told things exactly as they are. No beating around the bush with her, and she saw Mary Ann the week after we'd gotten her. She knows how much we loved her from the get-go."

Vicky had asked if she or Eldon knew a man by the name of Lou Bearing, and that had stopped the conversation. Vicky could almost hear the condensed quiet that had gathered on the other end. "It's not ringing a bell," Myra said finally. "Maybe Eldon knows him. Why do you ask?"

Vicky started to explain that Clint had interviewed him after he'd talked to Rosemary, then stopped. There were no notations, no indication Clint had actually spoken to the man. Only the name written under three different days. It was possible Clint had intended to interview Lou Bearing and, for some reason, had changed his mind.

Myra had jumped into the silence. "I have to get back to work. I'm leaving early this afternoon to take Mary Ann to the dentist's."

Now, Rosemary Little Shield was directing her to a love seat in the small living room and asking if she would like a cup of coffee. "That would be nice," Vicky said, perching on the edge of a cushion. Outside the temperatures hovered below freezing, and despite the warm air blasting through the Ford, she had been chilled on the drive across the reservation. She unbuttoned her coat and kept it on, huddling inside the warmth, listening to the clinking, splashing sounds coming from the kitchen.

Rosemary came through the archway into the living room, a

mug in each hand. She set the mugs on the small table in front of the sofa and settled herself into a faded pink upholstered chair.

"Like I told you on the phone," Rosemary said, "I don't have a lot of time. I'm on the early dinner shift at the diner today."

Vicky said she understood. Ulrich's Diner in Riverton. She had eaten there many times. She supposed she must have seen Rosemary Little Shield there, another Arapaho woman working in town, a long drive every day. Women on the rez would go wherever they could find a job. It was the work that mattered, not the distance.

"So you've taken over Mary Ann's adoption case?" The woman had an open, matter-of-fact manner. There wasn't much time; the polite preliminaries had to be skipped. "That other lawyer spent a good hour here asking questions. He hung around so long that Larry came in from the pasture to see what was going on, so then he interviewed both of us."

And that was strange, Vicky was thinking. In his notations, Clint hadn't mentioned Larry Little Shield. It seems there was a lot that Clint Hopkins hadn't mentioned.

"Would you mind telling me what you told Clint?"

Rosemary lifted her shoulders in an exaggerated shrug. "What you'd expect, I guess. How Myra called and said they had a new baby to care for. Naturally, I was surprised, 'cause they'd just lost their baby. So I was thinking, where did this new baby come from? She told me they were foster parents, and they hoped they'd have the baby for a long time, like the rest of her life. That evening, Larry and I went over to see the baby. I remember we brought some stew I'd made. You always need food with a new baby. And Mary Ann was real new, you could tell. Tiny little thing. But alert, with big blue eyes that followed you around, watching you, like she was trying to figure everything out."

"Did it strike you as unusual that she was white?"

"You mean a white foster child with an Arapaho couple? I guess, but Myra said they thought the mother was Arapaho, and the baby happened to look more white than Indian, which would probably change as she grew. You know, the Indian side would come out. All I know is what I told Clint. Myra and Eldon were as happy as I'd ever seen them. There never was a couple more in love with a baby. I was so happy for them, after what they'd been through. Larry and I, neither one of us, wanted to throw any cold water, so we kept our mouths shut. But we were both thinking, soon as social services finds a white couple to take Mary Ann, the Little Shields will lose her."

"But it didn't happen. Didn't you wonder why?"

"You sound like that other lawyer." She gave a throaty laugh. "Like I told him, it didn't happen, and pretty soon the whole family just accepted Mary Ann as one of us. We figured Eldon and Myra would adopt her, and that's what they are trying to do."

"Did you hear any rumors or gossip around the rez?"

"Rumors? Like what?"

"Clint didn't ask about rumors?"

Rosemary shrugged. "There's always busybodies that's got an opinion and can't keep it to themselves. Sure, there were rumors, some of them real nasty, like maybe Mary Ann was stolen, or Myra and Eldon bought her from somebody. Nobody paid any attention. Mary Ann had a good home. It was all that mattered."

Vicky was quiet. Everyone on the list was related to the Little Shields, all of whom had probably ignored the rumors. Clint had no way of knowing what people might have said behind the family's back, but a judge would want to know. A judge would demand hard evidence to prove Mary Ann had been left on the Little Shields' doorstep. She felt a downdraft of weariness. Is that what Clint had experienced? A sense of the impossibility of proving Mary Anne had been left on the Little Shields' doorstep?

"Why did you suggest Clint talk to Lou Bearing?"

"Who?" Rosemary had sprung upright and was pulling on a jacket she had yanked off the hook "I just realized the time. I can't be late for my shift."

"The man Clint interviewed after he spoke to you." Vicky got to her feet and started buttoning her own coat.

"You mean Lou and Debbie Bearing? Don't really know them. Keep to themselves. Never seen them at the powwows or farmers' markets. Why would I send Clint to talk to them?"

"I thought they might be neighbors."

Rosemary threw a scarf around her neck as if she were throwing salt over her shoulder and could read the future based on the patterns in which the crystals fell. "Neighbors? What are you talking about. The nearest neighbor is a mile away."

Vicky looped her own scarf under her chin and followed Rosemary out into the frigid air. A sheen of frost lay over the Ford. She was trying to picture Clint's calendar. In the jottings below Rosemary's name, he had written the word *neighbor*. The following day he had written Lou Bearing's name for the first time.

Except there was no one who could qualify as a neighbor, and Rosemary had not suggested Lou Bearing.

"Hope you have good luck helping Mary Ann," Rosemary called over her shoulder as she turned toward the pickup on the far side of the stoop.

"Thanks for your time." Vicky's voice sounded sharper in the cold air than she intended. She veered in the opposite direction, toward the Ford, and was about to get inside when she stopped. She must have misinterpreted the sequence of Clint's notations. Neighbor could have referred to Lou Bearing's neighbor.

She swung about and started back across the yard, waving at the woman maneuvering the pickup into parallel tire ruts that ran out to the road. Finally the pickup rocked to a stop and the driver's window began a slow, jerky motion downward.

Vicky grabbed hold of the door handle. Her breath floated into the cab, a cloud of stream. "Who did you suggest Clint talk to?"

The woman blinked several times, as if she were trying to comprehend. "I didn't suggest anybody. I'm going to be late."

"Please. It's important. You must have mentioned someone."

She looked away a moment, then turned back. The tip of her nose was red with the cold. "It was just conversation. We were talking about the adjustment Eldon and Myra had made to take care of a baby, and the baby wasn't even their own. It's not like babies know the difference between night and day, so they're up all night, crying. You don't know what's wrong. I told him what Dina said . . ."

"Dina?"

"Dina Fowler. Worked the same shift at the diner. She'd come to work looking like she'd been up all night, and she didn't even have a baby. It was her neighbor's baby. Crying all night. I remember Dina saying she hadn't even realized the neighbor's were expecting. Then, one night, the crying started."

*Neighbor.* Clint had jotted the single word, and Vicky realized she had assumed that Lou Bearing was Rosemary's neighbor. He wasn't; he was Dina Fowler's neighbor. She said, "Does Dina still work with you?"

"Left a couple years ago after she and Matthew moved to Lander. She opened her own place on Main Street. Like I say, we were just chatting. I never expected Clint would go find Dina." The window began creaking upward. "I really have to go."

Vicky stepped back and gave the woman a little wave of appreciation. Hard pellets of ice and snow sprayed from the wheels as the pickup ground forward. Clint Hopkins had been a good adoption lawyer because he was thorough. Nothing was unimportant, no idle chitchat. Every comment might lead to something.

# 18

FIRE CRACKLED IN the wood burning stove, a survivor from the nine-teenth century, glowing red and orange and emitting heat waves into the small room. Traces of gray smoke escaped from the metal chimney that rose through an opening in the ceiling. Shannon was conscious of her uncle standing close behind her in the small room. A few feet away, slumped in a chair in front of the stove, was an old woman bundled in a Pendleton blanket, with a lined, leathery face and a pink scalp covered with strips of thin gray hair.

"Grandmother." Thomas Horn bent over the woman. The gentleness in his tone surprised Shannon, as if he were speaking to a child or someone quite ill. "Are you up for visitors?"

The old woman stirred and shifted about inside the blanket. "I love visitors."

"Father John from the mission is here. He brought his niece." Shannon felt the man's eyes dance over her for a moment. "They would like to talk with you."

At that, Theresa Horn strained sideways and looked over her shoulder. Light flickered in her narrow black eyes.

Shannon watched her uncle move in a little closer, drawn to the warmth of the fire. The woman squared herself again in front of the stove. From somewhere in the folds of the blanket, she brought out a hand, speckled with spots and thin as paper, the fingers as crooked and fragile as dried sticks. Uncle John held her hand in both of his for a long moment. "How are you, Grandmother?"

Voice crackling like the fire, the old woman said she was as ornery as ever. Waiting for winter to blow away so her bones could warm up. "And who's this pretty thing?" She strained sideways again, and now Shannon felt the old woman's gaze traveling over her.

"My niece, Shannon."

"Oh, yes, so Thomas said. My grandson tells me what he wants me to know. He thinks I'm too senile to know what he's up to, so I always check." The old woman gave a little laugh that rumbled about the blanket.

Shannon stepped in closer to let the old woman take her in, make up her own mind as to what kind of heart beat inside this white woman. Good heart? Bad heart? A day on the reservation and its ways were taking hold of her. If Theresa Horn decided she had a bad heart, Shannon knew, they might as well leave, because the old woman would go as silent as an abandoned drum.

"I'm so pleased to meet you." Shannon leaned down—not too far, just enough to allow the old woman to bring her into focus. "Your grandson was kind enough to invite us over."

It took a moment, but gradually a smile worked its way through the old woman's expression. First the black eyes, then the mouth. She lifted a hand again, and Shannon took it, conscious of Uncle John watching her. Was her excitement contagious? She was holding a hand that had held Lizzie's hand. The small hand of a child then, when Lizzie was in her late fifties or early sixties. The hand of an old woman now, roughened and muscular.

"So you want to know about my grandmother." Theresa Horn retrieved her hand and hid it again in the blanket. "Thomas told me Father John called about bringing you by. You come from back east."

The old woman was sharp today; she hadn't missed anything. Shannon glanced up at Uncle John beside her. He was easy to read. Thomas hadn't returned his calls because his grandmother hadn't made up her mind whether she wanted to share her most precious possession—her stories—with a stranger. Even when Thomas brought them home, he probably wasn't sure how she would react.

"Chicago," Shannon said.

The old woman nodded. "Grandmother came from a place near Chicago. You have that in common, that and red hair. Oh, I remember reddish hair poking out of the calico cloth she wrapped around it. You'd better sit down." She motioned to the kitchen chairs Thomas had pulled over.

Shannon dropped onto one of the chairs and leaned forward, conscious of Uncle John taking the chair next to her and Thomas Horn hovering nearby in the shadows, close enough to hear everything. The old woman was saying something about her grandmother dying when she was seven years old.

Shannon felt a stab of disappointment. How much could the old woman remember? How much would be true?

"I remember how she hated her hair," Theresa said. "Hated her white skin. Used to try and hide them. My father got her light skin. His hair was light, not red like grandmother's. Never made any difference. He knew he was Arapaho, but I guess that was what bothered grandmother. She knew she wasn't Arapaho, no matter what her heart said."

"It's wonderful that you have those memories." Shannon could feel her whole being reaching toward the old woman. This was as close as she would ever come to Lizzie Brokenhorn, these people on the rez with Lizzie's blood in their veins.

"I may be old as the hills." Theresa gave another cracked laugh. "Some days I still got my marbles. What else you want to know?"

What else? Shannon threw another glance at the man beside her. Information is a gift. It was impolite to ask for a gift. Finally she said, "You actually knew her. I was hoping you could tell me if"— she drew in a long breath, then plunged on—"if you think she was happy."

The old woman sank further down into the blanket until her chin disappeared. "Nobody asked questions like that back then. You were alive, so you were happy. Grandmother worked hard. She did her chores. She cooked our food every day. We ate stew. Rabbit, deer, elk, if Dad and Grandfather got lucky. Beef when we got our rations once a year. Beef on the hoof."

Another laugh erupted from the blankets. "I guess they thought, let those Indians play at being Indians and slaughter their food. One beef for a family. The men killed the cow and Grandmother went to work. She had a big knife, sharp enough to take off your finger, and she got down on the ground and skinned and butchered the carcass. Up to her elbows in blood when she finished. She cut off big slabs of beef that she pounded with the berries us kids found on the prairie. She stretched the beef out to dry on racks grandfather built. We had beef stew on real cold days in the winter when we needed extra fat on our bones, she used to say."

"We saw her house." She'd been right, Shannon was thinking.

Lizzie had made the stew at the stove. "It looks like there was a stove inside."

The old woman shook her head. "Grandmother cooked over the big wood fire in the tipi. If we came inside to get warm, she put us to work. Go to the creek and get more water. Go clean the potatoes in the snow. She always had a bucket of wild potatoes and onions she dug in the fall. The dirt stuck to them like glue. By the time I got them clean, my fingers were frozen. Grandmother didn't take to excuses. If I complained, she told me to get back to work."

"She sounds very . . ." Shannon could sense the man beside her waiting—his breath suspended— while she searched for the word. "Disciplined." She had almost said *tough*.

"She survived, didn't she? The old people kept us alive. Hunting, trying to grow crops on this no-water land, working all the time to keep our bellies filled. You want to know if she was happy? I'd say she would've been happier living free on the plains in the Old Time. But when she came to the people, the Old Time was gone, and the people were sick and hungry. Weren't any good times before or after the rez."

Shannon gave Uncle John a quick glance. *When she came to the people.* As if Lizzie Fletcher had come on her own.

The old woman had tilted her head back until her chin emerged from the blanket. Her gaze trailed the chimney to the ceiling. "I remember how she taught me to make fry bread. 'Pinch off a piece of dough,' she'd say. Those white hands of hers were quick and strong. 'Pat it out.' The old woman patted at the blanket until Shannon could almost see a ball of dough taking shape, round and fat and smooth like the photos she had seen of Indian women working in the food booths at powwows.

"'See?'" the old woman said, her hand still patting the blanket.

"'Not like that. Like this!' Oh, she was a stickler for doing it right. Not worth doing unless you did a thing right. She'd toss the dough into hot oil and turn it with a stick until it was golden brown and sizzling. You could see the steam coming off it, and your mouth would start watering. She always kept pieces of fry bread in her necessary bag. When us kids got hungry and started crying, she'd pull out a piece of fry bread to shut us up."

Shannon sat back, reluctant to let the moment pass. Theresa Horn was deep in memories now, transported to another time. A child following her grandmother around, doing what she was told, hoping for another piece of fry bread. And where was her own mother? Tending to the crops, hunting for wild berries and vegetables, hauling water? Working. Working. She knew enough about tribal life to know it was the older women, the grandmothers, those whose work kept them closer to home, who raised the children.

"Lizzie sounds like a good grandmother," she said, wanting to keep the memories flowing, to hold the old woman in the past.

"We didn't think of good or bad. Grandmother looked after us. She taught us kids how to survive. How to tan hides and sew shirts and pants and dresses. She took us to the Sun Dance. Oh, I remember riding in the back of the wagon that bounced all over the place. Grandmother up on the buckboard handling the horses. They never gave her any trouble. She could turn and stop them whenever she wanted. She taught us to be respectful of the dancers 'cause they danced in the heat for three days without water or food. They made a sacrifice to the Creator so that He would take pity on the people. After the dancing ended, we helped Grandmother hand out the chokecherry juice so they could drink water and eat food without getting sick. She knew all these things, Grandmother did. She passed them on to us."

The old woman slumped downward until her chin disappeared again, and Thomas stepped forward, not saying anything. His look said it all: She's getting tired.

Uncle John stood up first, and Shannon rose beside him, reluctant to let go of the past. This old woman had known Lizzie Brokenhorn, held her hand, sat at her side, breathed in the essence of her. "Thank you," she said, but the old woman's eyelids had dropped down and she had receded into some other place. Perhaps she was still with Lizzie.

Shannon waited while her uncle shook hands with Thomas Horn and thanked him, then she did the same. The man crossed the room, opened the door, and Shannon stepped out first into the blast of cold air.

"SHE DIDN'T TELL me everything." Shannon watched the cabin, a dark smudge in the gray light, pass outside her window as they drove along Blue Sly Highway.

"What else would you have liked to know?"

"What else?" Shannon laughed. "E degio e posso," one of her favorite arias, was playing between them. "Everything else. Did Lizzie ever look at her white arms and legs and wonder who she was? Where she came from? Why was she different from her people? Why she resembled the white people in town? Did she wonder what they thought of her?"

"What do you think?"

"Of course she did. So did John Brokenhorn. He moved the family into the mountains at one point to hide her from white people who might take her. Recapture her." She slid sideways into the corner and stared at the man beside her, the clumps of reddish hair beneath the brim of his cowboy hat. They were alike; they were related; they came from the same tribe. What was it like for Lizzie to look at her Arapaho family—husband, aunts and uncles and cousins, all the people who gave her her place on the earth—and know she was different?

She straightened herself and stared out the windshield. It looked like snow again, the dark clouds hanging low, stationary and heavy, waiting to open up. She would spend the rest of the day writing out her notes, deciphering what she wrote, reading between the lines. Is that what history was about? The past that lodged between the lines?

And this evening? This evening she would see James Two Horses. Hamburger or pizza someplace. He would know a little restaurant with small tables that they could hover over, faces close, voices low, talking. She still felt the ripples of amazement that had run through her last night. She had never been able to talk to David like that, where she felt he was taking in every word, taking her seriously.

She turned into the passenger window and dabbed at her eyes. She didn't want Uncle John to see. God, she couldn't think of David without crying. It was as if his name turned on a faucet inside her. What a fool she'd been. She had always known it was coming. She had to give him that—he hadn't lied to her. But she had hung on, hoping for what? That he would change his mind, of course, fall in love with her, be unable to imagine life without her.

"Are you all right?"

She felt Uncle John's eyes on her. She couldn't hide from him.

She swallowed hard and tried to compose herself before she turned toward him with the most relaxed smile she could muster. "Sure. The research is going just as I hoped." She drew in a long breath, aware of the stuttering sound. "James and I are having dinner again tonight. I hope Elena and the bishop don't take offense."

Uncle John gave her a sideways glance. A glance, nothing else, but she knew that he knew everything.

She stopped the words crowding into her throat: *I might have been tempted to sleep with him last night if he hadn't said, "We'd better go. It's time I got you back to the mission."* It was the way it should be. The last thing she needed was to jump into another relationship after David. And James was different, so much more solid and real. Any relationship, if it happened, would be like that.

Uncle John understood. She saw the truth in the throb of a tiny blood vessel in his temple, the way he glanced over and smiled at her. She felt raw and exposed, all her secret hopes thrown into the road for everyone to see.

"I'll let Elena know," he said.

# 19

THE FRONT DOOR sighed open into the warm, muggy atmosphere of the diner halfway down Main Street in Lander. Odors of hot grease, fried meat, and coffee hung over the counter that stretched along the rear. A few booths lined the plate glass windows on either side of the door. The place was empty. The lunch crowd, if there had been one, had moved on, leaving behind wet traces of boot prints on the yellow vinyl floor.

The bell above the door jangled into the silence for a moment before cutting off as Vicky let the door bang behind her and slid onto a stool. Through the opened door behind the counter she could see a woman bent into scrubbing the metal surface of a trestle table. The shiny circle widened under her hand.

Vicky took the menu out of the metal holder and flipped it open. The realization that she was hungry had come out of the blue. Toast and coffee this morning before she'd gone to the office, then nothing, and it was almost time for dinner. Living off adrenaline, chasing after Clint Hopkins, trying to escape the image of the dark figure suspended over the hood of the black truck. She squeezed her eyes shut a moment, forcing away the thought that she was two blocks—*two blocks*—from where Clint had died.

She glanced at the menu: hamburger, steak sandwich, turkey sandwich, grilled cheese. There was another thought that stayed with her, an icy hand gripping her: the truck had been waiting for Clint Hopkins. She *knew* it to be true. Clint had been murdered. Somehow it all converged on the last name on the calendar, Lou Bearing. Clint had met the man, spoken with him, and something Lou Bearing said must have sent Clint elsewhere. A man obsessed with uncovering the truth behind an infant's sudden appearance on a doorstep, doggedly interviewing one person after another, day after day, and then? Nothing. A calendar with three days x-ed out. Where had he gone? What had he done? Taken a break in the midst of an investigation? Put his feet up by a fire and smoked a pipe? She didn't think so.

She had been staring at the menu, lost in her own thoughts, and now the woman from the back was on the other side of the counter. She had set down a glass of water, and now she was tapping a pencil on the notepad cupped in her hand. An Arapaho with the prominent cheekbones, the little hook in her nose, the black eyes that seemed to take in everything and gave nothing.

"What can I get you? Sorry, we're out of apple pie."

Apple pie. Vicky hadn't yet turned to the dessert section. "Are you Dina?"

The woman stepped back, something new in her eyes, a flicker of interest. "Dina's Diner. This is my place. What's it going to be?"

"Grilled cheese." A hot grilled cheese sandwich struck her as the most delicious item on the menu. "Coffee."

Dina slipped the pad into the pocket of a white apron streaked with ketchup and mustard stains and the shiny residue of grease. The order was not worth writing down. She had already turned back when Vicky said, "I'm an attorney here in town. Vicky Holden. I'd like to talk to you for a few minutes."

The woman swung back. "I heard of you. The Indian lawyer. Were you working with the lawyer that got killed?"

"I've taken over one of his cases."

"About time, I say. He came in here last week, asking questions. Had me digging into the past, trying to remember what happened five years past, like that wasn't a lifetime ago. 'You must remember,' he told me, and sure enough, I remembered. He was working on an adoption case for an Arapaho couple. Well, he didn't have to say anything else. I figured he was helping the Little Shields adopt that white girl they'd been taking care of. I told him, you need to talk to Vicky Holden, the Indian lawyer. She'll know about tribal adoptions." She studied the surface of the counter and drew in a breath that puffed her cheeks. "Too bad what happened to him. Run down in the street like that. He seemed like a good guy."

She glanced around the diner, as if she wanted to make sure another customer hadn't materialized, before leaning in closer. "Let me get your grilled cheese. I'll join you for a cup of coffee."

Then she was off. Through the door, out of sight in the back, a refrigerator door swishing open and closed, metal clanking against metal, a faucet running. After a moment, new odors floated out to the counter—hot, fresh coffee and melting cheese. Vicky sipped at the water, conscious of the empty space in her stomach.

Dina reappeared, balancing two mugs of coffee with a plate piled with a grilled cheese sandwich, potato chips, and a dill pickle. She set them on the counter, then walked around and settled on the adjacent stool.

"You go ahead." She nodded at the sandwich. "It's late for lunch. You must be hungry."

Vicky bit into the sandwich, then took another bite. Is this what came from working in a diner—feeding people all day long—the ability to sense hunger? She took a sip of coffee, aware of the woman's eyes watching her, waiting until the time was right to talk. Until they were both ready. It was the Arapaho Way.

She finished half the sandwich, took a long drink of coffee, and rotated toward the woman. "I spoke with Rosemary . . ."

Dina put up a hand. "And she told you about the crying baby. Clint came around wanting me to tell him everything I knew. Like I say, it took a minute to figure out what he was asking about. But when the memories started coming, they were real clear. We were living outside Fort Washakie, Matthew and me. Nearest neighbors a little way across the field. Lou and Debbie Bearing. Arapahos. Real standoffish, didn't want anything to do with anybody. Never saw them go anywhere. Lou worked in the barn out back. Kept to themselves. Didn't have any kids. All of a sudden they had a baby. How'd we know? Never heard a baby crying like it was in pain, screaming bloody murder all night long. We didn't get any sleep for a week. I went over once and knocked on the door. They didn't even answer, just shouted from inside: 'What do you want?' 'Is there anything I can do to help?' I had to shout back. I remember it was freezing cold, and I was leaning into the door trying to get some warmth. They shouted back that they were fine, just a little colic. They were taking care of her. It wasn't gonna last long."

"Her? They said *her*?"

Dina pulled her lips into a tight line and nodded. "That was the last night we heard the crying. The next night was quiet as a grave. After that, I started watching their house when I was home, you know, their comings and goings. She drove a little car, and he had a pickup. They'd drive off for a while, then come back. I didn't see any sign of a baby. I wondered what had happened to the baby. I thought I should call social services."

"Did you?" This would be something, a social services inquiry from someone else about a baby that had appeared out of nowhere. Like the baby dropped at the Little Shields', except Mary Ann had not disappeared.

The woman was shaking her head. "We talked about it and decided we should give them a chance to explain, before we dragged in the . . ." She let a beat skip before she said, "Authorities. We went over one evening after we'd seen them come home. This time Lou opened the door. Real friendly like, which surprised us. Says come on in, want some coffee? Matthew said we came over to see how their baby was doing. He said *their* baby even though we knew she wasn't theirs. Debbie never looked like she was pregnant, and we'd seen her outside a couple weeks before that crying started."

Vicky waited while the woman took a drink of coffee. Finally, she went on: "'Oh, wasn't our baby,' Lou said, like we was some kind of nincompoops didn't know the score. 'Some friends were visiting. Sorry their baby made so much racket. Yeah, we were real glad to see them move on.'"

"Did you believe them?"

"Clint asked the same question." Dina held the mug to her lips and peered over the rim, a faraway look in her eyes, as if, for a moment, she were back talking to Clint. "Now, I think, of course we didn't believe them. How could we? But at the time, what can I say? It seemed reasonable even though . . ."

"Even though?"

"We never saw any other cars at the house. No pickups or campers, the kind of thing you see when folks come visiting."

Vicky took another bite of the sandwich. Lukewarm now, the cheese congealing against the toast. She washed it down with coffee. "Did Clint say anything?"

The woman laughed. The mug of coffee shook in her hand. "I got the impression Clint Hopkins wasn't much for saying what was on his mind. He kept his own counsel. I imagine he went to have a talk with Lou and Debbie. Wouldn't surprise me if they denied there was ever a baby at their house. Maybe we were having hallucinations, me and Matthew. Wouldn't surprise me if that's what they told him."

"When was the last time you saw him?"

"Clint? Never saw him again. Just that one time. You could tell how much he wanted that little girl to be safe with the folks that loved her, like he was going to do everything he could to make it happen."

Vicky pulled her bag around from the back of the stool where she had hung it and was groping inside for her wallet when Dina set a hand on her shoulder. "It's on the house. I'd like to see that little girl safe, too, so no one can take her away."

OUTSIDE, THE TEMPERATURE was dropping, the cold settling over the parking lot. Vicky pulled her scarf around her neck and sank inside her coat. Her fingers stiffened as she pulled on her gloves. *I'd like to see that little girl safe.* The words bounced around inside her head. Clint had wanted the same thing. It had gotten him killed. And now it was what she wanted.

She slid into the Ford and shut the door. It made a hollow thud in the cold air. The engine balked for a second before it finally turned over, cold air exploding from the vents. The sky, gray clouds edged in black, fell all around. Spring seemed so far away this afternoon, it might have been November. She realized that the tiny buzzing noise, like that of a mosquito, was her cell. She rummaged through her bag among the lipstick, combs, notepads, pens, tissues, keys— the detritus of her life—and pulled out the cell. "Vicky Holden" appeared in the readout. She pressed the answer button.

"Oh, I'm glad I reached you." A mixture of relief and anxiety ran through Annie's voice. "Betty White Hawk called back. A so-called friend of Vince's sent her on a wild goose chase. Betty went to the house the friend told her about, and nobody there had seen Vince in a week or more. You ask me, they're helping him. Betty said she's going to lose her job because she didn't go into work today. All she can think about is Vince."

"Did she mention Lou Bearing?"

"The guy from the bar last night? She went to his house this after- noon. He ordered her off his property. Said she was harassing him."

Vicky took a minute. She could see her breath curling into the cold air. "What is she going to do next?"

"She's hoping you'd tell her."

Lou Bearing. The name kept appearing like thistles in a patch of grass. The clock on the dashboard read 4:24. It would take forty minutes to drive across the rez to the Bearing house.

"Anything else?"

"You had a couple of walk-ins this afternoon that Roger took. Are you okay?"

"Yes, of course." The questions took her by surprise. "Why wouldn't I be?"

"You seem so, I don't know, distracted, ever since the accident."

Vicky started to say it wasn't an accident, then checked herself. Was she the only one who believed it was murder? She told Annie to lock up when she left. She would see her tomorrow morning. Then she pressed the end button, put the gear into reverse, and backed out of the parking slot. She had to wait for a thin line of traffic to pass before she skidded onto the street. Exhaust from the truck ahead lay down black lines over the snow, like paint. There was nothing in Clint's notes except the name Lou Bearing. Nothing about him. Who he was. What kind of work he did. What he had told Clint.

*Why did you leave it all in your head?* The truck threw back chunks of snow that slid down the windshield. Vicky fiddled with the wipers until, finally, they swished the snow away. She was heading out of town into the reservation. The snow-streaked brown shoulders of the Wind River Range rose into the gray clouds.

Lou Bearing, wife Debbie, no children—that was all she knew. She drove to Fort Washakie and continued west, the mountains looming closer. The Bearings lived on a road outside town, with a big barn out back, Dina had said. "You can't miss it."

# 20

VICKY TURNED OFF the engine and scanned the house. A rectangular house, wooden stoop at the front door, a faint light inside turning the windows iridescent. Whoever was inside would have heard the Ford, engine growling, crunching the snow. If the Bearings wanted company, they would open the door.

She gave it another couple minutes, then got out. The snow was banked around the stoop and piled over the steps, and she had to grip the rail to keep from slipping. She could feel the snow trickling down into her boots. The door bucked under her fist when she knocked. Draughts of icy air blew across the stoop. Silence except for the swoosh of the wind.

She had started back down the steps when she heard it: the loud, heavy clank of metal on metal. She stood still, holding on to the rail. The sound came again, like that of railroad cars coupling, or a trolley banging against a metal bumper. Industrial, city sounds incongruous on the open, snowy plains that stretched into the dark distances.

Vicky walked around the house and down the side, the cold working its way through her coat. Across an expanse of churned snow in back was the dark cliff face of a barn. Dim arrows of light escaped around the double doors that shuddered with the thumping noise. It was getting dark fast, shadows thickening across the snow.

She made her way to the doors, waited for a break in the noise, and knocked. The noise stopped, leaving an eerie quiet that lasted a half minute, as if whoever was inside had run out another door. She removed her glove and knocked again, pounding hard, the wooden doors shivering sideways. From inside came the sound of shuffling footsteps and a low muttering before the doors finally rattled apart on their metal rails.

The man standing in the opening was slim and hunched forward, backlit by the bright lights inside. He had black hair, cut short above his ears, and deep-set eyes that gave his face the look of a mask. A red scar, like the teeth marks of a saw, pulsated on one cheek.

"Lou Bearing?"

"Who wants to know?"

Vicky went through it all, keeping her eyes on the mask: She was Vicky Holden, an attorney. Could she talk to him for a few minutes?

"I'm busy."

"I represent a friend of yours, Vince White Hawk. And there's another matter . . ."

He sliced a thin arm between them, as if he were chopping wood. "That Rap is no friend of mine. Who told you that?"

"You were seen drinking with him at the Buffalo Bar and Lounge a couple of nights ago."

"So what? I drink with a lot of people."

"Could I come in?" The wind, sucked through the opened doors, was whipping around them. The man started backing up, and Vicky followed him inside. Floodlights attached to metal poles in the corners lit the barn like a stadium. Tools and crumpled rags littered the benches against the walls. In the center, a sedan listed sideways on blocks two feet high. Next to the sedan was a black truck, the front facing the rear wall, hood up. The air was thick with the smells of paint and metallic dust. She had stepped into a garage and body shop.

Lou Bearing reached past her and yanked the doors shut. "Make it quick." He spoke out of the corner of his mouth, his lips stiff, as if they were glued on. The jagged red scar, which ran from the corner of his mouth to his temple, pulled his left eye downward. He stared at her out of the right eye.

"Vince could be in serious trouble," she said.

Bearing swung around and walked over to one of the benches, then turned back. "Don't see how it's my business."

"There's a warrant for his arrest on a robbery charge." She could feel the cold gripping her. The barn was like an icebox despite the lights beaming down and a space heater that crackled and glowed red in the far corner. She pushed on: "He's gone into hiding. I'm trying to help him. I was hoping you might know where I can find him."

Bearing rubbed his hands together, impatience pouring off him. He didn't say anything.

"Who else did Vince drink with at the bar? Did he say anything about a drinking house?"

"Time for you to push off." Bearing's expression remained flat, unreadable, except for the scar, which glowed purplish in the light.

Vicky stood her ground. Everything about the man's demeanor said he was hiding something. If he knew where Vince might be, why wouldn't he say so? Especially if what he claimed were true, that he and Vince were not friends. What difference would it make to him? The man was as nervous as a cat.

A new thought hit her as she watched him: Lou Bearing did not want Vince found.

Then he was shouldering past her and pushing back the doors. Frozen air stirred around them. What had made her think Lou Bearing would tell her anything when he had stonewalled Vince's mother and John O'Malley?

She stepped farther into the center of the barn, ignoring the opened doors. "There is something else."

"There's nothing I have to say to you." The scar jiggled when he spoke. He was rubbing his hands, as if he could work warmth into them. Little beads of perspiration glistened on his forehead.

"I've taken over the Little Shield adoption case that Clint Hopkins spoke to you about."

"Don't know anything about it." Bearing dodged sideways toward the bench, picked up a hammer, and walked to the front of the black truck. "Get out of here." He spit the words over his shoulder.

"Whoa! What's going on?" A woman stepped into the doorway, then came into the barn. Something familiar about her, and yet Vicky couldn't remember ever meeting her. Another face on the reservation, at the grocery store, the gas station, lost among hundreds of faces. Arapaho with straight black hair showing beneath a cowboy hat pulled low over her forehead. She had a dark complexion, red-flushed with cold or anger, and little pillows of flesh below her deep-set dark eyes. She wore a bulky jacket that gave her a stuffed look, shoulders and chest bulging. So this was Debbie Bearing.

"Who are you?"

"Vicky Holden."

"Oh yeah. The Rap lawyer in a fancy office in Lander. We don't need any more lawyers around here."

"I'm representing the Little Shield family . . ."

"Nothing to do with us. You better leave."

"I know Clint Hopkins came to see you."

"I was gonna tell her . . ." Lou began.

The woman put up a hand and moved deeper inside, head bent forward; the doors jiggered behind her in the wind. She threw a warning glance at her husband. "I'll handle this." Then she squared her shoulders a few feet from Vicky. "If you know that lawyer came around here asking a lot of stupid questions, you know what we told him. Five years ago? Who remembers five years ago? So some neighbor says she heard a baby crying. So what? We got relations. They come and visit. Sometimes they hang around. I told that lawyer to stop bothering us."

*Stop bothering us.* Debbie Bearing swallowed hard, as if she could pull back the words. It was obvious this was not something she had meant to say.

"Clint came to see you two days in a row." Vicky went for the opening. She could see Clint's calendar, the black Xs on the following three days. "Then he came back a third time. Where had he gone? What new questions did he have for you?"

Lou Bearing looked frozen in place, a statue next to the truck. His wife was breathing hard, shuffling her feet on the hard-packed dirt floor. She took her time before she said, "How are we supposed to know what that crazy lawyer was after? Asking a lot of questions that had nothing to do with us. What do we know about the Little Shields? What do we care if they adopt a kid or not? You lawyers get your jollies pestering people. Made Hopkins feel like he was earning his big fee. Lou threatened to throw him out."

And that was it. Vicky knew by the nervous lift of Debbie Bearing's voice, the nerve jumping at the edge of her eye. She glanced over at the thin, stooped man braced against the side of the black truck, hammer dangling from one hand. She doubted Lou Bearing could have thrown out a big, fit man like Clint Hopkins. Clint had left because he had run into a wall, and whatever he had glimpsed behind that wall had led him to call her.

That night he was murdered.

"I also represent Vince White Hawk." Vicky went on, grasping at thin air. From the tiny flicker of light in the woman's eyes, Vicky knew that Debbie Bearing knew her client.

Debbie curled her lips against her teeth. She looked over at her husband a moment, then settled her shoulders inside the bulky jacket. "How we supposed to know every Rap on the rez?" Keeping her gaze on Vicky, she said to her husband, "You told her that, right?"

"Right." Lou's voice sounded shaky and uncertain. "Just because I had a drink with the guy doesn't mean I know him."

Debbie turned sideways and glared at the man, who looked as if he wanted to fade into the truck. "You drink with a lot of guys."

"I told her."

Debbie turned back. Her gaze was level and steady, as if everything had been cleared up. "Get out and leave us alone." She tossed her head in the direction of the doors and the wind whistling through the cracks.

The doors banged shut behind her as Vicky went out. She picked her way through the pencils of light around the corner of the house and out to the front, the light getting dimmer. The night was black with dark clouds that obscured the moon and the stars that usually lit up the sky. She lurched for the handle and slid inside the Ford, grateful for the familiar feel of the steering wheel in her hands, the cough of the engine turning over, and the flare of headlights that washed over her footprints in the snow.

She backed across the yard, turning halfway around to make out the tracks, not wanting to attempt a U-turn and get stuck. The Ford crawled down into the barrow ditch and up onto the road, engine growling and tires spinning. She drew in a sigh of relief and drove toward Lander.

She had accomplished nothing. Nothing to allay Betty's fears, nothing that might help the Little Shields. And yet she couldn't shake the feeling that behind the stonewalling and the indignation of Lou and Debbie Bearing, there was everything.

# 21

THE CELL WAS ringing. A muffled noise that emanated from the depths of her bag on the passenger seat and jolted Vicky out of the rhythm of the tires on the snowy pavement. Vicky slipped her earpiece behind her ear, not taking her eyes from the flare of headlights on the road. The ringing stopped. "Vicky Holden here."

A jumble of sounds: clanking glasses, a distant roar of guffaws, the shuffle of boots on a hard surface. "Hello." She heard herself shouting over the noise in what was probably a bar. A surge of anticipation ran through her. Vince could be on the other end. "Are you there?"

"Vicky? I got to talk to you." It was a woman's voice, aggressive and depressed at the same time, slurring the words, stumbling over them. The voice of Betty White Hawk.

"Where are you?"

"At the Buffalo. Waiting for Vince."

"You heard from him?"

"No. No." The aggression surged forward. "I'm going to find him."

"How does that help Vince? Your drinking."

Loud, raucous laughter erupted in the background. It was a moment before Betty said, "I'm waiting for Vince. Sooner or later, he's gotta come in. He likes this place. He drinks here. So I got to thinking, there's some stuff you don't know."

"You think it will help locate Vince?" Vicky kept her eyes on the road, the yellow headlights bouncing on the snow. It was surreal, the silence of the snow around her, the hum of the engine, and the stream of warm air flowing from the vents interspersed with the noise of the bar, the drunken meanderings of Betty White Hawk, who had convinced herself that her son would show up if she waited long enough and drank enough to keep believing. And now she was reminiscing, calling up stuff she wanted to talk about.

Vicky knew the way it would go. The nights that Ben Holden had come home drunk, the old memories flooding in and Ben wanting to talk and talk and talk. *Sit down, Vicky. I'm talking to you.*

"Vicky? You there? I gotta talk to you."

"It can wait until tomorrow." Vicky tried to blink back the image of Betty White Hawk making her way across the bar and stumbling outside when Vince didn't show up. Driving herself home.

"I keep thinking . . . I keep thinking, what if Vince is dead? I can't stop thinking . . ." She was crying, soft mewling noises like those of an infant.

"Stay there," Vicky heard herself saying. "I'm on the way." She could feel the tiredness clinging to her, pulling at her legs and arms. In fifteen minutes she could be home. Her own apartment, familiar and warm. She would scramble eggs, make fresh coffee. Be alone. Think about her conversation with Lou and Debbie Bearing, try to figure out their connection to Vince White Hawk and the Little Shields. That there was a connection, she was sure. But nothing made sense. And there was Betty, drinking, wanting to tell her *something*.

"Did you hear me?" Vicky said. "I'm on the way."

The neon sign with *Buffalo Bar and Lounge* in white letters and a large, yellow glass of foamy beer glowed on the sign ahead. Vicky pulled into the parking lot. It had taken almost forty minutes to get to Riverton. The sense of uselessness was like a physical presence beside her. Betty had probably left by now.

She slammed out of the Ford and made her way to the front door, the icy pavement pulling at her boots, as if she were walking underwater. The pounding noise of music cut through the frigid air. Before she could open the door, it swung out and two cowboys staggered past in the blast of a guitar riff.

"Well, now. What have we here?" One of the cowboys stepped sideways toward her, head first, as if he were heading off a straying calf.

Vicky dodged past and caught the door as it was about to close. "Hey, pretty lady," the other cowboy called as she stepped inside and pulled the door shut. The air was dim and smoky, vibrating in the music that poured out of speakers set along the ceiling. It took a minute for her eyes to adjust. Groups of cowboys and women in blue jeans and boots—laughing and shouting, hoisting bottles of beer and glasses of what was probably whiskey with ice cubes clanking—formed and dissolved around the table. A few couples were dancing on a small floor in the center, moving drunkenly together at half pace to the music. She couldn't spot Betty anywhere.

Then she saw her, small and vulnerable-looking, straddling a stool, propping her head on one hand, an elbow set on the bar for support. A half-filled glass of whiskey stood next to her elbow. Vicky started around the tables, slipping away from a cowboy who reached for her arm. She slid onto the stool next to Betty. The smell of whiskey invaded her nostrils and sank into her throat. She swallowed hard to counter the reflex to throw up. "You had better let me take you home."

Betty managed to lift her head a little, then let it sink back onto her hand. With her other hand, she gripped the glass and took a long drink. "I didn't think you were coming."

"How long have you been here?" Vicky wondered how many glasses of whiskey Betty had put down.

"Vince could show up anytime." Betty swiveled a little on the stool, then grabbed the edge of the bar to steady herself. "He's all I got, Vicky. I have to wait for him."

"He had three bottles of whiskey," Vicky said. "He's drinking somewhere else. When he sobers up, he'll call you." God, how many times had she said this to Betty? And who was she trying to convince? This drunken woman or herself? "He's not coming to the bar. I'd better take you home. You can wait there for him to call."

"He's going to die." The woman's face crumpled into the kind of grief Vicky had seen at funerals. Betty White Hawk was already mourning her son.

"You mustn't lose hope." Vicky tried for a calm, optimistic note, and yet she had the sense that she was missing something. Betty had wanted to talk to her, to tell her *something*. The music thumped from the speaker overhead and drowned out the sounds of ice clinking in the glass that Betty set down. The bartender had moved across from them, and Vicky realized he was waiting for her order.

"Coffee, black." She faced him. "Make that two coffees. We'll be at the table." She nodded toward a vacant table against the far wall, a good twenty feet from the nearest speaker. Then she took Betty's arm. "Let's go where it's not so noisy," she said.

It was as if the woman had climbed out onto a cliff and stood staring down at the abyss. "Vince won't see me over there. I have to stay here."

"I'll watch for him." Vicky took hold of the woman's arm and tried to nudge her upward, but Betty remained immobile, holding on to her place a moment before she started to lift herself off the stool. She fell against the bar and clawed at the edge, breathing hard. For a moment, Vicky feared she might pass out.

"I'll help you," she said, grabbing Betty's arm hard and propelling her upward. Then they were stumbling, both of them, around the tables, past the guffaws and loud, drunken conversations, past a table of cowboys.

"What we got here?" A cowboy jumped to his feet. "Let me give you a hand." He took hold of Betty's other arm and, as if he knew where they were headed, guided her, toward the vacant table. "Better get some coffee in her." He winked at Vicky. "Call on me anytime."

The bartender walked over, waited for the cowboy to head back to his own table, and set down two mugs of coffee. "She didn't finish her drink."

"Coffee is fine." Vicky nodded, then sat down next to Betty, who was blinking at the log wall, as if she were trying to figure out how the bar had disappeared. "Drink this," Vicky said, handing the woman a mug. "You'll feel better."

Betty took a long drink of coffee before setting the mug down. "I keep seeing Vince dead, and I can't take it, Vicky. It's going to kill me. I couldn't just sit there waiting for Father John or some cop to knock on my door with the horrible news."

"Vince has gone on benders before. He'll sober up, and I can still try to get the judge to send him to rehab."

"You don't know."

"What? What don't I know? What did you want to tell me?"

"I watched his Daddy die. Rickie. The love of my life." Moisture swelled in the woman's eyes. She made fists and punched at her head. "You know what that's like? To listen to the man you love gasping for breath? I can't ever get that hissing sound out of my head. I kept shouting, 'Don't die on me. Don't you dare die on me.' But I couldn't breathe for him, I couldn't get him air."

Vicky waited a moment before she said, "You told me Rickie died in an accident. You didn't tell me you were there."

"The pickup turned over and I crawled out, but Rickie . . . he was trapped beneath the steering wheel. It pinned him down like a big boulder. I couldn't . . ." Betty set her elbows on the table and leaned into her fists. "I couldn't get him out. I tried and tried. I pulled so hard, but he wouldn't move, and all the time he kept hissing. I screamed for them to come and help, but they went on. They drove away and left him to die."

Betty was crying hard now, and Vicky found a tissue in her bag and handed it to her. She waited while Betty swiped at her eyes and nose, then nudged the coffee mug toward her. "Try to sip a little more."

It was a moment before Betty lifted the mug and took another drink. When she set the mug down, Vicky said, "Who drove away? Who are you talking about?"

Betty looked at her with wide eyes blurred with tears. "Lou and Debbie. I hate them. I've stayed away from them since it happened. Vince was young when his Daddy died. I never told him about Lou and Debbie because I didn't want him to grow up with the hatred I lived with. When I heard Vince had been drinking with Lou right here in this bar, I thought I was going to go crazy. Lou's going to do to Vince what he did to his Daddy."

"What did he do?"

"I've been trying to forget."

"I know. But if Lou is going to do the same thing to Vince, you had better tell me what it was."

Betty drained the rest of the coffee, and Vicky motioned the bartender for a refill. After the bartender had moved away, she waited while Betty took a sip of the fresh coffee, giving her time to organize whatever she was about to say.

Finally Betty set the mug down and looked at her. "We didn't have any money. And Vince was getting bigger. He needed things. A lot of food, and he was always growing out of blue jeans and boots. Rickie wanted to be a good dad. He loved that boy. He got to talking to Lou Bearing—they'd gone to school together—and Lou said he had a job for him. Five hundred dollars. Well, that was a lot of money. All Rickie had to do was drive Lou and Debbie over to a car lot in Casper. They had picked out a car they wanted, and Lou knew how to start it. He was gonna drive the car off the lot and back to the rez with Debbie in the passenger seat, like they were just a young couple going to the movies."

Betty took another drink of the coffee, and Vicky could see she was starting to sober up. She was saying how she had gone along because she didn't want Rickie to go alone. And it would look better if it was a couple in the pickup. The cops wouldn't be so suspicious. Lou and Debbie were scrunched together in the backseat, giddy with excitement. It wasn't a new car they intended to steal. Nothing fancy. Lou needed an SUV for the parts. He could cannibalize it, fix up a couple of other SUVs that, she figured, he had also stolen. Lou knew what he was doing, Rickie told her. He'd always been good at fixing up old cars, making them like new.

"What happened?"

"We went to the lot. It was Sunday night, nobody around. Didn't take long, and Lou and Debbie drove out through a chain that was about a foot high. Snapped it in two. We started back to the rez. Lou wanted us to follow, stay close behind, in case of trouble and they had to abandon the car. They figured they'd jump back into our pickup and take off. It was crazy, the whole idea, but Rickie had five hundred bucks in his pocket. We were on Seventeen-Mile Road, and Lou was driving fast. Too fast, and Rickie tried to keep up. We came around that big curve, and the pickup skidded out into the other lane. There was a truck coming, and Rickie tried to get back into our lane. That's when it happened. We were all over the road, back and forth, out of control. I don't know how we missed hitting the truck. I still see it whizzing past. Next thing I knew we were rolling down the barrow ditch and out onto the prairie."

She started crying, big, racking sobs that shook her chair. Vicky placed an arm around the woman's shoulders. "I'm so sorry," she said.

"I tried to pull him out. I tried and tried, and Lou and Debbie kept going. They didn't even stop. I can't watch Vince die like that, Vicky. I can't."

"Do you think they're still stealing cars?"

"What do you think? They got Vince to help, just like they got his daddy. They paid him some money. Those sons of bitches. When I went out to beg them to tell me what they knew about Vince, they threw me out!"

Vicky sat back in her chair. The music sounded far away, as if it came from across the street. The bar had started to clear out, only a few cowboys and their girlfriends still hugging the tables. Nobody was on the dance floor. Vince had been drinking with Lou Bearing, a man who repaired cars and trucks in a barn, and Vince had come into some money. It made sense.

"I'll drive you home," Vicky said. "I'll have your car brought to your house in the morning." Annie would handle it, she was thinking. She would hire a couple of her relatives to retrieve the car.

"What would you have said to Lou if he had come in?" Vicky guided the woman out of the bar and across the parking lot. She placed her arm around her waist and turned her toward the Ford.

Betty stopped and looked at her. "Didn't you hear what I told you? If that sonofabitch came in, I was going to kill him."

# 22

FATHER JOHN SET the phone next to the laptop on his desk where he could answer it right away. He had spent most of the morning staring at it, willing it to ring, picking up at the first jangle of noise. Two calls, so far. Lucinda Oldman, wanting to schedule the baptism for her new son, and Grandfather Black Wolf, letting him know Grandmother was back in Riverton Memorial. Could he visit her? Yes, of course. Later this morning for sure.

Nothing from Shannon. No call, no sound of James's truck plowing around Circle Drive. It wasn't his business, he kept telling himself. Not his business at all if his adult niece chose to spend the night with a young man. And who knew? The truck could have gotten stuck in the snow. Maybe the engine wouldn't turn over. What else could Shannon have done but spend the night and wait until morning?

He set both elbows on the desk and blew into his fists. He had caught the glances between Shannon and James, the quick, warm smiles, like the remembrance of a private joke. Hadn't Shannon told him how wise and mature James was? He tried to tamp down the sense of alarm. Shannon, coming off a breakup, trying to hide the disappointment, confusion and pain enveloping her like a cloud. Back and forth he went between worrying and telling himself it wasn't his business. She was his brother's child, an adult, which meant she was part of him, too, an appendage he'd seldom thought about, until he'd begun to sense something was wrong.

He kept his eyes on the phone. Surely, it would ring. He had considered calling James's house, but that seemed intrusive. He had no right. He had every right, he decided, to confirm that Shannon was safe. He picked up the phone, scrolled to James's number, and tapped the call button. It took a moment before the ringing started, then three long rings before James's voice was on the other end. "Two Horses."

"I've been worried about Shannon." Father John picked his way through the words; he didn't want to sound like an overbearing busybody. "Is everything okay?"

"Everything's fine, Father." They both knew the real reason for the call. "We're on our way to the mission now. See you in fifteen minutes."

Father John pressed the end button. He got up and went down the hall, following the clack-clack of computer keys. Bishop Harry was bent over the small laptop. "Have a seat," he said, his eyes on the screen.

Father John dropped onto the hard wooden chair the bishop kept for counseling sessions—guaranteed not to make anyone want to linger. He waited a moment until the clacking stopped and the bishop shut the laptop and looked up. He had blue eyes as shiny as new marbles, lit with intelligence and humor. He nodded, an acknowledgement of the real reason Father John was there. "You're worried about her."

"She's having a tough time. It looks like she made a mistake with her last . . . relationship." Father John swallowed the word. What in heaven's name did it mean? A commitment with strings and end dates? Hardly a commitment at all. "I'm afraid she may be making another one."

"We all have to find our way, John. Often the price is a mistake. Can you save Shannon from pain?" He waited until Father John shook his head. "You can be her friend, her uncle, part of her family. Families must love unconditionally. I would also suggest"—he nodded four or five times—"that you trust her."

"What about James?"

"Ah, James. We've had two very interesting discussions. I believe he is making progress in discerning his vocation."

"Do you believe he has a vocation?"

"Without a doubt. The calling came to him like a bolt of lightning. St. Paul struck down on the road to Damascus. He knows he must serve the people of God, go where the Lord leads him."

The wind had come up, and the bare branch of a cottonwood tapped against the window, making an eerie, rhythmic sound. The old building sighed and creaked. "You're saying James has a vocation, but not for all of it."

"Precisely." The bishop gave him the benevolent smile he had probably bestowed on students in the school he'd run in Patna, India. "James also has a vocation for a family. He very much wants to marry and raise children. He must find his way."

"The diaconate."

"Or the Anglican priesthood. He must decide."

Father John looked over at the window, the cottonwood branch scraping back and forth. He watched the wind unfurl and lift the snow across the space between the building and Eagle Hall and wondered if he'd had a vocation for all of it twenty-five years ago.

"I've been checking the online news bulletins from the province." The bishop sat very still. His voice had gone soft and inward. "The powers that be are gathering for what they call a planning meeting. Planning the future of the Jesuit missions."

Father John nodded. He supposed Father Jameson had called to let him in on what was going on. There hadn't been time to return the call. There would never be enough time, he thought, for the news that was most likely coming.

The front door opened and swooshed shut, sending a draft of cold air down the hall and into the small office. He got to his feet, conscious of the intensity of the old man's blue eyes on him. It was uncanny how the bishop could see through him, read his thoughts.

"You don't have regrets, do you?"

Father John turned around in the doorway. Regrets? How could he regret this? St. Francis Mission and the Arapaho people. He felt as if, all of his life, he had been on his way here. "No regrets," he said.


"JAMES HAS A wonderful idea." Shannon had already swooped her laptop off the desk in the closet-sized office and was in the corridor, laptop gripped to her chest, still bundled in her coat, gold-colored cap pulled down to her eyebrows. Red curls sprang from beneath the cap. Her eyes brimmed with enthusiasm. James stood behind her as if he had stepped back to give her center stage. "He's arranged for me to view an old movie Lizzie and her husband were in."

Of course, Father John thought. Dozens of Arapahos and Sho-shones had gone to Hollywood in the early nineteen-twenties to be in the first cowboys-and-Indians movies. The Brokenhorns had been part of the troupe.

"Almost two years in Hollywood! Imagine. I'll be at the library in Lander, in case"—she stopped, as if she couldn't imagine why he might want to know where she was—"you know, anybody calls here, in case they can't reach me on my cell."

Father John smiled at this niece of his and walked her and James to the front door. He closed the door behind them, shoving it hard against the wind, then went back to his desk. A sense of relief flooded over him. A wise man, the bishop. They would find their own way, Shannon and James.

He had just begun to pay a few bills—not all of the bills stacked in front of him, since there wasn't enough money in the mission account, but those that had worked their way into the highest priority—when he heard the dual growl of engines. Shannon and James, driving off; someone else arriving. He wasn't expecting any-one, but parishioners were always stopping in. A chat, maybe a little counseling, a cup of coffee. He finished writing the first check. The engine cut off, leaving the whistling noise of the wind. Then the clack of boots on the steps, the pneumatic whoosh of the door open-ing. He recognized the footsteps in the corridor and was on his feet when Vicky rapped on the door frame and stepped into his office.

"I took a chance I'd find you." Snowflakes sparkled in her hair and on the shoulders of her black coat. She looked flushed with fatigue.

"Let me take your coat." He was surprised at the ease in which she shrugged the coat into his hands, something weighing on her mind.

"Coffee?" He was already at the small metal table behind the door, filling two mugs with the coffee he'd made this morning. He shook some powdered creamer into his mug. Vicky liked her coffee black.

He handed her a mug, then leaned back against the edge of his desk. She wouldn't sit down, he knew, preferring to sip at the coffee while she trolled about the office. Window, door, back again. She thought better when she was moving. She had never actually told him this, but he knew it was true. He took a drink of his own coffee and waited until she turned to face him.

"What do you know about Lou and Debbie Bearing?"

"I've met them a few times." This wasn't what he was expecting. He'd thought she might have some news about Vince White Hawk. Everything about her warned that the news she did have wasn't good. He had tried to call Betty last night, but she hadn't answered. He intended to stop by the school where she worked. "What's going on?"

"I think the Bearings are involved with Vince White Hawk's disappearance. He still hasn't shown up, and Betty is worried sick. She's . . ." Vicky hesitated, then plunged on: "She's falling apart, John. She's been drinking. I met her at the Buffalo Bar last night. She'd convinced herself that if she hung around there, Vince would come in."

"You think Lou and Debbie Bearing know where he is?"

Vicky had started circling again, sipping at the coffee. "Betty thinks Vince got his drinking money from them." She stopped again. "Ten years ago, the Bearings hired Vince's dad, Rickie, to help them steal a car in Casper and bring it back to the rez. Betty went along. She and Rickie were following the Bearings back to their place, speeding on Seventeen-Mile Road, when Rickie's pickup turned over. He was trapped behind the steering wheel. He died there. The Bearings drove on. They didn't stop to help."

Father John took a moment. The accident, as everyone called it, that had killed Vince's father, had happened a few months before he'd come to St. Francis. "Does Betty think the Bearings had Vince help them steal a car?"

"She says it's what they do. Steal cars for the parts Lou uses in the shop he's set up in his barn. When I went to see them . . ."

"You went to see them?"

"Yesterday. I didn't learn much. Lou was working on a sedan and a truck. A black truck. He and Debbie claimed they didn't know anything about Vince." Vicky was pacing again, working out something in her mind. "They're lying. But there's more, John. I think they also know something about the Little Shields and their daughter."

She stopped pacing, and this time she walked over and leaned against the desk beside him. "The Little Shields had hired Clint Hopkins to help them adopt their daughter. I've taken over the case."

He nodded and started to say how sorry he was about the lawyer, but Vicky was going on, something about how she had been following Clint's investigation. "I'm running into brick walls, but I'm convinced that"—she took in a gulp of air—"he found out something that got him killed."

He didn't say anything, waiting for her to pick up her thoughts again, arrange them in some kind of order that made sense. He had counseled Myra and Eldon Little Shield a few times. They weren't parishioners, but they had come anyway, worried sick that they could lose their little girl. He had encouraged them to seek a legal adoption. They must have hired Clint Hopkins. The *Gazette* had said Clint's death was an accident. It was clear Vicky didn't think so.

A moment passed before she drew in a long breath and said, "I've talked to Dina Fowler. She and her husband, Matthew, used to live near the Bearings. She told me they didn't have children, but she had heard a baby crying at their house for a week. It was in March, five years ago. The same time the Little Shields got Mary Ann. Eldon said they told you about it. He gave me permission to discuss it with you."

Father John waited while Vicky went over to the table, poured some more coffee, and resumed pacing. "A baby left on their doorstep," she said. "Myra's cousin worked for social services. She gave them papers that made them think they had temporary custody. I suspect the relative was trying to help them out, since they had just lost their own baby. The point is, they love that little girl. They want to adopt her. I believe Clint must have stumbled onto something that could complicate the adoption." She turned around and faced him again. "Clint Hopkins, the best known adoption attorney in the county, asked me to be his cocounsel. An Arapaho lawyer. Whatever he learned, he believed the tribe would be involved."

"You're saying Clint could have learned where the child came from?" The Little Shields' biggest fear, Father John was thinking: that their child's natural parents existed somewhere, and cared.

"I'm saying that Lou and Debbie Bearing could know something about it." Vicky threw one hand in the air. "Five years ago, a neighbor heard a baby crying at their house. A relative's baby, the Bearings say, and who could disprove it? How could anyone connect Mary Ann to the Bearings?"

Vicky circled over to the window and looked out. "Lou is a nervous man. It's like he has something on his conscience that he would like to be free of. I got the sense he might have told me something if Debbie hadn't come in."

He'd had the same feeling the other night at the Buffalo Bar, Father John was thinking. Lou Bearing had shrunk away from him and Betty, holding on to the edge of the table, as if the table could protect him from their gaze, their accusations. A feeling was all it was, a second sense that came from years of watching people shift about in their chairs, avoid his eyes, clasp their hands together, and, finally, unburden themselves.

"I can go out to the house," Father John said.

Vicky gave him a quick smile. "I was hoping you would say that."

# 23

SHANNON STARED AT the image on the video. An ordinary-looking woman, leathered, wrinkled face with no makeup, no sign of concern about her appearance. *Take me as I am.* Staring out at the camera, unsurprised, as if this were normal, acting in a movie, pretending to be someone else. She wore a blouse embroidered with quills, a printed skirt that swished about her legs, and a headdress filled with eagle feathers she would have earned, Shannon knew, from the trials she had overcome. The headdress concealed her hair. Her eyes were light, her face pale.

Standing beside her was John Brokenhorn, wrinkled like Lizzie, but dark-skinned with narrowed, defiant black eyes. His eagle-feathered headdress listed to one side. On the chest of his dark shirt were beaded and quilled pendants, gifts from Lizzie, most likely. And a silver peace medal with the hard-to-decipher image of some politician who had promised the Indians peace.

All of this, plunked down in Hollywood.

"She looks old and tired." James rolled his chair closer to Shannon's and hunched toward the photo.

"In nineteen-twenty-two she would have been fifty-nine."

"She had a hard life."

"Is that what you think?" Shannon turned toward him and smiled. She didn't know where James Two Horses had come from. Out of the blue, confident and assured, settled within himself. He had a vocation to the priesthood, he'd told her. But there were other vocations, other callings, he couldn't ignore. He'd been talking to the bishop, and the old man had helped him to see that he would have to find the way to honor all of his vocations.

Her heart had sunk when he'd first mentioned the priesthood. How silly, she told herself now. What had she expected? A man she had just met, even though it seemed as if they had always known each other. They had talked for hours last night, talked about everything. It was great, taking it slowly, getting to know each other. She had never met a man like James. He seemed to be part of her, connected by some invisible thread she hadn't realized existed. She remembered the faintest light shining in the window just before she'd fallen asleep on the sofa. When she'd awakened, she saw that James had draped a blanket over her. She could hear him moving about the kitchen. Smells of coffee and bacon drifted through the sadness that permeated her. This man, who seemed part of her, was considering the priesthood. Well, maybe she was kidding herself. Soul mates didn't exist, except in romance novels and fairy tales—the *forever afters*. She no longer believed in all of that.

She was glad for his presence now, the way he found her work—her project—exciting and interesting. Unlike David. *Who cares about what happened a hundred years ago?*

She cared, and part of coming to the reservation, she realized, was to be with her uncle, an historian who cared, and to do research where Lizzie had actually lived and be with the people she had loved. To find more than history. To find the *story.* And she had found James. He had suggested they watch a video of *The Covered Wagon,* one of the movies Lizzie and John Brokenhorn had been in. He arranged with the librarian at the Lander Library to set up the video. They were alone in the small, glass-enclosed room. Beyond the glass, the librarian—Nancy somebody, who James had gone to school with—stood behind a counter, in an earnest conversation with a young woman. People milled about, wandering among the stacks of books on the far side of the counter.

He turned toward her and smiled. "Ready to continue?" When she nodded, he pressed the forward button, and the images started moving again across the small screen. Indian warriors racing past on horseback, the long, winding wagon train coming over the prairie, all accompanied by the tinny plunking of a keyboard. The images looked grainy and unstable, as if sand were blowing through. Lizzie, huddled with the other Indian women in front of a tipi, stooping over a kettle, a little fire dancing beneath it.

At one point, James reached for her hand and squeezed it. "It must have been hard for her."

She was struck by the sympathy in his voice. She studied his profile for a moment: the dark eyes, almost black. The bump at the top of his nose, the high forehead and the strong, wide chin, the generous mouth. Brokenhorn might have looked like this, so handsome that he had taken Lizzie's breath away.

"Living on the reservation?"

James shook his head. "Hollywood."

Yes, of course. She went back to watching the images flash past.

"An Arapaho woman." She kept her voice low, parsing her thoughts over the ripple of piano keys. "Not really Arapaho. A white woman, born into a white family, plunked down among her own people for a while. White people everywhere she looked. On the streets and sidewalks, on the movie lot. She was surrounded by white faces."

She shifted toward James. "She must have wondered how her life might have gone had she not been captured. How could she have looked at the cars and houses and shops and restaurants and all the rest of Hollywood and not thought, What would this have been like? What would I have been like?"

"You think that in the two years Lizzie spent in Hollywood . . ."

"She might have regretted the way her life had gone."

James was shaking his head, giving her that thoughtful look she was getting used to, as if he had heard every word and was turning what she'd said over in his mind. "It wasn't her world. She had never known white towns and crowds of white people. The only white people she'd had contact with lived in Lander and Riverton, and I doubt she went to town very often. There were signs on the shop windows then: No dogs or Indians allowed."

Shannon sat back. "She never wrote anything." The movie had ended, the screen shimmered gray, and James pressed another key.

"She would have been illiterate," James said. "Some Arapahos went to the school at St. Francis Mission, but most worked the ranches and farms. They had to work, or they didn't eat. Not many girls went to school." He gave a sharp laugh. "They had to do most of the work."

"It's impossible to know what Lizzie felt. All I have is conjecture and . . ."

"That's not history."

"Exactly. Besides, what was Lizzie supposed to do if she had felt regrets or longings? Leave Brokenhorn? Leave the only life she knew? Whatever she may have felt, I think she would have kept silent and gone on."

THE SUN HELD all the way across the reservation. It had broken out this afternoon, a red disc that flared against the gray clouds moving across the mountains. Always welcome, the sun: warming the frozen air, licking at the ice at the edge of the roads. Father John squinted in the brightness as he drove toward Lou and Debbie Bearing's place outside of Fort Washakie.

He had stopped by Riverton Memorial first to visit Grandmother Black Wolf, who assured him she would be up and about and home, where she belonged, in no time. After that he had doubled back to Wind River school, where he had found Betty White Hawk in the break room, gulping coffee, jittery as a cat. No, she hadn't heard from Vince. Every day she worried that this would be the day her son could die.

Coming around a bend, he spotted the house and barn rising against the Wind River Mountains in the background, like the painting of a winter's scene in a Western museum. Except for something odd: a woman with long black hair was stomping through the snow in front of the house, arms waving, beseeching, clutching at the air. She flung herself about, shrieking like a trapped animal. He pulled a sharp turn across the road, bumped over the barrow ditch and stopped a few yards from her. She paid no attention, lost in herself, shrieking and reaching for the sky, in some kind of primitive dance. A dance of grief.

Father John jumped out and ran to her. "What is it?" His own voice mixed with the woman's cries. "What's happened?"

She stopped moving and looked at him, eyes unfocused, skittering about. The shrieking died back into a gurgling noise. She wrapped her arms over her chest and started plucking at the sleeves of her jacket.

"Debbie?" he said, and the name seemed to grab her attention. She folded downward, sinking onto her knees in the snow, boots splayed behind her. She was sobbing.

Father John hunched down beside her. "Look at me, Debbie. I'm Father O'Malley from the mission. I want to help you. Tell me what's happened."

"He's dead." The woman spoke so softly, he had to lean forward, bracing himself with one hand in the snow. "Lou's dead."

# 24

FATHER JOHN PULLED his mobile out of his pocket and pressed 911. Crumpled beside him, Debbie Bearing seemed to be sinking deeper and deeper into the snow. There was one ring, then a voice asked what the emergency was. He gave his name and said he was at the home of Lou and Debbie Bearing west of Fort Washakie. Lou Bearing was hurt. Possibly dead. Debbie was in shock. "We need an ambulance." Which could take a while, he was thinking. There were few patrol cars, few officers to cover the miles of empty space on the rez. "It's the house with the large barn in back."

"Where is the injured man?"

"I'm not sure." He wasn't even sure if the hysterical woman beside him knew what she was talking about. He leaned closer to Debbie, trying to get her attention. She had drifted off, gone somewhere else. "Where is Lou?"

She blinked at him, the effort to concentrate printed on her face. "The shop," she said finally.

"I heard," the voice on the phone said. "I'll hold on while you check."

"I'm going to give the phone to Debbie," he told the voice. "Talk to her while I'm gone."

For a moment, Debbie didn't seem to understand. She recoiled from the phone, an alien object from outer space. "Tell the operator what you've told me, Debbie."

She nodded, as if the sound of her own name had brought her back again, and reached for the phone. Her fingers were red and stiff with cold, and the phone started to slip. He closed her fingers around it, holding them there a moment, willing the warmth of his own glove into her hand. "Lou's dead," he heard her say as he got to his feet and started around the house toward the barn.

A light-colored pickup stood close to the house. The snow all around had been disturbed. A lot of footsteps; he wasn't the first person to have walked about today. He stayed with the footsteps down the side of the house to the barn, where the footsteps had churned out big, messy circles, as if a tractor had run through.

One of the barn doors had been pushed open, and the sun glinted on the metal railings. Inside looked as dark as night. Just across the threshold, he could see smudges of snow prints on a hard-packed dirt floor that bumped into the darkness. "Anyone here?" He was shouting into a vacuum, the sound of his own voice echoing around him.

He moved farther inside. The shadowy hulks of vehicles rose in front of him. He patted the wall on the left, then the one on the right. Finally his fingers found a smooth plastic plate with a switch in the center. Lights flashed on, streaming down from metal poles in the corners, flooding over a black truck and a dark sedan lined up in bays. Tools spilled over the worktables alongside the vehicles.

More tools cluttered the benches against the walls and dangled from hooks on the walls.

He stepped toward the vehicles, scouring the areas in between, the spaces under the tables and benches, any place large enough for a body. Nothing out of the ordinary, nothing he wouldn't expect to see in a garage: little pools of oil here and there, glinting in the light; oil-smeared rags tossed onto the benches; coveralls hanging from nails.

"Anyone here?" He spotted what looked like a broken baseball bat lying next to the wall. He stooped over and picked it up, feeling his muscles tighten, bracing for the unexpected. Someone could be here, someone involved in Lou Bearing's death. Anything could have happened. A disgruntled customer, an argument that escalated into violence. Metal tools everywhere, easy to grab, slam into a scalp. My God.

He reached the wall and turned, moving down the side of the black truck toward the hood, his own heart pounding in his ears. Still nothing. Then, there, sticking out from below the bumper, was a boot, dirty and worn-looking, and, oddly, not out of place on the soiled dirt. Attached to the boot, a jeans-clad leg. Another leg angled under the truck. The body of a man sprawled facedown, light shining on the circle of scalp near the top of what was left of his head. Spreading around him was a dark, glassy pool of blood. Blood splattered the metal bumper like flecks of black paint and smeared the wall three feet away. The ashy smell of blood filled his nostrils, the smell of death.

It took a moment to absorb what he was looking at. The blue jeans and brown jacket, the outstretched arms, as if Lou Bearing had tried to save himself. There was a black revolver a few inches from his right hand. "God have mercy on your soul," he said.

He took a few steps backward, then swung around and started retracing his steps, walking slowly, searching the spaces and the shadows, gripping the bat, wanting to make sure no one else was here. He moved past the door and checked out the other side of the barn. Still nothing except the faint smell of blood and an odd change in the atmosphere the farther away he got from the body. He started along the side of the sedan and worked his way again toward the rear wall. A couple of brooms leaning against a table, metal pails stacked together, shelves lined with paint and aerosol cans, a container of brushes. He stooped down and looked underneath the vehicles, then glanced up at the rafters. Hiding places, but no sign of anyone, except for the body of Lou Bearing under the front of the truck.

Father John turned around and hurried out into the bright glare of snow and sun. He broke into a run around the house. Debbie Bearing was folded over in the snow. He could hear her moaning.

He knelt down beside her. She started rocking back and forth, moaning and mumbling, not making any sense. She gripped her knees to her chest, and he managed to pull the mobile out of her hand.

"Are you still there?"

"I'm here, Father." The voice came from far away, another reality.

"A man is dead in the barn. He was shot in the head."

"Lou Bearing?"

"His wife must have found him."

Debbie was still rocking back and forth. He leaned over and patted her shoulder.

"You're sure he's dead."

Yes, he was sure, he told the voice. He knew death. So many deaths since he had come to St. Francis. Accidents, fights, gunshots. "He's dead," he said again.

"Try to keep the wife calm until the medics arrive." The voice was steady and certain. How many times had the operator given this advice? Wife, mother, cousin, friend—keep them calm. "Do you want me to stay on the line?"

"No. We'll manage."

He ended the call, slipped the phone into his jacket pocket. The woman was wobbling now, trying to get to her feet, to get a grip on the earth. "An ambulance is on the way," he told her. "Shall we wait inside where it's warmer?" He started to take hold of her arm.

"No. No. No." Debbie swatted at his hand, then lifted her own hands overhead. The screeching began again, the besieging of heaven. After a long moment, she seemed to catch her breath. "Don't take me in there. I can't go back there."

"It's your home, Debbie," Father John said, trying for reason, logic. What was he thinking? "You can wait in my pickup," he said. It wasn't warm; he was never sure if the heater would turn on, and the engine had been cooling now for a while. Still, better than the snow.

She didn't protest. No screeching now, just low moaning and sobbing sounds. He held her arm and helped her onto her feet. She was surprisingly heavy for a small, compact woman. A solid build, thick arms he could feel through the weight of her jacket. She stumbled forward, boots skimming the snow, not connecting with the ground, and Father John placed his arm around her waist, holding her upright as they walked to the pickup. He lifted her into the seat, where she flopped back, breathing hard. Father John waited for the screeching to start again. It came at intervals, it seemed, the way grief came in waves. He reached behind the seat for the blanket he kept in back and pulled it around her shoulders, enfolding her in fleece. She was shivering.

"He left me." Debbie spit out the words, like something hard and bitter in her throat. "He promised he would never leave me. We were in it together . . ." She stopped, as if in that instant she realized what she was saying.

"In what together?" Father John kept his voice low.

"A team. The Bearing team, that's what we were," she said. "Lou and Debbie. Nothing was going to tear us apart. Oh God. Oh God."

"Take a deep breath," Father John said, and after a moment, that is what she did. Drew in a long breath, more docile now, following instructions, as if she had been lost out in the yard, circling and screaming, not knowing what to do, and now someone was telling her what to do. She let the breath out slowly, then drew in another.

"What will happen to me?" She looked up at him, then flicked her eyes away. "We had a pact. Why did he leave me? I was strong for both of us. God, he was drinking and going to bars, even though I told him I'd take care of everything. Don't worry. And everything was working out like I planned. Working out, working out." The words sounded like the click of a metronome.

"Debbie, what are you talking about?"

He wondered if she knew herself. She seemed rational and irrational at the same time, flailing at something that welled inside her.

When she didn't say anything, he asked if there was someone he could call. "Family or friends? They'll want to be with you."

She threw her head back and laughed. "I never thought he'd do it. I never thought he had the guts to do it. He told me lots of times he was done, fed up. This morning he started in. Shot his hand at the coffee mug, and spilled coffee, and said he was tired of it."

"Tired of what?" What was she trying to tell him, to get off her chest?

"Waiting. Tired of the waiting, and so end it. Shoot yourself, I don't care. He went out to the shop. He left so fast, I don't remember him going. He's sitting there with coffee dripping onto his jeans, and then he's gone, and I heard it. I heard the shot. I never thought . . . I never wanted . . . I killed him."

Father John patted the woman's shoulder again and told her to take another breath. This was as tough as it got. There were no words. *Don't blame yourself.* He expected her to start screeching again, reaching for heaven. This would take time. Years. "I'm very sorry," he told her. "There must be someone you want with you."

"Just us. Our team, Lou and me. We did fine, didn't we? Nobody else. Don't let anybody else in. We told each other we're enough."

Down the road, coming toward the house, coming fast, was the sound of sirens. A parade of vehicles: gray and white police cars, an ambulance, and a white van. They started to slow down. Father John stepped away from the pickup and waved them forward. One by one they turned, dipping into the ditch then up onto the yard, snow spitting beneath the tires, sirens fading and finally shutting off, leaving only a faraway echo.

# 25

THE HOUSE LOOKED deserted. Holding its place in a row of other houses, cars at the curb, pine trees bundled in snow, and yet something different about it, as if the life had been sucked out. Vicky managed to fit the Ford between two sedans, then made her way up the un-shoveled walk.

The door was flung open before she reached the porch. Lacy Hopkins leaned outside, face drawn, blanched with questions. "What is it?"

"Vicky Holden." A sheen of ice lay over the porch floor. Lacy stared around the edge of the door. No sign of recognition in her eyes, no memory of Vicky having been here the day after Clint's death. Another face in the crowd of people offering condolences. "I'm the lawyer who has taken over one of Clint's adoption cases."

Lacy nodded. A flicker in her eyes, like the effort to remember. Then she said, "I wasn't expecting company."

"I wanted to ask you about something." They were standing outside, like two women waiting for a bus, Vicky thought. Lacy looked disheveled, as if she hadn't slept in a long time. Sandy hair uncombed and ropy, hanging over the shoulders of her gray sweatshirt. Veins throbbed in the long neck rising out of the sweatshirt. Her face looked as dry as leather, her lips flaky.

She motioned Vicky inside, then reached around and pushed the door shut. The house was hot and closed-in, as if the air had coalesced into a tight ball. Vases of flowers stood about the floor and crowded the tops of two tables, permeating the air with the sweet, sickly odor of a funeral home. The French doors in the far wall were opened, and Vicky could see into Clint's study to the polished, empty surface of his desk.

Lacy was looking about, surveying the living room as if she were seeing the disarray for the first time—flowers, piles of laundry on the sofa, magazines jumbled with empty food cartons on the coffee table, boots and shoes kicked off on the carpet.

"It won't take long," Vicky said.

Lacy turned toward her. Surprise in her face now, as if she had just registered who Vicky was. "I guess you'd better sit down." She stepped over to the sofa, gathered up a pile of clothing and dumped it onto the floor. "I remember you now. You saw the accident."

Vicky nodded. "I'm very sorry."

"You don't believe it was an accident."

Vicky felt a little tremor of unease. "I told the police what I saw."

Lacy nodded. "It was you, then. A detective told me a witness thinks somebody murdered Clint. Asked me all kinds of questions. Who would want Clint dead? Any threats? Arguments or altercations? How was our relationship? Problems in our marriage? Oh my God." She was starting to cry, shoulders shaking. "It was an accident! Can't we leave it at that? Isn't that bad enough? Do I really have to deal with all the suspicions, the gossip?"

"I'm very sorry." There was nothing else to say. Vicky couldn't say she hadn't seen what she had seen.

"You're not the only one."

"What do you mean?"

"Some other witness, out of the blue, decided my husband was murdered. Why are you doing this to me?"

Vicky let the question invade the space between them. There were no answers, no platitdudes that might soften the blow. Finally, she said, "I'm trying to settle an adoption case Clint was working on. The Little Shields' case."

"You really believe I know about Clint's cases?" Lacy gave a hoarse laugh. "He kept them to himself. They were his life, all the little kids looking for homes. They were Julia and he was their"— she hesitated, staring at Vicky for a long moment before she plunged on—"warrior riding to rescue them."

"I've been following Clint's footsteps." Vicky picked at the words, moving through rocks and thistles. "I've talked to the people he talked to, and I've run into a dead end. There are several days unaccounted for on his calendar. I don't know where he went or who he talked to."

"My husband lived in his head."

A clock somewhere ticked in the silence.

"In his head. Always lost in a tangle of thoughts. Working things out. Planning. Plotting. Do you think he was easy to live with?" She gave another hoarse laugh. "It was like living with a robot."

Vicky flinched. Was that what she had become? A robot? Obsessed with her cases? With the people who found their way to her office? The drunks and addicts and petty criminals like Vince White

Hawk, needing her help, taking over her life? Is that how the people close to her would describe her? Lucas in Denver, Susan in Los Angeles, her own children sending texts, leaving voice mails?

She realized the woman was talking about Julia being settled at school in Laramie, living her own life. "Clint didn't have to worry about her anymore, and I was . . . well, hereabouts somewhere. He barely noticed me."

Lacy looked away, her face rigid, like a mask with tiny cracks breaking beneath the surface. For the briefest moment, Vicky allowed herself to wonder if the barely noticed wife had grown tired of being a cipher in her husband's life. She must have heard the gossip about Clint and his young secretary. Every lawyer in town knew, Rick Masterson had told her. Surely Lacy knew.

Vicky could feel the words skittering away. A coldness came over her, and she realized she was shivering in the hot, flower-drenched house. The woman slouched on the chair across from her, gray sweatshirt bunched around her waist, a clump of hair hanging over one eye, wondering . . . what? If the lawyer working on one of Clint's cases thought she might have arranged her husband's death?

"I didn't kill my husband, you know." Lacy blurted out the statement. "There was a blizzard, and the truck driver didn't see him. It was an accident, a terrible, cruel accident. And here I am"—she lifted both hands—"with nothing to look forward to."

"Do you have family, friends to talk to?"

"Do you really suppose it might do any good?"

Vicky leaned forward. "Your husband cared deeply about a child named Mary Ann Little Shield. He wanted to see her legally adopted by the parents who have raised her. I'd like to finish the work he was doing. I need your help."

Lacy didn't take her eyes away, staring without blinking. After a long moment, she said, "I have no idea where he went, if that's what you want to know. Just packed a bag, placed his laptop in his brief-case. It was like, 'Oh, by the way, I have to go out of town on a case for a few days.'"

"Out of town? Did he say where?"

"Ask Evie. I suspect he told her." Lacy shrugged. "She's probably at the office. A young lawyer from Casper will close Clint's practice. I have no idea whether he'll keep Evie on or throw her out in the street where she belongs."

So Lacy had heard the gossip. Vicky got to her feet. "I'll keep you posted about the Little Shield case."

"You do that." Lacy nodded toward the door, and Vicky under-stood she could find her own way out.

VICKY SENSED THE presence on the other side of the door. A move-ment, an almost imperceptible shift in the atmosphere. She knocked again. A small tremor ran through the hard wooden door followed by a punctuation of silence.

"Evie?" She leaned into the door. "It's Vicky Holden." A moment passed before she heard the sound of footsteps approaching. She had called the office from her mobile on the way over. There was no answer, and she had decided to take a chance that Evie Moran was still here.

The door swung inward a few inches. The secretary stood in the opening, bracketed by the edge of the door and the frame. "I wasn't expecting visitors," she said. "I'm about to leave."

"This will only take a minute."

Evie dropped her eyes and let out a long sigh, as if the excuse were too familiar to bother responding. "The new lawyer will take over next week. You should talk to him."

"He won't be handling the Little Shields' case." Vicky waited a beat before she went on. "May I come in?"

The secretary yanked the door back. She looked older than her years, slumped with worry. Her eyes were red-rimmed, like the eyes of a clown, and her hair stood out in patches, as if she had been pulling at it. She wore a pink blouse that hung over the top of her jeans, and she was barefoot, long painted toes splayed over the carpet. Behind her the office looked swept clean, everything in place: the surface of the desk clear, the side chairs squared to the front of the desk, magazines arranged on a small table against the wall, books stacked on a bookcase. She swung around, walked behind the desk, and dropped onto the chair. "I've been through everything," she said. "I gave you what Clint left on the Little Shield case."

"There's a three-day gap in his calendar." Vicky perched on one of the side chairs. "I thought he might have taken time off to sort through the information he had, but Lacy said he went out of town on business. She didn't know where he'd gone."

"What makes you think I would know?"

Vicky shifted in the chair. This wasn't going to be easy. Something had happened between the two women since she'd last talked to them. They had been in shock then; Clint not yet dead twenty-four hours. But now? They'd had time to think, connect dots. She wondered if Lacy had seized upon the rumors and confronted the secretary. And how had Evie responded? By accusing Clint's wife of arranging his murder?

"Clint might have mentioned something." Stay with the subject at hand, Vicky told herself. Rumors, speculation—let the police sort them out. All she wanted were legal parents for a little girl.

"I told you, Clint didn't talk about his cases."

Vicky nodded. Clint Hopkins, a lawyer who lived in his head, allowed his cases to take him over, consume him, so that nothing else mattered. Like a robot, his wife had said. Programmed to focus on whatever case he was working on.

She tried a different tack. "I know Clint spoke to Lou and Debbie Bearing on two occasions before he left town. The day after he returned, he went back to their place, and that night he was killed. I think he must have found something he thought they could explain. Something he asked them about. Why else would he have gone back?"

"Then you should ask them."

"I have. I'll have to find the answer somewhere else."

Vicky kept her eyes on the woman across the desk until, after a long moment, Evie Moran got to her feet. "This is my last day here," she said. There was a crack in her voice. "Everything's over. The new lawyer offered me a job, but I declined. Thank you very much."

Vicky stood up. "I think you know where Clint went."

The young woman was shaking her head. She squeezed her eyes shut against the moisture shining at the edges.

Vicky hurried on: "You don't want to tell me because you were with him." It was a guess, the kind of stab in the dark she'd taken when she could feel a client was holding back. "Tell me, Evie. Help me conclude the case Clint cared so much about."

Evie sank back into her chair, as if the air had gone out of her. She dropped her face into her hands and began sobbing, making little staccato noises. "Does everyone know? Lacy and you and everyone else in the world? Clint said it was our secret. He never told secrets. He never told anyone anything."

"Where did you go?"

"I was only there one night. He said he would be busy. There was someone he had to talk to." She dropped her hands and sat up straight, drawing on some new resolve. "He didn't say who it was.

'I'm still figuring things out,' he said. I knew if I showed up before Saturday, I'd never see him. He wouldn't even talk to me, he'd be so engrossed in whatever he was doing. So I waited and flew down Saturday night. We spent the night together and drove home on Sunday. It was beautiful. Snow everywhere. Just Clint and me alone in a white world. Then he was gone."

"Where, Evie? Drove home from where?"

"Denver."

# 26

VICKY COULD HEAR the beep inside her bag as she made her way down the icy sidewalk to the Ford. A new text message. The bright sun bore down onto the rooftops, but there was a chill in the wind that whipped at her coat. She dipped her head, tucked her chin into the collar, and tried to ignore the beeping noise, her thoughts on the three missing days. Two days driving back and forth to Denver; one day in Denver. But where in Denver? Who had Clint gone to see and why?

Clint had deleted everything on his laptop but the barest notes and names on his calendar. What had he found that he didn't want to come into anyone's hands, not even hers? Still, he had wanted to consult with her on the Little Shield case. He would have told her everything, Evie said. And what was that? What had he carried about in his head, unwilling to allow anyone to see?

Vicky gripped her coat close with one hand while she opened the car door with the other. She slid inside and started the engine. She was shivering. He had gone to Denver, Evie said, and Vicky had pushed the girl. There must have been something that would give them an idea of what he did there.

Evie had gone into Clint's office and retrieved the laptop. Vicky had waited while Evie had called up the file on the Little Shield case. Nothing, the secretary said, except the notes. Then Evie had skimmed the list of files. No sign of Little Shield, Wind River Reservation, Arapaho.

Vicky had been pacing the small area between the desk and the door, conscious of Evie still hunched over the computer, the keys clicking. "I told you Clint kept everything in his head. He was paranoid his files would be hacked."

Vicky had stopped pacing, a new thought presenting itself. "What about the Web sites Clint visited before he went to Denver? They could tell us what he was looking for."

Evie had pulled back, tapped a couple keys, then hunched forward again, eyes boring into the screen. "Nothing." She exhaled the word. "Clint erased his entire history."

"What did he tell you?" She had pressed the secretary again.

"Nothing. He told me nothing."

Inside the Ford, Vicky retrieved her mobile, her hand shaking with cold. An image of the dark figure starting across the street in the snow played across her retinas. A dark figure, carrying a briefcase. Paranoid, controlling, thorough. And something else: elusive.

She ran her finger over the button and tried to concentrate on the text message. Her hand was shaking with cold. Annie: "Shooting at Bearing's place. Someone dead. Thought you'd want to know."

Vicky felt her heart catapult inside her chest. A shooting at the Bearings'. My God. And this morning she had gone to John O'Malley and told him she suspected Lou Bearing was hiding something. She knew John O'Malley. He would have driven out there to talk to Lou. He would have gone right away. For her. To allay her concern.

She could see Lou Bearing skulking about the barn, nervous, eyes twitching, yearning to tell something. To unburden himself. Confess. The man's discomfort had been as palpable as another presence. She had defended clients like that, shifting in their chairs, wanting to tell everything, get it off their chests. Finally blurting out the sad, terrible truth.

Lou Bearing had been like that, until Debbie walked in, determination and resolve propelling the woman, enough for both her and for her husband. And everything had changed. Lou's demeanor, the yearning that had shone in his eyes, the longing to set down a heavy load.

Is that what happened? Debbie Bearing had walked in on a confession? And a man was dead? The man who had heard Lou Bearing's secret?

Vicky realized that, somehow, she had pulled away from the curb and was driving down Main. A blur of snow piled over the street and wrapped about the buildings. She swiped at the tears bristling on her cheek. She could feel her heart thumping. God. God. What if she had sent John O'Malley to his death?

She had to get ahold of herself. She was talking to herself out loud, her own voice echoing in the void of the car. Admonishing herself. *Get a hold on. Get a hold on.* Anything could have happened. Lou himself could have been shot. Someone else could have come to the barn. She fumbled in her bag for her cell and pressed John O'Malley's number. Three rings, then the familiar voice saying to leave a message. She tossed the cell on top of the bag.

John O'Malley could still be at the mission, in a meeting, a counseling session, nowhere near the Bearing place. She turned onto Seventeen-Mile Road and drove toward the blue billboard rising into the sunshine and blue sky. The words looked watery: *St. Francis Mission*. She swung left and sped down the tunnel of cottonwoods, rear wheels sliding in the snow, and turned toward the administration building, her heart pounding. Her mouth had gone dry. The red Toyota pickup was gone.

She jerked to a stop where the Toyota had stood, flung open the door, and ran up the steps. She slammed herself against the heavy oak door. "John!" She shouted into the corridor, into the emptiness of his office. "John. Are you here?"

"What is it?" The bishop listed down the corridor from the back office. "What's happened?"

"Is John here?" John O'Malley was not here; she could sense his absence. The Toyota pickup was gone.

"I'm afraid he's gone out." The old man couldn't quite hide his own worry. "Left a couple hours ago. Is everything all right?"

"I don't know. I don't know." Vicky had swung back toward the front door when the door across the corridor flew open. The tall, red-haired woman—a girl, really; the serious look on her face almost comical—blocked the corridor.

"What's happened to my uncle?"

"He went to talk to someone. There's been a shooting. I'm going over there."

"I'm coming with you," the girl said, and Vicky could hear the click of footsteps behind her as she yanked the door open and ran down the steps. She had started to back the Ford onto Circle Drive when Shannon O'Malley pulled open the passenger door and jumped onto the seat. A black jacket half on, half off. She wiggled about, jammed both arms into the jacket, and pulled the fronts closed.

"You think Uncle John's been shot?"

Vicky hunched over the steering wheel and peered past the windshield, barely registering the question, the girl's voice nothing but background noise.

"I don't know," Vicky managed. She was at the end of the cottonwood tunnel, sliding into the turn back onto Seventeen-Mile Road. A horn sounded, brakes squealed. She jammed her foot down hard on the accelerator and sped away from an oncoming pickup.

For a long, blessed moment, Shannon was quiet. Vicky was aware of the girl staring straight ahead, watching the road. It could take thirty minutes to get to the Bearing place. She had lost two minutes checking the mission. Two precious minutes. She wondered if an ambulance had been called. There was a chance the victim was still alive. Oh God. Let him be alive.

"It's dangerous here."

Vicky flinched. The girl's voice had startled her out of her own thoughts. She had forgotten the girl was here.

"Life is dangerous," she said.

"Uncle John is great." And then she went off about the research she was doing and how John O'Malley had been helping her, how he really cared about a captive white girl who had become Arapaho more than a hundred years ago. Background noise to the name pulsing inside Vicky's head. *John O'Malley. John O'Malley.*

"Why would anyone want to shoot a priest?" the girl said.

The road unfolded ahead, mottled gray asphalt plunging through the whiteness. The reservation looked deserted, empty, except for a trail of smoke rising out of chimneys here and there.

It took a moment before Vicky realized the girl was waiting for an answer. What an absurd question. No one would want to harm Father John O'Malley. He was a man of the people; he belonged here. "No one. No one," she said, trying to blink away the image of Debbie Bearing, the hot hatred in the woman's eyes.

"You think someone did."

"I want to make sure he's all right."

Shannon went quiet again. This time Vicky felt the girl's eyes boring into her. "You love him, don't you?"

"Everyone loves him." Vicky waited a moment, scanning the road ahead for the junction with Blue Sky Highway. Easy to miss with snow everywhere; more minutes would be lost. She slowed for the turn, then picked up speed again, heading southwest. She turned onto Highway 287. The rooftops of Fort Washakie appeared like dark smudges on the horizon ahead. She glanced over at Shannon O'Malley. "It's not what you think."

The girl took her time. Then she said, "Well, that's too bad."

Vicky felt her muscles stiffen. This girl came from another time, another world, where people did what they wanted to do and nothing else mattered. Nothing else was allowed to get in the way, not vows and conventions and expectations . . .

The noise of a siren grew louder. She saw the flicker of red and yellow lights, slowed down, and jittered to the side as the ambulance tore past. Shannon was up partway on her knees, stretching backward, eyes following the ambulance. "It could be Uncle John."

They were a short distance from the Bearing place, and Vicky made a decision: They would go on, find out who was in the ambulance. Then she would follow it. Follow it to hell.

She pulled out into the lane and kept going. Shannon was still twisted about. "We should turn around."

Vicky didn't say anything. Looming through the glare of sun and snow was the Bearing house and the barn behind it, a pair of dark buildings set back from the road with vehicles parked in the yard. She could make out a police car and a blur of people walking about. She slowed again, came around a short curve and swung left, bumping over the barrow ditch and up into the yard past a couple of sedans and other vehicles toward the red pickup. She jammed on the brake, slammed out of the Ford, and started running, barely aware of the surprise in the faces turned toward her. Past the little groups of people, around the cars. She stopped. The rear door of the police car hung open. There was a muffled squawk and a hiss of radio noise. And then she saw him: getting out of the backseat, his cowboy hat brushing the top edge. Coming toward her now. "Vicky," he said.

"Oh my God. You're alive." She was trembling; her legs felt numb, as if she were standing on air. She felt the warmth and strength in his arms as they wrapped around her and pulled her to him.

After a moment, she stepped back, and it was Shannon's turn, hugging him, sobbing. "We were so worried."

So many eyes on them, Vicky realized. At least a dozen people gathering around, boots shuffling in the snow. A plainclothes officer had gotten out of the other side of the car and was watching over the roof. A spectacle. Two women sobbing over a priest.

"Come over here." Vicky felt him lift her hand. Then he took Shannon's hand and led them toward the front of the house, away from the others. "Lou Bearing is dead. Debbie found him in the shop this morning. It looks like he shot himself."

"I knew you would come here . . ." Vicky began, wanting to explain, yet knowing it wasn't necessary. She could see in his eyes that he understood; the moccasin telegraph had the news already. She had tried his cell, but he hadn't answered. Then she had gone to the mission to find him. He wasn't there, and Shannon had insisted on coming with her.

"I was finishing the statement to the police." He gave a nod in the direction of the police cars. "Debbie's on the way to the hospital. She's in shock. I'm going over there." He looked at both of them a long moment, then he reached out, and Vicky felt herself pulled into his arms again. Then Shannon, crowding in. "You're all right?"

"We're fine." It was Shannon's voice, muffled against his jacket.

Vicky didn't say anything.

# 27

THEY WERE STANDING inside the door as if they had seen her turn into the driveway. Annie and Roger, expressions edged with anxiety. "You okay?" Annie said.

Vicky pushed the door closed. She could feel the dry heat blowing through the vents. Of course she was okay. Why wouldn't she be? She started to slip out of her coat, and in an instant, Roger was behind her, taking the coat, hanging it on the rack next to the door.

"We heard about Lou Bearing," he said. "Debbie's in the hospital with shock. The news is all over the telegraph."

How efficient the moccasin telegraph was. The news had reached the office before she had. She wondered what else Annie and Roger had heard. It wasn't just a matter of text messages and phone calls. Now it was videos. She closed her eyes for a second, trying to erase the video of herself throwing herself into John O'Malley's arms. That should stir up a lot of gossip.

"I went to the mission this morning," she began. A feeble effort to explain. What did it matter? People would believe what they wanted to believe. "John said he would have a talk with Lou. I was afraid I had sent him to his death." She drew in a long breath, feeling calmer now, more like herself. "He went to the hospital to check on Debbie."

Because Debbie had no one, she was thinking. No one she seemed to care about. No one who cared about her, except Lou, who was gone. But this was Vicky's family, Annie and Roger. And the kids, Lucas and Susan. Living far away, but part of her nevertheless. She had *someone*.

"Are you hungry?" Annie might have been addressing a small child. "Roger brought in sandwiches. Egg salad?"

Perhaps that was the emptiness inside her—hunger. Breakfast had been hours ago. She couldn't even remember what she had eaten before she'd left for the office.

"Egg salad sounds delicious." She gave them another smile, these two solicitous people—this family—and went into her own office. She had *someone*, she told herself again. John O'Malley was a priest. He cared for those who had no one.

Annie was behind her. She stationed herself at the corner of the desk and waited while Vicky sat down and turned on the computer. "What's the rest?"

"Lianna Blue Hawk canceled her appointment this afternoon. I guess she's not ready to divorce Joseph. They're trying to reconcile."

"And when will she be ready?" Vicky stared at the icons peopling the computer screen. "When he's knocked her senseless?"

Annie nodded, a blurred motion at the edge of Vicky's vision. "I told her you'd see her when she changed her mind. Lester Duwalt dropped in without an appointment. Claims highway department wrongly terminated him because he took time off for his grandfather's wake. Roger saw him. You have an appointment with Doris Rides Fast at five. She didn't say what about."

Roger materialized beside Annie and set down a paper plate with a sandwich and chips and a mug of coffee. The musty odor of hardboiled eggs mixed with the aroma of fresh coffee. Vicky glanced up and nodded her thanks.

"Let us know if you need anything else," Annie said. They were backing out of the office, around the opened beveled-glass doors, these two friends of hers.

Vicky swiveled about, giving them her full attention. "Thank you," she said. "For everything."

Roger pulled the doors shut, and Vicky went back to the computer. She was running up against mountains. Everywhere she turned, she encountered an outcropping of rocks. Vince White Hawk, still missing. He could be a thousand miles away. He could be in a drunken coma or dead. And Mary Ann Little Shield, lost in a place as gray and amorphous as a snow cloud, with parents not legally her parents. People who loved her and who might lose her.

She forced herself to concentrate on the new information Evie Moran had given her. Three missing days on Clint's calendar that weren't missing after all. He had been in Denver. A night there with his secretary, a day driving back to Riverton, and he'd told her nothing. And yet, he must have had a reason to go to Denver.

She held herself still, barely breathing. Clint had visited the Bearings before he left and had gone back to see them as soon as he returned. Something he had learned from the Bearings had sent him to Denver. Clint must have stumbled onto something. And he had been killed because of it.

It all came back to Denver. She typed in "Denver Wind River

Reservation 2011" and strained toward the screen, willing a connection to come up. A chamber of commerce site appeared, followed by things to do and see in Denver, festivals, and races. A similar site popped up for the reservation. Powwows, rodeos, parades, drumming groups, dancers. Nothing that might explain a connection between Denver and an infant left on a doorstep on the reservation.

Vicky sat back and tried to focus on something else: a shadowy thought circling in her head, something Shannon O'Malley had mentioned. She had pushed it away, her own thoughts focused on the fact that someone was dead at the Bearing house, and John O'Malley had gone there. Now she felt herself slowly coming to attention. Shannon's voice sounded in her head as clearly as if the girl were sitting beside her now: *Uncle John's been a big help to me. He gets it, you know? Not everybody does. My own father wonders why I care about a captive white girl who became Arapaho.*

Captive white girl! My God, the reality was as obvious as the Wind River Mountains looming over the reservation, and Clint Hopkins had seen it. Lou Bearing must have divulged something that made Clint scour the internet and go to Denver. Divulged too much! Whatever Clint had found, he had tried to erase it, except for his calendar and notes. Had he expected her to follow in his tracks, should something happen to him? Hoped she would latch on to the truth and help Mary Ann? If she didn't, Mary Ann Little Shield would remain in that gray, indefinite place.

She typed in "Missing Infant Denver 2011." A new set of Web sites, several pages long, materialized. Culled from stories in newspapers, radio and TV, two or three internet news sites, several blogs. She tapped on an account from the *Denver Post* and read down the page.

## MOTHER KILLED, INFANT ABDUCTED IN CARJACKING

*A tense carjacking Monday ended in the death of a twenty-nine-year-old Denver woman, Louise Adler Becket, and the abduction of her five-week-old daughter, Elizabeth Louise. Jason Becket, husband of the deceased woman and father of the infant, has offered a $25,000 reward for information leading to the safe return of his child. "I will never stop looking for her," Becket said.*

*Witnesses said the incident occurred in Cherry Creek North, the popular upscale shopping area. At about five p.m. Louise Becket parked her late-model Honda SUV in front of a series of shops. A pickup immediately pulled in alongside the SUV, and a man and a woman jumped out. They accosted Mrs. Becket as she was attempting to remove the infant from the rear seat. The man allegedly subdued the victim while the woman took her purse and got behind the steering wheel of the SUV. She backed out and drove down the street with Mrs. Becket hanging on to the rear door in a futile attempt to rescue her infant. Witnesses said the woman slipped under the wheels of the SUV. According to Denver Police Detective Tim Martinez, she was pronounced dead at the scene. The man fled in the pickup, following the SUV, and both vehicles headed east toward Colorado Boulevard.*

*Witnesses describe the carjackers as medium height with dark hair and dark complexions.*

*Police have issued an alert to law enforcement throughout Colorado and neighboring states. Anyone with information on the missing infant, the dark-colored SUV, or a light-colored Chevrolet pickup is urged to contact their local police immediately. Police are concerned that the longer the infant remains with the carjackers, the greater the danger she is in.*

Vicky read the article again. She felt as if the breath had been sucked out of her, as if the beveled-glass doors and the snow-covered ground framed in the window were closing in. Elizabeth Louise Becket, a white infant—a captive—stolen from her family. Whose father had offered a $25,000 reward for her return. Was that the story of Mary Ann Little Shield?

She glanced through the other sites. Repetitions of the newspaper article with something new added: police mockups of the two carjackers, according to the descriptions of witnesses. Dark hair and dark eyes, indistinct features. Indian, Hispanic, Asian. They could be Debbie and Lou Bearing or a thousand others.

There were pages of Web sites. Week after week, and still no news of the missing infant or the dark-complexioned carjackers. But no news in the months after the carjacking did not mean that Elizabeth Louise Becket—or her body—hadn't been found sometime in the past five years.

She closed the sites and typed in the same search string for Denver in 2012. An anniversary article popped up: "One year ago today, five-week-old Elizabeth Louise Becket was abducted in a carjacking in Cherry Creek North that left her mother, Louise Becket, crushed under the wheels of her SUV. Despite a five-state alert and ongoing search for the carjacked SUV and the Chevrolet pickup one of the carjackers drove, neither the vehicles nor the infant have been located. 'I know my baby is out there somewhere,' said Jason Becket, husband of the dead woman and father of the missing infant. 'She is all I have left. If anyone knows of her whereabouts, I beg you to contact the police.' He said the $25,000 reward he had offered following the incident will stand until his child is found."

Vicky repeated the search for the following years: 2013, 2014, 2015, 2016. Fewer articles appeared each year, a gradual tapering into a vacuum of inevitability and even acceptance, like the gradual tapering of grief.

She started a new search, this time for Jason Becket. He would still be in Denver, she was certain, and Clint Hopkins had gone there to talk to him. The search took only a few minutes, and she had located the man. The photograph showed a handsome man with a broad chin and curly hair and something undefined in his eyes, like a visible mote. Jason Becket owned several restaurants, including the Thirty-Second Street Bistro, judged the best bistro in Denver two years running. Vicky jotted down the telephone number, picked up the phone, and called.

She glanced at her watch while a phone rang somewhere in Highland, the northwest section of Denver, not far from where she had lived when she practiced law in a downtown skyscraper, before she'd come home to the reservation.

"Thirty-Second Street Bistro." The voice on the other end sounded cheery and enthusiastic. There was a faint background noise of clinking glasses and buzzing voices

Vicky asked to speak to Jason Becket. There was a muffled sound, as if a hand had been placed over the receiver: "Is Jason here?" A second passed, then the woman said: "Who's calling?"

"Vicky Holden. I'm an attorney in Wyoming."

She should hold, the woman said. Several minutes passed, the line inert, and Vicky had started to wonder if they had been cut off when a man's voice said, "This is Jason." There was an edge of impatience to his voice. "What is this about?"

"My name is . . ."

"Yeah, I got it. You're an attorney in Wyoming. Is this about Elizabeth?"

"Yes."

"You'd better have something definite. No more theories and possibilities, no more gossip. There was another Wyoming attorney here last week, asking a lot of questions. If you know something about my daughter, let's hear it."

"Mr. Becket, the lawyer you spoke to, Clint Hopkins, has been killed. I've taken over an adoption case he was working on. It's imperative that I meet with you." She should have checked the flight schedules, she was thinking. Flights out of Riverton in the winter could be erratic. She plunged on: "I can be in Denver tomorrow." She would drive, if she had to.

"Killed!"

"He was struck down by a truck. The police believe it was an accident. I saw it happen. I believe it was deliberate. Could we meet tomorrow?"

"God! Why would anyone kill him? He seemed like a nice man. A little tense and, frankly, a little confused. I wasn't sure what he was trying to sort out and put together."

"Can we meet tomorrow?"

"Yeah, sure. Come to the restaurant. You know where it is?"

Yes, she told him. She knew where it was.

She had just replaced the receiver when the phone rang. Annie, saying Rick Masterson was on the other line. Vicky waited for the clicking noise, then she said, "Rick?"

"How about dinner?"

Dinner! Another conversation between two people who had witnessed the same incident and seen different things. "Sorry," she said, starting to explain that she was leaving town tomorrow and had a lot to do.

He cut her off. "Look, Vicky. I've been thinking about Clint's death. I believe you're right. It wasn't an accident."

Vicky let a couple seconds go by before she said, "What changed your mind?"

"Clint, himself. Something he said at the meeting started to bother me. He told me he intended to bring you in on an adoption case to make certain the little girl would be settled with people who loved her, in case . . ." Vicky could hear the in and out of his breathing. "In case something happened to him."

"Something happened?"

"An hour later, he was dead. I realized I'd seen what appeared logical. An accident in a blizzard. I've told the police what Clint said. Look, Vicky, I'm sorry that you and I got off to a bad start, and I'm sorry we can't get together this evening. I have to go back to Cheyenne tomorrow, but I'll be here in a couple of weeks on another consultation job. May I call you?"

Vicky tried to picture the man who had sat across the table from her two nights ago. Sand-colored hair, earnest-looking face. A man who could reconsider, acknowledge other possibilities. "Of course," she said.

# 28

FATHER JOHN PEERED past the windshield wipers at Seventeen-Mile Road, blurred in the falling snow. He could barely see a car length ahead. It had started snowing sometime in the middle of the night and showed no sign of letting up. All around, the prairie and sky merged together, indistinguishable. Beside him, Shannon hunkered down inside her jacket with a scarf around her neck that billowed upward and connected with the knit hat, leaving a slit for her eyes. He jogged the heater knob, turning it on and off in an attempt to wake it up. Finally, the heater choked out a burst of warm air. "Giorni poveri vivea" played softly between them.

"Should warm up in a bit." He hoped that would be the case. All winter the heater had operated with a mind of its own. Inside all the layers of wool, Shannon was shivering.

"How far do we have to go?"

He glanced over and gave her a quick smile. "A Boston girl, complaining about the cold? Not far, fifteen minutes." Probably longer, he was thinking. He kept the pickup at a slow, steady pace, watching for oncoming vehicles to burst out of the white haze. He had just gotten to the office this morning and was making coffee, measuring out the grounds, when the phone had rung. He had darted over to his desk and managed to grab the receiver before the caller was shunted to voice mail.

"This is Daisy Blue Water . . ."

"Hello, Grandmother."

"Ah, Father. How's the weather at the mission?"

Always the polite preliminaries first, even in a phone call. Father John smiled. "It's still snowing," he said. Only a handful of people at Mass earlier, and he didn't blame them for staying home. In fact, looking out at the wrinkled faces of the elders, snuggling inside their jackets against the chill in the church, he'd wished they had stayed home.

Daisy was going on about how she had gotten home yesterday from visiting her granddaughter's new daughter in Billings and how her grandson's boy had come over to shovel the walks before he went to school and how he would pick up groceries for her this afternoon. When Father John said she had a good family, she gave a sigh of contentment. And then she came to the point: "My relation Wilbur says you want to talk to me about my grandmother."

He explained that his niece, Shannon, was doing research for her dissertation on the captive Fletcher girls. She was here to research Lizzie Brokenhorn.

"Lizzie," Daisy said. "Grandmother loved that name soon as she found out it was hers. When you want to come over?"

He had suggested later this morning, and the old woman had agreed. Shannon hadn't come to the office yet. He suspected James had brought her back late last night. They had been spending a lot of time together. Getting to know each other, Shannon had told him. He knew Shannon: the minute she came in and heard Daisy had called, she would want to see her.

And now Shannon sat with her hands encased in big, furry gloves, resting in her lap. She stared straight ahead. He could feel the thoughts building inside her, searching for an outlet. He waited.

"I hope you don't disapprove of me," she said.

He shifted his eyes toward her and gave her another smile. "I'm proud of you and the work you're doing. I'm proud you think history is worth devoting yourself to."

"Oh, come on, Uncle John." He could feel her eyes lasering him. "James and I are together as much as we can be. We're taking our time. I want you to know we haven't started an . . ." She hesitated. "What you would call an affair. Our relationship's not about sex. I mean, it's bigger than sex. It's not that we don't want to sleep together. It's not the time, yet."

He glanced over and gave her another smile. "I know you'll make the best decision for yourself."

"You like James."

"Yes, I do."

He glanced sideways again. She was shaking her head, dipping her face deeper into the scarf. When she spoke, her voice sounded muffled and blurred: "I got a text from David yesterday. He's already moved out. Packed up his stuff, which pretty much was everything in the apartment, and poof! He's gone. The rent is paid for the month. In other words, I have a month to get my stuff out of there. That ought to take about an hour." She lifted her chin, and he saw that she was crying.

"I'm sorry."

"Breakup by text. Isn't that the best? No big arguments, just, So long, it's been nice to know you. I think there's an old song about that."

She was running a furry glove over her cheek, mopping at the moisture. "I'm not that sad, really. I mean, we had already broken up. We had an understanding. We would only stay together while it was"—she paused—"convenient. It's just that I didn't expect it to be so . . . bloodless."

Turning onto the highway, gripping the steering wheel against the back tires that were slipping about, Father John took a moment. The outskirts of Riverton—warehouses, garages, trailer homes— punched through the whiteness. "What about James?"

She was quiet for so long, he feared he had overstepped the sense of intimacy she had established. He was not her father.

"I think I'm falling in love with him."

He looked over at her, and she caught his eye and smiled. "He is so not called to be a priest."

"Falling in love . . ." He let the words settle between them.

"He's a good man," Shannon said. "One of the best I have ever met. He's . . . well, he's mature. He's not looking for a convenient relationship. He wants us to be together, to love each other for the long term. He's a forever-after guy. You'd approve, wouldn't you? Forever after?"

Father John was about to say he was glad she and James were taking their time, when she said, "I can write my dissertation any-where, isn't that what you told me? I have all my research on the computer, the records and documents on Amanda Mary and Lizzie, the interviews with descendants. As soon as I finish the research on Lizzie, I can start writing. Two white girls captured by the Indians with completely different lives. Is it okay if I do it here?"

For how long? Father John was thinking. How long would there be a guesthouse and a mission? "The guesthouse is yours . . ."

She interrupted. "I told James you'd say that. I'll have a friend pack my stuff and send it. It won't be a big box, I promise. James and I, well, we can continue to get to know each other, see where we're going."

He was driving down the side streets of Riverton now, through a residential area: bungalows set back from the street, snuggled in snow, snow lining the curbs, banked against the parked cars. A forever-after guy, she had called James. That was what she wanted. Not the Davids who broke up by text. Not the commitments with strings attached, but the real thing. Maybe it wasn't really so different from the way it had been when he was Shannon's age. He had loved her mother then. He had wanted to marry her. Forever-after. He kept his eyes on the snowy asphalt ahead, aware of Shannon's presence filling up the cab: the daughter he might have had.

"You know she loves you, don't you?"

He felt as if Shannon had tossed a hard, icy snowball that caught him in the solar plexus. He didn't say anything, and she went on: "I saw the way she reacted yesterday when she thought you might have been killed."

He started to say they were friends, he and Vicky. They worked together. But Shannon shot out a furry glove. "Oh, please. I heard it yesterday from her. You're just friends and all that BS. There must be some way . . ."

"There is no way," he said. He found the brown-frame bungalow he was looking for, turned in alongside the curb, and gave his niece a reassuring smile. The commitment he had made was forever. "No way," he said.

\*    \*    \*

"I WAS TOUCHED when Wilbur called me." Daisy Blue Water sat upright in a chair with flower-print upholstery and worn armrests, a
small, ancient woman, fragile-looking, with a wrinkled face. She
held her head high, a duo of paleness—light-brown hair fading to
gray, cropped close to her head, and ghostly blue eyes. He would
have taken her for a white woman, if he hadn't known she was an
Arapaho grandmother. She kept her hands clasped in the lap of her
red skirt and crossed her feet, a prim and reserved posture left over
from the mission school, he thought. So many of the elders who had
gone to St. Francis School retained what the nuns would have called
"good deportment."

"I'm sure Grandmother would be surprised to think anyone
cared about her life. Apart from her family, naturally."

Shannon scooted herself to the front of the sofa cushion beside
him. He could feel her excitement. "I understand you knew her."

"Oh, yes. I have very clear memories, even though I was very
little, you know. She died in 1928. I was five years old."

Father John could see Shannon doing the calculations in her
head. Daisy was ninety-three years old. Living in the home she'd
occupied for fifty years, cooking meals as she had always done,
visiting her new great-grandchild. She had family close by, descendants of Lizzie Brokenhorn, looking out for her.

Shannon leaned toward the old woman, concentrating on her
story: how her grandmother used to pull her onto her lap and sing
to her. "She liked to bake cakes. Her cakes were terrible, tasted like
plaster and hard as stones. Naturally, all us kids ate them anyway.
They were sweet, and we had powerful cravings for sugar."

Shannon slipped a photo of Lizzie and John Brokenhorn from

her bag, a photo she'd found on the internet, she'd told him earlier. She popped to her feet, handed Daisy the photo, and sat back down. "Is this how you remember her?"

"Oh my." The old woman held the photo with her fingertips, as if it were a sacred object. "It's been years since I've seen this. It looks just like I remember her, and Grandfather, too. Only the photo makes her look darker. Her hair was very light and fine, like silk. I used to love to brush it. She had eyes like clouds, the faintest blue, and skin as white as winter. One time I asked her why her skin was so white, and she told me something was wrong with my eyes. She was brown, she said, like the rest of the people. But I had the same color of skin and light hair. I remember showing her my arms and asking why I had white arms. She would say, 'Don't think about it. You'll be brown soon enough.' She was right. In the summers I turned brown, but the brown would go away, and in the winter I looked white again."

Shannon glanced over at Father John, questions lighting her eyes. It wasn't polite to ask for the gift of information. He felt a surge of pride, the way she leaned back now and waited.

After a moment, Daisy said, "Oh, Grandmother knew she was white. She learned her story when Amanda Mary found her in 1902. She'd been looking for her for thirty-seven years. She never gave up hope. She wrote letters to the army, even wrote to Custer. It would get back to her that a trader had spotted a white child in an Indian camp, but when soldiers went out to look, the camp would be gone. Vanished into the plains. Amanda Mary kept at it. The woman had grit, I say."

Shannon waited a moment before she said, "I believe Lizzie also had grit."

"Oh, yes." Daisy was staring across the room, a distant look in her eyes as if she had gone somewhere else. "Especially when she finally met her sister. Amanda Mary rode the train to Casper and took a stagecoach to the reservation. A hundred miles, bouncing over the plains. Must have taken her back to her own time in captivity. It was brave of her to come. You want some coffee? I put a coffee cake in the oven."

The old woman pushed to her feet and steadied herself against the back of the chair a moment. Then she pushed off toward the kitchen. Father John stood up. "May we help?"

Shannon was close behind the old woman, and Father John followed. A few minutes later, they were seated at the dining room table, mugs of coffee and slices of coffee cake all around. Odors of warm cinnamon and sugar melted into the fresh coffee smells. "Thank you," Shannon said, sending a smile toward Daisy at the head of the table.

Father John could sense the urgency in Shannon's silence as they ate pieces of cake and sipped at the coffee. Finally, Daisy set her fork down and clasped her hands around her mug. She had long fingers with short, pale nails. There was a small gold band on her left hand.

"Grandmother never told me about meeting Amanda Mary, but my mother was there. She sat beside the interpreter that came from the agency. Grandmother never learned English, but my mother had gone to the mission school, so she knew English. She told me Grandmother was very upset. She didn't want to know she was white. Inside, she was Arapaho. Amanda Mary told her she was her sister. Grandmother's name was Elizabeth Fletcher, but their mother called her Lizzie. She was two years old when the Cheyennes attacked. Amanda Mary said they rose up out of the bushes along the creek, out of the ground. They were everywhere. She was holding her baby sister, Lizzie, in one arm. And she was holding their mother's hand when their mother slumped to the ground, and she saw the arrow in her chest. Next thing she knew, a warrior grabbed Lizzie. Mother said Amanda Mary cried when she told the story. "She had feared her baby sister was dead, but there she was, sitting beside her on a wooden chair Grandfather had made."

Daisy took another bite of cake, another sip of coffee. Letting the story live for a while, make its own way into their minds. After a moment, she went on: "Amanda Mary had come to take Lizzie home, back to her own people. She said Lizzie would live in a big house and wear pretty dresses and eat meat and potatoes every day. She would learn English and read books. They would be together again, two sisters, the way it was supposed to be.

"Grandmother started crying, Mother said. She talked so soft the interpreter had to keep asking what she said. She told Amanda Mary that she was home. She was with her people. She had her husband and children. She said something else . . ."

Daisy paused, sipping at her coffee, the pale eyes cloudy with memories. "She told Amanda Mary she was content. Well, it must've broken that woman's heart. Mother said Amanda Mary was real quiet. Just got into the stagecoach and went bouncing off."

Daisy set her mug down and smiled around the table. Back in the present now. "From then on, Grandmother called herself Lizzie."

# 29

VICKY HADN'T EXPECTED Lucas to meet her. She had called him last night to let him know she would be in Denver for a short time, to tell him she regretted not being able to spend more time.

"I get it, Mom," he'd said. "You're working on a case." She could hear the rest of it in his voice: she was always working on a case. He hadn't said he'd be waiting when she got off the airport train and followed the crowd up the escalators into the bright lights of the terminal. People everywhere, and there he was, standing just outside the railing. So handsome, like his father, that it took her breath away. She ran over and hugged him, then hugged him again. "What are you doing here?"

"I took the day off." He had already grabbed her bag and walked her across the terminal. "At least we can spend time together while I drive you around. Where to?"

By the time they were out of the airport and on the highway, warm air was filling the black BMW. She had told him the name of the restaurant she was going to in North Denver, and he had nodded. It made perfect sense that a case she was working on should take her back to the neighborhood where she had once lived.

"You okay, Mom? You look a little tired."

"I'm fine," she said. "And you look wonderful. Everything okay with you?"

"Better than okay." Lucas kept glancing between her and the highway. She could sense the turmoil inside him, the way he'd been when he was little, fidgeting to tell her something. And then he told her: Adrienne, the most wonderful girl in the world, had agreed to marry him. "You're going to love her, Mom. She's everything I ever hoped for, and what do you know? The crazy girl's in love with me."

Vicky stared at the highway, the open, snow-swept fields on either side, the flat-roofed commercial buildings spread ahead. The memories came crashing in. The vast, open plains; the hot summers on the rez; the rodeos and the bucking broncos; the hamburgers sizzling in the food booths; the smells of dust and coffee. And the cowboys—Indians from reservations all over the West—and none could ride a bronco or a bull longer than Ben Holden. And she, crazy girl, had loved him.

Now, beside her, was his son, an IT expert at a software company in Denver who sat at a desk in front of a computer all day. His sister, a graphic designer in Los Angeles, engaged to a white man. Ben would be proud of their accomplishments. He was always proud of his kids.

She shifted sideways so she could take him in, the whole reality of him. "You're so like your father."

"Mom! Come on." He looked over at her, wide-eyed. "I'm like you. I'm not like him."

He remembered too much, she thought. The drunken Ben, the shouting and the flying fists, and everything falling apart—their family, the way things should have been. "Wedding plans?" she said.

"We're thinking June, a year from now. You'll love her, I promise."

"I promise I'll love her."

He would bring Adrienne to the reservation in the summer, as soon as it was sunny and warm, so she could see it the way he remembered it, Lucas was saying. They would go to a powwow, ride horses across the plains. There should be a carry-in dinner at Blue Sky Hall—didn't she think?—with the elders and grandmothers and friends he'd gone to school with. Yes, Vicky said to all of it. It would be a trip into the past.

They had left the highway behind and were in North Denver. Stop-and-go traffic down Federal Boulevard, Victorians and bungalows set back behind pines dusted with snow, women pushing strollers down the sidewalks, all as she remembered.

Now they were on Thirty-Second Street, heading west, the mountains rising like ice floes into the sky ahead.

"Looks like the restaurant." Lucas had slowed down, searching both sides of the street for an empty space at the curb. A long line of cars snaked past the restaurants and shops that occupied the string of Victorian houses. The BMW rocked to a stop. "Call me when you're finished," Lucas said as she got out.

The restaurant was packed. Every table taken. Groups of people, impatient looks on their faces, jammed the desk inside the front door. Laughter punctuated the low hum of conversations as plates clattered together and waiters hurried about. Vicky managed to make her way to the desk and told the young woman with black hair wrapped about her head like a ribbon and crayon red lipstick and bored eyes that she had an appointment with Jason Becket. The woman flinched backward. She started to say something about Jason being very busy when Vicky interrupted. "Tell him Vicky Holden is here." She waited while the woman picked up a receiver and repeated her words.

A couple of minutes passed, then a good five minutes. Vicky had stepped back from the crowd waiting for tables. Across the restaurant were two doors. One to the kitchen that expelled waiters hoisting loaded trays, and one that never opened. She kept her eyes on that door and, finally, it swung inward.

She could have picked Jason Becket out of a crowd. Blond hair, light complexion, a long nose and prominent chin, and a familiar look about him. It hit her with a thud: the man was the large, masculine version of Mary Ann Little Shield. He worked his way around the tables, and she went to meet him, holding out her hand. "I'm Vicky Holden."

His grip was hard, his expression businesslike. He ushered her through the door into a hallway paved with gray vinyl. Beyond the window at the far end, she could see a red delivery truck parked next to a Dumpster. Another door on the right opened into a small office, files and papers stacked everywhere, a pair of side chairs, shelves, a desk.

In a quick, efficient motion, Jason swept a chair clear and pulled it closer to the desk. He gestured for her to sit down, edged past the desk, and dropped into the seat he had probably just vacated. A pair of silver-framed photos stood at the corner of the desk. One, an infant wrapped in a pink blanket. The other, a pretty, dark-haired woman and Jason with a small boy on his lap.

"What do you know about Elizabeth?" His tone was flat, blunt, as if he didn't believe she knew anything. So many starts and stops, so many hopes dashed over the years. *I will never stop looking for her.*

Vicky unbuttoned her coat and loosened her scarf. The ceiling vent made little rattling noises as it emitted waves of warm air. He had not offered to take her coat. Clearly, Jason Becket did not expect the meeting to last long.

She took a moment before she said: "I believe Clint Hopkins told you about a white child who came to the reservation around the time your daughter was abducted."

"How shall I explain?" he began. "I told Clint I can't allow myself to get excited. There have been too many false reports, too many false sightings." He picked up a pen and began jabbing it against the mouse pad next to the computer. "What happened to Hopkins?"

"He was run down in the street the night after he returned from Denver."

"Accident?"

She took a moment before she said, "I don't think so. I saw it happen."

"You think it has something to do with the child?" A faint note of hope sounded in his voice, difficult to conceal.

"I'm trying to piece together the information Clint had gathered. It would help if you could tell me what you told him."

"He knew the facts; he'd read the newspaper accounts. He asked me to go over them." Jason shrugged. "My wife was running errands in Cherry Creek. She'd taken Elizabeth with her. I've always suspected it was her last stop because she kept Elizabeth on a regular schedule, and in thirty minutes or so, she would have wanted to be home to nurse her. You must have read the newspapers."

"Newspapers don't print the whole story."

He shifted forward, looking out of the corners of his eyes, watching something unfold beside him. "The carjackers, a man and a woman, came up when she was leaning into the backseat to get

Elizabeth. They struck her on the head, knocked her down. The woman got behind the wheel and started driving. My wife managed to get up. She ran alongside the car and held on to the door. She was trying to save Elizabeth when she slipped beneath the wheels and was killed. The man drove off in a pickup. They kept going. They didn't even stop."

*They didn't even stop!* Vicky could hear Betty White Hawk's voice looping through her head. A rollover crash, her husband trapped beneath the steering wheel. Lou and Debbie Bearing had driven on.

"There were witnesses," Jason was saying. "They gave the police descriptions. Nothing helped."

"Did they say anything that wasn't reported?"

"The carjackers were Indians. Oh, they looked Indian in the police illustrations, but the police wanted to keep their options open. Hispanic. Middle Eastern. But one witness got a close look at them. Laura Clement. She came out of a store as they started driving away. She heard my wife screaming and saw her fall under the wheels. She ran over to her, but there was nothing anyone could do. She said she would never forget the carjackers' faces. She could identify them."

"Did you tell Clint this? That a witness could identify the"—she drew in a breath—"killers?"

Jason nodded, his gaze still turned sideways. Then he faced her. "I told Clint I need a connection. I need to know how the child got to the reservation. I need proof she is Elizabeth. I've been through hell. The FBI is still on the case. Nothing," He stopped, allowing the weight of the word to settle between them. "I have a new family now. Sarah and I were married three years ago. We have a little boy, Josh. I've found some peace. I can't put myself through the agony and uncertainty again, not without proof."

Vicky sensed the conversation winding to an end, that Jason Becket was about to jump to his feet. He said, "Do you have that proof?"

"No." Vicky had been about to say, "Not yet," but she had swallowed back the impulse. She may never be able to find the proof. She may never be able to connect Elizabeth Becket to Mary Ann Little Shield.

She hurried on, not wanting the conversation to end. "What did Clint say?"

"Clint Hopkins was a man of few words. I didn't get the impression he liked to give anything away. He said he would talk to people on the reservation and get back to me."

"With the connection?"

"I presume that's what he meant."

"There's one more thing," Vicky said. Jason Becket was on his feet, and she got to hers. "Did he say how he had found you?"

"It was the first question I asked him. I got a half answer, something about how he had heard some things on the reservation."

Heard some things. Had Clint put it together? A baby crying at the Bearings'? A woman leaving a baby on a doorstep, a man repairing cars in his barn? A man who needed parts? All it had taken was an internet search. Starting close to home, branching across Wyoming, then to neighboring states. He'd spent a lot of time on the internet, his secretary had said. It's where he did most of his research.

Another possibility slid into her mind: Lou Bearing, a man struggling with a secret, longing to unburden himself. What had he told Clint?

Jason Becket walked around the desk and set his hand on the doorknob. He turned to her. "If you find a connection . . ." He paused, searching for the words. "I will want tests, you understand? I will want definite proof. I want my child back. *My* child. I will do everything to get her back."

Vicky left the restaurant feeling weak and slippery-footed. She had called Lucas from inside and waited until the BMW pulled up before she let herself out into the cold air. She held on to the door for support as she slid onto the seat. Elizabeth's mother had held on to the door. This was what Clint Hopkins had run into, the possibility—the likelihood—that Mary Anne Little Shield was Jason Becket's daughter. She did not belong with the people who had loved her for five years. Clint had wanted the adoption to be final. For Mary Anne's sake, so she could never be taken. Abducted again.

And yet there was a white man who could be her father. She understood why Clint had come to her. How would the tribe react? A child who had been part of them turned over to a white man, a stranger she didn't know? Tribal adoption laws were clear-cut. No Arapaho child could be adopted outside the tribe without tribal permission. What about a white child who had been living as an Arapaho? Would the tribe enter the case on the side of the Little Shields?

"I take it your meeting didn't go the way you hoped."

Vicky could feel her son's eyes on her, and she tried to pull herself back. "It's complicated," she said.

# 30

TRACES OF SNOW clung to the kitchen window and shrouded the residence in silence, interrupted occasionally by the sounds of the bishop puttering about upstairs and Walks-On snoring in the corner. Father John poured coffee into a mug, stirred in a quarter cup of milk, and headed back to the study. The lights around Circle Drive glowed in the window behind his desk.

He dropped into the old leather chair that, over the years, had taken on the contours of his body and stared at the interview with Amanda Mary Fletcher on the laptop. Published in a review of American history more than a hundred years ago, a few months after she had met Lizzie. "Well, I can't say for sure the white woman I talked to was my sister. There is no proof. She calls herself Kellsto Time, which means Killing Horn, and says she is the wife of Brokenhorn. She says she is Arapaho, and denies any memory of our family. She doesn't speak English, so I was required to take the word of a half-breed interpreter. I wouldn't be surprised if that Indian, Broken-horn, hadn't bribed the interpreter to put words into Lizzie's mouth."

"What do you plan to do next?" the interviewer asked.

"I will wait, and I will pray, as I have done for thirty-seven years. I will pray that, if she is Lizzie, she will get word to me. I trust my sister knows I am waiting for her. If she is my sister."

FATHER JOHN GLANCED through the interview again. A sense of long-ing, disappointment, and even denial rang through Amanda Mary's words. And yet, she seemed certain that if the wife of John Broken-horn were her sister, she would find a way to come to her. She would wait.

Her sister never came. And yet, Daisy Blue Water had said her grandmother took to calling herself Lizzie after the meeting. For the first time, she had acknowledged she was white. Still, she had stayed on the reservation, a white Arapaho woman.

"There's a lot about Amanda on the internet," Shannon had told him on the drive back to the reservation. She had found whatever was there, all of it now on her laptop, all the research and inter-views. She had been filling in the gaps on the reservation, pulling in the human story left out of the records. The fact that Lizzie had cried when she met her sister—no record had mentioned that.

He shut down the laptop and swiveled toward the window. The wind drove the snow against the glass like shotgun pellets. His thoughts circled back to Shannon. Perhaps she would be another white woman married to an Arapaho. He smiled at the idea. It was an old story.

He couldn't shake the image of James in the sacristy getting ready to serve Mass, before Shannon had arrived. Earnest and con-flicted, pulled toward the priesthood and pulling away. The priesthood wasn't what he had expected. Oh, Father John understood. It wasn't what he had expected, either.

Aware of another presence in the small room, he swiveled back and watched the bishop drop onto a chair that listed sideways under the old man's weight. He gripped a mug of coffee in both hands, lifted it to his lips for a moment, then set it on a small table. "Thought I might find you here," he said. "Trouble sleeping?"

Father John supposed that was the case, although he hadn't yet gone upstairs. An unsettled feeling had taken hold of him, as if the day were still moving toward something. So much unfinished, hanging in the air. Vince White Hawk still missing. Lou Bearing dead, and Debbie in shock. An Arapaho couple trying to adopt a white child. All unconnected, and yet he couldn't shake the notion that, somehow, they were mixed up together.

"How is the widow?"

Father John snapped back to attention. The old man seated across from him had a way of reading his mind. He told the bishop that, by the time he had reached the hospital, Debbie Bearing had already been released. He had driven back to the house and parked outside. She didn't come out, even though he'd had the feeling she was there, which meant she did not want company. He tried to blink back the image unreeling in his head: the woman flailing about the yard, howling at the sky.

"Vicky thought you were the one who had been shot." The bishop had narrowed his eyes on him. "She was quite upset."

"Yes, I know." Father John started to explain that Vicky had asked him to stop by the Bearings' place, then swallowed back the explanation. The circumstances didn't really matter. It was the fact that Vicky feared he had been killed. There had been times when he had felt the same terrible dread about her.

"You're very close."

"We're friends." Dear Lord, the bishop and Shannon both knew the truth. Was it that obvious? He thought of the way Vicky had thrown herself into his arms when she saw he was alive, and all the people standing about, watching. The moccasin telegraph had probably been jammed.

"You are a good priest," the bishop said.

"I pray every day."

"Not that the love you feel for each other will be taken away, I hope. The love of another always blesses our lives."

"For the courage to honor my vows."

"The day will come when you will have to leave the mission." The bishop shook his head. "When we'll both have to leave. There are rumors . . ."

"I've heard them." He had logged on to the province newsletter himself earlier this evening. The meeting had been held, a gathering of Jesuits and benefactors, to discuss the direction to take in the future, to test the air. It was clear where the discussions would likely lead. "The Jesuit province may have to close the mission," he said. "Not enough priests. Not enough money. What else is new?" He tried to make light of it. "It's always been a possibility."

"It will be hard for you to leave."

"For you, too."

"Oh, yes, but I've packed up and left before." The bishop got to his feet and hooked the handle of his mug in one finger. "I feel sleep coming on," he said, shuffling toward the door. Halfway across the study, he turned back. "We must always be ready to go."

He was bent-shouldered, moving across the corridor, taking the stairs one heavy, purposeful step at a time. The bishop had fallen in love with St. Francis Mission, with its people and its history and its silent emptiness. They were alike, Father John thought.

He could hear Walks-On snoring in the kitchen, deep into whatever dreams the night would bring. It was as though the day had finally collapsed. Father John was about to snap off the desk lamp and head upstairs when the phone rang. He glanced at the name on the small screen: Betty White Hawk. His muscles tensed as he lifted the receiver. "Father John."

"Thank God you're there." The voice lifted in hysteria. "You have to come right away." She started sobbing, garbling the words. "They're going to kill him. You have to stop them."

"Betty, listen to me. Take a deep breath and tell me what's happened."

She was crying hard, gasping for breath. A couple of seconds passed before she gulped out her son's name and told him the police found the house where Vince was hiding. "Somebody snitched him out. They're going to kill him."

"The police are not going to kill him, Betty. They're going to arrest him."

"Don't you get it?" The hysteria reached a higher pitch. "Nobody's going to arrest Vince. I know my boy. He'll shoot his way out, and they'll kill him. You have to stop them."

"Where is he?"

She gave a tangled set of directions. Seventeen-Mile Road, Yellow Calf Road, the first cutoff. A shack by the river. "I'm almost there. I can see the police lights, all red and blue. Oh, God. God. Don't let anything happen to my boy."

"I'm on my way," Father John told her.


THE PLANE JUMPED and rocked in the snow falling outside. It had been late leaving Denver. At one point, it had looked as if the flight would be canceled because of the weather in Wyoming. Vicky had thought she might have to call Lucas and ask him to come back for her. Finally, the flight had been posted. Late, but still taking off.

Vicky clutched the armrests, as if the armrests might steady the bouncing plane. The man seated next to her was snoring. God bless him! A lucky man to sleep through this. She closed her eyes against the snow smearing the window and tried to ignore the creaking noises. The images came to her out of the darkness: A white girl growing up Arapaho. A dark figure with a briefcase flying over the hood of a truck. Lou Bearing longing to lay down a heavy burden. And now, a man grieving for his lost child.

Coincidences. Betty White Hawk said that Lou and Debbie Bearing stole cars for parts, but that didn't prove that they had carjacked a car in Denver. A witness claimed she could identify the carjackers. After five years? Any defense attorney could establish enough doubt to discount the identification.

She knew what she had to do. She had to inform the adoption court of the possibility that Mary Ann Little Shield could be Elizabeth Becket. Tests would be made. She felt an emptiness opening inside her. Either the Little Shields or Jason Becket could lose a child.

Vicky's eyes snapped open. The plane had begun lurching back and forth. The man beside her shifted in his seat. Vicky tried to ignore the rocking plane and focus on Clint Hopkins's actions after he came back from Denver. He'd called her, arranged a meeting, and gone back to see Lou and Debbie Bearing.

And that was what had been bothering her. What had he hoped for? That Lou and Debbie would admit to carjacking a car in Denver, killing a woman, and driving off with an infant?

They would never have admitted anything. Except that Lou . . . She could still see the image of the slim man with narrow shoulders leaning against the truck as if he had been caught in a tornado. How long would Lou have resisted the pressure to tell the truth? Is that why Clint had gone back? Hoping Lou would break down, unburden himself?

Now Lou was dead.

But Clint had died first. Clint, who had put the pieces together, the coincidences, all except for the last connection between a crying baby and a baby left on the Little Shields' doorstep. He must have confronted Lou and Debbie about the carjacking, the abducted baby, the witness who could identify the carjackers. What he knew could have sent Lou and Debbie Bearing to prison for the rest of their lives.

Vicky sat up straight. Another piece of the puzzle clicked into place. She could imagine Lou Bearing and Vince White Hawk, hunched over beer at the Buffalo Bar, Vince listening to a proposition, just as his Dad had done ten years ago. *Easy money. You need money, don't you? Take care of a little job.*

The pilot's voice boomed over the intercom. They would be on the ground shortly. Temperature twenty degrees, snow falling. A cold night out there, folks. The lights of Riverton flickered through the snow clouds, foggy and remote from the new image gripping her: Vince White Hawk with a stash of money, hiding out on the reservation, on the run from murder.

Vince would never surrender.

# 31

VICKY FOLLOWED THE man who had sat next to her down the metal steps and across a swath of snow-blown concrete. A blast of frigid wind went straight to her bones. Inside, the terminal resembled an aquarium in the bright lights. She was still shivering as she made her way through the small crowd beyond the baggage trough.

She didn't see them at first, but there they were: Annie and Roger, hurrying forward, worry etched on their faces. The roads must be terrible, Vicky thought. She had left her own car in the parking lot, but here they were, good friends, come to fetch her.

Then she understood it was something else by the way Roger swung her bag out of her hand and started for the door, and Annie fell in beside her. "It's Vince." Annie kept her voice low, throwing a glance toward the people milling about. Vicky could feel a knot tightening in her stomach. The sounds of greetings and conversations surged around them, and Annie didn't say anything else until they were through the door.

"They found him." Annie stayed close beside her, the two of them picking their way along the snowy trail that Roger stomped out toward the short-term parking. "He's been holed up in a drinking house. A so-called friend snitched him out. Police have surrounded the house, and Vince is refusing to come out. He has a gun, and he's threatening to kill himself."

Roger held the doors of his SUV open while Annie got into the passenger seat and Vicky lifted herself onto the rear seat. She pulled her scarf around her chin and snuggled into a little warmth.

"We figured you'd want to get out there right away," Roger said, turning on the ignition, looking over one shoulder as he backed the SUV out of the parking space. She could see the worry lines below the cap pulled halfway down his forehead.

"Betty's beside herself." Annie joined in, straining around to catch her eye. "She's scared to death Vince will either kill himself or come out shooting and let the police do it. He's terrified of going to prison."

"Where is she?"

"She's at the house by now, I'm sure. She must have called a half dozen times to see if you'd gotten back yet."

They were driving through Riverton, past the restaurants, shops, gas stations shimmering in the falling snow. Vince. Vince. She had worked out a deal with the prosecuting attorney. All he'd had to do was come with her and surrender. He would have been in rehab now. Safe in rehab.

But Vince had wanted to drink, and the force of it—the sheer need for alcohol—was stronger than anything else. Where had he run into Lou? At the bar where Betty had gone looking for him? And Lou had recognized the force of want in his eyes. He had *smelled* it. He'd offered Vince money for a simple job: follow a man with a briefcase, wait for the best opportunity, run him down.

Roger made a right onto the reservation. The windshield wipers made a lazy, droning noise against the snow at the edges of the cleared crescents. Ahead, the sign for St. Francis Mission looked blurred and wavy. Betty would have called John O'Malley, and he would have gone immediately. Vicky could feel herself relax a little. John would do everything possible to keep Vince alive.

THE BLUE AND red lights on a cluster of police cars swirled in the snow. Several yards behind the cars stood the house itself—a shack, really—a collection of logs and sticks left over from the days when the government believed shacks were good enough for Arapahos. Thick snow lay over a roof that might collapse at any moment, except the roof had held on through decades of winters. It would hold on tonight, unless a volley of gunshots blew it to pieces. Vicky shivered at the thought.

Roger maneuvered the SUV through the barrow ditch and into the yard. He stopped behind one of the police cars. An ambulance stood nearby, an ominous sign, preparation for the worst. Vicky got out and slammed the door, searching the little groups of people milling about, BIA police in bulky uniform jackets, ear flaps dangling from their caps, plainclothes officers bundled in sheepskin jackets.

She spotted John O'Malley over by a floodlight mounted on a metal tripod. As if he had felt her eyes on him, he broke away from a group of officers and started toward her. Voices all around were subdued and tight, and it struck her that the voices of the enemy in the Old Time must have sounded like that before the warriors swooped down on a village.

She had started toward John O'Malley, snow blowing in her face, aware of Annie on one side, Roger on the other, when Betty

White Hawk—hatless, hair streaked white, face twisted in hysteria—jumped in front of her. "You've got to stop them!" She was shouting, throwing her arms about, gloves dangling off her hands.

Vicky took hold of the woman's shoulders. "What's happened?"

"He's going to kill himself if they"—the words sounded like a long wail; she waved a flapping glove around—"don't go away. He wants them to leave him alone."

She was aware of John O'Malley beside her. Annie and Roger had stepped away to give him room and, behind them, she could see Michael Lefthand, the BIA police chief, and another officer start over.

"We've been trying to talk him into coming out," John O'Malley said. "He wants to talk to you."

"Then we have to go in."

"Not going to happen." The police chief shouldered in beside her.

"Vince is desperate, Michael. I'm his lawyer. I have the right to talk to him. Father John is his pastor. We have to convince him to surrender peacefully. He's facing a charge of attempted robbery. It's not worth a life."

"I get it, but Vince is not listening to anybody's pleas." The chief threw a glance sideways. "No offense, Father. We have a SWAT team ready to take that shack and bring him out."

"They'll bring out a dead body," John O'Malley said. "Is that what you want?"

"Nobody needs to die tonight." Vicky stared at the chief until she was sure she had his full attention. "Let us try."

The chief lowered his head, considering something about his boots. A clump of snow slid off the brim of his hat. A couple seconds passed before he looked up. "You get one chance. If Vince White Hawk refuses to talk to you, we go in. Got it?"

Vicky nodded, and she and John O'Malley followed the chief over to the floodlight. He took a megaphone from another officer and handed it to Vicky. "One chance," he said.

The megaphone was heavy, unbalanced. Vicky held it to her mouth and pushed it up with her other hand. "Vince, it's Vicky." Her voice boomed around the yard as if they were in an echo chamber. "Father John and I are coming in."

Silence. The shack might have been empty, left with nothing but ghosts.

"No going in unless he's on board," the chief said. "You could be walking into a bullet."

"Vince, can you hear me?" Vicky heard her own voice, swollen and shaky. "I have to know if you hear me. Open the door a little." She waited. The door remained fixed, shadowy and flimsy-looking. God, the SWAT team would overpower it in a second. "Vince! We can help you. Let us help you."

Still nothing. "Better let it go." It was Roger's voice behind her, joining in. "It's too dangerous."

She glanced up at John O'Malley. In his eyes was the same resolution that had gathered inside her. She tilted the heavy megaphone upward again. "It's just Father John and me, Vince. You know we're not armed. We're coming inside to talk to you."

"No, you are not," Chief Lefthand said.

Vicky pushed the megaphone into his chest and started across the yard after John O'Malley, who was already halfway to the shack. A flurry of movement and the sound of angry voices erupted behind them.

"Vince! We're coming." John O'Malley's voice came back to her in a freezing blast of wind. "Open the door. Nobody's coming in but us."

He had reached the door now, Vicky so close behind she could feel the warmth of his jacket. The door trembled under his fist. Nothing but the hushed silence that had settled over the shack and the yard, as if she and John O'Malley were alone. Two or three seconds passed—a lifetime—before she heard the clicking noise, and John turned the knob. The door creaked open. "Vince!" he called.

John O'Malley stepped inside, and she was right behind him, moving into a tiny space of shadows and gray light framed in the front windows. Over in the corner, a space heater emitted a red glow. A blanket, the only other sign of human habitation, had been tossed near the heater. Seated cross-legged on the bare wooden floor a few feet away, the red glow playing over his face, was Vince White Hawk, hands shaking, dangling off his knees.

Vicky got down on one knee beside him, conscious of John O'Malley sinking beside her. "Let us help you, Vince," she said. He wore the same dark sweatshirt he had worn the last time she'd seen him. Torn jeans, exposing bony, bruised-looking knees. Tucked inside the waistband of his jeans was the black metal handle of a pistol.

"You can't help me." The words came like a hoarse cough.

"I'm going to see that you are taken to the hospital." God, the man needed help, whatever he had done. Day after day of steady drinking. He could have been dead. "I'm going to try to work out the same deal with the prosecuting attorney. You'll plead guilty to harassment and he'll drop the attempted robbery charge. You'll be sentenced to jail, but you'll spend the time in rehab."

"It's your chance for another start," John O'Malley said.

Vince didn't move. He might have been a sculpture in a park. *Indian Sitting Alone.* Without looking up, he said, "You don't get it."

"Oh, I get it," John O'Malley said. "I've been where you are. I know all about second chances. And one thing I know for sure: you don't turn them down."

The floodlight burned through the window behind her, and white light striped Vince's face and sweatshirt. He might have been behind bars, she thought.

Vince lifted his face, blinked into the light, and tried to scoot backward. The effort tipped him sideways, and John O'Malley set a hand on his shoulder to brace him. Vince was shaking. The space heater was no match for the cold air that invaded the old shack. Vicky got to her feet, scooped up the blanket, and wrapped it around Vince's shoulders. He shuddered into it.

"Nobody's gonna make me a deal."

"There are no guarantees," Vicky said. "I'll do my best."

"They think I killed somebody."

"You tried to rob somebody," John O'Malley said.

Vicky took a moment before she said, "Did you?"

Vince rocked backward, as if she had struck him with an anvil, eyes wide with fear, jaw moving with the impact of words trying to escape. One hand reached for the gun. "You'd better get out of here. Get out, both of you."

"I'm your lawyer," Vicky said. "Whatever you've done . . ."

"Nobody's gonna believe me. Even you think I killed that man." He gripped the gun and yanked it out. "I'm warning you. Get out!"

"Take it easy, buddy." John O'Malley's voice was calm, normal. "Put the gun away."

Vince was waving the gun like a flag. He kept his eyes on Vicky. "The cops'll never believe me." Tiny bits of spittle peppered her face. "I'm not going to prison for a murder I never did."

"I know what happened to Clint Hopkins." And she did, Vicky realized, as if the figures in the scenarios she had imagined had reassembled themselves. It wasn't Vince behind the wheel of the black truck. Either Lou or Debbie Bearing had been driving, because Vince had taken the money and disappeared.

"You didn't kill him." Vicky sat down on the floor, not taking her eyes from the gun. Steadier in Vince's hands now. "Lou offered you money to do a job, isn't that right? You were desperate for a drink, so you took the money. But you didn't have it in you, did you Vince? You couldn't kill a man."

John O'Malley had turned toward her, and she could see in his expression that he understood part of it. She hadn't had time to tell him what she had learned in Denver. The same truth that Clint Hopkins had uncovered, the truth that had gotten him killed.

"Clint Hopkins knew enough to send the Bearings to prison," she said. "They wanted him dead."

Vince was blinking into the light again, all the muscles of his face creased in concentration. "Lou never told me what the guy did. Just said he'd be at a meeting in downtown Lander later that night. He always carried a briefcase. I was supposed to wait for him to come out . . ." He gulped, as if something hard had lodged in his throat. "Lou gave me a thousand dollars. Said there'd be another thousand after I did the job. I took the money and . . ."

"Disappeared," Vicky said.

"I'm not a killer."

"Give me the gun." John O'Malley held out his hand. "It's your second chance, buddy." A long moment passed—Vicky could hear her heart hammering in her ears—as the dance went on: holding out the gun, pulling it back, holding it again, and, finally, setting it into John O'Malley's hand.

"We're going out together," he said. "Vicky and I will go first. You'll be right behind us."

Vince moved his head in what passed for a nod, then made an effort to get to his feet, scooting forward, trying to push himself upward. A great effort that came to nothing until John O'Malley took hold of his arm and lifted him up.

At the door, John O'Malley shouted that they were coming out, that Vince was unarmed. There was a change of plans then, since Vince was stumbling and weaving about. Vicky stepped out alone into the flood of white light, the falling snow like black flies in the light. Walking behind her, John held on to Vince.

"Your mother's waiting for you," she heard him tell the young man.

# 32

THE WOMAN CAME out of the house and ran toward the car parked in front. Coat open, sides flapping in the breeze that stirred the snow and sent little white clouds spiraling upward, head bare, scarf flapping around her neck. Betty White Hawk, a dark figure against the bright sunshine that had emerged this morning and scrubbed through the last of the snow clouds.

Vicky pulled the Ford in behind the car. A mixture of surprise and expectation flashed across Betty's face. She stood in the opened driver's door, stopped in motion. Vicky slammed out and walked over, boots crunching the snow.

"I been waiting all morning." Betty sounded tense, accusatory.

"I've been at the prosecutor's office." Vicky closed in on the woman. "I came as soon as I could."

"How is he?"

"Vince is in the hospital. He's under arrest."

"The deal?" Betty looked as if she might jump out of her skin.

She slapped away the scarf that blew across her face and blinked into the brightness. The sun had set the snow ablaze.

"Peters withdrew the deal. He's upset over last night's standoff. Vince didn't help himself by hiding out and threatening to kill himself."

"I know. I know." Betty lifted both hands in supplication. "He's my son, and I love him. All he could think about was getting a drink. You said you'd help him."

Vicky let a long moment tick by. Betty didn't know the rest of it: her son had accepted money to kill a man, had declined to do the job, and had taken off with the money. Neither did Peters, which, if the truth ever came out, would mean charges of conspiracy to commit murder and probably a host of other charges Peters would be happy to come up with.

"I'll meet with him after he's had time to think. A guilty plea means Peters wouldn't have the expense of a trial. In exchange, Vince would serve his sentence in a treatment facility."

"Guaranteed?"

"It's what I'm asking for." And hoping to conclude, she was thinking, before Peters became aware of Vince's role in a homicide.

Betty swung around and looked away, through the glare of the sun at the blowing puffs of snow. "We both trusted you."

"I'm doing my best."

"I have to get to work. If I don't show up today, I'm toast." Betty started sinking onto the seat, her attention directed to the steering wheel, the ice-crusted windshield.

Vicky leaned into the opened door. "There is something I need you to do."

This interrupted the woman's attention, and her head jerked around. "Visit Vince? They won't let visitors near him."

"I want you to tell the fed what you told me about the Bearings and the death of your husband."

Betty's mouth went slack. She squinted into the sun. "I never told anyone, except you."

"It's important. A child's future is at stake."

"It happened a long time ago. What does it matter? I gotta go."

"It matters, Betty. There's something else I have to put together, then we'll go to see the FBI agent together."

The woman gave a quick, dismissive laugh. "I lost my husband that night. I lost Rickie. All I have left is Vince and my husband's reputation. He was a hero to folks around here, a great husband and a great dad. And he lost his life in a senseless accident. You want me to take his good name from him? Tell the fed he was a thief?" She started crying, her voice shaking. "My son's going to prison. Treatment facility, whatever. He's going *away*. And you want me to destroy all I have left? Everybody thinking how lucky I was to have had such a good husband?"

"Please think about it." Vicky felt the door yanked out of her hand. The subject closed now, the conversation over. The engine sputtered into life and the car jolted forward, then swung into a U-turn, and gunned across the yard, snow spitting from the tires.

ST. FRANCIS MISSION was quiet, drenched in the sun, the buildings sharp against the blue sky. The Toyota pickup stood nosed against the front stoop of the administration building. Vicky pulled in alongside and hurried up the steps. John O'Malley was coming across the office toward her as she came through the door.

He reached out and took her hand. "I've been expecting you."

Last night, so much had been left unsaid after Vince had finally agreed to surrender. What choice did he really have? And they had walked out together, the three of them, into the crowd that pulsed about the floodlight. The rest of it had happened fast: Chief

Lefthand pulling Vince's hands behind his back, clamping on handcuffs, and pushing him down into the police car. She remembered shaking with cold and uncertainty as the car drove off. Vince on his way to the Fremont County Detention Center, where it would be up to a doctor to decide if he needed hospitalization. But he was alive.

She had been aware of Annie and Roger moving in close. They would drive her home and, as they started toward Roger's SUV, she had nodded at John O'Malley and mouthed the words: "Thank you." Then they had driven off, and Vicky remembered shaking with cold all the way to her apartment in Lander. It had taken hours to warm up, hours before she fell into an exhausted, black sleep. By morning the Ford had materialized in the parking lot. She wasn't sure when Annie and Roger had picked it up at the airport.

Now she dropped onto a side chair and let her coat slip from her shoulders while John pulled up a twin chair and sat across from her. "How is Vince?"

That was all it took for the words to rush forward. She told him everything she had told Betty: Vince in the hospital, the prosecuting attorney reluctant to cut another deal, her own hope—faint, unrealistic—that he would come around and she could get Vince committed to a treatment facility.

John O'Malley hadn't interrupted, had just nodded, understanding it all. Finally she jumped up, brushed past him and walked over to the window. The mission grounds looked quiet and peaceful. Beyond, the reservation stretched into the blue sky, the sun beginning to sink, and the shadows turning the snow blue-gray. She looked back. John had abandoned his chair and was half sitting on the edge of his desk, waiting.

"Is it about the Bearings?"

She nodded and told him what she had learned in Denver. A man trying to pick up his life after his wife was murdered, his child stolen. She could still see the photo in the silver frame: Jason Becket, a dark-haired woman, and a small boy, and the other photo of an infant snuggled in a pink blanket. She told him about the carjacking in Denver five years ago, the young mother trying to get her baby out of the backseat and slipping under the wheels. The carjackers were a man and a woman, possibly Indian. They had driven on: the woman in the stolen car, the man in the truck.

"There was a witness who claims she can identify the couple," she said.

"It was five years ago."

"A traumatic event like that is probably etched in her mind." Vicky started circling the space in front of the desk.

"You think it was Lou and Debbie Bearing."

She didn't stop, just told him what Betty had said about her husband's death. "They were car thieves. That's how Lou got parts for the cars he fixed. Only in Denver, they got something more. An infant strapped into the backseat. They had killed a woman and driven on. Driven on! With an infant in the backseat!" She stopped. A chill began at the base of her spine and shot into her neck. "What if they had panicked and abandoned the baby? Left her in a trash barrel, thrown her into the weeds. Anything."

"But they didn't. They took care of her." She heard the touch of compassion in John O'Malley's voice, as if he had seized on a small, decent thing.

"And when their neighbor asked about the baby crying every night, Debbie told her not to worry. It wouldn't last much longer. My God, John. The baby had become a problem. She could link them to the death of her mother. They had to get rid of her. Drop her on a doorstep and drive off. But the Little Shields might have called the police. The Bearings took a huge risk, John. A huge risk."

Vicky started pacing again, wearing a circle around the center of the office, trying to corral her thoughts, all the coincidences, the connections. There was still a crucial gap, the piece she couldn't put into place.

"Why the Little Shields?" She stopped pacing and faced him. "Why take the infant to them? Myra told me they knew of the Bearings, but they didn't *know* them. They had never spoken to them. Yes, they had lost their own baby, and news would have spread on the moccasin telegraph, but other couples had lost children. They weren't the only bereft couple on the rez."

"Unless . . ." Vicky dropped onto the chair, feeling light-headed, the air knocked out of her with a new thought working its way into her mind. "Unless the Bearings hadn't gone car stealing at all. They had gone baby snatching. Baby snatching for a bereft couple. In Denver, a big city, far from the rez. No one would connect an abduction in Denver to the reservation."

John perched on the chair in front of her and leaned forward, everything about him tight with concentration. She could feel him trying to arrange this new theory into a plausible, cohesive order, some kind of logic. "There isn't any proof, Vicky." *A terrible thing to contemplate, to accuse someone of.* She could read the message in his eyes. "They didn't know one another. Why would the Little Shields believe the Bearings would do something like that?"

Vicky was quiet a moment, aware of John O'Malley watching her, seeing *into* her. "In any case," she began, arranging her thoughts, listening to them tumble out, word by word, "I have to tell the Little Shields what I learned in Denver. Tests will determine if any of this makes sense. Jason Becket may not be Mary Ann's father after all, and then . . ." She threw out both hands. "None of this speculation will matter."

# 33

*I AM COMING with you.*

John O'Malley did not have to say it out loud. Vicky knew he would go to the Little Shields' with her. They had confided in him, and he had counseled them. They had given her permission to bring him in on the case. And now he would go with her. What was it? Moral support, physical support, or just to let the couple know that she was not the only one who may have stumbled onto what could be a terrible truth.

She shrugged into her coat while he set his cowboy hat on his head and yanked his jacket off the coat tree behind the door, pulling it on as they headed down the corridor and into the afternoon, the pale sun stippling the grounds. "Let's take my car," she said. The Ford had a heater that worked.

They crossed the empty, white spaces of the reservation in long periods of silence, thinking the same thoughts: the ramifications of this latest theory, a possible deadly connection between the Bearings and the Little Shields. But where was the proof? She had to keep in mind there was no proof.

Two figures were in the yard, a man and a small child. Rolling balls of snow that grew in circumference and left narrow tracks of dirt that crisscrossed the yard. Yellow hair hung beneath the child's pink cap and fanned across her shoulders. The man's face looked flushed, reddish brown with the effort of pushing an enormous ball toward some kind of enclosure in front of the gray-sided house. A snow fort, Vicky thought. And in a corral on the side of the house, a small pony.

Eldon Little Shield looked up and waved as Vicky steered the Ford off the road and into the yard. The child did the same, a wide grin spreading over her face, as if they were friends, coming to help. A sinking feeling hit Vicky as she pulled in behind a gray pickup.

"Your secretary called to let us know you'd be stopping by." Eldon stood outside the door as Vicky swung it open. "I left the shop early. Didn't want to miss you."

Mary Ann huddled beside him—all pale skin and wide blue eyes—and Vicky wondered how much she knew. Children knew everything; they were spies, spying on adults, spying on their own lives. And yet the hesitancy, the worry frowns in Eldon's face were absent in hers. "Good to see you, Father." Eldon waved them both toward the house. "Myra's waiting."

The house had a tidy, lived-in feel, a newspaper tossed on a coffee table, a bronze framed photo of Mary Ann on a table, jackets hung on a rack behind the door, odors of hot chocolate radiating through the warmth. Myra emerged from the kitchen as Eldon took their coats, adding them to the pile on the rack, a large squishy outcropping that bumped against the door. "You bring us good news, I hope," he said.

The child had sprinted to her mother, who was removing her hat and scarf, the mittens crusted with ice, the pink jacket soggy with snow. Whispering something about hot chocolate and cookies, she steered the child into the kitchen. Mary Ann was giggling.

Eldon nodded toward the sofa and a pair of chairs with oak armrests, an Indian blanket folded over the back of one. "Coffee? Hot chocolate?" The affable host, the smallest sense of uncertainty in his voice.

"No, thank you," Vicky said. She exchanged a glance with John O'Malley, who also waved away the offer. She dropped into one of the chairs while he perched on the other. This was not a social call; the information she had gathered in Denver, the theories and conjectures, none of it good. Out in the kitchen the child gave a carefree burst of laughter; metal clanged against a hard surface.

"I have new information about your case," Vicky began. "I know you've spoken to Father John . . ."

"Yeah. Yeah." Eldon waved away the rest of it. "Any news you got, I want Father John to hear."

Myra was back, and the couple settled together on the sofa, Myra leaning toward the kitchen, half turning toward the child. She gave Vicky a conspiratorial glance, mother to mother. "Put her in front of the iPad and she'll sit for hours." She shot a glance at her husband. "She can't hear us. She's lost in a game."

Eldon leaned forward and clasped his hands between his knees. "What did you find in Denver?"

How did he know? Vicky tried to scramble through the last couple of days. There was only one way Eldon could have known about the Denver trip. Annie had said that Debbie Bearing called yesterday, and she had told her Vicky was out of the office. Out of the office. Following Clint Hopkins' trail. Debbie must have concluded she had followed the trail to Denver, and she had told Eldon.

"I'm afraid it's not good news," Vicky began, reaching for the words. "I've learned that an infant was abducted in a carjacking in Denver five years ago."

"That can't have anything to do with us." Myra worked her hands in her lap, kneading them together.

Eldon remained silent.

"It's possible that infant was your child, Myra," John O'Malley said.

"Crazy talk." Eldon jerked upright, a warrior on alert to an approaching enemy. "Denver's a long way from here."

"The family's name is Becket." Vicky pushed on. The whole story had to come out, light had to be thrown on the truth. "The father has never stopped looking for his child. He wants her back."

"You mean, he thinks Mary Ann is his child? He wants to take her from us? From her home? From her people?" Myra's voice cracked, and for a moment Vicky thought she would burst into tears. Instead she drew in a long breath, drawing on some inner reservoir of strength. "Mary Ann doesn't have anything to do with his baby. Her mother lived on the rez. She brought her to us because she wanted us to raise her. That man in Denver can't have her. He can't take her away."

A wild, high-pitched shriek broke across the room. Mary Ann stood in the kitchen doorway, arms flailing against the doorjambs. She shrieked again, mouth opened. "No! No! No! I won't go! Don't let anybody take me away!"

Myra jumped to her feet. "Oh my God," she said, gathering up the child, lifting her into her arms, cradling her, the child screaming now, face twisted in pain, wet with tears. Myra carried her into the kitchen, kicking the door shut as she went. The door gave a loud thwack that sent invisible waves through the atmosphere.

Eldon was on his feet. "Do you know what you've done? Do you have any idea!" He stepped forward, fists clenched, and John O'Malley got to his feet. Vicky stood up beside him.

"Take it easy," John said. The muffled sounds of a sobbing child came from the kitchen. "We're trying to find the truth."

"It's not her! Maybe some kid got abducted, but it's not her. There's no proof, no evidence."

"There was a witness," Vicky said. "The witness can identify the carjackers. They were Indian, a man and a woman." She hesitated, then plunged ahead. "I think they were Lou and Debbie Bearing."

Eldon didn't move, a statue frozen to the rug spread over the vinyl floor.

"You knew that, didn't you?" John O'Malley said, keeping his voice low and confidential, the confessor urging the penitent forward.

Then something happened: a crack in the man's composure and assurance.

Eldon drew in his lower lip and turned away. He stared across the room, past the window, out to the icy, white expanse that ran to the sky, the truth crashing around them.

"You don't know." His voice was shaky. "You don't know how it was. Coming home from the hospital alone. Our baby girl dead in some steel freezer, never to be with us, grow up in her home, let us love her, be our family, be everything." He started to cry, his words thick with tears. "Myra couldn't take it. She just couldn't take it. 'Why us?' she kept asking. 'What did we do that was so bad our little girl was taken away?' She got worse and worse, crying all day, staying in bed and crying. Then I found her in the kitchen, a big glass of yellowish liquid in her hand. I knocked it to the floor because I knew. I knew what it was. The bottle of bleach was on the counter."

The man shifted himself around until he was facing them. "I could never leave her alone. I called the relatives. They came over and stayed with her, so I could go back to work. Somebody here day and night. Never alone."

"You contacted the Bearings." John O'Malley pushed on, low, rational tone. "Was it Lou? A man who ran a body shop in his barn, repaired cars, the same kind of work you do. You must have known him. Did he come to your shop looking for extra work?"

The two men locked eyes for a long moment, then Eldon broke away. "Scavenger, that's what he was. Coming around begging for old parts we didn't want. The boss sent him out to the yard to get rid of him. Let him take the junk so we didn't have to haul it away. That's what he used on the cars he worked on. Mostly junk. The rest, he stole, I figured. How else did he get any new parts?"

"He stole cars, so you thought he could carjack an infant for you," Vicky heard herself say.

Eldon took a step sideways, into another persona. He gave a large, raucous laugh. "You can't prove anything. It doesn't matter what Lou might've told you. He was a drunk and a liar. Nothing but a scavenger. You pay him a few dollars, he'd tell you anything."

"Or do anything," Vicky said.

"You got nothing. Debbie says I had anything to do with what they did in Denver, I'll deny it. Her word against mine."

"Mary Ann's mother died trying to save her," Father John said.

Eldon dropped his head and leaned forward, as if a hard gust of wind had caught him in the back. "I don't know anything about it," he said. "You don't have proof. All I know is our baby was on our doorstep; somebody left her. That's all I know."

"The adoption court will want proof that Mary Ann was abandoned. I will have to inform the court about Denver. The court will order tests . . ."

"No!" Eldon stood straight, shoulders back, chest thrust out. "I will not allow tests on my child. Nobody's taking her from us, you hear me? No court. Nobody."

"There's a chance the court could order a joint custody," Vicky said. "The tribe could get involved since Mary Ann's being raised Arapaho and believes . . ."

Eldon lifted a fist, and Vicky flinched backward, half aware of John O'Malley moving between her and Eldon.

"You hear yourself?" Eldon was shouting now, barking out words. "Court. Joint custody. Like hell!" He checked himself, drawing in a long breath. The child was still sobbing in the kitchen, a muffled noise that wafted past the closed door. "This is my family we're talking about. They're all I've got, Myra and Mary Ann, my two girls." He moved sideways and fixed his gaze on Vicky. "We wanted Mary Ann safe, so nobody could take her away, and you come here with joint custody? We don't need you. You're not our lawyer anymore, understand? Get out of my house, both of you."

IT HAPPENED IN an instant, like a flash forward, Vicky aware of the weight of John O'Malley's arm around her, sheltering her from the angry, fist-clenched man, guiding her to the door, grabbing their coats and shrugging into them as they crossed the yard, the door slamming hard behind them. She was shaking, and John took the keys from her hand and said he would drive. Then they swung around and were out on the road that stretched ahead into the blue-denim dusk coming on.

Neither one spoke. Thoughts on the same track, Vicky knew. Revisiting the same pieces of information, plugging in the vacant spaces. "Lou and Debbie took care of the baby until the time was right," she said finally, blurting out another supposition. "They waited for instructions from Eldon. It had to be snowing, a blizzard, with no chance Myra would recognize the vehicle or Debbie Bearing running away."

"What about Clint Hopkins?" John kept his eyes straight ahead, steering the Ford down the narrow road.

"He must have figured out what took place in Denver and confronted Lou and Debbie. He was thinking about Mary Ann. I think he hoped I could convince the tribe to step forward on her behalf, so that she would remain Arapaho. At the very least, we might have worked out an arrangement where Mary Ann's biological father and the Little Shields shared custody. Of course, that assumes Clint never realized Eldon's part in the abduction."

"There's no proof, Vicky." She felt John's eyes on her. "Even if Debbie accused Eldon of hiring them, Eldon would deny it. It would be her word against his."

Vicky didn't say anything, her own eyes trained on the road unfolding ahead, nothing but empty space and sky. "She would deny that Lou hired Vince to run Clint down in the street like a dog. When Vince took the money and ran, someone else had to do it. And . . ." She took a moment, allowing the logical conclusion to present itself. "Lou was already weighed down with guilt. Debbie was the strong one."

Letting a few more seconds tick by, she watched the road, but she saw something else now: Lou Bearing leaning against the black truck. The hood lifted, the tool table nearby. He had been repairing the truck from whatever damage Clint Hopkins' body had inflicted. She said, "The truck is in the barn."

John had been quiet for some time, and she glanced over. He kept shifting his gaze to the rearview mirror. She turned sideways and looked out the back window. "How long has that black truck been there?"

# 34

FATHER JOHN DIDN'T reply. When *had* the black truck appeared out of nowhere? He'd noticed it a good five minutes ago, but when had it appeared? After he had pulled out of the Little Shields' yard and started toward Seventeen-Mile Road? Had it been parked down the road, waiting for them to leave?

"Did Debbie Bearing know you went to Denver?"

"I haven't talked to her," Vicky said, her voice tight with uncertainty. She sat twisted about, her gaze on the rear window. Then, a rush of certainty: "She called yesterday, and Annie told her I was out of the office. She must have figured I went to Denver and she told Eldon."

The truck was speeding up, gaining on them, the front bumper gray and solid-looking. The headlights had flashed on, yellow spotlights in the darkening dusk. He could barely make out the figure behind the steering wheel: jacket collar up, dark scarf bundling the lower half of the face, cowboy hat pulled low. It could be a man or a woman. He pressed down on the accelerator.

The truck shot forward, and Father John pressed harder, trying to maintain space between the two vehicles. He wasn't used to the Ford, the way it responded. It felt steady in his hand, but the road was patched in snow, ice glistening like puddles of rain. The truck didn't want space: it loomed in the rearview mirror.

"Hold on." He leaned onto the pedal, aware of the white needle shaking upward: seventy, seventy-five, eighty. The truck stayed close. Enormous, a black monster risen out of the empty white spaces. The Ford, small in comparison, a bumper car. Eighty-five. Ninety. Too fast for the road conditions. It was getting darker, harder to see beyond the headlights. The truck kept coming closer.

"She's trying to run us off the road." Vicky's voice was high, close to panic. He could feel the wheels slipping, hydroplaning, almost airborne, and he knew she felt the same sensation. "We can't outrun it."

The loud thud jerked the Ford sideways. The car started to spin out, and it took all his strength to turn the wheel into the spin until they were headed straight again, but down the wrong side of the road. The speedometer jumping at ninety-two now.

"Turn off ahead," Vicky shouted. "We have to go cross-country."

He couldn't speak, all his attention focused on the road and the truck coming in for another hit. He tried to spurt ahead, but the Ford was going all out, and this time the hit was square, encompassing the entire rear end.

The Ford jerked forward, shaking, wobbling. He gripped the wheel hard and let up on the gas a little. The truck stayed close behind. Then the Ford righted itself, and they flew ahead, steady and straight.

The truck had dropped a car length behind, but it was still there, relentless. Vicky was right. He was going to have to drive off the road onto the wide expanse of empty land. But a sharp move at this speed would turn them over. The truck was roaring in close again, and this time, the hit came on the right, a noise that shattered the air. He heard Vicky scream as they spun out, snow spattering the windshield. No time to turn into the spin. The Ford was on its own trajectory, like a bucking bronco, and they were soaring over the barrow ditch and plowing through the snow. Twenty, thirty yards before he managed to rein in the vehicle and bring it to a stop. His heart thumped in his ears. They were still upright.

He looked over at Vicky. She was blanched, driven back into her seat. "Are you okay?"

"I'm okay." She had been holding her breath, he knew, and now she let out an explosion of air.

Later, when he tried to work it out, he wasn't sure when he had heard the crash, the squealing brakes, the thumping tires, the grating scrape of metal against metal. When had he gotten out, expecting the black truck to be coming for them over the snow? But it was then that he saw the two vehicles: the sedan clinging to the road, the black truck overturned in the snow. Black plumes of smoke rose over the truck.

Vicky pushed herself out and started running toward the road, high-stepping through the snow, arms outstretched for balance. He took off after her, then passed her, the whole scenario passing again in his mind: spinning out into the oncoming lane, headlights bouncing ahead. Dear Lord, he never saw the other vehicle. The driver had seen them, though, and swerved into the other lane.

The black truck, going ninety, ninety-five miles an hour, had been coming in the other lane.

He was breathing hard, sliding down the side of the ditch, forcing his way up the other side and out onto the road. Vicky stayed close behind; he could hear her shouting into her cell: Accident. Seventeen-Mile Road. Send ambulances.

He ran to the sedan first, the right front accordioned into a jumble of metal shards hissing and sweating in the heat that radiated off the vehicle. The left side, the driver's side, was mangled. He could see the man slumped over the steering wheel; no one else inside. The man was moving, head lolling. Somehow he had managed to turn the sedan just enough—inches—so that the back took the brunt of the crash.

"Hold on!" Father John yanked at the door. Stuck, jammed into the frame. He yanked again, one boot propped against the lower frame, and felt it give a little with a sharp, squeaking noise. He tried again, throwing all his weight into the effort until the door came loose. He managed to open it a foot, enough to wedge his shoulder behind it and push. He could feel the man's eyes on him and sense the panic.

He leaned inside. "Where are you hurt?" The man was Arapaho, a familiar-looking face, most likely from one of the get-togethers, not one of his parishioners. Blood was running down his forehead.

"I don't know." His voice sounded stronger than Father John had expected. "Everywhere."

Father John pulled his handkerchief out of his jeans pocket and pressed it against the man's forehead. It started to fill up with blood. He refolded it and pressed again, adding pressure until the bleeding slowed. "Can you hold this?"

The man nodded. He gripped the handkerchief and clapped it to his forehead.

"I'm not going to try to get you out," Father John said. There could be spinal injuries, head injuries. "An ambulance is on the way. The medics will tend to you."

The man gave a little nod and seemed to settle back, bleeding and in shock but alive. Alive, thank God.

Father John slid down the ditch on the other side of the road, then clawed his way upslope to the truck. The wheels were spinning against the sky. Cab smashed, windows blown out, shards twinkling in the half light, and inside—Debbie Bearing, upside-down, dangling from her seatbelt, slumped sideways. Vicky was hunched close to the broken window.

"Help me," Debbie kept saying over and over, a kind of litany.

"The ambulance is coming," Vicky told her. She glanced up at him. "I've been telling her, but she doesn't understand. She's delirious."

"Help me."

The door had been jammed into the roof, the window space smashed to half its size. It would take a crowbar to open the door, and even then, it might not budge. For half a second he thought about reaching inside and releasing her seatbelt, but she would fall onto the crushed roof. The window was too small to pull her through.

"Try to hold on," he said, but he could see she was letting go. Letting go of life. He thrust his arm inside, found the woman's hand—cold and limp—and squeezed it. "Breathe with me, Debbie. In. Out." He exaggerated his own breathing, gulping in air, blowing it out. "In. Out."

Her breathing sounded labored and faint. She was looking up at him out of the corner of her eye, past the scarf tangled around her head and caught somehow on the steering wheel, tethering her to the truck. He could see the spasms in her neck muscles.

"Breathe, Debbie. In. Out." He glanced over at Vicky, and in her eyes, wide with shock and fright, he could see the truth: It was useless. The woman was dying.

"I'll pray with you." He turned his attention back to the woman dangling upside down. The wind made a low moaning noise around them. "Dear Lord, merciful God, forgive me my sins." He wasn't sure if her lips were moving silently or if it was part of the spasms in her neck. "I place my soul in your hands. I trust in you."

She went still. Lips not moving, eyes straight ahead, focused on something else, another reality. Father John could feel the life going out of her, and yet her hand remained the same, limp and cool. "God have mercy on your soul," he whispered.

He let go of her hand; she would have to go on alone. He retrieved his arm, aware of the glass shards catching and tearing at his jacket, and stood up. The sound of sirens came from the distance, but the wind could imitate that eerie, distant wail. They were in the middle of the reservation, miles from the nearest ambulance, the nearest patrol car. It would take a while before help arrived. He had to go back up to the road, see about the injured man and keep him company. He was a priest. Wasn't that what he did? Dig inside himself to find encouragement and hope for someone else?

He turned to Vicky, waiting beside him, eyes fixed on the lifeless body of the woman inside the truck, the woman who had wanted them dead. The woman who had killed and killed.

He put his arms around Vicky and drew her close, allowing the warmth of her to warm the coldness inside him. Thank God, they were both alive.

# 35

VINCE WHITE HAWK stood beside her, sleepy-eyed, drugged, bent forward, as if he were leaning into the wind, but he wore a suit, a snappy blue tie, and a white shirt with the collar jutting out from around his skinny neck, all of it the work of his mother. She had wanted her son presentable for the court hearing.

"Mr. White Hawk, you are charged with attempted robbery." A routine matter for the district court judge who shuffled through a pile of papers in front of him before looking up. "Mr. Peters?"

Jim Peters got to his feet. He took a moment to marshal his thoughts, then he said, "Your honor, prosecution and defense have reached a disposition of this case. We have agreed to ask the court to release Mr. White Hawk on a personal recognizance bond to be cosigned by him and by his mother, Betty White Hawk. As a condition, Mr. White Hawk will enter a sixty-day program of addiction recovery and rehabilitation. He will be taken to the rehab facility immediately.

"After he has successfully completed rehab, we have agreed to reduce the attempted robbery charge to a misdemeanor charge of disturbing the peace with a stipulated sentence of one-year probation, on the condition that he remain sober during that time. We have reached this disposition in view of the fact that Mr. White Hawk voluntarily came forward and provided the Lander Police Department with essential information that enabled them to clear up the murder last week of Clint Hopkins. In addition, Mr. White Hawk's mother has also provided information that enabled the FBI to solve a five-year-old abduction and murder case in Denver."

The judge worked his lips around silent words for a moment. "Ms. Holden?"

Vicky got to her feet. She could hear her heart pounding. In the meeting this morning, she hadn't been sure whether Peters would accept her request to ask the court for bond and rehab. After every argument she had made, he had reminded her that Vince could not be trusted. Finally Peters had agreed.

"Your honor, we agree with the prosecuting attorney."

The judge took his time before he said, "I'm also inclined to agree." He looked up and fastened his gaze on Vince for a moment. "The attempted robbery charge will stand until Mr. White Hawk successfully completes rehab and remains sober for thirty days. I am going to set a return court date for that time. If your client has met the conditions, I will grant the prosecution's motion to reduce the charge to a misdemeanor. He will enter a guilty plea, and I will accept the probation sentence. However, if he violates probation by substance use, he will be sentenced for such violation. Is that clear?"

"Yes, your honor," Vicky said.

"Mr. White Hawk, you will now be transported to the treatment facility in Rock Springs. Good luck, and don't let me hear of you in trouble again. This court is adjourned." The judge banged his gavel and swept through the doorway behind the bench, black robe swaying.

Vicky turned to her client. The sheriff's deputies were already approaching to whisk him to a van waiting outside the courthouse. "You have a second chance," she said.

Betty pushed past the deputies, grabbed her son, and started hugging him. "Thank you," Vince said, mouthing the words over his mother's shoulder, and Betty jerked around. "Yes. Yes. Oh, Vicky, thank you for giving me my son back." She let him go then, and kept her eyes on the deputies escorting him down the aisle and out the door.

Jim Peters stepped over. "Let's hope your client can stay sober and out of trouble." He shook his head at the improbability.

"He's going to be just fine." Betty threw her shoulders back and lifted her head, on sure ground now. "All my son needs is a chance."

Peters gave a mock salute and stepped back to the table. He gathered up the papers, slipped them inside a briefcase and left the courtroom.

Vicky walked out with Betty, who seemed calm, wrapped in a new reality she could accept. Vince off to treatment, sure to recover, come home, live a good life, be her son.

VICKY DROVE NORTH on Highway 287, through the bright noon sunshine, a feeling of spring in the air. Snow glistening in the fields. She lowered the window a few inches and breathed in the faintest smells of spring: wet soil, sagebrush stirring into life, the freshness of the wind.

The sedan was turning into the yard when she crossed the barrow ditch. A light-blue, sporty-looking car with green and white

Colorado license plates. Jason Becket had called two days ago. The FBI had concluded the investigation into the murder of his wife and the abduction of his child. The witness—a mother herself out shopping for a few things for her own children—had gotten a good look at the carjackers. She would never forget their faces, she said. They still appeared in her nightmares. She had positively identified photos of Lou and Debbie Bearing. Without paternity tests, there was no proof that Mary Ann Little Shields was Elizabeth Becket, but there was a preponderance of evidence.

Vicky had not been involved. Everything was confidential that Eldon had told her and Father John—a lawyer and a priest. The whole story—the human story that Eldon had blurted out—would probably never be told: his wife, suicidal; his desperation to replace a lost child; a scavenger and carjacker coming around the shop. Not anyone he *knew*, not a relative or connection that could be traced to him.

It had taken several phone calls and meetings to persuade Betty White Hawk that it could help her son if she told what she knew about the Bearings. Vicky had arranged a meeting with Ted Gianelli, the local fed. She had gone along, reassuring Betty every step of he way.

Vince had been eager to tell the truth, hoping for a deal that would keep him out of prison. He had talked to both Gianelli and the police in Lander, filling in the gaps. Vicky had held her breath when he admitted to taking money to kill Clint Hopkins, then going into hiding, but the prosecuting attorney had declined to file any further charges. Vince had come forth willingly; he had helped to solve Clint Hopkins's murder as well as a five-year-old crime, and he was already facing charges for his own clumsy attempt at robbery.

Vicky slammed the door behind her and started across the yard through the piles of snow and rivulets of water. Jason Becket got out of the car and came toward her, a dark shadow silhouetted against the grayish house. He held on to her hand a moment as if she were a connection to his child, then tossed his head back at the house. "So this is where Elizabeth lived," he said.

"I'm sorry." She left the rest unsaid: *They're gone.* She had told him when he called that the Little Shields had fled the reservation. The FBI had already notified him.

"When?"

"A week ago," she said. "I told them what I had found. I told them there would have to be tests. I believe they left that night."

"Before I could get to her." Jason looked about, taking in the wide, snow-stippled yard, the great empty spaces. Then he stepped over to the blocks of snow melting in the sun. "What's this?"

"A snow fort. The day I came, Eldon and"—she hesitated—"the child were building a snow fort."

He drew in his lower lip, eyes sunken in thought. "She could have everything. A big house with a swimming pool. All kinds of lessons—music, tennis, horseback riding. Does she like horses?"

Vicky said she didn't know, but there had been a pony in the corral out back, and she didn't know an Arapaho child who didn't love horses.

"She would be a beautiful debutante, like her mother." He tossed his head toward the house. "Can I see inside?"

Vicky walked over to the front stoop, wet from melting snow. The house belonged to Myra's aunt, according to the moccasin telegraph, a piece of information wedged among the speculations about why the family had abruptly fled the reservation. Myra's aunt threw them out? They moved to Denver? Oklahoma? L.A.?

Vicky tried the knob. Of course Jason would want to see the inside, and it had crossed her mind to call the aunt, but what would she have said? Mary Ann's natural father wanted to see the house his child had lived in? That would have sent a rush down the telegraph. Besides, no one locked their doors on the rez. Anyone should be able to find shelter in a storm.

The knob turned in her hand and she stepped into the living room, Jason Becket behind her, so still that she turned around to check if he had come in.

The furniture was still there: sofa against the wall, a couple of chairs and small tables, a deep-backed TV that jutted into the middle of the room, but no signs anyone had lived here. A vacant place on the table where the photo of Mary Ann had stood.

"She watched TV in here." Jason sounded distant, lost in thought. He crossed the room and leaned into the kitchen. For the first time, Vicky saw the vinyl flooring, popped at the edges; the worn tablecloth hanging around the thin legs of the table; the countertop, scarred and stained.

She heard herself saying that the child had an iPad and she liked to play games at the kitchen table.

Jason turned and started down the hallway. A glance into the first bedroom: double bed, washed-out chenille bed cover. He walked to the second bedroom at the end of the hall and stepped inside. Pink everywhere: pink bedspread and pink canopy with blue and yellow flowers that looked hand-embroidered, white dresser and small vanity, lamps with frilly pink shades. Everything else was gone. No stuffed animals or dolls or toys. The sliding door on the closet was open, the closet empty.

Jason was quiet for a long moment, taking it in. "They love her," he said as if he were talking to himself.

"They love her very much." The rest of the story, Vicky was thinking, would never be told: the man who loved her had arranged for her abduction.

"Then she's lucky. She has two families who love her." Jason backed out of the room, and Vicky followed: down the hall, across the living room, and into the warmth of the sunshine.

"I'll never stop looking for her." He swung about, as if he could preempt any questions she might ask. "The FBI is on their trail. They are looking in every state, watching flight and train reservations. I've hired my own investigators. I've found her now—God, it's been so long. I've come so close, so many times, but I've finally found her. I know who she is and I know who *they* are. Eventually . . . eventually I will bring her home to her real home with her own family. I will never stop."

"She's Arapaho," Vicky heard herself say.

"I know. She'll have to spend time with them. They love her and . . . she loves them. We'll work something out. Summers on the reservation." He threw out a hand and waved to the great, vacant spaces; the immense blue sky. Then he gave a little wave, walked over to the sedan, and got in.

The engine gunned and stuttered in the patches of snow, then the sedan bounced across the barrow ditch. Vicky watched it speed down the road spitting out rocks and ice until it was a tiny dot in the distance, a black fleck in the sun.

# 36

THE FRONT DOOR flew open, followed by the thump of footsteps. Father John glimpsed the brown van outside the window as he got up from his desk. He turned into the corridor as Shannon swept past.

"My things!" In an instant, she took hold of the clipboard the deliveryman held out and scribbled on the page. "They're here," she said, swinging around as the man in the brown trousers and jacket let himself out. "I told you, Uncle John, I travel light. Two boxes. Hardly enough stuff to notice."

He offered to take the cartons to the guesthouse, but she gave a little wave and shook her head. "James is coming by in a little while. Another counseling session, not that it's doing much good." She shrugged her shoulders in the direction of the bishop's office down the corridor. "All that talking about what James really wants. I can tell you what he wants. He wants us to be together!"

"Then I'd say James and the Bishop are making progress." Father John smiled. Who wouldn't love her? So open and disaffected, yet more settled than when she had arrived, deep into writing her dissertation, consumed with the stories of two sisters—one white, one Arapaho—and in love with James Two Horses.

Yes, James would take her cartons to the guesthouse. He would help her. He would look after her.

"I'm beginning to understand Lizzie." Shannon walked beside him along the corridor; they might have been strolling through the cottonwoods to the river on a sunny day. "It just came to me. You know how it is. You spend days and weeks and months living with someone in history, and you begin to understand what must have happened, how the person must have felt. You *know* the truth, even though it isn't spelled out in any historical record. But you know it."

They had passed the door to his office and were standing outside the storage closet he had set up for her. He could see the small desk wedged against the wall, layered with papers and folders, a scattering of pencils, pens, and paper clips, a coffee mug, the detritus of a dissertation. "Tell me about Lizzie," he said.

"Here's the thing, Uncle John. She wanted to go with her sister. She wanted to visit her own beginnings, see the home where she had lived, sit at the fireside where her parents had sat, walk the same grounds, gaze at the same stars. She wanted to touch that part of herself, but she was frightened."

"Frightened? Of Brokenhorn?"

"Oh no." Shannon shook her head, as if the idea were absurd. "Brokenhorn loved her. He was devoted to her, and from what the descendants have said, he never mistreated her. He was proud of her, and yes, he worried the whites would take her away. He vowed never to let that happen. He even moved his family into the mountains at one time where no one would find them. Yet Lizzie met with

Amanda Mary, and I believe Brokenhorn approved, because he knew Lizzie was frightened. He knew she wouldn't leave him and the children, not even for a short visit."

Father John could feel the excitement rolling off the young, red-haired woman beside him. It took him back to his own days as a graduate student, such excitement at finding something new, something no one else had ever realized, at comprehending. "You're saying Lizzie feared that if she went with her sister, she wouldn't be able to return."

"She wouldn't know how to return. Think of it: an Arapaho woman, living on the plains, riding a stage coach to Casper and taking the train all the way to the Midwest. She wouldn't know how to get back. There wouldn't be any horse tracks on the plains for her to follow."

"Nevertheless, you believe she wanted to go?"

Shannon shrugged and pushed on, full of the wonder of it, the contradictions and pain in a woman dead more than a hundred years. "She was changed after meeting Amanda. The descendants say so. She insisted everyone call her by her white name, Lizzie, not Kellsto Time. She bragged to the other women that she had a home somewhere else, other people who loved her. When she went to Hollywood, she went with Brokenhorn and a trainload of Arapahos and Shoshones. She got to see the white world, but Hollywood wasn't where she had come from. She wouldn't have been frightened. She knew Brokenhorn would bring her home."

"Interesting theory." He felt like a teacher again, discussing a student's paper. "You'll need evidence."

"You know how it is. Truth has a way of coming out. You discover it first because you *know* it, and eventually the evidence catches up, proves you were right all along." She looked up a moment, studying the ceiling. "Daisy Blue Water has agreed to meet with me again. I think she likes remembering her grandmother. Who knows? Maybe she'll remember how her grandmother had wanted to go with Amanda, but had been too scared." She gave him a wide smile. "Let's hope she remembers before I finish writing," she said.

Father John retraced his steps into his own office. The click-click of Shannon's computer started before he sat down at his desk. Another white girl, his own niece, falling in love with an Arapaho, living on the reservation, becoming Arapaho. He smiled at the idea. And James, who had thought he wanted to be a priest, wanted a life with her. James would conclude his counseling sessions, which would leave the bishop without a project. Yesterday, when he'd stopped in the office, he'd found the bishop reading a recipe book. The old man had glanced up, excitement in the watery blue eyes, and asked what Father John would think of pork ribs with plum chutney and roasted potatoes.

He had gotten a call later from a young couple thinking about getting married, circling around the pluses and minuses. He suggested they talk to the bishop, an expert at helping young people choose the path forward.

From outside came the thrum of tires on gravel and the steady roar of an engine. He swung around, went over to the window and watched the tan SUV pull in beside his pickup—the car Vicky had rented while the Ford was being repaired. She was out in a flash, shoulders forward, making her way to the front steps. He met her in the corridor.

"I heard the good news a little while ago." He was ushering her into his study, taking her coat. He hung it on the back of the coat tree and told her that Betty had called. He could still hear the voice at the other end of the line, thick with relief and joy.

"Vince is in a treatment center in Rock Springs. He has a chance."

Father John nodded her to the chair, but he knew she wouldn't alight. She would travel around his office, pacing out her thoughts. They were traveling people, she had once told him, the Arapahos.

"Coffee?" The coffee he'd made this morning had gone stale; it would take only a few minutes to brew a fresh pot.

"Thank you." She gave him a smile. It surprised him, her acquiescence. It meant she would stay awhile; something else was on her mind.

He retrieved the glass pot from the table behind the door and carried it into the miniature kitchen off the corridor. On automatic, the same routine every morning and again during the day, depending upon his visitors. By the time he perched on the edge of the desk, watching Vicky stroll about, the smell of fresh coffee filled the office.

"Let me," Vicky said. And she was behind the door, pouring two mugs, stirring powdered milk into one, which she brought over to him. "I just met with Jason Becket."

He sipped at the hot liquid and waited. She had told him earlier about the FBI investigation and the preponderance of evidence that a man in Denver named Jason Becket was the father of Mary Ann Little Shield. He remembered the cascade of emotions that had washed over him: a father about to find his child; a couple about to lose theirs. It hadn't surprised him that the Little Shields had disappeared; wasn't that what Brokenhorn had done when he thought the whites might take Lizzie? Disappeared into the mountains? The moccasin telegraph had the news before Vicky had called to tell him it was true.

"How is he?"

"Devastated." Vicky stopped at the window, looked out, and

sipped her own coffee. "To come so close! It must be like losing her all over again."

So close. In his mind was the image of Daisy Blue Water recounting an old sorrow. Amanda had come so close to finding her sister only to lose her.

"He'll never stop looking." Vicky turned toward him. "The world is a small place today. So much media. It's difficult to hide. Still, it could take time. Mary Ann may be grown up before he finds her."

"She may find him."

Vicky smiled at him again, and he knew she'd had the same thought. "One day she'll look into the mirror and see blond hair and light eyes and say, *Who am I? Where did I come from?* And Jason Becket will be waiting."

She started pacing again—the door, the chairs, the window, and back again—something else on her mind, working out the best way to bring it up. He waited, and after another tour about the office, she stopped. "Is it true, John?"

He knew exactly what she meant. "It's a rumor." He tried to shrug it off, a nuisance. "There are always rumors." He dipped his head toward the corridor lined with framed photos of the earliest Jesuits at St. Francis Mission, his predecessors, strong and courageous and faithful men he had tried to emulate. "I suspect they heard the same rumors in their time. The Jesuits are always worried about having enough priests, enough money for its missions."

"Is it true?"

Vicky would not be put off; he could not cajole her, pretend it was nothing to worry about, the way he had been pretending to himself. He pushed off the desk and went to the window. The afternoon sun flared over the mission grounds, a spring sun, pale yellow, not yet in full control of its powers. Walks-On was asleep in front of the residence.

He turned around, facing her. "I believe, this time, it's true."

"Which means, you will leave." The words hung like a heavy weight between them. "The people need you here. I need you. How can you leave?"

Father John looked back out the window. It was the question he had been wrestling with in the middle of the night. How could he leave? Oh, the actual leaving, the physical part, would be easy. Packing up—a couple of cartons, smaller than those that contained Shannon's belongings; the O'Malley's traveled light— mostly books and CDs, his old CD player, a change of clothes, an extra pair of boots, Walks-On's bed. He could pack in thirty minutes, drive around Circle Drive and through the cottonwood tunnel the last time, Walks-On seated beside him, staring out the window, never dreaming they wouldn't be home by dark. The easy part he could do. He wasn't sure how he could do the hard part, and he knew, when he looked around at Vicky, that she understood.

He perched again on the desk. "You know," he said, trying to make sense of it in his own mind, the story he had told himself in the middle of the night, "Whatever time we get with the people we love is precious, no matter how long it is. Fifty years, twenty-five, ten." He had been at St. Francis a little over ten years now. "A slice of precious time that belongs to us for a while, and then is gone. We are always going. All of us."

Vicky took her time finishing her coffee, then she set the mug on the table behind her and turned toward him. Pinpricks of light danced in her eyes. "I'm not one of your parishioners you can cajole with your logic and your philosophy. I don't care about slices of time. I don't care how precious it is. When it's over, it's over. What is important is now. It's all we have."

"Then we have what matters, Vicky. We have the present. Nothing will happen overnight. Closing a mission takes time, and this is a bureaucracy we're talking about. Bureaucracies move at glacial speed. I've learned not to worry—I've told myself: wait until you know whether you have something to worry about. We're here now, in the present."

"Waiting," she said.

"Yes, in the present."

# AUTHOR'S NOTE

The story of Elizabeth "Lizzie" Brokenhorn, her captivity and subsequent life as an Arapaho on the Wind River Reservation, is based on historical records. We know that Amanda Mary Fletcher Cook spent thirty-seven years trying to find her sister, that they were briefly reunited in 1902, and that Lizzie was deeply affected by the reunion and by learning of her background. Still she chose to remain with her husband and children and to live out the only life she had known. The records are also clear that John Broken-horn was a good husband who cared for his wife, worried that white authorities would take her away, and tried to protect her.

But records are thin on how Lizzie might have felt about her situation—what Shannon calls "the outside of history." While actual descendants of Lizzie and John Brokenhorn no doubt exist, the descendants you meet in this story are fictional. The stories they relate about Lizzie's day-to-day life are not found in the historical records about Lizzie but are consistent with the life of a traditional Arapaho woman in Lizzie's time.

Did Lizzie Brokenhorn actually butcher cattle, make fry bread, attend to the dancers at the Sun Dance, look after the grandchildren, as the fictional descendants relate? As Shannon would say, it might not be in the historical records, but we know it is true.

RUPERT CHRISTIANSEN

# *Prima Donna*

## A History

VIKING

VIKING
Viking Penguin Inc.,
40 West 23rd Street,
New York, New York 10010, U.S.A.

First American edition
Published in 1985

LIBRARY OF CONGRESS CATALOGING IN PUBLICATION DATA
Christiansen, Rupert.
Prima donna.
Bibliography: p.
Includes index.
1. Opera.  2. Women singers.  I. Title.
ML1700.C56  1985  782.1'088042  84-48828
ISBN 0-670-80482-7

Printed in the United States of America by
The Book Press, Brattleboro, Vermont
Set in Ehrhardt

# CONTENTS

# LIST OF PLATES

# *Introduction*

This book is a history of a line of women who for nearly 300 years have been at the centre of the magnificence and scandal of opera, ridiculed, reviled, and worshipped.

The *Oxford English Dictionary* gives 'the first or principal female singer in an opera' as its major definition of 'prima donna', and records examples of the usage in English from the end of the eighteenth century. Although it is commonly assumed that the term arose in Italian around 1650, in fact *'virtuosa'* was the ordinary way of referring to a principal female singer until about 1800; *'cantatrice'* (meaning simply 'female singer') was also internationally used. Such words were neutrally descriptive, and in the earlier phases of opera a prima donna was the *cantatrice* who sang the greatest number of arias in the course of any particular work.

Not until the middle of the nineteenth century and the highly publicized and promoted careers of Grisi and Patti did 'prima donna' come to bear an innuendo. In 1862, for example, Henry Mayhew, in his survey *London Labour*, identifies the prima donna as a sort of courtesan, idling her way through wealth and fame; and by the twentieth century, particularly in English, the term had stuck as a label of abuse on a level with virago, shrew, or bitch. To be a prima donna was not so much to be a great interpreter of operatic music as to be an outrageous *grande dame*, 'exacting, torrential, and exasperating', and often lazy, greedy, stupid, conceited, and 'impossible' as well. It has proved a powerful stereotype. A woman who wants her own way is a prima donna. A woman who makes a complaint is a prima donna. A woman who changes her mind is a prima donna.

The truth about the real prima donnas is more complex, and rather than treating them as either gorgons or freaks, I have tried to put their lives and their art into the contexts of operatic and cultural history. Many of the women in these pages worked their way up from unprivileged backgrounds, fought tooth and nail to get a hearing in a male-dominated world of ruthless intrigue, braved enormous risks, and accepted the necessary sacrifices. The rewards —fortune, independence, public acclaim, the chance for self-expression beyond the roles of wife and mother—were incomparably high, but so were the odds against success, let alone happiness. Opera has always been a highly-strung profession, running on dynamic and creative clashes of will and temperament. Given such a gamble in such circumstances, a woman had to be alert and aggressive to survive. 'Acting the prima donna' may have been the only way to avoid exploitation, and a prima donna's greed was often the hard-headed refusal to work for less than her market value. Her celebrated whims, too, often had solid reasoning behind them: not only were there artistic standards to maintain, but the singing voice is a sensitive physical instrument which requires careful handling and husbanding. A woman who refuses compromises is a prima donna. A woman dedicated to her talent is a prima donna.

It would be possible to make a feminist defence of the prima donna. She proved that women of no inherited rank or moral virtue could stand up in public—something Jane Austen or Emily Dickinson never had to do—and make their lives for themselves.[1] However, feminist writers have shown no interest in prima donnas, despite massive and justified attention paid to their sister painters, writers, and scientists. Why should this be? Not, I think, because all lastingly successful operas to date have been written by men and largely present women in passive or dependent situations; but perhaps because prima donnas are, almost by definition, *successful*. They have not been the victims of oppression and intimidation, they have grabbed at the glittering rewards of their success; they often fought against the very women they should have helped. (When asked to comment on Grover Cleveland's dictum that 'a woman's place is in the home', the American prima donna Emma Eames replied that it might be appropriate for 80 per cent of women, but that was no reason to stifle the other 20 per cent.) And if prima donnas have been mocked, they have also been worshipped. Like the sirens of the *Odyssey*, their voices were sexually alluring

[1] Why women in music have had so much more success as performers than as composers is another fascinating question.

and morally dangerous. In the nineteenth century a prima donna also became a *diva*, a goddess. The idea behind this is empty-headed, but potent—flowers, diamonds, applause, flattery, glamour are all aspects of exactly the sort of womanhood that feminism deplores.

But there are other ways of looking at the phenomenon. With the idealizing of the *diva* came all the journalistic emphasis on charisma, genius, and mystique, and a consequent under-emphasis on the technique, intelligence, musicianship, and plain hard work which make a first-rate singer. A prima donna is also a product of her musical epoch—there were no 'Wagnerian' voices in the eighteenth century, for instance, simply because the musical idioms of the time did not require them—and the changes in ideas about vocal style and the constitution of good singing are matters that I have tried to elucidate. At the same time, it must be appreciated that the prima donna has a central and creative role in the development of opera—*Norma* and *Anna Bolena*, for instance, are as much an expression of Pasta's genius as they are of Bellini's and Donizetti's; the capabilities of Schröder-Devrient, Stolz, and Jeritza were vitally inspiring at various times to Wagner, Verdi, and Richard Strauss; while in our own day, Berio gave Cathy Berberian music which trusted a great deal to her own improvisation, rather as the eighteenth-century prima donna would completely transform a written melody with fantastic embellishments. In other words, a prima donna has never been a dummy in costume.

We have been talking so far about The Prima Donna, when the reality is a variety of women who have made their livings by singing. Beyond the generalizations, each of them has had her own struggles, frustrations, virtues, and vices. Some found teachers and patronage quite easily; some were born in the theatrical trunk. Others faced the climb on their own and found that they had to give up their lives to achieve their art. Some, like Callas, found the price too high; many made disastrous marriages to men who either exploited them (Nordica, Tetrazzini) or deplored their ambition (Melba)—most of their better unions have been made with other musicians or to men directly involved in, and with an understanding of, opera and its pressures.

The aim of this book is to suggest the rich individuality of prima donnas as both women and singers, without resorting to either strings of anecdotes or abject *diva*-worship. I am afraid that limitations of space—and the reader's patience—have inevitably meant that many fine singers are not even mentioned, and others find less than their fair share of space: I am particularly aware that the prima donnas of Eastern Europe and South America are under-represented. My apologies to them all, but it has seemed more important to provide a broad cross-section, including some not strictly eligible castrati and mezzo-sopranos (in some periods a prima donna was invariably a soprano), than to cram in names and facts just for the sake of being encyclopedic. For similar reasons, I have excluded singers whose careers have been almost exclusively in *lieder*, concert, or operetta. I have also avoided technical terms and analysis, while assuming a reader acquainted with the basics of musical vocabulary. Anyone wanting more detailed comment on specific recorded performances than I have provided can do no better than J. B. Steane's *The Grand Tradition* (1973), a book I have found truly inspiring.

I can only claim this to be a preliminary mapping-out of a neglected but fascinating area of cultural history. The limited exploration I have done in museums, archives, and libraries suggests that there is a lot of room for further writing and research on the subject: if my efforts provoke any such work, I should feel amply rewarded.

# *From* Opera Seria *to Mozart*

'The Dutchis of Molbery had got the Etallian to sing, and he sent an excuse, but the Dutchis of Shrosberry made him com, brought him in her coach, but Mrs Taufs huft and would not sing because he had first put it ofe; though she was thear yet she would not, but went away . . . I wish the house would al joyne to humble her and not receav her again.'

In this semi-literate letter written in 1708 by one Lady Wentworth to her daughter is perhaps the earliest recorded instance of 'prima donna' behaviour—'Mrs Taufs huft'. Caprice, bad temper, greed, hauteur—Mrs Taufs, or Tofts, as she is ordinarily known, embodied the popular and enduring image of the female opera singer, and her career certainly contains many elements and situations which will occur repeatedly in the course of this book. Already we see an ignorant public gleefully creating a *monstre sacré*, oblivious of the sensitivities necessary for singing. Lady Wentworth, for instance, never considers the possibility that Mrs Tofts was rightly affronted at the 'Etallian's' failure to appear at the right time: what most concerns her is that Mrs Tofts's impudent presumption broke the codes of social deference. The prima donna is already a noisy threat to female decorum ('let your women keep silence in the churches' enjoined St Paul in Corinthians) and Mrs Tofts realized that she could afford to withhold her labour. It made her unpopular among the aristocrats who patronized her. When Mrs Tofts went mad, people of fashion giggled: it was her deserved come-uppance.

Katharine Tofts's origins are obscure: she was probably born about 1685, and emerged in London musical life at the beginning of the eighteenth century, when the vogue for Italian opera was just beginning there. Lady Wentworth's 'Etallian' was the famous castrato Nicolino, making his English début. On the occasion at which they were present—a gathering of aristocrats for a private recital in the rehearsal room of the Queen's Theatre—he and Mrs Tofts were to sing from a new opera, *Pirro e Demetrio*, probably a *pasticcio*, a piece cobbled together from various sources and typical of its time. Nicolino would have sung in Italian, Mrs Tofts in English, a common and much-ridiculed practice. Italian finally won the day, perhaps as much because of the chic attached to a foreign language as because of its wonderfully singable vowel sounds.

Mrs Tofts first came to fame singing songs in concert at the Drury Lane Theatre. Of her voice and its qualities we know next to nothing. She was a soprano, probably with a degree of agility unusual for her time and place, although soon to become a necessity. The infamous hack dramatist Colley Cibber wrote that, 'The beauty of her fine proportion'd figure and exquisitely sweet, silvery tone of voice with the peculiarly rapid swiftness of her throat, were perfections not to be imitated by art or nature'—which is about as far as the contemporary vocabulary of music criticism can take us. But something more of her career can be determined. In December 1703 she cancelled an appearance 'by reason of a great cold', an announcement which then, as now, probably met with incredulity. Then in early 1704 another singer made a highly successful first appearance at Drury Lane. This was Margherita de l'Épine, an Italian resident in England, longer established than Mrs Tofts and considered a very fine artist. During her second appearance on Mrs Tofts's territory a violent outbreak of hissing and orange-throwing occurred and an arrest was made, the culprit being embarrassingly identified. The following letter was published shortly afterwards, originally addressed to the manager of Drury Lane:

> Sir, I was very much surpriz'd when I was informed that Ann Barwick, who was lately my servant, had committed a rudeness when Mrs L'Epine the Italian gentlewoman sung.I hope no one can think that it was in the least with my privity, as I assure you it was not. I abhor such practises and I hope you will cause her to be prosecut'd, that she may be punish'd as she deserves. I am, sir, your humble servant Katharine Tofts.

We may doubt the sincerity of this repudiation, but it is known that the two ladies continued to sing in the same performances, even if never in duet.

Madame L'Épine was extremely plain, and was publicly known

as the 'Tawny Tuscan'; Mrs Tofts was a beauty, and had the added advantage of being British. Fashion, chauvinism, and political faction played their parts in the subsequent partisanships.

> Music has learn'd the discords of the state
> And concerts jar with Whig and Tory hate.
> Here Somerset and Devonshire attend
> The British Tofts and every note commend . . .
> There fam'd Lepine does equal skill employ
> While listening peers crowd to the ecstatic joy:
> Bedford to hear her song his dice forsakes
> And Nottingham is raptured when she shakes[1] . . .

So wrote the poet Hughes; while the newspapers carried further epigrammatic and poetic compliments to the ladies, one of which has been attributed to Pope:

> So bright is thy beauty, so charming thy song
> As had drawn both the beasts and their Orpheus along,
> But such is thy avarice, and such is thy pride
> That the beasts must have starved, and the poet have died.

What gave Mrs Tofts real glamour, however, was her association with Italian opera. In 1705 she appeared in *Arsinoe, Queen of Cyprus*, a piece by Thomas Clayton, now, like the majority of early operas, vanished. It has its significance as the first English attempt to emulate the Italian style, and it had a certain popular success, but critical feeling was hostile, one authority finding 'nothing in it but a few sketches of antiquated Italian airs, so mangled and sophisticated that instead of *Arsinoe*, it ought to be called the Hospital of the Decrepit Old Italian Operas'. Before *Arsinoe*, the English operatic tradition had been theatrically rooted with isolated exceptions, notably Blow's *Venus and Adonis* (c. 1685) and Purcell's masterpiece *Dido and Aeneas* (1689). Interpolated songs and incidental music had been common since Shakespeare's day, and the masque and varieties of court entertainment were also remembered, but the Italian conception of opera which began in the late sixteenth century as an attempt to recreate what was thought to be the mode of Greek tragedy and which soon became, roughly

1 A shake, or trill.

speaking, a series of elaborate songs linked by accompanied recitative, had not caught on till then.

In Italy the female singer had long been familiar as the object of honours and flowery compliments. In Renaissance courts, the singing of songs and madrigals was considered an estimable occupation for ladies, and the d'Este palace in Mantua was particularly celebrated for its 'golden-throated nightingales', including the Duchess Isabella herself. The earliest female opera singer we know of is Vittoria Archilei (1550–c.1618), who sang and danced in many of the first operas performed in Florence, where she was attached to the court of the Medicis. We know somewhat more about another Mantua-trained *virtuosa*, Leonora Baroni (1611–70). She did not sing in opera, but in the courts, where her recitals would be accompanied on the *lira* by her mother Adriana, who had also been a singer. She was said to be 'highly accomplished ... graceful, frank and full of intelligence' and her renown spread abroad: in 1644, at the behest of Cardinal Mazarin, she sang in Paris. The young John Milton heard her in 1638–9 during his Italian tour, and was impressed enough to write three conventional Latin sonnets in tribute to her:

> *Nam tua praesentem vox sonat ipsa Deum . . .*
> *Quod si cuncta quidem Deus est, per cunctaque fusus,*
> *In te una loquitur . . .*

> (For the sound of your voice makes it clear that God is
>     present . . .
> If God is all things and omnipresent, nevertheless
>     he speaks in you alone)

It was in Venice that opera grew into a commercial entertainment, and the first public opera house opened there in 1637; but we know virtually nothing about any of the singers from this period, and it is only in London with Mrs Tofts that the historian first finds a prima donna adulated, exploited, fought over, fighting back, publicly discussed, and probably libelled. Such was her *éclat* in fact that she was soon in a sufficiently strong position to wrangle over her contract with Drury Lane. But here again we must be careful not to fall unthinkingly for the notion that she was simply motivated by Pope's 'avarice and pride'. A lot of her demands seem perfectly justifiable, although it has to be said that her fee for a performance in 1705 was £16 13s. 4d., over four times as much as that of Mrs Bracegirdle, the leading actress of the day. Eventually Mrs Tofts pleaded for redress with the Lord Chamberlain, the court official who licensed the theatres, claiming that the manager 'tooke all the Opportunitys he could to be Revenged on her: which was in calling on her to sing oftener than she was able to performe', thus causing her to lose her voice and require expensive medical attention. She also demanded money for costumes and stage ornament, as well as two bottles of wine to refresh 'the Gentlemen that practice with her'. She won her case, and went on in 1706 to the great triumph of her career in the title-role of Bononcini's *Camilla*, an Italian opera that was played repeatedly over the next few years and which remained popular throughout the century. A scene in which Mrs Tofts as Camilla shoots and kills a wild boar passed into contemporary theatrical legend—*The Spectator* even published a letter, purporting to come from the shade of the unfortunate animal: 'Camilla's charms were such that beholding her erect mien, hearing her charming voice and astonished with her graceful motion, I could not keep up to my assumed fierceness, but died like a man.' Soon she is again petitioning the Lord Chamberlain for better terms, on the basis of 'this climate being much worse than any other for voices, and in short the misery . . . if seiz'd with a cold'. She also threatened not to sing again until she received reimbursement for the eighty guineas she had spent on gowns for *Camilla*. Again Mrs Tofts got her way, but in 1708 she left Drury Lane and signed up with the new Queen's Theatre in the Haymarket, where she and Madame L'Épine each received a fee of £400 for the season. She supplemented her already large income by giving private recitals like the one Lady Wentworth attended. The theatrical gossip Chetwood records how in 1709 she went to the Duke of Somerset's 'where there were about thirty gentlemen, and every kiss was one guinea; some took three, others four . . . but none less than one'. In the twentieth century, plenty of prima donnas have been prepared to sing in night clubs or musical comedy, but of her kind only poor Mrs Tofts seems to have sunk as low as this. Two months later she made her last British appearance in an opera called *Love's Triumph*. *The Tatler* shortly issued a report that Mrs Tofts:

> . . . has had the ill-luck to break before her voice, and to

disappear at a time when her beauty was in the height of its bloom. This lady entered so thoroughly into the great characters she acted, that when she had finished her part, she could not think of retrenching her equipage, but would appear in her own lodgings with the same magnificence that she did upon the stage. This greatness of soul had reduced that unhappy princess to an involuntary retirement, where she now passes her time among the woods and forests, thinking on the crowns and sceptres she has lost, and often humming over in her solitude

> I was born of royal race
> Yet must wander in disgrace.[1]

But for fear of being overheard, and her quality known, she usually sings it in Italian.

We know nothing else about this nervous breakdown, and we can only conjecture at the pressures which might have caused it or the reality of her mental state. The music historian Dr Charles Burney (1726–1814), writing towards the end of the eighteenth century, considered the story exaggerated. It is certainly true that Mrs Tofts reappears in Venice in 1712, singing 'in all the great Assemblies that were held at the Electoral Prince of Saxony's', apparently with great success. *The Spectator* devised a 'letter from Camilla', which shows, if nothing else, that people had not quickly forgotten her.

> I live here distinguished, as one whom Nature has been liberal to in a graceful person, an exalted mien, and heavenly voice. These particularities in this strange country are arguments for respect and generosity to her who is possessed of them. The Italians see a thousand beauties I am sensible I have no pretence to, and abundantly make up to me the injustice I received in my own country, of disallowing me what I really had. The humour of hissing, which you have among you, I do not know anything of, and their applauses are uttered in sighs ... P.S. I am ten times better dressed than ever I was in England.

Does this hint at the possibility that Mrs Tofts retired from the London stage, not because she was mad, but because she had

1 A well-known air from *Camilla*.

suffered from some stormy audience behaviour and could not recover her nerve? In Venice she never sang in opera again— strange if *folie de grandeur* was her complaint—only in concerts. In 1716 she married—her original 'Mrs' was probably meaningless, and Tofts her maiden name—one Joseph Smith, a faintly shady consul in Venice, who was busy acquiring, perhaps with his wife's earnings, Canalettos which came to form the basis of the royal collection now in Windsor Castle. She again fades from sight, residing in the Palazzo Balbi, where she was said to live in great state until her death in 1756. An unreliable source, Sir John Hawkins, later repeated the *Tatler* story—in her Venetian seclusion Mrs Tofts had suffered a relapse: 'Sequestered from the world [she] had a large garden to range in, in which she would frequently walk, singing, and giving way to that innocent frenzy which had seized her in the earlier part of her life.' Even more fanciful was the news that, having turned Roman Catholic, she sang for the Pope, who had subsequently paid her scandalous attentions. The blend of fantasy, deliberate falsification, vindictiveness, and detached amusement which make up this tale will be another recurrent factor in the following pages.

But first, what were early prima donnas such as Mrs Tofts singing? It was a difficult period for the operatic form, and no amount of special pleading can make even its best works fully alive today, for we have lost the idea of theatre they were composed around—an idea indifferent to naturalism in speech, deportment, gesture, and plot, but centrally concerned with putting forward a strong moral case for one of the approved virtues—constancy, clemency, honour—which made men and women noble. The Baroque opera presents an interesting contradiction: on the one hand, the action on stage showed aristocratic or mythological personages, allotted a definite prominence in the plot and a certain number of arias appropriate to their status in a system of hierarchies which operated from the king's court right down to the seating arrangements within the opera house. On the other hand, performances were conducted in a state of near-uproar, with noisy audiences, under-rehearsed stagings, and the singers allowed a since unheard-of degree of liberty to interpret or embellish the music as they wished. What in the mere printed score now appears to be an intolerable monotony of formula was subverted in performance by a spirit of licence and improvisation. The chief vehicle for this freedom was the *da capo* aria—in which the initial melodic idea would be repeated with runs, trills, and all the other ornaments associated now with the term 'coloratura'. Of course, many used the opportunity just to show off high notes or staggering breath control, but the greatest singers were always recognized for their ability to make their inventions dramatically memorable and relevant, an intensification of the aria's basic emotion—anger, jealousy, relief, joy, grief—which the 'original' composer had set out in skeleton form. Some singers changed their ideas from performance to performance, others were more consistent. And it was only the better musicians who devised their own decorations. The run-of-the-mill prima donna hired a hack. The Italian composer Marcello satirized the practice: 'The singer . . . will at the first possible moment take all her arias . . . to her Maestro . . . so that he may write in the passages, the variations, the beautiful ornaments etc.—and Maestro Crica, without knowing the first thing about the intentions of the composer [will write in] everything he can think of.' This improvisatory principle has recently been revived, but in a manner perhaps rather genteel and academic— we probably get a better idea of its exhilarating effect from 'scat' singing in jazz.

Perhaps the Baroque opera house is better compared to a night club than to the modern darkened and silent temples of art. In the eighteenth century audiences would come and go throughout the performance, in and out of auditoriums kept fully lit, talking, eating, drinking, conducting amorous intrigue, and generally treating the entertainment with what in some ways was a healthy lack of respect. In such an atmosphere the singers had to work hard to shock the audience into attention. Sometimes they would themselves behave with a corresponding disdain of audience and drama. 'All the while the *ritornello* [orchestral introduction] of his air is being played the singer should walk about the stage, take snuff, complain to his friends [seated in stage boxes] that he is in bad voice, has a cold, etc.' wrote Marcello in his ironic account of the common practices of the time.

The decorum of opera in this period was a strange mixture of high formality, great casualness, and semi-hysteria. Many early critics found it an idiotic farrago, mainly because of the eternal language problem—the operas being sung either in incomprehensible Italian or nonsensical translation. Financially it depended on capital earned from a sort of seasonal subscription system. Nowadays the great complaint about such systems is that casting and repertory are geared to the average subscriber's tastes, and this effectively ties managements' and artists' hands: in the eighteenth century 'persons of quality' were more concerned with buying their way into a place where they could be seen by their social peers. Opera was not an entertainment for all classes, and it was always very expensive, partly because of the market value of great singers, for whom demand always vastly exceeds supply. Admission was over four times what it was for the playhouse, and the theatre in the Haymarket (variously called the Queen's, King's, and Her Majesty's) was built at an appropriate distance from the city centre by a committee of noblemen, and ultimately watched over by the Lord Chamberlain. A box subscriber in 1721 paid twenty guineas to hear fifty performances. Many would attend every night—one must bear in mind the dearth of alternative public diversions—but the engraved ivory or silver ticket was transferable. The pit was more like the orchestra stalls of today than the hard benches of the playhouses, and was filled with young gallants who liked to cruise up and down the aisle known as 'Fop's Alley'. The gallery was usually known as the 'Footmen's Gallery' and was largely populated by that class, waiting on their masters. The amount of seating was variable, the general principle being to cram in as many as would pay. Another oddity was the habit of allowing standing room on the stage. This was frequently condemned as a nuisance but seems to have lasted throughout the eighteenth century.

The popularity of Italian opera in London was initially sporadic, and profitable only when a fashionable foreign singer could pack the place out. A major setback was the immense success of Gay's *The Beggar's Opera* (1728), a play in English set in the pits of London low life, the music of which is made up from folk-ballads and street ditties and which can be seen as a straight satirical inversion of the pretensions and conventions of Italian opera, to the point where they were no longer viable. For instance, the duets between Polly Peachum and Lucy Lockit, rivals for the hands of the highwayman Macheath, commemorate a performance of Bononcini's *Astianatte*, given in the presence of the Princess Caroline, at which the respective partisans of the two prima donnas, Faustina and Cuzzoni, caused a near-riot with their cheering and booing. The story soon developed that Faustina and Cuzzoni themselves had gone for each other in the ensuing fracas, and it was this apocryphal fight that Gay immortalized:

> Why how now Madam Flirt,
> If you thus must chatter
> And are for flinging dirt,
> Let's try who best can spatter!

This sort of crudely pricking satire burst a delicate bubble: even Handel, the greatest operatic composer of his time, and resident in London, gradually turned to oratorio and the English language.

Handel's Italian operas still hold the stage on account of their wonderful melodies, passages of genuine intensity and their often imaginative orchestration, but it is doubtful whether they can ever again be part of the mainstream of the repertory. As 'music dramas' the operas of Monteverdi, active almost a century earlier, are more satisfying. One significant reason for this is that Handel did not use the free and flexible *arioso*—a form of continuous musical declamation, half-way between dry recitative and melodic song, which gives Monteverdi's *L'Incoronazione di Poppea* so much of its thrust and expressive variety, and which Wagner and Verdi also pursued in their very different idioms. Handel's operas are hidebound by the Baroque pattern of a succession of long solo arias preceded by recitative, contrasting in mood and interspersed with orchestral interlude, chorus, or duet. Continuous dramatic impulse is not easily won through such a static principle, but the audiences did not want that anyway. It was the arias that mattered, and we can safely say that the reason why people went to the Italian opera was to hear sopranos, mezzos, and castrati sing them, whether they were simple or elaborate, fast or slow, elegiac or spectacular. Little attempt was made in *opera seria* to distribute leading roles among the various voice ranges, for the tenor part was usually secondary, while baritone and bass were scarcely exploited at all. Not until *opera buffa* was the balance adjusted: compare Mozart's *Idomeneo* with *Cosi fan tutte*.

Faustina and Cuzzoni were the first in a great line of rival prima donnas which includes Grisi and Viardot, Lehmann and Jeritza, Tebaldi and Callas. These feuds have always been very popular with the public, and the press has remained happy to feed the real and often inevitable conflicts of personality by inventing inflammatory remarks and slanders. The tale of Faustina and Cuzzoni is one in which all the virtue, and the reward, was seen to be on one side.

Francesca Cuzzoni was born in Parma in 1698, and began her career in the Italian opera houses, as well as being court singer to the Duchess Violante of Tuscany. She was, wrote Walpole, 'short and squat, with a doughy cross face, but fine expression; was not a good actress; dressed ill; and was silly and fantastical'. Others found her 'of turbulent and obstinate temper', governed by 'ingratitude and insolence'. On her arrival in London in 1723, her singing in Handel's opera *Ottone* created a sensation. In rehearsal she proved fractious, and according to Burney, 'treated the composer with but scanty respect; making alterations in the passages he had written, and affecting inability to sing them in their original form'. This is interesting as it shows Handel protective of his compositions and not happy with the prima donna's assumed prerogative to alter and ornament at her discretion, even though he was prepared to insert new arias designed to show off her technique. Composers of lesser eminence would not have been able to pull such weight, and Handel only got his way, it was said, by seizing Cuzzoni round the waist and threatening to throw her out of the window unless she sang what he had written.

Cuzzoni was the rage—her salary was £2,000 for the season, handsomely supplemented with private and provincial appearances. Black market tickets for her benefit performance (a gala at which all takings accrued to the star honoured) went for as much as fifty guineas. Her extravagance was said to measure up to these vast sums. In Handel's *Rodelinda* she appeared in a 'brown silk gown, trimmed with silver', which was much imitated by ladies of fashion, among them the Countess of Pembroke, leader of her band of aristocratic admirers. Cuzzoni's only rival in London, where she lived for five years until 1728, was the castrato Senesino: until, that is, the arrival of her fellow-countrywoman Faustina Bordoni in 1726.

Faustina, as she was always known, was one of those rare prima donnas who seems a darling of the gods. Born in Venice in 1700 of patrician family, she was beautiful, charming, a fine actress, and a great singer. She had a brilliant career, made an excellent marriage and lived to enjoy a vivacious old age. Cuzzoni was always either on her trail or one step ahead of her: but their quarrel cannot have been caused by competition for the same parts—Cuzzoni was a soprano, Faustina a mezzo. They had first sung together in Venice, but the trouble came to a head in London, where the audiences were fiercest. It was during an opera by Handel called *Alessandro*, according to Burney, that 'they began to kindle the flames of discord among the frequenters of the opera and patrons of the art, which increased to a more violent degree of enmity than even the theological and political parties of high church and low, or Whig and Tory, which then raged in this country'. Lord Hervey wrote:

> No Cuzzonist will go to a tavern with a Faustinian. And the ladies of one party have scratched those of the other out of their lists of visits. I was t'other night upon the water, and heard nothing till three o'clock in the morning but invocations of one and execrations upon the other.

Horace Walpole tells how the Prime Minister's wife Lady Walpole bravely invited them both to sing at one of her *soirées*:

> . . . an assemblage of the first people in the kingdom were present . . . Finding it impossible to prevail on the one to sing while the other was present, she took Faustina to a remote part of the house under the pretext of showing her some curious china, during which time the company obtained a song from Cuzzoni, who supposed that her rival had quitted the field. A similar device was practised in order to get Cuzzoni out of the room while Faustina performed.

At subsequent grand dinner parties, they were seen to behave 'politely . . . and relieved their hostess by mutual concessions'. The situation was eventually resolved by a sordid financial expedient. The opera house managers realized that one or other of them had to go, and Cuzzoni was indisputably the greater headache. She had sworn never to accept a smaller salary than Faustina, and they had till then been equally paid. Faustina was now offered an extra guinea, and Cuzzoni left London in high pique: perhaps exhausted by the continual tension, Faustina almost immediately fell ill and the opera season came to a premature halt. The year was 1728, and *The Beggar's Opera* was considered more novel and exciting than the Italian opera—the theatre of the Royal Academy of Music, to which Handel was contracted, collapsed shortly afterwards.

Cuzzoni's subsequent progress is an unhappy one: she priced herself out of the Viennese opera market by demanding a salary of

24,000 florins, but toured Naples, Venice—where Faustina was also passing through—Florence, and Genoa. Handel, working for another opera house, refused to have her back to London, but she eventually returned in 1734 for a further three seasons, when she sang at the opera house in Lincoln's Inn Fields, established in opposition to Handel. Although the castrato Farinelli was enthralling everyone, it was a time of general disenchantment with the Italian opera, and Cuzzoni made less impression than before. She returned to the Continent, singing in the major cities, but things now went very wrong. In 1741 a report reached London that she had poisoned her husband, a harpsichord-maker, and was to be beheaded. However, she reappeared in 1745 as a court singer in Stuttgart, where she settled until 1748, and where her contract held the proviso that if she lost her voice it would be made void. Perhaps in absconding to Bologna, leaving massive debts behind her, she was anticipating the worst. Certainly her voice seems to have collapsed thenceforth. When she made a final trip to London in 1750–1, she gave a benefit concert which was regarded 'less as a musical entertainment than as an act of charity'. Dr Burney was there, and recorded an evening that must have been even more pathetic than comparable efforts by Pasta and Callas: 'Her voice [was] reduced to a mere thread; indeed her throat was so nearly ossified by age, that all the soft and mellifluous qualities, which had before rendered it so enchanting, were nearly annihilated.' A couple of months later she was arrested for debts of £30. The Prince of Wales bailed her out, and in 1751 she had one final benefit appearance which she advertised to the public as 'the last I shall ever trouble them with, and is made solely to pay my creditors'. Burney wrote that 'there was but little company', and she left England 'more miserable than when she came'. In Holland, she was again thrown into prison for debt, working her release by giving concerts on parole. Her last years were spent in Bologna, living in extreme poverty as a button-maker and dying in 1770.

It is pleasanter to commemorate Cuzzoni as a great singer. Handel may have hated her, but she excelled in his music—during a performance of his *Admeto* there was a cry from the gallery, 'Damn her! She's got a nest of nightingales in her belly!' Burney translated a more considered Italian critic thus:

... so grateful and touching was the natural tone of her voice, that she rendered pathetic whatever she sang, in which she had leisure to unfold its whole volume. The art of conducting, sustaining, increasing, and diminishing her tones by minute degrees, acquired for her among professors the title of complete mistress of her art. In a *cantabile* air, though the notes she added were few, she never lost a favourable opportunity of enriching the *cantilena* with all the refinements and embellishments of the time. Her shake was perfect; she had a creative fancy, and the power of occasionally accelerating and retarding the measure in the most artificial and able manner by what the Italians call *tempo rubato* ...

There is something almost cruel in Faustina's smooth path through life, given her rival's nemesis and the wonderfully complementary qualities of their two voices. After London, Faustina made successful appearances in all the major Italian opera houses and in 1730 married the prominent operatic composer Johann Hasse. For more than thirty years the couple lived at the Saxon court in Dresden, where Hasse was *kapellmeister* and for which he wrote numerous pieces in the classic *opera seria* form. Their two daughters trained there to be singers, while Faustina continued a fêted international career, promoting her husband's operas. After the upheavals of the Seven Years' War, they went to Vienna and finally Venice, where she died at the age of eighty-one. Burney visited her in Vienna, and found her 'a short, brown, sensible and lively old woman ... with good remains, for seventy-two, of that beauty for which she was so much celebrated in her youth, but none of her voice'. That voice had been a penetrating mezzo-soprano, with a wide range. Whereas Cuzzoni had excelled in the slow and pathetic, Faustina was a virtuoso. Here is Burney again:

She in a manner invented a new kind of singing, by running divisions [fast florid passages] with a neatness and velocity which astonished all who heard her. She had the art of sustaining a note longer, in the opinion of the public, than any other singer, by taking her breath imperceptibly ... her professional perfections were enhanced by a beautiful face, a symmetric figure, though of small stature, and a countenance and gesture on the stage which indicated an entire intelligence and possession of the several parts she had to represent.

And yet Faustina and Cuzzoni, both as women and as singers, were and remain eclipsed by the glory of one of the most bizarre phenomena of European culture—the castrato.

'It had all the Warblings and Turns of a Nightingale, with only this difference, that it was much finer and did not a man know the contrary, he would believe it impossible such a Tone could proceed from the throat of anything that was human.' This description of a castrato, written by an anonymous Englishman in 1718, is typically awe-struck at singing which, at its best, combined unearthly beauty of tone, the flexibility of a coloratura soprano, phenomenal breath control, and enormous power. We may assume it had a womanly sound, yet it also had some quality which put it beyond definite sexual identity. More helpful is a contemporary Frenchman, Charles de Brosses: 'The timbre is as clear as a choirboy's, and much stronger . . . their voices almost always have something dry and piercing in them . . . but they are also brilliant, light, full of sparkle, very strong and extensive.'

The sound of the castrato just survived into the era of recording. One Alessandro Moreschi, who conducted and sang in the Sistine Chapel choir, made some records of sentimental religious music in 1902–3, but they are apparently little more than tantalizing—Moreschi was middle-aged when they were made, and had a mediocre technique. John Steane, in his authoritative review of recorded vocal music, *The Grand Tradition*, found their impact 'sadly comical'. But in the eighteenth century the great castrati were the wonder of the civilized world, and a history of the prima donna has to pay tribute to them, because, in the words of Brigid Brophy, 'the reign of the castrati was actually the period of utmost triumph for the female voice'.

In terms of salary, status, glamour, the castrati were the true prima donnas of their time and, for the only time until Caruso and Chaliapin, male singers were a greater box-office draw than female. 'As the male singer was at once more respectable and more thoroughly artistic than the singing actress,' wrote Vernon Lee, a nineteenth-century commentator on eighteenth-century Italy, 'it was he who had all the social advantages of the art for himself . . . when he sang people remained silent and breathless, and occasionally went into hysterics; when he ceased the applause was perfectly frantic; everyone possessed his printed portrait . . . the ladies wore miniatures of him, sometimes four at a time; and the wits of the coffee-houses and lecture rooms wrote sonnets in his honour.'

Eunuchs had long been common and convenient in Eastern courts, but the practice of castrating boys to create this extraordinary vocal situation dates possibly from the end of the Roman Empire and was certainly known in Byzantium. In the sixteenth century, Spanish 'falsettists'—who were either what we today know as counter-tenors, or true castrati—became popular in the choirs of the Catholic church, where women were not allowed to sing. By the end of the sixteenth century Pope Clement VIII had sancti-fied the use of castrati in the Sistine Chapel choir, and the rise of Venetian opera soon gave them an even more spectacular arena.

The exploitation of castration was confined to Italy. The oper-ation itself was strictly illegal, and those who perpetrated it faced death, their accomplices (parents included) excommunication. However, various blind eyes belonging to various interested parties were turned, and while many indulged in nominal moral outrage, many more were happy to accept the sad 'accident' that had befallen the child, and to relish its happy side-effect. It has been estimated that by the mid-eighteenth century as many as 4,000 boys a year, mostly from poor or peasant backgrounds, were thus assaulted, the parents sometimes receiving a sum from a singing teacher, who in turn would take a percentage in his protégé's career. Of all these, a mere handful would mature to make a decent living as singers. The operation itself was easily performed. The victim was drugged with opium and the vas deferens leading from the testicles to the urethra painlessly severed together with the cord structures. The testicles, deprived of 'the vein that conveyed their Proper Aliment and Support . . . grow lank and flabby, till at last they actually dry up and come to nothing'. To have a fully inhibiting effect this had to happen before puberty: sometimes it was done in infancy.

The consequent hormonal imbalance had many strange physical effects: an enormous amount of hair on the head but none on the body, a tendency to grow extremely tall and in later life obese and very wizened, were some of them. Castrati's speech remained pipingly boyish, while their gait was often so loping and awkward that in compensation they cultivated a variety of affectedly elegant postures on stage. Most significant was the fact that the vocal cords did not thicken,[1] and that the chest developed to the point where the rib cage came to look almost busty.

The castrati's breath control was their greatest technical asset— their lung capacity allowed them to exhale for a minute or more. This, allied to an intense conservatory training starting at an early age, gave them their edge over the ladies. Many castrati spent their lives as church singers, but it was in opera that they became big business. Those of the second rank would often take up long-term contracts at one of the smaller German courts, where the Italian opera was the centre of artistic and social activity—Hasse and Faustina's appointment in Dresden is a remarkable instance of this sort of patronage. The most famous names had international careers and commanded enormous sums of money. They would travel with their 'suitcase arias' or *aria di baule*, a form of signature tune which they would insert into whatever opera they were appearing in, regardless of dramatic context. Their vanity sometimes went further —Luigi Marchesi, wrote Scudo, liked to

> ... play the part of someone who could wear a gilded helmet crowned with red or white feathers. He wanted to make his entry descending a hill, from the top of which he could cry, *'Dove son io?'* ('Where am I?'). Then he demanded that a trumpet gave forth a blast, after which he could declaim *'Odi la squillo della tromba guerriera'* ('I hear the blast of the war-like trumpet'). Having sung this, he advanced to the front of the stage and invariably sang the same rondo ... in which he lamented his cruel lot.

Much of the vanity is surely excusable in anyone involuntarily deprived of certain normal human fulfilments.

Some of the castrati's effect on eighteenth-century society came from their sexual ambiguity, both on and off stage. Some were homosexual. Obviously they were peculiarly attractive to married women looking for liaisons which could not result in pregnancy. Voyeuristic curiosity provided a further *frisson*: sniggering innuendo must have been another occupational hazard. Forbidden to marry though still able to perform sexually, they took advantage of a licence sometimes granted to anomalies. In opera they were called

[1] For a discussion of the mechanics and physiology of singing, see Ch. 6.

upon to play women's roles, and some habitually wore women's clothes. This became even more complicated when, to avoid the papal ban, women in Rome took to the stage masquerading as castrati dressed as women. Balzac was to write a short story, 'Sarassine', on these lines, and Casanova's memoirs report some embarrassing encounters. Sitting in a café, he noticed an attractive man:

> At the appearance of his hips I took him for a girl in disguise, and I said so to the Abbé Gama; but the latter told me that it was Beppino della Mamana, a famous castrato. The abbé called him over, and told him, laughing, that I had taken him for a girl. The impudent creature, looking fixedly at me, told me that if I liked he would prove that I was right, or that I was wrong.

The first internationally famous castrato was Baldassare Ferri (1610–80), about whom relatively little is known, but who is reported to have visited London around 1670; and we have already mentioned Nicolino, one-time partner of Mrs Tofts and the first to establish himself in London. Nicolino was more appreciated for his acting than his singing, although his success, especially in Handel's music, did much to further the initially shaky cause of Italian opera. Even the thoroughly cynical *Tatler* praised him for 'the grace and propriety of his action and gesture, [which] does honour to the human figure . . . There is scarce a beautiful posture in an old statue which he does not plant himself in.' This sort of deportment would have been very appropriate in the static stylizations of *opera seria*—'naturalistic' behaviour has never settled happily into opera, and modern efforts by theatre-based directors to make singers run around can often look ridiculous, as well as being detrimental to good vocal production. Nicolino was succeeded by Senesino, whose relations with Handel were stormy, but who sang alongside Faustina and Cuzzoni in some of his operas. One evening in 1734, another young Italian castrato made his London début. Senesino sang opposite him as a furious tyrant, but was so overcome by the beauty of the newcomer's singing that he completely forgot his character, rushed over to the young man and embraced him. Senesino was prickly, but he had the good sense that night to acknowledge one of the noblest names in the history of singing—Farinelli (or Farinello; his real name was Carlo Broschi).

Senesino was not the only fellow professional to be overcome. The aspiring Gizziello fainted with despondency on first hearing Farinelli, convinced that he could never sing again after encountering someone he considered so superior to himself.

Farinelli was born in Apulia in 1705, possibly of a patrician family that had fallen into disgrace. He was taught by both his brother Riccardo, later the composer of some of his 'suitcase arias', and in Naples by Nicolo Porpora, himself a pupil of the elder Scarlatti and indisputably the greatest singing teacher of the eighteenth century. Farinelli made his first public appearance at the age of fifteen in a serenade composed by Porpora for the birthday of the Habsburg Empress of the day. It was in opera in Rome that Farinelli first became famous, and a story told of him at the time (later transcribed by Burney) demonstrates something of his breathtaking—or non-breathtaking—technique. Farinelli had a bravura aria with an accompanying trumpet obbligato. Singer and instrument engaged in fantastic competition:

> ... after severally swelling a note, in which each manifested the power of his lungs, and tried to rival the other in brilliancy and force, they had both a swell and shake together, by thirds, which was continued so long, while the audience eagerly waited the event, that both seemed to be exhausted; and, in fact, the trumpeter, wholly spent, gave it up ... when Farinelli, with a smile on his countenance ... broke out all at once in the same breath, with fresh vigour, and not only swelled and shook the note, but ran the most rapid and difficult divisions ...

Farinelli's early days were spent mostly between Naples and Rome, often appearing in vehicles specially tailored for him by Porpora. In 1726 Frederick the Great's flute-teacher, Quantz, described the voice as 'a penetrating, full, rich, bright and well-modulated soprano ... His intonation was pure, his trill beautiful, his breath-control extraordinary, and his throat very agile ... But the fire of youth, his great talent, the general applause and his ready throat brought it about that at times he proceeded in too spendthrift a fashion.' Passing on to Vienna at the end of the decade, the Emperor Charles VI confronted him with Quantz's reservation. 'If you wish to reach the heart,' he said, 'you must take a more plain and simple road.' Farinelli took the royal judgement very seriously, and purged his singing of excesses. By 1734, when he arrived in London for what became two and a half years' residence, he was probably at his peak.

Farinelli was pure singer and although tall and handsome, clearly made no attempt to act. Like a Flagstad or Melba, his genius lay in the perfect production of a glorious sound, built on a rock-solid musical foundation. Burney wrote of his London performances that 'without the assistance of significant gestures or graceful attitudes, [he] enchanted and astonished his hearers by the force, extent, and mellifluous tones of the mere organ . . . though during the time of his singing he was as motionless as a statue, his voice was so active, that no intervals were too close, too wide, or too rapid for his execution.' A tiny doubt creeps in that he might have been a little dull after a while.

London fell: the opera orchestra were so thunderstruck when they heard him that they could not play; a noble lady in the audience cried out after an aria, 'One God, one Farinelli!'; Hogarth represents him in 'The Rake's Progress', surrounded by hangers-on; the Prince of Wales sent him 'a fine wrought gold snuff-box, richly set with diamonds and rubies, in which was enclosed a pair of brilliant diamond knee-buckles, as also a purse of one hundred guineas'. In all, he probably made about £5,000 a year while in London. Handel, in the rival opera house, was virtually ruined, but even Farinelli could not long stem the rot that had set into the Italian opera in London. The public were at bottom tired of it, and by 1737 the sensation of 1734 was said to be singing to £35 worth of takings.

Nevertheless, he left England fully intending to return: London must have been a charming haven from the suffocating provinciality and intrigue which infested the opera in Central Europe and Italy. But his life now took its strangest course. Philip V of Spain was neurotically withdrawn, and his court in decline. Philip had already abdicated once in favour of his son, but the boy had died, forcing his father to reassume the throne. Washing, shaving, and changing his clothes were as much anathema to him as attending to matters of state. Nothing engaged his interest, and his scheming Italian wife Elizabeth Farnese was terrified that he would die, leaving her to dowagerhood, and her unpleasant stepson Charles to the throne. Farinelli was the last hope, or at least an outside chance, and Elizabeth lured him to Madrid in the hope that he could work a miracle—which he did. The British ambassador sent this dispatch to London:

> Philip was struck by the first air sung by Farinelli, and at the conclusion of the second sent for him [he was singing from a room next to the King's bedchamber], loaded him with praises and promised to grant whatever he should demand. The musician, who had been tutored by the queen, entreated him to rise from his bed, suffer himself to be shaven and dressed and attend council. Philip complied, and from that moment his disorder took a more favourable turn.

Farinelli was to stay in the Spanish court for over twenty years. He immediately became the victim of his own success. His salary was enormous, but his duties insufferably monotonous. Philip lived another nine years, kept from catatonia by the beauty of Farinelli's singing. It was said that the King was only interested in hearing the four same arias, and that Farinelli had to sing them all every night between midnight and 5 a.m., interspersing them with soothing and elegant conversation. If this is true, he would no doubt have taken advantage of singer's licence and varied the ornamentation— Philip may have found this part of the fascination. After the King's death he stayed on under Ferdinand V as an *éminence grise*, gathering power and influence like a beneficent musical Rasputin. No one had a bad word for him: he was above political and amorous intrigue. Vernon Lee speaks of him as 'modest and self-respecting in the most corrupting position, unselfish and forgiving amidst baseness: something which makes him appear like almost an idyllic hero among the artificial worthless people around him'. The truth may be that he was just intelligently diplomatic, and knew when not to open his mouth. He was now in effect retired, and so took over not only the direction of royal church music and opera— which he conducted with exemplary firmness and to a very high standard—but also concerned himself with the canalization of the River Tagus, with the interbreeding of Spanish and Hungarian horses, and in the cause of the Prime Minister Ensenada, who had quarrelled with the Queen. Paintings of the period depict him with all the regal trappings, surrounded by cherubim and trumpets, garlanded with laurel. But then everyone was ready to make a myth out of Farinelli. First came the myths about his singing; then came the stories of his magnanimity and largesse, such as this pretty tale.

A tailor who had made Farinelli a superb suit of clothes for a court gala refused payment from him, but asked instead to hear him sing. Farinelli, accompanying himself at the harpsichord, willingly obliged and 'exerted himself in every species of excellence'. When he had finished, the tailor thanked him and made to leave.

> 'No,' says Farinelli, 'I am a little proud; and it is perhaps from that circumstance that I have acquired some small degree of superiority over other singers. I have given way to your weakness, it is but fair, that, in your turn, you should indulge me in mine.' And taking out his purse, he insisted on his receiving a sum amounting to nearly double the worth of the suit of clothes.

If we refuse to believe in such unmitigated virtue, Farinelli's personality remains somewhat mysterious. His surviving letters to his lifelong friend, the librettist Metastasio, are gushing, formal, and unexceptionable, but hardly vivid.

In 1759, Farinelli finally left Spain—against his will, but forced out by the conflict of loyalties inevitable in the Seven Years' War. He retired to Bologna, living in a villa he had been planning for years, with a fortune, a handsome pension, and a fine collection of keyboard instruments. He became melancholy: Casanova claimed to have visited and found him 'bored and boring . . . One day while I was speaking to him of Spain, he burst into tears: his heart was still set on the high position he had lost.' Other visitors included Gluck, Mozart, Burney, and the Emperor Joseph II. He died in 1782, a year before his most considerable contemporary, the mezzo-soprano castrato Caffarelli. As is so often the case with these operatic 'rivalries'—as indeed with Faustina and Cuzzoni—one party is made out to be all virtue and the other all vice, while the two voices in question are so different as to be properly incomparable. In fact, these two seemed to have got on well, and Farinelli engaged Caffarelli to sing in his opera house in Madrid.

Caffarelli, born in 1710, was another pupil of Porpora, who hated him, but also considered him a greater singer than Farinelli. His career was centred in Naples, and his only visit to London in 1738, in the wake of Farinelli's departure and the doldrums of operatic activity, was a failure, although Handel there composed for him the famous so-called Largo, 'Ombra mai fù'. Considered reports of his voice are few: it is his temperament that has been passed down to posterity. He fought a duel, one of many, with a double-bass bow;

spent a night in a cistern having been surprised *in flagrante* by a jealous husband; was given three days to leave France after a duel over the relative merits of French and Italian music; and was briefly imprisoned in 1741 for 'disturbing the other performers, acting in a manner bordering on lasciviousness with one of the female singers, conversing with the spectators in the boxes from the stage, ironically echoing whichever member of the company was singing an aria, and finally refusing to sing in the *ripieno* [ensemble]'. He is even known to have sulked in the lavatory. In latter years his singing became erratic, but at his peak, he must have been very exciting—what descriptions of his voice there are suggest that it had a dark and dramatic timbre. Metastasio wrote to Farinelli that in Rome 'numerous critics' had found his voice 'out of tune, strident, and uncontrollable: so that he can make no effect without forcing it, when it becomes harsh and unpleasant'. This reminds one of the later Callas, and that perhaps gives a fair idea of his wilful individuality. For all his success he was persistently querulous. Unlike that friend to the great, Farinelli, he seems to have had a rooted distaste for nobility and royalty—when Louis XV sent him a gold snuff-box, Caffarelli disdained it; on being informed that similar gifts had been gratefully received by ambassadors, he retorted, 'Let the Ambassadors sing!' He was however absurdly high-handed himself. The pompous inscription above his palazzo in the Calabrian dukedom he bought himself—*Amphion Thebas, Ego Domum* ('Amphion built Thebes, I built this house')—gave rise to the neatly deflating rejoinder, *Ille cum, tu sine* ('He with, you without'). Yet in retirement, away from the aggravation and pressures of a performer's life, he became much nicer, giving large amounts of money to charity and taking to religion. Burney met him in 1770 and found him 'very polite', entering into 'conversation with great ease and cheerfulness'.

With Gaetano Guadagni (*c*.1725–92) we come to a singer whose singing did not fit the standard style and accomplishment. He is instead a singer representative of the general reaction against contemporary *opera seria* that set in about 1740, and to which Gluck's was the most lasting contribution. Guadagni's training and earliest years are obscure, but his first prominent engagement was not in a church choir or in *opera seria*, but in the eighteenth-century equivalent of musical comedy. *Opera buffa* developed out of the great traditions of Italian *commedia dell' arte*, and its light, usually premarital, intrigues perpetrated by a variety of stock characters. In Italy, the *buffa* was originally played in the intervals between the acts of the *seria*; later it became an afterpiece. Musically, *buffa* was predominantly swift and bright with, like Gilbert and Sullivan operas, patter songs and much attention paid to musical setting which allowed the words to come through clearly. The bass voice played an important part, being used for old codgers, crotchety fathers, and the forces of authority, while ensembles were much more common, extended arias much rarer, than in *seria*. The triumph of this form is Mozart's *Le Nozze di Figaro*, and its principles can still be felt through Verdi's *Falstaff*.

Guadagni sang juvenile lead, and came to London with an Italian company in 1748. He was considered to have no technique, and the management of his contralto voice was 'wild and careless'. But he was good-looking, 'his countenance replete with beauty, intelligence, and dignity', and a strong actor. He attracted the attention of both the elderly Handel, who gave him the mezzo part in *Messiah*, and of the actor-manager David Garrick, who 'took great pleasure in forming him'. All this encouraged Guadagni to become a 'serious' singer, and he began to study with Gizziello (the castrato who had fainted on hearing Farinelli), coming out with a stronger sound in a wider compass. In 1762, in Vienna, he created the role of Orfeo in Gluck's opera and thereby won his place in history.

Gluck's 'reform' operas were part of the general cultural move away from Baroque excess towards more restrained Neo-classicism. At first influenced by the independent and insular French opera, which had never surrendered to the supremacy of the aria and never accepted the castrato, and then by the theory of the Italian musicologist Algarotti, Gluck sought to purify Italian opera. Like so many operatic reforms—be they the early Florentines' or Wagner's—this one was an attempt to bring opera closer to drama. Ornament and elaboration gave way to simplicity, singer's licence to composer's law, and the music became the servant of the text, faithfully reflecting and intensifying human feelings. Gluck did not quite fulfil his own best ideals, and there are still elements of older styles in his operas, but he managed to break a mould. So did Guadagni. He was the singer Gluck needed, possessing, wrote Angus Heriot in *The Castrati in Opera*, 'the grandeur and nobility that Gluck demanded, [while] his powers of execution were not great enough to tempt him to introduce unsuitable *fioriture* [decorations] or cadenzas, and thus mar the Neo-classic severity of the conception'. His personal demeanour was correspondingly uncompromising. In the name of dramatic propriety, he refused to break from his character and take bows after an aria, or to encore anything. Audiences were often angry at being so ignored, but Guadagni believed in 'the dignity of the singer's calling'. Burney wrote that, 'He had strong resentments and high notions of his own importance, which revolted many of his warmest friends and augmented the malice of his enemies.' And yet when he returned to London in 1769, he sang Orfeo in a version which included extra music by J. C. Bach and others, as well as interpolating an aria composed by himself. This fact should warn us against the mistake of overestimating the completeness of Gluck's 'revolution' —if he had broken the mould, there was still life in the shattered pieces. *Orfeo* was popular, but audiences continued to flock to bravura singing, rather than to severe conceptions. Guadagni never had the drawing-power of Farinelli, and his voice, though 'perfectly delicate, polished, and refined', was always too thin and weak. Burney remarked that his most notable technical accomplishment was his 'artful manner of diminishing the tones of his voice like the dying notes of an Aeolian harp'. He continued to travel round Europe until 1776, finally retiring to Padua, where he last sang Orfeo behind the scenes in a domestic marionette performance of his own devising.

In retrospect, Guadagni heralds the demise of the castrato. At least he was the first of what are now called 'singing-actors'—a dubious recommendation, which too often means third-rate singing and second-rate acting. Guadagni may not have been that, but he is eclipsed by one figure who came after him and who consciously upheld the great vocal style of the previous generation.

Gasparo Pacchierotti was born in 1740 and may have trained at San Marco in Venice, where he certainly began his professional life. The unusual longevity of his voice may well have been due to the fact that he did not start singing publicly in his teens. In 1770 he passed into opera, taking up an appointment in Palermo.

From Sicily he moved steadily northwards through the opera houses of Rome, Florence, Milan (where he sang in the inaugural performance at La Scala) Padua, and Genoa. His repertory included Gluck's *Orfeo* and other 'reform' operas, but he was unusual in his taste for music of the old school, especially the arias of Handel. His great friend Bertoni also wrote operas adapted to his gifts and accompanied him to London.

In London Pacchierotti was to find his finest eulogist, Richard, Earl Mount Edgcumbe, whose musical reminiscences are among the most valuable of their kind. Mount Edgcumbe is categorical in his insistence that Pacchierotti was 'the most perfect singer it ever fell my lot to hear'. He continued:

> Pacchierotti's voice was an extensive soprano, full and sweet in the highest degree; his powers of execution were great, but he had far too good taste and too good sense to make a display of them where it would have been misapplied, confining it to one bravura song (*aria di agilità*) in each opera, conscious that the chief delight of singing, and his own supreme excellence, lay in touching expression, and exquisite pathos . . . As an actor, with many disadvantages of person, for he was tall and awkward in his figure, and his features were plain, he was nevertheless forcible and impressive: for he felt warmly, had excellent judgment, and was an enthusiast in his profession. . . . As a concert singer, and particularly in private society, he shone almost more than on the stage; for he sung with greater spirit in a small circle of friends, and was more gratified with their applause, than in a public concert room, or crowded theatre.

If history had played fair, what a singer of Schubert's *lieder* he would have been! Mount Edgcumbe also details his amazing powers of sight-reading, his talent for improvisation, and the expressive power of his recitative—an aspect of singing neglected by the early virtuosi, but which became more vigorous and subtle after Gluck. Burney also records that his voice ranged over more than three octaves from the tenor pitch up to a soprano top C.

Burney never heard Farinelli or Caffarelli, but he was a close friend of Pacchierotti, and his daughter, the novelist-precursor of Jane Austen, Fanny, made a pet of him. She also paid him the supreme novelist's compliment—putting him into one of her books, *in propria persona*. In *Cecilia* the heroine attends an opera rehearsal as part of her initiation into polite society: the opera was *Artaxerxes*, the theatre the King's, Haymarket, and Pacchierotti was the singer. In her fascinating journal, Fanny Burney recorded the progress of this 'very grave and very sweet man' through his triumphant seasons in London between 1778 and 1780.

First we gather that Pacchierotti was no Guadagni: being on stage and in character was no excuse to omit social courtesy: 'Pacchierotti found me out and gave me several smiles during the performance: indeed, he could never look either to the right or the left without a necessity of making some sort of acknowledgement in return to the perpetual bows made him from almost every box in the house . . .' Later we see him the subject of female adoration at a *soirée* of Lady Mary Duncan's, who became notorious for sending him a scandalously large sum of money. Although lanky and awkward, he had numerous female admirers, who, one suspects, exploited his good nature and innocence: 'Oh how the Miss Bulls do idolise him! They profess thinking him quite angelic, and declared that they should even look upon it as a favour to be beat by him! I laughed violently at this extravagance . . .' In a conversation with a friend of the Burneys', he is shown in an even more vulnerable light:

'This is a climate' said Pac, 'never in the same case for half an hour at a time; it shall be fair, and wet, and dry, and humid forty times in a morning at the least. I am tired to be so played with, sir, by your climate.'

'We have one thing, however, Mr Pacchierotti', he answered, 'which I hope you allow makes some amends, and that is our verdure; in Italy you cannot boast that.'

'But it seem to me, sir, to be of no utility so much ever-green; is rather too much for my humble opinion.'

'And then your insects, Mr Pacchierotti; those alone are a most dreadful drawback upon the comfort of your fine climate . . .'

'I must own,' said Pacchierotti, 'Italy is rather disagreeable for the insects: but is not better, sir, than an atmosphere so bad as they cannot live in it?'

'Why, as I can't defend our atmosphere, I must shift my ground and talk to you of our fires, which draw together society.'

'Oh, indeed, good sir, your societies are not very invigorating! Twenty people of your gentlemen and ladies to sit about a fire, and not to pronounce one word is very dull.'

Fanny's comment on this is interesting: Pacchierotti became very animated during this exchange, since most of the people he met in London 'affect a superiority to conversing with him, though he has

more intelligence, ay, and cultivation too, than half of them'—
which suggests that, for all its 'lionizing', society did not take singers
very seriously.

Pacchierotti returned regularly to London, but spent most of his
remaining active years in Venice. On his last visit to London, he
coincided with Haydn, who persuaded him to perform his solo
cantata 'Arianna a Naxos', the composer playing the pianoforte
part. 'It is needless to say,' wrote Mount Edgcumbe, 'that the
performance was perfect.' Pacchierotti finally retired to Padua,
living in a villa furnished in the English style and surrounded by
an English garden. He studied English and Italian literature and
worked on a treatise on the art of singing which by the time it was
published in edited form in 1836, had become an anachronism, a
commemoration of a lost art. The French invasion of Italy upset
him deeply, but he came out of retirement to sing before Napoleon
in 1796, and made a final appearance in 1814, at the age of
seventy-four, singing in a Requiem for Bertoni. In 1817 Stendhal
visited him and was very moved, finding him 'still sublime when
he sings a recitative . . . I learnt more about music in six conversations with this great artist than from any book.'

After Pacchierotti, the art of the castrato went into irreversible
decline. As so often, this was due to a complex of causes rather
than a single one. The new spirit of liberalism and republicanism
condemned castration as an aberration of pampered tyrants and
their decadent courts, while the full-blooded tastes of Romanticism
preferred voices that were 'natural', rather than fabricated by
surgery. Changes in musical composition and the inevitable wither-
ing of *opera seria* left the castrato redundant. The last of the operatic
line, Velluti, who will appear in the next chapter, had to compete
with a new vogue for the tenor voice, as well as a magnificent
generation of female singers, capable of assuming the roles, male
and female, that the castrati had previously monopolized. But the
dream of the castrato voice, its power and beauty, lingered on: it is
known that Wagner wanted a castrato to sing the wizard Klingsor
in *Parsifal*, and approached the Sistine Chapel, where the type
survived the strenuous efforts of the Napoleonic government to
eradicate the operation. He was forced to abandon the idea, though
the association of the castrato with preternatural power became a
familiar Romantic notion.

The Elizabethan falsetto counter-tenor voice, popular since the

1950s and useful in productions of Baroque opera, probably bears little relation to the castrato tone, none to its flexibility and volume. Then in 1966, at the height of a major revival of florid singing, the following letter appeared in an American gramophone magazine:

> I have many friends, some of them quite prominent in musical circles, who agree with me that if there is to be a serious and widespread revival of Baroque and *bel canto* opera, there must necessarily be a return of the *castrati* to sing the roles they alone can handle with dramatic and vocal legitimacy . . . I definitely do not advocate force, but if a young singer should possess a fine voice which he wishes to preserve, I can sympathize with no reason for discouraging him . . .

Few women singers reached a dominating position during the great era of the castrati. The sweet clear tone nurtured by teachers of the time was simply no competition for the unearthly magic and variety of castrato timbres. Caterina Gabrielli (1730–96) was one of the few to create a stir, as much because of her unquenchable self-will as because of her talent. She was the daughter of a cardinal's cook and through the patronage of her father's employer, and despite the Church's disapproval of women singers, she became yet another pupil of Porpora's. Her voice was a light, brilliant soprano, and she was a compelling actress. In 1770 in Palermo, when Pacchierotti was singing opposite her, Gabrielli 'exerted herself in so astonishing a manner, that, before it was half done, poor Pacchierotti burst out a-crying and ran in behind the scenes, lamenting that he dared to appear on the same stage with so wonderful a singer.'

Burney found her 'the most intelligent and best bred virtuosa with whom I had ever conversed'. Her love life was complicated and uninhibited—'she was supposed to have achieved more conquests than any woman breathing', whispered one contemporary —but what made her scandalous was her constant refusal or failure to sing when contracted to do so. She once alleged that the reasons for this were physical and genuine, and it is as well to respect this. Opera singing requires a delicate physiological equilibrium, and many people are not aware, for instance, that women find it difficult to sing in pitch while menstruating, owing to the relaxation of abdominal tension. Audiences tend, equally naturally, to feel slighted when an advertised favourite cancels at short notice, especially as some strongly constituted singers never miss a performance. But Gabrielli was in a class of her own.

Some years ago [the viceroy of Sicily] gave a great dinner to the principal nobility of Palermo, and sent an invitation to Gabrielli to be of the party. Every other person arrived at the hour of invitation. The viceroy ordered dinner to be put back, and sent to let her know that the company awaited her. The messenger found her reading in bed. She said she was sorry for having made the company wait, and begged he would make her apology, but that really she had entirely forgotten her engagement. The viceroy would have forgiven this piece of insolence, but when the company came to the opera, Gabrielli repeated her part with the utmost negligence and indifference, and sang all her airs in what they call *sotto voce*, that is, so low that they can scarcely be heard. The viceroy was offended; but as he is a good-tempered man, he was loth to make use of authority; but at last, by a perseverance in this insolent stubbornness, she obliged him to threaten her with punishment in case she any longer refused to sing. On this she grew more obstinate than ever, declaring that force and authority should never succeed with her; that he might make her cry, but never could make her sing. The viceroy then sent her to prison, where she remained twelve days; during which time she gave magnificent entertainments every day, paid the debts of all the poor prisoners, and distributed large sums in charity . . . (Sutherland Edwards)

Reading between the lines this sounds as though Gabrielli ('reading in bed') might have been ill; what one also notices is the appalling condition of a singer beholden to a patron with law on his side. (Gabrielli was later incarcerated again for screaming at the pestiferous Infante of Parma, '*Gobbo maledetto*,' 'Accursed hunchback.') Outside Italy, she sang for Catherine the Great in St Petersburg and with Farinelli's company in Madrid. In London, she made little effort and frequently replaced herself with her sister Francesca, a vastly inferior singer who was her constant companion.

Of the next generation of prima donnas, three of the most famous excited an extraordinary amount of abuse, in a generally tempestuous but *louche* period.

Brigitta Banti was the roughest of them. She was born in 1756 and began, like Piaf, as a street singer in Paris, never losing the air of a *femme du trottoir* and finding it quite unnecessary to make any concessions to gentility. No one could teach her anything—one of those who tried and failed was Piozzi, whose marriage to Mrs Thrale so mortified Dr Johnson—and many said that she could not even read music, learning everything by sharpness of ear and instinct. Mozart's librettist Lorenzo da Ponte loathed her, calling her a 'musical Messalina'. He worked with her in London in 1794 and his memories of the experience were not pleasant. 'She could make any theatre at which she was engaged tremble at the sound of her name . . . she brought to opera, where her voice alone had introduced her, all the habits, manners and customs of an impudent Corsican. Free in her speech, still more in her actions, given to debauchery, licentiousness and drinking . . .' Yet there must have been more to her personality than this. In the noble role of Gluck's Alceste her acting was judged 'sublime'; and if the discriminating Mount Edgcumbe had found Pacchierotti the most perfect singer he had ever heard, Banti was the 'most delightful', 'her voice, sweet and beautiful throughout, had not a fault in any part of its unusually extensive compass. Its lower notes, which reached below ordinary sopranos, were rich and mellow; the middle, full and powerful; and the very high, totally devoid of shrillness.'

Slightly older than Banti was Mara, born Gertrud Schmeling in 1749, and the first German prima donna. Her biography was written in her own lifetime, and we have an unusual amount of verifiable facts about her career and experiences. Mara's childhood was cruel. She suffered both a tyrannical violinist father and rickets, from which she never fully recovered. As an infant, she once snapped one of her father's violin strings, and as punishment was made to learn the instrument: later she ascribed her perfect intonation to her violin training. Soon she was good enough to be trapped in that heavily exploitable form of child labour, the infant prodigy. At the age of six she was playing publicly in Vienna, but in 1759 in London the pathetic little bubble burst, leaving father and daughter stranded and penniless. They set out to tour the more gullible provinces, little Gertrud by now having shown signs of vocal ability. Somehow they reached the quiet cathedral town of Wells, where the father played the flute to his daughter's soprano and guitar. Fortunately they were heard by a local musical dilettante, who was impressed by the girl's voice and arranged for a concert in more glamorous nearby Bath, from which they earned enough to get back to Germany.

One of Mara's first engagements was in Leipzig, where Goethe heard her. In 1771 she bravely made her way to the court of Frederick the Great in Berlin, with a letter of recommendation from the Electress of Saxony. Bravely, because Frederick was notoriously averse to the idea of German singers, and patronized only Italians. The one-time friend of Voltaire and enlightened despot had become a crabbed old man, running his court opera like a department of state. He conducted the orchestra himself on occasion, and had been known to lash at the players with his baton. The King received the girl coldly. Her nerves must have been steely, because her initial reaction was to walk round the room examining the paintings. Then, her spirit inflamed by his silent sarcasm, she gave a flawless display, and won both his admiration and a contract.

The arrangement was not happy. At first all went well enough. She took lessons from Porporino, Frederick's court castrato, and foreign visitors, including Burney, were impressed with her. But her very success became the problem, since Frederick became possessive of his prima donna to the point of keeping her under close surveillance lest she escaped to the fleshpots of the international scene. She was aware of her own value too, and within a year of arriving in Berlin had attempted to enlist Frederick's support in an unattractive quarrel with her father.

She then fell in love with Giovanni-Battista Mara, a court cellist, who resembled her father in being lazy and drunk. Frederick opposed the match, and even locked her up in Spandau fortress when she tried to elope, but they were eventually married on the condition that they remained in Berlin. The King now had a third party to play with in the battle of wills, and whenever there was trouble Herr Mara was sent off to play in the band of a front-line regiment.

Mara now tried to get herself dismissed, and refused to sing music commanded by the King. During a state visit by the Grand Duke Paul of Russia she announced that she was ill and took to her bed. Frederick needed her for the entertainment, and sent eight dragoons who carried her off on the mattress. She at first sang without enthusiasm and almost inaudibly, until natural vanity reasserted itself. The Maras became a byword for impertinence and *lèse majesté*, and when they eventually did escape from Berlin —in 1780, on the pretext of taking a spa cure for an attack of pleurisy—Frederick released her without vindictiveness and perhaps with relief. The story is a sad instance of the perils of patronage, in which security of tenure hardly compensated for the restrictions on personal liberty.

Over the next four years Mara sang in Vienna, Munich—where Mozart was appalled by the couple's arrogance and unimpressed by what he found over-artful singing—and Paris. In 1784 she arrived in London, where she was to settle for the next eighteen years. Her husband became impossible—she divorced him and he drank himself to death in Holland—but her career prospered. She sang in opera with Pacchierotti, and 'I know that my Redeemer liveth' in the grand Handel commemoration concert of 1784 in Westminster Abbey. Mount Edgcumbe has this to say of her:

> Mara's talent as a singer (for she was no actress, and had a bad person for the stage) were of the very first order. Her voice, clear, sweet, distinct, was sufficiently powerful, though rather thin, and its agility and flexibility rendered her a most excellent bravura singer, in which style she was unrivalled; but she succeeded equally well in some of Handel's most solemn and pathetic songs, though there appeared to be a want of that feeling in herself, which, nevertheless, she could communicate to her hearers.

By 1790 her voice was beginning to lose its strength, and she made the mistake of singing the part of Polly Peachum in *The Beggar's Opera*, to which she was hardly suited. In 1802, 'in the maturity of her charms, which had never been great', she left London with a young flute-player and made a farewell tour of Europe, settling first in Moscow, where she lost everything in the 1812 conflagration, and then in Tallin, where she taught. Then, continued Mount Edgcumbe:

> When she was almost forgotten, she re-appeared as suddenly and in as singular a manner as she had vanished. A very few years ago, 1819, an advertisement from Messrs. Knyvett announced for their concerts a most celebrated singer whom they were not yet

45

at liberty to name. This mysterious secret was soon after explained by another announcement, that *Madame Mara's* benefit concert would take place at the King's theatre on an evening specified, no one being at all aware of her return to England, or even of her existence. She must have then been at least seventy; but it was said that her voice had miraculously returned, and was again as fine as ever. But when she displayed these wonderfully revived powers, they proved, as might be expected, lamentably deficient, and the tones she produced were compared to those of a *penny trumpet.*

She returned to Russia, wrote her memoirs, and lived to the age of eighty-four. Goethe sent her two poems on her eighty-second birthday, paying tribute to her singing in 1767, sixty-four years earlier.

One of the most significant facts about the third of these women, Mrs Billington (1768–1818), was that, for all the operatic activity in London, she remained until the 1920s the only English prima donna to achieve real European fame. Her life appears an unhappy one, and one biographer claimed that she suffered throughout from a neurotic depressive condition; but many claims were made for her, including those of the gutter press. In 1792, a book was published which showed Mrs Billington 'immersed in the horrible depths of human depravity', deflowered by her father, and saddled with both an impotent husband and venereal disease. On the other hand, Reynolds painted her as Saint Cecilia, and she received the tributes of doggerel:

> With beauty's soft blandishments arm'd to delight
> Resistless and charming, she bursts on the sight;
> From her eyes issue rays of voluptuous mirth,
> And she catches applause, ere the judgment has birth.[1]

Born Elizabeth Weichsell, she was the illegitimate daughter of a German wind player and a mother who had studied with J. C. Bach and sang in Vauxhall Pleasure Gardens. The young Elizabeth was also taught by Bach, but started off, like Mara, as another tiresomely talented infant instrumentalist. At the age of twelve, two sets of her pianoforte sonatas were published.

---

1 Pasquin's *Children of Thespis* (1792).

46

She married her second teacher, James Billington, and made her first stage appearance in Dublin. In 1786 came success at Covent Garden, which she consolidated with further intensive study in Paris. Interestingly, Mrs Billington continued to take voice lessons throughout her career, and she seems to have been exceptionally conscientious. Her repertory was never distinguished, but it was the pretty pastoral music of Arne, Shield, and Arnold that the public wanted.

Haydn, then resident in London, became a tremendous admirer of hers, and in his biography of the composer, Stendhal reports a meeting between the composer, Mrs Billington, and Reynolds, at which Haydn commented on Reynolds's portrait: 'You have painted her listening to the angels: you should have painted the angels listening to *her* divine voice.' Mount Edgcumbe judged her voice, 'though sweet and flexible', to be 'not of that full nature which formed the charm of Banti's, but was rather a *voce di testa*, and in its very high tones resembled a flute ... she possessed not the feeling to give touching expression, even when she sung with the utmost delicacy and consummate skill.' George III privately criticized her for excessive ornamentation of 'pathetick songs', when taste was moving towards something simpler. She also constantly used her brother as orchestral leader when she was singing, doubtless to ensure sympathetic *tempi*.

After the publication of the scurrilous attack on her morals, Mrs Billington left England in 1794. She answered the accusations and sued the publishers, but the scandal stuck. Making her way to Naples, where 'her only desire was to live in seclusion', in a climate recommended as beneficial to her mental condition, she was persuaded by the English ambassador, Sir William Hamilton, to sing before the royal family. Some say that she became Hamilton's lover, others that she was the intimate of the notorious Emma Hamilton, Sir William's wife and a fine amateur singer herself. Whatever the truth, she made a strong impression in her début at the Teatro San Carlo in an opera written for her. Almost immediately her husband died of an apoplectic fit after a large dinner with the Bishop of Winchester; there was also an eruption of Mount Vesuvius. A female Protestant heretic was vulnerable to blame in such circumstances, and many thought she had poisoned her husband, with whom she was known to be unhappy.

Mrs Billington proceeded to tour the major Italian opera houses, and in Milan was received by the Empress Josephine. She re-married there, a young Frenchman called Félissent, and bought an estate near Venice. When Félissent maltreated her, she returned to England in 1801. He followed and harassed her for money, but was arrested and deported as an alien. London found her even better than remembered, and she took contracts at both Drury Lane and Covent Garden simultaneously. In her first season back home she must have earned in the region of £15,000. She sang at the farewell performances of both Mara and Banti in 1802, and remained supreme until her retirement in 1811, when her voice was still at its peak but her spirit broken. She had become comically fat, and her first child had died in infancy. A second, probably illegitimate, had been placed in a Brussels convent. Félissent re-appeared in 1817 and took her back to the Venetian estate. Her unstable life ended, possibly at the hands of her husband, less than a year later. *The Times* commented in its obituary: 'Into whatever human errors she might have fallen, she possessed an excellent heart and a truly benevolent disposition ... it is impossible to describe the anxiety with which her numerous friends implored her not to leave the country with a husband who, after having lived separate from her abroad for 16 years, came to England, and declared he could no longer live without her.'

Towards the end of the eighteenth century opera seemed ready to collapse into utter banality, at least in England. Standards were generally as low as public taste, and there was still an obsession with *pasticcio*—the stitching-up of popular tunes, in the absence of copyright, from various sources, irrespective of musical or dramatic integrity. As we have seen, even Gluck's operas received this treatment, and *Orfeo* is still performed with a florid interpolated aria by Bertoni at the end of Act I. Banti, Mara, and Mrs Billington were prima donnas with nothing of much worth to sing outside oratorio. The great operatic music of the time hardly reached them; which is to say, Mozart hardly reached them.

Mozart's operas are accessible to us today in ways that those of other eighteenth-century composers cannot be. In them we find that ambiguity and anxiety, a sense of tragedy in comedy, and the complexity of human feeling and motive, that we find in neither the austerities of Gluck nor the cheerful energies of *opera buffa*. Yet Mozart inherited these traditions and genres, developing and working with the possibilities they offered. His early operas are distinguished only by the youthful genius in the music: theatrically, they look pretty much like anyone else's product.

But with the mature Italian operas, *Don Giovanni*, *Figaro*, *Così fan tutte*, he takes the surface subject-matter of farce and *opera buffa* —courtship, seduction, the cynical old against the cunning young, the servant outwitting his master—and gives it a depth and pace that it had never previously had: *Figaro* is the first opera to be developed intelligently from a good modern play (Beaumarchais' *Les Noces de Figaro*); while the old story of Don Juan is used not to point a finger at the fate of libertines so much as to create an atmosphere of dangerous confusion in which the villain might also be a hero and the victims take their share of the satire. In *Così* another familiar farcical situation is turned inside out by the emotion Mozart invests in it. With *Die Zauberflöte* he manages an even more staggering transformation. The pantomime entertainment and spectacle which distinguished the German *singspiel* is taken as a basis for an exploration of some of mankind's most solemn questioning of moral conduct and religious truth.

None of these works offer the prima donna easy options. Ensemble and recitative, unrewarding in terms of applause, require as much effort and artistry as the arias. They offer no easily achieved effectiveness: rather, they mercilessly expose the fraudulent. Mozart had the incomparable gift of making the smallest nuance in the vocal line sing with meaning, and the ability to articulate that detail is perhaps the ultimate test of a Mozart singer.

Mozart's music is both uniquely gratifying and cruelly testing to sing. It lies very well for the voice, and does not strain the vocal equipment—in fact, singers very often say that it 'refreshes' the voice. But it poses complex technical challenges, and the Mozart arena is strewn with corpses. The operas also demand a variety of vocal style and type, especially from the soprano. Elektra in *Idomeneo* and Donna Anna in *Don Giovanni* both require a heroic dramatic compass that can effortlessly scale itself down to produce a liquid legato. Donna Anna's first aria, 'Or sai chi l'onore', for example, needs a Brünnhilde's aggressive force, and stamina and accuracy in negotiating wide intervals; while the second, 'Non mi dir' starts in icily smooth calm before launching into the sort of supple coloratura that most 'dramatics' cannot muster. Then there are the infamous arias of the Queen of the Night in *Die Zauberflöte*, and Constanze's bravura 'Martern aller Arten'. However, the Mozart that is most deeply loved by both singers and listeners is found in the more lyrical roles—the Countess, Susanna, Donna Elvira, Zerlina, Pamina, Ilia in *Idomeneo*—where the challenge is in sustaining and interpreting a melodic line rather than in virtuosity. Today we associate such parts with singers such as Schwarzkopf, Jurinac, Te Kanawa, Margaret Price, and Lucia Popp, all great exponents of the purified Mozart which has developed since the Second World War. Precise in intonation, clean in execution, stricter in tempo than previously, but allowing a limited amount of decoration, usually at the discretion of the conductor rather than the singer, the enlightened modern Mozart style has cut out the slurring and swooping which pre-war Mozart singers employed to make the music sound more 'romantic' and emotional. But style in Mozart is never enough. Mozart's operatic music uniquely conveys *personality*: Susanna is wonderfully differentiated from the Countess or Cherubino—or Zerlina or Despina—and the singer has to understand that psychology, to convey it in her phrasing and tone. If she cannot communicate a particular human being, she is not singing Mozart well. Mozart did not see women in terms of symbol or stereotype. Nothing human is shut out of his imaginative world, and in the Italian operas in particular his music bespeaks a variety of female desires, strengths, and failings. Donna Anna granted a moment of genuine grief by the orchestra at the end of her Vengeance aria; the pathos of Fiordiligi's yielding to Ferrando— 'Fa di me qual che ti par', 'Do what you like with me'; the Countess's weary forgiveness and Pamina's assertion of 'Die wahrheit', 'the truth': to realize such things, the prima donna must understand something more than style.

Mozart's feeling about singers and their capabilities were predictably mixed: the demands his music made were considerable, and he had many struggles with the inadequate and recalcitrant. Yet inasmuch as he wrote carefully for individual voices and was prepared to insert extra music as required, he was a composer of his time—to survive, he had to be. His ideal was a castrato of the *vieux école*, Manzuoli, who taught him singing when he was a boy in London, and he found no one in adulthood to measure up to him. By the time Mozart's mature operas were being written in the 1780s, a good castrato was hard to find. The role of Idamante in *Idomeneo*, the most beautiful and moving of all *opera seria*, was taken by one Vincenzo dal Prato, who infuriated the composer: 'I have to teach him the whole part as if he were a child,' he wrote to his father: he had 'no intonation, no method, no feeling'. With prima donnas he had better luck. He was in love with two of them. The English singer Nancy Storace was the first Susanna in *Le Nozze di Figaro*, and for her Mozart composed a lovely aria for concert singing, 'Ch'io mi scordi di te?'; Aloysia Weber, elder and initially preferred sister of Mozart's wife Constanze, also had such arias written for her in a florid style.

The outstanding contemporary Mozart singer was indisputably Catarina Cavalieri (1760–1801). In *Die Entführung aus dem Serail*, Mozart sacrificed dramatic credibility, and composed a long, heroic and fiendishly difficult aria, 'Martern aller Arten', to show off what he called her 'flexible throat'. With a long instrumental introduction, it is a producer's nightmare, and often the prima donna's too. Cavalieri also sang in the first performance of *Der Schauspieldirektor*, a one-act squib which satirizes the folly of two rival prima donnas, each trying to outbid the other vocally and financially. Mozart clearly enjoyed poking fun at these ladies and the music they sang: *Così fan tutte* contains an aria, 'Come scoglio', which, with its ridiculous sentiments of constancy, its gigantic leaps and meaningless runs, is a superb parody of *opera seria* at its silliest. For Cavalieri Mozart inserted an aria—Donna Elvira's 'Mi tradì'—into *Don Giovanni*, and in a revival she also sang the Countess in *Le Nozze di Figaro*, a role requiring the utmost control and smoothness of line. Even though she was the mistress of his rival Salieri, Mozart remained on very cordial terms with her until his miserable end. A few weeks before his death he took her and Salieri to see *Die Zauberflöte*: in a letter to Constanze, Mozart reported their verdict that 'they had never seen such a delightful show'.

Only *Figaro* and *Don Giovanni* survived Mozart's death as popular works (although *Die Zauberflöte* appeared sometimes as *Il Flauto Magico*), and it was not until the middle of this century that his other masterpieces won the central place in the repertory that they now hold. The first Mozart opera to be heard in London was *La Clemenza di Tito*, in which Mrs Billington sang in 1806. A work of great virtues and some originality, it was also a throw-back to the ethics and structure of conventional *opera seria*. London considered it 'modern' at first, because of the unfamiliar sophistication of its harmony and orchestration. Within twenty years, however, it would look and sound hopelessly old-fashioned. For out of the unprecedented turmoil of the revolutionary and Napoleonic period a new culture was growing, in which opera found new fresh roots and shapes. The great age of the prima donna was about to begin.

# *Romantic Opera*

John Keats once admitted that 'there is a tendency to class women in my books with roses and sweetmeats—they never see themselves dominant'. One of the fascinations of early Romantic opera lies in the fact that at one level it deals in the standard 'roses and sweetmeats' female fantasy-role—woman as passive victim and virginal innocent; as intercessor, the bearer of pity and mercy; woman waiting and praying—while at another, it gives women that domination which Keats found lacking in his poetry. In many of these operas women become genuinely heroic, put in positions of power and made agents of their own destinies: Beethoven's Leonore or Bellini's Norma and Cherubini's Medea, modelled on classical tragedy, are notable examples of this. Opera provides the strongest image of woman in any Romantic art form. Neither the novel nor painting gave women such an open field of action, such a number of revolutionary possibilities. Nowhere else was a woman put so firmly at the structural centre. The great prima donnas of the period both seized and forged these possibilities, performing with an intensity and individuality unknown in the eighteenth century.

The political and intellectual upheavals of the time had had their inevitable radical effect on public taste. The *ancien régime*, with its fixed moral and class codes, had been unsettled, not just in France but throughout Europe. From the turn of the century, war, or the prospect of it, became a norm. The fixed form of *opera seria* became as anachronistic as the absolutist monarchies under which it had flourished, and a new music developed for a new social dispensation.

But revolutions are never thorough or clean, and the new era began, ironically enough, with two magnificent relics, Angelica Catalani and Giovanni-Battista Velluti, who became dinosaurs in their own time. Mount Edgcumbe spoke of Catalani as 'the last great singer heard in this country whose name is likely to be recollected in musical annals'. His was the older connoisseur's feeling that nothing could be quite as good as it had been in the days of Pacchierotti, but that Catalani was a last link with his vocal style and accomplishment. Unfortunately for art, she was an extremely silly singer, without any apparent musical taste or adventurousness.

> Her throat seems endued (as has been remarked by medical men) with a power of expansion and muscular motion by no means usual, and when she throws out all her voice to the utmost, it has a volume and strength that are quite surprising, while its agility in divisions, running up and down the scale in semi-tones, and its compass in jumping over two octaves at once, are equally astonishing. It were to be wished she was less lavish in the display of these wonderful powers, and sought more to please than to surprise; but her taste is vicious, her excessive love of ornament spoiling every simple air, and her greatest delight (indeed her chief merit) being in songs of a bold and spirited character . . . in which she can indulge in *ad libitum* passages with a luxuriance and redundancy no other singer ever possessed, or if possessing ever practised, and which she carries to a fantastical excess. (Mount Edgcumbe)

This extraordinary coloratura soprano was born in Sinagaglia in 1780 and had little musical education. In early days she sang with Mrs Billington and the castrato Marchesi in Italy, where she was always regarded with a degree of scepticism, and then spent about six years in Lisbon. In France she became a favourite of Napoleon's, but even the blockade of the Channel could not stop her from getting to London, where she made her début in 1806 in Portogallo's *Semiramide*. The *Morning Post* was beside itself in search of superlatives. Her first performance was good enough: 'There never was perhaps a singer of any age or country, who possessed such powers of voice and execution, as this Lady . . . we must notice her bravura at the end of the first act, which exceeds all possibility of description'; but her second far exceeded 'any description that is within the scope of language to justly characterize'; while 'on Saturday she exceeded her former efforts beyond all description'. So much for the ineffable nature of music!

Catalani's repertory was largely nonsense, and became progressively more ridiculous. When she did sing Mozart (she was the first

54

London Susanna in *Figaro*), the results were considered excellent, but nothing could wean her away from bravura showpieces specially composed for her by contemporary hacks. 'It was no matter how unmeaning or preposterous these displays were: it was quite enough if they were astonishing.' Two of the ultimate idiocies were an arrangement of Figaro's aria 'Non più andrai', in which she would drown 'by the force and volume of her organ, the whole brazen instruments of the orchestra', and, much to Mount Edgcumbe's distaste, a vocalized version of some variations for violin.

Catalani was a woman of immense amiability, unspoilt by her success and extremely generous. She was also very beautiful. Mount Edgcumbe found 'the outline of her features . . . decidedly tragic (almost Siddonian), yet she can relax them into the most charming smile, and assume the character not merely of gaiety, but even of *niaiserie*, and of arch simplicity.' Her husband, a French army officer, Paul Valbrèque (or Vallabrèque), acted as her manager and did the dirty work of negotiating exorbitant fees, leaving the prima donna free to charm one and all. 'No woman,' wrote Michael Kelly in his *Reminiscences*,

> . . . was ever more charitable or kind-hearted, and as for the quality of her mind, I never knew a more perfect child of nature. At Bangor she heard the Welsh harp for the first time. The old blind harper of the house was in the kitchen; thither she went, and seemed delighted with the wild and plaintive music which he played. But when he struck up a Welsh jig, she started up before all the servants in the kitchen, and danced as if she were wild. I thought she never would have ceased.

She was in London regularly until 1814 and became a staple feature of fashionable life. It has been estimated that she amassed £50,000 while in England, but it was not always easy. Once she went on strike when the management's payments to her fell in arrears: this provoked a riot in the theatre—chandeliers and musical instruments were smashed and it had to be closed for a week. The size of her fee was also a major cause of the 'Old Price' riots at Covent Garden in 1809. But beyond the charge of avarice, no breath of scandal was ever attached to her: 'She pursued her course with undeviating propriety,' wrote one commentator approvingly. Valbrèque eventually tried to buy the King's Theatre as a permanent base for his wife, but failed. The couple left for Paris, and London may have felt some relief when in 1815, amid the drama of Napoleon's return from Elba, the French state handed them the Théâtre-Italien, along with a generous subsidy. Four years of fiasco ensued, as Catalani gave way to tendencies already noted in London. Not only could she not endure any sort of rivalry, but she deliberately surrounded herself with ninth-rate singers in supporting roles and sacked half the orchestra and chorus in draconian economy measures. 'My wife and four or five puppets—that's all you need,' replied Valbrèque, when asked on what principle he ran his opera house. In performance nothing much mattered except the display pieces, and the repertory was consequently abysmal, with rehearsal and production cut to a minimum. The monotony soon overpowered the French, and Catalani seems to have sensed that her time on stage was up. She began a grand series of concert tours. Stendhal reported her visit to Milan:

> Signora Catalani is come to town with the promise of four recitals. The tickets are to cost ten francs each, and the whole of Milan holds up its hands in horror. (The price of a seat at *la scala*, on a regular subscription, is precisely six and thirty centimes) . . . Everyone who heard her concurs in the verdict: for pure vocal quality, Signora Catalani has no rival within living memory . . . What marvels then, were it our fortune to witness, had nature but seen fit to bestow upon her the gift of a *soul*! But, alas! in the event, she sang every single aria on the programme *in exactly the same style* . . . It is fully eighteen years now since Signora Catalani first came to Milan and sang 'Ho perduto il figlio amato' and she has not made an iota of progress.

In Naples, she charged seven times the usual amount and billed herself unequivocally as '*prima cantatrice del mondo*'. In 1824 she returned to London and to opera, appearing in a comic piece to which her considerable (when she bothered) acting talent was well suited. Her voice was deemed to have retained all its glory, and in four months of London performances she made over £10,000. As a portent of the times, Pasta and Rossini were also in London and the composer and Catalani sang a duet together at a music festival in Cambridge.

Catalani sang on regardless until she retired in 1828, and Valbrèque continued to get her the best possible terms. A Catalani contract of 1826 (not, incidentally, accepted by the management) contained the following clause:

> Madame Catalani shall choose and direct the operas in which she is to sing; she shall likewise have the choice of the performers in them; she will have no orders to receive from anyone; she will find all her own dresses.

Shortly, further down, we gather that she would also expect to receive half the total takings. Valbrèque also insisted that a large number of free tickets, presumably for a claque, should be made available to him. In fact, it would be possible to regard Catalani's entire career as a monument to exploitation and artistic malpractice. Yet she commands respect. However intransigent and narrow-minded, she was aware of her strengths, and she did not disappoint her audiences. The composer Spohr records a touching sign of weakness in her otherwise near-flawless vocal equipment, a characteristic which immediately makes her a more sympathetic performer: she suffered terribly from nerves and was observed before a concert to 'tremble from head to foot . . . hardly able to breathe'.

Her retirement was marked by one final immense gesture in the endowment of a school for aspiring prima donnas. There were no fees, but a stipulation was made that every pupil had to adopt 'Catalani' into their surname. In her latter days, Catalani sat in Paris in genteel poverty, knitting obsessively. She was visited by the 'Swedish Nightingale' Jenny Lind a few weeks before she died, and a correspondent of *The Musical Times* interviewed her: 'I hate music,' she exclaimed. 'Fifty years of humble invocation to the Virgin not for a blessing on my dearly beloved children, not for the health and happiness of myself, but for a benediction on my crotchets and quavers.'

Catalani was one of those singers whose greatness was thrust upon them by virtue of a unique physical organ: she was not interested in making concessions to the art of music. Our second dinosaur, the castrato Giovanni-Battista Velluti (1781–1861), tried harder, to no avail. He arrived in London at the same time as the notorious 'Living Skeleton' Claude Seurat, and society went from staring at one physical freak to listening to another. Velluti was an epigone, and capitalized on his extraordinariness—London had not heard a castrato for a quarter of a century when he appeared there in 1825. The sniggering was widespread, and he was the subject of 'scurrilous abuse', some of it probably justified. Extremely handsome, he was notorious for his dalliance with ladies of quality. 'Childishness,' wrote Stendhal, who admired his art, 'is the predominant facet of his character, and a footman can lead him around like a bear on a string.'

Even more than Catalani, he suffered from his own obsolescence. For one thing, his voice was not particularly strong or opulent. Mount Edgcumbe, admittedly hearing him only late in his career, was disappointed: 'His general style is the *grazioso*, with infinite delicacy and a great deal of expression, but never rising to the grand, simple and dignified cantabile of the old school, still less to the least approach towards the *bravura* . . . there is a great want of variety in his performance, as well as a total deficiency of force and spirit.' He had to compete with a new fashion for tenor heroes and with the superb Rossini travesty parts for women. His response was largely defensive, and the operas written for him were largely old-fashioned, pallid, and replete with ornaments and antique vocal effects. When in 1813 Rossini (who as a child had himself narrowly evaded Velluti's fate) wrote a part for him in *Aureliano in Palmira*, there was an argument—Velluti had an enormous success with his principal aria, but Rossini was furious at the way his original simple melody had been decorated and embellished out of all recognition. On that occasion young composer had to yield to established singer, but Rossini was soon in a position from which he could enforce his insistence that what he wrote was meant to be sung, without the singer's creative collaboration. Stendhal understood the momentous significance of this transference of power when he wrote that, 'The revolution inaugurated by Rossini killed the gift of originality in the singer.' Perhaps 'killed' is too strong a word, and 'restricted' more accurate: throughout the nineteenth century prima donnas decorated at their pleasure, though never to Catalani's extent.

In 1824 Meyerbeer wrote the last role for a castrato, Armando in *Il Crociato in Egitto*. It was, as Mount Edgcumbe puts it, 'quite of the new school', and Velluti took it to London. Among the other singers at his début was the seventeen-year-old Mlle Garcia, soon to be famous as Malibran. *The Times* maintained that a male soprano, or representative of the 'epicene gender', as he was delicately referred to, was a nasty foreign thing, and 'will never suit the unsophisticated palate of that people who for years fought the battles of Europe and came from the contest victorious'. Velluti himself was 'distinguished by a melancholy placidity', his face speaking of 'a heart that knows no joys. It is a painted sepulchre.' Mount Edgcumbe was more dispassionate: 'At the moment when he was expected to appear, the most profound silence reigned in one of the most crowded audiences I ever saw, broken on his advancing by loud applauses of encouragement. The first note he uttered gave a shock of surprise, almost of disgust, to inexperienced ears, but his performance was listened to with attention and great applause throughout, with but few *audible* expressions of disapprobation speedily suppressed.' His success, founded in curiosity, never consolidated itself, and he continued to be something of a joke. One evening, having sung the words 'il nostro casto amor', 'our chaste love', a gallery wit shouted, 'What else could it be?', which caused hysterical mirth. He could have prolonged his stage career had he been willing to sing opposite Pasta—which he wasn't —although she must have made him look and sound rather foolish. In 1826 he took over the musical direction of the King's Theatre, where he was noted for his attention to historical accuracy in costume. At forty-five, he was ready to bow out gracefully, but his professional end was ignominious. The ladies of the chorus successfully sued him for non-payment of a promised bonus, and he left the country in disgust. His long retirement was spent farming in the Brenta, using his fortune to try out novel agricultural methods. He and the also-retired Rossini mellowed into friends and giggled at the *avant-garde* peculiarities of Berlioz.

Far more suited to Rossini's mature style was a Spanish soprano, Isabella Colbran. There have been many great Spanish Rossini singers, perhaps because the characteristic Spanish sense for subtleties of rhythm relieves his music of its frequent four-square predictability. Rossini worked at a staggering pace, and liked the short-cut of his chosen formulas, frequently sweeping up material from his last unsuccessful serious opera and dumping it surreptitiously into his next comic one. At the same time, he was a true liberator, learning from the example of Mozart in matching the flexibility and swiftness of *opera buffa* to dramatic subjects, as well as increasing the amount of effect gained from the orchestra and from vocal ensemble, particularly in his famous finales. Rossini's music is very noisy—Mount Edgcumbe objected to it for that very reason. It uses a lot of brass and percussion, a lot of martial rhythms, a lot of *crescendo, accelerando,* and *sforzando.* It retains a lot of the verve and melodiousness of *opera buffa,* but it has a cruder energy as well, whipping its audiences into little fits of excitement. In sum, Rossini established a new set of operatic clichés and brought to an end the long-drawn-out death pangs of *opera seria,* even though he often used the time-honoured classical plots in works such as *Maometto Secondo* or *Semiramide.* His success was remarkable for a mere composer, and Stendhal begins his gloriously ramshackle biography with a tribute to his eminence. 'Napoleon is dead; but a new conqueror has already shown himself to the world; and from Moscow to Naples, from London to Vienna, from Paris to Calcutta, his name is constantly on every tongue. The fame of this hero knows no bounds save those of civilization itself; and he is not yet thirty-two!'

Rossini first encountered Colbran as a boy of fifteen in Bologna. She was seven years older than he, and already well known. Her startlingly theatrical presence is described by Stendhal:

> It was a beauty in the most queenly tradition: noble features, which, on the stage, radiated majesty; an eye like that of a Circassian maiden, darting fire; and to crown it all, a true and deep instinct for tragedy. Off-stage, she possessed about as much dignity as the average milliner's assistant; but the moment she stepped on to the boards, her brow encircled with a royal diadem, she inspired involuntary respect, even among those who, a minute or two earlier, had been chatting intimately with her in the foyer of the theatre.

Queenly, noble, fire, majesty, 'true and deep instinct for tragedy' —these became the familiar attributes of the new race of prima donna, and Colbran was the first of the breed.

In 1815 Rossini went to the recently rebuilt Teatro San Carlo in Naples and signed a long-term contract with its impresario, Domenico Barbaia. This man became the greatest power in early nineteenth-century opera, managing at various times opera houses in Milan and Vienna as well. He began life as a waiter and was said to be the first to put whipped cream on to coffee or chocolate. He made a fortune out of gambling concessions in opera house foyers and elsewhere. More significantly, he had real artistic instinct, and knew that to commission good composers was as important to opera as engaging good singers. Colbran also had a contract with Barbaia, or probably two, as she appears to have been his mistress as well as his prima donna. She was also favoured by the King of Naples, which made her extremely unpopular with the Republican element of the audience.

Rossini's reputation, then as now, was largely based on his comic operas, but Colbran was no comedian, and she weaned Rossini away from *buffo* librettos to matter more noble, fiery, and majestic. They began with *Elisabetta, Regina d'Inghilterra*, a bizarre distortion of the Queen's involvement with the Earl of Leicester, an early instance of the new 'historical' opera, which caught on in the wake of the vogue for the novels of Scott. Stendhal's impassioned description of Colbran as Elisabetta gives a good idea of her arrestingly economical style. She

> . . . used no gestures, did nothing melodramatic, never de-scended to what are vulgarly called *tragedy-queen poses*. The immensity of her royal authority, the vastness of events which a single word from her lips could call into being, all this lived in the Spanish beauty of her eyes, which at times could be so terrible . . . it was the unmistakable absence of the least shadow of doubt concerning the devoted obedience which would greet the most insignificant and capricious of her commands, which characterized the acting of this great artist; all this wealth of exquisitely-observed detail could be read into the statuesque calm of her every gesture. And when, rarely, she did move, it was as though the breaking of the stillness were forced upon her from within . . .

Between 1815 and 1823, Rossini wrote nine further parts for Colbran. But according to Stendhal from 1816 onwards there was a major problem: 'Signorina Colbran revealed a marked tendency to sing either above or below the required pitch, and her singing became what (in inferior mortals) would certainly have been termed execrable; but God forbid that one should have suggested anything of the kind in Naples . . . This, to my mind, represents one of the most flattering victories achieved by rank despotism . . .' Stendhal probably put her decline unfairly early. The problem of poor intonation was, interestingly, a common one among Romantic prima donnas, probably the consequence of both the fervour of their histrionics and the fashion for forcing the voice to create a violent or arresting effect. In any case, Stendhal and the Neapolitans reacted strongly:

> If we found that she was firmly resolved to sing out of key, we likewise took a firm resolve and chatted away ostentatiously among ourselves until it was all over, or else escaped into a coffee-house and ate ices. After a few months of these and similar excursions, the audience began to grow bored with the whole thing, gave up the pretence of deluding itself that poor Signorina Colbran was all she had been in her younger days, and waited expectantly for the management to get rid of her. Nothing happened . . . In 1820, one thing alone would have made the Neapolitans happy: not the gift of a Spanish constitution, but the elimination of Signorina Colbran.

Rossini and Colbran married in 1822, having lived together for some years. It was not a happy idea, even though it was a partnership built on great mutual respect. Some said that he had married her for her money—not a fortune by Catalani's standards, but still a lot more than a composer could hope to earn. They left Naples, and Rossini's version of *Semiramide*, with Colbran as the eponymous heroine, the last part he composed for her, was premièred in Venice in 1823. Passing on to London in 1824, Rossini was fêted by royalty and high society, the fame of his operas preceding him. Colbran made little impact, however—Mount Edgcumbe found her 'entirely *passée* : . . her powers are so diminished that she is unable to produce any effect on the stage'. Her career swiftly disintegrated, and when in 1830 Rossini finally opted to settle in Paris, she stayed behind in Bologna, demoralized and listless. Her extravagance became neurotic, and she developed—perhaps an inheritance from her days with Barbaia—a taste for gambling. To cover her losses she started giving singing lessons. Rossini's father, deputed to oversee and hand out her monthly allowance, fulminated to his son, 'a spendthrift who looks only for ways to show spite, and that because one doesn't want to kowtow to her grandeurs and insanities'. Colbran herself was clearly desperate. She wrote to a friend, 'When fortune is remote from you, everything conspires against you. I must tell you that my health is always bad, that my affairs go from bad to worse, and in order to distract myself I have turned to gambling, with such disaster that I cannot take a card that doesn't become a victim.' Rossini meanwhile had found a new and less demanding companion, the *demi-mondaine* Olympe Pélissier, and in 1837 he was legally separated from his wife. She died in 1845, the composer at her bedside.

The utter collapse of Colbran's career in London was not only due to whatever vocal deficiencies she may have had. The problem in 1824, as for Catalani and Velluti, was the triumph of Giuditta Pasta, greatest of all Italian prima donnas, who, said the critic Henry Chorley writing in 1861, 'has printed deeper impressions on the memories of those that heard her than any other female singer'. Not that Chorley ever heard Pasta in her vocal prime—he came to her art late, when she had begun to sing consistently out of tune. For the Pasta of the 1820s we have Stendhal, a friend as well as her most articulate admirer.[1] He had originally toyed with the idea of falling in love with this woman of genius, but soon contented himself with regular visits to her *salon* in Paris's rue Richelieu. He used to stay so late that the porter, who had to get up to let him out of the building, began to hate him. Eventually, he moved into an apartment above Pasta's, whiling away the small hours in her company, playing faro and talking to visiting Milanese: in this building, Stendhal wrote his *Life of Rossini*, which contains the encomium to Pasta.

The liaison was innocent, and Pasta's married life remained perfectly respectable. In fact, one wonders whether Stendhal was ever allowed to get very close to his goddess—for such a great analyst of women, his picture of her personality is oddly one-dimensional and idealized: 'She was in my view without vices or faults, a simple, consistent, just, natural person.' On the qualities of her singing, however, he is vividly suggestive.

> Madame Pasta's voice has a considerable range. She can achieve perfect resonance on a note as low as bottom A and can rise as high as C# or D ... the true designation of her voice is *mezzo-soprano*, and any composer who writes for her should use the *mezzo-soprano* range for the thematic material of his music ... one of the most uncommon features of Madame Pasta's voice [is that it] is *not all moulded from the same metallo*, as they would say in Italy [i.e. possesses more than one timbre]; and this fundamental variety of tone produced by a single voice affords

[1] Did he name the heroine of *La Chartreuse de Parme* after her daughter Clelia?

63

one of the richest veins of musical expression which the artistry of a great *cantatrice* is able to exploit . . . Without such a palette of breath-taking colour deep within her own being, and without such an extraordinary and compelling natural gift, Madame Pasta could never have achieved the over-mastering force of natural expression which we have learnt to associate with her—a miracle of emotional revelation, which is always true to nature . . . always alive with that unmistakable, burning energy, that extraordinary dynamism which can electrify an entire theatre.

One important fact emerges here—Pasta was not a true soprano, but some sort of mezzo: did she, in her long and rigorous apprentice-ship, force her voice up to the C#s and Ds against its natural inclination, and was it that forcing which caused her particular failures of intonation? Against this shortcoming are ranged the splendours of her art, its superb line and *portamento*; the austerity and meaningfulness of her ornamentation; the voice's facility at changing from 'head' to 'chest' voice; and her subtle rhythmic instinct. What made her style 'modern' was the ability, as Stendhal implies, to 'colour' her voice, to give the same note different emotional overtones. Her singing lacked the purity of Mrs Billington's or Mara's, but it was infinitely more interesting. For Chorley, Pasta's greatest 'grace' was her 'depth and reality of expression . . . Her recitative, from the moment she entered, was riveting by its truth . . . the impression made on me was that of my being always subdued and surprised for the first time. Though I knew what was coming, when the passion broke out, or when the phrase was sung, it seemed as if they were something new, electrical, immediate.' She was indisputably a great tragic actress, and, like Callas, the power of her performances lay in their complete commit-ment to the highest ideal of opera—the expression of human emotion through music. Her acting was as linked to singing as a Shakespearean actress is to her speaking voice. She presented a severe and noble intensity that women have rarely been allowed in art outside classical drama, and which found its fulfilment in Bellini's *Norma*.

Giuditta Negri was born near Milan in 1797—her Christian name and her mother's, Rachele, suggest that she had Jewish blood, which would make her another sort of rarity among prima donnas. She started singing in Milan and in 1816, sponsored by the

1. Jacopo Amigoni (1682–1752), Portrait Group, c.1752, oil on canvas. Farinelli sits in the centre; the woman to whom he hands the music has been thought to be Faustina. One of the most relaxed and attractive of the many pictures of Farinelli.

3. Mara as Gluck's Armida.

2. Mrs Billington in 1801, the year of her return from Italy.

4. Angelica Catalani as Susanna in *Le Nozze di Figaro*. Water-colour sketch by Chalon, 1815.

5. Isabella Colbran in the 'cantata' *Il Sogno di Partenope*, which she sang at La Scala in 1817.

6. The great Giuditta Pasta.

7. The young Giulia Grisi, who sang with Pasta in the first performance of Bellini's *Norma* in 1831.

composer Paër, joined Catalani's company at the Théâtre-Italien in Paris. It was not an auspicious beginning and, according to Chorley:

> ... her voice was originally limited, husky, and weak, without charm, without flexibility, a mediocre mezzo-soprano. Though her countenance *spoke*, the features were cast in that coarse mould which is common in Italy. Her arms were fine, but her figure was short and clumsy. She walked heavily, almost unequally. No candidate for musical sovereignty ever presented herself with what must have seemed a more slender and imperfect list of credentials.

Her will was superior to her endowment, however, and she continued to slave at her technique. After an unremarkable season in London, she retired to Italy with her husband, the lawyer Giuseppe Pasta, and had a baby. She then sang in secondary Italian opera houses. A fascinating letter from this period survives, written to Pasta by the composer Nicolini, who was writing an opera for the Roman winter carnival season, in which Pasta was to appear. Like a dressmaker asking for measurements, he asks her for 'the music of two arias which suit your voice well so that I can get a fair idea of your method and skill'. She returned to Paris and the Théâtre-Italien in 1821, a transformed artist. At first her chief vehicles were the operas of Rossini; Desdemona in *Otello*, Colbran's role of Elisabetta, and the title-role of *Tancredi*, in which she sang the famous 'Di tanti palpiti', at the time virtually Rossini's signature tune. Her *salon* became famous too, and a large number of letters survive written to her by male admirers. Some were prostrate with infatuation, of course, but many are simply and strikingly friendly. Pasta's relationships with men appear truly adult, and make one suppose that her *salon* was a place of real frankness, intelligence, and mutual respect, with the singer as a comrade rather than a goddess.

In the timely year of 1824, Pasta braved London again. Disappointed by Colbran and Velluti, bored by Catalani, the city of Kean and Macready was ready for a new grandeur. Pasta repeated Desdemona, as well as Semiramide and Romeo in an operatic version of Shakespeare's play by Zingarelli. Her success was such that the management of the King's Theatre offered her a contract worth £14,000 for the season, but went bankrupt before they could fulfil the sum. Back in Paris, she significantly took over the part written for Velluti in *Il Crociato in Egitto*: her repertory also included a Mary, Queen of Scots, Otello himself, and the Medea of Mayr's not-quite-forgotten *Medea in Corinto*, which gave her great histrionic, if not musical scope. Her relations with Rossini were cordial, but although he frequently conducted her in his operas, he never wrote anything substantial for her. That privilege was reserved for Donizetti and Bellini, whom she inspired to produce some of their finest music, in collaboration with the efficient librettist Felice Romani. Donizetti's *Anna Bolena* gave Pasta a great historical character, suitably romanticized, and a superb final *scena* which, as William Ashbrook has written, 'vividly presents the stages of Anna's retreat from unendurable reality, through longing for release, to triumph, once her reason is restored, as she finds the spiritual strength not to curse but to forgive those who have brought her to her death'. Donizetti wrote much of this opera at Pasta's villa on Lake Como, with the voice on hand, as it were, to refer to. Bellini's talents were both gentler and deeper than those of Donizetti, whose historical melodramas are well turned but hardly moving. Bellini died young, and his harmony and orchestration are thin and unsophisticated compared to those of his major rivals. He is most admired for his long-spun melodies, which had their effect on Chopin's Nocturnes, and were valued by Wagner, but there is more to his operas than beautiful tunes. The music for Pasta in the bucolic *La Sonnambula*, the story of a village maiden who sleepwalks her way into trouble that impairs her good reputation, may now seem pretty and anodyne, but *Norma*, which followed it in the same year of 1831, has a power that no other opera of this school possesses. The title-role is at the very acme of the soprano's repertory, considered more challenging than Brünnhilde or Isolde and rarely sung even competently. Its range and stature is an impressive indication of Pasta's genius.

Norma is a Druid high priestess who has borne two children to a Roman proconsul, Pollione, only to discover that he now loves her friend and junior priestess Adalgisa. After struggling against feelings of vengeance, she is persuaded by Adalgisa not to kill her children. Norma then exposes her own personal treachery against her oppressed people before the assembled Druids and commits herself to the pyre: Pollione, moved by her sacrifice, dies with her. Underlying this is a not very subtly modified version of the Medea story, which also exploited Italian nationalistic feeling in the Druidic animosity against the occupying Roman forces. No self-respecting tenor would volunteer to sing the part of Pollione, and Adalgisa fades from the drama unsatisfactorily. It is in Norma herself that the impressiveness is found. Her opening scene involves the test of 'Casta Diva', with its spacious dreamy line and exquisite chromatic cascades, followed by a *cabaletta* which is not brilliant and angry but a sweet musing on the joys of love—and much the more difficult for that. This aria requires from its singer the utmost control of tone and rhythm at a very early stage in the evening; later she has two long-breathed lyrical duets with Adalgisa; a ferocious and florid part in a long trio-finale; and stretches of declamatory *arioso* and recitative. Nothing in Norma's music is simple or emotionally neutral: there is a powerful scene of frenzy and remorse as Norma comes close to killing her children, and bitter scorn and hard-edged irony in her confrontation with Pollione. In the last act finale Bellini demands one more marshalling of resources in Norma's moving plea, 'Deh! non volerli vittime', which flowers into a vast climax.

Simply to pass muster, then, a Norma needs power, stamina, flexibility, beauty and variety of tone, as well as theatrical presence and intelligence. Even Pasta doubted whether she could measure up. She complained to Bellini that 'Casta Diva' was not suited to her abilities, but he made her promise to work on it for a week. A few hours before the première, she sent the composer a parchment lampshade decorated with flowers surrounding warriors and maidens, a bouquet of cloth flowers, and a note: 'Allow me to offer you something that was some solace to me for the immense fear that persecuted me when I found myself little suited to performing your sublime harmonies, this lamp by night and these flowers by day witnessed my studies of *Norma* and the desire I cherish to be ever more worthy of your esteem.' After an initial fiasco at La Scala, the opera became very popular and was repeated there thirty-nine times in the first season. But it finished Pasta as a singer, and by the time she sang the part in London, in 1833, one reviewer claimed that 'It would not be exaggerated to say that not a single phrase of the entire opera was sung on the correct pitch . . . it required her power as an actress to save her from disaster.'

The English singer Adelaide Kemble, who studied the part of Norma with Pasta, has some interesting observations on Pasta's difficulties with pitch:

Even at her best, she had always sung false upon three notes in the middle of her voice—the C of the third space, with the D and E which follow, were invariably considerably too flat. One day that she was teaching me to sing 'Casta Diva', the great air of the 'Norma', when I came to the words 'spargi in terra', which falls upon these particular notes, she suddenly stopped me. 'Crescete, mia cara' ['Too sharp, my dear'], said she. I began again, and was again stopped at the same place. Anxious to ascertain the fact, about which I had my doubts, I repeated the passage for the third time, very gently touching the piano at the concluding note, and finding myself in perfect unison with it . . . [She] then herself sang the notes a full quarter of a tone too flat . . . a very curious proof that her falseness of intonation was an imperfection of the ear, and not of the voice, for these three notes of the scale—a most remarkable peculiarity which I have never since met with in any one. . . . Over her bedroom door hung innumerable birds in cages. 'J'aime à les entendre le matin' she said; adding, with a comical shade of bitterness, 'Ces petits coquins, ils chantent toujours si juste' [I like to hear them singing in the morning . . . the little rascals, they always sang in tune'].

In 1833 Bellini unsuccessfully asked for Pasta's daughter's hand in marriage, and also honoured her with the title-role in *Beatrice di Tenda*, her last creation. By now, although she maintained all her command and exceptional musicianship, she simply could not be relied upon to sing in tune. Her unsparing commitment was her downfall. Reluctant to retire, perhaps partly because she had lost most of her money in the Guymuller bank crash, she gave some more performances in London in 1837 and made a trip to St Petersburg in 1840, by which time her voice was in a miserable state. Adelaide Kemble heard her during the last but one of her engagements in England: 'I remember while I was sitting in my stall worshipping this great goddess and thanking Heaven for a new revelation of happiness, hearing a well-known old dandy [ancestor, no doubt, of the modern opera queen] who was just before me exclaim, while he applauded her with a sort of good-natured condescension, "Oh, poor dear old thing! How stumpy she is! How old she has grown, to be sure! She oughtn't to have come back again!" ' Then, ten years later, when she was fifty-two, she was seduced back to London to sing some scenes from *Anna Bolena*.

Chorley's account of this tragic occasion is magnificent. In the audience were the great French actress Rachel (who was overtly sarcastic about the proceedings) and Pauline Viardot, Malibran's sister, a great singer herself, then at her peak. 'Nothing more inadvised could be dreamed of,' began Chorley: the voice's 'state of utter ruin on the night in question passes description . . . Dismal as was the spectacle, broken, hoarse, and destroyed as was the voice, the great style of the singer spoke.' She attempted Anna Bolena's final *scena*:

> By that time, tired, unprepared, in ruin as she was, she had rallied a little. When, on Anna Bolena's hearing the coronation music for her rival, the heroine searches for her own crown on her brow, Madame Pasta wildly turned in the direction of the festive sounds, the old irresistible charm broke out; nay, even in the final song, with its roulades, and its scales of shakes ascending by a semitone, the consummate vocalist and tragedian, able to combine form with meaning—the moment of the situation with such personal and musical display as form an integral part of operatic art—was indicated: at least to the apprehension of a younger artist, 'You are right' was Madame Viardot's quick and heartfelt response (her eyes full of tears) to a friend beside her; 'You are right! It is like the *Cenacolo* of da Vinci at Milan—a wreck of a picture, but the picture is the greatest picture in the world!'

Prosper Mérimée visited Pasta in retirement on Lake Como, and found 'Git', as she was familiarly known, happily growing cabbages. She loved gardening and the country life. In her heyday there had been Pasta fêtes on the lake, with fireworks and famous 'Pasta arias' played throughout the night by a band on a boat, but the life of this incomparable prima donna ended quietly in reduced circumstances. George Sand saw her once in Venice: 'In her old hat and coat, Pasta could have been mistaken for a box attendant. Yet she made a sign to the gondolier to indicate the direction she wanted to take, and in that gesture the great Queen, if not the *diva*, reappeared.' J. E. Cox, an English music critic, was sailing across Lake Como in 1861, and caught sight of her chasing some turkeys with a switch; Sutherland Edwards quotes from the account of some other English visitors:

We did not see her at her best, for having just risen from her siesta, in which we had disturbed her, she was only half awake. We found her very friendly and evidently gratified by our visit. Her mouth and teeth are still lovely, the great eyes full of fire, her black hair in a dishevelled state, and her dress an extremely original medley of oddities. She never ceased talking of old times, and told us that she had given up living in the villa because both her mother and her husband had died there. She afterwards wrote something for our albums, and gave us some beautiful flowers.

Devoted to her family, warm-hearted and sensible, Pasta nevertheless rarely emerges to history as a vivid human being, nor do portraits suggest any startling individuality. Perhaps, like so many great actors and actresses, her magnetism was reserved for the stage. None of which could be said for Maria Malibran. If, as one French critic put it, Pasta embodied the spirit of Sophocles and Racine, Malibran embodied Shakespeare and Victor Hugo. To Chorley, she was just 'thoroughly, fearlessly original'.

It has become a cliché of operatic journalese to compare Callas with Malibran, but this is not fair to either. Callas was closer to Pasta, imperious and grand, a tragedienne of instinctive nobility and reserve. Malibran was wild, impetuous, and uninhibited. She loved to improvise and to play around on stage, to the point of both embarrassing her colleagues and of making a fool of herself. In the middle of love scenes, she tickled her tenors or pinched their behinds; she introduced absurd dances at inappropriate moments, once falling flat on her face; she even sang the part of an old hag in Cimarosa's *Il Matrimonio Segreto*, just for the joy of dressing up. She was deadly competitive—'The idea that the fame of any living artiste could approach hers, was enough to eat her heart away,' wrote one of her observers—and performed in a spirit, not of dedication to art, but of doing one better or that much more than anyone else. Compared with Pasta, a lot of her effects were simply startling and even cheap: in his journal, Delacroix, of all painters, remarked on the way in which she ripped her handkerchief and gloves to pieces in a fraught moment of Donizetti's *Maria Stuarda*:

> She thus achieved moments full of energy and seemingly full of truth, but it also happened that she would seem exaggerated and faulty in her timing . . . I do not recall ever having seen her *noble*.

When she came nearest to the sublime, it was only to such a conception of it as a bourgeoise might possess; in a word, she was completely lacking in the sense of the ideal.

Her singing, however, was of the same school as Pasta's. Both had instruments made great by will, rather than by nature, and both lacked Catalani's vocal opulence and physical impressiveness. Chorley describes Malibran's voice clinically:

> It was not naturally a voice of first-rate quality. It was a mezzo-soprano, extended upwards and downwards by that hardy and tremendous exercise the introduction of which has been ascribed to the appearance of her father . . . the girl was early put into possession of an instrument two octaves and a half, if not more, in compass, weakest in the tones betwixt F and F—a weakness audaciously and incomparably disguised by the forms of execution, modification, and ornament which she selected. Her topmost and deepest notes were perpetually used in connected contrast . . .

Ernest Legouvé is more evocative:

> Malibran's voice was like gold, but like gold it had to be dug from the bowels of the earth; it had to be separated from the ore; it had to be forged and beaten, and made pliable like the metal under the hammer . . . One day in Rome when she was to play Rosina, I heard her study the shakes of her *cavatina*. Every now and then she stopped short to scold her own voice saying 'Obey me! I'll make you obey me!' The struggle therefore was a necessity.

The necessity of struggle began early, pathetically early. Malibran's childhood must have been agony, and she was allowed no space for natural growth. To the end of her short life, she retained a weird naïvety of temperament. She always loved playing with dolls, but farmed out her own child. She stayed up all night, rode bareback all morning, sang all afternoon and evening, before collapsing into a trance of sheer exhaustion. Her frenzied intensity battled with a frail constitution, but she had been taught to ignore all such limitations.

Her father was Manuel Garcia, founder of the greatest of operatic families, and himself an important figure in the history of singing.

The son of Spanish gypsies, Garcia became the first of the newly liberated batch of tenors, given, in the operas of Rossini, a prominence they had not known before. He created the part of Almaviva in *Il Barbiere di Siviglia* and was Otello to Pasta's Desdemona. His singing was florid, loud, excitable, and immensely popular in Naples, London, and Paris. Maria was born in 1808, and could read music before her alphabet. She made her stage début at the age of five in an opera by Paër: the first of many Malibran stories has it that when the prima donna of the evening suffered a memory lapse, the child immediately filled in her part. Apocryphal or not, the little girl was tyranically drilled by her father, who did not stop at brute force. Paër was once walking past the Garcia apartment with a friend. Screams were heard, and the friend exclaimed, 'Someone is being murdered!' Paër walked on calmly and replied, 'It's just Garcia beating trills into his daughter.' This unremitting trauma, inflicted on her by a father she loved deeply, formed her voice and her personality. If Garcia takes the credit for schooling a rough and uneven instrument, he must also take reponsibility for her manic self-destructiveness and desperate need to be loved. 'If I were near you, you would have neither face nor body, because I would eat all of you. Love me, love me as I love you, and if you have the chance, *for the love of God*! write to me even though it be two lines,' she wrote to Pasta, whom she worshipped. Pasta never replied to this or further similar adolescent outpourings.

Maria's childhood was itinerant, and she consequently spoke French, Italian, Spanish, and English. She made her first proper public appearances in London in 1825, singing opposite her father in *Il Barbiere di Siviglia* and with Velluti in *Il Crociato in Egitto*. Garcia, nearing the end of his vocal life, then had the idea of taking his family and the Italian opera to New York, where both were entirely unknown. The American impresario was one Dominick Lynch, who had been fired by hearing Pasta. He and Maria tried to persuade Pasta to lead the troupe, but a tendency to sea sickness, and a reluctance to leave her family for a long period, made her refuse. The whole enterprise smacked of that well-known American phenomenon, the quick buck, but it gave Maria solid stage experience and some easily won adulation from a gullible audience, ready to approve of it all as another genteel European import. One of her admirers was a middle-aged French-born merchant, Eugène Malibran. When she announced that she wanted to marry him, Garcia only gave his permission on condition that Malibran promised a large sum of money in compensation for removing his thoroughly bankable daughter from his company. Garcia and family left New York for Mexico. Free from the stifling presence of her father, Maria married and retired from the pressures of the operatic stage. Problems began soon afterwards. Malibran lost all his money and proved to be something of a charlatan. Maria resumed her career in a loyal effort to save him from embarrassment and grossed large sums in New York and Philadelphia. By the end of 1827, the marriage had obviously deteriorated, and the most respectable way of separating was for Maria to return to Europe and for Malibran himself to follow when business improved. She does not seem to have undertaken to send him money, although she may have agreed that anything she earned might be deducted from the money he still owed to her father. In Paris, Maria began by singing at fashionable *soirées*, where even Colbran 'who in her whole life never gave a compliment to anyone, approached, arms open, before a numerous group to embrace me, to pay me a thousand compliments'. After the departure from the Théâtre-Italien of the reigning prima donna, Henriette Sontag, Maria was ready to take her place. She triumphed in two of Pasta's Rossini roles, Semiramide and Desdemona, and then wrote to her husband to say that he need not bother to leave New York—she was happy where she was and as she was, living a respectable chaperoned life and presiding over a cheerful-sounding *salon*, full of pranks and party games. In 1829 she attacked London again, where, according to Chorley, she was initially found 'unequal, bizarre, and fatiguing'. Her Zerlina, for instance, in *Don Giovanni* was not the usual demure Petit Trianon shepherdess, but 'a coarse, vulgar country lass, agog for enjoyment', who at the ball 'jumped and jigged about, out of time and out of place'. Authenticity in costume was important to her. She sang the sleepwalking scene in *La Sonnambula* not in a muslin négligé, but a peasant's coarse gown, woollen stockings, and night cap; for Donizetti's *Maria Stuarda*, she sketched from tombs in Westminster Abbey.

There can be no doubt that Maria Malibran irritated a section of public taste. She was not, as has sometimes been implied, a harbinger of naturalism, but a vehement over-actress, who would throw into her interpretations extraneous detail and an excess of emotion. A Parisian friend of Pasta's, Albert Stapfer, wrote to her that Malibran 'hadn't the strength of mind to resist the death-dealing acclaim of the Parisian public. Day by day, she becomes more mannered and exaggerated.' She was often inspired, but she was occasionally ridiculous and even, as Delacroix thought, 'unbearable'. Yet it was this 'over the top' quality which must have made her so exciting. Like Judy Garland, she seems to have communicated a sense of danger, a sense of someone pushing her own resources beyond all reasonable limits and who was prepared to risk failure in the attempt. How long her magnificent voice and hard-earned technique could have stood up to the anarchic schedule of her life is an unanswered question; but, as Gautier put it, 'she had the genius to die very young'.

Malibran's off-stage personality was completely at one with this, and for all her fervent kindness and generosity, one imagines that she was hardly a relaxing companion or someone for the close sympathies of intimate friendship. She was lucky to find, in 1829, Charles de Bériot, a famous Belgian violinist, darkly handsome, shy and diffident, who provided her with steady moral support as well as being an object in whom she could satisfy her thwarted desire for love. Unlike most prima donnas, she was faintly prim about sex, and she longed to be publicly acknowledged as Bériot's wife—which is how she privately presented herself. For the next five years the drama of trying to get rid of Eugène Malibran (who had returned to Paris and who, under the Napoleonic Code, was entitled to all his wife's property) brought further tension into her life. It was not until 1836, with the patronage of General Lafayette and a change in the hitherto inflexible law, that she won an annulment and could remarry.

Until 1832 Malibran sang chiefly in London and Paris, alternating between frenzy and collapse. Apart from her theatrical engagements, she also sang in concert and at private parties, and if she did drink heavily, as was rumoured, it was hardly surprising. She became notorious for cancelling performances at the last minute, but also sang in the most painful circumstances—a broken arm, pregnancy, lips scalded by sal volatile—nothing could stop her when she chose. In 1832, on a whim, she left for Italy and sang in Rome (where she was heartbroken to receive the news of her father's death), Bologna, and Naples, accompanied throughout by Bériot, who adapted his own engagements to hers. Back in London in May 1833, she sang in English one of her very finest roles, Amina in *La Sonnambula*, a performance which quite besotted Bellini. The manager of Drury Lane, Alfred Bunn, was forced into paying her £2,000 for fifteen performances and comments in his memoirs on her 'inordinate love of money . . . it would be sheer humbug to say she had not that passion'. But avarice went with truly massive donations to friends and to charities, gifts that were often anonymous. Somehow she managed to give her time too, and one of the silliest and most charming Malibran stories concerns a visit to a hospital for orphans. Malibran, swathed in inconspicuous black, toured the wards. A dying child needed a bath and was making violent resistance. Malibran: 'If I sing to you, will you get into the bath?' Malibran sings a *bolero*, so exquisitely that the nuns' eyes fill with tears. The child continues to screech, but Malibran has a further inspiration, takes all her clothes off, gets into the bath herself, and is soon followed by the child, stunned no doubt into acquiescence.

Alfred Bunn was another who was stunned into acquiescence, as he dredged up ever larger sums of money to keep Malibran at Drury Lane. Their relationship was a lively one, and one of the letters he reproduces in his memoirs gives an idea of Malibran's entrancing childishness and manic mental energy: it concerns an operetta she was trying to learn.

St James's Street, Mardi

Again and again, alwais me, and eternally me, my dear Mister Bunn. I have been tormenting poor Chelard out of his wits. I want to have my part to practise it, know it, and be able to play it in 10 days the latest. I am sure if you give proper orders for the copy of the parts, *we* shall be all ready, at least I will be ready in 8 days . . . but—rehearsals, parts, orders, rehearsals, no rehearsals without parts, no parts without orders, and no orders without my eternal hints, and my never ending letters, since it appears you will not do me the high honour of comming at my house for a quarter of an hour to have a little settling chit-chat. However it may be, I wait your pleasure, noble cousin, and humbly beg for an answer when it may suit your Majesty. Nonsense apart, pray say YES or no . . .

To A Bunn !!!!!!
Esquair!!!!!!

Back in Naples, Malibran repeated *Sonnambula* and, again measuring herself against Pasta, sang *Norma* for the first time:

75

unfortunately no coherent description of her in this latter role survives. It is easy to imagine her charm as the sleep-walking maiden, but less easy to conceive how she coped with the simplicity and restraint necessary to a Norma. With a signal lack of tact, she chose the part for her début in La Scala in 1834. The Milanese identified the part with Pasta, and one of a lunatic fringe of 'Pastists' threatened her life. Pasta herself was in the audience, and was greeted with ferociously partisan applause. Even the fearless Maria Malibran was overcome with nerves, and the 'Casta Diva' *scena* was disastrous, although she redeemed herself later in the evening. After the second performance, there was what the Italians call a *furore*, and the police were called in to evacuate the theatre. A huge crowd escorted the prima donna back to the Visconti *palazzo*, where an orchestra and chorus waited to present a cantata in her honour. The next major addition to Malibran's repertory was Leonore in *Fidelio*, a role associated with her Teutonic counterpart, Wilhelmine Schröder-Devrient, and in which Malibran indulged her leanings towards melodrama, flourishing two pistols at the climax of the dungeon scene, where everybody else flourished one. Back in Milan she sang the eponymous heroine of Donizetti's *Maria Stuarda*, which was not a success, despite the high possibilities of Mary's situation. She was 'voiceless' at the première, and the censors considered the subject-matter sufficiently inflammatory to demand debilitating cuts. The opera seemed quite dead after its first five performances, but was successfully resuscitated in the 1960s as a vehicle for Sutherland, Caballé, Sills, Janet Baker, *et al.*

Malibran never created a major repertory role, and it is sad to realize how much of a unique talent was spent on second- or third-rate music. Her last new assumption is a case in point. *The Maid of Artois*, a bastardized version of the Manon Lescaut story, was written for Drury Lane by Balfe, the only nineteenth-century English opera composer of European standing. It contains pretty melodies and an action-packed plot, both designed to show off the prima donna, but it hardly extended or challenged Malibran as *Norma* did Pasta—except that she needed a pint of porter, variously conveyed to her while on stage, in order to get through a last scene which required a top E and a trill on a high C!

In the middle of 1836 Malibran, now legally married to Bériot, was pregnant, not for the first time—her one surviving child, brought up by Malibran's mother, became a pianist and died in

1914. She nevertheless accepted an invitation to an aristocratic hunting party in Surrey, and, with customary bravado, insisted on riding the roughest mount in the stable. In a truly hideous accident, she was flung head first to the ground after her foot had slipped through the stirrup. A superficial recovery was followed by bursts of manic depression, blinding headaches, and an intensification of activity in all spheres. Bériot had discouraged her from the expedition in the first place and she never dared tell him the true origin of her malaise. Her last months were spent in Belgium, her nominal home, France, and England. She finally collapsed in Manchester after a concert in which she had insisted on singing an encore, and died in the Mosley Arms Hotel a few days later. She was twenty-eight.

A Romantic for any age, Malibran had been admired by Verdi, Liszt, Rossini, Chopin, Mendelssohn, Hans Christian Andersen, and George Sand. Fifty thousand people lined the streets of Manchester to watch her funeral cortège; Alfred Bunn recited his own commemorative ode from the stage of Drury Lane:

> Enchantress of the nations! She who breathed
> The sweetest notes that ever music wreathed . . .

and Alfred de Musset wrote some finer, if untranslatable lines:

> *C'est ton âme, Ninette, et ta grandeur naïve*
> *C'est cette voix du coeur qui seule au coeur arrive*
> *Que nul autre, après toi, ne nous rendra jamais . . .*

It is difficult not to feel a touch of scepticism after this brief and magnificent explosion—can she really have been that good? But the question is pointless. Like Nijinsky, Rachel, or Paganini, the myth of the personal phenomenon of Malibran is more important than a balanced, comparative, and historical assessment of her achievement as an opera singer. 'If life is not a crime, it is at least an expiation,' she mysteriously told Ernest Legouvé, and perhaps the lingering emotion on pondering personalities such as Malibran's is a sense of pity for the harsh and inexorable hand that they were dealt, with no choice but to exhaust their lives through their genius, denied the joys of being ordinary.

The Garcia dynasty, however, had further to go, and lasted into the twentieth century. Garcia's son, also called Manuel, died in 1906 at the age of a hundred and one. After some unsuccessful appearances in opera, he became one of the greatest of all singing teachers, his pupils including Jenny Lind and Mathilde Marchesi, who herself taught Melba. His first wife and their son were also successful opera singers. The Garcia method, as laid out in *Traité complet de l' art du chant* (1847) is still actively respected today, and is notable for its scientific approach to the physiology of voice production. He also invented the laryngoscope, a mirror apparatus which allows the throat to be observed in action.

His sister Pauline, thirteen years younger than Maria and born in 1821, was one of the most remarkable women of the nineteenth century, a prima donna of intelligence rather than instinct, and a woman who, like George Eliot or George Sand, her closest female friend, triumphed over the irregularities of her personal position to become a social figurehead and an embodiment of women's noblest potential. George Sand told her, 'You are the priestess of the ideal in music and your mission is to spread it, to make it understood, and to reveal to the recalcitrant and ignorant the True and the Beautiful.' That she was to some extent able to fulfil this high injunction was not due to extraordinary vocal resources, and her career in opera lacked the hysterical *éclat* of Malibran's. Her advantages were the Victorian belief in the religion of art, and a repertory far more sophisticated and interesting than her sister's had been.

Pauline Viardot-Garcia came to consciousness in Mexico, whither, in 1826, her father had taken the family on an operatic tour after their fateful visit to New York. When civil war broke out, the Garcias tried to escape the country, but they were waylaid by brigands who robbed Garcia of the entire takings of the trip. They made their way back to Paris and the patronage of the now wealthy Maria. By the age of seven, Pauline could play the piano well enough to accompany her father's pupils, and herself eventually became a pupil of the young Liszt, with whom she was infatuated —perhaps the only occasion in her life when she fell out of emotional control. She also took singing lessons from her mother after Garcia's death, but rarely came into close contact with her peripatetic sister, who was none the less intensely interested in her burgeoning talent. After Maria's death, her considerable gift as a pianist fell into the background as she was inevitably pushed forward as Malibran's younger sister and heir. The roles she initially took reflect this—Desdemona, Rosina, Amina, Norma, even the old hag in *Il Matrimonio Segreto*, among them: all Malibran vehicles—and they were not well suited to her. Chorley tells the familiar story:

> It was to be felt that nature had given her a rebel to subdue, not a vassal to command in her voice. From the first she chose to possess certain upper notes which must needs be fabricated, and which never could be produced without the appearance of effort. By this despotic exercise of will it is possible that her real voice —a limited mezzo soprano—may have been weakened.

She would probably have had a steadier career if she had not taken on such parts. But as it was, Gounod, who was later in love with her, found her at thirty 'already nearing her end, and singing out of tune all the time'. The longing among mezzos to extend their range upwards into the more glamorous and lucrative soprano bracket is a common operatic phenomenon: with mixed results, Christa Ludwig, Shirley Verrett and Grace Bumbry have recently essayed such an ascent. It is a tricky business, and as with everything about vocal technique there are few fixed rules. Every voice has its own quirks, variabilities, 'dead' notes, and unlikely strengths. Plenty of mezzos can reach the odd B♭ or even C happily, even if they are not comfortable singing in the accepted soprano *tessitura*. But Pauline Viardot was one who later realized that she had made a mistake, and told one of her pupils, 'Don't do as I did. I wanted to sing everything, and I spoilt my voice.'

Yet her early years were successful enough. Some found her not quite as forthright as they wished, and she was once, interestingly, criticized as following 'psychological inspirations derived from novels of the day'. One of her more unlikely admirers was the elderly Duke of Wellington, who commented on her London début, 'The impulse is in her to be great, and great she will be, whoever lives to see it.' He was magnificently right.

Rossini was the first composer to treat the possibilities of the dramatic coloratura mezzo, and was graced with two fine exemplars of the type—the hideously pock-marked Benedetta Pisaroni and, later, Marietta Alboni—Marilyn Horne is their phenomenal modern counterpart. Pauline Viardot extended this spectacular but limited repertoire into the style of French Grand Opera, and the inspiration of her art was a factor in the creation of such mezzo parts as Dalila in Saint-Saëns's *Samson et Dalila*, Cassandra and Dido in Berlioz's *Les Troyens*, and perhaps even Carmen. More directly, she worked with Meyerbeer, the most successful opera composer of the period. However eclipsed now, Meyerbeer remains a pivotal figure in the evolution of operatic form. He and his librettist Eugène Scribe wrote unashamedly for the rich bourgeois audience of the rampantly commercial and cynical society we know from Balzac's novels. This audience wanted something showy and effective, something Romantic—but only in a reassuring way. It wanted value for money and immediate gratification, not an art for connoisseurs. The Italian audiences always had a genuine interest in music and singing: in Paris they wanted a superior floor show, a good evening out, exciting without being disturbing. Auber's *La Muette de Portici* (1828) and Rossini's *Guillaume Tell* (1829) established the conventions which Meyerbeer so adroitly exploited. The plots are historical, usually on themes of the Middle Ages or the wars of religion, and the action is vivid and heroic. Variety was very important, hence the frequency of ballets, tableaux, processions of clergy or royalty, crowd scenes, and scenic *coups de théâtre*: the Triumph Scene in Verdi's *Aida* is a late and famous example of this, while Meyerbeer came up with a midnight orgy of ghostly nuns in *Robert le Diable*, the Massacre of St Bartholomew in *Les Huguenots*, and a shipwreck in *L'Africaine*. Musically, extended arias play less part than ensembles; orchestral effect and harmonic gimmick replace sustained or developed melody; a degree of sheer noise, bright orchestration, and five long acts (it is almost impossible to perform a complete Meyerbeer grand opera in under five hours) made up the slick and glittering package. The sensational success of the lurid *Robert le Diable* in 1831 established Meyerbeer's supremacy after the premature retirement of Rossini, and although the Théâtre-Italien continued to fill seats with the older Italian pieces, Meyerbeer at the Opéra itself in rue Le Peletier made everything else look and sound a little *passé*.

What did such vulgarity offer to an artistry and sensibility as refined as Pauline Viardot's? Chiefly, vocal lines far less taxing than Italian opera and the histrionic possibilities of sophisticated melodrama, with its wide range of extreme emotions emerging in striking situations. Viardot seized on this new repertoire, playing leading roles in *Robert le Diable* and *Les Huguenots* as well as Rachel, who dies in a boiling cauldron, in Halévy's *La Juive*. In 1849, at

Meyerbeer's particular request, she gave the first performance of Fides (who meets her end in the conflagration of the palace of Münster) in his *Le Prophète*. Playing this simple burgher woman, filled with maternal love yet forced to renounce her son and, at one point, forced to beg for alms, Viardot was found deeply affecting. It was in such parts that she had her most undisputed success at the major operatic centres. In Italian opera she was overshadowed by Grisi, and during the early 1840s, when she was in her vocal prime, she performed mostly in Berlin, Dresden, and St Petersburg, where she was idolized. But perhaps her finest role was Orfeo, or Orphée in the French version, edited by Berlioz, of Gluck's opera. The melancholy and simple dignity of the piece was balm to the truly musical public of Paris, sated by a long diet of Meyerbeerian excess, and in Viardot's sensibility it found a noble interpreter. Between 1859 and 1861 she sang the part over 150 times. Dickens went to one performance and found himself in her dressing-room afterwards, his face 'disfigured with crying'. Chorley here found her shortcomings an advantage:

> The peculiar quality of Madame Viardot's voice—its unevenness, its occasional harshness and feebleness, consistent with tones of the gentlest sweetness—was turned by her to account with rare felicity, as giving the variety of light and shade to every word of soliloquy, to every appeal of dialogue. A more perfect and honeyed voice might have recalled the woman too often to fit with the idea of the youth. Her musical handling of so peculiar an instrument will take place in the highest annals of art.

It was as Orphée that she made her last operatic appearance, in Weimar in 1870. Berlioz describes her interpretation in some detail: by modern standards of Neo-classical style, it sounds rather frenzied. She sang 'J'ai perdu mon Eurydice' at first in a slow tempo, 'then after the adagio "Mortel Silence! Vaine esperance!" in *sotto voce* (*pianissimo*, with a trembling voice, choked with a flood of tears); she finally took up the theme in a more animated tempo, withdrawing from the body of Eurydice, beside which she had been kneeling, and rushing away with mad despair towards the other side of the stage, the very picture of frenzy in her outcries and sobs.'

Pauline Viardot's latter years are full of musical novelty. She was the first London Azucena in Verdi's *Il Trovatore* (a part modelled on Meyerbeer's Fides) and sang his Lady Macbeth in Dublin—

cruel stuff for even a voice of steel, and she transposed almost all the music down, a frequent practice of the time. Then there was a revival of Gluck's *Alceste*, Gounod's first opera *Sapho* (the title-role written for her), a concert première of extracts from Berlioz's masterpiece *Les Troyens* in which she sang Cassandra, and a private recital with an audience of two, one of them Berlioz, of the newly composed Love Duet from *Tristan und Isolde*, Wagner taking the part of Tristan: an outstandingly unsuccessful occasion. Finally, in 1870, she gave the first performance of Brahms's Alto Rhapsody.

Parallel to all this activity was a personal life of some complexity. Throughout she was supported by the necessary streak of blinkered selfishness in her relationships. For all her fascination, she does not seem to have had any of her sister's desperate warmth, and in the name of her mission to art she was capable of using people without giving much back. She personally knew almost every name of musical, literary, and artistic distinction of the mid-nineteenth century. Romantic love seems never to have overcome her: Alfred de Musset found his passion for her unrequited, and the lovesick Gounod was only flirted with; Berlioz had one of his brief obsessions for her, but was ultimately disappointed at her coldness. She played the game skilfully. On the advice of George Sand, who was worn down by her unsatisfactory affair with Chopin, she had married in 1840 Louis Viardot, then impresario of the Théâtre-Italien. He was middle-aged, level-headed, and reliable, a man of principle and patience, who provided the calm and stable conditions in which her art could best flourish. The marriage survived even the extraordinary intrusion of Ivan Turgenev, the most persistent of Pauline Viardot's admirers. He first fell in love with her in St Petersburg, and through his mediation she introduced Russian music to the West: later in her career she made a speciality of Russian songs, and Tchaikovsky wrote 'None but the lonely heart' for her. Another happy side-effect of the relationship is the play *A Month in the Country*, to some extent inspired by the situation with Gounod, of whom Turgenev was wildly and unjustifiably jealous: Pauline may be seen as Natalya, Viardot as Islayev, Turgenev as Rakitin, and Gounod as the callow young tutor Beliaev.

Turgenev followed her back to France and remained in love with her for the rest of his life. He and Viardot became great friends, and their last years were spent *à trois*: the two men died within a few months of each other. It is perfectly possible that, although

Turgenev and Pauline frequently lived under the same roof, they never had any sort of physical relationship. It would be equally plausible to assume that one of her children was his, and she brought up his illegitimate daughter in her own household. Pauline destroyed most of her significant letters to him, and Turgenev's surviving correspondence is ambiguous. One moment he addresses her respectfully as his 'dearest beloved, best friend'; the next he is more extravagant: 'My God, I could lay my whole life, like a carpet, under your dear feet, which I kiss a thousand times.' Shortly before he died in 1883 he cried out that she surpassed Lady Macbeth in her wickedness. Henry James, who visited the Viardot *salon*, wrote that 'she has made him her property'; Flaubert branded him as 'a man in leading-strings'.

Pauline Viardot worked on. From 1863 onwards, she cut back on her operatic appearances, singing only in concerts or small provincial opera houses and basing herself for some years in Baden-Baden. She taught, played the piano or organ, composed operettas (some to librettos by Turgenev) and songs to Russian texts. Most important she continued to patronize younger composers, including Brahms, Saint-Saëns (who characterized her voice as 'not velvet or crystal ... but bitter-sweet oranges'), Massenet, and Fauré. She died in 1910, in the Paris of Proust and the Ballets Russes.

If Pauline Viardot was one of the major exceptions, then Giulia Grisi (1811–69) fulfilled the popular archetype and proved the rule. She was imperious, exacting, and devious: if she liked you as she did the English impresario Mapleson, she could be 'most obliging: full of good nature'. Others found her 'irritable and ambitious'. The young Queen Victoria adored her, but was upset when her singing teacher Lablache, Grisi's colleague, expressed reservations: 'I do not think he quite *likes* her,' the Queen admitted to her journal. Lablache also pointed out the bad habit she had of swallowing before starting a *roulade*, 'a habit she has contracted from fear of failing'. This was a small flaw, however, in a strong and true dramatic soprano voice which had no need of the elaborate faking cultivated by Pasta and Malibran. And if Grisi lacked their interpretive genius and musicality, she had a compensating stamina and reliability. Chorley witnessed all her major assumptions and described her voice as

... rich, sweet, equal throughout its compass of two octaves ... without a break, or a note which had to be managed [viz. produced by means of some acquired trick], capable of any required violence, of any advisable delicacy ... I have never tired of Madame Grisi during five-and-twenty years: but I have never been, in her case, under one of those spells of intense enjoyment and sensation which makes an epoch in life, and which leave a print on memory never to be cancelled by any later attraction, never to be forgotten so long as life and power to receive shall endure.

The implied comparison is with Pasta, who actively encouraged Grisi at the outset. The young Giulia sang with the great prima donna in *Anna Bolena* and as Adalgisa in the first performance of *Norma*—'*Benissima! bene, très bien—pas mal, la piccola,*' Pasta exclaimed in rehearsal, later giving her informal lessons. When in 1832 Grisi reached the Théâtre-Italien in Paris, replacing Malibran who had refused to sing in the city until her marriage to Bériot was ratified, an *aficionado* wrote to Pasta: 'I want to tell you about Madame Grisi, a young and pretty woman who imitates you as much as she can in several of your favourite roles, *Semiramis, Anna Bolena*, etc. etc. Costume, deportment, gesture, intonation—she takes them from you, except the inspiration which gives life to it all.' Or, as Chorley put it, 'Madame Grisi has been remarkable for her cleverness in adopting the effects and ideas of others more thoughtful and originally inventive than herself.'

Giulia Grisi came from another remarkable musical family. Her father was a Napoleonic general who lived to over a hundred, but her aunt Josephina Grassini was a noted contralto of Mrs Billington's time, Pasta's teacher, and rumoured to be, at various times, the mistress of Napoleon, Wellington, and Castlereagh; her elder sister Giuditta had a brief but considerable career as a mezzo; while her younger cousin Carlotta, who also began as a singer, became one of the greatest ballerinas of the nineteenth century, the lifelong love of Théophile Gautier, and creator of the role of Giselle in 1841. Giulia's early vocal development was rapid and unproblematic—hers was clearly a naturally strong and facile instrument. She made her début in Bologna at seventeen and at the age of nineteen was put under contract to La Scala. When her reputation increased, she broke her terms there on the grounds that she had been a minor when the agreement had been made. She never sang in Italy again, but shrewdly—Grisi was almost invariably shrewd—concentrated her efforts on Paris and especially London, where she missed only one season between 1834 and 1861.

Grisi had a regular and imposing beauty which contributed considerably to the effect of her grander portrayals, further enhanced by the bearing of her tenor partner Mario. Gautier was reminded of '*un tableau de Titian ou Giorgione*'. In the 1830s she was a figure of some notoriety, and bore an illegitimate child to Lord Castlereagh's son. Her marriage to an indolent French nobleman was brief and unsuccessful. She was unable to divorce him, indeed she had to pay him an annual allowance of £2,000, a fact which infuriated her. '*Porco infame*,' 'infamous pig,' she later exclaimed in a letter to her lawyer: 'Let the devil take him, I'll not give him another penny.' Her subsequent personal union with Mario was one of the most glamorous matches of the time. They became matinée idols or, one might say, the operatic Laurence Olivier and Vivien Leigh. They made a devoted couple, despite Grisi's outbursts of irrational jealousy over the possibility that some member or other of the female opera public might be paying Mario untoward attention.

The most bizarre of his fans was one Miss Giles from Gloucestershire, a lady of private means who had already made a name for herself by following the actor Charles Kean around. She was very ugly and fantastically dressed. Grisi detested her, decided that she was casting the evil eye, and referred to her as 'the Skull'. 'There she sits,' wrote a newspaper columnist, 'alone in her spacious box, dressed in the costliest of lace and brocades, perfectly indifferent to everything but Mario . . . lorgnettes are levelled towards the place where she sits from all parts of the house . . . but she heeds nobody, and when not looking over the fringe of her splendid fan . . . at the object of her burning passion, she sits like a sphinx.' She went to the incredible length of stowing away on the ship that took Grisi and Mario to America in 1854, and was discovered by Mario under a tarpaulin over which he had tripped, a story one imagines Grisi found highly implausible. In Paris she mortally embarrassed Mario during a performance of *Faust* by showering him with rose petals from her box, thus causing hysterical mirth among the rest of the audience. A few days after this, a lamp in her hotel room fell over and she was burnt to death: Mario paid his respects to the corpse.

Grisi and Mario's domestic life was otherwise dull and blameless, passing between the fabulous Villa Salviati above Florence, in which they were visited by heroes of the Risorgimento, a French *château*, and a series of West London mansions. Their commitments included their three daughters, Grisi's fanatical homeopathy ('Her medicine chest,' reports Mapleson, 'held, besides orgeat and other syrups, brandy, whisky, hollands, port-wine, and bottled stout'), little society, charitable donations, and regular habits—all very good for the preservation of the voice, and all run on staunchly Anglophile lines. Mario himself was the son of a general and lineal descendant of the Borgias. Born a Cavaliere di Candia, he only became a singer to escape financial embarrassment, but was so ashamed of tainting his family name with the stain of the stage that professionally he used only one of his many Christian names. Like Grisi, he had a naturally strong voice and only suffered from never having to try very hard. He was the most successful tenor of the period, despite his nonchalant manner and chain-smoking of cigars. In her petty and vicious campaign against Pauline Viardot, he served as Grisi's key weapon.

In the Italian dramatic repertory—a Norma so convincing that tenors singing opposite her took her fury personally, Semiramide, Anna Bolena, Donizetti's Lucrezia Borgia—Grisi was unrivalled. If she lacked what Chorley called 'the originating faculty', she had sterling vocal equipment which rarely let her down and a fine stage presence. Her reputation and popularity were immense: she even had the great Mario as well. But she could still not tolerate Pauline Viardot and her success in the new operas of Meyerbeer. She herself failed in the modern repertory, and made something of a fool of herself in *Le Prophète*—but then Viardot could not have sung Lucrezia Borgia. Matters reached a head in the first season of the Royal Italian Opera at Covent Garden. Pauline Viardot had been kept out of London by Grisi between 1839 and 1848, for she had never liked the idea of Malibran's brilliant sister. But Viardot returned in the latter year to sing Amina in *La Sonnambula*—a poor choice, both because it was not a role which gave her much scope, and because it had been one of Grisi's favourites in her younger days. Mario was due to sing opposite her, but he was suddenly and inexplicably withdrawn, leaving Viardot with an inexperienced and unrehearsed tenor. The same tactic was repeated on the evening of Viardot's benefit performance. *Les Huguenots* was scheduled but it was announced on the morning that Mario was too ill to sing. Grisi, with double-edged graciousness, offered to appear that night in *Norma*, should the management agree to the substitution. What she meant, of course, was that she would be prepared to steal Viardot's evening by taking the title-role, leaving Viardot to the secondary position as Adalgisa. Viardot outpointed her: thanking Grisi for her kindness, she announced that, if all else failed, she would be happy to sing Norma herself to Grisi's Adalgisa, but that she had found a tenor who could stand in for Mario. *Les Huguenots* was normally sung in Italian, and the tenor only knew the part in French, so Viardot re-learnt her every line by curtain up. The excitement was intense, and the performance was a complete triumph for the tenor and for Viardot. And yet Grisi tried again in 1850, pulling Mario out of the London première of *La Juive* at the ninth hour. Viardot was ready with another substitute tenor, the performance was again a triumph. Grisi, sitting prominently in a box, was furious.

This is not the only story of Grisi's machinations. From the mid 1830s to 1840s she was the ring-leader of a tight little cabal of singers who united themselves to extort the maximum amount of money out of managements and exert a self-perpetuating stranglehold. This quartet, also known as the *vieille garde*, consisted of Grisi, Mario, the baritone Tamburini, and the great *buffo* bass Lablache: the tenor Rubini and the coloratura soprano Fanny Persiani were also involved. The central quartet were most famous for Donizetti's *Don Pasquale*, of which they gave the first performance in 1843; Bellini's *I Puritani* was their other major vehicle. The manager Benjamin Lumley bitterly describes how they announced 'their determination to resist every effort of the director to vary the composition of the phalanx, by declaring that not one of them would engage singly—in other words that M. Laporte, then manager of Her Majesty's Theatre, must agree to take them collectively or not at all. The *prima donna*, who was looked upon as the "head and front" of the coalition, had confessed as much to the manager, although she declared that she had reserved herself the right of acting separately when she chose.' In 1840 Laporte refused to engage Tamburini. He was a brave man—the defection of four such stars could have been as disastrous to his receipts as their collective presence was to seat prices. A modern equivalent might be a hypothetical team of Callas, di Stefano, Gobbi, and Christoff: no one could complain about mediocre standards, but the situation was clearly undesirable. At the end of one Tamburini-less perform-ance, a riot took place, vividly reported by Dick Doyle in his Journal of 1840:

> There was a party of noblemen in the omnibus box who, with Prince G[eorge] of Cambridge (so says the paper) were the ringleaders. The orchestra attempted to play the overture to the ballet but was quite smothered in the deafening cries for Tamburini and Laporte ... Mr Laporte at length made his appearance amid a most desperate volley of screams which the majority of the house cried down every time he tried to speak. Others called out 'No Tamburini, no intimidation'. The manager in the mean time was carrying on a conversation with the occu-pants of the omnibus box, but did not seem to come to a satisfactory conclusion. He retired, the drop curtain rose, and the dancers appeared but just as the orchestra struck the first note, one of the most terrible outcries that were ever given vent to rang through the house. The manager was again forced to appear and attempted to make a speech, but his voice was drowned amid the cries of 'Engage Tamburini!' 'Yes or no. No conditions.' This game was kept up till one o'clock when Mr Laporte, having promised that he would engage Tamburini, the whole pit and the boxes that conveniently could do it, rushed simultaneously onto the stage to the great bodily fear of any of the corps de ballet who happened to be there, and waved their hats in token of their triumph.

When Lumley himself became manager he took a harder line, but Grisi and Mario did not toe it, and eventually defected to Covent Garden.

Grisi did get her come-uppance, in the grand style. She made an over-long business of giving up, and came to grief. Her 'fare-wells' began in 1849: by 1860 *The Times* music critic was asking, 'Does the word *last* bear an esoteric idiom in operatic parlance other than that ordinarily accepted?' In 1861 she sang in *Don Giovanni* with the young Adelina Patti, and in *Norma*, *Les Huguenots*, and *Lucrezia Borgia*. J. E. Cox was present at her farewell concert in the same year and reported her humiliation:

On retiring from the orchestra, after a peculiarly cold reception —as unkind as it was inconsiderate, seeing what the career of this remarkable woman had been—there was not a single person at the foot of the orchestra to receive her or to accompany her to her retiring-room! I could imagine what her feelings must have been ... I could not resist the impulse of preceding her, without obtruding myself upon her notice, and opening the door of the retiring-room for her ... Her look as I did this and she passed out of sight is amongst the most painful of my Recollections, for it uttered more than words could speak, how sweet that small drop of consolation had been to her at such a moment.

But as if this was not enough, she returned five years later and gave one final performance of *Lucrezia Borgia*, which descended to farce:

At the end of the first act ... Mdme Grisi, accustomed to the stage of the Royal Italian Opera, remained too far in front ... and when the curtain came down the Lucrezia of the evening found herself kneeling on the ground ... and cut off by the curtain from the stage behind. This placed the unfortunate singer in a ludicrous and, indeed, painful position; for she had a stiffness in one of her knees, and was unable on this occasion to rise without the help of the stage attendants.

After recourse to homeopathy, she finished with only the added indignity of failing to reach a high A. She was played out, and died of cholera in Berlin three years later, on her way to join Mario in St Petersburg.

# 3

# *The Victorian Nightingales*

It is important to remember, especially in a book of this nature, that opera is not simply a matter of outstanding personalities. The prima donna exists only as institutions allow her to exist, be they state-subsidized opera houses or commercial recording companies. And, of all theatrical forms, opera has the most complex and misunderstood sociology. Its public image has long been dominated by the idea of an entertainment for a moneyed and philistine élite which sits through the evening in a state of near-coma or incessant fidgeting, and which only comes to life when fighting its way to the bar in the interval. Above all, opera is very expensive, its prices inflated by the tyranny of the star foreign singer.

There is more than a little truth in this, but it is a partial and distorting simplification. Before we look at a strain of prima donna peculiarly suited to the Victorian sensibility, it will be as well to give a rough picture of the nature of the business we are dealing with in an age which saw a revolution in communications, spanning the introduction of the railway and the gramophone. We concentrate on London, not only because it is the best-documented operatic centre of the nineteenth century, but also because it is the most interesting, inasmuch as it never knew the public or court subsidy that existed in Europe. Private capital and public demand were the twin pillars between which the prima donna balanced herself, and there were plenty of moments, then as now, when the entire structure looked ready to collapse.

The second King's Theatre (called Her Majesty's after 1837), built after a fire had destroyed the first in 1789, was the centre of opera in London. Drury Lane and Covent Garden both held occasional seasons, and Drury Lane was particularly noted for its English opera, but the King's was the regular opera and ballet house. It was a little larger than the present Covent Garden and rather smaller than La Scala, probably holding about 2,500 people.

Its early years were beset by endless legal wranglings over leases and sub-leases, constant changes of management, and eventual closure. The notion that an entrepreneur could make large sums of money out of opera was current, but there was little evidence of this. Only with the arrival of a publisher/bookseller, John Ebers, in 1821 was any sort of order restored, and in his seven-year stint as tenant-manager even he lost £44,000 and was declared bankrupt. Ebers concentrated on improving the standard of ensemble and production, sticking out against the more outrageous of Catalani's financial demands—Pasta, who at £2,365 for about twenty performances, did not come cheap, was nevertheless better value.

After Ebers came a French actor, Pierre Laporte, another man of artistic acumen and financial incompetence, who was at one point imprisoned for debt. His release was engineered by a young Jewish solicitor, Benjamin Lumley, who then became Laporte's right-hand man and successor. Lumley was tough over money and contracts, and by 1845 had re-established the theatre's liquidity, bringing it out of litigation for the first time since the 1780s. Unfortunately, he lacked much musical initiative, playing safe in terms of repertory and giving more attention to the ballet. In 1847 a permanent company, the Royal Italian Opera, was established at Covent Garden, taking Lumley's musical director and the *vieille garde* (with the exception of Lablache), with whom Lumley's relations had progressively deteriorated. The defection was a blow, a relief, and a challenge to Lumley: he found his trump card in Jenny Lind. When she abruptly retired, he seized on Henriette Sontag, who made a triumphal comeback. Lumley was offered the management of La Scala, which he refused, although he did make a brief and disastrous incursion on Paris. In 1852, he boldly tried to turn Her Majesty's into a joint-stock company, thus relieving himself of some of the financial burden, but his plans were thwarted by legal complications. A lean season followed Sontag's death and the scandalous default of a German prima donna, Johanna Wagner. Musical standards had fallen irreparably. In 1853 the theatre was left empty and it only reopened in 1856 after Covent Garden, under the management of Frederick Gye, had burnt down after a masked ball. Lumley had handed over the lease to Lord Ward for safe-keeping, and Ward assigned Lumley a sub-lease in 1856 to allow a reopening under his management. Despite the new popularity of Verdi, the pretty Marietta Piccolomini and the magnificent Therese

Tietjens, Lumley could not raise the arrears of rent, and Ward foreclosed on him: the theatre again went dark in 1858. Then followed the remarkable E. T. Smith, a restaurant owner and lessee of Drury Lane, later a tin merchant, who, it was said, could not tell the difference between 'La Troviata' and 'Il Traviatore': he, in his turn, delegated to Colonel James Mapleson, a violinist, unsuccessful tenor, and, most interestingly, London's first full-time concert agent, who sought out and signed up singers for both Lumley and Gye. Mapleson took over Her Majesty's in 1862 and through this and other ventures dominated the English and American operatic scene for the next twenty-five years. His long-serving musical director Luigi Arditi described his success thus:

> I have known prime donne enter his office infuriatedly, vowing that they would not depart from his presence without a 'little cheque' or hard cash, and these same irate ladies would sally forth, after waiting his leisure for some considerable time, with their angry looks transformed to absolute serenity . . . there never lived the man whose suave, gentle art in calming the irrepressible creditor was more conspicuous or effective.

So much for the prima donnas' *éminences grises*, who wrote their memoirs and articulated their grievances: we know much less about their ultimate paymasters, the public. There were no market research surveys in Victorian England, and we can only guess at the constitution of the audience. An early turning-point was the increase in 1807 of the subscription price of boxes from 180 to 300 guineas. This put them out of the reach of even many of the nobility and meant that boxes were increasingly rented out for single performances only, thus causing a distinct lowering of the general tone. It is interesting to note, in Lumley's memoirs, that the Duke of Wellington sat in the pit in an orchestra stall, not in a box. 'Fop's Alley', as the aisle through the pit was known, remained a prominent feature of the auditorium, even in Lumley's day: 'All that was aristocratic, distinguished, fashionable, or (still more) would-be fashionable, met, swarmed, greeted, babbled in an ever-seething, ever-varying crowd.' But commercial considerations came first, and fashion alone could not keep the opera solvent. There was not enough cultured aristocracy to fill Her Majesty's two-hundred-odd boxes at up to fourteen guineas each, especially after Covent Garden had opened: rich tradesmen had to be made welcome too. Tickets were on sale not only through the box office, but through booksellers who, acting as agents, seem to have bought block bookings at a concessionary price: in 1852, Lumley sold £10,000 worth of seats to a Mr Mitchell. It is safe to say, then, that the mid-nineteenth-century opera audience showed a far wider distribution, socially and geographically, than the narrow metropolitan one of the pre-railway era. Trains and tourism were two salient factors in this—London was a centre of both, particularly after the Great Exhibition of 1851—and Lumley rather snobbishly deplored the alteration:

> The Opera House—once the resort and the 'rendezvous' of the *élite* of rank and fashion, where applause received its direction from a body of cultivated, discriminating 'cognoscenti', and the treasury of which was furnished beforehand by ample subscriptions in reliance upon the provision to be made by the manager —now mainly depends for support upon miscellaneous and fluctuating audiences; audiences composed in great part of persons who, in hurried moments of visits to the metropolis, attend the opera as a kind of quasi-duty, in order to keep pace with the musical chit-chat of the day.

This period also sees the start of labour problems in the opera house: both chorus and orchestra were roused by the spirit of trade unionism. Just before the 1867 conflagration of Her Majesty's the all-male orchestra went on strike against the employment of a female harpist, and in 1861 Mapleson had sacked the entire chorus after they struck over what he called an 'exorbitant claim'. He re-employed more docile Italian immigrants, a practice which continued in London until the First World War. The disparity in salary between the prima donna and everyone else in the establishment must have been thoroughly inflammatory. Pasta's 1827 fee of £2,365 for a summer season is nearly a thousand pounds higher than anyone else's, while some soloists earned as little as £75 or £100. This sounds shocking but it was not necessarily extortionate. A prima donna sang at her market value, relative to her drawing-power. Managers were only too thankful to secure her services and fill the house.

The Victorian prima donna is a frailer and more impressionable creature than her early Romantic counterpart. Compared with the heroic characters of Medea, Norma, Semiramide, or Anna Bolena, the Victorians turned to a more anodyne femininity and to a vocal style which in some ways was a throwback to that of Mrs Billington —pure silvery tone without *vibrato*, firm in intonation but limited in colour and emotional range, with a spectacular top register and an easy coloratura, but nothing in the chest to give out the splendid rage of a Pasta. The parts the 'nightingales' preferred—Zerlina in *Don Giovanni*, Lucia di Lammermoor, Amina in *La Sonnambula*, later Gounod's Juliette and Marguerite in his *Faust*—were those of innocent victims, sweet-tempered, yielding, and duped. They are the virgin maidens of old men's sexual fantasy; in parts such as Marie in Donizetti's *La Fille du Régiment*, Rosina in *Il Barbiere di Siviglia*, or Zerlina, a hint of the little minx gave further spice. In general, they answered the Victorian male culture's obsession with women as ministering angel. The dichotomy between the dramatic singer—a Pasta, Grisi, or Tietjens—and the nightingale is made clear in George Eliot's great novel *Daniel Deronda*, with its two contrasting singers. Mirah Lapidoth is all sweetness and light, with a voice 'not strong enough for opera', while the Alcharisi is a woman of 'desire, will, and choice', who acted as powerfully as she sang.

The development of the maiden or nightingale prima donna was probably much encouraged by the popularity of the Romantic ballet in the 1830s and 1840s. Dancers like Marie Taglioni danced in *La Sylphide* or *Giselle* with the utmost ethereality of movement, swathed in white gauze and illuminated by the new glow of gas lighting. Soft, malleable, a pure object of desire and mystery, they gave the illusion of weightlessness as their male partners scooped them off the ground into exquisite lifts, their point shoes and willowy arms allowing them the same sort of flexibility of manoeuvre as a coloratura technique gave the soprano.

None of the singers in this chapter perfectly fits the stereotype, but none of them contradicts it either. Fanny Persiani (1812–67) may serve as a point of introduction. In 1835, while at the Teatro San Carlo in Naples, Donizetti wrote his most famous 'tragic' opera, *Lucia di Lammermoor*, for her. Lucia is orphaned, fey, and given to feverish imaginings—a far cry from the grand passions of a Norma or Medea. She is easy prey to the manipulations of her ambitious brother, who forces her into a profitable but loveless marriage. Her plighted lover Edgardo interrupts the wedding ceremony and, unaware of the scheming, denounces Lucia, who goes mad, kills her husband and then dies herself after the most popular of all 'mad scenes', in which the voice echoes a flute obbligato and which contains poignant reminiscences of the earlier love duet and other arias. It is a long virtuoso showpiece which can be successfully negotiated by a light voice. With notable exceptions, the role has now largely been appropriated by heavier voices like Callas's or Sutherland's with a wider range of tone, but this was not what the composer wrote for. Persiani's timbre was white and silvery and Lucia is intended to sound girlish, both in her opening *scena* and in the famous sextet with its piping top notes. The role became one of the nightingales' calling-cards. It has opportunities for all the vocal tricks, requires little acting ability beyond conveying a virgin abused, and the situation, rather brutally adapted from a Scott novel, has plenty of atmosphere. Persiani sang Lucia throughout Europe and became identified with it. She was plain and sickly, but a fine musician much appreciated by connoisseurs and admitted by Grisi into the all-powerful *vieille garde*. It was her husband, a composer, who put up much of the initial capital with which the lease of Covent Garden was secretly bought in 1846.

If Persiani lacked charm and grace, these qualities were held in abundance by Henriette Sontag. Her career was a strange one. She was born in 1806, in the proverbial theatrical trunk, her father a *buffo* bass and her mother a provincial actress, neither of them at all respectable. Henriette appeared a few hours after her mother had been on stage in Koblenz, and was christened Gertrud Walpurgis, a name she wisely forgot. After her alcoholic father's death, her mother moved to Prague, where little Henriette played numerous juvenile roles. She entered the Conservatory there, and in 1821 made her adult début to considerable acclaim. From the beginning everything about her was pretty—big blue eyes, pouting little mouth, a demure smile, mild temperament, and a voice sweet, pure, and accurate, backed up by what was probably the soundest technique of her era, Catalani always excluded. The great Neapolitan impresario Barbaia immediately engaged her for his opera house in Vienna, where she sang Mozart and Rossini, and where she was given the title-role in the first performance of Weber's bizarrely plotted opera *Euryanthe*. Amazingly, she also sang in the first performances of Beethoven's Ninth Symphony and *Missa Solemnis*, much to the composer's pleasure—amazingly, because Sontag's was never a very powerful voice and Beethoven is a

8. Maria Malibran, in a drawing by Léon Noel which extraordinarily catches her vulnerability and charm. 9. *above right* Malibran's sister Pauline Viardot as Gluck's Orphée, an interpretation of melancholy passion extolled by Berlioz and Dickens.

10. Grisi at the height of her career as the first true dramatic soprano: the winsome beauty has become handsome and formidable.

11. Therese Tietjens, Grisi's successor in roles like Lucrezia Borgia and Norma, as well as a powerful singer of Verdi.

12. Henriette Sontag, first of the nightingales, engraved in a style popular in the 1820s and 1830s. 13. *above right* A photograph of Jenny Lind taken during her American tour.
14. *right* Adelina Patti, the child prodigy.
15. *below* A postcard of Craig-y-nos, Patti's Welsh castle, now an old people's home.

notoriously awkward vocal composer, who never made the usual concessions to natural limitations of breath or range. It is a considerable tribute to Sontag's underlying strength as a singer that at the age of eighteen she could tackle such music without ruining that sweetness, purity, and accuracy. Sontag also sang Donna Anna in *Don Giovanni* and Semiramide, roles for dramatic soprano, but refused to sing Spontini—none of which adds up to a readily identifiable vocal type. In 1825 she was engaged for the season in Berlin and became the darling of the town. One German writer observed:

> One might put the prize of a hundred ducats on the invention of an adjective that has not been used for Sontag, and none would win the prize. She has been called 'the indescribable, the heavenly, the incomparable, the divine, the universally admired, the matchless, the adorable, the adored, the delicate pearl, the dear Henriette, sweetest of maidens, darling little girl, the heroine of song, divine child, the champion of melody, the pride of Germany, the pearl of opera . . .'

Outside the German-speaking world she had, like Mara, the initial hurdle of prejudice against Teutons singing Latin music. Her success in Paris from 1826 onwards was nevertheless enormous, despite the rival presences of Pasta and, later, Malibran. But there were plenty who found her irritating. Pasta's friend Stapfer wrote to her that 'Even with her fine deportment, pretty figure, charming foot, etc. . . . she [Sontag] somehow finds a way of making herself utterly disagreeable . . . with her simpering and mannerisms . . . no expression—even musical—no verve, no soul, no intelligence.' Doubtless Sontag was not a singer of great emotional range, nor a very impassioned actress, but she embodied the 'nightingale' type to perfection. There was no aggression in her voice, just a fragile artless charm. Put at its bluntest, old men could and did slaver over her, as they slavered over a sexless yet totally 'feminine' ballerina like Taglioni. 'On she carols,' rhapsodized Berlioz, 'higher and higher, like the lark at heaven's gate, so soft, so clear, so wonderfully distinct that, like the silver bell from the altar, it is heard through the pealing organ.' The *Harmonicon* more intelligently noted her trick in florid passages of sacrificing volume so as to keep accuracy: 'She executes *arpeggio* passages with the neatness of a good finger on the pianoforte, and her *staccato* notes are not less finished; they are like drops of sound, each a whole in itself and completely detached; but when playing thus wonderfully on her vocal organ, she abates its power, all such passages being given a *mezza voce*.'

When Malibran came back to Paris from New York, it was Sontag she had to meet and match. She was thunderstruck at the German's accomplishment and, being Malibran, felt that she had to do better. The press was anxious to uncover a deadly rivalry between the two, but, as so often, it is difficult to find any solid evidence for it. They sang together in *Semiramide, Don Giovanni,* and *Tancredi* in both Paris and London, making elaborately deferential gestures to each other when bouquets were thrown. The rivalry, if anywhere, was off-stage. Charles de Bériot, Malibran's second husband, had previously proposed marriage to Sontag and been devastated at her refusal. More insidiously, Sontag's demeanour made her acceptable in high society, whereas Malibran's vehemence often left her *de trop*, much to her chagrin. In London Sontag was courted by the Duke of Devonshire and a caricature of 1829 associated her with Golbourn, the current Chancellor of the Exchequer; in Paris, Sir Walter Scott presented her with a souvenir album filled with literally hundreds of signatures from members of the *beau monde*. 'The Sunday papers,' wrote Chorley, 'told of Dukes dying for her, of Marquises only waiting to offer her their coronets at her feet. Royalty itself was said to mingle in the dance.'

Then from Paris appeared a strange report: Mademoiselle Sontag, having slipped on a cherry stone in her boudoir, had twisted her knee, and would not be appearing in public, either socially or professionally, for a certain period. This kind of story could only mean the embarrassment of pregnancy and Sontag's reputation in polite society plummeted. Malibran was full of righteous indignation, and a touch of glee. 'She has dropped in public favour like a fallen soufflé,' she wrote, 'I am very angry about this, but very angry, for she was very nice.' Sontag lost her baby and returned to the stage looking wan and pale. The question of paternity was endlessly discussed in every *salon*. In 1830 the story came out. Sontag had been 'secretly married' since 1827 to Count Rossi, a young diplomat from the Sardinian court in Turin. She was now to leave the stage and marry Rossi in public—in other words, she had never been married at all. The King of Sardinia had refused to sanction the marriage and three years of negotiation had been necessary to secure his permission, Sontag's retirement being a primary condition. According to Chorley, the King of Prussia helped 'and made his wedding present by bestowing on her a patent of nobility. The daughter of the people was extinct. She had her escutcheon and quarterings and a "von" to her maiden name—as was only befitting one who was henceforth to figure in court circles.'

Over the next twenty-odd years, she made various private or charity appearances in concerts in the cities to which she and her husband were assigned—The Hague, Frankfurt, St Petersburg, and Berlin. She took to the study of composition, and brought out a cantata, *Il Naufragio Fortunato*, for herself and chorus. In St Petersburg she once sang at the court opera for Tsar Nicholas I, but the rebuke from Turin was swift and absolute. In Berlin, she sang duets with the royal princes and princesses of Prussia. Other noble amateur after-dinner singers were eclipsed, and her natural vanity must have been mildly gratified. But Chorley suspected that she was unhappy, bored by the 'regulation nothings' of diplomatic functions and keen to talk about her days as a trouper. The theatre had been her whole life and seven children were not compensation enough. At least she kept her voice alive, and fate was to take its turn.

The next of the nightingales came from an unexpected source— Sweden. She was Jenny Lind, a figure perfectly attuned to the middle-class morality of the age, whose career was the most sensational of the nineteenth century. Above all, she was respectable. She brought pure Protestantism to a profession tainted with Catholicism and made her private conduct part of her public appeal. Nowadays it is difficult not to feel impatience or even suspicion at her thoroughly Victorian narrow integrity. We look for, and find, a degree of hypocrisy in her massively publicized charities, her ecclesiastical connections, her white gowns, and unadorned person. A modern writer, Henry Pleasants, thinks that 'The insignificant, snub-nosed, plain, simply dressed, hesitant, unassuming, poor-little-me, pining for the northern homeland, pure of heart and noble of thought, was the greatest of her roles.' But her contemporaries found her angelic in the purity of her sentiments, and she never failed to say the proper thing. Thus in the middle of her American tour, managed by the ruthless showman Barnum, from which she spun $176,675, the Swedish Nightingale wrote to a friend, 'Few people realise what an inwardly beautiful and quiet life I lead, how infinitely little the world and its vanities have intoxicated my mind! Herring and potatoes, a clean wooden stool and ditto wooden spoon to eat porridge with, would make me happy as a child and set me dancing with joy.'

Jenny Lind's childhood had its share of wooden spoons but little joy. She was born illegitimate in Stockholm in 1820, and never managed to form a stable relationship with her mother, who continued to plague her through her years of fame. Variously farmed out to relations and foster parents, the little girl's natural exuberance and desire for maternal love were never answered. However, at the age of nine, the maid of a ballerina at Stockholm's Royal Opera heard her singing at an open window, and via her mistress arranged for an audition at the Royal Opera School. Despite her mother's distaste for the stage, she was immediately admitted, and from the age of ten sang, danced, and acted in a number of juvenile roles. At seventeen, she sang Agathe in Weber's *Der Freischütz*, soon followed by Lucia, Donna Anna, and Norma, imbuing them all with the soft wan tenderness and pathos which from the first made her acting style so distinctive. The young Wagner was to speak of her 'curious pensive individuality'. She identified herself with her roles in what we would now think of as 'Method' style: 'It seems to me when I act that I feel fully all the emotions of the character I represent. I fancy myself—indeed believe myself—to be in her situation, and I never think of the audience.' Not surprisingly, by the time she was twenty-one her voice was showing signs of being over-taxed: she had already given over four hundred performances in Stockholm. Further tension was caused by the husband of the family with whom she was then lodging. Lind loved both the composer Adolf Lindblad and his wife. She sang his songs and thought of herself as their daughter. But when Lindblad declared his passion for her and hinted at the possibility of a *ménage à trois*, she received a considerable moral shock. The only solution was to leave Stockholm.

In 1841 she made for Paris, to take lessons from Malibran and Viardot's brother, Manuel Garcia. 'Mademoiselle, you have no more voice,' he told her, in what she later described to Mendelssohn as the worst moment of her life. He advised her, literally, to keep her mouth shut for three months. When she came back, he set to work with science, correcting her breathing technique and building up her control of dynamics. He found her hard-working and

intelligent, but doubted her ultimate success. By the standards of
the day she had none of the bearing of a prima donna. Paris was
anathema to her, anyway, and she was desperately lonely. She heard
Grisi and Persiani, and saw Rachel act: 'The difference between
Mlle. Rachel and me,' she wrote back to Sweden,

> is that she can be splendid when angry—but tender she cannot
> be. I am desperately ugly, and nasty too, when I am angry, but
> am better at being tender, I believe. Of course I do not compare
> myself with Rachel. Heaven preserve us. She is infinitely greater
> than poor me!

With Garcia's help, she not only recovered but developed her
instrument. The return to Stockholm was triumphant, and over the
next few years her reputation grew steadily throughout Northern
Europe. In Copenhagen Hans Christian Andersen fell in love with
her, but she would call him only 'dear brother'. He sent her copies
of 'The Ugly Duckling', 'The Emperor's Nightingale', and 'The
Snow Queen', which severally dramatized the position. In Berlin
Meyerbeer treated her like 'the tenderest father' and Henriette
Sontag was deeply impressed ('modesty forbids me to repeat what
she is said to have said'). It was Mendelssohn who came close to
breaking her moral self-possession and her modern biographer
Joan Bulman is convinced that with him 'she found a companionship
deeper and more satisfying than anything she was ever to know for
the rest of her life'. He was happily married, however, and his
manifest influence on her remained musical. He did not live to
write the opera he promised her, but she was the inspiration
for the soprano part in his oratorio *Elijah*, which became the
corner-stone of her repertory in later life and which exploited the
peculiarly beautiful tone of her high F#s.

She had become famous, but she had still not ventured beyond
the secondary opera circuit. The thought of the London–Paris
nexus daunted her, and by 1845, with her customary mixture of
diffidence and arrogance, she was talking about giving up the stage,
with its freight of draughts, fatigue, and nerves. Then began the
Bunn Affair. Alfred Bunn, manager of Drury Lane Theatre, offered
her a not very generous contract for twenty performances in
London. Urged on by Meyerbeer and the British ambassador's
wife, she signed in the interval of a performance, later claiming

that she had been *distrait* and hampered by her lack of English. She then panicked and tried to negotiate an annulment on various grounds. Thanking Mr Bunn for his compliment to her 'trifling talent', she announced that she would not meet London standards: 'I possess neither the personal advantages, the assurance, nor the charlatanism of other *prime donne.*' Moreover—and perhaps this was the real crunch—she could not sing in English as was the custom at Drury Lane. Bunn understandably refused to release her. Some months later, desperate for someone to fill the gap left by the *vieille garde*'s defection to Covent Garden, Lumley entered the fray. After consulting Mendelssohn, she signed a very generous contract worth £4,800 for the season, plus expenses but minus the right to sing in concert anywhere else. Lumley also undertook to settle with Bunn. An equivalent contract with Berlin had been worth about a quarter of this. Then, in a fit of terror and without warning Lumley, she wrote to Bunn and offered him £2,000 if he would release her. Again, he refused. Enormous amounts of publicity were accruing, and London burned not just to hear Lind, but to know whether she was coming at all, and, if so, where she would sing. Chorley had already wearied of her. He was irritated at the 'herald-trumpets' which 'spoke of charities done, in a tone as if charity was the exception not the rule among musical artists'. The long anticipation 'had racked our opera world into a state of fever, and elevated it into a firm faith, moreover, that that which had cost so much trouble to secure must be, indeed, something unspeakably precious'. She delayed her arrival in London to the point at which Lumley had to go to Vienna to collect her—someone had told her that she risked imprisonment should Bunn decide to strike. When she did finally appear in April 1847, she was appalled at the size of the theatre and refused to give Lumley a date for her début. Lumley was beside himself, but the press coverage continued to fuel the romance of the timid Swedish songbird. *Punch* published the lament of Mr Bunn:

> Thy talents I would fain requite
> Though Lumley gives thee more,
> They say thy salary is, per night,
> One six six thirteen four.
> The Haymarket may hear thy strain
> But discord to thy mind

Whispers will come from Drury Lane
Of faithless Jenny Lind.

Finally, she sang, in Meyerbeer's *Robert le Diable*.
Orchestra stalls went for five or six guineas, boxes for twenty. The Queen and Prince Albert led an audience that included the Duke of Wellington, Prince Louis Napoleon, Mendelssohn, and Lablache, as well as the crush of nobility and fashion. Lind was not making her début in a familiar opera, like *La Sonnambula* or *Il Barbiere di Siviglia*. She had chosen the 'modern' music of Meyerbeer, which would be less immediately telling of her technique. But after a superb trill at the end of her first solo, Lablache let forth a stentorian '*brava*', and the rest of the audience followed suit. By the end of the evening the enthusiasm was maniacal, and the Queen herself threw down a bouquet. Chorley sceptically noted that he had 'never seen anyone so composed as Mlle. Lind was on that night . . . the absence and the semblance of emotion, at once, in the midst of such overcoming excitement, were strange.' In the ensuing months she sang in *La Sonnambula*, *La Fille du Régiment*, and the unsuccessful première of Verdi's *I Masnadieri*, her popularity spreading far beyond the ordinary opera audience. Her private virtue was as much praised as her singing. Horses, dogs, dolls, a tulip, a pub, and a whistling kettle took her name in vain. She rode along Rotten Row with the Duke of Wellington and was repeatedly received at court. Bunn meanwhile had instigated legal proceedings against her.

Did her singing justify the fuss? Thackeray found her 'atrociously stupid. I was thinking of something else the whole time she was jugulating away', and he could not wait to get out 'and have a cigar'; J. E. Cox, in his *Musical Recollections*, says little more than that he was 'extremely disappointed'; the columnist 'Fast Man' in *Punch* moaned: 'We have had enough of Jenny Lind. She don't suit us . . . We admire an actress who comes out, and is jolly. Jenny Lind does the gentle, and the interesting, and the angelic. So do young people in a consumption. We call that sort of thing spoony.' This, of course, is just the voice of the artistic philistine, and Chorley is again perhaps the best guide. He paid tribute to what Garcia had nurtured—her extraordinary breath control, glorious top register with its peculiarly beautiful *pianissimo*, and general technical mastery. She was, however, limited in dramatic range to the lyrical and pathetic, and even in the thickening atmosphere of adulation her Norma was considered pallid in a London with living memories of Pasta, and Grisi still in command at Covent Garden. She was inhibited by Italian, which she never pronounced with 'finished clearness'. Chorley also felt that the other side of her creditable 'resolution to offer the very best of her best to her public' was a certain 'over-calculation' in her performances, an excess of earnestness. Yet what finally gave Lind her appeal as a singer was a unique colour in the voice, an unmistakable and recognizable sound, which, like that of Supervia or Lotte Lehmann, immediately evoked a particular personality. Chopin described it as 'a kind of Northern Lights': others babbled of woodland freshness.[1]

After the London season had ended, she went on an extensive tour of the provinces by railway.

Trains not only brought in audiences from outlying parts. They also sent out singers in relative comfort and vastly increased the possibilities of touring schedules. In a comparatively small country like England with relatively good roads the railway made less difference—Catalani had made extensive tours of the English provinces, reaching deep into the West Country. But in Europe and, later, America the effect was revolutionary. The most eccentric of nineteenth-century prima donnas, Ilma di Murska, had her own special view of it. She

> ... never thought it worth while, when she was travelling from some distant place on the continent, to announce that she had started ... Her geographical knowledge, too, was often at fault, and some of the routes—'short cuts' she called them—by which she reached London from Vienna, were of the most extraordinary kind. She had taken a dislike to the railway station at Cologne, where she declared that a German officer had once spoken to her without being introduced; and on one occasion, partly to avoid the station of which she preserved so painful a recollection, partly in order to get to London by a new and expeditious route, she travelled from Vienna to St Petersburg, and from St Petersburg took a boat to Hull, where she arrived just in time to

1 On the subject of the comparison of voices to natural phenomena, Lumley records a friend of his who found that voices he disliked variously conjured up 'snails, stale beer, sour milk, curry powder, rhubarb, mud splashes, and tea leaves from which the water has been strained'.

join my opera company at the representations that I was then giving in Edinburgh. We had not heard of her for weeks, and she came into the dressing-room to find Madame Van Zandt already attired for the part Mdlle di Murska was to have played, that of Lucia. She argued, with some truth, that she was in time for the performance . . . (Mapleson)

The climax of Lind's railway tour was a visit to Norwich where she was invited to stay with Bishop and Mrs Stanley. Cathedral bells pealed to welcome her, and the church establishment was outraged at the liaison of the cloth and the stage, however impeccable the latter in this case was. The spirit of Trollope hovers deliciously over the incident. But for Lind it was a turning-point, consolidating her desire to quit the impure world of the theatre for something with more uplift. She had liked London and the English from the first, but at the Stanleys', in Joan Bulman's words, 'she had come face to face with Victorian ecclesiastical England, and it touched something very deep in her . . . Never had her religious yearnings found such encouragement. With the Stanleys she could discuss her inmost thoughts and feelings.'

Other factors combined to determine her. Late in 1847 her mentor Mendelssohn died, and a few months later Bunn's suit against Lind was decided in favour of Bunn, with the award of £2,500 damages. Considerable and humiliating doubt was cast on Lind's perfect purity of motive, and Bunn later published a book containing the papers of the case. She was also encouraged by Queen Victoria, who expressed approval of her moral delicacy. The Queen loved 'the dear opera' and attended regularly until Prince Albert's death, recording her views in her diary and in letters. She was devoted to Mario and Grisi, but as she wrote to the King of the Belgians, 'Poor Grisi is quite going off, and after the pure angelic voice and extremely quiet, perfect acting of J. Lind, she seems quite *passée*. Poor thing! She is *quite* furious about it, and was excessively impertinent to J. Lind.' Grisi, we know, was at this time engaged in a vendetta against Pauline Viardot, yet it is difficult not to side with her here.

Lind returned to Lumley and Her Majesty's after operatic farewell visits to Stockholm and Berlin. She added Lucia and Elvira in *I Puritani* (very much Grisi's property) to her London repertory and repeated last season's favourites, following it up with another concert tour and another visit to the Stanleys in Norwich, where the proceeds of two of her concerts went towards the establishment of the still extant Jenny Lind Hospital. She dithered over making a straightforward public announcement of retirement from opera, partly because she was anxious not to let Lumley down, but finally made her last appearance, in *Robert le Diable*, in May 1849. She was close to breakdown after over-work and two broken engagements, one to a dull Swede and one to an even duller Englishman whose strict piety even she found hard to take.

At this point she was contemplating complete retirement, when she was approached by an agent of Phineas T. Barnum, the American impresario who until then had specialized in freak shows and was most famous for the exhibition of a midget known as General Tom Thumb. For all his chicanery, Barnum was a genuinely imaginative showman who rightly realized that he could sell Lind as a curiosity, putting a Swedish Nightingale on a par with Tom Thumb and the Feejee Mermaid. He knew nothing about music and had never heard her sing, but what signified was his command over American credulity and the railroad. The money he offered her was a fortune in itself, enough for a lifetime of that favourite Victorian combination, capital and charity. An advance of $187,500 was deposited in a London bank and Lind consented. She would sing only in concert, retaining complete control over her repertory and associates.

Barnum was the first impresario to exploit the value of advance newspaper publicity and he personally propagated a number of stories to herald her arrival. It was said that she had 'changed all men's ideas of music as Bacon's system revolutionised philosophy'; that her primly dressed hair disguised the fact that she had no ears; that she had secretly married the Duke of Devonshire. When she actually arrived in New York, huge crowds gathered at the harbour: cheers, serenades, bouquets, flags, and speeches were all carefully stage-managed. The campaign worked triumphantly, and in the ensuing fever for tickets Barnum decided to auction seats for the first concert—bidding reached up to $225. Then there was the merchandising spin-off, as commemorated in a doggerel song of the time:

> Yes, all is Jenny Lind now,
> In ev'ry shop she's found;

Jenny Lind you get there retail
By the yard, quart, pint, or pound.
We've Jenny Lind shirt collars,
And round my neck—Oh fie!
I've fastened lovely Jenny Lind,
A charming op'ra tie.

Under Barnum's efficient management Lind went on to sing a total of ninety-five concerts throughout the eastern and southern states. The tour is a fascinating prototype of the high-pressure, high-profit exercises of later years, where an unheard prima donna was sold on massive and systematic 'pre-publicity'. Barnum grossed a total of over half a million dollars *after* he had paid Lind's fees and was a happy man, but for her the strain and irritation was ceaseless.

Conditions were often uncomfortable: in Madison, Indiana, she was even required to sing in an abattoir. As a sympathetic journalist recorded, she had to receive a constant flow of visitors every day, starting with

... the lady beggars, who, in some instances, have 'put the screws on her' ... To such unexamined and unexpected applications, Miss Lind has usually offered twenty or thirty dollars, as the shortest way to be left to herself. In almost every instance, she has had this sum returned to her, with some reproachful and disparaging remark, such as 'We did not expect this pittance from you!' 'Excuse us, we came for a donation, not for alms' ... With one or two such visitors, on the morning we speak of, were mingled applicants for musical employment; passionate female admirers who had come to express their raptures to her; a dozen ladies with albums; one or two with things they had worked for her, for which, by unmistakable tokens, they expected diamond rings in return; one who had come indignantly to know why a note containing a poem had not been answered; and constant messages meantime from those who had professional and authorized errands requiring answers ... This sort of 'audience' lasted at Miss Lind's rooms all day. To use her own expression, she was 'torn to pieces'—and it was by those whom nothing would keep out. A police force would have protected her, but, while she habitually declined the calls and attentions of fashionable society, she was in constant dread of driving more humble claimants from her door.

It is scarcely surprising that reports of the Swedish Nightingale's brusque wilfulness and peremptory bad temper filtered out.

After she and Barnum had amicably terminated their arrangements, Lind resumed a less exhausting schedule, but the novelty was wearing off. Without Barnum's tough tactics, her image became tarnished and receipts plummeted. The situation was exacerbated by the man she married in Boston, Otto Goldschmidt, a short and serious German Jew, nine years younger than Lind, who had been a pupil of Mendelssohn's. He had no glamour or publicity value whatsoever, except as 'a model of virtue, industry and domesticity' (thus did his wife describe him to a friend), and the way in which his second-rate pianism was blatantly pushed forward at every Lind concert infuriated audiences. For his part Goldschmidt simply did what he was told, serving his wife with a dog-like devotion which gratified her innate sense of spiritual superiority. He also gave her life the steady anchorage it had lacked, and when in 1852, after eighteen months in America, Lind sailed back for Europe, she was finally in the domestic position to make the withdrawals she had long professed to want.

London had missed her, and it was hard for the opera-house managers to know what to do after she had left.

Then something extraordinary happened: Lumley's desperate stroke of genius. He had suffered a disastrous Lind-less season, and something radical had to be done. As soon as Lind's departure had become definite, he sent to Berlin as his agent the pianist Thalberg with the idea of approaching the Countess Rossi, Henriette Sontag. Many thought her dead, but reports had steadily come through of her private appearances and the miraculously good state of her voice, kept in trim but not over-taxed. Thalberg wrote back that 'The prospect of returning to the stage seemed to affect the Countess greatly: she even shed tears at the thought of it.' And in 1848 anything was possible. It was the year of revolutions, and with a new regime in Turin, Rossi was in danger of being dismissed from his ambassadorship, leaving his wife free to do what she pleased. The political situation see-sawed, Countess Rossi hesitated, Lumley waited. Finally, Rossi was stripped of office and his wife became Sontag again, returning to London on a contract worth

£6,000 over six months. She was now in her mid-forties and had not been a professional singer for nearly twenty years. Such a return is surely unparalleled in operatic history, and Lumley was taking a risk. The press was incredulous and a report even circulated to the effect that the public was in fact going to hear Sontag's daughter. But all went extremely well. She appeared as Donizetti's Linda di Chamounix: 'the cheering was universal, genuine, unusually prolonged'. Remarkably, she went on to master the 'new' (to her) repertory of Bellini and Donizetti, rather than merely repeating her earlier impersonations. The romance of the situation was not the only reason for her success. If anything, she seemed to have developed her artistry. Conditions had changed during her absence, particularly in regard to the expansion of the orchestra. She had been a contemporary of Catalani's and was now one of Viardot's. Chorley thought her superior to Lind in *La Fille du Régiment* and she was as happy in *La Sonnambula*. She went on to sing in Paris and Brussels, and kept Lumley's London receipts buoyant for two further seasons. He also organized for her a gruelling provincial concert tour of which the high point was a visit to Stonehenge, at that time assumed to be Druidical, where Sontag was inspired to sing 'Casta Diva' from *Norma*; and the low point, her near-death from exposure when the train had to be abandoned in a snowstorm between Glasgow and Aberdeen.

In 1852 Sontag collapsed completely from exhaustion and spent the summer recuperating at a German spa. She announced a second retirement from music in Europe, but the Rossis still needed money, and again following in the wake of Jenny Lind's success, they decided to brave America. The schedule was as hectic as the material rewards were great, and she was singing in opera, not just concerts—the first great soprano to do so since Malibran's youth. Henry James remembered her as 'supremely elegant in pink silk and white lace flounces': her concert taught him the meaning of public acclamation, 'the vast high-piled auditory thundering applause at the beautiful pink lady's clear bird notes'. At least once she was *une fille du régiment* in the afternoon and Lucrezia Borgia in the evening. In 1854 she died of cholera in Mexico City.

The search for nightingales continued. There were plenty of silly gimmicks, like the Black Malibran, a Cuban lady who sang to a small guitar and caused transitory enthusiasm. Marietta Piccolomini, popular in the mid-1850s, made Verdi's *La Traviata* famous. She may be compared to the film-star prima donnas of the 1930s like Grace Moore—wonderful ankle, smile, teeth, hair, publicity agent, etc., but fatally lacking in one needful quality. 'As for singing,' wrote J. E. Cox, Piccolomini 'had not an idea of what the meaning of that accomplishment really was . . . If it had not been an insult to common sense, whenever she came in contact with a difficulty, the manner of her shaking her little head, making a dash at it, and then scrambling helter-skelter through it, would have been amusing . . . On one occasion she was known indeed to have said "They call me little impostor, and they give me bouquets, applauses, moneys: why not be a little impostor?" ' Lind was not to be won back to opera. She eventually settled with her husband in England, singing in concert and oratorio, usually for charity, rearing three children, teaching at the Royal College of Music, and becoming ever more severe.

Her charities became as burdensome to her as her voice. Here, from the end of her life, is a letter complaining of an importunity. The Lind tetchiness is very evident.

Dear Miss Pearson,
I must take for granted that you are one of the daughters of [illegible] although you give no address or date on your letter. I am very much occupied—I always work for others—and I have been so particularly busy before our first performance of Bach last Wednesday that I could not answer the threescore letters addressed to me from all sorts of people. I return the letter you sent me. Numbers of applications from perfect strangers to me arrive every week—and of course I take no notice of them . . . I have already more duties in that line than I am capable of, yet I will gladly send you a post office order for two pounds if you think that this family is still in need . . . but in sending this—I only do it for your sake, as I have been obliged to lay down the rule not to send money to people who are perfect strangers to me. I am too overwhelmed with similar cases . . .

Lind died in 1887 at her last home in the Malvern Hills. More than any other prima donna, she helped raise the moral and social status of performers. The purity of her singing was interpreted as evidence of the purity of her soul, and her Victorian audiences were happy to be applauding the two simultaneously. But she was also a fanatic and, as the above letter shows, the fervour in her charity left no room for the spontaneous and easy-going generosity which characterizes theatre people at their best.

The undisputed prima donna of the second half of the Victorian age had something of that quality. Adelina Patti was as expensive as Catalani and her intractability made her the despair of managers, but she was fundamentally amiable. Her egotism was always naïve, the natural response to a lifetime in the hothouse of public adulation. Getting what she wanted was all she was ever to know. The critic Hanslick described her as a 'child of nature, half-timid and half wild, what the French call *sauvage*, good-humoured and violent, inclined to sudden quickly passing fits of temper'. Even into her forties her appearance remained touchingly girlish, her face dominated by dark, eager, and inquisitive eyes.

Like Sontag, she was born to theatre. Her Italian mother gave birth to her in 1843, just after singing Norma in Madrid, and family lore insisted that Adelina's first scream was a perfectly pitched high F. Her father was an impresario, who took his wife and children to New York in 1846, settling in the Bowery. He was fruitlessly engaged in establishing an Italian opera company in America, along the lines of the Garcia effort. In 1848 he was joined by the enigmatic Maurice Strakosch, an ex-pupil of Pasta's turned impresario. He married Patti's sister, but it was clearly the wilful and naturally gifted Adelina who engaged his fullest attentions. The young Henry James heard her as a child prodigy, dressed in plaid with long white drawers, and a red hussar jacket, 'mounted on an armchair, its back supporting her, wheeled to the front of the stage and warbling like a tiny thrush'. Strakosch exerted a Svengali-like influence over her earliest professional years, touring her round the States and promoting her with the calculation of a Barnum, but retiring her at twelve so that the voice could develop without strain. He also taught her Pasta's ornamentation and cadenzas, and quite possibly made her his mistress as well. In 1861 she came to London under his management and tutelage. She had been singing in opera in New York and New Orleans for about two years, but it was still in Europe that reputations were made.

Patti and Strakosch arrived at the office of Mapleson, who was sufficiently excited by her rendition of 'Home, sweet home' to engage her on the spot. He rushed off to organize a company and a season, as well as a theatre to put her in, but returned to Patti and Strakosch's hotel to find them in possession of a £50 personal loan from Gye at Covent Garden, 'which intelligence reduced my height by at least two inches'. They had signed up with the Royal Italian Opera. Patti began a twenty-five-year reign at Covent Garden; Mapleson was left with a company, a theatre, and an announced season, but with Patti as his opposition. It was the beginning of a long battle.

Patti's repertory was large but fairly unadventurous. She made her London début in *La Sonnambula*, and continued through the gamut of Rossini, Bellini (though never *Norma*), Donizetti, and Verdi up to *Traviata*. It could be said that she and her imitators 'held back' public taste in the era of *Tristan* and *Otello*, but this is not altogether fair. The nightingales did take up new roles in the second half of the nineteenth century on the less exalted plains of French opera. Lyrical and sentimental romances like Gounod's *Faust* and *Roméo et Juliette* or Thomas's *Hamlet* or *Mignon* suited them admirably, with sweet soprano parts written with all due consideration to their style and type of voice. Patti loved Wagner's music, and late in her career sang a little of it in concert, but she lacked the necessary heroic temperament as much as the technique. Some worthless showpieces written for her died the death, and her only two real gambles in new music were Carmen and Aida. Her Carmen was a total miscalculation, but her Aida was successful. She was coached in this enormously challenging role by Verdi himself, who admired her unreservedly, despite her cavalier cuts and transpositions. She could be a good actress, especially in comedy, but no one could claim that she advanced the cause of music drama. She disliked the strain of rehearsals, and even in the early days Strakosch would often attend them on her behalf: later she sent her maid along to find out something about the new sets or what the tenor looked like. In the 1880s she wrote her exemption from these tiresome functions into her contracts, along with a demand that the size of her name on the billings should be at least a third higher than anyone else's.

But she was no fool, nor was she irresponsibly idle. Patti's overriding principle was vocal health, and her life was dedicated to it. She never drank tea, coffee, red wine, or spirits, nor ate bread, sweets, or cold food. Her daily routines when she was performing, wrote a French journalist, were rigorous: 'chocolate in the morning, at eleven o'clock lunch of eggs and white meat, a few hours' siesta, and a walk towards four o'clock; on her return, some vocal exercises, and then, after some consommé, departure for the concert or theatre ... Nothing could make this singer deviate from this regularity to which she attributed the preservation of her organ.' Of her technique, she knew nothing, beyond that she had to avoid stress. At the slightest hint of a cold, she cancelled. 'I sing comfortably,' she once said.

Patti's emotional life may have been under less control than her voice. Her first marriage was to the French Emperor's equerry, the Marquis de Caux. He was considered something of a blackguard and the match was not approved, but Patti would have her way. According to her companion Louisa Lauw she pined in the Marquis's absence and would sit up all night in her room, playing 'fantastic strains on the guitar'. After she had married him they 'soon found that there was scarcely a question upon which they were of one mind', and Patti began to flirt with a married French tenor, Ernest Nicolini. The Marquis was inflamed with jealousy, to the point at which he and Patti came to blows. Much to the delight of the newspapers Patti then eloped with Nicolini, but like her godmother Grisi she at first found it impossible to obtain a divorce, and for some years she and Nicolini openly lived together, her celebrity allowing her to ride the social embarrassment. Nicolini was a boor and a third-rate singer, but he was very good at keeping unpleasantness at a distance, so Patti went on singing while the rest of the world ran around keeping her comfortable.

As with Jenny Lind, one wants to know whether somewhere, sometime, a mental constitution like Patti's experienced blind panic, terrifying *ennui*, desperate loneliness, or anything deeper than stage nerves or a fit of pique. Perhaps Patti was as inwardly calm as she appeared; perhaps, suggested her contemporary Clara Louise Kellogg, it was the secret behind her singing: 'A great deal is heard about the wonderful preservation of Patti's voice. It *was* wonderfully preserved. How could it have been otherwise, considering the care she has always taken of herself? Such a life ... she has allowed herself few emotions. Every singer knows that emotions are what exhaust and injure the voice.' Hanslick went further and noted Patti's complete lack of moral or intellectual imagination. He once gave her Dickens's *Great Expectations* to read, but she threw it back at him after a few chapters: 'That an old woman wouldn't give up her old bridal dress and old wedding cake can't be true and isn't possible,' she complained of Miss Havisham. 'I am no longer a child to whom one can give such things to read.'

In the twenty years following her London début she sang all over Europe, winning over even those like Hanslick who despised her 'empty and ineffectual' repertory. The elderly Rossini was infuriated by her ornaments for one of his arias, but charmed enough to write her some new ones. In 1868 she and the great contralto Alboni sang the *Stabat Mater* at his funeral. In St Petersburg the Tsar allowed her to call him 'Papa': one of her visits is commemorated by Tolstoy in Part V of *Anna Karenina*. In 1881 she returned to New York, and in 1882 Mapleson finally caught the bird for some transcontinental tours. Six years later he published his memoirs. Brought to a peak of exasperation by the failure of his American fortune-making schemes, he revenged himself in print on Patti, whose decision not to renew her contract lost him a chance of lasting success. The stories he tells are irresistibly funny, classic prima donna anecdotes, but they do not necessarily give accurate accounts of real events. Instead, he gave the public a parody of prima donna behaviour that it has still not forgotten: 'Madame Adelina Patti,' wrote Mapleson, 'is beyond doubt the most successful singer who ever lived. Vocalists as gifted, as accomplished as she might be named, but no one ever approached her in the art of obtaining from a manager the greatest possible sum he could by any possibility contrive to pay.' What he failed to add at this point is that without Patti he would have had no audience at all.

Mapleson's company toured in a special train, in which Patti had her own sumptuously appointed carriage. One of her constant companions was a parrot called Ben Butler, which according to Mapleson shrieked 'Cash! Cash!' every time he crossed the portal. The fee she demanded was £1,000 a performance and she had to have it by 2 p.m. on the day of the performance. On occasion Mapleson had to stand at the box office, waiting for the last monies to come in, but, fortunately, the Americans were universally mad to hear her. 'Amongst the numberless inquiries at the box office several were made as to how long Mdme. Patti remained on the stage in each of the different operas; and the newspapers busied themselves as to the number of notes she sang in each particular work; larger demands for seats being made on those evenings when she sang more notes.' In *Lucia*, for instance, it was calculated that

Patti was paid 42½ cents for every note she sang. It may have been worth it: according to her, one night in San Francisco, during a performance of that opera, a lunatic threw a home-made bomb on to the stage. It exploded, panic ensued, and a riot was imminent. Patti advanced to the footlights, began to sing 'Home, sweet home' and order was immediately restored.

Apart from cash and the delicate state of Patti's health there was, records Mapleson, another serious problem on one of the tours, in the form of a coloratura soprano in the company, the Hungarian Etelka Gerster, who was later treated by Freud's colleague Charcot for hysteria. After a humiliating incident at a curtain call, Patti conceived an unquenchable loathing for poor Gerster.

> If anything went wrong, from a false note in the orchestra to an earthquake, it was always, according to the divine Adelina, caused by Gerster and her 'evil eye'. 'Gerster' was her first exclamation when she found the earth shaking beneath her at San Francisco … Whenever Gerster's name was mentioned, whenever her presence was in any way suggested, Mdme Patti made with her fingers the horn which is supposed to counteract or avert the effect of the evil eye; and once, when the two rivals were staying at the same hotel, Mdme. Patti, passing in the dark the room occupied by Mdme. Gerster, extended her first and fourth fingers in the direction of the supposed sorceress, when she found herself nearly tapping the forehead of Mdme. Gerster's husband, Dr Gardini, who, at that moment, was putting his boots out before going to bed …

Gerster had her revenge when Patti was kissed in public by the overcome Governor of Missouri. A journalist asked Gerster for comment on this scandalous incident: she replied simply, 'There is nothing wrong in a man kissing a woman old enough to be his mother.' Despite all this, Patti gratified her American audiences to the hilt, receiving the most fulsome tributes graciously, but preserving the distance proper to a *diva*. Her life remained basically simple —she sang, smiled for the press, and took the money. No other prima donna radiated so little effort.

A spirit of the crassest commercialism and snobbery runs through Patti's American tours and their depressingly fabricated razzmatazz, repeated *ad nauseam* in every visited city. Theatrical conditions and acoustics were usually totally unsuitable for opera, and the level of performance can have been nowhere near as high as the level of publicity. It was a phenomenon worthy of Mark Twain's witheringly sceptical eye. The mistake would be to see such tours as an attempt to make opera a genuinely popular art-form: what mattered to the audiences was the social cachet attached to witnessing yet another European cultural import. London and Paris, St Petersburg and Vienna also exploited the class connotations of opera, but in the officially classless society of the United States the scale of the exploitation, at various levels, was quite different. In San Francisco, one of America's great opera cities, the rage to hear Patti caused a sort of latter-day Gold Rush.

On the day of the performance it took the whole of the police force to protect the theatre from the overwhelming crowds pressing for tickets, although it had been announced that no more were to be had. Long before daylight the would-be purchasers of Patti tickets had collected and formed into line, reaching the length of some three or four streets; and from this time until the close of the engagement, some four weeks afterwards, that line was never broken at any period of the day or night. A brisk trade was done in the hiring of camp stools, for which the modest sum of 4s. was charged. A similar amount was levied for a cup of coffee or a slice of bread and butter . . . Ticket speculators were now offering seats at from £4 to £10 each, places in the fifth row of the dress circle fetching as much as £4, being 400 per cent above the box-office price . . .

To describe the appearance of the house at the performance would be impossible. The toilettes of the ladies were charming. Many were in white, and nearly all were sparkling with diamonds. In the top gallery people were literally on the heads of one another, and on sending up to ascertain the cause, as the numbers were still increasing, the inspector ascertained that boards had been placed from the top of an adjoining house on to the roof of the Opera-house, from which the slates had been taken off; and numbers were dropping one by one through the ceiling on to the heads of those who were seated in the gallery. (Mapleson)

As a result of all this speculation, Patti built up as grand a fortune as any Victorian industrialist, and she spent it as they did, becoming the *châtelaine* of a large and ugly Victorian country house called Craig-y-nos, in a superb position some miles north of Swansea.

Over £100,000 was spent on improvements, although it is interesting to note that only three bathrooms served thirty-four bedrooms! There were electric lights in the reception rooms and an elaborate system of electric burglar-alarms designed to protect the Patti treasury and her wardrobe of over 300 gowns. Forty servants were permanently employed. Among the installations were a billiard room, a conservatory, a winter garden, a tennis court, a chapel, and a huge orchestrion organ ('It was with the aid of her splendid orchestrion,' cooed Hermann Klein, 'that Mme Patti first began to comprehend the intricacies of Wagner's more advanced works'); but most spectacular of all was the construction of a private theatre seating a hundred which by means of a hydraulically lifted floor doubled up as a ballroom. The drop curtain depicted Patti as Semiramide in a chariot driven by four white horses. She gave some small-scale operatic performances there, but her greatest joy, oddly enough, was to take part in plays mimed to musical accompaniments—a fashionable genre at the end of the nineteenth century—and she even appeared in such an adaptation of Sardou's play *La Tosca*, made popular by Sarah Bernhardt and later used by Puccini.

After marrying Nicolini and buying Craig-y-nos, Patti's career became less energetic and more profitable. In 1885 she abandoned Covent Garden for concerts, and in 1887 made her operatic farewell to New York. She then visited Montevideo and Buenos Aires, where her fee reached new heights, and sang in various other less exposed operatic centres. Her last significant effort for opera was her Parisian appearance in a new version of Gounod's *Roméo et Juliette*, conducted by the composer. Patti sang opposite the great tenor Jean de Reszke, and together they made the piece a popular favourite. But as she approached fifty she began to husband her resources and carefully contract the scale of her operations. The shrewdest commentator on this part of Patti's progress was George Bernard Shaw, then a music critic writing as Corno di Bassetto, and an ardent Wagnerian dedicated to the idea of opera as intellectually challenging music drama, but also a lover of fine Italian singing. Thus his feelings about Patti were genuinely mixed. He deplored her stage manners and the endless courting of, and responding to, applause—'Patti will get up and bow to you in the very agony of stage death if you only drop your stick accidentally.' In 1893 he went to hear one of her Albert Hall concerts, which had already become annual institutions. These occasions consisted of Patti singing a couple of arias and a couple of ballads interspersed with a variety of supporting musical acts. As programmes that were quite without any logic or coherence, save that of focusing attention on Patti, they typified for Shaw everything that was most mindless in London musical life.

> On Saturday afternoon the Albert Hall was filled by the attraction of our still adored Patti . . . It always amuses me to see that vast audience from the squares and villas listening with moist eyes while the opulent lady from the celebrated Welsh castle sings Oh give me my lowly thatched cottage again. The concert was a huge success: there were bouquets, raptures, effusions, kissings of children, graceful sharings of the applause with *obbligato* players—in short, the usual exhibition of the British bourgeoisie in the part of Bottom and the *prima donna* in the part of Titania.

But his admiration for her singing could be almost unbounded. He was happy for middle age to take away some of her topmost notes and limit her repertory to ballads and 'standards' rather than coloratura showpieces:

> I never fully appreciated Patti until one night I heard her sing, not *Una voce* or anything of that sort, but God save the Queen. The wonderful even soundness of the middle of her voice, its beauty and delicacy of surface, and her exquisite touch and diction, all qualify her to be great in expressive melody, and to occupy a position in the republic of art high above the pretty flummery of newspaper puffs, flowers, recalls, *encores*, and so forth which makes it so difficult for people who take art seriously to do justice to the talent and the artistic pains with which she condescends to bid for such recognition.

Her dabbling in Wagner brought a similar tribute: she attacked the 'Prayer' from *Tannhaüser* 'with the single aim of making it sound as beautiful as possible; and this being precisely what Wagner's own musical aim was, she goes straight to the right phrasing, the right vocal touch, and the right turn of every musical figure, thus making her German rivals not only appear in comparison clumsy as singers, but actually obtuse as to Wagner's meaning.' Shaw regarded Patti's career as a waste of a great voice and musicianship on over-played war-horses and a bad old system in which 'it was still possible for a *prima donna* to bounce on the stage and throw her voice at the heads of the audience with an insolent insistence on her position as a public favourite, and hardly the ghost of a reference to the character she is supposed to impersonate'.

But the system had plenty of life in it—it still does—as was witnessed by the excitement generated by Patti's return to Covent Garden in 1895 for six 'farewell' performances in three of her most famous roles, *La Traviata*, Zerlina in *Don Giovanni*, and Rosina in *Il Barbiere di Siviglia*. The timing was perfect. She was in magnificent voice and had been away from opera in London long enough to cast enormous glamour over the proceedings. At Flora's party in *La Traviata*, Patti emblazoned her bosom with over £200,000 worth of diamonds, and two costumed detectives lurked round on stage to protect them. After this, Patti's operatic career was virtually over. She planned to sing Elsa in *Lohengrin*, but perhaps wisely, perhaps sadly, never did.

Craig-y-nos had become famous for its lavish hospitality and Patti wanted to spend as much time there as possible, entertaining foreign nobility, ambassadors, musicians, and journalists. The music critic Hermann Klein described her house parties as:

> ... always full of interest and variety. It was an inestimable privilege to enjoy the daily society and conversation of Adelina Patti; to hear her ever and anon burst into song; to catch the ring of her sunshiny laugh; to come under the spell of a personal charm such as few women possess ... Her memory is extraordinary. She tells a hundred stories of her early life in America ... how they used to stand her upon the table to sing; how she first rendered 'Casta Diva' by ear without a single mistake; and how, when her eldest sister, Amalia, was striving hard to master the shake, the tiny Adelina stopped her and asked, 'Why don't you do it like this?' therewith executing a natural and absolutely irreproachable trill.

Patti's own letters reveal her simple self-centredness, as well as considerable charm: here she writes in 1896 to an American niece, Marie Brooks:

> ... I am so frightfully busy, that it is almost impossible for me to do my letter-writing just now, but I will not allow another day

to pass without sending you these few lines, to tell you how much I appreciate your kind thoughts of me—I can well imagine how terribly anxious you must feel about your sons and your property in Cuba, with all this dreadful fighting going on there—I hope most sincerely that the disturbances will soon end, and your anxiety be over . . . My season here in the South [Nice] has been a series of colossal triumphs—I only wish I had more time to tell you all about my success in 'Traviata', 'Lucia', the 'Barber', 'Don Giovanni', and 'Mirka' [mimed play] which we gave for the Czarewitch, and of the autographed portrait he gave me of himself . . . two concerts I had arranged to give in London at the Albert Hall proved such an enormous success that I was obliged to return and give an extra one, and even then it was found impossible to seat all the people who struggled for admission . . . I am going to give my Charity concert at Cardiff, which I think will be an exceptionally grand affair, as it will be the first time I have sung there for charity—my concert was to have been given in Swansea, but owing to the impertinent interference of some of the Swansea Committee, who upset all the arrangements I declined to sing there, and am giving the concert in Cardiff instead, but I have arranged that part of the proceeds of the concert shall go to the Swansea hospital and the poor of the district as I do not want them to suffer for the stupidity of the Swansea Committee . . .

After Nicolini's death, Patti's health declined somewhat, and Craig-y-nos closed its doors as her third husband Baron Cederström, a celebrated masseur, owner of a military gymnasium, and barely twenty-eight when she married him, disapproved of any over-excitement. Farewell and charity concerts saw her into the first years of the twentieth century. Her last operatic appearance was in 1907 at Jean de Reszke's private theatre in Nice, but as late as 1914, when she was seventy-one, she sang for the Red Cross at the Royal Albert Hall.

The great fact of these last years is, however, her recordings, made when she was sixty-two. The story of the gramophone's technical evolution has been so authoritatively told by Roland Gelatt in his book *The Fabulous Phonograph* that it seems pointless to give even a resumé here, although its importance to the prima donna cannot be over-estimated. Yet it must also be emphasized that these early recordings can mislead. Many indisputably great singers can sound almost comically inadequate on record, leaden, expressionless, off-pitch, or terribly rushed. Often this is due to transcriptions made at fractionally the wrong speed or to the limitations imposed by the four-minute 78 rpm disc. Some voices —Nordica's and Fremstad's, for instance—were just too big for the equipment recording them. Others hated the recording situation and the discomforts of the studio, and in subsequent chapters a number of prima donnas will give vent to their dislike of the whole recording business.

Nor should it be thought that the early gramophone brought opera into every lowly thatched cottage. Records alone were enormously expensive—Patti's pink label records cost one guinea for about seven minutes of music. At such prices, the industry grew slowly, but its potential was never in doubt, and the capture of Patti's voice was one of its greatest coups.

Like several other singers, Patti was slow to be won over to the idea of recording, and her initial reluctance may have been further fuelled by the poor critical reception of her 1903 farewell American concert tour. When after long negotiations she finally agreed in 1905 to receive the Gramophone Company at Craig-y-nos, she was still apprehensive. The crew waited for days, as Patti prowled about the machine with a small girl's curiosity. Then, after dinner one evening, the accompanist Landon Ronald (from whom the following account comes) was playing from *Tristan* on the piano: Patti began to sing along softly, 'just to see if she was in voice'. The next morning she agreed to record, and first sang Mozart's 'Voi che sapete'.

When she had finished her first record she begged to be allowed to hear it at once. This meant that the record would be unable to be used afterwards, but her wish was immediately granted. I shall never forget the scene. She had never heard her own voice, and when the little trumpet gave forth the beautiful tones, she went into ecstacies! She threw kisses into the trumpet and kept on saying, 'Ah! mon Dieu! maintenant je comprends pourquoi je suis Patti! Oh oui! Quelle voix! Quelle artiste! Je comprends tout!' . . . Her enthusiasm was so naive and genuine, that the fact that she was praising her own voice seemed to us all to be right and proper. She soon settled down and got to work in real

earnest, and the records, now known all the world over, were
duly made.

They are indeed lovely records, even if one cannot be as sublimely
uncritical about them as Patti was herself. The faults are manifest.
The voice has clearly frayed with age. In the parlour songs and
ballads she can sound arch, as in the bracing jollity of 'Comin'
through the Rye' or in the exaggerated dolefulness of 'The Last
Rose of Summer'; in the art songs and arias she is often over-taxed
and plain over-ambitious—she scampers through 'Batti, Batti' from
*Don Giovanni* and loses the pianist towards the end in her attempt
to sing it at the fast tempo common in her day; elsewhere her
intonation can suddenly turn sour, while her *portamento*, scooping,
and over-emphatic attack on climactic notes are not to modern taste.
But what wonderful, almost reckless exuberance, what pleasure in
singing, what riches of detail and phrasing! Not for a minute is her
singing dull or pompous. In the comfortable middle of her range,
she combines clean diction with beautiful tone, and she can colour
her sound to bring out the implications of a word or change of
mood. In an aria from *La Sonnambula* or Thomas's 'Connais-tu le
pays?', she sounds warm and dreamy, the tone veiled and withdrawn; in Lotti's 'Pur dicesti', she is graceful and witty, giving out
a trill which sounds natural and spontaneous, rather than a mere
special effect; while in concert songs like 'Il bacio', 'La Serenata',
and the Spanish 'La Calasera', she is boldly extrovert—the Baron
was reputedly shocked at her Hispanic whooping in the latter—
singing with youthful rhythmic crispness. 'Hearing, one can believe,' says John Steane in his previously cited review of singing,
*The Grand Tradition*—but the story of Patti could never have
suggested a singer of such abandon and involvement, of such
imagination and originality.

Patti's sovereignty was undisputed. No other singer of her era
had the same longevity or drawing-power, the same glamour or
salary level: perhaps no other singer was as good as she was either.
But if Patti was queen there were plenty of royal princesses.
We have already encountered the Eastern European coloratura
sopranos Etelka Gerster and Ilma di Murska, and there are other
sopranos whose biographies would all merit exploration, among
them Pauline Lucca, famous for her Meyerbeer and romantically
'linked' with the Kaiser; the second Swedish Nightingale, Christine

Nilsson, a woman of disconcerting beauty and 'undisciplined genius' according to Shaw, popular in London and New York, where she sang in the opening performance at the Metropolitan Opera House; and the French Canadian Emma Albani, who was the regular alternative attraction to Patti at Covent Garden and who also excelled in the early Wagner repertory.

The prima donna became a grander creature towards the end of the century, more womanly in person and more statuesque in manner, although silvery pure 'choirboy' tone remained in fashion. Some of these singers could act quite powerfully when they chose, yet any attempt at presenting ordinarily credible or consistent human behaviour on stage was generally eschewed, as the prima donna regularly broke out of character to acknowledge applause and any other sort of tribute. There was little respect for accurate musical texts. Cuts and wanton transpositions were common. The prima donna could sing much as she chose, and conductors and colleagues had to follow suit. Touring, the voracious new American market, and, later, recording doubled her money. Her social position consolidated itself, simply because she was unassailable: no one could gainsay her. Talent, money, and popularity made up for birth. In short, the prima donna had reached the height of her power—no longer just a free woman, she became a positive tyrant. No singer took firmer advantage of this situation than Dame Nellie Melba.

Melba was anything but fey or vague, and she could not be bothered with the finesse of Patti's velvet gloves. She was brusque, business-like, organizing, sometimes downright rude. 'I am Melba,' she would announce categorically to anyone who threatened to cross her will in any way. She was totally uninhibited. After a royal command concert at Windsor Castle at which a number of distinguished musicians performed, she turned to the Lord Chamberlain and complained in a loud voice, 'What a dreadful concert this would have been if I hadn't come.' To those who pleased her, she could be regally patronizing—issuing Melba warrants to favoured tradespeople and distributing Melba tiepins, graded in splendour, to those who had served her well. She adopted a series of young musicians who were generously treated while they remained absolutely loyal. She could equally be absolutely dismissive of the claims of others who came into her domain. The accompanist Gerald Moore remembers her as 'the terrible Melba'.

On concert tours in her latter days, he recalled, she put great store
by flattering lighting, but only got round to testing the effects 'while
her assisting artists were performing: during the first group of
violoncello solos . . . lights were raised and lowered, spots, foots,
flashed on and off until the diva was satisfied with the result. That
cellist and audience were disturbed was of small moment . . . Dame
Nellie was not personally inconvenienced.'

On stage, she moved pieces of scenery and discarded props
which offended her. 'What's this bloody thing?' she would exclaim,
and fling the unhappy object into the wings. The writer Beverley
Nichols, who 'ghosted' her prim and mealy-mouthed autobiography, *Melodies and Memories*, was once dragooned into helping her
change round the furniture in a hotel foyer. When challenged by
the hotel management as to what on earth she was doing, she gave
her customary reply of 'I am Melba,' then graciously added, 'But
don't worry, I'm not going to charge you for it.'

But the primary fact about Melba is, of course, her nationality,
which to an unusual extent identified and explained her. She was
one of the first Australians to give her country any sort of glamour
or appeal—as she was fond of saying, 'I put Australia on the map'
—but her own attitude to the place was always ambivalent. She
was both worshipped and reviled when she returned there, and
she was characteristically frank about what she considered its
shortcomings. Melba the prima donna had been made in the teeth
of Australian values and opportunities.

Her beginnings were not romantically outback, but solidly middle
class. She was born Helen Mitchell in 1861, and was brought up
in a respectable suburb of the respectable city of Melbourne,
whence 'Melba' was later derived and which she aptly described
as full of 'parsons, pubs and prostitutes'. Her father, a Scots
Presbyterian, was a prosperous building contractor to whom she
remained devoted, despite his initial scepticism of her ambitions,
and she inherited from him a tough and canny business sense which
later helped her to turn her enormous earnings into a solid fortune.
As a child she hummed and whistled incessantly, a practice which
she later considered as having provided her basic vocal training. At
her Girls' College she also took singing lessons from an Italian,
Pietro Cecchi. The teenage Melba therefore had the natural musical
equipment and a good Italian teacher: what she lacked was a social
climate which could nurture her into art. The amount of opera, or

indeed of any sort of orchestral music, in nineteenth-century Australia was small, and Ilma di Murska was the only prima donna of note to visit the continent in Melba's youth. Nor was the idea of professional, independent, middle-class women prevalent, and at first Nellie Mitchell looked like meeting an ordinary destiny. At the age of twenty she followed her father north to Queensland, where she married Charlie Armstrong, a handsome black-sheep adventurer from England. This, however, proved a mistake from the start. Her father did not approve of Armstrong and gave the couple no money. Armstrong himself had not bargained for a woman with a will, let alone an incipient prima donna. In despair, Nellie wrote to Cecchi:

> I do not mind telling you that times are very bad here, and we are as poor as it is possible for anyone to be. We have both come to the conclusion that it is no use letting my voice go to waste up here, for the pianos are all so bad it is impossible to sing in tune to them . . . I am anxious to leave Queensland as soon as possible. *I must make some money.* Could not you form a small company and let us go touring through the colonies, for of course I should like to study for the opera . . .

This, according to Melba's most recent biographer, is the first evidence of her ambition to be anything much more than a polite after-dinner singer. In fact, she had quarrelled violently with Armstrong and had decided to return to Melbourne with her baby. Supported by Cecchi's belief in her potential, she worked like a fury and was soon earning her living by singing in concerts throughout the state of Victoria. Her father neither helped nor hindered her; her husband stayed up in Queensland farming. Then in 1886 her father was sent to London as a delegate for a Colonial Exhibition: Nellie with her baby went too, armed with a sheaf of introductory letters. Sir Arthur Sullivan told her to come back in a year and he would consider her for the D'Oyly Carte chorus. Others were even less encouraging. Her last straw was Mathilde Marchesi, a pupil of Manuel Garcia's, who herself taught in Paris and numbered Gerster and di Murska among her protégés. Marchesi was fortunately overwhelmed and took the girl on immediately. It was only on this trip to Paris that she entered an opera house for the first time.

In later life Melba liked to make out that Marchesi had done everything for her singing, and she appears to have been one of the very few women Melba really loved. The truth is a little more complicated. Nature had given her a fabulous sound and Cecchi, over six years, had drilled her with basic technique. Marchesi came in at the last stage, and could be said to have exploited Melba (as she now became) for her own glory, presenting her to the operatic world as her own creation. Another contemporary pupil of Marchesi's, the American soprano Emma Eames, put it thus: 'This brilliant new soprano had little to learn and in truth was well along the road to vocal sophistication before Madame ever saw her, and lacked only taste and imagination and musical intuition.' These last three qualities would be a lot for any teacher to provide, but many would say that they were precisely what Melba's singing *always* lacked.

Yet Marchesi was obviously an inspiring teacher, as well as one who could arrange useful introductions: through her, for instance, Melba met Gounod, Thomas, Massenet, and Delibes, in all of whose operas she would perform. The trademarks of the Marchesi style were purity of intonation, evenness of scale, clean, forward diction, and a free upper voice. It is the true style of *bel canto* (a term now misapplied to the Pasta era, or confused with coloratura) in which tone and line take precedence over expressivity, and it is appreciated in the now-familiar metaphors—Marchesi herself described Melba's voice as more like that of 'a bird than of a human creature' and 'as clear as a silver bell'.

Marchesi introduced her successfully into Parisian *salons*; and Maurice Strakosch, Patti's mentor, offered her a contract but shortly afterwards dropped dead. She made her real début in 1887 at the Théâtre de la Monnaie in Brussels when she was twenty-six. It is worth noting that compared with Sontag, Lind, and Patti, this was relatively late: nowadays it would be considered a little early. Her success as Gilda in *Rigoletto* was instant, and only marred by the unpleasant reappearance of her husband, whom she now determined to discard. In 1888 she sang Lucia at Covent Garden, but things did not go well, and she returned first to Brussels and then to Paris. She was soon lured back to London, however, partly through the offices of one Lady de Grey, a powerful figure of the time who exerted influence over the opera house and who liked Melba as both woman and singer. She was properly launched in a prestigious production of Gounod's *Roméo et Juliette* with Jean de

Reszke, a singer she adored and respected; without any acting ability or any great beauty, she won the power she craved through the indisputable physical superiority of her voice.

Melba's triumph as a singer went hand in hand with her speedy social climb. By the 1890s the London *haut monde* was sufficiently relaxed to admit representatives of the arts as something more than entertainers, and Melba saw no reason to be daunted. She revelled in money, chic, and titles, candidly announcing, 'I'm a damned snob.' Lady de Grey was her guide, and in her memoirs Melba tediously relates the splendours of her drawing-room:

> The Duchess of Leinster, robed in white satin with marvellous sapphires round her neck, holding her head like a queen. Lady Dudley, with her lovely turquoises, so numerous that they seemed to cover her from her head to her knees; and Lady Warwick, then at the height of her beauty, the old Duchess of Devonshire, making somewhat pointed comments on those around her, the brilliant Duchess of Sutherland . . .

But it wasn't all ladies. In 1890 she fell in love with the twenty-two-year-old Duke of Orléans, Bourbon Pretender to the French throne, then exiled in England. Melba was thirty, a commoner, still married, and a Protestant. There was little hope of anything permanent emerging from such circumstances, but their affair was intense and glamorous while it lasted, and he accompanied her to Vienna, St Petersburg, Paris, and Brussels. Highly discreet but also much talked about, it probably won Melba a certain *cachet* among those spangled duchesses, even if the Queen stopped inviting her to sing at Command Performances. Real ruinous scandal threatened, however, when Armstrong served a divorce writ, a hearing of which would have brought the liaison firmly into the public eye. The writ was later mysteriously withdrawn, but the Duke found it all too hot, went off on a long safari, then came back and married an archduchess. Melba was left alone and never found anyone else to whom she could commit herself. Armstrong, from whom she was finally divorced in 1900, even took their son away to America. But if at bottom she was a lonely woman, there was little else that her life lacked. She was an Edwardian rather than a Victorian by temperament, and described the King's reign as 'an immense week-end party in which everybody was intent on getting the most out of life'. Her own London house in Great Cumberland

Place was furnished in the manner of Versailles: she was pleasure-loving and self-centred, spending lavishly on comfort and show, and scoffing at conventional or timid morality.

Yet the professional Melba was tight-fisted and sharp-eyed. In John Hetherington's words, 'She remembered how hard the climb had been, and she had no intention of letting all that effort go for nothing. She never committed the deadly sin of being complacent.' She knew that her real power lay not in having desserts named after her (Pêche Melba, as devised by Escoffier), but in her voice; just as her real palace was no *ersatz* Versailles, but Covent Garden. No one there crossed Melba, and her disapproval, expressed with a trooper's command of expletives, was said to have stifled the careers of Selma Kurz, Emma Eames (both Marchesi pupils), and Geraldine Farrar, though it is hard to find concrete evidence of this. If she did operate to get rid of rivals, she must have employed subtle rather than overt means. What did matter to her were her unique privileges. She had her own dressing-room to which she kept the key—'MELBA. SILENCE! SILENCE!' was inscribed across the door; and her own fee—Caruso had to be content with £399 per performance as only Melba was permitted to earn £400. Her real power base was the loyalty of her audience, particularly its fashionable end, and from 1890 onwards 'Melba Nights' at Covent Garden were one of the major events of the fashionable calendar, on a par with the races or charity balls. Shaw was a jaundiced observer of the earlier of such occasions, noting tartly how Melba 'received flowers in those large baskets which English ladies and gentlemen invariably carry with them in the theatre, and which they present to singers in moments of uncontrollable admiration'. Appropriately enough, the last Melba Night before the outbreak of the First World War was attended by two kings, four queens, and a dowager empress.

These were the conventional trappings of prima donna-hood, but Melba was not a conventional singer, and her operatic repertory was substantially more contemporary than her nightingale predecessors. She sang no Mozart, no Bellini; Rossini and Meyerbeer only a little; Lucia was her sole major Donizetti role. The Italian nexus was fast giving way to the modern French one. It could be said that Gounod, Thomas, Delibes, and Massenet gave the world updated Donizetti, with efficient plots softened with plenty of pathos, waltzing melodies in place of coloratura, lushly orchestrated sentimentality in place of rough-edged energy. Melba studied with all these composers and made their music a corner-stone of her repertory. The only two roles she created, in now forgotten pieces, were also by Frenchmen, Saint-Saëns and Bemberg. She even sang some of the new *mélodies* of Debussy and Reynaldo Hahn. In late Italian opera, she briefly assumed Aida and Nedda in Leoncavallo's notorious *I Pagliacci*, but her two most famous parts here were Desdemona in Verdi's *Otello* and Mimi in Puccini's *La Bohème*— both of which, again, she studied with the composers, and which she sang until the very end of her career. In the 1890s there was also Wagner to reckon with. In its high seriousness as well as its harmonic language his music posed radical questions about the future of opera and the future of singing. The initial compromise was to sing the early operas—*Lohengrin* and *Tannhäuser* in particular —in Italian, and a lyric soprano could manage this without disaster. But Melba went further, partly because she genuinely loved Wagner's music and partly because she must have foreseen a time when Wagner would be as essential to a soprano as Rossini had been seventy years previously. The irritating example of Lilli Lehmann, who could apparently sing anything, must also have goaded her on. In 1896 she tried to sing Brünnhilde in *Siegfried*. The part consists of one very long scene with a crucifyingly taxing climax, and it was quite beyond Melba's vocal capacities. Despite the support of her beloved Jean de Reszke as Siegfried, she had a bad cold and scarcely got through the forty-minute ordeal. After that one evening she suffered a severe vocal collapse, developed a nodule on her vocal cords, and was advised not to sing for some months. The baritone David Bispham witnessed the fiasco and noted how ludicrously old-fashioned her stage deportment became in such an opera: she 'was apparently forgetful of the Wagnerian tradition to remain well within the scene, and Jean de Reszke, in the heavy fur coat of Siegfried, was kept busy patrolling the forward part of the stage to keep the white-clad Melba from rushing into the footlights, over which she had so many times sung to delighted audiences'. She was probably also trying to prevent her voice being drowned by the Wagnerian orchestra.

Melba did not need to worry: what she could do was enough to keep her in power. Covent Garden was her 'artistic home', but she was also supreme in New York, and even won over the thoroughly chauvinist audience of La Scala, Milan, when she sang Lucia there in 1893. Her returns to her native Australia began in 1902 with a concert tour; in 1909 she set up house in the state of Victoria; in 1911 and 1924 she was chief mover and attraction of an Australian touring opera company. She herself made enormous sums of money there, netting £2,350 from one concert alone in 1902, but equally ploughed a considerable amount back into Australian music, closely involving herself in two Melbourne music conservatories. As she got older, she spent more time in Australia, both singing and recuperating, but she was unable to settle there for very long. According to Blanche Marchesi, she introduced the taxi-cab into the continent. A scandalous and baseless newspaper report of her alcoholism was the first of many trials by which she was dogged, but the last Melba story has remained the most notorious. In 1928 a biography of the contralto Clara Butt appeared in which Melba was quoted as advising Butt on her forthcoming Australian tour: 'All I can say is—sing 'em muck! It's all they can understand.' Melba furiously denied the remark and insisted that the publishers delete the page in question. But Australia could not forget the insult, and 'sing 'em muck' passed into the common currency. Melba was right to be indignant inasmuch as she had always tried in a small way to educate public taste, but she had often spoken more politely to the press of her disappointment at the Australian failures of musical appreciation, and 'sing 'em muck' does have an authentic ring to it. Melba could not resist one final dig: 'It would be quite unnecessary to advise Clara Butt to sing muck, since that's all she sings anyway.'

During the First World War Melba raised over £100,000 for the wounded, and was created a Dame of the British Empire for her efforts. But post-war society was not as diamond-studded as she would have liked. She returned to Covent Garden after its five-year closure to find her dressing-room repainted without her permission and men in 'shabby tweed coats' sitting in orchestra stalls once occupied by those in full evening dress. Although now fat, sour-faced, and well past her peak, she continued to sing in opera. In 1926, at the age of sixty-five, she made her Covent Garden farewell, singing scenes from her Desdemona, Juliette, and teenage tubercular Mimi. There is a fascinating recording of the evening in which we can hear not only Melba's still intermittently impressive singing, but also her farewell speech. 'A long farewell to all my greatness!' She thanks audience, orchestra, management, stagehands, stage-doorman, but it is the thought of the opera house itself that most seizes her—'I love it more than any place in the world,' she announces in a warm speaking voice, boldly charged with emotion, even though she had not sung there much since 1913. By the end of the speech she sounds close to breaking down, and her last words are mercifully drowned in applause. It is hard not to be moved at the thought of what such a moment must have meant, even to someone as hard-boiled as Nellie Melba. She continued to visit Covent Garden as Queen Dowager. Many stories are told of her in this new role, the most innocuous of them being that of her delight at a performance of *La Bohème*, when the audience began shouting for the tenor Martinelli. Melba, now slightly deaf, turned to her companion. 'Listen,' she said. 'They're still calling for their Auntie Nellie!' She had her fortune, a mass of friends and enemies, and an unassailable reputation, but singing was the great thing in her life, and once she had given up public appearances, her iron constitution gave way and she died shortly afterwards in 1931.

There is a certain mystery and a lot of controversy about Melba's singing that her recordings, spanning over twenty years, cannot resolve. What is beyond doubt is that it had an extraordinary natural radiance of tone, magnificently projected. This quality is suggested in two of the most quoted descriptions of its character. The American critic W. J. Henderson emphasized that 'It had splendor. The tones glowed with a starlike brilliance. They flamed with a white flame.' From the box-like acoustics of the early recording studio, one gets the whiteness and the brilliance, but not the splendor or the flame. Mary Garden, the great Scottish-American prima donna, carries it further. Speaking of the last floated high C with which Mimi closes Act I of *La Bohème*, Garden found Melba's

> . . . the strangest and weirdest thing I have experienced in my life. The note came floating over the auditorium of Covent Garden; it left Melba's throat, it left Melba's body, it left everything, and came over like a star and passed us in our box, and went out into the infinite. I have never heard anything like it in my life, not from any other singer, ever. It just rolled over the hall of Covent Garden. My God, how beautiful it was. . . . Since then I always wait for that note . . . they reach and reach for it,

and then they scream it, and it's underneath and it's false, and it rolls down the stairs . . . That note of Melba's was just like a ball of light. It wasn't attached to anything at all—it was out of everything.

She recorded the scene with Caruso and the note in question is indeed very beautiful in a lunar sort of way. From records, one can also appreciate the precise articulation of both word and note, and the evenness of tone. There are no weak moments, nothing smudged or breathy. Everything is truly and cleanly sung, without tremulousness or *vibrato*, and with near-impeccable accuracy of pitch.

But here one's reservations begin: that precise articulation often becomes reminiscent of a music box's mechanical rigidity. In 'Ah, fors' è lui' from *La Traviata* Melba's phrasing is absolutely square and literal, the emotional dynamics—halting, then yearning, then ardent—reduced to mere *crescendo* and *diminuendo*, learnt rather than felt. Her singing always has tremendous determination and aggression. It knows what to do, where to go, and why it's going. Other shades of feeling are hard to find—her 'Lo! hear the gentle lark' never merits the adjective; her 'Caro nome' has no wistfulness; Juliette's waltz-song sounds as if it is meant for puppets to dance to; and compared with Patti's infinite coquettish charm, her 'La Serenata' has no lilt or allure. 'I do not think anything in the world could have hindered me from becoming a singer,' claimed Melba, and this ruthless wilfulness cuts through her singing, which in that sense is highly expressive of her personality—even her Mimi can sound hectoring. And yet, the Melba sound has a drug-like effect. Listen to it for half an hour, and even though no impression of depth or sensitivity is left, the tone will ring on in the head, obsessively insistent. It would be pointless to deny Melba greatness. Hers was a magic voice, as magic as that of Trilby in George du Maurier's famous novel of that name, published in 1894, in the first years of Melba's fame. Trilby O'Ferrall is a simple Irish lass who cannot even sing in tune until mesmerized by the charismatic Svengali. Then she becomes the paragon of nightingales:

Every single phrase is a string of perfect gems, of purest ray serene, strung together on a loose golden thread . . . waves of sweet and tender laughter, the very heart and essence of innocent, high-spirited girlhood, alive to all that is simple and joyous and elementary in nature . . . all the sights and scents and sounds that are the birthright of happy children . . . All this, the memory and the feel of it, are in Trilby's voice as she warbles that long, smooth, lilting, dancing laugh, that shower of linked sweetness, that wondrous song without words . . . a clear, purling crystal stream that gurgles and foams and bubbles along over sunlit stones; a wonder, a world's delight. And there is not a sign of effort, or difficulty overcome.

# 4

# *The Wagnerians*

No revolutionary is ever quite consistent with himself, or lives up to the implications of his ideals, and Richard Wagner (1813–83) is no exception. His attempt to overthrow the Meyerbeerian conception of grand opera, 'forced down people's throats by the spirit of speculation, and lazily swallowed by the social *ennui* of the dwellers in our large cities', was sincere, even if fuelled by personal animosities. He was a high Romantic, standing for pure Art in an age of commercialism and exploitation; he was made, and to some extent made himself, an outcast from the bourgeois norms of success that Rossini or Meyerbeer had happily embraced. Wagner had his vision, and because he knew himself to be a genius, he saw it as the duty of others to sacrifice themselves to achieve it. No singer at the first Bayreuth Festival was to receive any payment beyond living expenses: 'A lot of use to me a singer would be who came to me only for the sake of a silly salary. Such a person would never satisfy my artistic demands.' Equally, no one would be charged to attend a performance. Equally, rich people had a duty to finance the operation, and, equally, Wagner, as a genius, exempted himself from the ordinary exigencies of debt repayment.

Yet when one looks coolly at Wagner's operas, there is less purity of purpose. In his voluminous prose polemics he proposes the idea of the *Gesamtkunstwerk*, a union of music, drama, and the visual arts: opera should be a communal celebration, like Greek tragedy, deeply expressive of the people's dilemmas and best spiritual values. But, as Shaw originally pointed out, he was more than ready to exploit the despised trappings and conventions of French and Italian opera to gain his effects. Theatrically speaking, Brünnhilde's immolation on Siegfried's funeral pyre and the destruction of Valhalla is pure Scribe-and-Meyerbeer, as is the Venusberg orgy in *Tannhäuser* or the procession of the Knights of the Grail in

*Parsifal.* A sickly sort of Christianity, sado-masochistic eroticism, and an idealization of the female pervade *Tristan* or *Parsifal* much as they do *Robert le Diable* or Gounod's *Faust.* We have already seen how, when translated into Italian, *Lohengrin* and *Tannhäuser* became vehicles for the 'nightingale' prima donnas.

Where, then, is Wagner the revolutionary to be found? This question is not easily answered. We cannot examine closely here his harmonic practices and their impact on twentieth-century music, nor his scoring, nor the development of those ever more complex webs of orchestral themes, built up throughout the later operas and individually known as *leitmotivs*, which act on the listener something like an authorial commentary in a novel—judging, reminding, pointing ironies and parallels, sometimes dominating the action, sometimes burrowing deep into the subconscious. The major issue for the prima donna was what Wagner did to the vocal line. In his own words, he 'elevated the dramatic dialogue itself as the main substance of the musical production'. The most significant word here is 'dialogue', for Wagner sought to eliminate all formal musical divisions, such as that between recitative and aria, and to create a continuous flow of speech, heightened in beauty and meaning by being set to music. He deplored the repetitions, paddings, and clichés of expression in Italian libretti. In his operas the drama was not a mere peg on which to hang a succession of musical numbers, nor was the orchestra just accompanist and colorist—it too was given, through the *leitmotivs*, what Wagner called 'a faculty of speech'. Thus the Wagnerian singer had to master two things above all: the art of intelligent musical declamation, of 'talking to music'; and how to ride a sometimes ruthless and unprecedented volume of orchestral sound which at times could contradict, rather than support, the vocal line. Wagner was not interested in catering to singers: rather, it was singers who should cater to him and his art. And so they did, as voices of new types and powers were trained.

What early Wagner audiences most missed was definite melodic contour, regularly phrased and repeated often enough to become what is popularly known as a tune. One of his most formidable critics was Eduard Hanslick, whom Wagner resented violently enough to satirize in the figure of Beckmesser in *Die Meistersinger von Nürnberg.* Hanslick tried very hard to appreciate Wagner and the 'music of the future'. He was happy to pay tribute to his energy, originality, and masterly instrumentation: there were passages he acknowledged as lovely or exciting. But he also found most of it insufferably tedious: 'the intentional dissolution of every fixed form into a shapeless sensually intoxicating resonance; the replacement of independent articulate melody by vague melodization . . . those extended scenes in which one takes in little more than a continuous fluctuation of featureless, fluid tonal matter. Melody, self-sufficient melody from which alone the intrinsic musical body can be constructed, is lacking . . .' It was precisely the last point that Wagner would have taken up, much as he loved melody in Mozart, Rossini, and Weber. He mourned contemporary German music's unmelodiousness—'Song, song, and again I say song, you Germans!' he exhorted in an early essay on the virtues of Bellini—but his idea of what constituted melody was wider ranging than Hanslick's. Melody was not necessarily 'self-sufficient': indeed, in opera it had suffered from being irrelevant, and Wagner was aiming at melody constantly bent towards fulfilling the drama, rather than towards vocal display, pretty tunes, or any other sort of immediate audience gratification. George Eliot, a cultivated amateur musician, saw further than Hanslick. She was in Weimar in 1854, where she heard Wagner's three early major works, on which she reported in her journal:

> I had not the patience to sit out more than two acts of *Lohengrin* . . . The declamation appeared to be monotonous, and situations in themselves trivial or disagreeable were dwelt on fatiguingly . . . With the *Fliegende Hollander* I was delighted—the poem and the music were alike charming. The *Tannhäuser* too created in me a great desire to hear it again. Many of the situations and much of the music struck me as remarkably fine. And I appreciated these operas all the better retrospectively, when we saw *Der Freischütz*, which I had never before heard and seen on stage. The effect of the delicious music with which one is so familiar was completely spoiled by the lack of recitative and the terrible *lapsus* from melody to ordinary speech.

In an essay written shortly afterwards she admits that Wagner 'has pointed out the direction in which the lyric drama must develop itself', and concedes that 'It is just possible that melody, as we conceive it, is only a transitory phase of music.' Love his music, however, she could not: 'You long for the sound even of a street organ to rush in and break the monotony.'

For everyone except the rabid, some of Wagner's music always remains monotonous. We can all pick our own dead spots: few, I think, could honestly say that they find Wotan's monologue in Act II of *Die Walküre* gripping, for instance. I myself find much of *Parsifal* difficult, and sometimes feel desperate in Act I of *Meistersinger*. Everyone also has their favourite passages—'Winterstürme' or 'Du bist der lenz' from Act I of *Walküre*, the love duet from *Tristan*, Walther's prize song in *Meistersinger*, as well as the orchestral chunks such as the 'Ride of the Valkyries'. In sum, Wagner did not really achieve his ideal of constant flow, and, ironically, it is the 'anti-Wagnerian' *Pelléas et Mélisande* of Debussy which is most nearly a true 'play set to music' without a musical rise-and-fall being imposed upon it. There is plenty of song in Wagner, and plenty of recitative, however much he tried to redistribute the interest and however much we seem to hear something between the two. For the prima donna there are as many wonderful vocal challenges as in any of the great Italian operas and a series of demands on her stamina and power as testing as any flight of coloratura or mad scene.

Wagner's first crucial operatic experience was hearing Wilhelmine Schröder-Devrient sing the title-role of *Fidelio*. He was an impressionable boy of sixteen, in the first flush of a passion for Beethoven, but he was never to forget

> ... the almost satanic ardour which the intensely human art of this incomparable actress poured into [my] veins. After the performance I rushed to a friend's house and wrote a short note to the singer, in which I briefly told her that from that moment my life had acquired its true significance, and that if in days to come she should ever hear my name praised in the world of Art, she must remember that she had in that evening made me what I then swore it was my destiny to become. This note I left at her hotel, and then ran out into the night as if I were mad ...

This extraordinary woman was born nine years before Wagner in 1804, the daughter of a baritone and one of the finest tragic actresses of her time, Sophie Schröder, sometimes labelled the German Mrs Siddons. She passed on to her daughter an acting style of heightened naturalism, teaching her the gesture, diction, and ability to project intense emotion characteristic of the new Romantic school. At fourteen, Wilhelmine was already playing

Shakespeare and Schiller in Vienna. Her vocal training, on the other hand, was relatively casual. Good teachers were hard to find in Germany: many were Italian, and there was a lot more money to be made in London or Paris than in the backwaters of Germany. Schröder-Devrient had no Garcia to drill her into accuracy and agility or the steady emission of tone, and she was always to rely too much on the rasping and emphatic exaggeration that has dogged bad Wagner singing ever since.

German opera was not yet the popular international commodity that Italian opera was, and Schröder-Devrient was never happy with the latter's vocal requirements. Her *Norma, La Sonnambula, Anna Bolena, Otello*, etc. did not match up to the contemporary competition from Pasta and Malibran, and the blatant inadequacies of her singing restricted her career abroad. But apart from her theatrical genius she did have one other great advantage, in the form of the German role with which she was always identified and in which she so thrilled Wagner—Leonore in Beethoven's *Fidelio*, which she first sang in Vienna in 1822 at the age of seventeen and an opera which she did much to make popular. Beethoven himself rehearsed her and was sufficiently moved to promise to write her another opera, which he sadly never did. In London Chorley was dismayed at her singing of Leonore—'Her tones were delivered without any care, save to give them due force. Her execution was bad and heavy. There was an air of strain and spasm . . .'—but he paid tribute to her portrayal of the woman who risks all to save her unjustly imprisoned husband: 'There was a life's love in the intense and trembling eagerness with which she passed in review the prisoners when they were allowed to come forth into the air—for *he* might be among them! There was something subduing in the look of speechless affection with which she at last undid the chains of the beloved one, saved by her love—the mere remembrance of which makes the heart throb and the eyes fill.' One of her most famous moments as Leonore was at the phrase 'Noch einen schritt und du bist todt' ('One more step and you are dead'), when she flourishes the pistol at the prison governor Pizarro. The last word 'todt' ('dead') would be barked out with a convulsive laugh, rather than sung at its proper pitch. But this *parlando* became one of her worst mannerisms and an easy way out, as Chorley noted, of any vocal difficulty: 'She cared not whether she broke the flow of the composition by some cry, hardly on any note, or in any scale—by even speaking some word for which she would not trouble herself to study the right musical emphasis or inflexion—provided only she succeeded in continuing to arrest attention.' Berlioz felt even more strongly about it:

> She would have considered herself to have failed if she did not monopolize the attention of the house, rightly or wrongly and by whatever piece of stage business, in every scene she appears in. Her whole manner suggests that she sees herself as . . . the only character with whom the audience need concern itself. 'What? Listening to that fellow? Admiring the composer? Interested in that chorus? How can you be so misguided? Look over here, this is what you should be attending to . . .' Her singing, as I have said, is often wanting in accuracy and intonation and taste. The cadenzas and the numerous alterations which she now inserts into her roles are in poor style and clumsily managed. But her spoken interjections are in a class apart. Madame Devrient never sings the words, 'Dieu! o mon dieu! oui! non! est-il vrai? est-il possible?' etc. She speaks the whole passage, or rather shouts it at the top of her voice.

Wagner was outraged on reading this, but not because he thought she was a great 'pure' singer: 'She had no voice at all,' he candidly admitted, 'but she knew how to use her breath so beautifully and let a true womanly soul stream forth in such wondrous sounds, that we never thought of another voice or singing.' He saw that 'her tendency to exaggeration was at times almost painful'. But he compared her with the run of prima donnas, or 'female castrati', as he scathingly called them, and extolled her powers of expression and 'womanliness' against their mindless *bel canto*.

In 1835 Wagner, now launched on his musical career, had conducted his goddess when she visited the small town of Magdeburg. Among the operas in which she appeared under Wagner's direction was Bellini's version of *Romeo and Juliet, I Capuleti e i Montecchi*, in which she sang Romeo. Many years later Wagner told his wife Cosima that the memory of her ardour in that role had inspired him to the second act of *Tristan*. She, for her part, recognized Wagner's talent, if not his genius, recalled his adolescent letter of 1829, and was flattered by his attentions, becoming his patron and friend. Wagner was deeply affected by her interest in him: when on his first visit to London, he dropped a snuff-box she had given him into the River Thames, he nearly drowned trying to retrieve it. The power of his experience of her continued long after her death: Cosima's diaries of her life with Wagner in the 1870s record the number of dreams in which she figured, and their house in Bayreuth, Wahnfried, had a *sgraffito* above the portal depicting Schröder-Devrient as Tragedy. Yet he was never in love with her. She had become blowzy and plump by the time he knew her, and altogether lacked the delicate mystique that he found so attractive in women: he was particularly appalled by her theatrical coarseness of language.

The opera house with which she was most closely associated, for more than a quarter of a century, was that of Dresden, and it was here that Wagner and she came together again in 1842. *Rienzi*, Wagner's third opera, was to be given its première and Schröder-Devrient agreed to sing the *travesti* part of Adriano. *Rienzi* is written squarely in Meyerbeerian format and was originally intended for production at the Paris Opéra. It is a five-act historical drama set in fourteenth-century Rome, with a strong theme of 'people against the nobles', a large role for the chorus, and some spectacular stage effects, culminating with Adriano's suicidal ride into the burning Capitol. Schröder-Devrient had great difficulty with it all. She was well past her peak, and found the idiom of the music difficult. At one point, after failing to master some unexpected modulation of key, she flung the score at Wagner's feet and stormed out. Wagner showed unusual (for him) forbearance and tact. The opera was fortunately an immediate and stunning success of an unproblematic kind that Wagner never again experienced. His next work, *Der Fliegende Holländer* (1843), shows the influence of the other great German opera of the early Romantic period, Weber's *Der Freischütz* (1821), in which Agathe was another of Schröder-Devrient's most famous parts. Weber was himself a considerable operatic reformer, many of whose ideas Wagner inherited and developed. *Freischütz* is based in folk-lore, full of imaginative orchestration, with some gorgeous melody and the *frisson* of the supernatural. *Fliegende Holländer* follows it in these respects, and with its movement towards a continuous musical flow, as well as the embryonic use of the musical *motif*, it also contains features of Wagner's mature style. At the middle of the opera stands Senta, the Norwegian village girl obsessed by the legend of the ghostly Dutchman doomed to wander the sea until a woman's love redeems him. She would be prepared to make any sacrifice to save him, and when he does appear, kills herself to prove it. This nexus of ideas—woman-love-death-salvation—is one of Wagner's persistent themes, both in his art and in his life, and we shall return to it. Schröder-Devrient was the first Senta. Rehearsal was a terrible time. Wagner privately referred to her as a sow and a bitch, for she was in a permanent state of near-hysteria. Her love-life was notoriously complicated and unhappy, involving three marriages, four children, and a succession of infatuations with thoroughly unsuitable younger men. Her first husband divorced her for adultery and won custody of their children; her second embezzled her money. After her death an anonymous pornographic book appeared entitled *A Singer's Memoirs*, which she was widely thought to have written. Stylishly composed, with a certain amount of insight into sexual psychology and featuring lesbian orgies and an English milord named Sir Ethelred, it is a good example of elegant erotica. There is, however, very little indication of her career as a singer in it, and if it does derive from papers or journals she left, the elaboration must be considerable. What is interesting about it is the simple fact that Schröder-Devrient should be associated with uninhibited expressions of libido.

In the rehearsals for *Fliegende Holländer*, this association manifested itself to Wagner's ultimate benefit. The cause of her mental unrest was the abandoning of one long-standing liaison for a passionate and ill-advised one. Racked with guilt and uncertainty, she ate nothing and looked deathly. Confiding in an egoist like Wagner cannot have been very reassuring, and he regarded her carryings-on with a mixture of amusement, sorrow, and contempt. She in turn mocked him as an innocent in matters of illicit passion —'Oh, what do you know about it, tied to your wife's apron strings?' she complained, little knowing that she was talking to the future composer of *Tristan und Isolde* and one of the most scandalous adulterers in Europe. Finally, the only cure was work. She flung herself into the role 'as a matter of life and death', and her high pitch of emotion, thoroughly suited to Senta, was exacerbated on the first night by the presence of her new lover in the audience. The opera was not a success, but Schröder-Devrient evidently gave a staggering performance and saved the evening from disaster.

In 1845 Wagner produced *Tannhäuser* at Dresden. This romantic opera set in medieval Germany carried his style a stage further.

Although it contains some definite arias, there are also passages of freer musical dialogue and monologue that were highly original. Such sustained and complex music made impossible demands on singers and orchestras of the time. Schröder-Devrient sang Venus, the goddess of sensual love who tries to keep Tannhäuser from his nobler spiritual life. She did not understand her music at all and was by now absurdly fat for the role. In rehearsal she warned Wagner that the public would not appreciate his innovations, especially in such an inadequate production, and she was right. A further problem was her jealousy of Wagner's adopted niece, the nineteen-year-old Johanna, who sang the hero's other love, Elisabeth. Still in a highly nervous state over her love affair, she was convinced that Wagner had deliberately set Johanna up in the same opera with the intention of humiliating her. In revenge she decided to call in a loan she had generously made Wagner for the publication of his operas and which he could not conceivably repay. When she instituted legal proceedings, Wagner had to take a further loan from somebody else, and was thus flung deeper into a spiral of debt from which he was never to extricate himself. It marked the end of their relationship—Wagner saw her only once more, when she made an inflammatory public speech during the 1848 revolution for which she was nearly imprisoned. She retired from opera in 1847 and devoted herself to *lieder* singing: Schumann dedicated the great chin-up song 'Ich grolle nicht' (from *Dichterliebe*) to her, and one can imagine how heroically she must have interpreted its stern and hectoring phrases. In 1850 she married a Livonian baron and made an attempt to domesticate herself. 'She would wear a big apron and an immense bunch of keys hanging at her waist, insist on dusting the drawing-room, and even sweeping the floor, especially when visitors were coming; she would go to the kitchen and stir the scrambled eggs.' This particular performance did not last long: nor did her efforts to teach. 'The poverty of heart and spirit was too great,' she wrote to Clara Schumann in 1850, 'the soil too barren, to nourish the strong roots torn from my own heart.' She died in 1860. Wagner bore her no grudge for the considerable trouble she had caused him. In his autobiography, he talks of the 'turbulence and force' of her 'inner daemon, combined with such genuine femininity, lovableness and kindness of heart'. Few of the others who crossed his will met with such indulgence.

Wagner had also taken up with the revolutionary cause in 1848, and was obliged to leave Germany when the Dresden uprising collapsed. He moved to Paris, then to Zürich, and the première of his next opera, *Lohengrin*, was given in his absence, at Weimar, in 1850 under the direction of Liszt. Over the next fifteen-odd years Wagner lived in exile, his life taken up with his prose writings, conducting, the gestation of the enormous *Ring* project, and with growing estrangement from his wife Minna, a woman sadly ill-equipped to cope with his egotism and ambition. In 1857 they were living together in a cottage on the Swiss estate of a wealthy silk merchant, Otto Wesendonk. Here he began work on *Tristan und Isolde*, fuelled by an ultimately disastrous affair with his host's cultivated wife Mathilde. He set some of her poems to music— one of the rare occasions on which he used anyone else's texts. These secret hymns to an unfulfillable passion, known as the *Wesendonk Lieder*, are unrelievedly yearning and plangent, and contain some of Wagner's kindest and most purely lyrical writing for the female voice.

*Tristan* takes up many of their musical themes and expands on their ideas about love—renunciation, the conflict of night and day, the desire for oblivion. It is easy enough to see these as the future clichés of a thousand novels, films, or fantasies, and the opera's originality as erotic philosophy has been overrated—no one ought to claim that *Tristan* tells us as much about adult sexual relationships as *Phèdre*, *Antony and Cleopatra*, or *Anna Karenina*. Its power lies not in its 'message'—the impossibility of perfect union between two people outside death—but in the hypnotic sensuality of the music, with its notorious lack of harmonic definition; the vast single impetus of each of the three acts; and its relentless concentration on absolute emotional state—'One thing alone left living,' wrote Wagner, 'longing, longing unquenchable, a yearning, a hunger, a languishing forever renewing itself.'

The part of Isolde requires a soprano capable of projecting two radically opposed personalities, and few of the great Isoldes have ever held the perfect balance. As we have seen, Elsa in *Lohengrin* or Elisabeth in *Tannhäuser* can be sung by lyric sopranos with a pure line and sweet tone: but Isolde requires much more. Act I presents Isolde the sorceress, determined on vengeance, self-deceived and even slightly crazed, suffocating with suppressed rage at her humiliation, sarcastic in her dialogue with Tristan, impatient with her servant Brangäne. Fury has to ring out scaldingly from her first utterance, and even the softer passages must have something insinuatingly sinister to them. The tone must be supremely confident and unfailing, since any hesitation or insecurity ruins the dramatic illusion of her obsessiveness. But from the drinking of the potion onwards a rapturous warmth has to flood through the voice, melting the ice, cracking the steel, releasing a pulsating desire which culminates in a graphically orgasmic climax. In her relatively brief appearance in the third act, Isolde is transfigured, gentle and tender with the dying Tristan, then rising to the *Liebestod* in 'calm of mind, all passion spent'. This, at least, is the Isolde of one's aural dreams: no singer could be humanly expected to encompass such a range—but then, Wagner's later operas were not written with a tremendously realistic sense of anyone's musical or theatrical capabilities.

*Tristan* had its first performance in 1865 in Munich, under the new-found patronage of Ludwig II of Bavaria. Wagner's fortunes had sunk even lower after the Wesendonk episode and the disastrous performance of *Tannhäuser* at the Paris Opéra in 1861, for which the composer had refused to make alterations necessary to please an audience with definite notions of what it wanted for its entertainment. Ludwig's lavish financial support and hero-worship were what he needed to survive; he had also won the fanatically complete devotion of Cosima von Bülow, Liszt's daughter and a married woman, who later became his second wife. Over the next few years Wagner lived happily at Triebschen on Lake Lucerne, where he completed *Die Meistersinger von Nürnberg*, which was triumphantly produced in Munich in 1868, and continued work on the *Ring*.

Wagner's impatience with the restrictions and unimaginative management of existing opera houses had long been simmering. Ludwig had promised him a theatre in Munich, but the scheme was blocked by the King's opponents and Wagner had to organize his own solution to the problems of staging his operas. In 1872 the north Bavarian town of Bayreuth gave him a site on the top of a hill, and work began on what would incidentally become the largest free-standing timber-framed building in the world. More importantly, it was to be a temple to Wagner's art, purified of all financial motivations and run by neither impresarios nor prima donnas. Money was raised by public subscription and a massive subvention from Ludwig. Worlds away from Patti's Covent Garden, Wagner stated his principle:

> It would be well to keep in mind the fact that this undertaking has nothing to do with a money-making theatrical enterprise, the performances will be attended only by invited guests and the patrons of the undertaking: no one will be allowed to pay for admission. On the other hand, I have already provided for a sufficient number of seats to be placed at the disposal of the citizens of Bayreuth—these to be distributed free of charge.

Needless to say, it did not work out quite like this, but by 1876 Wagner was in complete artistic control of the most advanced theatre of its time. The opera composer had, as it were, finally left the servants' staircase.

The admirable features of the auditorium are well known— the sunken orchestra pit, the superb acoustics, the simplicity of decoration and the spartan seating arrangements, ranged as in an amphitheatre, without the usual tiers of boxes. There was a huge stage, elaborate machinery, and remarkably sophisticated lighting equipment. The lowering of the house lights during performance was not quite as unprecedented as is usually made out—Wagner took the idea from the Vitinghoff Theatre in Riga, also deeply raked and wooden, where he had been a conductor in 1837–9. But despite all this advanced technology and noble thinking there must have been something faintly comical about the first festival in 1876, even if only, as poor Nietzsche found, the reality was so very far from the ideal. Over the years great curiosity about the project had been aroused throughout Europe and the town was quite unable to accommodate the influx of visitors. The pilgrims, who included Grieg, Liszt, Bruckner, and Saint-Saëns, spent much of their time trying to find something to eat—'throughout the whole duration of the Festival,' wrote another, Tchaikovsky, 'food forms the chief interest of the public; the artistic representations take a secondary place. Cutlets, baked potatoes, omelettes—all are discussed much more eagerly than Wagner's music.' An air of bathos hung over the proceedings, and even today there is still something pompous in the conception of Bayreuth—as dishonest in its way as the sensationalism of the Paris Opéra.

Nothing, however, can detract from the greatness of *Der Ring des Nibelungen*, which was first presented in its entirety at this first festival. Although the *Ring* takes its ambience and some of its plot and characters from Norse mythology, its ethics and structure are based in Greek tragedy: specifically, in the dynastic working-out of justice after an initial wrong, which Aeschylus had explored in *The Oresteia*. It is a work which bites deep into the spirit of its age, but also raises some of the basic questions about moral and social life which pose themselves, in some form or another, to every epoch and culture. For the prima donna it offers first and last the supreme and exhausting challenge of Brünnhilde as a test of endurance and also a test of intelligence. Brünnhilde's development is a complex one, and to think of her simply as a sort of whooping Viking policewoman is to miss everything. She begins as her father's obedient daughter, blindly fulfilling the militarist notions of Valhalla, until Siegmund shows her the real loneliness of the hero, and the tragic but necessary consequences of defiance. She sides with the outcast rebels against her father's weary assertion of the old law, and is duly punished, her godhead taken away. Reborn as an isolated mortal, she falls in love with Siegfried, a wild boy of the woods, who knows no fear and is completely open to experience— qualities which might save the world. The ring he gives her is a pledge of love, and not the poisoned crux of a desperate power struggle: she refuses to give it up, even to save her father. When she believes herself betrayed by Siegfried, she becomes mad for vengeance, in music similar in idiom to that given to the Isolde of Act I. Then, when every treason is uncovered and the boy she loves is dead, she reaches her own plateau of ecstatic acceptance, gladly sacrificing herself to whatever comes after the curse on the ring has been lifted. This is a simplified retelling, but it may give some indication of the part's strange mixture of passivity and activity. As vocalist, a Brünnhilde has to meet the animal yelps of 'Ho-jo-to-ho', which must be accurately pitched, not screeched; the solemn unearthly stillness of the *Todesverkündigung* scene with Siegmund; the long modulations of emotion of the last scene of *Siegfried* (which prostrated Melba), building towards its final reckless laughter. In *Götterdämmerung* there is no shirking the sheer volume required in the opening duet or the ferocious second act, and the opera ends with what the *Guinness Book of Records* claims as the longest aria in the repertoire—the 'Immolation' scene—which must seem like a marshalling of all that has gone before, a strong, meditative, and exalted final statement. Successful Brünnhildes, like successful

Normas, can be counted on the fingers of perhaps two hands. It is not so much a matter of high notes—indeed Birgit Nilsson has pointed out how much of it lies in the lower-middle of the soprano range—as of unfailing nerve combined with inflexion. A Brünnhilde cannot get through on sheer brutal accuracy of attack.

There are other fine women's roles in the *Ring*, although *Das Rheingold* ought to be in the *Guinness Book of Records* as well, as the only nineteenth-century opera without a prima donna. Fricka, Waltraute, and Erda are not dominating figures in the plot, but they do each have superb scenes which give the mezzo-soprano noble opportunities, and the same is true for the mixed-voice ensembles of Norns, Valkyries, and Rhinemaidens. The loveliest music and the most immediately sympathetic personality is that of Sieglinde, the lonely and unhappy wife of Hunding, who is drawn into a fateful union with her twin brother Siegmund. A Sieglinde is often trying herself out for Brünnhilde, but the latter's music is far more declamatory, and it is the *contrast* between the two women in *Walküre* which is important: similarly in *Götterdämmerung* (which, as Shaw claimed, is the most conventionally operatic episode of the *Ring*, complete with a chorus, a trio, a march, a marriage, and a conflagration), Brünnhilde stands immense against the mincingly graceful fluting of Gutrune.

It could not be said that the first Bayreuth Festival was a success in any ordinary sense of the word, but it was certainly amazing that it happened at all. By the end, Wagner's debts had rocketed still further, and he seriously considered emigrating to America to escape his creditors, the sickness of Germany, and the Jewish influences which he so feared and hated. But his music was slowly making its way out of the *avant-garde* into the standard repertory. In 1875 the first Wagner opera had been presented at Covent Garden—*Lohengrin*, in an Italian translation by Marchesi's husband. A company from Leipzig toured the *Ring* round Europe. Bayreuth closed for lack of funds, but Wagner decided to stay in the domestic calm of his mansion Wahnfried ('Peace from delusion') and worked on his last opera *Parsifal*, which he completed in Palermo and which reopened Bayreuth in 1882, a year before his death in Venice.

Wagner's relations with prima donnas were mixed. After Schröder-Devrient, there was none he held in any great awe. He had an edgy time with Pauline Viardot, with whom he had sung the *Tristan* duet in front of an unimpressed Berlioz, and finally he quarrelled with her over the Jewish question. He wanted Therese Tietjens for Isolde, but could not get her, and the part went to Malvina, wife of the first Tristan, Ludwig Schnorr, who died shortly after the first performance moaning, 'Farewell, Siegfried! Console my Richard!' Malvina Schnorr later became an agent in the revelation to King Ludwig of the adulterous relations between Wagner and Cosima, with difficult consequences for all. A soprano from Vienna, Amalie Materna, sang the first Bayreuth Brünnhilde and Kundry in *Parsifal*. She suffered from what became a familiar Wagnerian problem: although a fine and strong singer, her appearance was homely and quite devoid of the spiritual beauty that should shine forth from Kundry in particular. But Wagner's 'favourite child' was a young lyric-coloratura soprano from the Court Opera at Berlin.

Lilli Lehmann (1848–1929) came from a family of professional singers, and her mother was an old friend of Wagner's. In the first Bayreuth *Ring* she was cast as a Rhinemaiden, a Valkyrie, and the carolling Woodbird of *Siegfried*—all parts lying at the lightest and brightest end of the vocal spectrum. Her account of the rehearsal period (the only one to survive from any of the singers) is unfortunately stronger on adulation and rapture than precise detail:

> These days were, in their way, unique and never to be repeated —Wagner in his full creative power, the splendidly liberating ambience and those particular artistic and stimulating performances that are gone forever. There was the sound of the orchestra, made up only of the greatest players; and the music itself which lifted us up to the great genius—all combined to produce a state of inspired exaltation. It was a powerful and strange magic spell that remains in my memory and, all pettiness gone, still works on my emotions . . .

She does, however, describe how Wagner wept with joy when he first heard the Rhinemaidens sing their trio; how vividly he assumed various characters in rehearsal; how he told her of his plans to perform other composers' great operas at Bayreuth; how he 'sat on the stage, his legs crossed and the score on his lap'. After the festival was over he wrote to her expressing his gratitude—she was also one of the artists who had not insisted on a fee:

Oh Lilli, Lilli! You were the most beautiful of all—and you are right, dear child—it will never come again. That was the magic of it all—my Rhinemaidens! Fidi [Wagner's son Siegfried] sings their song all the time . . . And now you are really engaged—my congratulations!

The engagement proved, in fact, a minor disaster for Wagner. Lehmann was maltreated by her fiancé, later Bayreuth's technical director, and broke off the liaison. In 1882 Wagner summoned her back to Bayreuth to lead the Flower Maidens in *Parsifal*. She accepted, and took over the responsibility of rehearsing the ensemble. Wagner was again enraptured by the result, but at the eleventh hour she withdrew, feeling that she could not stomach the proximity of her ex-fiancé. Since 1870 she had been restricted to Berlin by an imperial contract which only allowed outside performances with a special dispensation from the Kaiser. Now her international career had just begun, with appearances in Vienna and London. She probably benefited from the enforced stability of her early years, for despite her enormous repertory (170 roles in 119 operas), she was no infant marvel. Her gifts were a tenacious will and a patient musical intelligence. In utter contrast to Schröder-Devrient, she sang after the best classical models. Preparing Isolde she sought, in her own words, 'a beautiful legato in the fine Italian style; for after all there is only one perfect art of song', rehearsing 'every phrase hundreds of times . . . gradually increasing my physical and vocal endurance'. She was in the process of making an extraordinary passage, from being a singer of the 'nightingale' mould and timbre to one who could master Wagner's sternest music. Her achievement turned out even more extraordinary than that, for somehow she managed to keep her voice slim and firm enough to continue singing coloratura parts. She did not have the massive natural endowment of some of the later Wagnerian sopranos, but she did have a deep understanding of the technicalities of singing, and her book on the subject, *Meine Gesangskunst* (translated as *How to Sing*) shows a thorough grasp of the physiology of voice production. Few prima donnas have had such a strong intellectual awareness of their art.

Lehmann's first Isolde was sung in 1884 in London, a city which did not meet with her approval. She roundly deplored the carryings-on of Mapleson's management, the prima donna Christine Nilsson, and the fogs which even in spring 'smothered every pleasure'—they must indeed have been a deadly hazard to singers' delicate throats, and their prevalence in winter must have been one consideration in generally starting the opera season in May. Contemporary verdicts on her interpretation are oddly mixed: Wolf objected to her making a virago of Isolde, while Hanslick urged her to be cautious—'Her far from heroic voice is no match for the merciless surf of the Wagnerian orchestra.' Caution was not, however, in Lilli Lehmann's nature. In the words of Henry Pleasants, she 'revelled in the accomplishment of the impossible; she accepted challenges with the self-destructive zest of a Malibran, with the advantage that hers was a more resilient constitution'. Her next bold move was in the direction of New York and the newly opened German-oriented Metropolitan Opera House. To get there for a decent period she had to break her Berlin contract, incurring the Kaiser's wrath, an enormous fine, and an order banishing her from all German opera houses which lasted until 1891. It was well worth the trouble, for she got exactly what she wanted at the Met, becoming their first regular dramatic soprano. She sang Brünnhilde there for the first time, as well as her other major roles of Isolde, Leonore, Aida, Donna Anna, Norma, Carmen, and Violetta—the latter in Italian as well as German when the Met modified its language policy.

Lehmann loved the Americans, finding their high moral tone and earnestness sympathetic. She was a fanatic vegetarian and anti-vivisectionist, and nothing pleased her more in New York than the fact that the whipping of horses was forbidden. Society ladies who appeared before her with feathers or plumes in their hats were treated to a stern lecture. She also became known for the austerity, bordering on stinginess, of her personal life. The chambermaids in her New York hotel were shocked to discover that Madame Lehmann washed her own stockings and handkerchiefs and even hung them up to dry in the bathroom. She refused to tip the liftboys and preferred to stand on the streetcar rather than hire a cab and waste a dime on comfort.

In 1891 she began teaching, and two of her pupils, Geraldine Farrar and Olive Fremstad, became the outstanding American prima donnas of the pre-war years. Lessons were conducted in conditions of Prussian discipline: the over-emoting Farrar had her hands tied behind her back—'Now express your feelings with your voice!' commanded Lehmann. One day Lehmann threw a book at

Fremstad, who then stormed out in tears, vowing never to return. On the stairs she met Lehmann's soon discarded husband Paul Kalisch, a second-rate tenor she had peremptorily married in the vain hope of drilling him into a great Siegfried and Tristan. 'What are *you* worried about?' he said to Fremstad on hearing her story, 'She does that to me the whole time.'

In 1896, Lehmann met her real match when she returned to Bayreuth and came up against Wagner's widow Cosima, who now governed the place like a beleaguered high priestess defending the purity of the cult. In 1886 Cosima had invited Lehmann to sing in the first Bayreuth *Tristan*, but Lehmann had furiously declined when she learnt that the role she was being offered was not Isolde, but Brangäne. Cosima's zeal, as so often in such situations, had led to a hardening and narrowing quite alien to Wagner's pioneering theatrical sense. She did not lack her own production ideas, but in the event of any argument, she referred back to the authority of her dead husband, often seeking confirmation from her son Siegfried, who had been aged six at the time of the first festival. Absolute and exclusive rights were kept over *Parsifal*, performances of which became the centre of the Bayreuth mystique. The opera could be seen nowhere else, and owing to its elements of Christian ritual, applause was forbidden. This in itself was an unjustifiable tradition, as Wagner had actually encouraged the first audience to applaud at the end of the opera and was even said to have let out a loud 'bravo' at the end of the Flower-maidens' scene in the second act. More lastingly serious in its effects was the growth of a Bayreuth-sanctioned conception of Wagner singing. It flourished under the tutelage of the chorus-master Julius Kniese and consisted of bringing Wagner's vocal line as close as possible to speech, at the expense of rhythm and tone, rather than allowing it a natural musical flow. Wagner, on the contrary, had always insisted on his music's melodiousness and appreciated the legato that Italian singers brought to it. But Kniese's coaching led to rasping, barking, forcing: Shaw found the 1894 *Parsifal* 'an abomination . . . German singers at Bayreuth do not know how to sing: they shout; and you can see them make a vigorous stoop and lift with their shoulders, like coal-heavers, when they have a difficult note to tackle, a *pianissimo* on any note above the stave being impossible to them.'

Lehmann came back to Bayreuth as the most famous Brünnhilde in a world obsessed with Wagner. After his death, the controversy faded and his status was undisputed. For the *fin de siècle* generation, he was the great image of the Artist—titanic, uncompromising, visionary. It was not only the initiated writers, artists, and composers who worshipped him, but the mass of music lovers. Ordinary public taste adjusted to his originality to the point at which Shaw in 1889 could write:

> Oh Bayreuth, Bayreuth, valley of humiliation for the smart ones of the world! To think that this Wagner, once the very safest man in Europe to ridicule, should turn out the prime success of the century. To be reduced to a piteous plea that you always admitted that there were some lovely bits in *Lohengrin*! . . . Yes, the cranks were right after all. And now—now . . . it is not merely a question of whether he or Offenbach is the more melodious, but of whether he is to be accepted as the Luther of a new Reformation, the Plato of a new philosophy, the Messiah who is really to redeem the fall and lead us back to the garden of Eden . . .

Queen Victoria herself commanded a performance of *Lohengrin* at Windsor Castle and wrote in her diary, 'I was simply enchanted. It is the most glorious composition, so poetic, so dramatic, and one might also say, religious in feeling and full of sadness, pathos and tenderness.' Young ladies played piano arrangements of the Ride of the Valkyries and the Good Friday Music from *Parsifal*. Cosima's staging even made it all eminently respectable, and Shaw found Rhinemaidens swimming about in muslin tea-gowns, giving 'a strong impression that they had forgotten their gloves and hats'. The romance of opera was German and Wagnerian: Italian opera now seemed meretricious, slightly vulgar, even laughable. Without the continuing patronage of the prima donna it would have been even more scorned.

Lehmann was deeply offended by Cosima's slighting attitude to her present eminence as well as her authority as a member of the original 1876 cast. There was a tight-lipped quarrel between the two women over a red wig, which neither won. Lehmann's pique is evident in her account of the events, from which one gets the distinct impression that she would very much have liked Cosima's job herself.

> I suffered to see how the form of the *Ring*, which we had all so lovingly absorbed and taken away with us, together with our

thoughts of its creator, was now being dislocated in the very place that was its home ... All roads may lead to Rome but to the Bayreuth of today there is but one—the road of slavish subjection. There is no true conception of how valuable individual artistry can be ... Cosima was not only very clever and well-informed. She had also assumed the authority of judgment peculiar to the aristocracy, so that what she announced was accepted as infallible.

Ironically, Shaw was reluctant to judge Lehmann's Bayreuth Brünnhilde the exemplar of 'individual artistry': 'She acts intelligently, sings effectively and in tune, and is attractive enough, attaining in all these respects a degree of excellence that makes it impossible to call her commonplace; but for all that she is conventional, and takes the fullest advantage of the fact that plenty of ideas suggested by Wagner will attach themselves to her if she only stands her ground impressively.'

Shaw's final comment on this Brünnhilde was that she would doubtless make a very good Marguerite in Gounod's *Faust*, a role she did indeed sing. This is telling. One suspects that Lehmann, for all the praise given to her versatility, was not a true Wagnerian soprano—or rather she became one by training and will-power, not by the exploitation of a physical resource as was the case with Flagstad or Birgit Nilsson. Her fame as a Wagnerian was due to the fact that there were very few singers at the time capable of understanding how to sing his music at all. When her recordings were made in 1907, when she was almost sixty, she bequeathed only one Wagner extract—a bumpily phrased 'Du bist der lenz' which most lyric sopranos can match up to—and the outstanding items come from the more familiar repertory of Mozart, Bellini, Verdi, and even Meyerbeer. Oddly enough, the singer she most suggests is Melba—a Melba with more piercing attack and intelligent colouring. But there is the same limpidity of tone and smoothness of production, apart from the odd jerk between head and chest register, attributable to age, the same brilliance without weight, and the same no-nonsense forthright briskness. Anything nostalgic, wistful, or seductive finds her lacking: Marchesi's daughter, herself a well-known singer, thought her icy-hard on stage. Her 'Casta Diva', for instance, is extraordinarily accurate and secure, but it fails to suggest a veiled high priestess: she cannot slide down those chromatic runs in a trance or suggest a woman with a secret passion.

What is truly magnificent is her scaling of the harsher reaches of Mozart's music. The coloratura is amazing—far neater and truer than Patti's efforts at the same era of life. Her 'Martern aller Arten' in John Steane's words 'meets every technical demand, and has power and majesty beyond comparison'; Donna Anna's long narrative and aria beginning 'Don Ottavio, son morta' is truly arresting and grand in conception—here is a woman well able to bludgeon her fiancé into submission and fight back against her seducer. The fact that she had suffered from asthma as a child makes her technique all the more astonishing.

Mozart played a large part in the long twilight of Lehmann's career. She found the opportunity to satisfy her autocratic tendency in Salzburg's early Mozart festivals, where she managed to sing, produce, assemble casts, and dictate artistic policy. Nothing daunted her: she disapproved strongly of Mahler's 1906 *Don Giovanni* and brought forth her own competing version for Salzburg, which she rehearsed in her Berlin home. Mahler found the result absurdly amateurish. In 1910 she left Salzburg and opera, but continued to sing publicly until her seventy-second year. She paid eloquent and justifiable tribute to her own sterling achievement in her autobiography:

> I have gone my own road proudly, the way of the will, of knowledge, and of capacity, in accord with my aspirations and abilities. Thanks to my education, my talents and industry, I have been able to pursue it with increasing authority. I quickly grasped what availed in art, and gladly learned of everything, with the firm resolution to attain the greatest possible perfection in the realm of art.

Writers like Henry Pleasants have probably made too much of the 'versatility' of prima donnas like Lehmann, in comparison with the 'specialized' prima donnas of today. The fact is not that a phenomenal flexibility of voice has died a mysterious death, but that singers were thrown into a ferment by the popularity of Wagner, without really appreciating the peculiar nature of his demands. Survivors like Lehmann were the exception: early casualties fell thick and fast, as they still do. Nothing in opera seems to evanesce like a new Siegfried or Brünnhilde. 'Sound technique' was no guarantee of success—we have already seen Melba out for months after forty minutes of *Siegfried*.

By the beginning of the twentieth century, a number of definite types and career patterns had emerged from the Wagnerian soprano. There was the great might-have-been, Hedwig Reicher-Kindermann, who died at twenty-nine; the latter-day Schröder-Devrient, Katharina Klafsky, persistently out of tune but 'elemental, tremendous in everything'; the steely-voiced Rosa Sucher, favoured by Cosima at Bayreuth; and above all these, the Croatian Milka Ternina. Her performances of Isolde with Jean de Reszke as her Tristan in London and New York were written into legend, and her Brünnhilde, Tosca, and Fidelio were equally celebrated; but she was cut short in her prime by a muscular disease which had the embarrassing side-effect of making one side of her face twitch in a manner which made her appear permanently lascivious. The next generation had been trained with the possibility of Wagner from the start, but their records do not reveal a Golden Age beneath the hissing. John Steane's verdict is of 'a higher proportion of plodding ungainliness then than now, more choppy phrasing, less attention to detail and less understanding of the need for light and shade . . . careless over the precise length of notes and occasionally getting intervals wrong'. In time, the baneful absolutism of Cosima at Bayreuth lost much of its influence. The festival closed at the beginning of the First World War, when the copyright on *Parsifal* expired, and it only reopened in 1924 under Siegfried Wagner, whose policy was cautiously liberal. Bayreuth became a symbol of Wagnerism rather than the opera house which set standards and arbitrated style.

In the inter-war years Wagner performance came to maturity with an incomparable generation of singers and conductors, whose nobility is evident in the surviving records of Frida Leider (1888–1975), the most celebrated Isolde and Brünnhilde of her time. What the New York critic W. J. Henderson said of Lehmann's Brünnhilde is also good for what we hear on record of Leider's: 'She was possessed of that rare combination of traits and equipment which made it possible for her to delineate the divinity in womanhood and womanhood in divinity, the mingling of the unapproachable goddess and the melting, pitying human being.' There is no sense of strain at any part of the range of Leider's voice, and she sounds as rich and full in the vital lower reaches as in her glowing top notes. She hadn't the sharp brilliance or agility of Lehmann, but the voice's 'natural' tone was weighted with more colour and feeling. Even more remarkable is its liquidity—the ability to move through long phrases with the values of good Italianate legato kept prominent throughout. Second-rate Wagnerians always make the listener aware of the edges and corners in the music, points at which the singer snatches a bit of breath or fudges one note to get to another on schedule. Leider never loses her poise or sonority: her fault, if anything, is the opposite. The recording situation gave her, she admitted, a sort of inverted stage-fright, and she found it much easier to sing moving about a stage in costume than standing still in an empty hall at eleven in the morning. She reports one occasion when the first half of the *Fidelio* aria was recorded in one hall, from which she had to move to finish in another hall, with completely different acoustics and atmospheric conditions. There are times, such as her 1928 recording of Brünnhilde's Immolation, when verbal point and urgency are absent, and a disengaged smoothness of line takes over. Yet this slight dullness never affected her in the theatre: 'Leider was quite incapable of a routine perform-ance,' wrote Vincent Sheean. 'She was good or bad, she was often great, but she was never mediocre.'

In her quaint and unrevealing memoirs, she describes her modest Berlin upbringing and a brief early career as a bank clerk. Her aspirations were initially charged by the acclaim showered on visiting prima donnas like Emmy Destinn or Geraldine Farrar, but Lilli Lehmann's autobiography soon put her on the straight and narrow path of artistic idealism. Her teachers included Alban Berg's sister, and she made her provincial début at the relatively late age of twenty-six. Unlike Materna, Lehmann, or Flagstad, she did not skip about for a while in operetta: Venus in *Tannhäuser* was her first role, and she never ventured far out of the dramatic soprano repertory. Apart from her Wagnerian roles, she was also admired as Donna Anna, Leonore, Strauss's Marschallin, and Amelia in *Un Ballo in Maschera*; in her early years she even sang a few Normas. By 1923 she was prima donna at the Berlin Staatsoper, and in 1924 she first went to London, where she sang in the golden Bruno Walter seasons with Lotte Lehmann, Maria Olczewska, Lauritz Melchior, and Friedrich Schorr. Her popularity at Covent Garden was immense and lasting. In 1927 she sang Brünnhilde in Italian at La Scala, which she significantly considered 'extremely beneficial to my technique. In using the open Italian vowels, my throat expanded without effort, my breath moved more freely. I succeeded in carrying this over into my German performances . . .' In 1928 she sang for the first of four years in Chicago, until the company there fell victim to the Depression. Leider's success had been uninterrupted but exhausting, her only holidays being the enforced leisure of transatlantic liners.

Then, in 1933, Hitler was elected Chancellor of Germany. Leider's violinist husband was Jewish: 'I was completely unprepared for this news, which caused me great distress. But artists are too easily inclined to ignore what might otherwise disturb their art, so, after the first excitement, I threw myself into my work even more intensely.' She paid dearly for her naïvety. Wagner became a standard-bearer of the Nazi ideology of German culture, and to sing his music under the new régime was seen, in America especially, as a political act. Hitler was a regular visitor to Bayreuth and a close friend of the English-born Winifred Wagner, who had inherited control from her late husband Siegfried. She won all sorts of exemptions from the tyranny which stifled everyone and everything else in Germany, and Hitler personally guaranteed the festival's financial security. In 1933 Leider sang Brünnhilde in a new Bayreuth *Ring* lavishly produced by Heinz Tietjen, who also ran her home opera house in Berlin and who brought his singers from there up to Bayreuth for the summer. When she had first sung there in 1928, she found the approach old-fashioned, although she learnt much from Bayreuth-trained singers. It was at Bayreuth that she considered herself to have mastered the role of Kundry for the first time, and when Tietjen (the first person outside the Wagner family to have control of production) was appointed, he did away with many of the more antiquated conventions of staging. But by 1938 the festival had been turned into a glorified political rally, with swastika flags in the Festspielhaus and Hitler in formal residence at Wahnfried. Leider's husband was forced into exile in Switzerland, and she herself suffered a nervous collapse which effectively ended her operatic career.

Leider had few vocal problems in her later years, apart from the natural contraction of her topmost register. However, in her first season at the Met, during that fateful year of 1933, there was an electrifying incident of which Vincent Sheean gives an eloquent account. The occasion was a performance of *Die Walküre*:

She was on her knees before Wotan (Friedrich Schorr), with her noble head humbly bent and her left hand at her throat . . . She had reached the point where she had to sing '*War es so schmachlich?*' She sang the first two words and notes—that is, '*War es*'—after which a strange, very small sound came out of her throat and no note followed. That weird small sound is quite impossible to describe and if I had not been sitting so close I could have not heard it; I suppose most of the three thousand people there present did not. The click (if it was a click) seemed like the electrocution, the murder of the great voice . . . Leider kept her head down and I saw her shake it in a kind of fury . . . She had been singing the whole performance over a bad cold, so bad that she could not even speak. Now the voice itself, the very sense of her existence, refused its divine grace, and there she was, on her knees, with the ruin of a great career in plain view in front of her. Such a concentrated ordeal seldom befalls an artist. I felt, or imagined I felt, the struggle of her will to conquer her body. Then she threw back her really grand head and looked out beyond all the three thousand of us to some utter truth beyond us, opened her mouth with confidence, it seemed to me, and by some power (I could see her throat quivering) the voice was given again. From then on to the end of the act Leider sang with everything an artist has to give, although the sacrifice of her voice must have been tragic.

As Sheean goes on to consider, this sense of knife-edged excitement, tension, and awe are all fundamental to the experience of Wagner's music, and it was the induction of so much over-wrought emotion that led Nietzsche to pose his 'physiological objections' to it. An artist like Leider could bring her audiences to a pitch of silent hysteria, as Sheean also demonstrates: 'Isolde and Brünnhilde were hers, and there are no moderate ways of expressing how deeply she could move us in them . . . I have been so shaken by her Isolde, again and again, that I could no longer stand up, and had to go and sit on the floor of the house in that area at the back where the standees go. Some of those *Tristan* performances·left me very uncertain of my own surroundings—so dazed that it was physically difficult to get out of the crowd and into the cold, wet street where reality slowly returned.' Wagner himself had understood the nature of the monster he had given birth to, writing to Mathilde Wesendonk during rehearsals that 'This *Tristan* is turning into something *dreadful* . . . only mediocre performances can save me. Completely good ones are bound to drive people crazy.'

Leider recovered her voice, although Sheean claims that she was 'never restored to full vocal power'. She herself does not even mention the incident in her memoirs. The Met re-engaged her in 1934, but after that she remained in Europe, for reasons that are not clear: she claimed that anti-German feelings were running high, while the Met archives suggest arguments over fees.

After the beginning of the war, Leider gave only *lieder* recitals, and then retreated to her country estate in what is now East Germany. Her memoirs give a long and harrowing report of the last days of the hostilities, which she was clearly amazed to survive. There was a grotesque incident when the advancing Russian army passed through and a party requisitioned her house: 'They noticed a picture of me in my *Walküre* costume with helmet, shield and spear, whereupon the chauffeur, pointing at it, cried "Soldier!" and aimed his pistol at me. The officer immediately knocked it out of his hand.' Later the soldiers found a trunk full of her wigs and stage accoutrements and cavorted around dressed as Valkyries.

Leider's withdrawal opened the American door for another singer, about whom Leider sagely says nothing in her book and who was herself to suffer from the humiliations of war. Kirsten Flagstad (1895–1962) is the second Nordic phenomenon of opera. Like the first, her ordinariness was transfigured and made glamorous, even superhuman. 'When I am not dealing with art I am the most commonplace person in the world. I am not a bit mysterious or unusual or complex. I am an absolutely average Norwegian,' she claimed in all sincerity. Whereas Lind was calculating and deeply self-aware, Flagstad always appeared faintly bewildered by her immense gift. Her voice was uttered like a torrential force of nature, something beyond her own reason or control. Before going on stage, she played patience, as if innocent of what was about to befall her. 'I see her now,' wrote Vincent Sheean, 'in her dressing room at the Metropolitan . . . calm and majestic, smiling kindly, braiding her hair with a vocal score of the opera open on the table before her, an Isolde who had never suffered humiliation of spirit or the wish to die. She had been knitting and put the work down beside the *Tristan* score while she talked to us. After we left I imagine she

16. Wilhelmine Schröder-Devrient, *c*.1830: her immense personal magnetism is barely hinted at in this engraving.

17. The invincible Lilli Lehmann, with dog.

18. Her rival Lillian Nordica, the first American Brünnhilde. 19. *right* Frida Leider as Isolde, an interpretation still remembered with awe.

20. *left* Olive Fremstad, photographed by Mishkin as Isolde. 21. *above* Birgit Nilsson rehearsing for the famous 1962 Bayreuth *Tristan und Isolde* with Wieland Wagner.

22. Kirsten Flagstad attained a popularity that no other Wagnerian soprano has ever approached: here the press catch her with a bevy of Girl Scouts paying their respects.

resumed her knitting . . . No more tranquil approach to unbridled passion has come under my observation.' Her family background was strongly musical and she had undergone a sound and steady provincial training, but she had no burning motivation: there was no great dedication to singing or the theatre, and a few lessons in Dalcrozean *plastique*[1] gave her all the ideas about acting she thought she needed.[2] 'I don't know anything, really, about my voice . . . why it behaves as it does I have no idea,' was another typical Flagstad disclaimer. All she wanted, she said, was a husband, a family, and a quiet, comfortable life.

In her operatic backwater of Oslo, she had sung everything from Tosca and Aida to musical comedy, and over twenty quiet years her voice had slowly increased in size and weight. In the early 1930s, without any sense of approaching her destiny, she began to sing some of the lighter Wagner roles—Elisabeth, Elsa, and Eva in *Meistersinger*. Even though she had been given a score of *Lohengrin* for her tenth birthday and had immediately learnt parts of Elsa's music, Wagner played little part in her life, and as late as 1930 she had almost fallen asleep with boredom at her first hearing of *Tristan*. But in 1932 she herself sang Isolde in Oslo with enough *éclat* to win a recommendation to Bayreuth, where she sang in the 1933 and 1934 *Rings*. A talent scout from the Met had heard her as early as 1929 and had evinced interest, but it was only after Bayreuth that they followed it up. She was summoned to St Moritz, where she underwent a gruelling audition in a heavily curtained room that muffled the splendour of her voice. The Met had lost Leider and were anxious for a new soprano who could satisfy New York's insatiable Wagner-lust, but they do not seem to have had any high hopes of a raw and gauche Norwegian who had only just begun to sing in German. She was accepted diffidently and bundled off to Prague for some intensive coaching under George Szell. Her début was as Sieglinde in February 1935. It was an instant, overnight, copybook sensation of the sort that sends New Yorkers reeling with excitement. Four days later she sang Isolde; by the end of the

---

1 'Rage: clenched fist and five steps downstage in a majestic manner; sexual passion: hands clasped on breast and head turned away' is how Sheean describes her stage manner.
2 What do you need to sing Wagner? she was asked: 'A pair of comfortable shoes,' she replied.

month she had appeared as the *Walküre* and *Götterdämmerung* Brünnhilde, and in April she was Kundry in *Parsifal*—all three operas being quite new to her.

Flagstad did not have Leider's intensity or Lehmann's personality and intelligence. There were always plenty, Toscanini among them, who thought little of her interpretative power. What she had was the ability to sing Wagner with calm, literal accuracy. She was an absolutely faithful singer of music that had previously seemed to deny that possibility. As the *New Yorker* put it, 'Madame Flagstad has the superlative gift of being able to do her job.' She was fortunate in having perfect pitch, but her musicianship went deeper than that: W. J. Henderson remarked at the time of her first New York appearance that 'There are no evasions of the demands of the music. She does not alter rhythms, introduce questionable tone-qualities or indulge in any of the other tricks which some singers use.' Vincent Sheean wrote that her voice was the greatest he had ever heard, 'the greatest in volume, range, security, beauty of tone, everything a voice can have, and all of one piece, never a break in it, all rolling out with no evidence of effort or strain even in the most difficult passages. The only defect to be found in her remarkable performances was that they did not express what Wagner wrote.' The qualification is, of course, somewhat crippling. It is not just the fact that German was not her native tongue—in her autobiography she describes the painstaking way she found out 'what it all meant', at least in terms of the dictionary—but the lack of an entire dimension of passion and urgency. Her singing is placid through music which bespeaks rage and obsession. We complain about the tonal imperfections of other Wagner singers and shake our heads at the thought of the Bayreuth 'bark', but Flagstad's straightforward perfection—for it is something near that—is not the answer either.

Until 1941, she maintained an effortless supremacy in the Wagnerian repertory. The gap between supply and demand was such that she was given little opportunity to try anything else, although Edward Johnson, the manager of the Met, begged her in vain to sing Norma. She was married to a lugubrious Norwegian lumber merchant and hotel-owner, Henry Johansen, whose wealth meant that she need only sing what, when, and where she wanted. Most of her professional year was spent in the major North American centres and it is no exaggeration to say that her box-office drawing-power saved the Met from bankruptcy in the final phase of the Depression. She loved Hollywood and movie magazines and the thought of herself as a celebrity: despite Garbo-like protestations of a desire to be left alone, anonymous, etc., she relished every last handclap of public adulation with a pleasure of which only the naïve in heart are capable. And like Jenny Lind, she did achieve a general fame beyond the opera-going audience. Ogden Nash wrote comic verse celebrating the singer from Scandinavia, 'land of peace and sane behavia'; she sang on the Bing Crosby Show and in the movies. Again like Lind, her appeal came from a well-projected simplicity of manner which, after sophisticated prima donnas like Maria Jeritza or Lily Pons, made her seem wholesome and 'unspoilt by success'.

It was this very aspect of her public image which left her so cruelly exposed during the Second World War. She immediately suffered from the automatic association of Wagner with Hitler and from the revulsion from any aspect of German culture. By 1940 and the fall of Norway, she declared herself 'exhausted to the verge of hysteria' by five years of American fame. Everyone expected the unsullied Flagstad to do the right and noble thing—fight the Nazis —but she took the craven course of returning to Norway and her husband, a member of the extreme right-wing and later collabor- ationist Quisling party. She had 'no idea' about politics, she had 'no political views at all': she just wanted to get back to her husband as a private citizen, not as a national symbol. Norwegians in America tried to get her to stay, arguing that her return would be a propaganda victory for the occupying régime, and the ambassador himself stepped in. It was oddly and aptly like Waltraute's plea to Brünnhilde to return the ring to Valhalla, when Brünnhilde renounces every claim, every power, except that of her love for Siegfried. Such ironies were academic, however, and Flagstad left herself pathetically vulnerable. Her passage back to Norway took her across Germany, and she was widely suspected in America of having secured a visa through friendly Nazi contacts. It was even claimed that she had sung Wagner in Berlin. In fact, once back in Norway, she had persuaded her husband to resign from the Quisling party and had rigorously refused any public engagements in occu- pied territory, singing only occasionally in neutral Sweden and Switzerland. 'Like millions of others,' she later explained, 'I had no choice but to sit it out. There was nothing I could do, nothing my background and temperament had prepared me to do but to wait.' After the war, however, she began to show quite exceptional courage and determination in salvaging her reputation.

Her husband had died while awaiting trial for collaboration and she needed to resume her career. The beneficial side effect of her withdrawal was a wonderful Indian summer for her voice, which remained at its peak until she was well over fifty. London reaped the reward of tolerance. Her pre-war performances at Covent Garden had been very successful, despite the continuing presence of Leider, and a début marred by a bad cold and a wound caused by a powder-compact falling from a box on to her head while she was watching a performance of *Götterdämmerung* that featured Leider and Melchior and was conducted by Sir Thomas Beecham. After the war, Covent Garden reopened without much money and cleverly re-established its international reputation by engaging singers such as Flagstad, Hotter, and Schwarzkopf who were politically dubious and whom other houses were initially reluctant to engage. All three relearnt some of their roles in English, and Flagstad sang Wagner in four fondly remembered seasons. In America things were very different. Her first return there was primarily a private visit to her daughter, married and living in Arizona, but the protests began almost immediately. The Met had refused to have her back, but although their reasons were not altogether political—Helen Traubel had since assumed Flagstad's roles, and the management could not simply dispose of her—this gave a sort of official confirmation to the public's suspicions of her integrity. Before the war she had had her little vanities, problems with unsympathetic conductors, and pique if her appearances were not sold out. She now faced a barrage of hostility unparalleled in opera history. Apart from a flood of press allegations against her, friends and colleagues, including her regular partner Lauritz Melchior, with whom she had quarrelled violently in 1938, publicly wanted nothing to do with her; recitals at Carnegie Hall were picketed; in Philadelphia, a businessman hired a claque of college boys at $15 each, who booed her from the first note and hissed 'Nazi' while she was singing. Stink bombs were thrown and when fisticuffs broke out, the police were called into the concert hall. But she persevered, for as Henry Pleasants put it, 'She could be small in small matters, not so much childlike as childish. But in big matters she was big.' And there were plenty who stood by her, notably the young conductor and pianist Edwin McArthur, whom she assiduously patronized.

By 1951 she had won her way back to the Met. Her singing for a Jewish relief charity undoubtedly mollified her opposition. The tumult of applause which greeted her as Isolde lasted right the way through the Steersman's song, at the end of which a lone voice shouted, 'Welcome back'—but Rudolf Bing, the new manager of the Met, also reported a letter from the Broadway impresario Billy Rose comparing the re-engagement of Flagstad to the hypothetical appointment of Ilse Koch (the extermination camp official who had made lampshades out of human skin) as wardrobe mistress. Flagstad herself was dry-eyed throughout. She accepted the invitation to return to the Met not because she wanted to sing, but because she wanted to complete her moral rehabilitation. Having won this battle, she faced another, albeit much lesser, scandal. A recording of *Tristan und Isolde* conducted by Wilhelm Furtwängler was made, with Flagstad giving a superb account of herself. For some years in the theatre she had missed out Isolde's top Cs—yet in the recording they sounded gleaming and forceful. It eventually leaked out that incidents of the note had not been contributed by Flagstad at all, but by Elisabeth Schwarzkopf, whose husband Walter Legge had produced the recording. Flagstad had shown her appreciation with the gift of a superb diamond necklace. There was a good deal of outrage at this fairly innocent trick, and Flagstad was accused of artistic dishonesty. The incident, trivial as it was, had a peculiarly demoralizing effect, and hastened her retirement.

In her last years in the opera house, Flagstad broadened her repertory to take in two classical roles—Gluck's Alceste, with which in 1952 she took her farewell to the Met, and Dido in Purcell's *Dido and Aeneas*, which she sang for nothing but love in the tiny Mermaid Theatre in the London back garden of her friend the actor-manager Sir Bernard Miles. She expressed regret that she had not sung more Mozart and Strauss—she gave the first perform-ance of his *Four Last Songs* at a London Promenade concert of 1950, also under Furtwängler—but it was typical of her to have turned down the opportunity to sing Strauss's Elektra on the grounds that the text was 'coarse and indecent'. In the concert hall she could range wider, as long as she included the obligatory chunk of Wagner, and some of her loveliest records are of songs by Grieg and Sibelius.

Her years of semi-retirement do not seem to have been very happy. She settled in Norway where she coped with an undercurrent of unpopularity caused by her wartime conduct. She did, however, become the first director of a newly founded Norwegian opera company and continued to make a few records for Decca. Their producer John Culshaw persuaded her in 1958 to learn the mezzo-soprano part of Fricka in *Das Rheingold*, for what was to be the first studio recording of the *Ring*, and the cool slow majesty of her voice is still evident there at the age of sixty-three. Then a long and lonely struggle against cancer began. Culshaw sent her records of Gilbert and Sullivan to convalesce with, hoping to the very end that he might get her for the *Walküre* Fricka: but she died painfully in 1962.

Flagstad was a popularizer, the most famous of all Wagner singers, in Britain and America at least, with a reputation beyond the ranks of opera-lovers. She was also very much the type of singer who carried her interpretation in her luggage, as it were; Flagstad's Isolde was the same in London as in New York and differences of production affected it minimally. This was not wanton sloppiness on Flagstad's part: she was simply following standard operatic practice. At this time, the idea of 'production' was generally slight in any case, consisting more of strategic marshalling and positioning of forces against the geography of the set than the realization of the director's ideological vision of the opera in question. No one changed this state of affairs more than Wagner's grandson Wieland who, in collaboration with his brother Wolfgang, reopened the Bayreuth Festival in 1951 after the post-war years of disgrace.

It is today even more common to speak of Chéreau's *Ring* or Visconti's *Don Carlo*, than of Boulez's *Ring* or Giulini's *Don Carlo*, for it is now fashionable in opera to let theatrical considerations dominate musical ones, and Wieland Wagner was the first producer aggressively radical enough to revolutionize the old orthodoxies of staging. A new Germany had to look at its old heroes in a new light, and the Wagner stable had to be cleaned out. Wieland's singers not only had to act, they had to act in a style which fitted his approach. A Flagstad's small repertoire of attitudes and poses would have been no good to him. Cosima had aimed at once-and-for-all definition, but Wieland constantly explored possibilities: his later productions often contradicted the implications of his earlier ones. In 1951 Bayreuth had little money and Wieland made a virtue of necessity by sweeping away spears, helmets, forests, and the detritus of realistic presentation, replacing them with austere 'timeless' settings and sophisticated lighting—with the effect of emphasizing the universal mythic content of his grandfather's works, rather than their roots in Germanic folklore. None of Wieland's first prima donnas were singers of Flagstad's or Leider's stature, but they performed with unfailing commitment and intelligence. Astrid Varnay and Martha Mödl were early and distinguished exponents of the 'singing actress' type, that favourite companion of producer's opera whose sometimes chronic vocal inadequacies we are asked to excuse on account of an overriding dramatic credibility. Schröder-Devrient and Pauline Viardot are earlier names which might come to mind here, but they were blazing exceptions: in the post-war period, the good actress whose singing wobbles, screams, or dries up has become a regrettable norm.

Perhaps it is unreasonable to expect any generation to nurture more than one truly magnificent Wagnerian soprano, and an era that has had Birgit Nilsson can hardly feel cheated. The primal Wagnerian gifts of security, volume, and stamina were granted her, and if she lacked Mödl's or Varnay's impulsive manner, she was an impressive actress. But the most extraordinary thing about Nilsson was her continual development, her steady capacity to learn, even when her position was assured. 'I think I can say that each of my 208 performances of Isolde ... has in some way differed from all the others,' she claimed. She was the opposite of complacent, and her granite features conceal what is evidently a complex personality. Schuyler Chapin, manager of the Met, described her as 'a very self-contained person, extremely sensitive and easily hurt'; the record producer John Culshaw found her 'not easy to get close to', outwardly jovial and sociable, but untrusting in herself and others. She managed herself and drove a hard deal; her fees were very high; no one got the better of her.

A farmer's daughter from western Sweden, she was born in 1918—some books give 1922: either way, the power of her last performances is almost unbelievable. Her father hoped that as his only child she would take over the farm, and the night before her audition at the Stockholm Academy of Music made her milk ten cows. She won her place, but the first years were unhappy, with a teacher who did not understand her voice and a début at the Stockholm opera in 1946 which left her close to suicide. But eight solid years of consolidation followed in Stockholm, singing heavy roles like Aida, Tosca, and Donna Anna, which she continued to sing, even when firmly identified as a Wagnerian. She claimed that having to master her voice over a bad head cold put the seal on her technique. In the mid-Fifties she began on the major Wagnerian parts, first in Stockholm and then internationally: Munich, Vienna, San Francisco, Covent Garden, Bayreuth, and, from 1959, the Met. Canny, hard-working, independent, and persevering, a part of Nilsson has clearly never left the farm, but her essential serious-ness has been overshadowed by her much-publicized knockabout wit. There were clashes with conductors, Knappertsbusch and Karajan especially; and a long-standing and good-humoured battle with Rudolf Bing, the manager of the Met, led to various incidents, including her putting him down as a tax-deductible dependant on her Internal Revenue form—it did her no good, and in 1975 she had to abandon America for a few years when a dispute with the IRS came to a head. During a performance of Puccini's *Turandot* the tenor Franco Corelli sulked in his dressing-room after being drowned by Nilsson at the end of 'In questa reggia'. Bing humoured him by suggesting that in the clinch that closed the final love duet he gave her a small sharp bite on the neck. Corelli cheered up at once and followed Bing's notion. Bing shortly received a phone call from Nilsson: 'I cannot go on. I have rabies.' At Bing's farewell gala, she sang the closing scene from *Salome*, during which the severed head of John the Baptist, presented to her on a tray, was modelled on Bing's own.

Nilsson's early performances were often criticized as 'cool', and 'the icy Birgit Nilsson' became a cliché of operatic criticism. There certainly is something chilly about the cutting force and occasional sharpness of her tone, especially compared to Flagstad's kindlier and sweeter sound. But Nilsson was an infinitely more intense singer than Flagstad, a singer born for extremes of emotion, for the peaks that leave the rest of us breathless. Her Brünnhilde, compared with Leider's or Helga Dernesch's, is relentlessly the Valkyrie: she fails to dramatize vocally the contrast between the unawoken goddess of *Die Walküre* and the woken mortal of *Siegfried*. Her Isolde, on the other hand, a part which does require a constant grandeur, was a performance which grew to profound truth. She had sung Isolde 87 times when in 1962 Wieland Wagner asked her to re-create the role for a new production at Bayreuth. Wieland regarded her as something of a *pis aller*, for in 1960 Anja Silja, a lithe twenty-year-old beauty had arrived at Bayreuth to sing Senta. She had a modernity of temperament which fascinated Wieland as an angle for his productions, and she became his muse as well as his lover. Silja might have been a reincarnation of Schröder-Devrient: she too came from a theatrical and musical background and was a child prodigy, making her concert début at ten, and her operatic one at sixteen, as Rosina in *Il Barbiere di Siviglia*. Her singing was wild and wayward—sometimes enthralling, sometimes plain ugly and off-pitch. For Wagner's music she quite lacked those necessary gifts of stamina and security, and she was never allowed much time for calm growth. Wieland wanted her for everything he did, at Bayreuth and elsewhere, and she did too much too soon. There was nothing statuesque or restrained about her acting style —as Fidelio, she would fling off her cap at the moment of revelation in the Dungeon Scene, letting long blonde hair tumble over her shoulders, making nonsense of the idea of 'disguise as a man', but creating a tremendous *frisson*; as Salome, she lay on her back, her head dangling over the edge of the stage. She was openly and convincingly erotic, with something strangely evasive behind her arresting stage manner. Against her Nilsson may at first have appeared conventional, inflexible, uninteresting, but Silja was not remotely ready at twenty-two to sing Isolde at Bayreuth, and Nilsson it had to be. There was initial tension and disappointment on both sides, but she and Wieland went on to forge a production that lasted for eight summers and which witnesses would rank among the greatest operatic experiences of their lives. Nilsson later said of Wieland, 'I get down on my nose to him,' and he seems to have opened some floodgate in her art: the live recording made from performances in 1966 communicates much of her splendour in the role.

Perhaps her most shattering achievement was as Elektra in Strauss's gruesome opera, again memorably recorded under Georg Solti. Here is awe-inspiring singing. In Elektra's monologue, one can hear the variety and subtlety of which Nilsson was capable, as well as a power that cuts the air like a sword ripped out of its sheath. There is yearning in her cries to her dead father, madness in the imperturbable steadiness of tone as she remembers his murder, and a winsome softness as she recalls her childhood. In the dialogue with Clytemnestra, she is light and frosty, simpering, mocking, and insinuating; in the greeting to Orestes there is a searing tenderness. Somehow she can bring all this to a climax of vengeful fury and ecstasy, the voice rolling through and over the orchestra tumult. Nor is this the fabrication of the recording studio. I came away from an actual performance of Nilsson's Elektra with a splitting headache and a shaken soul.

Since Nilsson, there has been nobody decisively and consistently in command of the Wagnerian repertory. No one could pretend that we are in a golden age of Wagner singing. There have been some wonderfully warm and sensitive Brünnhildes, like Rita Hunter and Helga Dernesch, but they have been short-lived, and Dernesch, a potentially major singer much patronized by Herbert von Karajan, has been forced to give up soprano roles altogether, the top of her voice having disintegrated. Linda Esther Gray, a Scots girl of noble mien and with a vibrant joy in her singing of Wagner, has raised hope among the despairing; Hildegard Behrens and Jeanine Altmeyer, one of Lotte Lehmann's last pupils, are also both very exciting—one hopes not too exciting for their own vocal good. Some other quite respected interpreters seem to confine the technical challenge of Wagner to taking a deep breath and hoping to arrive at a rest before it gives out—their misconception being that Wagner's is 'expressionistic' music, which needs only to be 'deeply felt' or sung 'with soul' to be effective.

It must be difficult to be a Wagnerian prima donna, and the jokes about heaving bosoms, spears, helmets, and 'Ho-jo-to-ho', with the Ride of the Valkyries crashing away in the orchestra, must get very boring. No other representative of the species has such a strong stereotype to contend with, as put, for instance, in Anna Russell's famous spoof version of the *Ring*. But Wagner himself dealt in female stereotypes, and to return in *Ring*-like fashion to our starting place, he did not present the prima donna with a set of dramatic possibilities substantially more complex than anything in Donizetti or Bellini. In some ways, less so. Most of Wagner's heroines are maidens of the sentimental tradition, with the single sublime mission to save men through the power or example of their love. In this Wagner was thoroughly the Victorian, and it was left to Richard Strauss to provide opera with broader images of womanliness.

# 5

# *Great Names of New York*

When Henry James returned to New York after a twenty-year absence in Europe, his mind saturated with the complex and hierarchical culture of the old world, he was intrigued by the paradoxical escalation of an *haut monde* within a democratic society. No royal court, no rights afforded by birth existed in the United States, but the Very Rich had to cultivate fields in which to display their ever-burgeoning wealth. Money was made to be conspicuous: the style with which this could be managed gave claim to aristocracy. Charity, art collecting, balls, all played their part, but nothing at the beginning of the twentieth century had quite the immediate cachet of a box at the opera. 'The opera function,' wrote James, was 'the only approach to the implication of the tiara known, so to speak, to the American law.' But who was there to curtsey to? he wondered.

James went on to talk of the 'general extravagant insistence' on the opera, and its role as 'the great vessel of social salvation . . . the whole social consciousness thus clambering into it, under stress, as the whole community crams into the other public receptacles, the desperate cars of the subways or the vast elevators of the tall buildings'. Opera in New York still feeds off this hysterical atmosphere. Crisis, scandal, triumph, spectacle: New York loves its opera at the *n*th degree of excitement, and no applause is worth having if it is not a thirty-minute standing ovation.

New York audiences are both fiercely loyal and cruelly fickle, sentimental about overnight sensations and old favourites. Quiet respect and patient interest are not in their temperament. They want big voices, top notes and gut-busting intensity. They love their opera to involve a risk or ultimate feat—Melba's Brünnhilde, Schumann-Heink's septuagenarian Farewell, Jeritza's prostrate 'Vissi d'arte', or Ponselle's début. In the Met standing-room queue,

171

heart of the New York opera audience, the long hours of waiting are whiled away with such tales, elaborated, exaggerated, and passed on from generation to generation.

The bad side of this is clear enough, and for the prima donna New York is a dangerous place. Like everything else in America, the prima donna becomes a commodity to be exploited and capitalized upon. The financial temptations are extreme, but there is a price to be paid in return. Many great operatic careers have been dissipated in fortune-making continental tours, movie contracts, and Broadway musicals.

Yet underneath so much that is plainly silly or trumped-up, opera in New York has always had one fundamental quality—excitement. One cannot be an opera-goer for long in New York without succumbing to the sheer physical stimulation afforded by its scale and fervour. Like the city itself, it has energy even when it is exhausted.

There had been regular seasons of Italian opera in New York since 1854 and the establishment of the Academy of Music on 14th Street. Malibran, Alboni, Sontag, Grisi, Tietjens, and Patti had all sung opera in the city before the Met was even built. From its beginnings with Garcia's little troupe, Italian opera was a fashionable artistic import, an example of the aping of European style which beset the aspiring nineteenth-century American. The old 'Knickerbocker' families had filled the boxes of the Academy of Music for over a quarter of a century before they realized a revolution in high society was upon them.

The flood of money-making which followed the Civil War had bred a generation of *nouveaux riches* for whom there were no boxes available in the existing opera house. A cabal of these parvenu millionaires, led by J. P. Morgan and representatives of the Astor and Vanderbilt clans, decided that they, their wives, and their wives' jewels should shine forth in a brighter and better auditorium which they themselves would build. New money would be seen to outclass old money, and each shareholder in the scheme would have the right to his own box.

The opera house which opened on Broadway and 39th Street in October 1883 was modelled on Covent Garden and La Scala, with a passing nod at the splendours of Garnier's Opéra in Paris. This first Metropolitan Opera House was peculiarly unsatisfactory in a number of ways: its sight-lines were poor and its backstage facilities primitive, but the boxes (which made up a quarter of the total seating capacity) were properly prominent. The shareholders kept a form of control over artistic policy by leasing the opera house to an impresario who remained accountable to them. They wanted someone efficient who could negotiate with the stars and provide a standard repertory—Morgan himself was said to be partial to *Il Trovatore*—but beyond that they were not unduly bothered. There was, of course, the (perhaps not apocryphal) lady who tapped the conductor on the shoulder in the interval of a performance of *Meistersinger* and asked whether he would mind playing the third act before the second, as she and her friends always left early, and she had therefore never heard it—but such instances of musical passion were rare.

The Swedish prima donna Christine Nilsson sang Marguerite in the house's opening performance of Gounod's *Faust*. She received $1,000 for her efforts, more than ten times what the average orchestra member earned in a month, but the real success of the first season was the Polish soprano Marcella Sembrich. Between them, Nilsson and Sembrich accounted for two-fifths of the Met's total payroll and contributed substantially to the $¼-million loss sustained by the manager Henry Abbey.

This initial lack of success can be ascribed to two major impediments: one was the all-surpassing attraction of Adelina Patti, singing under Mapleson's management at the old Academy of Music; the other was the fact that, although the boxes were full, the upper regions remained empty. The Met's most recent historian Martin Mayer has pointed out that the $2 required for the cheapest seat was about what an average workman would have earned in a day: the equivalent sum in 1983–4 might be $75, or about four times the actual current price of a cheap seat at the Met.

Apart from its autumn-winter orientation, the pattern for this first year was modelled on much the same lines as the spring-summer season at Covent Garden—the same repertory and many of the same singers were presented in a similar style. But then something bizarre happened. Abbey withdrew and his place was taken by Leopold Damrosch, a German immigrant of high standing in the New York musical scene. Damrosch proposed a season of German opera (strictly, opera in German, for Verdi and Meyerbeer were performed but in German translation), with modestly priced and hard-working German singers who would provide a high standard of ensemble and rehearsal. For the boxholders this meant long evenings sitting in the dark in an atmosphere of unremitting earnestness, yet it worked. Glamour gave way to artistic fervour; seats for the public became much cheaper; the critics, most of them of German extraction anyway, applauded, as the romance of Wagnerism settled in Manhattan.

Damrosch died after one year of heroic labour, but his place was immediately taken by his twenty-three-year-old son Walter, who continued the assembly of a remarkable team. From Bayreuth came Anton Seidl, Wagner's erstwhile assistant and tireless international champion, as conductor; Amalie Materna, the first Bayreuth Brünnhilde; Albert Niemann, the ageing but imposing *heldentenor*; Marianne Brandt, a powerful mezzo from Vienna; Max Alvary, a matinée idol Siegfried; and most significantly Lilli Lehmann, determined to conquer the heavy Wagnerian repertory, and the prima donna who would stand as Minerva to all American aspirants.

This regime lasted until 1891, buttressed by the support of New York's large German population. But finally the boxholders decided that they had had enough. Boredom set in, and stern measures were taken to combat the result. The following notice was posted:

> Many complaints having been made to the directors of the Opera House of the annoyance produced by the talking in the boxes during the performance, the Board requests that it be discontinued.

The management was transferred back to Abbey with Maurice Grau, on the understanding that Italian opera in Italian with a good list of stars would be produced. Conversation in the boxes could resume.

Then in 1892 a fire gutted the building. It was time for a complete reassessment. The opera house was reconstructed with improvements, including electric light. Only nineteen of the original shareholders remained, and Morgan and Vanderbilt closed their grip on the vacated boxes. Grau, a man of strong financial instinct, took the helm firmly, and under his steerage the Met committed itself to star singers at the expense of all else. The same old war-horses would be trotted out night after night, execrably decked up and accompanied by an orchestra not much better than that of the vaudeville pit. But the stars were refulgent: Melba, Calvé, Sembrich, the de Reszke brothers, Lassalle, Scotti, and Plançon among them. Grau made over $½-million for himself and plenty of singers topped Nilsson's $1,000 fee. In the boxes, society had settled into a charming routine. Two bejewelled and Worth-coutured ladies would sit in the front of the box, with four white-tie gentlemen behind them. On the fashionable Monday night, the leader of the pack, Mrs Astor, would appear promptly at 9 p.m., regardless of the performance, and receive guests in the next intermission. After she left, her imitators felt that they too could go—the real show was over.

For the prima donna's prestige these were golden years and circumstances, and it is in the last years of the nineteenth century that the female American singer finally established herself as a serious musical proposition. The standard of music teaching in America had been immensely improved by the influx of German and Italian immigrants, and the Met's tours across the States set many young provincial hearts palpitating with ambition. But as for Henry James's heroines, the education that mattered still began in Europe. Americans like Sybil Sanderson and Emma Eames both started their careers in Paris after studying with Marchesi: Sanderson, a beautiful Californian with a small silvery voice, captivated Massenet, who wrote *Esclarmonde* and *Thaïs* for her; while Eames, described by Shaw as 'well educated, and with no nonsense about her', went on to become Melba's arch rival at Covent Garden and the Met—'Good day to you, Eames,' Melba would say if their paths crossed, sweeping past her without a backward glance. According to Max de Shauensee, who discussed the matter with Eames's husband, Melba was completely indifferent to Eames and certainly had no vendetta against her. It was Eames who suffered the pangs of jealousy, referring to Melba only as 'MY ENEMY'. The most famous Carmen of the era before Calvé, Minnie Hauk, was a native New Yorker who toured the States with Mapleson, but whose sole Met appearance was a failure. She ended her days living in Wagner's villa at Triebschen.

The finest émigré American prima donna, and one of the finest women of her time was Lillian Nordica, born Lillian Norton in Maine in 1857. Hers was good old New England farming stock, and her grandfather had been a Revivalist preacher. In her family circles the stage was considered an improper destiny for a young woman, but Lillian Norton was never one to be discouraged, and accepted the drudgery of being a clerk and seamstress so as to pay for singing lessons. While studying in Boston, the great dramatic soprano Therese Tietjens heard her and gave real praise, but one feels that her Yankee grit was such that she would have got there entirely on a 'Teach Yourself Great Opera Singing' manual, had all else failed. 'A young person with a chin so expressive of determination and perseverance,' wrote another early American prima donna, Clara Louise Kellogg, 'could not be downed. She told me at that early period that she always kept her eyes fixed on some goal so high and difficult that it seemed impossible, and worked towards it steadily, unceasingly, putting aside everything that stood in the path which led to it.'

She won her way to the impossible goal without natural musicality. Rehearsal for her was a matter of endless repetition. 'There are plenty of singers with voice and talent equal to mine. But I have *worked*,' she claimed. She began professionally by singing in churches and concerts, and later joined Gilmore's American Band, singing ballads and arias on long whistle-stop tours. She reached London with the band in 1878, passing on to Paris and Milan where she continued her crash-course studies. Having changed her name to Giglio Nordica ('lily of the North'), she began in opera, singing the Patti repertory in Italy and Germany. In 1881 she had great success in St Petersburg and in 1882 went back to Paris to study Marguerite in *Faust* and Ophélie in *Hamlet* with their respective composers, Gounod and Thomas. She then made the first of three disastrous marriages to Frederick Gower, a speculator in telephones, who insisted that she retired from the stage. Gower was a bully and a shark: fortunately for Nordica he vanished over the English Channel in a balloon and was assumed dead.

Her career recommenced in America with a Mapleson tour and in 1887 she made her first appearance at Covent Garden in *La Traviata*. London high society fêted her fresh and vital personality, while the critics praised her sterling efforts—'courageous to the point of audacity', wrote Shaw—even more than her achievements. 'She was a most wonderful coloratura singer and had a perfectly placed voice ... She could have gone on, I am sure, many years longer than she did, had not her tremendous ambition to sing in German opera overruled her judgment,' wrote the contralto Ernestine Schumann-Heink, one of her greatest friends from these years. But the fashion for Wagner caught her, as it caught every other prima donna of the age. At first she sang only Elsa in *Lohengrin*, which fitted well enough into her French-Italian repertory. Shaw was cutting on the subject, labelling her 'Elsa of Bond Street', because of her 'well-corseted waist' and 'bumptious, self-assertive' manner. For the first Bayreuth presentation of the opera in 1894 she studied the part in German with Cosima Wagner, who found her gratifyingly co-operative. Her success there was the watershed: she would work to become a dramatic soprano in the mould of Tietjens and Lehmann—and work she did.

In 1895 at the Met she sang Isolde to the Tristan of Jean de Reszke in a memorable performance which set new vocal standards for Wagner interpretation, as well as decisively showing that 'French-Italian' singers could keep their purity of style while singing in German. Nordica 'simply amazed those who thought they had measured the full limit of her powers'. Yet even now her star began to fall. After this triumph, she was eager to tackle Brünnhilde at the Met and felt a justifiable claim to the role—only to discover that her friend Melba was scheduled to sing the part in *Siegfried*, apparently at the personal request of Jean de Reszke. It was an inexplicable and inexcusable insult to a native singer, and Nordica was mortified. She tore up her contract with the Met, publicly accused de Reszke of plotting against her, and stormed off to sing elsewhere. Melba's subsequent *débâcle* has already been discussed: whether de Reszke did recommend Melba to sing Brünnhilde is unclear, but it is possible that he was worried that Nordica would drown him in the final duet, Siegfried having been on stage for about two and a half hours before Brünnhilde is awoken. Nordica may have been vindicated, but she was still miserable, and in the same year of 1896 she took her second husband, a hopeless gigolo and drawing-room tenor of charm and military good looks called Zoltan Döme. In her story about Nordica, 'The Diamond Mine', Willa Cather remarks that her heroine 'tried to give good fortune to an unfortunate man, *un misèrable*; that was her mistake. It cannot be done in this world. The lucky should marry the lucky.' Döme was a loser, who attempted to ride his way to success on Nordica's shoulders. He was also intolerably lazy and a womanizer. Nordica finally and sadly announced that she would sue him for divorce. As a newspaper report caustically put it: 'at the sight of the soprano, whose income is so great, the husband fainted'. Nordica made her escape, only to be informed later the same day that he had made a rather feeble effort to kill himself. She persevered in her resolve, however, and rid herself of him. After the divorce, Döme took to the disconcerting habit of sending her notes before concerts, informing her that he would be sitting in a box with a gun and would shoot her while she was singing.

Nordica's relations with her colleagues were much more satisfactory. She and Melba had risen at Covent Garden together and felt mutual respect and affection which survived the Brünnhilde episode, and de Reszke soon became a friend and partner again. Her direct rival was Lilli Lehmann, who at first regarded her efforts to emulate her with contempt. At Bayreuth one summer Nordica had a mutual friend ask Lehmann whether she might pay a social call, as one prima donna to another. 'Tell her I am not taking any pupils this season!' Lehmann snapped back. Two years later at the Met they were singing in the same performance of *Don Giovanni*. Lehmann's dresser sent out a frantic request for a pair of black stockings—Lehmann had left hers at the hotel. Nordica could easily have taken the opportunity of returning the Bayreuth snub, but was not so petty-minded. The next day she received a touching note which serves as an object lesson in the ease with which the paranoiac sensitivites of a prima donna can be dispelled.

> My dearest Mrs Nordica!
> With heartfelt thanks I send back the stockings you lent me last night; I washed them myself so you can be sure they are clean.
> I already told your husband that I was glad to hear your voice is so much better better [*sic*] now as two years ago, I hope you will be pleased.
> With much love and thank [*sic*], yours sincerely and affectionately,
> Lilli Lehmann Kalisch

Lehmann became positively affable. One day she emerged from the stage door with Nordica, who stepped into a waiting carriage. Lehmann pulled up her skirt to reveal a pair of stout and sensible boots. 'You ride,' she called out, 'I valk!'

Nordica was particularly generous with the time she gave to young singers, remembering kindnesses done to her in her youth by Tietjens and others. When the New Zealander Frances Alda made a début which the critics slammed, Nordica at once wrote to her: 'There was never a young singer who appeared at the Metropolitan who wasn't severely criticized on her début. Melba,

Sembrich, Farrar, myself . . . all of us have gone through what you are going through today. Have courage.'

Nordica certainly lived by her own precepts. After ten years in the major centres as a dramatic soprano, singing the heaviest of Wagner and Italian roles, as well as making the odd return to her earlier repertory, her voice was wearing thin. In 1907 she left the Met for Hammerstein's new but short-lived Manhattan Opera, where she was shabbily treated and virtually dismissed when attendances at her performances did not reach the required level. Her records date from this later period and fail to reveal a voice which must have still had enormous trumpeting power and accuracy: the first recording equipment was defeated by voices of such size. She herself was bitterly disappointed by her failure in the studio, and instead embarked on a useful project to record vocal exercises for students—a very good idea, which foundered as sadly as did her scheme to found a 'Bayreuth-on-the-Hudson', something along the lines of a modern arts centre.

In 1909 she sang Isolde for the last time and never again appeared at the Met. In what was interpreted as sour grapes, she then attacked the domination of the house by Italians and the casting of a non-American singer (Destinn) for the première of Puccini's *La Fanciulla del West*. Her third marriage, to a banker who 'borrowed' nearly half a million dollars off her to buttress some failing operations, soon terminated. With the decline of her operatic status, she had embarked on some devastatingly exhausting tours. She travelled in her own railway carriage, 'The Brünnhilde', which had a music room, a salon, three bedrooms, a bathroom, kitchen, and servants' quarters, but such comforts were purely external. She had acute rheumatism at all times and sometimes other worse ailments. The baritone David Bispham toured with her, and relates her reaction to an attack of bronchitis: 'I have never seen any woman in such abject despair, walking up and down the little dining-room of the car like a caged tigress, every now and then touching a note on the upright piano which had been placed therein, and trying her voice . . . tears and misery had ravaged her comely face so that it was hardly recognizable.' But at 8 p.m. she would emerge in her concert toilet and sing her programme—very, very badly. 'During that entire week, this tragi-comedy would repeat itself every day. Her bronchitis never left her, and from my room I could hear this poor woman, as she entered the dining-room, touch the piano furtively and sing a few notes.' Once she faced Bispham with the truth: 'Do you think, now I am getting old, I should be doing this if I didn't have to?' Between 1910 and 1913 she suffered a series of nervous collapses.

She became an active campaigner within the suffragette movement, took to cycling, and spoke up for equal pay and a female President. 'If I thought I would help the cause of woman suffrage by going out and throwing a brick through a window or adopting any other militant tactics I would do it,' she asserted in an interview. Such feelings of solidarity with their sex are very rare among prima donnas, who have to regard other women as hostile to their always precariously held positions. Nordica, however, always sought friends. She was a lonely woman who had created a golden cage for herself, furnished with all the luxuries but without a key by which to let herself out: she could understand that other women's cages were not of their own making.

In 1913 at the age of fifty-six she embarked on a final concert tour which was to take her round the world. In Australia she had a complete physical and emotional collapse: then, *en route* for Java, her ship foundered on a reef off Thursday Island and the passengers were forced up on deck. Nordica caught pneumonia as a result of the exposure and died in hospital in Batavia. For her funeral, she wanted 'some great speaker' who could say 'she did her damnedest'. It would have been the appropriate epitaph, but there was more to commemorate. Thirty years later, reviewing the début of Kirsten Flagstad as Isolde, the veteran New York critic W. J. Henderson cast his mind back to Nordica and paid her a handsomer tribute.

> She sang Isolde so intelligently, so opulently in respect of gradation, subtlety of tint and significant treatment of text that she left the hearer convinced that she was the real Irish princess of the drama . . . the singing was . . . beautiful in tonal quality, sustained and exquisitely moulded in phrasing and nobility of style.

While American singers were passing into Europe to win their first necessary laurels, European singers could hardly wait to sail out in the opposite direction. Like the millions of immigrants of these years, they saw America as a passport to freedom and fortune —which indeed, for singers trapped in the provincial opera houses of Italy or the court theatres of Germany, it often was. But the market conditions in America were quite different from elsewhere, and the rapidly developing communications technology—wireless, movies, recording, amplification—all meant that it was possible for an opera singer to make a career outside the traditional arenas of opera house and concert hall.

Whether this worked to the detriment of art and technique is a moot point: it certainly involved singing a lot more ninth-rate music than the Lehmann-Melba-Nordica generation ever bothered with. We live at a time when the spheres of 'light' and 'serious' music are much more rigidly separated than they were at the beginning of the century, and a properly trained singer of aspirations would certainly not have felt a loss of caste when tackling a 'popular' ballad—yet it is depressing to look back at the American years of, for instance, a contralto as rarely endowed as Ernestine Schumann-Heink and see how much time she spent in America with music that could get along without her quite nicely, while others hooted and bellowed their way through Verdi and Wagner.

*'Ich bin nichts als eine gewöhnliche deutsche Hausfrau,'* 'I am nothing but an ordinary German housewife,' was Schumann-Heink's favourite self-disclaimer, and it became her public image. She was not a glamorous soprano, displaying her diamonds over Worth gowns, but a hard-working, cooking and sewing mother of seven. She had the common touch: her singing was aimed at the woman with her hands in the washtub and the soldier longing for home. It was all triumphantly successful, but it obscured the real nature of her achievement.

Ernestine Schumann-Heink was born in 1861 as Ernestine Rössler, the daughter of a soldier of fortune, and had a rough peripatetic childhood. Her family had strong musical connections and Italian blood, and like Patti she communicates the feeling of having been born to sing, of someone for whom singing was as natural as breathing. In fact, she underwent a long and rigorous training, followed by a four-year apprenticeship in Dresden and a fifteen-year contract in Hamburg, where she clashed violently with her regular conductor, Gustav Mahler. She sang everything from Katisha in *The Mikado* to the Third Boy in *Die Zauberflöte* to Carmen and Amneris in *Aida*. At first she struggled through real poverty and hunger, bringing up the first four of her children on a meagre salary after her first husband had deserted her. Her breakthrough came in the 1890s when she made a name for herself as the finest interpreter of the contralto and mezzo Wagner roles, such as Brangäne in *Tristan*, Ortrud in *Lohengrin*, and Erda, Fricka, and Waltraute in the *Ring*. In 1896 she began her long association with Bayreuth, where she managed Cosima consummately and even won her affection. Once she complained to the 'Frau Meisterin' that the armour she had to wear as Waltraute was too heavy for her to sing in. Cosima was outraged at the thought, but Schumann-Heink managed to get her to try it on herself and admit the justice of the case—no small feat.

In the later 1890s she alternated between Bayreuth, Berlin, Hamburg and London, where she sang at Covent Garden and at a Windsor Castle Command Performance of *Lohengrin*, with a cast which also included Nordica, Bispham, and the de Reszkes, given to celebrate Queen Victoria's eightieth birthday. It was Nordica, a staunch friend and ally, who suggested America to her, and in 1898, heavily pregnant with what was to become George Washington Schumann-Heink, six other realized children, and her ailing second husband, she set sail.

For four successful seasons at the Met she repeated her Wagner roles and added to her repertory what was probably her favourite part, the distraught mother, Fidès, of Meyerbeer's *Le Prophète*. When Grau left the Met in 1903 his replacement as manager, Heinrich Conried, did not meet with Schumann-Heink's approval, and it was from this time that her career took its distinctively American turn. Her Met appearances petered out, she broke her imperial contract in Berlin, and virtually stopped singing opera in Europe. In 1905 she became a naturalized American and set up home in the Villa Fidès in New Jersey with her third husband (the second, whom she deeply loved, having died), a Chicago lawyer named William Rapp, who soon disappeared.

What made her take this course was her success in a musical comedy called *Love's Lottery*, which ran on Broadway and on tour in 1904–5. Schumann-Heink played a German washerwoman, and clearly relished the whole exercise. She then began on the round of concert tours and recording, and by the end of the decade she had a following outside urban musical circles comparable to that of Caruso, with whom she memorably recorded the duet from *Trovatore*, 'Ai nostri monti'. Everywhere she went, a little bevy of local press would foregather and Schumann-Heink, making an embracing gesture, would boom forth some sentiment to the effect that here, at last, was her true home—with the result that she was said to be honorary citizen of half the cities in the USA.

Her last significant operatic appearance was as Clytemnestra in the first performance of Strauss's *Elektra* in 1909 in Dresden. 'It was frightful,' she later recalled. 'We were a lot of mad women. There is nothing beyond *Elektra* . . . We have come to a full stop.' Strauss commented bluntly that she was miscast, although one can imagine the splendour with which she endowed the music of this Freudianized demented mother-figure. Back in America, the First World War gave new meaning to her role as a singer to the nation. The troops called her Mother Schumann, and eyes filled with tears as she sang 'Just Before the Battle, Mother', 'The Star-Spangled Banner', and 'When the Boys Come Home' at endless fund-raising functions. The irony of this was that sons of hers were fighting on both sides, and the one in the German army was killed in combat.

After the war she became one of the first musical stars of wireless, and is still remembered today for her annual singing of 'Silent Night' on Christmas Eve. She even made guest appearances in a comic radio soap opera, *The Goldbergs*. In 1926 she returned to opera for the first time in ten years and to the Met in twenty to sing the Earth-Mother Erda in the *Ring*, a role she repeated again in 1932 at the age of seventy, and of which a recording exists. A couple of years earlier she had made a studio recording of Waltraute's narration to Brünnhilde, the moving description of the desolation of Valhalla, and although the music is cut and the tone of the voice is worn to a ravelling, it reveals singing of the deepest understanding.

Unfortunately Wagner could not pay the bills. Schumann-Heink's investments were wiped out in the 1929 crash, leaving her with twenty-eight dependants. She had now passed into the realms of the old joke, and her tours became desperate efforts to keep afloat. She returned to Katisha in *The Mikado*, and sank as far as singing in movie houses between the features, finishing up performing four times a day in vaudeville with an outfit known as 'Roxy and his Gang'. Finally, in 1935, after she had moved to Los Angeles, she made a film, *Here's to Romance* with Nino Martini: the next year she died of leukaemia.

She had given honest pleasure to millions—of that there can be no question—and half of her over fifty professional years had been spent in opera, but it is surely not snobbery to lament the dissipation of the other half. Schumann-Heink has been called the American Clara Butt, but her singing is more than lush, plummy *portamento* geared to the lachrymose and patriotic, as Butt's is too. It has none of the usual lugubrious limitations of a contralto voice: there is immense wit and delicacy, as well as superb coloratura and a staggering high register. Her Brindisi from Donizetti's *Lucrezia Borgia* is quite uplifting, warmly playful in style, with a firm trill and some fabulously sustained top notes. Every memory of her Wagner praises its grandeur and conviction. How wonderful then if in her latter days she had recorded Brahms's Four Serious Songs or some Mahler rather than another version of 'Danny Boy'! America may not have torn her to pieces, but it distracted her from a mission far finer than national anthems and musical comedy.

In stark contrast to the jovially outgoing and publicly familiar figure of Schumann-Heink stands that of Olive Fremstad (1871–1951), a woman who did not understand the meaning of the word distraction and of whom her biographer wrote, 'The one thing for which there was never any room in her life was mediocrity.' She was reclusive and enigmatic, perhaps something of a mystic. 'Through suffering,' she said gnomically, 'I have learned to seek the light to guide me through dark waters, and in that search, as humbly as a small child, I am seeking an understanding of life.'

Needless to say, it was Wagner that she mostly sang, and Fremstad conveniently embodied all the most Romantic notions of Wagnerism. Lady novelists took her story (as far as it was ever known) and made extravagant fictions about it, the most famous being Willa Cather's turgid *The Song of the Lark*. Far more enjoyable is Gertrude Atherton's *Tower of Ivory* (1910), which tells of Margarethe Styr, formerly Margaret Hill, who arose from the depths of destitution and prostitution to become a prima donna. Singing at Bayreuth is the height of her exultation:

> When I stood on the greatest stage in the world with all my being set to the music soaring from my throat, not a nerve out of tune, I knew that I no longer was of common clay, that nothing that had ever happened to me before mattered in the least. Ah, what matter the charnel rooms in the soul when such memories blaze for ever above. Poor women! poor women!—that have no such blinding moments . . .

When the man she has dared to love deserts her for a pert American heiress, her panacea is a blazing performance as Isolde: 'What is mere human passion to art, what indeed, but its necessary but inferior partner?' she ponders. 'Nurse this, nurse this!' Atherton's novel is part of a 'spiritual' feminist literature which appeals for acknowledgement of the power of the outstanding woman's emotions and abilities in areas other than sexual love. The dross of womankind are venal in their desires, but some hold the sacred torch: Styr can give up passion and marriage, but she cannot surrender her art. Painful as the responsibility is, it is her appointed mission.

> There are many disappointments in my profession, and bitter, bitter contempts . . . If you love the good thing vitally, enough to give up for it all that one must give up, then you must hate the cheap thing just as hard. I tell you there is such a thing as creative hate! A contempt that drives you through fire, makes you risk everything, makes you a long sight better than you ever knew you could be.

Rather more polished and ironic, though no nearer conventional feminism, is Marcia Davenport's novel *Of Lena Geyer* (1936), which conflates elements of the careers of Melba, Nordica, Farrar, and Lotte Lehmann, as well as the author's mother Alma Gluck. But the core of the character of Geyer—a lonely, intense, unworldly dramatic soprano, sacrificing love and making do with lady companions, incapable of relating to ordinary life—is still Fremstad. In some ways the real Fremstad emerges as an unintentionally comic character—an aspect emphasized in Mary Watkins Cushing's memoir, *The Rainbow Bridge*—but she was indisputably an artist of extraordinary nobility and presence. Carl Van Vechten called her the Pasta of German opera.

Fremstad was born illegitimate, and was adopted by a Swedish father and Norwegian mother who emigrated to Minnesota. Her father was a surgeon turned evangelical missionary, and Olive's musical career began at prayer meetings, where she sang and played the harmonium. At the age of twelve she was giving piano lessons to adults, but in her teens she turned to singing. Cather's *Song of the Lark* makes much of the stifling small-town ignorance and philistinism which the heroine had to combat, but there must also have been a certain amount of encouragement as well. And

185

Fremstad's will was immense. She studied singing in New York for three years, sang regularly in St Patrick's Cathedral, and saved enough money to take a two-year course with Lilli Lehmann in Berlin. It was later said that she became involved with Lehmann's tenor husband, and certainly neither teacher nor pupil ever evinced much affection for each other in later years. Nevertheless, as Lehmann's pupil, she was given a hearing. She sang in the 1896 Bayreuth *Ring* and in Vienna as Brangäne and Adalgisa in *Norma* —all with Lehmann.

Although she sang in predominantly mezzo roles in this first stage of her professional life, she claimed to possess what she referred to as a 'long voice', and from her return to New York in 1903 onwards she sang as a soprano. Critics sometimes doubted the wisdom of this, but the occasional weaknesses of her top register, like the flaws of Lotte Lehmann or Callas, somehow became an integral part of her vocal personality. On record the voice sounds anything but huge or brilliant, and even bearing the falsifications of the recording trumpet in mind, she was obviously not an icy or hard-edged singer. She detested singing in the studio and was appalled at the results, but there is more to what she has left us than has commonly been acknowledged. Her art comes across as an introverted one. In, for example, Tosca's 'Vissi d'arte', no one—not Muzio, Destinn, Callas, or Scotto—quite captures as Fremstad does the immense sadness and essential privacy of the plaint that Scarpia is not meant to hear; and in Eboli's 'O don fatale' from *Don Carlos* she begins not with the attention-grabbing chesty declamation of most Italian mezzos, but with a quiet bitterness and melancholy that is arrestingly beautiful. All her Wagner excerpts have much to offer, although discomfort and constraint is also evident.

Fremstad's success at the Met conveniently came at the time when Nordica's exhaustion was beginning. Although she sang some of the standard repertory roles such as Tosca, Carmen, and Santuzza in *Cavalleria Rusticana*, it was for her Wagner that she was most valued. Not for her the statuesque proprieties of Lilli Lehmann: Fremstad's magnetism was not impersonal or monumental. 'The opera glass will never betray any of Mme Fremstad's secrets,' explained Willa Cather in the course of an interview.

The real machinery is all behind her eyebrows. When she sings Isolde, no one can say by what means she communicates the conception. A great tragic actress, her portrayal of a character is always austere, marked by a very parsimony of elaboration and gesture.

Henderson wrote further of her as 'no raging Isolde, but a woman smothering a devastating love which presently was loosed from its restraint and poured itself out in longing, sighing accents. There was little of the majesty traditionally associated with the role, but an abundance of . . . feminine lure.' There is a frustrating lack of more concrete documentation of Fremstad's theatrical style, but one remarkable piece of evidence has been revealed by Mary Watkins Cushing, who has deciphered the notes scrawled all over her score of *Tristan*. As with Pasta, everything in Fremstad's performances was calculated, rehearsed, and thought through: her interpretations did not change so much as intensify. ' "1-2-3 wide step—4-5-6 half-turn . . ." "Head up" is repeated over and over,' writes Cushing. 'The right or the left hand, even their fingers, have their special instructions, as well as the shoulders, the chest, the spine, the knees . . . perhaps most characteristic is her repeated reminder to herself "stand quite still".' Sometimes she is simply practical: at Brangäne's return from delivering the message to Tristan, she marks, 'Rush toward her, but *Caution* . . . don't arrive too soon because danger of bumping.' Elsewhere, she is more reflective, as at the opening of Act II, where she tells herself to gaze 'longingly into the forest where all her thoughts now are . . . *whole* body expecting the loved one . . . Here she *thinks* of torch,' then, 'just sing beautifully, gestures not necessary'; for the *Liebestod*, she is rather more blunt: 'take great breaths like a horse'!

About her other interpretations we can surmise less, although we know that her Brünnhilde was the first to emphasize the Valkyrie's girlishness. She personally commissioned Mahler's designer Alfred Roller to make her a costume which would allow her more freedom of movement than the traditional chain-mail cuirass, and then startled audiences by leaping about from rock to rock during the 'Ho-jo-to-ho' passage.

Fremstad's attention to the details of her performance and her fanatical dedication made her a difficult, even eccentric, colleague.

When in 1907 she sang the sole performance of Strauss's *Salome* to be given at the Met until 1933 (J. P. Morgan's daughter was so shocked by its lasciviousness that she made her father use his influence to have it removed), she was noted to stagger while carrying the plate bearing John the Baptist's head. When questioned on this, she admitted that she had been to the morgue and spent some time rehearsing with the real thing—all 12lbs of it!

Those she worked with found her exacting. Mahler, himself uncompromising, admired her enormously and she sang her first ever Isolde when he made his début at the Met on 1 January 1908 —also the first time New York had heard the opera played without cuts. Toscanini, however, deplored her refusal to rehearse the day before a performance. Finally, Gatti-Casazza, then manager of the Met, seems to have tired of her and let it be known that he would be engaging another singer to share her roles in the 1914–15 season. Fremstad immediately resigned. Her last performance, as Elsa in *Lohengrin*—Gatti refused her request for a *Tristan*—was greeted by one of the longest and most fervent ovations in the history of the house. 'May we all meet again in that far beyond where there is eternal peace and harmony,' she called over the footlights, bowing out at the height of her powers. She was only forty-three: at her age, Flagstad was only two years into her Wagnerian career. Gatti's action was a terrible tactical error: Fremstad had no successor, and the quality of Wagnerian sopranos at the Met did not recover for nearly twenty years. Gatti remembered her in his memoirs as 'a woman with a great sense of responsibility, thoroughly serious in her approach to her tasks, and sensitive to the point of being quixotic [but] rather nervous and difficult to keep happy'. That the Met could not accommodate such a temperament is a sad indictment of its priorities.

Fremstad sang on in Chicago for two years, and Gatti seemed to be on the verge of inviting her back for the 1917–18 season, had it not been for the cancellation of all German opera during the period in which America was at war. Her final public appearance was at a concert in New York early in 1920. Later the same year she wrote Gatti one of the most painful letters imaginable. Bowing to anti-German feelings caused by the war, a plan was announced for the Met to perform Wagner in English only. Fremstad played her last card:

There was a time during the War when it seemed almost impossible to convert Wagner into English without a tremendous artistic
loss. However, I am now convinced that it is the only way
at present of giving Wagner to English-speaking audiences.
Therefore, I am learning the operas in English—*Tristan,
Parsifal, Lohengrin,* and *Tannhauser*—I am also adding *Forza
del Destino* to my repertoire, making in all for the present, with
Tosca and Santuzza, seven roles.

I expect to do better work than I have ever done before, and,
naturally, in the event of your having a place for me, I should
like to do that work at the Metropolitan, on the stage which has
seen so many of my life's successes. Could you make this possible?

Gatti's reply is not on record, but it must have given him an
awkward moment. However he phrased his refusal, its effect on
Fremstad was decisive. She retreated completely, and for nearly
thirty years lived on in New York State as a recluse.

Her personal life had scarcely existed outside the opera house.
'I spring into life when the curtain rises,' she said, 'and when it
falls I might as well die. The world I exist in between performances
is the strange one, alien, dark, confused.' Even the most violent
impingements of reality did not seem to affect her. When caught
in the 1906 San Francisco earthquake, she insisted on returning
to her hotel room to salvage some crimson roses. Hours later she
was discovered calmly sitting in a small park on Van Ness Avenue
distributing them to refugees. She was briefly married twice, once
to a man who 'owned all the gold mines in Tierra del Fuego', but
her strongest personal relationship appears to have been with Mary
Watkins Cushing, a girl she employed as her living-in secretary
and buffer from the world. Cushing's book about Fremstad reveals
a woman who lived at an intolerable pitch of tension. In bed
Cushing would have to sleep with a piece of string tied round her
toe, which Fremstad pulled from the next room if she woke up in
the night and felt the need for company. Even on walks she could
not relax, but would improve the shining hour by measuring the
number of lamp posts she could walk past without drawing breath.
'Friends are not for me . . . Think of me as a stage creature only,'
says the heroine of *Tower of Ivory*—but Fremstad was even more
estranged and isolated than the fictional characters she inspired.

This in itself gave Fremstad her glamour, albeit of a rarified kind. The contemporary prima donna who had 'a hold on the baseball type of American' (as Willa Cather smartly put it) was Geraldine Farrar. Hers was the comforting kind of sophistication achieved by a clean-cut healthy all-American female that anyone could see the point of. You couldn't have taken Fremstad home to meet the folks—she would have stared into the ether and refused offers of refreshment. But Farrar was recognizable to any reader of *Little Women* as a female of vivacity and candour. She took the trappings of stardom in her stride and enjoyed them extravagantly—her dress account at Henri Bendel was said to run up $80,000 a year. Farrar had, with all possible capital letters, personality. The exposure she experienced in her period of fame was the sort that film stars became accustomed to: indeed, she became a film star herself. Her fans knew all her movements, her measurements, what she had for breakfast, lunch, and tea. She was canvassed for her views on matters great and small, and her life was an endless source of public interest. When the cameras were there, Farrar never forgot to smile.

The driving force behind this success story was Farrar's mother, a woman who had married at seventeen and felt vicariously ambitious for her daughter, born in 1882 in Melrose, Massachusetts. Farrar's father was a store-keeper who pitched for a Philadelphia baseball team, and both parents had good voices. Geraldine was a determined child with a strong histrionic bent. She later remembered how once she went out and 'purchased a pair of lurid plaid stockings and told her family and friends that when she had these on she was not to be spoken to or taken any notice of whatsoever'. At the age of ten, she impersonated Jenny Lind in a school pageant and decided to cultivate the role further. Her mother pushed her hard, and for that she was always deeply grateful. When it came to writing her autobiography, *Such Sweet Compulsion*, she claimed to have communicated with her mother's dead spirit, and a third of the book is related by a voice from beyond the grave—a deeply embarrassing device which allowed Farrar to pay herself some astonishing compliments.

Farrar began to study seriously in Boston, where she was heard by Nordica who recommended her to make her way to Berlin, and by Melba who recommended Paris. At this her mother decided that only the best was going to be good enough for her Geraldine. With financial subsidy from a local lady of means—Farrar scrupulously repaid her a debt of $30,000—mother and daughter went to teachers in New York and Paris. In 1901 Farrar made a successful appearance in *Faust* at the Berlin Opera, and after a number of unacknowledged letters of self-introduction, Lilli Lehmann summoned the Farrars to an audition.

> On arrival my mother thanked Mme Lehmann for receiving us but added that her daughter had already written two or three times without receiving any answer. 'I know,' came the severe reply, 'but I could not read the handwriting. It is too big and illegible.'
>
> I said I always wrote that way, which brought no further comment. Then I sang for her. But I felt she was not greatly impressed, and so I said, 'Mme Lehmann, will you *please* take me? I am intelligent and I am very hard-working. But you will never know that unless you give me a chance.'

Lehmann took Farrar on and, against all the odds, the relationship proved a great success. They clashed constantly but not bitterly, for Lehmann admired the girl's pluck and Farrar wheedled out Lehmann's frustrated maternal instinct. There was, however, never any question of emulating Lehmann's own accomplishment, Farrar's voice being expressive but physically limited. 'Technical control to her meant everything,' she wrote of Lehmann, 'while emotional colour was my natural asset and delight.' In a letter to the music critic Henry T. Finck, she admitted, 'I do not long to, nor do I believe I can, climb frozen heights like the Great Lehmann.' But Lehmann made Farrar into a real singer: when John Steane notes the 'bracing vitality and precision' of her singing, he is praising the Lehmann aspect of her training. Farrar may not have been an interpreter of Fremstad's stature, but she was certainly not an impostor.

At the Berlin Opera she became enormously popular. She was regularly seen in the highest court circles, and the Crown Prince paid her such persistent amorous attentions that her father had to knock down a man who cast aspersions on her honour. All this was duly reported in the American press. One of her humblest German admirers was the young Frida Leider: Farrar's appeal was always as potent to girls as it was to men. To girls who had very little, she exuded the fantasy of having very much: wealth, talent, beauty, fame, admirers, independence. 'It was said,' Leider recalled, 'that when singing Marguerite she wore really and truly genuine jewelled buckles on her shoes. She seemed to me the most elegant and bewitching creature, and I used to colour all the sepia postcards which showed her in a long evening gown, a little diadem of pearls in her gently waved hair, with long white kid gloves, her head gracefully rested on one hand.'

Over five years Farrar built herself up in Europe, developing her repertory and making some appearances in Paris, Monte Carlo, and at Salzburg as Zerlina to Lehmann's Donna Anna. In 1906 she returned to New York to a public burning with curiosity. Her début at the Met in Gounod's *Roméo et Juliette* brought a certain inevitable critical resistance—Henderson reported that 'largeness, power, brilliancy, are what this young woman has sought instead of mellowness, liquidity, and perfect poise'—but her stardom was irresistible. For over fifteen years she dominated the French and late Italian repertory: with Caruso as her most frequent partner, her presence would guarantee a full house.

Her manner on stage had naturalistic immediacy that compensated for a lack of vocal excitement. 'I am an actress who happens to be appearing in opera,' she said. 'I sacrifice tonal beauty to dramatic fitness every time I think it is necessary for an effect, and I shall continue to do it. I leave mere singing to the warblers. I am more interested in acting myself.' She played up to her audiences with an energy bordering on vulgarity. Caruso baulked at having his face slapped by Farrar's Carmen; as the music-hall singer Zazà in Leoncavallo's opera of that name, she created a scandal by 'raising her skirt to perfume the panties with an atomiser'; as the Goose Girl in Humperdinck's *Königskinder*, she would take her curtain call carrying one of the birds under her arm. Her most famous role, despite Puccini's initial disapproval, was Madama Butterfly, which she sang nearly a hundred times at the Met and of which she made recordings with Caruso and Scotti, whence her warm and intimate tones, combined with a firm line and intonation, are still pleasurable, even if she falls short of the dignity of Scotto or Los Angeles. Both Henderson and Schumann-Heink also single out her achievement as the pure-minded Elisabeth in *Tannhäuser*, but most of the rest of her time was spent conveying degrees of coquettishness.

The teenage girls who screamed and waved flags at the stage door on Farrar nights were christened the 'Gerryflappers', and

23. *left* Geraldine Farrar as a glamorous Madama Butterfly. 24. Rosa Ponselle, possibly as La Gioconda in Ponchielli's opera.

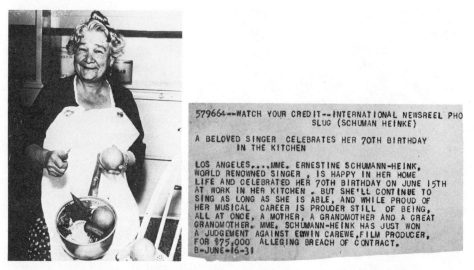

579664--WATCH YOUR CREDIT--INTERNATIONAL NEWSREEL PHO
SLUG (SCHUMAN HEINKE)

A BELOVED SINGER CELEBRATES HER 70TH BIRTHDAY
IN THE KITCHEN

LOS ANGELES....MME. ERNESTINE SCHUMANN-HEINK,
WORLD RENOWNED SINGER , IS HAPPY IN HER HOME
LIFE AND CELEBRATED HER 70TH BIRTHDAY ON JUNE 15TH
AT WORK IN HER KITCHEN . BUT SHE'LL CONTINUE TO
SING AS LONG AS SHE IS ABLE, AND WHILE PROUD OF
HER MUSICAL CAREER IS PROUDER STILL OF BEING,
ALL AT ONCE, A MOTHER, A GRANDMOTHER AND A GREAT
GRANDMOTHER. MME. SCHUMANN-HEINK HAS JUST WON
A JUDGEMENT AGAINST EDWIN CAREWE,FILM PRODUCER,
FOR $75,000 ALLEGING BREACH OF CONTRACT.
B-JUNE-16-31

**25.** *above* Ernestine Schumann-Heink, one of the first singers to exploit successfully the resources of the American publicity machine. **26.** Grace Moore impersonating Jenny Lind, receiving the tributes of the nobility after a performance of *Norma*, from the film *A Lady's Morals*.

their antics became something of a nuisance at the Met, which was fast losing its dignity. There were those who found the lady herself even worse than a nuisance. In an open letter she expressed her distrust of the newly appointed manager Giulio Gatti-Casazza, demanding that a second consul be appointed to govern with him; and like Melba she insisted on the key to her own dressing-room. With Toscanini, the great conductor of the Met during the years 1908–15, her relations proved catastrophic. After a first notorious skirmish—'I am the star,' asserted Farrar, in a quarrel over tempo; 'The only stars I know are in heaven,' retorted Toscanini—they became embroiled in a long and passionate love affair, kept a close secret from the press. Farrar finally demanded that Toscanini leave his wife and marry her: Toscanini, with his Italian conception of *la famiglia*, refused, and Farrar terminated the relationship. Toscanini's sudden and apparently unmotivated departure from the Met is now thought to be largely explained by his pain at the unavoidable encounters with his lost lover. Many years later Farrar invited him to dinner, at which caviare was served. Toscanini was furious, and whispered to his neighbour, 'I slept with that woman for seven years. Wouldn't you think she'd remember that I hate fish?'

From 1915 Farrar's life followed new directions. Her annual spring trips back to the Berlin Opera had been curtailed by the war, and instead she took to the movies once the Met season had ended. None of her fourteen pictures—which included a version of *Carmen*, *Joan the Woman* (about Joan of Arc) for Cecil B. de Mille, *The Woman God Forgot*, and *Flame of the Desert*—were of any distinction, but it was in Hollywood that she met a handsome actor, Lou Tellegen, a former stage partner of Sarah Bernhardt's, whom she swiftly married. Unmitigated disaster followed. Tellegen was lazy and spendthrift, and his own career was inexorably collapsing. He drank heavily and involved himself with other women. Farrar was not used to being treated so lightly, and within a few years divorced him. When some years later he committed suicide, Farrar showed no mercy on his memory. 'He had the perceptions of a moron,' she wrote in her autobiography, 'and no morals whatsoever.' As her mother's spirit put it, Geraldine was not made to be 'good material for tandem-going', and she never tried marriage again.

The strain of it all was beginning to tell. In 1918 Farrar developed a node on her vocal cords, and for six months was unable to sing, the silent procedures of the film studio being useful to her in her months of recovery. In fact, she does not seem to have regained her full powers, although she refused to diminish her work-load at the Met and continued to sing rumbustious *verismo* music which she had always found vocally exhausting. Vincent Sheean remembers Farrar's last years in the opera house:

> Her personality was more remarkable than her voice by the time I heard her. The voice had grown wiry thin in all its upper reaches and it never could have had much to offer in the lower part. By compensation there were wonderfully expressive tones still at her command in the middle voice [even though she] had pushed out her repertoire in all directions without regard for her special gifts.

Fortunately she could save face, in that she had always publicly, and probably sincerely, proclaimed her resolution to retire at the height of her powers. 'I have one very decided ambition,' she told an interviewer. 'I wish to develop my powers to the fullest extent and most complete beauty, and then—I wish to have the courage, when physical strength no longer responds to the creative demands, *to abdicate in favour of youth!*' Various factors conspired to make her fulfil her wish. Vocal problems, the stresses surrounding her divorce, and the advent of her fortieth birthday joined with the even more crucial advent of Maria Jeritza. The Met was captivated by this beauty from Vienna, with her new repertoire of startling theatrical tricks and a voice bigger than Farrar's had ever been. Without crossing swords with the newcomer, Farrar announced a short series of farewell performances. Just as he had refused Fremstad an Isolde, Gatti refused Farrar a last fling as Tosca, a role already assumed by Jeritza, and at a Saturday matinée in April 1922 she went out as Zazà, perfumed panties and all. 'I don't want any tears in this house,' she said in her traditional curtain speech. 'I am leaving this institution because I want to go.' The Gerryflappers then clad her in crown, sceptre, and robes, and she was borne aloft on to Broadway through an enormous cheering crowd.

Surprisingly, she did not make for Hollywood—in fact, her films had not proved particularly successful at the box office and Sam Goldwyn had terminated her contract. Instead she embarked on ten years of concert tours from which she made a good deal more money than she had made at the Met. On one such tour she sang a truncated version of *Carmen* 123 times in 125 days! There were constant whispers of a return to opera or a break into the legitimate theatre, but none of the schemes materialized. Promptly, at the age of fifty, she retired from performance altogether. She did make a return of sorts to the Met, but only as the interval commentator for the famous Saturday matinée radio broadcasts, and it was she who was on the air to announce the miraculous first appearance of Kirsten Flagstad in 1935.

In her long retirement in Ridgefield, Connecticut, she became a pillar of the community, involved with worthy causes such as the Girl Scouts and the women's voluntary service. Her fate was to become a spinster *grande dame* with unforgettably piercing blue eyes, respectfully visited by those with long and loyal memories, but there could well be a lot more to Farrar's story than has emerged in this sketch. At her death in 1967 she bequeathed her letters and papers to the Library of Congress, where they await an imaginative biographer.

Farrar was the first and most substantial of the American 'glamour' prima donnas, with a solid vocal talent to underpin her well-projected charms; but New York has also paid court to a series of lesser singers who could not have made their way without certain more venal and sensual endowments.

The most sheerly beautiful of them was indisputably Lina Cavalieri (1874–1944), who arrived at the Met in 1906, the same year as Farrar, but who failed to establish herself in a comparable repertory. Cavalieri let it be known that she was the barefoot daughter of a Roman washerwoman and a newspaper vendor, that she had slept in the gutters and sold oranges in the Piazza Navona, that she had begun by singing outside cafés. It may have been true, but supposition becomes verifiable fact in the mid 1890s when she became the mistress of Prince Alexander Bariatinski and then, from 1900, a prima donna. At the Met she sang with Caruso in the first house performance of Puccini's *Manon Lescaut* and Cilea's *Adriana Lecouvreur*, but her art was a fragile thing. By 1909 she was concentrating her activities on a Fifth Avenue *atelier* where she sold cosmetics made according to the recipes of Catherine de Medici, and in 1910 she married one of the Astor clan, from whom she was separated less than three months after. A brief film career was curtailed by the damage that studio lights did to her eyes. With the outbreak of war, she returned to Europe and lived off her jewels and divorce settlement. There were two more marriages, out of a total, she claimed, of 840 proposals.

Cavalieri had an insubstantial but pretty little voice which went well with her diaphanous beauty. As a singer she could not be taken very seriously, but as a late manifestation of the courtesan—a courtesan with a career and a press agent—she was magnificently successful. But perhaps the outstanding instance of a prima donna building her status on a combination of inferior musicianship and mass public appeal is that of Grace Moore. Born in 1901 in Slabtown, Tennessee, she made her way up through musical comedy and Broadway to make her début at the Met as Mimi in *La Bohème* in 1928. According to Vincent Sheean, she had a nice warm soprano, but no memory, imagination, or stamina, and 'she lived in terror twenty-five hours a day of her own shortcomings'. None the less, she lasted in opera until she was killed in an air crash over Copenhagen in 1947, singing a minuscule repertory and rehearsing with futile persistence.

Moore's ambitions did not lie in the direction of art. She wanted to be rich, famous, and admired, and she used her voice to attain the glittering end. 'She expected music to serve her,' wrote the recording producer Charles O'Connell, and had little interest in it beyond what was absolutely necessary or relevant. Her one estimable achievement was the title-role of *Louise*, which she had studied with the aged composer Charpentier.

It was the movies which gave her the exposure and publicity she craved, as well as keeping her afloat in the opera house. In a succession of musical romances, starting in 1930 with a 'biopic' of Jenny Lind and continuing through, among others, *One Night of Love*, *New Moon*, and *Love Me for Ever*, she became Hollywood's first true singing film star. As such, she was often regarded as the sinister portent of a new vulgarity. When the Covent Garden management attempted to hire Moore, Thomas Beecham and his partner Lady Cunard were roused to fury at the compromise of standards the engagement would represent. Miss Moore was much more concerned, according to a letter from her agent, that 'she should make her début night on the best and most fashionable one of the week; she also hopes that it will be possible to arrange a performance attended by the King and Queen'. In the event she was denied the royal presence, but she filled the house, as she always did, with a lot of people who had never been to the opera before—and probably never came again. Between performances she fluttered her eyelashes at eligible scions of the aristocracy, indulging the outrageously naïve snobbery for which she was notorious. 'What she did to this world in the way of snooting,' commented Sheean, 'was good for us poor folks to witness.' In other words, she fulfilled the popular image of the prima donna without contradiction.

Farrar, Cavalieri, and Moore represent the prima donna as 'star personality'. All three specialized in the sentimental and sadistic operas of the turn of the century—Massenet, Puccini, *verismo*—which gave them maximum opportunity to fulfil sexual fantasy, and all three allowed their lives to be fed into an inexorably voracious publicity machine. A satire of the whole phenomenon is contained in Welles's and Mankiewicz's film *Citizen Kane*, in which Kane's second wife Susan has an opera house built for her meagre talent. She makes her disastrous début in an exotic French opera (faked by Bernard Herrmann) entitled *Salammbô* and is never heard again. According to Pauline Kael, Welles and Mankiewicz may also have had in mind both Randolph Hearst's one-time fiancée Sybil Sanderson, later the creator of Massenet's Thaïs, whose parents sent her to Paris so as to keep her from Hearst's clutches; and also Samuel Insull, who built the Chicago Lyric Opera inside a skyscraper block of offices before his empire collapsed spectacularly in the Depression.

But the most pathetic of the ephemeral prima donnas of this period was Marion Talley, a 'girl-next-door' prima donna whose fate was nothing but a 'where are they now?' article. Her father was a telegraph operator in Kansas City, Missouri. As a boy his best friend had been Walter Chrysler, who became a motor tycoon. In 1922, the chubby fifteen-year-old Marion had auditioned for the Met and was told to go away and study. She duly departed for Milan, financed by some benefit concerts held in Kansas City, and returned to the Met. Someone was foolish enough to engage her, and in 1926 amid a barrage of press coverage, this wretched eighteen-year-old made her début as Gilda in *Rigoletto*. Trainloads from the home town came to New York to cheer her on. A telegraph line was specially installed backstage for Talley's father to tap out a report on the performance back to Kansas City. The press reunited him with Walter Chrysler: now, in the great melting-pot of American democracy, they could meet on equal ground.

The critics naturally deplored the whole incident, and as Talley went on to sing a variety of coloratura roles including Lucia, the Queen of the Night, and the title-role in Stravinsky's *The Nightingale*, they did not spare comment on her 'hard, pinched manner', 'hollow' middle voice, and 'harsh and strident' top register. The public, however, continued to be entranced by the idea of the 'Little Red Riding Hood of the Met', whose 'only vice was candy'. Her face was plump and inexpressive, her temperament placid and priggish: more important, she had a voice quite unripe for serious singing. After a coast-to-coast concert tour from which she was claimed to have made $350,000, her tender instrument had virtually collapsed. Further appearances at the Met were disastrous, and by 1929 she was a dead letter.

Perhaps Talley was taken on because someone remembered an even greater risk that had been taken back in 1918 with a girl of twenty-one and which was now paying off triumphantly. We have now come to one of the giants—one of the very greatest names, in fact, in the history of Italian singing: Rosa Ponselle.

The story of Ponselle is full of distortion and simplification: the poor Italian girl singing in lowly vaudeville, spotted by Caruso, and then shot to stardom after an untutored performance, certainly existed but the truth of the matter makes it all look a little less surprising. Rosa Ponzillo was born in Connecticut in 1897 into a typical first-generation Italian immigrant background: her father was a baker and small-town operator who never showed any pride or interest in his daughter's music unless money was being discussed. In fact, it was Rosa's elder sister Carmela who first went out into the metropolis, singing between reels in the nickelodeons, while Rosa was still being asked to keep her voice down and stop drowning everyone else in the school choir. 'I never had what I would call a "girl's voice"—the light, breathy-sounding, high-pitched voice we normally associate with young children. My singing voice was always big and round, and even as a teenager I could sing almost three octaves,' she wrote in her autobiography. She heard Tetrazzini, Calvé, and Melba in concert, and then quarrelled with the local priest at confirmation when he refused to allow her to take Melba as her saint's name. The singer who most influenced her, however, was Schumann-Heink, whose warmth of tone and fluency in range would find their way into her own style.

Like her sister, Rosa Ponzillo began her career in the movie house, before graduating to the Café Malone in New Haven, where she accompanied herself on the piano and sang standard arias from opera and operetta. Her great hit was Victor Herbert's 'Kiss me again'. Carmela meanwhile had found her way into a Broadway musical and it was decided that a sisters act would go down very well in vaudeville. Together Rosa and Carmela proved enormously successful with their duet rendition of the Trio from *Faust*, and were soon 'headliners' on the prestigious Keith circuit, touring the nation with Harry Lauder, George Burns, Sophie Tucker, Jack Benny, and the Marx Brothers.

There is thus no question of her being an untried unknown when the Met approached her in 1918. Carmela had gone for lessons to William Thorner, a fashionable voice teacher whose studio was frequented by agents and impresarios, and Rosa again tagged on after her. Both of them wanted to get out of vaudeville. Rosa had only been to the opera twice, but Caruso and Farrar in *Butterfly* and Muzio in *L'amore dei tre re* was no mean initiation. One day Caruso himself appeared in the studio, and asked to sing some duets with Rosa. He was sufficiently impressed to mention her name to Gatti-Casazza, who was looking for a soprano for the Met première of Verdi's *La Forza del Destino*. (It would be interesting to know why the resident *spinto* soprano at the time, Claudia Muzio, did not take the role.) Gatti auditioned both sisters, and even though she fainted half-way through, it was Rosa who was eventually offered a contract for the forthcoming season. It was a significant act, for as Gatti told her, 'If you make good, I will open the door to American talent as long as I am here. You will be the first American to appear at the Metropolitan without having been to Europe first.'

Ponselle, as she was now to become, was then closeted away for five months with Romano Romani, a *protégé* of Puccini and Mascagni's who was to remain her lifelong teacher, mentor, and close friend. Everything went extraordinarily well until the day after the dress rehearsal, with Ponselle riding high on the sudden realization of her miraculous natural capacities. Then she read a newspaper review in which a respected Met singer was severely criticized, and for the first time contemplated the possibility of her own failure. 'All I could think was, *just what have I gotten myself into?*' she remembered. Overcome with the crippling nerves that would dog the rest of her career, she was dragged to the opera house by sister, mother, and Romani. When she finally got to the wings, she looked pleadingly to Caruso for encouragement, only to find him in as bad a state as she was. No two singers on record communicate a greater sense of spontaneous technical mastery than Ponselle and Caruso; no two singers suffered more agonies of uncertainty before a performance. And *Forza* is not easy for anyone, even a Ponselle.

> As an opera, *Forza* is supremely difficult . . . The one thing that stands out . . . is my constant thinking 'Top, top, top. Up, up, up,' to keep my voice light and sustain that extremely high pitch Verdi established for the tone of the opera . . . I always felt that the duet with the basso was the most difficult part of the opera. By the time I got to the Vergine degli Angeli at the end of the act I was in seventh heaven, for I knew that the worst was behind me. In that scene with Padre Guardiano, Leonora has to be a lyric, dramatic and near mezzo-soprano. She must express fear, fatigue, piety, desperation, remorse, relief, and a dozen other assorted emotions—all in phrases placed all over the scale and above and below it as well!

Having been pushed on to the stage, her success on that evening in November 1918 was decisive, although perhaps not the sensation that history has generally consecrated. Every critic was impressed, but urged caution and sustained study: 'She has an arduous road to travel before she can call herself a finished artist,' wrote Richard Aldrich. The next five or so years did indeed turn out to be arduous ones, and in the view of many she slipped back and failed to fulfil her initial promise. In retrospect, it was the necessary period of consolidation during which she worked steadily with Romani on developing a type of voice unparalleled among her contemporaries, neither lyric, dramatic, nor coloratura, but capable of embracing all three. Her repertory was highly unusual, and did not follow the pattern which we would expect from comparable post-war singers such as Leontyne Price or Rosalind Plowright: a lot of later Verdi, some Puccini, Strauss, and Donna Anna in *Don Giovanni*, with perhaps the odd Donizetti or Wagner role. Ponselle sang no Puccini, Strauss, or Wagner on stage, nor did she undertake Verdi's *Ballo* or *Otello*; even though she considered it 'the greatest opera ever written', she only sang *Aida* twice at the Met, so terrified was she of the exposed high C in the Nile Scene. All this may have been partly to avoid clashes of repertory with Jeritza, Rethberg, and Florence Easton, the three other leading lyric-dramatic sopranos of the 1920s and 1930s—and she was clearly very influenced by the tastes and advice of Romani. Nerves and caution were other factors, but whatever the reasons, the result was some interesting revivals and reassessments.

She worked slowly, always with Romani, and prepared new roles over a period of years rather than months. In 1925 she assumed the taxing title-roles in Ponchielli's *La Gioconda* and Spontini's *La Vestale*, an almost forgotten early Romantic opera, statuesque and grandiose in idiom. The fullness of Ponselle's 'natural' endowment —an opulent timbre, seamlessly even throughout its range, surprisingly flexible in coloratura—was now matched to a deep musicality with a subtle sense of phrase and response to the composer's dynamic marking, as well as a real ability to communicate theatrically. Like Caruso's or Schumann-Heink's, Ponselle's tone *floats* —it never sounds pushed. It is like a liquid that does not freeze or congeal or evaporate. Victor Gollancz recalled it in Proustian fashion: 'I was given the other night a wine that tasted beautifully equable, yet was quite devoid of an exaggerated *velouté*. That was what Ponselle sounded like.' The cutting edge of a Nilsson is not there, nor is her coloratura as brilliant as a Sutherland's: Ponselle had a 'short top', and frequently transposed down to avoid high Cs and Ds. Otherwise, her singing is of a matchlessly satisfying completeness. In 1927 she triumphantly put herself to the ultimate test of *Norma*, a work not heard at the Met since Lilli Lehmann sang it in 1891. There was also a superb Donna Anna in *Don Giovanni*, Selika in *L'Africaine*, and roles in some then little-known Verdi operas such as *Ernani* and *Luisa Miller*. In 1930 she sang, at Covent Garden, her first Violetta in *La Traviata*. The collapse of commercial recording in the Depression years means that the only faint echo of this interpretation which survives is an amateur pirate tape from 1935, on which the distortion is almost intolerable. Fortunately, the splendour of the singing remains blazingly evident. This Violetta is no nightingale exponent of *bel canto*. She begins a little loud and sharp—the effect, no doubt, of nerves—and in the first act one does not hear the sickness which Callas etched into her singing of the role, nor the fragility in Cotrubas'. This Violetta is a good-time girl, who knows how to enjoy life, and in a stunning 'Sempre libera' grabs excitedly at it. The second-act duet shows a wonderful range of emotion—anger and bitterness as well as grief and self-sacrifice—while the splendour of 'Amami, Alfredo' seems to overpower the pirate tape-machine altogether. Ponselle was not beyond the occasional extravagant vulgarity, as in the screeching noises she makes when Alfredo denounces her in the third scene, but how fully she braves the extremes of this great part, its ecstasy and despair as well as its purely technical challenges. What these records conclusively prove is that Ponselle was so much more than an obedient musician with a natural vocal gift: she was an enthralling performer, whose art also had a rare power and excitement.

Apart from three glorious seasons at Covent Garden, during which she did much to restore the good reputation of Italian opera —'I do not think I have ever heard anything to surpass or perhaps even to equal it,' wrote Francis Toye of her Violetta—and one visit to Florence in 1933 for *La Vestale*, she never sang opera outside the United States, and indeed rarely left the Met company at all. The thought of new audiences and new opera houses paralysed her. Her enchanting letters to Covent Garden's managing director Eustace Blois are full of pleas, requests, apologies, and worries. Here among other things she tries a rather desperate means of avoiding those dreaded top notes:

> I hope you'll give us plenty of stage rehearsals for Traviata, as I won't have a chance to prepare it here. *You will won't you???* I do want to do it well you know . . . I do want to put it over *big* . . . I forgot to mention to the designer the colour of the *walls* in the bedroom scene, last act—if possible please have them a real mysterious lavender, more on the orchid shade. This color with my costuming of white is very impressive. Another great favor I ask of you is to get after the *orchestra pitch*. Have your German director keep pulling it down until you get it to 435 and *keep* them down. Get them to adjust their instruments before beginning your season.

Then in 1935 she sang Carmen, and everything suddenly went horribly wrong. Although the part lay very comfortably within her vocal range (Carmen is notoriously useful for sopranos worried about top notes), 'she played fast and loose with time and rhythm' and 'showed a cheerful disregard of laws of good singing for which she has won richly deserved eminence'—thus Olin Downes in the *New York Times*. Her acting was also considered an embarrassing miscalculation, the nadir being a vampish dance in the tavern scene which apparently had its origins in the Black Bottom and the Charleston rather than anything authentically Hispanic. She stuck by her interpretation and a minority claimed to be convinced by it, but there is no doubt that her confidence was badly shaken. She asked the Met management for a revival of Cilea's lyrical *Adriana Lecouvreur* and was refused, on the grounds that it was not a box-office attraction. She offered to sing it for nothing and was still refused. Outraged and exhausted, Ponselle announced her retirement. Her last performance at the Met was as Carmen in 1937. After the annual provincial tour and a few concerts, she never sang in public again. She was barely forty.

Some months earlier she had put paid to years of gossip and speculation by marrying Carle A. Jackson, the son of the mayor of Baltimore. For all her dedication, Ponselle had none of the asceticism of a Fremstad. She had had a string of romances and was known to enjoy herself uninhibitedly. Her great hobby was cycling, and Gatti-Casazza is said to have banned her from riding down Broadway to the Met from her apartment on Riverside Drive, lest she was involved in an accident. At a Met gala, she and Carmela once presented an acrobatic cyclist act left over from vaudeville days. In personality she was volatile and sensitive, quick to react to pressures or criticism. She argued with Jeritza, and once threw all her belongings out of their shared dressing-room; she argued fatally with her manager and long-serving secretary; and she argued with Carmela, who sang sporadically at the Met as a mezzo, without ever establishing herself as much more than Ponselle's sister.

Marriage to Jackson did not work well, despite the building of the famous Villa Pace (from the aria 'Pace, pace, mio dio' in *Forza*) near Baltimore, which is now the Ponselle Museum. The war took him away on active service, and Ponselle was also faced with the death of Romani, the conversion of Carmela to fanatical born-again Christianity, and a series of threats and demands from her mad brother Tony, who also had operatic aspirations. Shortly after Jackson's return, Ponselle, in a deep depression, took an overdose and spent a long convalescent period in hospital. Jackson then left her.

Music seems to have played relatively little part in her life during this dismal period, but after her divorce in 1950, some sense of purpose seems to have been re-ignited. She became artistic director of the small Baltimore Civic Opera and achieved some excellent results with limited resources; her guidance, formal and informal, of singers such as Beverly Sills and Sherrill Milnes, was inspirational; and her opinion of every aspect of American operatic life was sought after and respected. Perhaps most important of all, she became less reluctant to sing, and in 1954 songs and arias from her concert *soirées* were recorded at the Villa Pace. After nearly eighteen years of retirement, the voice had retained its *grandezza*. At either end of her range the tone may be a little frayed and edgy, and the breaks in register are audible. Sometimes her style sounds archaic or unidiomatic, as in a swooping 'Liebestod' from *Tristan und Isolde* and a ludicrously stately rendition of 'Là ci darem la mano' from *Don Giovanni*, in which Zerlina '*vorrrrrrei*'s and '*non vorrrrrrei*'s like a Gioconda. But the 'Vergine degli Angeli' is loveliness itself, and the two arias from *Adriana Lecouvreur*, delicately shaped and sustained, reveal why she so coveted the role.

Ponselle died in 1981. She remains a shining guiding light for every prima donna who aspires to the Italian repertory, although it was not until the emergence of the black soprano that anything approaching her splendour was heard from an American singer. The necessary exception is the case of Helen Traubel (1899–1972), a strapping six-foot-tall soprano, flamboyantly costumed by Adrian of Hollywood, who assumed the Wagnerian niche at the Met during Flagstad's wartime absence. 'Nobody knows the Traubels I've seen,' lamented Rudolf Bing, punning on the spiritual: Traubel spelt trouble. Her voice was invaluable—huge, firm, and accurate, if unlovable. Like Flagstad herself, she had no difficulty in negotiating and enduring Wagner's challenges. The problem was her lack of commitment. 'I can admit that opera bored me,' she announced in her autobiography, and she sought a number of ways to alleviate the tedium, one of which was playing games with her regular partner, Lauritz Melchior, who by this late stage of his career could have sung Tristan or Siegfried in his sleep. In performance, they habitually competed to see who could get the other to 'crack up' first: Melchior would appear in the wings while Traubel was on stage, wearing a hula-hula skirt over his chain-mail and launch into a Highland Fling. In the next act Traubel would parry by pulling funny faces during a love duet.

'All culture has is hard seats' is another gem from Traubel's memoirs, and shortly after Flagstad's return and a front-page quarrel with Bing, she left the Met for the plush sofas of the Chez Paree night club in Chicago, making further cabaret appearances in New York and Las Vegas. Here she sang what Bing quaintly referred to as 'programmes of folk music': opera—but not only soprano arias—'Vesti la giubba' and the Toreador's Song were aired as well, the St Louis (her hometown) Blues, musical comedy, and numbers from the hit parade. She then took to Rodgers and Hammerstein, where her impersonation of a brothel madam in *Pipe Dream* was a major factor in the show's collapse. She also made television appearances with Jimmy Durante and Jerry Lewis which usually involved some obvious guying of the conventions of opera. It was as though she wanted revenge: she even wrote a bad thriller entitled *The Metropolitan Opera Murders*.

The *reductio ad absurdum* of the prima donna aping herself and her art was the bizarre Florence Foster Jenkins. The unmistakable dreadfulness of her singing has remained a joke for forty years, although in fairness it ought to be remembered that when her infamous record was made in 1944 she was seventy-six, an age at which even Ponselle would have sounded distinctly unimpressive. It is conceivable that she may once have been able to sing competently, and it is more than conceivable that the whole thing was a hoax, perpetrated by someone who was well aware of the commercial potential in such a preposterous noise.

Little is known of Foster Jenkins's background, although her nobility is attested by her membership (as recorded in her obituary) of the Colonial Descendants of America, the National Association of Patriotic Women, and the American Huguenot Society. It has been said that she was the daughter of a rich attorney who cut her off when she announced that she wished to become a singer. It has also been said that she lived for thirty-eight years in a common law marriage with a ham Shakespearean actor, St Clair Byfield, while teaching the piano and—here we run into verifiable fact—running something called the Verdi Club, under whose auspices she would give her annual private recital at New York's Ritz-Carlton Hotel. Madame Jenkins preferred a light coloratura repertory, which she delivered in a variety of eccentric costumes. Winsome dances and *tableaux vivants* representing 'Grief', 'Dawn', and so on, were other features of the occasion. Her one public recital at the Carnegie Hall was an enormous success and is reported to have grossed $6,000. Unfortunately the artiste died from a heart attack only a month after giving it, mortified, so it is said, at the constant laughter which accompanied her singing and which she attributed to the claques of rival prima donnas.

Florence Foster Jenkins was the unwitting founder of a tradition that extends through Anna Russell and Peter Ustinov's Madame Beethoven-Finck to the modern cult of the drag queen. Such acts can be witty and stylish; more often they are trite and offensive. By now, one might have thought that the joke would have worn as thin as that of the mincing *ballerino*—but it hasn't. The prima donna is still an easily exploited laugh.

Since eighteenth-century comic squibs such as Mozart's *Der Schauspieldirektor*, there has been a tradition of presenting prima donnas as avaricious monsters, unable to tolerate rivalry or criticism. By the 1920s the image had consolidated to that of a middle-aged lady, Junoesque in build, imperious in manner, but also ridiculously susceptible to flattery. Presumably this was conditioned by the appearance of figures such as Melba, Tetrazzini, and Schumann-Heink; it certainly bears no relation to Ponselle, Jeritza, or Garden. A popular caricature in this vein is Madame Castafiore in Hergé's 'Tintin' series of cartoon adventure books, originally published in Belgium from the 1930s onwards.

Through the 1930s another stereotype developed, chiefly through the popularity of musical films and the musical taste of a generation brought up on Galli-Curci. This was the young blonde ingénue with the voice of a nightingale and a sweetness of heart to match. The thwarted fiancée played by Kitty Carlisle in the Marx Brothers' *A Night at the Opera* (altogether a fascinating document of operatic life in America) provides a good example of this, but the most famous names were probably Jeannette MacDonald, Grace Moore, and Miliza Korjus ('rhymes with GORGEOUS', proclaimed her publicity material).

These two types have lived on. The fresh-voiced Julie Andrews in her *Sound of Music* incarnation continued the ingénue tradition into the 1960s, while Miss Piggy of the Muppets is a last gasp of the more traditional style of prima donna. Among popular singers, Barbra Streisand is still regarded as an embodiment of the prima donna syndrome. The most interesting modern variant on the myth is visible in films like Bertolucci's *La Luna* and Bendeix's *Diva*, both highly coloured and elaborate melodramas which use opera to suggest a world of abnormal emotional obsession.

This is a cult to which the French have been particularly susceptible (and *Diva* is a very French film), encouraged by the invisible presence of Callas in the avenue Georges-Mandel during the final period of her life. The English and Americans have a more robust attitude, and the prima donna style has long been a popular feature of 'camp' popular culture.

What is sad about this is the narrowness of the image received by the uninitiated public of the nature of a prima donna. A romantic novel like Gertrude Atherton's *Tower of Ivory* may now seem over-intense, but at least it suggests that a prima donna could be serious about her art, that real sacrifices are involved, that her motives might be something finer than vanity and greed. New York idolizes a prima donna—and sometimes debunks her—but in the maelstrom of attention and enthusiasm, she may still find that it does not give her a fair hearing.

## APPENDIX

Owing to the kindness of Mr Robert Tuggle of the Metropolitan Opera Archives, I was able to look at the house's paybooks for the years between 1898 and 1957. The following is a brief comparative table, culled from these fascinating documents, relating to the fees paid to prima donnas. All figures are for a single performance unless otherwise stated.

In 1898–9 Melba earned $1,650; Lehmann, $1,250 plus hotel expenses; Nordica, $1,000; and Sembrich, $800. However, the highest earner was Jean de Reszke at 11,000 francs or $2,101. His brother Edouard took $668, while the other great bass of the time, Pol Plançon, sang for $220.

1899–1900: Schumann-Heink, $9,000 for 90 performances (later renegotiated at $16,000 for 80 performances, then $24,000 for 100); Eames, $1,000, payable in gold the morning after a performance; Sembrich, $1,000 plus two orchestra stalls (a fee that remained the same until 1906, when it became $1,200); Calvé,

$1,719, with a dressing-room as near the stage as possible (in 1903 this rose to $1,920 for appearances outside New York).

1905–6: Melba was promised $2,000 but never appeared; in 1907 Oscar Hammerstein at the rival Manhattan Opera paid her $3,000; Nordica, $1,250; Eames, $1,500; Fremstad, $1,382 for ten performances a month. An average family's annual income in New York was estimated at *c.* $850.

1907–8: Caruso, $2,000; Farrar, $800; Fremstad, $750; Chaliapin, $1,344.

1908–9: Fremstad and Farrar level-pegged for one season at $1,000; Mahler earned slightly less at $5,050 a month for six performances, while Toscanini got only $4,800 for twelve perform-ances a month.

1909–10: Destinn, $900; Farrar, $1,200 (making a total of forty appearances, and singing at least twice a fortnight); while Fremstad stayed at $1,000 (also for forty appearances); Nordica kept to her 1905–6 fee of $1,250. Hammerstein at the Manhattan paid Tetrazzini $1,500 and Mary Garden $1,400.

1911–12: Destinn, $1,200; Farrar, $1,250; Fremstad, $1,000. Toscanini was still down at $7,000 a month, averaging twelve performances in that period. Seats at the Met were priced, as they had been for some years, at between one and five dollars.

1914–15: Caruso, $2,500; Destinn, $1,300; Melanie Kurt, Fremstad's replacement, $500.

1919–20: Muzio, $625; Farrar, $1,500; Ponselle's second season —she had started at $150 for up to three performances a week— $100, with guaranteed fourteen days' rehearsal: the norm was seven.

1921–2: Jeritza's first season, $1,500; Farrar the same. Muzio, $800. Ponselle, $1,000 per week, singing 24 times in 15 weeks; Galli-Curci, $2,000; Chaliapin, $3,000.

1926–7: Galli-Curci on tour commanded $3,500, in New York, $2,250, with Jeritza a whisker ahead at $2,300; Schumann-Heink's return cost $500; Talley, $500 per week, three performances. The tenor Martinelli took $1,700, the baritone Ruffo $1,500; Gigli, $16,000 per month for approximately eight performances. In the mid-Twenties a motor car cost *c.* $1,000, a gramophone record $1, and a round-the-world cruise *c.* $2,000. A seat at the Met could cost up to $8.25 in 1929.

1930–1: the Depression had begun, but had not yet bitten into the upper end of the earnings scale. The charming and stalwart lyric soprano Lucrezia Bori, $1,400; Jeritza, $2,500; Ponselle (after her Covent Garden triumph), $1,700; Rethberg, $1,200.

1935–6: the Depression had hit. Flagstad and Lotte Lehmann, $750; Grace Moore, Ponselle, Bori, $1,000; Melchior, $1,000; Rethberg, $900; Martinelli, $800—less than half what he earned in 1926–7. Average earnings in 1929, $1,300; in 1935, $850.

1956–7: in the intervening twenty years, fees had not increased either in real or inflated terms. Tebaldi, Milanov, and Callas all earned the $1,000 top. By comparison in 1931 it took an average wage-earner 580 hours to earn enough to buy a refrigerator; in 1956, 168 hours.

# 6

# *Verdi and a*
# *Variety of Sopranos*

The prima donna's art is based in a science of astonishing primitive-
ness and confusion. Very little about the production of the singing
voice is fully understood, partly because it is impossible to observe
a 'throat' in action. Any sort of mirror device, like Garcia's laryngoscope, inhibits the musculature and cannot reflect the underside of
the vocal cords. Singing teachers all have their own ideas, their
own metaphors and peculiar tricks for schooling what in physical
essence remains nothing more than a form of expiration. Singers
themselves usually have little to say about their methods—Patti and
Flagstad both claimed that they had no idea at all how they could
sing as they did. The American bass Jerome Hines compiled a
series of interviews on the subject with a number of eminent
practitioners and concluded that 'most of the interviewees had
difficulty at first in verbalizing their universe of vocal experience.
This does not mean that they don't understand it, it means that
they are accustomed to thinking about it in the non-verbal language
of kinesthetic sensation. As a result they tend to describe their
private world of vocalism by gesture, shaping the hands and fingers
to represent laryngeal and pharyngeal configurations, or using arms
and elbows to demonstrate use of the diaphragm.' In textbooks one
often finds only what for a non-singer is sheer gobbledegook: here,
for instance, is a much-mocked passage from Lilli Lehmann's *How
to Sing*—'In order to make the vowel sound ā, the larynx is with
energy brought in closer relation with the nose. By dilating the
nostrils a preparation is made. The sensation is then as if the larynx
were under the chin.' Try it and see . . .

An important step towards accepting the mystery is, I believe,
the recognition of the miraculous and abundant variety of voices
which exists among singers. Just as no two speaking voices can be
exactly identical, so no two singing voices are either, and whatever

one's preferences, it is useless to apply one standard of perfection in listening to them. An individual voice itself will change in range, timbre, and control over the years. Contraltos become sopranos, coloraturas become 'dramatics', Brünnhildes become Lucias. Birgit Nilsson could sing the Queen of the Night's aria with its top Fs and literally breath-taking runs, but only *after* she had warmed her voice up through a performance of *Götterdämmerung* or *Tristan*. The conductor Karl Böhm refused to believe this, until he was summoned to Nilsson's dressing-room to hear for himself. Similarly, the standard categories of soprano, mezzo-soprano, tenor, baritone, and bass are not adequate or permanent classifications. Much depends on fashion and the demands of the composers of the day. Contraltos and *bassi profondi* have become rare; we have seen how the Victorians disliked *vibrato* in sopranos; the 1960s brought forth a sudden wave of first-rate coloratura techniques, which fifteen years earlier would have been unthinkable.

Every voice has its eccentric weaknesses and strengths. Pasta and Malibran, like a number of 'sopranos', were stronger at the top and bottom of their ranges than in the middle; Montserrat Caballé has a very weak trill; Rosa Ponselle could not be relied upon to hit top C; while Jenny Lind's F# (just at the point where most singers have trouble in focusing the tone) was universally considered glorious. The singing voice is dogged by historians who bemoan declining standards and past golden ages, but it is much more realistic to think in terms of constant modifications, in which one strength compensates for another weakness. This may not be a great age for Wagner, but it certainly is for Mozart.

What can be unequivocally asserted is this: that each voice has its own nature, and to force it beyond its natural capacities—as Melba did when she tried to sing Brünnhilde—is to court disaster. Forcing is not the same as developing, and a perceptive teacher can train a 'lazy' voice into fulfilment, or pull it up or down into a more 'comfortable' range. Part of a voice's nature is a cycle of growth, change, and decay, and a singer who lasts the course will be sensitive to the inevitable alterations in her or his equipment: Joan Sutherland is an excellent example of a prima donna whose voice has been through a number of stages, and who has always known when to leave well alone.

The physical mechanism of singing is based in the controlled expulsion of air through the vocal cords, two highly sensitive vibrating membranes stretched across the larynx. Resonators such as the larynx itself, the pharynx, palate, and sinus, pick up the sound created and amplify it: here the voice finds its unique timbre and character. The exploitation of this natural process begins with deep and gentle breathing into a relaxed system, then a smooth emission which leaves the singer with enough 'supporting' air in the lungs on which to 'float' the sound and finish a phrase comfortably. A good legato line depends crucially on this. Nervous tension or any gustiness in breathing out soon produce the common faults of tremulous tone and aspirates ('haah' instead of 'aah'). Melba is a model here: her 'commencement' (otherwise known as 'attack' or *prise du son*) of a note was without breathiness or any sense of thrusting or grabbing at the sound—it simply arrives, whereas Lotte Lehmann's breathing and attack were noticeably imperfect. A major area of controversy among singing teachers is the issue of the 'registers'—breaks of tone in the voice at which some claim that the larynx decisively changes its shape and position. Chest, middle, and head registers are the terms that have been used in this connection since the thirteenth century, although the scientific evidence for their existence is exiguous and many say that the feeling of a decisive gear-change is illusory. Nevertheless many sopranos, for instance, have difficulty knowing quite what sound to make around E and F at the top of the stave. Teachers struggle to 'equalize' the registers so that the voice sounds seamless and homogeneous, like Ponselle's or Leider's, all the way through its range, an achievement which involves working hard on the passage-notes which link the so-called registers. The voice must also be 'placed'; that is, the air must be directed, at least mentally, towards the appropriate resonating cavities which will give the sound full and firm tone. Some singers centre it all at the back of the mouth, others concentrate on their sinuses: most agree that the tongue must not block or deflect the sound. Intonation, or the maintenance of correct pitch, is another problem, particularly in an age where *vibrato* is prevalent. It is impossible for a singer accurately to hear the sound she or he is making, and within any audience there will be surprisingly different reactions to a singer's intonation. Very few singers sing at a perfect regularity of pitch, and a small degree of sharpness or flatness is part of a voice's personality. However, a singer who cannot keep steady is a sorry thing, and a real problem with pitch, like Pasta's, is excruciating. Diction, especially at the top of the voice, agility, and stamina are other primary hurdles that some singers remain more successful at surmounting than others.

There is so much that can get in the way. A sneeze can release a lot of phlegm and block paths of sound. A stomach upset can impair the breathing. Menstruation affects the abdominal muscles and can cause flatness. Ponselle could not sing near any artificial heat and would telephone the stage-door manager before entering the opera house to make sure it was suitably freezing. Perhaps the most common nightmare comes from the idea of nodes, small growths on the vocal cords which among other things are ruinous of a singer's ability to sing *diminuendo* and *piano*. They are probably caused by strain, can sometimes be cured by surgery or prolonged silence, and affect sopranos more than any other sort of voice. A celebrated victim was Lucrezia Bori, who for two years after an operation to remove a node did not raise her voice above a whisper. If nodes are avoided, a more inevitable fate awaiting the vocal cords is sheer exhaustion. The right amount of exercise keeps them in trim, but there is a point beyond which they simply become flabby and unresponsive. For a top C they are estimated to vibrate at something like a thousand times per second, and that is a pitch that cannot be kept up indefinitely.

Few singers, least of all sopranos, would dispute that the healthiest vocal diet is provided by the operas of Verdi. His is music that feeds the voice like honey, even though his writing is not necessarily easy to negotiate or interpret; in particular two of his most famous creations, Violetta in *La Traviata* and Aida, contain radical difficulties. But in opera no one (except perhaps Mozart) has composed music which requires so little forcing or faking and which contains so much gratifyingly expressive and beautiful melody. His career and achievement stand as one of the marvels of musical history.

Giuseppe Verdi was born in 1813; his first surviving opera was produced in 1839, the last in 1893, and throughout his great span he showed an astonishing capacity for growth and self-renewal. As a citizen, he stood at the centre of his society, its aspirations and struggles, and a fervent liberal patriotism runs through his works up to *Otello* in 1887, by which time Italy was free of invaders and united as a nation. As a composer, he instinctively maintained the directness and simplicity of a rich popular musical tradition, and although he was intelligently sensitive to contemporary innovations, he kept his own counsel, immune to vogues, patiently developing his art at his own pace in a spirit of stubborn peasant tenacity.

Not that he was reactionary or complacent: in his own way, he was as dedicated to the reform of operatic abuse as any Wagnerian. From his first opera onwards he was fighting with hard-nosed managements, narrow-minded censors, and lazy prima donnas, all of whom treated his scores much as it suited them. Verdi was nobody's lackey, and as early as 1843 he refused to supply the soprano Sophia Loewe with the showpiece aria for the finale of *Ernani* which she considered her due. He also spent much of his life battling for a system of copyright protection which would prevent opera houses making random cuts, alterations, and substitutions, as well as ensuring the dignity and income of the composer.

The young Verdi, however, did not command the terms, and his survival entailed compromise with singers' capacities and audiences' tastes. Later he talked about his 'years in the galleys', churning out operas to order on harshly commercial principles and following helplessly many of the standard bad practices of the time. Nor was he invariably successful. For a long time his music was considered rumbustious, noisy, and ugly, especially in England, where connoisseur critics such as Chorley regarded even *Rigoletto* as symptomatic of the decline of Italian music into sheer vulgarity. Now, with the hindsight of *Otello* and *Falstaff*, it is easier to appreciate the virtues of works such as *Ernani*, but the modern reaction in favour of early Verdi has surely been excessive. It is refreshing to find the leading Verdi authority Julian Budden admitting that *Attila* is not a rough-diamond masterpiece, but 'blunt in style, daubed in thick garish colours; full of theatrical effects with no depth to them and containing more than its fair share of brash *cabalettas* . . . despite a genuine strength of construction much of it remains no less than *Alzira* on the level of commonplace vigour.'

It is in the music for the prima donna that these first operas most often show distinction. Two female stereotypes recur: there are the noble and pure-hearted ladies such as Amalia in *I Masnadieri* (written for Jenny Lind) and the eponymous Giovanna d'Arco (Joan of Arc), who are given music of Bellinian grace and the sort of wide-arched melody the Italians call *cantilena*; then there are the fiercer more energetic schemers like Abigaille in *Nabucco* or Lady Macbeth, whose roles demand powerful lower registers and some fiendish top notes. Lady Macbeth rises to a *pianissimo* top D flat at the end of her sleep-walking scene: many singers like to get off-stage and sing it *mezzo forte* from the wings—but it is still not easy to reach. Both these types of heroine remain basic to Verdi's operas.

Like all major opera composers, Verdi's feelings about prima donnas were equivocal. In his youth he heard Malibran and it was a memory that was never effaced. No contemporary prima donna offered him comparable inspiration, and he was scathing about the latter-day 'caricatures of Malibran who have only her oddities without any of her genius'. Bellini had worked closely with Pasta, but Verdi missed out on the strongest soprano of his day, Giulia Grisi, who had crossed the Alps and made for the money of Paris and London, never to return to Italy.[1] Of the various sopranos he encountered, Giuseppina Strepponi (1815–97) was the most important to him, even if she was far from the best singer. She came from a well-connected musical family, and when Verdi was still a novice, she was an established prima donna in the dramatic repertory of Bellini and Donizetti. Her encouragement and patronage of the young composer was practical and genuine. In 1842 she created the role of Abigaille in Verdi's first real success, *Nabucco*: unfortunately, it proved the final nail in her professional coffin. She had sung too much over ten exhausting years and borne two illegitimate children as well as undergoing an abortion. The part of Abigaille was very taxing, and although she continued to sing it for a few years in the provinces, it must have finished her voice. At the age of thirty-one she retired from the stage and set up in Paris as a singing teacher. Verdi encountered her there by chance, and in 1849 they set up house together on the farm at Sant' Agata that remained Verdi's base for the next half century. Ten years and a lot of scandal later, they were married. Strepponi's correspondence reveals a splendid woman, warm-hearted, intelligent, and devoted to a man who with all his honesty and integrity could be moody and irascible.

Romantics like to believe that Verdi's experience of Strepponi's status as a 'fallen woman' seeking out happiness in rural retreat brought a new sympathy and emotional intimacy into his creation of the courtesan Violetta in *La Traviata* (1853). The idea is not altogether satisfactory. For one thing, although Violetta has passion,

1  She did sing a few performances of *Il Trovatore* very late in her career.

dignity, and independence of spirit, she is still primarily motivated by the ideal of noble self-sacrifice in the name of love which governs so many nineteenth-century operatic heroines. What does distinguish the role is the peculiar difficulty of singing it—a fact obscured by the opera's enormous popularity. Even a soprano as accomplished as Patti had to cheat by making cuts and transpositions, and in the twentieth century perhaps only Callas and Ponselle have fully commanded its technical problems, however easy it is to make an effect in the role. Most sopranos either garble the hectic coloratura of the first-act 'Sempre libera' or have to speed up the wonderful 'Amami, Alfredo' passage, which needs a true *spinto* to give it its full weight and breadth. The orchestra is not overpowering, the opera is not long, the notes involved are not unduly high: it is just very difficult to sing it all as written.

Violetta's successor, the veiled court lady Leonora of *Il Trovatore* (also 1853) is much more straightforward. This is a role that makes no dramatic demands whatsoever, and the stoutest soprano can walk through it all without a moment's embarrassment, so long as she can sing two gorgeous and stately arias in Verdi's most elevated style, each capped by the last of Verdi's old-fashioned *cabalettas*. These fast and brilliant passages tacked on to the end of each leading character's major arias usually had no purpose beyond showing off technique and stimulating wild applause: there was no other feature of conventional Italian opera that Verdi was so anxious to be rid of. In Violetta's Act I aria, he manages to make the *cabaletta* an expression of the character's nervous and self-deceiving love of worldly pleasures, but from the mid 1850s he managed to do without them altogether, developing a far more integrated aria structure.

Verdi's liberation from the *cabaletta* came at a time when he was moving decisively towards the model of French Grand Opera. He spent some years in Paris and wrote for the Opéra after the Meyerbeerian fashion. Sometimes he shows an awkwardness in reconciling the Italian and French traditions, but from *Les Vêpres Siciliennes* to the culmination of *Aida*, we can hear Verdi's steadily growing mastery of a more sophisticated and fluid technique. The orchestration becomes warmer and more varied, and the relentless energy of the early operas is replaced by more measured contrasts and colours. Situation and character are more expansively portrayed.

It is here that we must mention the *spinto* soprano. This term—properly *lirico spinto* or 'pushed lyric'—will be applied to several singers in the following pages (although Tietjens, Destinn, and Turner are better described as *soprani drammatici*) and it refers in particular to the type of soprano needed for the middle and late operas of Verdi. Gone are the agility and top E♭s exploited by Rossini and Donizetti: now a different conception of virtuosity prevails. In operas such as *Un Ballo in Maschera, Don Carlos, La Forza del Destino*, and above all *Aida* the soprano needs rich, full tone over a wide range, with a perfect *piano* on high notes and strong projection in the lower reaches; breath control which can sustain and colour a long modulating *cantilena*; and the ability to make straightforward emotional dilemmas powerfully vivid. The feelings of Aida, for example, as she weighs *'amor'* against *'patria'* are generalized enough, and her psychology is not explored in any modern sense—but her music is exquisitely refined and full of the most taxingly delicate effects, ruthlessly contrasted with passages demanding much more brazen and splendid tone in the middle of the voice. Thus after the infamous exposed ascent to a *diminuendo* top C in 'O patria mia' (a phrase that petrified Rosa Ponselle to the point where she would not sing the role), the soprano within minutes has to change *tessitura* and find a harsh, metallic edge for the confrontation with her angry father, before changing colour and range again for the love duet with Radamès. In the final entombment scene, at the end of a long evening, comes music involving wide and unfamiliar intervals, in a difficult key, which should be sung so as to convey a gradual ebbing of life and breath. Even Aida's first aria, 'Ritorna vincitor', depends entirely on the force of the switch between hysterical declamation and an exhausted prayer for pity. Technically then, Aida is a role of constant changes of gear, and it is rare to find a soprano who claims to sing it without trepidation. A successful Aida, like a successful Norma or Isolde, need fear nothing else.

Far less problematic for the *spinto* is Desdemona in *Otello*, a role which aspirants often use as a confidence-boosting trial run for Aida. Verdi wrote of Desdemona as 'the type of goodness, resignation, self-sacrifice. There are beings who are born for others, who are quite unaware of their own egos . . .' This characterization could equally be applied to the other *spinto* ladies, and one has to admit that there is a disembodied monotony about the presentation of these victimized and generally passive women which all the grandeur of their music cannot eradicate. For female wilfulness, energy, and anger we have to go to the three dramatic mezzo-soprano roles that Verdi created in the Azucena of *Il Trovatore*, the Eboli of *Don Carlos*, and the Amneris of *Aida*. In these operas Verdi was in effect setting off the two female types of his early phase (maidenly Giovanna d'Arco and wicked Lady Macbeth) against each other, although the music assigned to them both is radically different in style. The soprano line arches, soars, and falls in comfortable harmonic relation to the orchestra, while the mezzo is more explosive and combative. The dramatic mezzo is another distinctly middle-late Verdi vocal type, a modification of the old Rossinian contralto (itself a replacement of the castrato) with the range pushed higher and the upwards strain used to great effect. The dramatic mezzo originates in Meyerbeer's Fidès in *Le Prophète*, of which Pauline Viardot was the great exemplar. The *spinto* soprano grew out of another phenomenon of French Grand Opera, the *falcon* voice.

Marie Cornélie Falcon (1812–97) belongs to a tragic band of prima donnas whose apparently powerful instruments have prematurely collapsed after a few years of overwork (Ljuba Welitsch provides a modern example of this). Falcon left her mark, however. After Malibran's marital problems caused her to stop singing in Paris, Falcon filled the gap, albeit in a French rather than Italian repertory. At twenty she made her début at the Opéra as Alice in *Robert le Diable*, and went on to create Rachel in Halévy's *La Juive* and Valentine in *Les Huguenots*. She had a withdrawn and intense personality, and a presence on stage which was later compared to that of the actress Rachel. Her voice was of a new and extraordinary character with, as one contemporary described it, 'an incomparable metal, a timbre like nothing that has ever been heard'. She did not have the easy coloratura or top register of an Italian-trained prima donna, but there was something dark, strong, and womanly in her voice, something that suggested both ardour and grief. Falcon came to represent the romanticism of French Grand Opera, and her name is still used to indicate its range of soprano roles. Her name conjured up a mysterious but potent figure of immense dignity and restraint, and this was the image strongly received into Verdi's middle-period operas—*falcon* is, as it were, French for *spinto*.

Falcon herself met a swift nemesis. In 1838, not six years after

her first success, her voice collapsed in the middle of a performance.
There was consternation in Paris. Such a thing was unheard of—
but then so was such an exhausting weight of singing. Falcon went
to Italy for a long holiday and some lessons. In 1840 she returned
to the Opéra, where she was greeted by such rapturous applause
that a combination of nerves and emotion made her faint. When
she recovered, the audience heard a singer whose top and bottom
notes were still in their prime, but a middle voice that was worn
and erratic. Falcon retired immediately, and never sang in public
again.

After Falcon, one might note the interestingly transitional voice
of Grisi, a soprano deeply influenced by Pasta, who attempted
without conspicuous success to enter the *falcon* repertory. It is an
odd fact that few first-rate *spintos* have been Italian, and the muse
that Verdi found for his later operas was Bohemian. She was Teresa
Stolz (1834–1902), whose reputation was made in the eastern opera
houses of Odessa and Constantinople. In 1865 she came to La
Scala, where she was to sing in *Un Ballo in Maschera*, *La Forza del
Destino*, *Don Carlos*, the Requiem, and, most of all, *Aida*—as well
as the *falcon* roles in *Robert le Diable* and *La Juive*. Her manner was
commanding and impressive, and one may assume that she gave
these rather nebulous characters theatrical definition. The
American Blanche Roosevelt reports thus on her singing: 'The
power she gave a high C is something amazing . . . the tone swells
out bigger and fuller, always retaining that exquisite purity of
intonation, and the air seems actually heavy with great passionate
waves of melody.'

Her relations with Verdi are shrouded in mystery, despite exhaus-
tive detective work published by Frank Walker in *The Man Verdi*,
and it is impossible to tell whether or not she was his mistress. All
we have are Strepponi's letters, full of jealousy and misery at the
attentions Verdi paid to Stolz, who came to live at Sant' Agata for
an uncomfortable length of time. Strepponi wrung her hands, but
tried to maintain friendly relations with Stolz, who in turn appears
to have been fond of Strepponi. The situation righted itself eventually, and it is perfectly possible that the affair only existed in
Strepponi's head. It is also equally possible that she was being
forced to accept an unsatisfactory *ménage à trois*.

There is no doubt, however, about the power of Stolz's vocal
endowment, and in her day there was only one other soprano to

match her in the *spinto* repertory: a singer whose voice united 'great volume with rare sweetness . . . sufficiently powerful to fill the largest house. It was soft as velvet, and even when it grew weaker there was no flaw to be detected in its mellowness, none of those qualities which, miscalled "wiry" and "silvery", cover in reality ill-disguised attempts to enforce a pretence which no longer exists.' This is a description by the French critic Brémont of Therese Tietjens (or Titiens), who dominated the London opera scene much as Stolz dominated Milan: neither singer ever trespassed into the other's territory.

Tietjens was born in Hamburg of Hungarian extraction in 1831. Her background remains obscure, and her father has variously been recorded as of 'ancient and noble family' and as the keeper of a *bierkeller*. She sang in Central Europe until 1858, when the impresario Lumley wooed her from Vienna to Her Majesty's in London. It proved to be his last and most steadily profitable managerial coup. She arrived 'horribly nervous', and made her début as Valentine in *Les Huguenots* before an audience led by Queen Victoria, who was to become one of her greatest admirers. The conductor Luigi Arditi recalled that 'ere she had sung half a dozen pages of music, significant looks passed amongst the audience, murmurs of approval grew into exclamations of pleasure'— and Tietjens went on to triumph. She became a naturalized Briton in 1868, living with her mother in St John's Wood. She was believed to be a lifelong spinster, but in 1896 *The Times* carried a report that a man claiming to be her husband had just died in Montevideo, the last refuge of the Victorian scoundrel.

A contemporary tribute by Sutherland Edwards shows how well her qualities suited the temper of the time: she was not just a fine singer, but a noble, earnest soul, more robust than Jenny Lind, and much more likeable.

Nor will it be by her artistic merits alone that Mdlle Tietjens will be remembered. The qualities that go towards the making up of a really great prima donna are many and varied. Besides a fine and powerful voice, a perfect style, and high dramatic ability, she must possess great physical strength and that particular kind of force, half physical, half moral, which is known by the name of 'nerve'. This species of courage enabled Mdlle Tietjens to do her duty, and more than her duty to the public at times when many a vocalist, of perhaps equal merit in a purely artistic point of view, would have given way.

Compared with Patti (the obviously implied 'vocalist' who 'would have given way'), her demands were modest and matronly. She was noted for taking an excessive amount of luggage on tour with her, but her fee—£800 for four performances—was never in the Patti league. She devoted her Sundays to charitable causes—'singing in a poor neighbourhood . . . many persons actually stopped to kiss the ground where she had trodden'. Lumley's successor Mapleson admits that he was kept solvent by her steady appeal and utter reliability. Again unlike Patti, she was a staunch trouper and easy to deal with professionally—she is certainly the shining light in the otherwise dark world of Mapleson's memoirs. She was also extremely hard-working, and Arditi tells how after a performance they would repair to his home for supper, and at 1.30 a.m. start rehearsing again. As late as the 1870s, when her supremacy was unassailable, she had the humility to go to Marchesi in an effort to rejuvenate the brilliance at the top of her voice.

Her repertory was extensive, although Lumley was of the opinion that the now old-fashioned 'florid music of the Italian school' suited her far less well than the more modern 'declamatory dramatic style'. But her range was remarkable, embracing Rossini's Semiramide and the mezzo role of Fidès in *Le Prophète*, as well as the first London Amelia in *Un Ballo in Maschera*, Leonora in *La Forza del Destino*, and Marguerite in *Faust*: she also valiantly championed works of neglected merit. *Aida*, of which she would have been superbly capable, did not appear in time to catch her, but on the strength of her performance as the evil Ortrud in *Lohengrin*, Wagner wrote to her in 1864, offering the part of Isolde in his forthcoming opera and even prepared to negotiate cuts in the score to win her over. Unlike some more easily seduced sopranos, Tietjens wisely refused.

Donizetti's Lucrezia Borgia was Tietjens's most famous assumption, as well as her last. Already suffering from the cancer from which she was to die, she gave her last performance at Her Majesty's Theatre in 1877. Mapleson reported on the event: 'As the evening progressed she felt she could hardly get through the opera. Her voice was in its fullest perfection, but her bodily ailments caused her acute agony.' In the final scene when Lucrezia sees that it is her son who is dead, Tietjens uttered a terrible scream of agony: 'As it rang through the house the audience shuddered. Only the initiated knew how much reality there was in it.' At the end of the opera, Lucrezia collapses: when the curtain rose for applause, Tietjens continued to lie insensible on the floor. Having become extremely stout, it required four men to lift her. She died some months later: on the night before her death she received a personal message of sympathy and encouragement from Queen Victoria. Her funeral in Kensal Green cemetery caused something close to a riot, 'amid tokens of public grief such as no artist before her had ever been vouchsafed on English soil'.

By the 1890s that great iconoclast George Bernard Shaw was heartily sick of the Tietjens myth. She had become 'obsolescent':

> Imagine being inured from one's cradle to the belief that the sublime in music meant Titiens singing the Inflammatus from Rossini's Stabat Mater; that the tragic in operatic singing, far overtopping anything that Mrs Siddons could ever have done, was Titiens as Lucrezia Borgia ... that Valentine in *Les Huguenots*, the Countess in *Le Nozze*, Pamina in *Die Zauberflöte*, all weighed eighteen stone, and could not be impersonated without a gross violation of operatic propriety by anyone an ounce lighter ... in spite of her imposing carriage, her big voice, her general intelligence, and, above all, a certain good-hearted grace which she never lost, even physically, the intelligence was not artistic intelligence; the voice, after the first few years, was a stale voice; there was not a ray of creative genius in her; and the absurdity of her age, her pleasant ugliness, and her huge size ...

Shaw was barely twenty-one when Tietjens died and he can only have heard her in her last years, but he was reacting against a piety which held people back from appreciating a new generation of singers. Another critic of the period wrote that 'a certain number of operatic characters may be said to die with Mdlle Tietjens. For a time, at least, it will be very difficult to find a Norma or a Lucrezia Borgia.' In a sense, there was no need for another Norma or Lucrezia Borgia. There was a new Verdi and Wagner repertory for the dramatic soprano, and the only operas of the old Italian school whose popularity survived the turn of the century were *Il Barbiere di Siviglia* and *Lucia di Lammermoor*. The art of coloratura singing was no longer part of every prima donna's training—instead it would become the province of specialists such as Tetrazzini and Galli-Curci.

Tietjens's truest successor emerged twenty-five-odd years after her death, but for all the similarity we can assume between their respective vocal equipments, Emmy Destinn sang none of the 'old Italian' roles of Grisi, which Tietjens had kept alive and flaming. Destinn's voice is dark, heavy, and ardent, never brilliant or flexible. Desmond Shawe-Taylor described it as 'a voice full of meaning, a strongly emotional voice to which the sensitive listener cannot remain indifferent'. For the young Victor Gollancz, crouched up in the Covent Garden gallery night after night and growing to love opera through her singing, Destinn communicated 'a sort of spiritual urgency that can never be explained to anyone who hasn't heard her'. On record, her singing can now sound leaden and over-emphatic, even crude in its effects: she clearly had problems with her intonation and her singing is often unpleasantly flat or wobbly. What should rise and fall smoothly (like the end of Aida's 'O patria mia') can sound clumsy and effortful. But the more one listens to her, the more what Gollancz referred to as 'spiritual urgency' does shine out. It was this intense emotionality, as well as an underlying fullness of power in the voice, which made her such an outstanding interpreter of the *spinto* repertory and the first great Puccini prima donna.

Her art embodied the spiritual urgency in her life. She was a Romantic in the grand style, a woman of immoderate feelings, interests, and appetites—a recent film has needlessly falsified what needs no exaggeration. She was born Ema Kittl in 1878 in Prague: her family owned mines and breweries. As a child, she showed marked literary leanings and throughout her life she produced poems, novels, and a drama, *Rahel*, which has been occasionally revived. She studied singing under Marie Loewe-Destinn, and took her name in gratitude. In 1898 she made her début in Berlin where she soon became prima donna. For such a weighty voice, she sang a very mixed bunch of roles—Pamina in *Die Zauberflöte*; the lyric title-role in Charpentier's *Louise*; the *falcon* Valentine in *Les Huguenots*; and one of the heaviest of all Italian soprano parts, Ponchielli's La Gioconda. She also undertook Strauss's *Salome*, and she was that composer's first choice for Ariadne in *Ariadne auf Naxos*. In 1901 she sang at Bayreuth, and in 1904 she arrived in

London, which became her second home in the pre-war years. She took a Nash terrace house in Regent's Park and sang at Covent Garden for eleven consecutive summers. Over half a century later, in *Journey Towards Music*, Victor Gollancz reminisced about her art in these golden seasons when her tenor partners included Caruso, Slezak, and Martinelli.

> The apogee, I suppose, was the Nile scene in *Aida*, interpreted by Destinn, Caruso, and Dinh Gilly. No young opera-goer of today could possibly realise what it was all like; all the beauty and drama came to life for us in those incomparable voices, not as an occasional rarity, but in note after note and phrase after phrase . . . I adored Destinn: we used to say that her twiddly bit in the first act of *Tosca* was alone worth our whole half-crown 'and then some', and she accomplished the change of register in 'Vissi d'arte' with almost inconceivable mastery. But best of all were her soft high notes. They were like exquisitely rounded pearls, suddenly appearing, perfectly poised, out of nowhere: and were specially breath-taking when they opened a phrase, as with 'Un bel dì' in *Butterfly*.

Her voice had by now firmly settled in the *spinto* regions, and Aida, Tosca, and Butterfly became the centre of her repertory. One oddity that she sang was an ephemeral adaptation (in Italian) of Hardy's *Tess of the D'Urbervilles* by Baron Frédéric D'Erlanger, a banker whose money shored up the Covent Garden deficit. In 1908 she abandoned her contract in Berlin and made for New York, the Met having offered her a four-fold increase in salary. Here she was Minnie in the world première of Puccini's *La Fanciulla del West*, as well as singing more Verdi and Wagner.

With the outbreak of the First World War, Destinn's fortunes changed. She returned to Czechoslovakia, then a non-existent nation, its territories part of the Austro-Hungarian Empire. Destinn's nationalism was fierce, and the embattled Austrians interned her in her castle in Stráž, which some like to claim was used as a secret Resistance cell. The authorities refused to let her out, even to fulfil a contract at the Met, unless she agreed to sing for the Austrian Red Cross—which as a Czech patriot she refused to do. The castle, fortunately, was not dull. It contained a large aquarium and a choir of frogs, each of them named after a prima donna, who croaked at different pitches. There was a room full of relics of

Napoleon and a huge library mostly consisting of books about 'alchemy, astronomy, black magic, necromancy, mantology, witchcraft, flagellation, sonnambulism, spiritualism, and the occult'. There was even a ghost room containing a skeleton, fake tropical spiders dangling from the ceiling, and a coffin full of worms. A newspaper report listed Destinn's other hobbies as 'cats and collecting antiques', but there is no doubt that her ruling passion was sex. She lacked straightforward beauty, but occasionally there is a photograph which hints at the allure and sensuality that coloured her singing as well. Always desperate in search of the ideal, she made do with promiscuity, taking what she needed wherever she could: in her novel, *In the Shade of the Blue Rose*, the heroine finds that 'the desire for a man and his hot embrace were as necessary to her as a draught of liquid to one whose lips are dry and parched and to whom the vessel from which the drink came was of no importance'. Her lover in Berlin was the conductor Karl Muck; in New York, Caruso asked to marry her, and Puccini and Toscanini were besotted; but during the rehearsals for *La Fanciulla del West*, in which all these three were involved, she fell instead for the French Algerian baritone Dinh Gilly, who often sang opposite her as Aida's father. Together they lived in internment at Stráž, deeply but tormentedly in love. Eventually, Gilly could stand it no longer —Destinn took up, *à la* Lady Chatterley, with a forester on the estate, and Gilly spent the remainder of the war in a camp. Later he railed to the accompanist Ivor Newton against the whole breed of prima donnas:

> They should all be burnt at the stake. I detest them all, I lived with one for five years. In the old days, if they hadn't lovers around them they used to drag the scene shifters into their dressing rooms before their mad scenes.

Destinn's public eminence did not survive the war. In the years following the armistice she returned to Covent Garden and the Met, celebrating Czech independence by rechristening herself Ema Destinnová and refusing to utter a word in German, but her career soon lost momentum. Why this should have been is not clear—she was scarcely forty and the enforced years of silence left her voice, according to more than one critic, better than ever. There are several possible factors which contribute to an explanation. The collapse of her affair with Gilly must have left her bitter and demoralized. In New York, the fresh glamour of Jeritza and Ponselle counted against her, especially as they poached on areas of her repertory. She may also have fallen victim to the more general desire for novelty which inevitably followed the war. Even Victor Gollancz found that his enthusiasm had waned.

Back in Czechoslovakia she married a young air force pilot, and became enormously fat and very indolent. Food and drink were other passions of hers, and her expenditure proved considerably more lavish than her income. She sold her collection of jewels, took pupils, and occasionally sang in concerts, increasingly confining herself to Czech music. In 1930 at the age of fifty-one she died of a massive stroke. The beautiful city of Prague, now sadly returned to foreign dominion, still commemorates its Destinnová with a museum dedicated to her life in the Smirice Palace.

Listening to Destinn on records is, as I have implied, something that demands effort and imagination on the listener's part. One has to distinguish between what is plainly and permanently bad in her singing, what is the effect of recording, and what is simply the effect of a style now anachronistic. Shaw wrote off Tietjens with the callowness of youth: it would be all too easy to do the same with Destinn, especially given the eclipsing magnificence of Ponselle who came after her, and whose virtues are recognizably those of modern taste.

Ponselle (whose life and art are discussed further in Ch. 5) set technical and stylistic standards for the singing of the *spinto* repertory which have yet to be surpassed. Her recordings show what Destinn's most conspicuously lack—a real legato, with a smoothness of emission and tone throughout the range. Destinn is often arresting, but in the Verdi *spinto* regions individuality of character does not count for as much as the purely, lucidly, effortlessly musical realization of the score. Ponselle's ghost haunts the Verdi singing of Milanov, Callas, Leontyne Price, and the young Rosalind Plowright, even though that mellow ease—often compared to the textures of cream, velvet, or port—must often seem the most distant and unattainable of chimeras.

However, Ponselle was not the only great exponent of *spinto* roles in the Twenties and Thirties. There was Rosa Raisa, the first Turandot, and the elegant, well-schooled Elisabeth Rethberg, who sang both German and Italian lyric-dramatic repertories in New York, carefully avoiding direct comparisons with Ponselle. The revival of Verdi's lesser-known operas which took place in Germany in the 1920s had its spearhead *spinto* soprano in Meta Seinemeyer, who died young of leukaemia. Perhaps the most interesting figure is that of Dame Eva Turner, born in 1892 in the bleak Lancashire cotton town of Oldham—which also fathered the composer William Walton—another musician who opted for the Italianate. For a nation with such a persistent and significant tradition of patronizing Italian opera, Britain has produced extraordinarily few internationally famous Italian-opera singers, at least until the 1960s. Between Mrs Billington and Turner, there were really only Adelaide Kemble (1814–79), daughter of the actor Charles Kemble and a pupil of Pasta's, who sang Norma throughout Italy and was greatly admired by Liszt but retired into marriage after only four years of success; and the contralto Mary Shaw (1814–76) who was in the first performance of Verdi's *Oberto* at La Scala in 1839, but who also prematurely retired after her husband fell seriously ill. Both these singers were stars of the 'opera in English' seasons at Covent Garden in 1841–2.

Eva Turner also began with 'opera in English'. After studying at the Royal Academy of Music, she sang between 1916 and 1924 with the valiant Carl Rosa Company who toured grand opera round the British provinces for over eighty years. Neither Turner's voice nor personality were made to languish in obscurity. 'I wasn't a Lancastrian for nothing,' she said. 'Even in the chorus I said to myself, "I must get to the front." ' By 1924, she was firmly at the front of the Carl Rosa and was heard by Ettore Panizza, Toscanini's assistant, during a London performance of *Madama Butterfly*. Panizza persuaded her to audition for Toscanini at La Scala—a tremendous step, even though the way had been paved for English-speakers by the success there of a pretty Irish soprano, Margaret Sheridan. At the audition Turner boldly sang Aida's first aria: Toscanini was impressed, and engaged her to sing two Wagner roles. She lived on in Italy until the outbreak of the Second World War, building herself a villa on the banks of Lake Lugano, and centring her career on the northern Italian opera houses, Turin in particular. What made her reputation was the short but crucifying title-role in Puccini's last opera *Turandot*, which only the most heroic of *spintos* should dare to undertake. Ponselle, for instance, could not have coped with the burgeoning volume and rising pitch of the aria 'In questa reggia', but Turner's voice was huge, and expanded magnificently to that unforgettable climax at which most singers have to pull back. She sang Turandot in Chicago, South America, and elsewhere in Europe. Alfano, who completed the unfinished score after Puccini's death, thought her 'perfect' as the dead-hearted, fanatical, and ruthless ice-queen, and Turner's voice had the enthralling power to sustain the role in a way that perhaps only Birgit Nilsson has since matched. Elsewhere on her sadly few recordings she is a little over-weening and unyielding, a little too grand and sweeping in scale to be as beguilingly melancholy as an ideal Aida or Leonora should be: but everything else is there in singing of towering accomplishment. Apart from her Italian roles, she was not surprisingly an accomplished Wagnerian, and in her long post-retirement teaching career taught Amy Shuard, Rita Hunter, and Linda Esther Gray, her three leading British suc-cessors in this area. She remains an awe-inspiring and honoured figure in London musical life, serving the cause unswervingly. At ninety, she still stood erect as a guardsman, her speaking voice orotund and precise, her faculties thoroughly marshalled.

What is never said is that Turner should have gone even further. She should have recorded more, she should have sung at the Met and returned regularly to La Scala, working with the great conductors of the day. Even at Covent Garden, she was sometimes overlooked; on Coronation Night in 1937, an Italian singer was preferred as Aida, Turner being assigned the inferior task of leading chorus and audience in 'God Save the King'! The shortcomings of her career are emphasized by comparison with that of Zinka Milanov, a far less exceptional singer, albeit a very fine one.

In 1962, on the twenty-fifth anniversary of Milanov's début at the Met, 'the usually staid Monday night audience (Monday is "fashion night" at the Metropolitan) was beside itself . . . Radiant and deeply moved, Miss Milanov suffused the house with the glow of her emotions. She has one of those elemental temperaments whose very naivety is a great strength.' This last sentence, from a report in *Opera* magazine, politely hints at the truth—Milanov was very imperious and very determined. Even in retirement she remained indomitable: when the comedian Lily Tomlin announced in the programme for her one-woman show on Broadway that her standby (understudy) was Zinka Milanov, the prima donna was humiliated by the joke to the point of suing for $2 million. Through-out her years at the Met, she kept a close eye on potential rivals.

When Callas made her début there in 1956, she chose the part of Norma, in which Milanov had flopped two seasons earlier. As the second act was about to begin, Milanov made a slow pointed entry into the auditorium, gathering as much applause and attention for herself as possible. This remained a favourite habit of hers—I myself remember seeing her, long after she had retired, advance regally down the aisle before a performance of *Adriana Lecouvreur* with Montserrat Caballé. The applause was respectful and intimidated—we all knew at once that it was Milanov who had come to pass authoritative judgement, and that hers was the truly significant presence. At the Met's Centennial Gala, she was still there, sitting in a place of honour on the stage and surveying the proceedings with an icy and imperturbable stare.

She was born in Yugoslavia in 1906 and studied with Milka Ternina. In the early 1930s she took, like Turner, the best possible apprenticeship, singing regularly with the same company in a variety of roles. In 1937 she left her Zagreb nest, and again like Turner had her first international success under Toscanini, in the Verdi Requiem at the Salzburg Festival. From December of that year (in which Ponselle had retired) until the closure of the old house in 1966, with only one real break of three years after the war, she sang at the Met.

Milanov's early performances were marred by an uncertainty of pitch and a lack of general confidence, giving, as the Met historian, Irving Kolodin, put it, 'alternate sensations of pleasure and pain' —partly due, perhaps, to her difficulty with the Italian language. She continued to take lessons and worked hard with her accompanist brother, who clearly exerted considerable musical influence over her. By the 1950s everything had fallen into place. She married a Yugoslav general; she sang at La Scala and Covent Garden; she made LP recordings of her major roles with distinguished colleagues such as Jussi Björling and Leonard Warren; and, apart from the mistake with Norma, she stuck firmly to what she could do well—*Tosca, Trovatore, Aida, Un Ballo in Maschera, Andrea Chénier, La Gioconda,* and a very few others. She never bellowed or throttled her tone; her *pianissimo* was ravishing; she sang sparingly on her chest voice, so as to keep a pure soprano sound. She knew her limitations: 'A dog is a dog,' she told one interviewer portentously, 'and remains a dog even if he wishes he were a cat. The laws of nature cannot be changed. You are what you are.' She was cautious at all times and adamant about what she would not and could not sing: thus the Marschallin, Butterfly, and Turandot she had sung in Zagreb never passed her lips at the Met.

The result of this, confirmed by records, was a copybook art without much edge or flavour, apart from the wonderfully floated soft singing. One can start by finding Milanov relaxing but end up feeling a little bored. She can make a night-time reverie like 'D'amor sull' ali rosee' (from *Il Trovatore*) evanesce into the heavens, but any climactic open-throated cry—'Maledizione!', 'Suicidio!', 'Ritorna vincitor!'—finds her ladylike. The grand and sudden contrasts and modulations of mood upon which depends so much of Verdi's drama, and of *Aida* in particular, are not fulfilled.

Milanov epitomizes a certain idea of refinement and 'good taste' in Verdi singing, but it was Leontyne Price who broke the mould and brought back an uninhibited splendour. Price's voice has an unmistakably individual fragrance—husky, dusky, musky, smoky, misty (on a bad day, foggy!)—and a palpitating pagan sexiness. It is not the voice of a good girl. When she sang Puccini or Strauss the sheer opulence of sound became almost too much, like cream on top of a rich chocolate pudding. Living with such a gorgeous instrument it is hardly surprising that she told one interviewer:

> It's terrible, but you know I just love the sound of my own voice. Sometimes I simply move myself to tears. I suppose I must be my own best fan. I don't care if that sounds immodest.

She described her voice aptly as 'juicy lyric', rather than 'dramatic' (as one might describe Turner's): the juice is warm and sweet and tropical.

One can imagine Price bridling at that last word, since the first thirty-five years of her life were dominated by the fact that she is black. 'My career was simultaneous with the opening up of civil rights,' she complained. 'Whenever there was any copy about me, what I was as an artist, what I had as ability, got shoveled under because all the attention was on racial connotations.' She was born in 1927 in deep south Mississippi to parents who were active in the music of the local church. At the age of nine, Leontyne heard a recital given by the black American contralto Marian Anderson and decided that she wanted to sing for her living. The fact that a rich white family helped her with the money for lessons was later played up by the press, to the point where Price had to reassert the encouragement she had also had from her parents. She won a scholarship to the Juilliard School in New York, and studied with Florence Page Kimball, a pupil of Marcella Sembrich's.

In the early 1950s a serious black singer could only hope to follow Anderson into a career in concert and recital. A hundred years after the 'Black Malibran' and fifty after the 'Black Patti', Sissieretta Jones, the notion of a black prima donna had still not gained acceptance in the major opera houses. Price heard Welitsch sing Salome and was entranced; it would be opera or bust. She spent her first years as a professional in Broadway productions of the next best thing—'all black' American operas, such as Virgil Thomson's *Four Saints in Three Acts*, and *Porgy and Bess*. In 1955, Bing opened the Met door to Marian Anderson, against considerable conservative opposition, and engaged her to sing the relatively small role of Ulrica in *Un Ballo in Maschera*.

A barrier was down and a precedent established: the event heralded a decade in which blacks would fight for a full role in the world's greatest democratic society. Price made her way steadily, although her token-black status meant that, as she put it, she had 'to walk on my tippy-toes'. She sang Tosca on American television and in *Dialogues des Carmelites* in San Francisco, but her real breakthrough was in Europe. In 1958 she sang Aida, the black soprano's inevitable *carte de visite*, in Vienna, the Verona Arena, and at Covent Garden. In 1960 she sang at Salzburg and La Scala. Karajan patronized her assiduously; her success was unremitting. Finally, in 1961, seven days after Kennedy's inauguration, at the dawn of a new America, Price made her début at the Met, in *Il Trovatore*. For all the immediate and lasting glory that she found there, it was never her happiest theatre. One night she cracked in the middle of *La Fanciulla del West*—an opera for a Nilsson or a Turner rather than a Price or Ponselle—and had to be replaced. In 1966, as America's undisputed prima donna *assoluta*, she was chosen for the première of Barber's *Antony and Cleopatra*, which was to open the new Met in Lincoln Center. The massive publicity culminated in anti-climax and Price herself was swamped by Zeffirelli's leadenly lavish production. In later years the Manhattan critics remarked on the blandness of her characterizations and decided that her singing was mannered. The rest of opera-going humankind has had little chance to test their verdict, for since the mid 1970s, she has been reluctant to travel far from her home in Greenwich Village and her professional appearances have been sadly infrequent.

Throughout the 1960s, cut-Price imitations followed her thick and fast, as the black prima donna became fashionable rather than merely acceptable, but the *spinto* repertory is never going to be well stocked with adequate voices. The temptation is for lyric sopranos to push themselves into the louder, higher, lower, and better-paid bracket, with short-lived or stillborn results, and a deleterious effect on the quality of sound they produce. Of course such experiments have to be made, and without them we would not be able to hear the major achievements of Italian opera. It should be said again that the human voice is not hard and fast. In one sense, Milanov was wrong—a dog is not always a dog, or at least a mezzo is not always a mezzo, nor a lyric a lyric. A large number of prima donnas have at some time radically changed their range or repertory. But all too often one's inescapable feeling is that the wrong considerations have prevailed.

To round the story off, we can look at two black dramatic mezzos who have decided to sing *spinto* soprano. Shirley Verrett (born 1931) has even tried to have it all ways, by continuing with her mezzo repertory alongside Tosca, Amelia, and even Norma. 'I wish Verrett would listen to plain common sense,' wrote Walter Legge, while the change was being negotiated. 'She is by achievement the best mezzo in the world. She should be forbidden to sing Norma . . . I adore her as an artist, her application, natural acting ability, lovely velvety timbre, agility and brilliance. These particular qualities are so rare in one beautiful young woman that someone should lay down the law.' Verrett has in fact survived impressively enough, but her style has become, in the opinion of many, hard and over-projected, as though she was trying to prove her point through sheer will-power rather than spontaneous endowment.

An even more difficult case is that of the felinely glamorous Grace Bumbry (born 1937), another extremely popular figure. Prince Charles admitted that she was his favourite singer, and she had a flamboyant taste for motor racing which won her a lot of press coverage. By 1981, she had moderated her life-style. 'I have a tiny little Fiat 500, which sits in the garage of my house in Lugano, and a Cadillac Sedan de Ville which has about 1,000 miles on it, and a small Rolls [*sic*] in Europe. And I have far too many furs. In all sincerity, I don't need nine of them. How do you travel with nine furs?'

She studied with Lotte Lehmann (who prophesied that she would one day sing Brünnhilde and Isolde), but made her name as a superb exponent of the Verdi mezzo roles—Amneris, the Requiem, and especially Eboli in *Don Carlos*. In 1961, as Venus in *Tannhäuser*, she was the first black singer at Bayreuth, another decisive and much-publicized breakthrough for her colour. With her vibrant voice and electrifying appearance, she had wildfire success, and many saw the seeds of a mature greatness in her. Later came a spate of Carmens, some under Karajan at Salzburg. After Carmen, every mezzo naturally asks herself: what next? Bumbry became bored with the role—'Carmen is the same sickness for the black mezzo that Aida is for the black soprano,' she claimed. The answer came: sing soprano. She had always used vocal exercises which took her up to high C; Lehmann had seen her soprano potential. Milanov encouraged her too, and gave her some lessons. So, in 1970 at Covent Garden, she sang Salome, an unambiguously soprano role, and the new Bumbry was launched. She soon dropped her mezzo repertory, except for Eboli, which has a very high *tessitura*.

Considerable criticism ensued, however, and at the Met Bumbry lost out badly to Renata Scotto, whom Bumbry publicly criticized for taking on roles too heavy for her. In an effort to rejuvenate her reputation in New York, she boldly moved across the Lincoln Center Plaza to the City Opera for the 1981–2 season, where she sang Medea and Abigaille in *Nabucco*, to distinctly modified rapture. It is often remarked that the top of her voice does not inspire confidence, but the real problem, I suggest, is that she became obsessed with emulating Callas, or rather an aspect of Callas. Bumbry never saw her on stage, but listened hard to her recordings and took on the dramatic end of her repertory. Everything Bumbry did bespoke the angry, scornful tigress, of imposing presence and commanding gesture. She seemed to cultivate the same sort of vocal quality as well, harsh, chesty, sometimes plain loud and aggressive. Callas's genius, whatever its flaws, was much more subtle and complex than this. Bumbry's performances could degenerate into an odd mixture of the coarse and the studied, filled with broad melodramatic strokes but forgetful of the exquisite detail and musicality which informed Callas's art. All this being said,

Verrett and Bumbry are often very exciting singers, with temperament and presence: they both get an undeniable A for effort. Reports of their mutual rivalry were effectively belied by some extremely successful joint recitals, which involved some bewildering swapping of ranges.

The shortage of true *spinto* sopranos is one of the constant casting problems of every opera house, a situation emphasized by the fact that Verdi is the staple diet everywhere, a composer with the same capacity as Shakespeare of surviving countless incompetent or mediocre performances. Verdi's vigour and tunefulness may be infinitely durable and immediately available, but the deeper glory of his music is more evasive. To hear Verdi well sung is a rare privilege, and the prima donna who undertakes one of his *spinto* roles faces the greatest possible challenge to her technique and understanding.

# 7

# *Strauss and*
# *the Prima Donna in Vienna*

It would be possible to live in London or New York and remain quite unaware that the city contained a thing called an opera house, but in Vienna one has no such option. The opera house dominates city life, both geographically and spiritually. It is as inextricably associated with Vienna as coffee and cakes, the Prater wheel, kitsch, and Siegmund Freud, presenting the Viennese with an unfailing source of controversy. As a symbol of the city, it is not an inert monument like the Eiffel Tower or the Golden Gate Bridge, but an institution whose personnel, character, and achievements are varying. Every performance puts someone's reputation at stake; every new production or appointment is a politically charged act. The opera provides Vienna with more than entertainment—it gives the city its honour, and after the bombing at the end of the Second World War, its survival in some form was regarded not as a luxury, the cream for the coffee, but as a precondition of decency.

Vienna's operatic tradition goes back to the seventeenth century and was long in a difficult relationship with the imperial court. Gluck, Mozart, and Beethoven all wrote for Vienna, and in 1821 Domenico Barbaia brought Rossini with him from Naples, when he took over the management of the Theater an der Wien and the Kärntnerthor. Colbran, Sontag, Schröder-Devrient, Lind, and Patti all had significant success there, but our starting-point is 1869, when a new opera house was opened as the centre-piece of a massive urban redevelopment, along what is known as the Ringstrasse, which continues to embody the pomp and pretension of the doomed Austro-Hungarian Empire and its ruler Franz Josef. Six years later Paris was to open its own similarly grandiose opera house. Unlike the 'guest-star' oriented system of London, Vienna always maintained a permanent ensemble of artists, under long-term restrictive contracts as court servants. The prerogative of the prima donna did not obtain and perhaps more than any other opera house the history of Vienna is the history of its chief conductors rather than its leading singers. Musical standards were always abnormally high. Wagner found many of his singers for the first Bayreuth *Ring* here, and his operas were regularly and competently performed, sometimes under the composer's supervision and conducted by Hans Richter, at a time when most opera houses were still trembling at the strain of putting on even a cut version of *Lohengrin* or *Tannhäuser*.

The first unforgettable figure of the new Vienna Opera was undoubtedly Gustav Mahler, who in his lifetime was far more revered as a conductor than as a composer. He was chief conductor and artistic director there from 1897 to 1907, an appointment that caused immense controversy and which was violently resisted by Cosima Wagner on anti-Semitic grounds, despite his brilliant interpretations of her husband's works. Mahler enforced the Wagnerian etiquette of opera-going—dimming the house lights, refusing admission to latecomers, and warring against the claques. 'Tradition is slovenliness' was his militant watchword as he ruthlessly revolutionized every aspect of opera performance, restoring passages normally cut and insisting on respect for the composer's written intentions. Melba, however, once bested him: in a guest appearance, she was permitted to give the entire Mad Scene from *Lucia di Lammermoor* as a tailpiece to *La Traviata*. Otherwise the prima donna was thoroughly subordinated to ferocious rehearsal and musical discipline. One of his most significant reforms was changing the position of the conductor's podium. Before Mahler, the conductor of Italian opera had stood up against the stage, as close to the singers as possible, the orchestra following him from behind: Mahler moved back to the modern position in front of the orchestra, where it could receive the full force of his electrifyingly volatile and expressive gesturing. In partnership with the designer Alfred Roller, Mahler also created restrained and beautiful stage-pictures, which in their use of simple colour schemes and subtle lighting effects heralded a new attitude to operatic spectacle.

His taste in singers was particular and his control over casting draconian. He had no great love of the sort of purely beautiful effortless tone represented by Melba, and put his energies into building up an ensemble of voices with power and expressive variety. It was unfortunate that his name was amorously linked with three of his prima donnas, since the coffee-houses and *salons* were all too eager for any aspersion against him, and the casting-couch smear was as irresistible as it was unjustified. The only serious relationship he had was that with Anna von Mildenburg, a heroic Wagnerian soprano of great intelligence and dark, melancholy presence. Mahler had fallen in love with her while conducting in Hamburg, where they were both contracted, and in 1897 she followed him to Vienna. To avoid scandal, the liaison was carried on in the utmost secrecy and discomfort, and soon broke under the strain, although she continued to sing for Mahler in Vienna throughout his tenure. Mahler's formidable wife Alma was later to write off Mildenburg's passion as 'wholly self-seeking', but if anything it seems to have been the opposite—a complete submission to Mahler's destiny, artistic principles, and temperament. Marie Gutheil-Schoder and Selma Kurz were also the subject of amused whispers with little fact to ratify them. Gutheil-Schoder's style was harsh, vivid, and forceful and she was initially dubbed 'the singer without a voice', but Mahler loyally nurtured her and she remained a feature of the Vienna Opera until 1926, a celebrated Carmen and the first Viennese Octavian in *Rosenkavalier*. Selma Kurz had a similarly long career in Vienna as a coloratura soprano with a staggering trill, still to be heard on record; Melba was said to be inflamed with jealousy by her acclaim at Covent Garden.

After Mahler left Vienna for New York and the Met, his heart condition fatally exacerbated by the intrigue and malice directed against him, there was an inevitable lull, followed by the First World War and the collapse of the Habsburg monarchy. Austria emerged as a republic and Vienna's court opera became a state opera. The aftermath of war left the city impoverished and hungry, beset with inflation, strikes, and political unrest, but it won itself another conductor who was to send waves of excitement through the opera house. In an unhappily ill-defined arrangement Richard Strauss (1864–1949) was appointed co-director with Franz Schalk in 1919 and remained until 1924, when he too was prematurely pushed out. After Mahler's idealism and high seriousness, Strauss's regime appears indulgent and hedonistic, but his impact on the opera repertory has, to date, been greater than that of any other twentieth-century composer.

Strauss might a century hence prove to be the modern Meyerbeer —that is, an immensely self-assured and productive composer, who made a fortune and fulfilled the middle-class musical tastes of his time with ease, but whose lack of real sincerity, honesty, high purpose, call it what you will, eventually sank his reputation when taste changed. As yet, Strauss remains fashionable as the opera composer of sophisticated romances and two out-and-out melo-dramas, all brilliantly orchestrated in an idiom which remains for most opera-goers an acceptable version of 'modern music', harmonically dissonant, sometimes bombastic but conveying reco-gnizable moods and emotions in interesting situations. In *Elektra*, one responds to the over-heated neurotic restlessness, the fantastic range of colour and dynamic, right down to the final crashing C major chords which close the work; in an opera like *Rosenkavalier* or *Arabella*, we all wait for the soaring ecstasy of the soprano passages, which swoop or droop over the passing of beauty, the smell of a rose, or the coming of Mr Right. Strauss's is music of pure—or impure—sensuality, sometimes physically assaulting, sometimes (as in the Four Last Songs or the *Rosenkavalier* Trio) spine-tinglingly lovely. Whether it is any more than this is a matter for personal taste or high musical debate.

What is beyond dispute is Strauss's love of the female singing voice spinning out a long, smooth, high-lying melisma. He felt and communicated an inherent loveliness in the female condition, which seems to have outweighed his sympathy for the misery in the female plight—an unhappy woman is always a beautiful thing in a Strauss opera. Yet at least the Wagnerian mould was broken, and a Strauss heroine does not have to be branded angel, martyr, or virgin. She can let out her stays and uncover her cleavage without being thought a whore. Her sexual longings can be open and frank, her temper impulsive and melancholic rather than heroic and obsessive. Tricked or baffled by men, she can look in the mirror and keep a sense of proportion about life.

Strauss's first two major operas are notorious exceptions to this generalization. His early career had been dominated by the composition of narrative orchestral tone-poems in which he played fancifully at the 'depiction' of everything from a baby in the bath to mountain landscapes. The classicist Brahms devastated him by declaring that one of these pieces was 'too full of thematic irrelevancies', but Strauss continued to be a twentieth-century Baroque composer, in love with ornament, flourish, and gilded façades. In his operas the orchestra is always furiously busy making effects, and nowhere is this more overwhelming than in *Salome*, which Fauré described as a 'symphonic poem with added vocal parts'. Taken directly from Oscar Wilde's play, *Salome* was a sensation from its first performance in Dresden in 1905. Mahler then tried to get it for Vienna, but the censors forbade it as a distastefully lascivious treatment of a biblical subject; while in 1907, New York found its 'moral stench . . . abhorrent', and the Met did not perform it again until 1933. The shock value has now evaporated, but *Salome* still provides a marvellous opportunity for an imaginative prima donna capable of combining a Wagnerian's power with the naïve tones of an unpleasant spoilt girl. Whatever one's view of Salome's moral awareness, she is always a virgin, and coy prurience is strongly drawn in her music. Great interpreters of the role like Ljuba Welitsch bring an ironic lightness and sweetness into their voices when singing it, and it is interesting that Strauss pestered Elisabeth Schumann, famous as the nice silly convent-educated Sophie of *Rosenkavalier*, to sing the role, even offering to reduce the orchestral counterblast to accommodate her. Without the severed head, *Salome* could easily be turned into a Viennese comedy—the story of a petulant rich girl who wants to kiss the high-minded but ineligible John the Baptist and flirts with her stepfather to get his permission. The decadent apparatus of the work now looks tawdry or ludicrous, but its successor, *Elektra* (1909), remains a genuinely terrifying study of the obsessive pathology of hatred, for which Strauss wrote his most dense, viscerally gripping and plain loud music. The libretto was adapted by Strauss's great collaborator, the Viennese poet and playwright Hugo von Hofmannsthal, from his own 1903 version of the Sophocles play. Its psychology, full of Oedipal situations, bad dreams, and sublimated sexual frustration, makes it a product appropriate to Freud's Vienna, and perhaps no other operatic part demands from the prima donna such a purely intellectual grasp of the implications of the text, such an amount of verbal inflection, or presents her with such an amount of words to sing: this, as much as the length of the role and the volume required, sets it on its own. This Elektra is neither heroine nor victim, but a female Hamlet—unremittingly possessed by a mother's betrayal and a father's murder, driven by a suicidal tendency. Elektra is also a wit, and an interpreter who embraces the character's complex of moods should bring out the farcical aspects of her situation, her grovelling absurdity as well as her pathos. This is a brutally painful and exhausting opera for conductor, orchestra, the three women principals, and the audience. Strauss himself, easygoing by nature and bourgeois in his private life, was exhausted by composing it, and he never returned to any comparable subject-matter. Later he would write to Hofmannsthal of his ambition to be the Offenbach of the twentieth century—he had stripped off his Wagnerian armoury.

Strauss and Hofmannsthal's next opera was *Der Rosenkavalier* (1911), a roaringly popular success everywhere from its first performance in Dresden. More sentiment accrues to *Rosenkavalier* than to any other twentieth-century opera. It is 'loved' in the way that *Le Nozze di Figaro*, *Traviata*, or *La Bohème* are loved: the Marschallin's monologue, the Presentation of the Rose, the final Trio and Duet are listened to when all else seems lost. In this opera, Strauss and Hofmannsthal were determined to be charming. Every element and effect was carefully assembled to make up a pastiche of everyone's dream of the romance of old Vienna. There is a hint of Mozart in the period setting and the casting of lustful Count Octavian as a mezzo-soprano, a soupçon of Johann Strauss in the anachronistic waltzes, an Italian tenor to sing some mock-Verdi, and even a little black page. The milieu is aristocratic but *louche*, and a married noblewoman is allowed her adultery without incurring any subsequent humiliation. The orchestra sweetens, spices, comments on, and imitates it all, from the startlingly graphic representation of sexual intercourse in the prelude to the final little joke coda. The core of its musical appeal, however, is surely the ravishing blending of three female voices in various combinations and timbres, contrasted with the rough *buffo* bass of Baron Ochs —a beauty pursued by the beast principle, and one that Strauss returned to, partly to avoid having to deal with the tenor voice, which he disliked. The opera's emotional focus is the figure of the Marschallin, unhappily married, facing the end of her youth, involved with a younger man, perfectly well aware how it must all end, and facing that end, when it comes, with magnanimity and self-restraint. Towards the end of Act I she reflects on the inevitability of losing Octavian '*heut oder morgen*'; the passage of Time, '*ein sonderbar ding*'; her daily round of church, lunch with an old uncle, a drive in the Prater—and a Lehmann, a Schwarzkopf, a Crespin can engrave the poignance of it all on even the most cynical ear. The Marschallin is a symbol of the grace of aristocratic womanhood in an opera that depends a lot on nostalgia for the delights of the old order. If one is impervious to this appeal, *Rosenkavalier* is an oddly patchy work, which in anything less than a very good performance soon becomes intolerably over-long and futile: at its London première, Ernest Newman described it as 'one-third worthy of Richard Strauss, one-third worthy of Johann Strauss, and the remainder only worthy of the waste-paper basket'.

With *Rosenkavalier* Strauss reached a peak of fame and success. None of his later operas ever matched up to it in terms of public favour and he was to search in vain for the rest of his life for an equally happy formula. His next opera with Hofmannsthal, *Ariadne auf Naxos* (1912; second version, 1916), was considered too clever by half, although the pastiche is more economically contrived than its predecessor's, requiring only a small orchestra and ten singers. Originally, *Ariadne* was designed as a one-act opera to follow a spoken performance of Molière's *Le Bourgeois Gentilhomme*, but this proved impractical. After alterations it became an opera about putting on an opera, with another trio of high-voiced ladies in the leading roles. There is another breeches part for high mezzo-soprano in the Composer of the second version's Prologue, who lyrically defends the art of music against the philistines in some of Strauss's most pulsating and ardent pages; a grand prima donna part for the Ariadne, who has a grand monologue and a very grand aria and duet to negotiate; and finally the tiresome role of Zerbinetta, for a coloratura soprano who has to prance around giving the soubrette view on the proceedings. *Ariadne* was followed by *Die Frau ohne Schatten* (1919): its complex allegorical libretto delving into the mysteries of marriage and infertility inspired Strauss to a gorgeous and opulent score, but it was hardly designed for instant appeal in a society shattered by four years of war. It was the only Strauss opera to be given its première in Vienna, since Strauss ordinarily preferred to expose himself first in the smaller and kindlier opera house at Dresden. The first cast of *Die Frau* included Lotte Lehmann and Maria Jeritza, Vienna's two leading young soprano prima donnas, who were not on the best of terms. As such rivalries go, theirs was a sadly serious matter, fanned not by the press but by an artistic competitiveness centring on Strauss.

They entered the opera house by different doors on the nights on which they sang together, in *Die Frau, Ariadne, Carmen*, or *Die Walküre*; Lehmann refused to sing in a later opera of Strauss's, *Die*

*Aegyptische Helena*, because Jeritza had cornered it before her, while Jeritza always claimed that Strauss had offered her either of the leading parts in *Die Frau*, and Lehmann had been handed her cast-off. Later, their territories separated: Lehmann never reached the Met until past her operatic prime, in the season after Jeritza had completed her thirteen-year sojourn there, and Jeritza never sang at Covent Garden after 1926, during Lehmann's legendary seasons. In her autobiography, Jeritza makes no mention of Lehmann whatsoever; Lehmann, in one of her many books, makes much of Jeritza, granting her genius but making a number of back-handed comments on her general deportment. She finally recalls how, many years into retirement, she and Jeritza were brought together for a radio interview, broadcast from the Met, in which they discussed the rehearsals for the second version of *Ariadne*. They 'exchanged remarks that in our youth would have been cause for blistering hostility or open battle . . . we were even served champagne, which I sipped with delight while Maria, in an astonishing display of abstemiousness, confined herself to ginger ale. Which, perhaps, was all to the good, for there is no way of telling what she would have said or done if the champagne had gone to her head.' The jibe is light-hearted enough, but it unfortunately ignores the fact that Jeritza was an avowed teetotaller: whatever Jeritza may have done, it was not done under the influence of alcohol!

Much of the Lehmann-Jeritza feud went on unpublicized, but in 1925 Jeritza caused a real public scandal, when she clashed with the notoriously sensitive and excitable contralto Maria Olczewska during a performance of *Die Walküre* in Vienna. Jeritza stood in the wings with another singer, Hermine Kittel, waiting for her second Act II entry. Olczewska was on stage singing Fricka, deep in her debate with Wotan, sung by her fiancé who was widely suspected of dallying with Jeritza. In the circumstances, it was not surprising that Olczewska became thoroughly distracted by the sound of Jeritza's laughter and conversation. She hissed at her to stop, but Jeritza continued her merriment. Finally Olczewska marched towards the wings while Wotan was addressing her and spat at Jeritza. Unfortunately the force of the insult landed on the innocent Kittel, who was understandably outraged. Olczewska was immediately dismissed from the Vienna Opera, and according to Marcel Prawy a joke went round to the effect that the incident was symbolic of the new Austrian Republic—'The big powers quarrel and the small ones get it in the neck.'

Jeritza was certainly a big power, the only prima donna in the grandly authoritarian style of a Grisi or Melba which Vienna ever produced. She was born in the industrial city of Brno in 1887 and made a sensational début at the Vienna Opera in a forgotten opera, *Aphrodite*, in which she appeared in an unprecedented degree of nudity. She had a robust peasant beauty, with wonderful hair and a *retroussé* nose. Her voice was large, glowing, and somewhat ill-disciplined, and her acting style was instinctive and energetic. Strauss and Hofmannsthal adored and indulged her. In rehearsal for *Ariadne* (she created the title-role in the second version), she was observed to be departing somewhat from the written score. 'Stop her?' replied Strauss to an anxious *répétiteur*. 'No, leave her alone, she knows what she's doing.'[1] Her unavailability for *Die Aegyptische Helena*'s première precipitated Hofmannsthal to blind panic, as the suggested substitute was without Jeritza's essential erotic aura.

She also stands with Mary Garden as the last 'star' prima donna to concentrate her repertory on modern operas. Apart from her Strauss, she was famous in Vienna and New York for the double role of Mariette-Marie in Korngold's *Die Tote Stadt* and Janáček's *Jenufa*, as well as taking part in a lot of ephemeral flops like *Siberia* and *Quo Vadis?* She complained about contemporary composers' preoccupation with the 'degenerate, neurotic, mad or imbecile', and it is interesting to read her opinion of an opera in which she sang by the *avant-garde* Schreker as being full of 'unvocal shrieking' —not the last time a prima donna was to opine thus about the operatic music of the twentieth century. On the whole, however, her memoirs—which rejoice in the title of *Sunlight and Song*—are unilluminating as to her musical experience, and by far the longest chapter is devoted to a fawning description of her relations with the imperial Habsburgs: 'The archdukes and archduchesses—with some of whom I stood on a footing of intimate personal friendship —were the most amiable, unaffected persons one might wish to meet.'

[1] 'He makes phrases which go from here to Brook-e-Lyn. They make me choke,' Jeritza said of Strauss in the Met radio interview, to Lehmann's evident delight!

From 1921 she went every autumn and winter to the Met, where she replaced the retiring Geraldine Farrar as the glamorous star attraction: the Gerryflappers turned into Jerryflappers and women's magazines published her beauty tips—'How does Maria Jeritza keep the most beautiful elbows in the world? She soaks them daily in grapefruit juice', etc. Yet she continued hard vocal studies with the revered soprano Marcella Sembrich, as well as maintaining a fearsome keep-fit programme of Swedish gymnastics, swimming, and mountain-climbing.

Vincent Sheean gives his reasons for her popularity in New York: 'a fresh, strong voice, an eager awareness of the public, a sort of all-out unreserve . . . There was not a trace of subtlety in her voice or acting, but what she had to give was given so lavishly, so honestly and *de bon coeur* that no audience could resist her.' Her physical energy was inexhaustible. As Santuzza in *Cavalleria Rusticana*, Turiddu's push would send her rolling down a huge flight of steps, and when Alfred Piccaver revenged himself for some slight by refusing to administer the push, she simply rolled down anyway. As Carmen, writes W. J. Henderson, 'she was very busy. She made a vigorous attempt at a Spanish dance; she sprawled on tables and chairs, put her feet on men's laps, jumped on tables and off again and smoked cigarettes even while singing.' Her most sensational effect came as Tosca. When rehearsing in Vienna with the composer, who admired her enormously, she fell accidentally to the ground just before the aria 'Vissi d'arte', and discovering she had a nose-bleed, decided to stay there. Puccini approved the idea as a means of sustaining the dramatic impetus at a point where it is otherwise dissipated. Jeritza worked it up into a complicated piece of grovelling business, her hair falling over her face and her head sinking over her hands in a fit of sobbing. At first, wrote Lotte Lehmann severely, 'the effect was electrifyingly natural. Later on, however . . . that shock of hair always coming undone at precisely the same moment began to seem awkward and embarrassing because the artifice, the practised gesture with which she removed her hair-pins, became so obviously contrived.' Geraldine Farrar, herself a great Tosca, was even terser: 'I obtained no view of any expressive pantomime on her pretty face, while I was surprised by the questionable flaunting of a well-cushioned and obvious posterior.'

Her records give little idea of her abilities: they are sound, competent, but uninspired to the point of sounding perfunctory. In view of her description of a typical recording session, she is not to be blamed:

> The records were made in a small room, a room so small that the members of the little orchestra of ten or fourteen men which accompanied me had to sit close together, knee to knee. With the orchestra so close to the singer the sound of the instruments is so overpowering that it drowns the voice and I could not hear myself sing ... I found myself able to overcome this difficulty by holding my hands over my ears ... Then there is the matter of adjusting your position as you stand and sing, so that you are at exactly the right distance from the receiver. For deep register tones one comes closer, for high register tones one moves further away.

Like Leider's, her art was one which was cruelly inhibited by this situation, and Jeritza does not seem to have been born with the caul of inhibition. Strauss was probably right not to stop her in her tracks: far better to lose or gain a quaver than cramp such flamboyant self-projection, even if there were times when the sloppiness of her singing verged on the disastrous.

In 1932 the Depression-stricken Met decided that they could no longer justify her exorbitant fees, and she was not re-engaged. With a new American husband, she settled in America, making regular return trips to Vienna. After the Second World War she made some embarrassing farewell appearances there, donating her fees to the rebuilding of the bombed opera house. By this time her voice was frayed, but although over sixty she still sang 'Vissi d'arte' lying on the floor and rolled down the steps in *Cavalleria Rusticana*; she braved Salome and her Seven Veils and rode bareback in *La Fanciulla del West*. The third of her four husbands (the first had been the grandson of Melba's singing-teacher Marchesi) was a rich American umbrella manufacturer. Umbrellas were then a rarity in Austria and with a prima donna's largesse Jeritza distributed a huge stock of them, flinging them from her hotel balcony to fans waiting below. In retirement outside New York, she bred Lipizzaner horses imported from the Spanish Riding School in Vienna and was frequently conspicuous in the Met audience in a uniform of dark glasses and large floppy hat. She died in her nineties in 1982.

For all the excitement associated with Jeritza, the memory of Lotte Lehmann (1888–1976) is a far warmer one. Her recordings are still extraordinarily vivid documents which communicate something of what everyone who witnessed her recalls as a radiant exultant intensity. There was no posing, no faking, no imposition of false effect in Lehmann's performances, and she must have made Jeritza seem stagey. In her autobiography, she spoke of an actor's 'faculty of forgetting himself entirely, of utterly losing himself in the part he has to play, of giving up his everyday self for the wonderful illusion of some strange destiny which, in the moment of living it, becomes his own, for weal or woe . . . The best teacher of all is life.'

Lotte Lehmann was no relation to her namesake Lilli: in style and personality, apart from a shared devotion to animals, they were as chalk and cheese. Prussian by birth, she was the antithesis of Prussian by nature. She had a difficult early passage, brought up in the family of a minor civil servant who disliked the theatre on moral grounds, and she was never to conquer technical inadequacies in her singing left by a variety of teachers in Berlin. She was expelled from the school run by Patti's former rival Etelka Gerster, where they signally failed to transform the grainy, earthy timbre of her voice into the nightingale mould, and went on to study with Mathilde Mallinger, the first Eva in *Die Meistersinger*, with whom she was happier. Yet she remained one of those singers with evident physical problems, miraculously exploited to expressive effect. Lehmann had a strange pinched attack on high notes and suffered from shortness of breath. She compensated for the latter 'by taking advantage of every comma in the text and by a skilful "catch-breath" that not only concealed breaks in phrases, but was even converted frequently into a characteristic Lehmann-effect—that of a sudden heightening of emotional tension.' If one has a heart of stone and can listen that objectively, this may be clearly heard on her famous recording of Act I of *Die Walküre*. She continued, like Jeritza, to be careless over small notated points, and above the stave glory came and went: her friend Elisabeth Schumann (as Sophie) often sang the Marschallin's top B for her at the climax of the *Rosenkavalier* Trio—but Strauss would not have minded.

She candidly admitted all this, and her autobiography also makes plain how difficult her first years as a professional were. Gauche, over-eager, and easily upset, she had only been to the opera twice in her life, when in 1909 she won a contract at Hamburg and took all the customary small roles. When *Rosenkavalier* was brought into the repertory, Lehmann was promised Sophie, but on the insistence of another member of the cast the part went to her superior of a few years, Elisabeth Schumann. Lehmann's feelings of bitterness were exacerbated by a personal rivalry with Schumann for the love of Hamburg's young lion of a conductor, Otto Klemperer. When Lehmann finally got the part of Sophie, in London in 1914, she went quite unnoticed. For all this, she won her way to the mecca of Vienna, where Strauss's operas were the favourite escapism of an opera public eating off ration cards.

Lehmann was at first thoroughly uncomfortable, surrounded by formidable competition, but her time came when Marie Gutheil-Schoder fell ill while rehearsing the newly composed part of the Composer in the second version of *Ariadne auf Naxos*. Strauss was so overwhelmed by the dedication of the understudy that Gutheil-Schoder was pushed aside and Lehmann was given the première. She became famous overnight in a role that she adored: even when she had moved on to sing Ariadne, she would stand in the wings to breathe in the sound of the Composer's generous but thwarted idealism. Her golden years in Vienna followed. If her fan club (and her fee) was smaller than Jeritza's, it was as vociferous, and the two prima donnas vied for everything, as the Mahler generation of singers declined into middle age. Lehmann's repertoire was broad, as the Viennese system of presenting about fifty operas every season necessitated. Apart from her Strauss—she became Vienna's regular Octavian in *Rosenkavalier*—and the lighter Wagnerian roles, she sang Verdi, Puccini, Mozart, French and Russian opera—all in German, as was customary. However, her excursions into contemporary opera were less extensive than Jeritza's, and she turned down an offer to create Marie in Berg's *Wozzeck*, the finest and most lastingly radical German opera of the 1920s.

These were also Strauss's golden years at the Vienna Opera. He was more *laissez-faire* in approach than Mahler and perhaps rather too full of his own operas, which he loved conducting. He didn't rehearse over-much, his conducting style appeared slack, and he never worried about detail. 'All he wanted,' wrote Marcel Prawy, devoted to his memories of this epoch, 'was that his work should come to life, here and now, in the glamour of an evening at the theatre, and any deviation from the score that enhanced the brilliance of the occasion was not only tolerated but welcomed . . . One could quote hundreds of observations of this kind at rehearsals of his own works, for instance: "If you can't hit that note, sing another. Whatever's easiest, it doesn't matter." ' But the casualness had inspired results, and everyone except the pedants and backstage bureaucrats were happy.

Strauss's next opera after *Die Frau ohne Schatten* was a domestic comedy, *Intermezzo* (1924), which represents a significant change in pace and style. The work is remarkable for its construction out of short 'cinematic' scenes and its light conversational vocal line, carefully imitating speech intonations and rhythms, which in an unaggressive way (for Strauss was no manifesto revolutionary) anticipates the more whole-hearted experiments of Berg's *Wozzeck* or Schoenberg's *Erwartung*, produced within the same few months. Strauss wanted to escape from the giantism of his early works into music that was sharper, clearer, and closer to his beloved Mozart. Temporarily also rejecting the elaborate fictions of Hofmannsthal, he based the plot firmly in a ridiculous incident in his own life and Lehmann, with some trepidation, accepted the delicate task of creating the central role of Christine, closely modelled, warts and all, on Strauss's bizarre wife. Jeritza had refused the dubious honour. Pauline Strauss-de Ahna—the daughter of a general, she was ashamed of Strauss's bourgeois origins and insisted on asserting her family name—requires a little explanation. She is the joker in the pack of prima donnas, but she wins some sort of place in the pantheon on comic grounds.

As a singer, she was probably not of the first rank, although she did take a leading role at Bayreuth, and in their courting days Strauss conducted her as Isolde and in his own early opera *Guntram*. On their wedding in 1894 he composed for her four of his most rapturous *lieder*, including the tear-jerking 'Morgen'. Up to the end of the First World War, husband and wife gave *lieder* recitals together, during which Pauline did not spare on histrionics. Sweeping on to the stage, she would unwind and toss aside an astonishingly long scarf; at the end of singing any song with a piano postlude, she would bow extravagantly to the audience, thus precipitating applause and drowning her wretched husband's efforts as accompanist. Everyone detested her, or at least kept as far away as possible, which fortunately suited Strauss's dislike of socializing.

Mahler and Hofmannsthal could not bear even the briefest encounter, and Alma Mahler records her distaste for Pauline's vulgarity and material outlook. ' "Oh, men," ' Alma heard her say, ' "keep them on a tight rein, that's the only way"—and she went through the motions of holding the reins in one hand and the whip in the other.'

In fact, she did a lot more than hold the reins. She listened outside the study door to make sure Strauss was busy composing and bullied him mercilessly. She had no hesitation in humiliating him in public, and after the première of his second opera *Feuersnot*, loudly declared in front of the Mahlers that she held such music in contempt and refused to accompany its wretched composer home.

Lehmann spent a summer rehearsing at the Strauss home in Garmisch, where she observed that 'Pauline . . . derived an almost perverse pleasure from proving to her husband that no amount of fame could alter her personal opinion of him as essentially nothing but a peasant, a country yokel . . . she explained in great detail, how and why their marriage constituted a shocking *mésalliance* . . . nor was his music, as she readily explained to all who would listen, anywhere near comparable to that of Massenet.' Her other obsession was hygiene. All visitors to the house were immediately instructed to wipe their feet or take off their shoes, and when Strauss was stricken at the news of Hofmannsthal's death, Pauline screamed at him about some mud on the carpet. She once paid a call to Lehmann's house: while waiting for her to appear, she inspected all the cupboards in the drawing-room and ordered the maids to make changes. She was unintimidated by anyone, and remarks she made to high-ranking Nazi officials, mostly connected with the difficulties of collecting royalties during the war, caused Strauss considerable anxiety.

*Intermezzo* presents Pauline, as Christine, unflinchingly, but without viciousness. She was said to have enjoyed the opera. A character describes her as 'absolutely terrible', and she is shown as rude, hysterical, overbearing, and self-contradictory. Yet after the quarrels and farcical misunderstanding the real strength of the marriage is finally celebrated, for Strauss was devoted to this strange creature whose bluster concealed heaven knows what depths of inadequacy and vulnerability—the music conveys those qualities too, in passages of full Straussian emotions. Lehmann insisted that *Intermezzo* was 'a magnificent declaration of love', and played the part with as much charm as she could muster.

In the same year of 1924, Lehmann first took the Strauss role with which she will always be identified. Bruno Walter asked her to Covent Garden to sing the Marschallin in *Rosenkavalier*, and although she had never sung her before, she accepted for fear of losing a prestigious foreign engagement. She at once became a favourite in London, and returned in Wagner, Mozart, Verdi, and both Johann and Richard Strauss. With colleagues such as Elisabeth Schumann (now her dear friend), Frida Leider, Maria Olczewska, Friedrich Schorr, Richard Mayr, and Lauritz Melchior, German opera has probably never been better served or appreciated outside Germany or Vienna than it was during the pre-war seasons at Covent Garden, and one of its treasures was Lehmann's Marschallin. Her appearance in the part became a sort of annual summer fixture, a musical equivalent to Wimbledon or Ascot. Over the years she grew deeper and deeper into the character and its nuances of feeling; in later years, she was to write a long-pondered account of her interpretation. She was still singing the Marschallin at Covent Garden in 1938, the year of the Anschluss, when one evening she broke down. As the *News Chronicle* reported it:

> Throwing up her hands and exclaiming in German 'I can do no more,' Mme Lotte Lehmann suddenly staggered to the wings at Covent Garden last night and left the stage. The glittering audience was dumbfounded. The curtain was rung down—in the middle of Act I of *Rosenkavalier*. Herr Erich Kleiber, the conductor, carried on for a few bars, then the orchestra ceased playing. Thus was enacted one of the most amazing dramas in the history of opera.

A replacement was luckily available and the performance continued: but what makes the incident interesting is the two different explanations on offer. Lehmann's own version is that the wonderful old team had disappeared, and the cast surrounding her was full of Berliners, some of them hard-line Nazis hostile to an unequivocal opponent of Hitler. She had just been informed of her husband's tuberculosis, and she was terrified as to what would become of his children, half-Jewish by his first marriage. The audience was told that Madame Lehmann was suffering from seasickness, but a doctor diagnosed hysterical paralysis of the vocal cords. Walter Legge, then Assistant Director at Covent Garden, remembers it rather differently. 'Next day, Lotte, in good spirits, gave a small lunch party. She said she needed a rest and explained privately . . . that a few minutes before the performance she had been told that relations of hers who were trying to smuggle valuables out of Austria had been held up at the customs, but now she knew they were safely through.'

Whatever the truth, Lehmann certainly suffered in the Nazi era. In Vienna, things had been going badly for her since the early Thirties. Her last new Strauss role, *Arabella* (1933), proved an altogether unhappy experience and she sang it very few times. This opera was the last of the collaborations with Hofmannsthal and for Strauss was something of a retreat from the innovations of *Intermezzo*. *Arabella* is a period comedy of a bright young girl's courtship and its attendant complications: the intrigues are fantastic, and Lehmann found some of it implausible. The vocal writing sounds mostly like a return, if not a repeat, of Strauss's earlier romantic idiom, and the work has often been labelled as a second and inferior *Rosenkavalier*, without the same restlessly glittering orchestration. Lehmann was not selected for the Dresden première. Hofmannsthal for one, a hideous snob, found her too 'middle-class' in manner, and it may have been thought that she was a trifle old to impersonate an *ingénue*, but her most dangerous enemy was the conductor Clemens Krauss, who had led the Vienna Opera since 1929. He was determined to patronize a new crop of singers, and gave special attention to the Romanian soprano Viorica Ursuleac, whom he later married. The old guard felt slighted and pushed out before their time: an economic crisis also led to their salaries being cut substantially. Krauss was supported by Strauss, who thought Ursuleac the most 'faithful' of all his sopranos and gave her the first Arabella, specially written to exploit a top voice with more silvery glow than Lehmann's. Lehmann was still given priority in Vienna (Ursuleac was singing in Berlin at the time), but on the morning of the first performance, she received news that her mother had died. Being Lehmann, she went on to save the evening, insisting only on avoiding the curtain calls. The piece had only a *succès d'estime*.

The silver lining to all this was the presence in the audience that night of Arturo Toscanini, who had never heard Lehmann before. She became one of the very few singers for whom he felt unqualified admiration. In 1935–7 she sang *Fidelio* under his baton at Salzburg: of her performance as Leonore, history records only superlatives. It was, wrote Walter Legge:

> . . . her most profoundly moving achievement . . . encompassing every facet of the character—its nobility and tenderness, pity and force, humanity, anxiety and courage, and, in the closing scene, 'nameless joy'. Scores of phrases, sung and spoken, echo down the corridors of memory after forty years as vividly as her acting of the part. That five cruel bars in the great aria have sometimes been more exactly vocalised by others is beside the point: Lehmann was Leonore.

Normally tyrannically demanding of singers, Toscanini made some rare concessions to accommodate Lehmann's vocal shortcomings. It was said that they eventually became lovers, but the only evidence to this effect is the fact that before their respective deaths they both destroyed their mutual correspondence.

By now the lights were going out all over Europe. People like Krauss and Ursuleac had ingratiated themselves with the Nazis, and would spend the next years making skilful compromises to survive and even to prosper. Lehmann, however, had made an instant enemy of Goering by laughing at his wife's pet lioness and refusing to sing in Berlin as instructed, despite promises of high fees and captive critics: from 1934 she was banned from singing in Germany. Ursuleac later remembered it differently, claiming that Lehmann had been chronically jealous and a ruthless intriguer. Goering's offer had only been refused because she discovered that she would be sharing Sieglinde and Arabella with Ursuleac. There could be a degree of truth in this, despite Ursuleac's self-righteousness. In 1938 Lehmann decided to emigrate to America, and she was to spend most of the rest of her life as a happy exile in the charming California resort of Santa Barbara. Europe was never to hear her in opera again.

Her operatic career in America was not what it might have been. She first sang in Chicago in 1930, but by the time Jeritza had vacated her spot at the Met Lehmann was almost forty-six. Any success she had in her Wagner roles was soon overwhelmed by the miracle of Flagstad, and she also made a rare error of judgement in singing Tosca for an audience that had long been accustomed to the excesses of Jeritza.

The fact that the management offered Flagstad anything and everything first annoyed her: after the Norwegian had been given a revival of *Fidelio*, Lehmann refused the part ever again, probably nervous of those 'five cruel bars in the great aria' which got more difficult year by year, and the fact that comparisons would be made with Flagstad's effortlessness. As the Marschallin, however, she remained unassailable, and with a little help in ensemble from kind young Sophies, she continued to sing the part throughout the war as a melancholy and beautiful reminder of a culture now decisively shattered. In 1946, in San Francisco, she gave her last stage performance as the Marschallin.

Lehmann was far from finished. Since the early 1930s she had been giving regular *lieder* recitals of the type pioneered by Elena Gerhardt and Marcella Sembrich at the beginning of the century. Previously *lieder* had generally been given either at informal salon affairs, or as a group of items in a musical variety concert, at which the prima donna would sing only two or three times in the course of the evening, her appearances separated by a 'supporting programme'—this was the format favoured by Patti and Melba, for instance. Lehmann was one of the first to make popular the idea of singer and piano alone in a well-balanced programme of, say, Schubert, Schumann, Debussy, and Strauss. The mood was serious, and operatic gestures of the kind espoused by Pauline Strauss were eliminated: audiences were expected to listen hard and forget the spectacular gratifications of the opera house. *Lieder* has always been the province of the 'maturer'—but not necessarily older— singer, who likes to make a full range of effects without battling against orchestra, costume, stage lights, and upstaging colleagues. *Lieder* demands sensibility and intelligence rather than youthful power and virtuosity, and in properly intimate circumstances a recital can communicate a wonderfully vivid and varied impression of a singer's art. Lehmann's *lieder* embraced song cycles intended for male voice, like Schubert's *Winterreise* and Beethoven's *An die ferne geliebte*, as well as French *mélodies*—at that time a genre hardly known. With her regular accompanist Bruno Walter she made recordings of which one can only say that so close is their intimacy that they seem to reach out and take the listener by the hand.

In 1951 Lehmann gave a quite unannounced farewell recital at New York's Town Hall. Vincent Sheean was there: she 'said that she had been before the public now for forty years and reminded us of the words of the Marschallin: "*Jedes Ding hat seiner Zeit*", everything has its time. The howls of protest did not disturb her. She had Toscanini's orchids—he sent her orchids for each song recital, year after year, since she was "the greatest artist in the world"—and her mind was quite made up.' As a last encore, she sang Schubert's hymn of praise to music 'An die musik': understandably overcome, she was unable to sing the last phrase.

The remaining twenty-five years of Lehmann's life were packed with activity. She painted furiously but not very well, and wrote somewhat better. Apart from her autobiography, published before the war, and a number of rather disappointing books on interpretation, she also wrote fiction—her novel, translated as *Eternal Flight*, is an action-packed saga of two sisters, one a ballerina, the other a prima donna called Aimée Françoise. An amusingly whimsical story featuring Richard Strauss in heaven, playing endless rounds of his beloved card game *skat* and worried as to whether Pauline has ended up in the other place, is almost worth reading.[1] In 1955 she returned to Vienna for the first time in seventeen years for the opening of the rebuilt opera house and received an overwhelming welcome. But she was not one to live off memories. Her public master classes in the late 1950s provided another unforgettable round of Lehmann evenings, her students there including Grace Bumbry, Marilyn Horne, and Janet Baker. Among her earlier pupils had been Jeanette MacDonald, whom she coached for her sole operatic appearance, in *La Bohème* in Chicago. In 1962 she returned to *Rosenkavalier* at the Met, rehearsing a new cast that included Régine Crespin as the Marschallin.

Lehmann has often been cast as a noble soul who bravely resisted the corruptions of the 1930s. In fact, as she readily admitted, she did little against the Nazis beyond denying them her presence. In personality she was excitable, exacting, and sometimes quite cruel. Yet it is hard to think slightingly of her. Her records alone tell of a passionate spirit. Vincent Sheean, who knew her art as well as anyone, does not feel that they do her any sort of justice, but for those of us who never heard her 'live', they serve as an arch and corner-stone: like Callas's records, they embody a power and intensity of expression against which all others are measured. Lehmann's voice was not large or tireless, and although she longed

[1] It was published in *Opera*, February 1968.

27. A surprisingly pretty Nellie Melba in a title-role written for her, Saint-Saens's Hélène: later photographs show her immovable and granite-faced.

28. Emmy Destinn, another great pre-war favourite at Covent Garden, seen here as a seductive Carmen, a role she sang during her Berlin years at the turn of the century.

29. *left* Eva Turner's first Turandot, Brescia, 1926. 30. *above* Zinka Milanov rehearsing with a stage director for *Il Trovatore* at the Met. The reasons for her nickname '*la donna immobile*' are not hard to gauge.

31. *top left* The castrato
caricatured: Velluti in 1825.
Note the obvious symbolism of
the double bass. 32. *above right*
Catalani caricatured, quite
unfairly, as a prima donna free
with her favours. The occasion
was the Cambridge Musical
Festival of 1824. 33. *above* Patti
caricatured in Paris in 1880 as
a cat spewing forth money into
an impresario's hat: the artist
could equally have shown her
swallowing the coins herself.
34. Groucho Marx interviewing
Margaret Dumont in *Duck
Soup*: Dumont embodies a
popular idea of the prima-
donna type—stupid,
susceptible, and ridiculous.

to sing Isolde ('I loved it with the stubborn tenacity of the unlucky in love,' she claimed), the advice of Melchior and others dissuaded her from it. Of her Wagner, we are lucky to have a recording of Act I and part of Act II of *Die Walküre* under her beloved Bruno Walter. On stage her Sieglinde had shocked Kirsten Flagstad into the immortal remark that 'She behaved as a woman should only do with her husband,' and one can indeed hear a keenly sexual note in Lehmann's singing here, as well as a terrible despair and an abandoned ecstasy: the gripping urgency with which she tells Siegmund the story of her wedding, followed by her recognition of the freedom now at hand, is equally enthralling. Someone who wants an instant idea of what the fuss is about could well listen to Elisabeth's aria 'Dich teure halle' from *Tannhäuser*, where the joy of the music is realized in singing of spontaneous, almost reckless excitement. For the *Rosenkavalier*, follow a score or libretto, and mark the maternal kindness, the playfulness and wry humour, the held-back desire, the stillness of the resignation, the sudden assertiveness with which she invests music that can so easily sound limp and aimless.

A third major Viennese soprano of the Strauss era was, appropriately enough, a direct descendant of Henriette Sontag: Elisabeth Schumann (1888–1952) inherited much of her sweetness and charm. Hers could never have been the heroic musical destiny of her friend Lotte Lehmann—as John Steane puts it, Lehmann is at 'the centre of the spectrum . . . at the heart of human experience', while Schumann is confined to 'the qualities and colours of sunlight'.

Schumann's voice had little weight or sustaining capacity and under any pressure it could sound sadly frail. There are those who argue that her technique was fundamentally weak, and Michael Scott (judging from records alone) claims that by the time she was forty, her voice had 'no more than a wisp of tone'. Today her Mozart sounds much too slow and squarely phrased, and no one could think that her articulation of florid passages was crystalline. Occasionally, as Victor Gollancz wrote, 'she trembled on the edge of a Viennese archness'. Her repertory in opera was limited, and her stage career circumscribed. After her early days in Hamburg, she was in Vienna from 1919 to 1937, at Covent Garden 1924 to 1931, with some appearances in Salzburg and Munich, and one brief visit to the Met in 1915.

Yet all this seems quibbling when set against the sheer happiness and freedom in Schumann's singing. Her voice was bright and silvery in tone, and she appears to have eschewed altogether the dark colours of a chest register. In opera she was usually the soubrette—Mozart's Susanna or Zerlina, Adele in *Die Fledermaus*; Eva in *Meistersinger* was her biggest assignment—but always a soubrette with character, wit, and feeling. As Sophie in *Rosenkavalier* she is as fondly remembered as Lehmann is as the Marschallin, and her entranced singing of the phrase where Sophie breathes in the attar-soaked perfume of Octavian's silver rose is the indelible signature of her art.

Strauss loved the timbre of her voice, and it was he who brought her to Vienna for the first time. As mentioned above, he tried to persuade her to sing Salome, thinking no doubt of her girlish freshness, and offered to reduce the orchestration and make transpositions. Reluctantly she agreed, but then announced that the effect on her voice might be such that she could never sing Mozart again. Strauss withdrew at once. In 1921 he and Schumann toured North America giving *lieder* recitals. At every hotel, Schumann recalled, they were greeted by a band playing 'Tales from the Vienna Woods', and great disappointment ensued when it emerged that Richard Strauss was not the same thing as Johann.

As a *lieder* singer, and especially as a singer of Schubert's brighter songs, she ranks among the greatest. Perhaps no other *lieder* singer seems to take such a radiantly simple pleasure in singing. Lehmann used to beg her to stay away from her recitals if she was singing Schubert, so awed was she by her mastery of that composer's genius. Their approaches were very different: to resume an inadequate metaphor, if Lehmann takes you by the hand and stares emphatically into your eyes, Schumann pulls you out of your chair and tells you a story or leads you off on a delightful walk—she is more companionable than communing.

She too left Austria for America at the Anschluss with her Jewish conductor husband, Karl Alwin—her early love for Klemperer had culminated in a scandalous elopement from her first husband: Klemperer was publicly humiliated and terminated the affair. She finished her career singing *lieder* and teaching in Britain and America. For those not handicapped by race or disgust, the Vienna Opera remained a haven throughout the Second World War for both singers and audience. The Nazis attempted to leave it alone, whereas the auditorium at Bayreuth was hung with swastika flags, shrewdly realizing that opera as usual, as long as it was firmly Aryan in tone, mollified many of the Viennese bourgeoisie. For Strauss and many of the major conductors of the period like Furtwängler, Karl Böhm, or Clemens Krauss, it was all a matter of playing the game and keeping out of trouble. We look back and judge their behaviour as sadly lacking in principle, based in the sacrificing of larger issues to maintain a smaller modicum of independence. Some valued Jewish artists or employees were won the right to continue working, but there was also a good deal of shabby time-serving. Strauss himself was a self-proclaimed 'non-political' man who, by reason of his international eminence, would have been useful to either side of the propaganda battle. He later excused his sidestepping on the grounds that he had to protect his Jewish daughter-in-law and his grandchildren, but he never lifted a finger to protect anyone whose survival was not in his own direct interest. Otherwise the war does not appear to have concerned him as more than a chronic inconvenience.

Something of this small-mindedness finds its way into his music. At melodrama, romance, fable, or farce, he excelled, but the call to compose for the higher emotions found him at a loss. An opera written in the mid 1930s, *Friedenstag*, a story, like *Fidelio*, of heroic resistance to tyranny ending with a choral hymn to peace and brotherhood, brought forth music widely considered as lamely bombastic.

The prima donna for this and most of Strauss's later operas was Viorica Ursuleac (born 1894) who sang over five hundred performances of twelve Strauss roles. Trailing in the wake of her elegantly diplomatic husband, Clemens Krauss, who now domi-nated the performance of opera in Germany and Austria, this cool and competent soprano, a pupil of Lilli Lehmann's, was a glamorous figure of the Third Reich. She and Krauss became Strauss's most important allies at a time when his instinct was to isolate himself. Through them and their cordial relations with the Berlin authorities, Strauss managed to circumvent many tiresome restrictions and kept abreast of the latest policy requirements— Hofmannsthal was 'technically' a Jew, for example, which could have been an excuse for proscribing most of Strauss's operas. Pauline Strauss, whom the war had made more than usually irri-table, was not suitably grateful: when Ursuleac paid a call at the

Strauss villa in Garmisch, she was refused admittance on the grounds that she was wearing a fur coat given to her by Goering, a character of whom Pauline was not fond.

Strauss's last opera *Capriccio* was premièred in 1942. Krauss wrote the libretto in partial collaboration with Strauss and conducted, Ursuleac took the leading role of the Countess who must choose between her two suitors, a poet and a composer who are themselves collaborating on an opera. Set in eighteenth-century Paris, at the time of Gluck's operatic reforms, it is nothing more than a conversation piece, with interludes of light relief, debating the claims of words and music to primacy in opera. The matter is still unresolved in the final monologue, in which the Countess, staring into a mirror, reflects on art, life, and love. With its obvious echoes of *Rosenkavalier*, its opportunities for wit and pastiche, as well as for another sweetly melancholic soprano *scena*, its long dying falls bathed in an orchestral 'mild blue light', Strauss was in his favourite element. It is a weirdly calm and sophisticated work to have come out of a time of such consuming crisis, and opinion is still split between those who find it a sure cure for insomnia and those who regard it as Strauss's most perfectly moulded and finished work. The Countess is certainly a grateful role for a prima donna who wants to indulge a bent for expressive and mellifluous *portamento*. As a character, she resembles the Marschallin in combining a mature aristocratic charm and a private vulnerability, but Hofmannsthal's conception is by far the more touching— the situation in *Capriccio* does not provide a very heart-rending dilemma.

One singer who has been able to extract the maximum of interest out of the role is Elisabeth Schwarzkopf, one of the dominating figures of the post-war era. Unlike Lehmann or Jeritza, she was never an improviser or one ready to skate over difficulties of detail. Following her recordings with a score, one is at once impressed by her immaculate and scrupulous observation of the composer's markings—note-values, rests, dynamics, tempo. Nothing is shirked, everything is realized. Her regular accompanist Gerald Moore has written of her fanatic self-criticism, relentless rehearsing, and obsessive concern with accurate intonation. Her own scores were described by Edward Greenfield as 'covered with coloured pencillings, so close that she alone could read their meaning'. She was, one might say, a Prussian singer, the worthy heir to Lilli Lehmann's rigour and formidable inability to suffer fools gladly.

She was born near Poznań in 1915, the daughter of a classics master, and had two false starts as a singer in the Berlin of the late 1930s—first as a contralto, then as a soprano soubrette. From the beginning of the war she went for lessons to Maria Ivogün, a distinguished coloratura soprano of the Berlin Opera, and her husband Michael Raucheisen, a famous pianist and accompanist. These two seized on what André Tubeuf has called Schwarz-kopf's 'demanding and proud nature, her intransigence, her capacity for monastic self-discipline'. Ivogün brought nobility into her voice, while Raucheisen introduced her to the *lieder* repertory: Schwarzkopf emerged as a singer with more than flexibility and high notes. In 1942 she won a contract at the Vienna Opera, but immediately suffered a year-long collapse with tuberculosis, contracted in damp air-raid shelters. She sang with the German equivalent of ENSA, but could not get back to Vienna until 1945. By 1946, she was singing leading roles in the Theater an der Wien, which was 'standing in' pending the reconstruction of the bombed-out opera house. The liberating Allied authorities tangled everything in administrative muddles. According to Marcel Prawy, Schwarzkopf was 'once banned by the British but cleared by the French, and later banned by the Russians and cleared by the Americans'. At that time an English recording executive from His Master's Voice named Walter Legge was roaming central Europe in a ruthless effort to snap up musicians who had either begun their careers during the war years or who were now languishing in poverty and uncertainty. Many of them had been Nazis, some of them active in the party and under official investigation, but Legge was only interested in their talent. He was brilliantly successful— Schwarzkopf, Karajan, Furtwängler, Hotter, Flagstad, Lipatti, and later Callas were all among his trophies—and he was subsequently criticized for indiscriminate opportunism. Schwarzkopf herself was his most complete protégé, Trilby to his Svengali, it was said, and the closeness with which they combined their careers caused considerable resentment among other singers: Schwarzkopf was nicknamed Her Master's Voice, and Legge not only managed her engagements and produced her records, but later married her. He began by making her listen to records, so as to widen 'her imaginative concept of the possibilities of vocal sound'. Patti never heard the sound of her own singing until her career was over, but Schwarzkopf was able to learn from listening to herself over and over again, as well as using all the great singers of the past—Melba, Ponselle, Lotte Lehmann, Schumann, Leider—as her tutors, incorporating different aspects of their arts into her own highly wrought synthesis. Unlike so many prima donnas, she found the patient construction of a record uniquely satisfying, comparing it to the process of sculpture. Gerald Moore later wrote that Legge overestimated his formative influence on Schwarzkopf but the idea of using records was intelligent and original. It made Schwarzkopf into a uniquely self-conscious interpreter: it was perfectly natural to her that when asked on the BBC radio programme 'Desert Island Discs' to select eight recordings to be shipwrecked with, she should choose only her own!

In 1947 she left Vienna and for five years based herself at Covent Garden, where she sang the standard 'lighter' repertory—Mozart, some Verdi, Wagner, and Puccini—in near-impeccable English for a starting salary of £60 a week. Over the next fifteen-odd years, she was closely associated with the Salzburg Festival—Flagstad once said that the way Schwarzkopf opened the *Fidelio* quartet at Salzburg was the most beautiful thing she had ever heard. She was the very first singer at post-war Bayreuth, taking the small but honourable role of the First Rhinemaiden in *Das Rheingold*; in the same year of 1951, she created Anne Trulove in Stravinsky's *The Rake's Progress*. She also sang regularly under Herbert von Karajan, commuting with him between La Scala and Vienna in productions shared by both opera houses. All this went hand in hand with a careful balance of concerts and recitals, as well as a regular recording schedule. The only blot was America: although she had operatic success in San Francisco, the Met refused to hire her, on unconfirmed grounds that she had been a member of the Nazi party, and for similar reasons, Schwarzkopf's records were banned from Israeli radio broadcasts. Until 1964, New York only heard her in *lieder* or oratorio.

Her voice continued to develop, and when the coloratura went, the timbre became fuller in compensation. By the late 1950s she was only singing six operatic roles on stage. Three of these were Mozart—Fiordiligi in *Così fan tutte*, Elvira in *Don Giovanni*, and the Countess in *Le Nozze di Figaro*. Her principle of fulfilling the score as closely as possible made for a style more subtly shaded but less forwardly emotional than had been the pre-war case. Influenced by the conductor Josef Krips, Schwarzkopf phrased cleanly, singing with a firm vibratoless tone which became a standard on which the great Mozartians of the next generation have continued to model themselves. About her Strauss one can feel some reservations. It has often been said that Schwarzkopf is a 'mannered' singer, but here 'over-literal' is the more accurate adjective. Compared with Lehmann's, her Marschallin is an impeccable aristocrat, much too proper to have affairs with teenagers. The text is picked and pecked at to the point at which hardly a single word does not get some special emphasis or colour. The free sensuality and generosity of spirit that Lehmann's looser singing communicates is absent from Schwarzkopf's tight-lipped interpretation, which is finally meaningful but unmoving. She is, I think, happier in her other Strauss stage role, the Countess in *Capriccio*, a figure who does not have the Marschallin's depth of feeling, but must seem sharply aware and responsive. In her much-praised recordings of Strauss's Four Last Songs, written shortly before his death in his most glowing and flowing idiom, one may feel a lack of sheer tonal richness, in music which is more than anything a celebration of the glory of the soprano sound. Where she is quite irresistibly delightful is in comedy. Her sixth lasting stage role was Alice Ford in Verdi's *Falstaff*, which she sings on record with sharp wit and lightning playfulness and grace, while her series of Viennese operetta recordings, marketed by HMV Angel as the 'Champagne Operettas' deserve the accolade: Schwarzkopf has all that beverage's fizz and pop, dry, heady lightness, and strength of after-taste. Her portrait of the outraged Prima Donna in a recording of *Ariadne auf Naxos* is a perfect vignette of her comic gift, sung with relish and broad humour. Many singers do a good Schwarzkopf parody, but Schwarzkopf herself does the best of them all.

All these qualities and more emerged in her *lieder* singing, especially in the subtle and complex songs of Hugo Wolf, for whose revived modern reputation she and Legge take a large amount of credit. Schwarzkopf continued giving recitals until the later 1970s, when she switched decisively to teaching, and as Dr Elisabeth Schwarzkopf has given inspirational public master classes for young professional singers throughout Europe and America, which incidentally serve as a fascinating revelation of the powerful and dedicated mind which constructed her singing. In Legge's memoirs he tells the wonderful story of an early pupil of Schwarzkopf's who demanded an impromptu lesson in the restaurant of Biffi Scala in Milan. This was none other than Maria Callas, who had been having trouble with her top register during a recording.

> Callas walked in as if unconcerned, pecked my wife's cheeks and without sitting down said, 'Show me how you sing top As and Bs and make a diminuendo on them. Walter says mine make him seasick.' When Schwarzkopf demurred, Callas, ignoring the astonished diners, sang with full voice the notes that were giving her trouble, while Schwarzkopf felt her diaphragm, lower jaw, throat and ribs. Waiters froze in their stride, while guests turned to watch and hear the fun. Within minutes Schwarzkopf was singing the same notes while Callas prodded her in the same places to find out how she kept those notes steady. After twenty minutes or so she said, 'I think I've got it. I'll call you in the morning when I've tried it out,' and sat down to supper.

Schwarzkopf was a good person to ask for advice: from *schmaltz* to Schubert, she was a singer who did everything right.

The same cannot be said for Ljuba Welitsch, whose name means, literally and appropriately, 'Love Great'. This Bulgarian soprano, born in 1913, was virtually a contemporary of Schwarzkopf's, and they started at the Vienna Opera at the same time. Welitsch's success was mercurial. She was compared to Jeritza, but her wildly extrovert behaviour is more reminiscent of Malibran, 'instinctual, impulsive, greedy and generous with no defences'. In 1944 she first sang her most famous role—Strauss's Salome, which she was to repeat almost six hundred times in the course of her short career: a New York critic described her performance as 'a crescendo of passion and neuroticism'. The elderly Strauss himself was the first to acknowledge that she had everything for the part—the sensuality, the innocence, a lithe and shapely figure, a shock of red hair, and a voice of spontaneous silvery freshness and power. It was too good to be true. Welitsch conquered London and New York, her Salome was sensational everywhere: she also sang Tosca, Aida, Musetta in *La Bohème*, Donna Anna in *Don Giovanni*, a heartfelt Tatyana in Tchaikovsky's *Eugene Onegin*, and her recordings of extracts from all these show just how exciting she must have been. The problem was her lack of caution and restraint. One night she sang with an inflamed larynx, and started the slow murder of her voice. By 1950, it had shrunk in size and capability to the point of causing audiences familiar with her brief prime acute embarrassment. She was soon forced to retire from leading roles altogether, although to this day she occasionally puts in 'character' or small part appearances. Welitsch was not crushed by her first demise. She had her beloved poodles and a traffic policeman for a husband, and now began a new career as a television and film actress, as well as making cameo appearances in operetta.

Welitsch's extravagant personality made her a glorious exception to the general national diet of austerity and hard reconstruction, but behind the flash of her stardom, a stronger and softer light was being cast by an exceptional generation of younger prima donnas who would lead the ensemble back into the reconstructed State Opera House in 1955. There was the lyric soprano regarded by Lotte Lehmann as her truest successor, Sena Jurinac, eloquent and dedicated in a large repertory, but best loved in Mozart; Leonie Rysanek, as admired in New York and Bayreuth as in Vienna, her powerful top register making her a superb exponent of the 'Jeritza' Strauss roles; Irmgard Seefried, another outstanding Mozartian and *lieder* singer; and Lisa della Casa, a beautiful Swiss woman, whose watery clarity of voice made her Arabella enormously popular. All except Rysanek were to some extent overshadowed internationally by Schwarzkopf and the dominance she achieved through her long recording career, but in Vienna their delicately differentiated virtues and personalities were savoured by an audience of connoisseurs.

From 1956, Vienna was rocked by another conducting genius, whose tactics made him highly controversial. Herbert von Karajan took over from Karl Böhm, whose appointment to the new opera house was rescinded after a disastrous first season. Karajan insisted on Italian opera in Italian, a radical alteration in the old repertory system, and, like Mahler, control over production. Neither of these were universally popular measures. His Mahlerian inability to deputize or compromise caused even deeper frictions, and his departure in 1964 was spectacular, although he has since returned as a guest conductor, as did the sacked Strauss. The results of his strength of purpose were, of course, mostly magnificent, especially in the area of Italian opera, and he nurtured yet another school of prima donnas. Unlike Mahler, Karajan favours voices with an instrumental beauty of sound, rather than those of vivid dramatic force and distinctive humanity. Two outstanding exemplars of his taste are Christa Ludwig, a bottomlessly rich-toned mezzo, who has taken some soprano roles, and Gundula Janowitz, whose voice has the purity of a boy treble's.

These breathless lists evince the historian's panic—so much to say about so many in so little space. The Viennese *aficionado* hangs above like the Sword of Damocles. Where is Rose Pauly? What about the Konetzni sisters? Or Maria Cebotari? There is one more name, however, that I will not neglect, for it conveniently embodies the best of modern singing, as well as being representative of the Viennese tradition. Lucia Popp was born in 1939 in Czechoslovakia, motherland of a number of great Viennese singers including Jeritza. She first became famous on the strength of a miraculously well-articulated Queen of the Night in *Die Zauberflöte* at the State Opera in 1963, and over the next few years sang the part all over the opera world. At first she seemed cut out to be a successor to Elisabeth Schumann: with her pudgy, cheeky smile and charming demeanour, she inspires the same sort of undying affection in her audience. Then she found the measure of Sophie in *Rosenkavalier* and became a delightful Susanna and Despina, impeccably sung without the usual soubrette exaggeration or mincing. She has also become, like Schumann, a lovely Eva in *Die Meistersinger* without further Wagnerian ambition.

Yet Popp's technique is inherently stronger than Schumann's—comparing their recordings of the same Mozart arias is a good way to illustrate the soundness of the best modern schooling. Popp's voice has a distinctive piquance, which has been likened to the timbre of an oboe. It is not opulent or majestic, but it is very firmly under control, even throughout its range, accurate in intonation, and the breath is unobtrusively managed. Schumann could not have competed with Popp's command of coloratura, nor her linguistic versatility—she speaks Czech, German, Russian, English, and Italian.

Popp is currently building on the security of her technical foundations by venturing slowly into a more ambitious Strauss repertory—the Four Last Songs, Arabella, *Daphne*, Christine in *Intermezzo*, the Countess in *Capriccio*, the Marschallin. Perhaps one day, given her glorious Mozart and her still-developing prowess in *lieder*, she will prove the Schwarzkopf rather than the Schumann of our era.

Strauss is now as much a part of every German soprano's horizon as Rossini and Bellini were for Pasta or Malibran. Much as the Italians, Strauss wrote very specifically to suit the capabilities of singers and he has been rewarded with a series of outstanding interpreters. His operas have their shallows; they sacrifice truth for effect and reason for romance, but they wonderfully realize a particular dream of the female voice. In the twentieth century Strauss has kept the musical force of the prima donna alive.

# 8

# *National Style,*
# *or the Lack of it*

The detection of national characteristics, even at the most generalizing level, rarely amounts to more than a parlour game. We like to think that we can find some common denominator which infallibly distinguishes a Brazilian from an Argentinian, but a glaring specific exception invariably pops up to disprove it. Singing presents a peculiar jumble of problems in this respect: perhaps one should simply stop here and acknowledge that every great voice is a freak of nature. The central nineteenth-century tradition of vocal schooling neatly illustrates the confusion. What was widely known as the 'Italian' style had its most famous teacher in Manuel Garcia II, a Spaniard who lived in Paris and then London, whose most distinguished pupil was a Swede, Jenny Lind; and Garcia's chief disciple was the German-born Mathilde Marchesi, whose model product was the technique of Nellie Melba, herself an Australian of Scots descent.

The conclusion to be drawn from this is that a singer is made more by how and for what she or he is trained than by climate or diet. Perhaps racial types of facial bone structure can make for certain effects of vocal resonance, but it is hard to take the idea of 'national endowments' further than that. If Slavonic sopranos are fierce and wobbly or English contraltos plummy and booming, that is because they have been taught particular means of tone formation, not because of some good or bad national fairy.

In Chapter 6 we saw how a variety of Slavs, Anglo-Saxons and Black Americans have successfully interpreted the most demanding prima donna roles in the Italian repertory; now let us try and put some order into the complex picture presented by the French prima donna.

French operatic tastes have always been insular, even chauvinistic. For all the lush melodiousness we associate with Gounod and

Massenet, the majority of French composers—and audiences—
have been prepared to sacrifice beautiful tone to verbal clarity. The
Italian style of vocal display has never much interested them: even
the vogue for the castrati passed them by. The first great French
opera composer, Rameau, kept close to the purest ideals of the
early Florentines, writing pointed and austere declamation for his
singers while his contemporary Handel followed the Italian Baroque
form of the arias, with all its artifice of repeats and coloratura. As
the eighteenth-century critic Charles de Brosses put it, 'Italian
music can only trifle with syllables and lacks the expression which
characterizes feeling.'

Thus the early French prima donna had to make her way more
by passionate acting and strength of diction than by purity or
flexibility of voice; and in the nineteenth century with Rossini's
invasion of Paris, the French prima donnas were characteristically
dramatic sopranos with techniques inferior to their 'Italian'
rivals Pasta and Malibran, let alone Catalani. Joséphine Fodor-
Mainvielle, Laure Cinti-Damoreau, Henriette Méric-Lalande,
and Cornélie Falcon were all of this mould, and both Fodor-
Mainvielle and Falcon suffered early vocal catastrophe as a result
of singing music which made fatal demands on their ill-prepared
instruments. In the middle of the century there emerged Marie
Miolan-Carvalho, a sweet and elegant lyric soprano who created
Marguerite in Gounod's *Faust* and the title-roles in his *Roméo et
Juliette* and *Mireille*. This continued to be a popular type of voice,
used by Bizet for Micaela in *Carmen*, Offenbach for Antonia in *Les
Contes d'Hoffmann*, and by Massenet for his Manon—but for Emma
Calvé, the greatest French soprano of the nineteenth century, such
material did not offer enough histrionic possibilities.

Calvé had a voice capable of sweetest 'nightingale' tone, produced
with all the effortlessness one might expect from an erstwhile
Marchesi pupil and suited to the expression of every modest and
maidenly sentiment. Her inspiration, however, was not Patti or
even Viardot: in fact it was not musical at all. 'The spark that set
my art alight,' she wrote in one of her two volumes of memoirs,
was the Italian tragic actress Eleonora Duse, from whom Calvé
learnt the intensity characteristic of the new naturalistic school of
acting. 'I could never have thought it possible that anyone could
have given so much of themselves,' she continued, 'she seemed to
belong to a humanity more vibrant than our own. What accents!

What communicative emotion! . . . no artist is more involving, more enveloping, and no artist possesses such an ability to induce emotion.'

Calvé followed Duse from theatre to theatre, saturating herself in every gesture and intonation and in particular modelling her operatic interpretation of the abandoned Sicilian peasant Santuzza in Mascagni's *Cavalleria Rusticana* on Duse's legitimate stage performance. Such emulation paid off, as Calvé's intensity of style was not only sensational in itself, but was also influential on a younger generation of 'singing actresses' including Garden, Farrar, and Jeritza—none of whom could match Calvé's classic vocal schooling.

Calvé was no sophisticated Parisian. Her roots were in Provence and she kept to them. When she first returned to her native village at the beginning of her fame, she gave an impromptu outdoor concert after which a peasant came up to her nodding his head sadly. 'Poor girl,' he said. 'How you scream! How it must hurt you! You are wearing out your life! Such a waste of strength! It's dreadful!' She was born in 1858, of farming stock in the Aveyron region, but in early childhood her father moved to Spain on a business venture, and Spanish became her first language. There too, in unconscious preparation for her most popular role, she fell under an infant fascination for the gipsies and once invited herself to dinner at an encampment, much to her mother's horror.

Like Melba, to whom she is in so many ways comparable, Calvé hummed incessantly as a child, while the chants and canticles of her convent education further nurtured her voice. Moving to Paris, she went to a variety of voice teachers. Her early professional years were slow: she was unsure of herself and dissatisfied with her art. In 1882 she made her début in Brussels, then returned to Paris for lessons with Marchesi, who must have had a greater effect on her singing than Calvé ever gave credit for. Then followed three consolidating years at the Opéra-Comique, where the manager was Miolan-Carvalho's husband and where Victor Maurel, Verdi's first Iago and Falstaff, fervently urged her on. In 1887 she was hissed at her début at La Scala and returned to Paris for further study with a new teacher. Only with the revelation of Duse did everything fall into place. Lying ill in bed with the image of her idol in her mind's eye, Calvé studied *Cavalleria Rusticana*, until, in the words of Marchesi's daughter Blanche, 'She felt she had overcome the natural shyness that stood like a barrier between her will and her execution.' The performance was to break many conventions of operatic decorum. Calvé's costume consisted of some clothes she had bought off an Italian peasant woman; her gestures were 'spontaneous and apparently unstudied'. But the result was an unqualified triumph, and by the 1890s Calvé was established as a prima donna completely without the histrionic inhibitions or indolence of a Patti or Melba. Her tone and phrasing, moreover, remained properly disciplined, and she never made her effects through the rough chesty sound which was becoming fashionable among Italian interpreters of the role.

After Santuzza, Calvé began to work on the part with which she was to be most strongly identified, that of Bizet's Carmen. This masterpiece, first performed in 1875, with its simple plot, blazing orchestral colours, and miraculous succession of marvellous tunes, has shown a protean resilience to a broad variety of interpretations. Like Hamlet or Don Giovanni, Carmen herself can be seen in any number of ways. Prior to Calvé, singers like the American Minnie Hauk had exploited a picture-postcard image of the Spanish gipsy; later, Farrar and Jeritza would present her as a sort of silent-movie vamp, at the opposite pole from the chaste and fatalistic conception of the part held by Lilli Lehmann and Fremstad. Since the war, we have had Carmen as 'free woman' and feminist, valuing independence above security. Carmen the temperamental slut is always with us.

Yet no view of the character has had quite the extraordinary shock value that Calvé's had, memorably described by Shaw, who was deeply shaken by the naked display of animality.

> There is no suggestion of any fine quality about her, not a spark of honesty, courage, or even the sort of honour supposed to prevail among thieves. All this is conveyed by Calvé with a positively frightful power of divesting her beauty and grace of the nobility ... which seems inseparable from them in other parts ... To see Calvé's Carmen changing from a live creature into a reeling, staggering, flopping, disorganized thing, and finally tumble down a mere heap of carrion, is to get much the same sensation as might be given by the reality of a brutal murder ... It was the desecration of a great talent. I felt furious with Calvé.

Calvé herself actually disliked the part. 'Carmen has only two redeeming qualities. She is truthful and she is brave,' she wrote.

**35.** Lotte Lehmann as Sieglinde in Act I of
*Die Walküre*. **36.** *right* Maria Jeritza, one of
the great beauties among prima donnas,
possibly as Jenufa.

**37.** In 1963, Lehmann and Jeritza, brought together to discuss *Ariadne auf Naxos* with John
Gutman, buried the hatchet with a hysterical good humour that belied the violence of their
animosity during the Vienna years.

**38.** Emma Calvé in Massenet's *Hérodiade*.

**39.** Conchita Supervia.

**40.** *left* Mary Garden's scandalous Salome in Strauss's opera. **41.** *above* Garden at her iciest, with the psychologist Professor Coué, whose methods briefly amused her.

The problem may have been boredom: she claimed to have sung in the opera over three thousand times, and although the figure is highly unlikely, it may well have seemed as many as that. The clamour for Calvé's Carmen was universal. Queen Victoria commanded a performance at Windsor Castle, rewarded her with the gift of a dog, and commissioned a marble bust of the singer which still stands there today. At the Met her début in the role was acclaimed by an audience including Ellen Terry, Henry Irving, and Tommaso Salvini. Such was the infallible effect on the box office that managements were loath to let her do anything else, and over the years up to 1904 when she sang the part repeatedly in most of the great opera houses, the interpretation filled up with exaggerated and excessive business. One of her regular Don Josés, Jean de Reszke, particularly objected to the way in which she would suddenly park herself in his lap while he was trying to sing. 'Calvé's Carmen went to artistic pieces,' recalled W. J. Henderson. 'The prima donna could not stand her enormous success. She became extravagant, whimsical, erratic, irresponsible. She did anything that occurred to her to accomplish a passing situation.' Whether she was similarly cavalier with the music is disputable. Shaw claimed that she carried 'her abandonment to the point of being incapable of paying the smallest attention to the score,' but other critics have contradicted this. Her own considered view of the matter was that, 'Unfortunately for me, no one dared utter a word of criticism: and in consequence, I was carried away by my passion for realism. It became an obsession, and occasionally I overstepped the mark.'

Everything about Calvé suggests restlessness and volatility. At one point she considered quitting opera altogether to become an actress—anything to get away from the Carmen for which she was paid ever more irresistible fees! Her repertory was never large. Massenet wrote for her the title-roles in what was intended as the French answer to *Cavalleria Rusticana*, *La Navarraise* (in which Shaw wrote of her as 'a living volcano, wild with anxiety . . . mad with joy, ecstatic with love, desperate with disappointment') and *Sapho*, a strange piece with a contemporary setting about an artist's model; otherwise she was largely restricted in her years of fame to Santuzza, Marguerite in *Faust*, and Ophélie in Thomas's *Hamlet*.

In 1904 she announced her retirement from opera, although impresarios who opened their coffers wide enough dragged another few performances of Carmen out of her. She continued to sing in recital, where, apart from the inevitable Carmen arias, she made a speciality of Provençal folk songs. On a recording of one of these, 'Ma Lisette', she finishes with a top D of extraordinary soft purity and steadiness. It is widely supposed that this is evidence of what she called her 'fourth voice', a method of voice production she learnt from an aged castrato in the Sistine Chapel choir and which apparently involved keeping the mouth virtually closed, as if humming. It took her three years to perfect and she never succeeded in communicating the technique to any of her pupils.

Calvé's voice was an altogether unusual instrument, with a genuine and unforced extension in the lower regions beyond the scope of the other Marchesi-trained sopranos. Accompanists, however, would be driven mad by her persistent but inconsistent demands for transpositions. In the morning she would feel comfortable singing high; come the concert, everything had to come down. In the recording studio, she was even more eccentric. Before her first session, she refused to enter the door of the Gramophone Company's back-street London studio. 'Never in my life will I enter such a place,' she exclaimed from her carriage to her accompanist Landon Ronald. 'It is a tavern—not a manufactory. I shall be robbed there. You have brought me to a thieves' den.' Only when her fee of one hundred guineas was brought forth did she relent. Once in front of the horn, there were further problems. According to Roland Gelatt, 'She had the disconcerting habit of commenting on her performance in the midst of a recording—even uttering shrieks of joy or groans of disgust, depending on whether she had turned a particular phrase to her liking—and in the "Séguedille" from *Carmen* she insisted on dancing in front of the recording horn just as she was wont to do on stage.' None the less what we hear from Calvé's recordings is a voice of real loveliness, with a warmth that Melba's quite lacked.

Calvé was a prima donna who kept a simple love of the physical act of singing. She continued to give recitals into her vocal dotage, and during the First World War toured North America raising money for the French wounded. In one concert hall she noticed a party of innocent Germans, doubtless anxious to transcend the limitations of nationalism and hear a great singer. Calvé, however, could not restrain herself and half-way through her rendering of the *Marseillaise* spat in the direction of the enemy contingent. Such was her instinctive sense of theatre.

'Instinctive' is an important word in treating of Calvé. She was not interested in the conventional social success so highly valued by Melba. She lived the life of a manic depressive, and her memoirs alternate between the joys of music, painting, literature, travel, and references to long periods full of 'overwhelming catastrophes' and illnesses 'of which I still cannot speak'. She was married definitely once and possibly twice, although the memoirs contain absolutely no reference whatsoever to either the definite Signor Gaspari or the possible M. Boellman. She was a highly susceptible woman, and at one time fell deeply under the influence of a guru, Swami Vivi Kananda, who passed on to her the secrets of yogi breath control. All varieties of mysticism fascinated her, especially those of the East, and a friend recalls her singing her mantra: 'She became very calm, very serious too, and, closing her eyes, began in a voice deep, rich, full, and powerful: "*Om, om, Hari Om, tata sat*".'

Her other source of peace of mind was the castle she bought at Cabrières in her native Aveyron, no elegant country house, but a rough stone fortress perched on top of a crag. She continued to be restless, however, keeping up studies in Paris and Nice where she took pupils to relieve her growing financial embarrassment—and she continued to sing into her seventies. Colette encountered her in 1934 in a restaurant in Nice. She looked frail, and Colette wanted to order her a cab. 'What for?' Calvé asked. 'I have good legs. At home every morning, I climb, I climb. When I have enough, high up there, I sing, I sing for my mountain . . . For my mountain and also for some little shepherd boy. For a girl who beats out the washing . . . For a ploughman who stops his team and listens to me.' She died in 1942, shortly after losing the remains of her money in the aftermath of the German invasion.

The next great prima donna of French opera, Mary Garden (1874–1967), was not French at all, and in fact both spoke and sang the language with unmistakable American intonation. In a sense, she represents no style or school or even nation: if her art was French, her birthplace was Aberdeen, her passport always British, and her upbringing largely American. As a singer and a personality, she defeats all categories and comparisons: 'Mary Garden, as difficult of classification as a French verb,' wrote one journalist; 'a condor, an eagle, a peacock, a nightingale, a panther, a society dame, a gallery of moving pictures, a siren,' waxed another. It was almost as though she had already transcended the mortal condition. Whereas Calvé's life, as revealed in her memoirs, bespeaks a recognizable human being with ordinary enthusiasms, appetites, and failings, Mary Garden's is a glacial and flawless catalogue of achievement. She enjoyed neither food, nor sex, nor curtain calls. She was the complete egoist, ruthlessly self-aware and self-centred, utterly cold-eyed and imperturbable. 'I believed in myself,' she proclaimed, 'and I never permitted anything or anybody to destroy that belief . . . I wanted liberty and I went my own way.'

Garden's parents had taken her to America when she was six, and the family had settled in Chicago, the city with which the name of Mary Garden remains indelibly associated. Liberty began in earnest when a wealthy family paid for her to continue her musical studies in Paris, where she walked out on teacher after teacher—including Marchesi, whose insistence on the Melban virtues of pure tone and agility she found antipathetic—before her sponsors received a not-proven report of her lax moral behaviour and cut off their subsidy. Fortunately Garden was then taken up by Sybil Sanderson, a beautiful American soprano for whom Massenet had written *Thaïs*. In 1900 Sanderson introduced her to Albert Carré, director of the Opéra-Comique, who, like everyone else, was impressed by the girl's breezy self-assurance. She was told to learn the title-role of Charpentier's wildly successful new opera *Louise* and bide her time. In April of that year, on a day on which she recalled 'feeling particularly depressed over the death of a dog that had been run over by an omnibus', the original Louise fell ill in the middle of the performance and within minutes Garden had calmly stepped in and taken over without any stage or orchestral rehearsal: 'I have never been nervous in my life and I have no patience with people who are,' she asserted. Her feat brought her immediate fame, which she handled consummately. Over the next few years she consolidated her reputation and repertory at the Opéra-Comique, incurring the jealousy of Carré's soprano wife as she blithely carried on the *jeune fille Americaine* tradition established by Sanderson and her predecessors in Paris such as Marie van Zandt and Minnie Hauk.

In 1902 she was chosen by Debussy to create the part of Mélisande in his *Pelléas et Mélisande*. 'You have come to me from the mists of the north to create my music,' he told her. On the surface it was an unlikely piece of casting, for Garden was already notorious for her suitors and brisk, restless wit. Mélisande is a creature from nowhere, lonely, child-like, unawoken. Yet Garden was herself not quite of this world, at least in terms of feelings— 'I never really loved anybody. I had a fondness for men, yes, but very little passion and *no need*,' she admitted—and perhaps she brought something of her own unfeelingness into her interpretation. 'She hardly moved her hands and arms for long stretches of the action: her head was usually bowed in submission, but when it moved it had something to contribute to the composition . . . The voice had the pallor of the tomb at times; it was difficult to understand how such misty rose-gray and blue-gray notes could spin from a human throat.' Thus Vincent Sheean: a fellow prima donna, Frances Alda, whose compliments were few and far between, also emphasized this ethereality. 'She was so still. Just that one little phrase, "Il fait froid ici", as it came from her lips, and you shivered under the chill winds that blow between the worlds of the real and the unreal. Contrasted with it, [Lucrezia] Bori's rendering of the line sounded like a schoolgirl who steps out of bed without her slippers.'

Debussy fell in love with Mary Garden, promising to write her a *Romeo and Juliet* opera if she accepted him—but she laughed him off and told him how charming his wife was; the conductor of the first *Pelléas*, André Messager, was also brushed away. To Mélisande alone did Garden remain loyal, and the impact of her performance was an important element in what initial success the opera had. It is not an easy work, and the first audiences were bemused and sometimes bored by its delicacy and understatement, as well as its brief explosions and searing climaxes. The vocal line, made up of brief, thwarted interchanges and little recognizable melody, is not immediately gratifying. There is no ballet, no spectacle, no *scandale* in the plot. A certain sort of temperament has continued to find the whole thing a sure cure for insomnia. Yet to others it represents a peak of opera's expressive potential. Imagine Wagner writing an opera to a libretto by Henry James, full of the mysteries of innocence and guilt and bottomless unexpressed tragedies, a dream rather than an apocalypse, with music that conceals more than it reveals and suggests more than it states—and there you have something of *Pelléas*'s quality. Mary Garden understood it all intuitively and Debussy recorded that she needed almost no direction during the long and painstaking rehearsal period. 'All of my creations went into me and out,' she later said. 'They were inside of me, and I threw them out to the public. I never really worked over them, not in the usual sense—I just knew them . . . I just had it in me, all of it . . . I was Mélisande . . . That was all there was to it.'

In 1907, Garden left the Opéra-Comique and Paris. She returned to New York and Oscar Hammerstein's new Manhattan Opera House. To avoid too much direct competition with the Met, Hammerstein sought out not only new stars but a new repertory, and Mary Garden in French opera became a corner-stone of his success. Louise and Mélisande were two of her earliest roles here, but she became equally celebrated in the operas of Massenet, making her Manhattan début as his Thaïs, the Egyptian courtesan turned nun. Eyebrows were raised at once and gentlemen dropped their monocles, for there was nothing healthy about either Garden or Massenet: for good clean naughty fun Geraldine Farrar was New York's prima donna, but Garden excelled in conveying the more sophisticated and exotic varieties of eroticism. Massenet himself, according to Garden, was 'the yes-man par excellence' who wrote 'endless letters dripping with the most sickening kind of sentiment, everything underlined not once, but two, three and four times': his later operas are composed on equivalent musical principles. Garden gave even his attempt at pious simplicity, Le Jongleur de Notre-Dame, a sexual frisson by taking the tenor title-role and dressing herself in a short jerkin and tights. Strauss offered her the travesty role of Octavian in Rosenkavalier, but she refused on the grounds that it would have bored her to make love to a woman on stage. His Salome was more in her line: she sang it in French, à la Massenet as it were, and performed the Dance of the Seven Veils herself, swathed in layers of diaphanous tulle. In Chicago, the police banned it as an affront to public morality.

But she was to go a lot further than biblical virgins caressing severed heads. As Massenet's Cléopâtre, 'the queen, disguised as a boy, visits an Egyptian brothel and makes love to another boy'. 'Mary was very startling,' was the critic Carl van Vechten's thunderstruck comment! When Février's Monna Vanna appears before her captor clad only in a fur mantle, she is asked whether she is naked underneath: 'Oui,' replied Garden, and made everyone believe it. Most meretricious of all was her involvement in D'Erlanger's Aphrodite, which included the crucifixion of a negro slave, overt lesbianism, and a multiracial orgy. It was hardly surprising that the evangelical Billy Sunday preached against Mary Garden's lascivious incitements, or that a girl killed herself rather than suffer the pangs of unrequited infatuation for her prima donna.

Sadly, Garden's records communicate nothing of this fatal allure. In general, her singing makes a pleasant, correct, and unmemorable impression. There was always a faction that claimed she could not sing at all, and it is certainly true that in a 'heavy' role like Salome she was not beyond cheating by omission or abbreviation. At the same time, a recording of Violetta's first-act *scena* from *La Traviata* shows that there was some substance to her technique. Others noted her extraordinary ability to colour her voice to suit the character she had undertaken. Garden was in no doubt of the facts. Apart from a glass of milk with ten drops of iodine after a performance, her voice required no attention, let alone improvement. 'I did what I liked with my voice; I was always its master and never its slave. It obeyed me, and not I it . . . I never had to rest because it was tired—never, never, never. At all times, my voice was absolutely at my command.'

After the closure of the Manhattan Opera in 1910, Garden struck out west with many of Hammerstein's personnel and established a company on similar lines in Chicago. Here, over the next twenty years, Garden became as infamous as any gangster. Every year she would appear in a novel French (or at least Frenchified) opera, each of them flimsier than the last, as well as a few more conventional vehicles like *Tosca* or *Carmen*, and her established roles. She seems to have had very little musical discrimination: what attracted her was the chance to present some striking new variation on the old romantic dilemmas. To the *cognoscenti*, she was simply the greatest actress in America, with an imagination and originality which radiated through her bizarre repertory. She may not have been profound, but off stage as well as on, she astounded.

The Garden year began on her return to Chicago from a summer vacation in Europe, when she gave a press conference in her hotel suite, just before the opera season opened. She effortlessly publicized herself as the acme of sophistication and provided a feast of good copy. One year she was engaged to a Turkish pasha; the next she announced categorically that she did not wear corsets (she was scarcely five foot high, and *petite* in build). Then Coué, the apostle of auto-suggestion, had cured her of bronchial pneumonia; or she had met Mussolini whom she deemed 'the incarnation of Napoleon'. As the embodiment of modern womanhood her views on men and the question of sex took centre place. 'It is fine that women do no longer love as they did,' she said. 'It will be even finer if they can win absolute freedom. Formerly we were under the man's heel. Now just his little toe is on us. Yet how conscious we are of that little toe.' In Chicago her opinions and presence were ubiquitous: when a man who tried to assassinate her was asked why he had wanted to do it, he replied only, 'She talks too much.'

In 1921 pressure from the male little toe was finally lifted. Garden won herself greater worldly power than any prima donna had previously had when for one season she was made director or (as she insisted) directa of the Chicago Opera. Some magnificent artistic coups, including the première of Prokofiev's delightful *L'Amour de trois oranges*, were achieved at the expense of an administrative fiasco. 'I went as often as I could,' wrote Sheean, 'and reveled in the originality of the arrangements. An opera might be given once only—two performances was rather a long run—and a singer might make a debut which was simultaneously a farewell. These singularities are most often the prerogatives of failure . . . [but] Garden conducted her whole season through a tooting of success like the triumphal scene in *Aida*.' A large number of singers were engaged at large salaries and then given nothing to sing while the directa went on two or three times a week, though, to be fair, she received no fee for her services beyond what she earned as a performer. No attention whatsoever was paid to proper budgeting and the final deficit was ruinous. Garden was quite happy with the result, announcing, 'If it cost a million dollars, I'm sure it was worth it.'

Garden last sang in Chicago in 1931 and in Paris in 1934. She made a fortune—fees in Chicago were even higher than the Met, at which she never appeared. In the summer she augmented her income playing the casino at Monte Carlo where, being Mary Garden, she consistently won. She also made two silent films, including one of *Thaïs*, for which she was reported to have been paid $125,000. Olive Fremstad visited her on the set and was appalled. 'My God, Mary, you must be quite mad,' Mary Watkins Cushing heard her whisper. 'Why do you let yourself in for anything like this?' Miss Garden answered by tracing with one stiff finger in the icy air the cabalistic sign of the dollar. ' "Only that and nothing else," she declared, adding, "But even so it's not worth it, so DON'T." '

In semi-retirement (she continued to give lectures until her eighty-first year), she remained amazing and astounding. At the outbreak of the Second World War, she returned to Aberdeen and set up a military convalescent home with her sister. 'Gosh! How great it is to be British,' she wrote to an American correspondent. How great to be Mary Garden, she might have added. 'Eccentric' is too weak an adjective for this flawlessly armoured personality, but even in the ranks of prima donnas she stands out beyond the human rule.

Although she was identified almost exclusively with French opera, Garden represents only a feeble and commercially compromised branch of the French tradition in its post-Wagnerian phase. Today, of her major roles, only Mélisande still commands credence, however often something like *Thaïs* or *Louise* is dusted off and polished up. As a vocalist she clearly managed to do extraordinary things with an essentially limited instrument, but her example was a dangerous one to follow—not that anyone dared. A more solid line of French singing has been provided by their heavy dramatic sopranos. Calvé taught the Paris-born Gina Cigna, a famous Norma and Aida of the 1930s, while the half-Russian Félia Litvinne, a pupil of Pauline Viardot's, had a mastery of Wagnerian declamation. In her turn Litvinne taught Germaine Lubin (1890–1979), a gleaming heroic soprano who has been unfairly overshadowed by her contemporaries Flagstad and Leider. Her reputation was also affected by her sad 'collaboration' with the Nazis. In 1939 she sang in both Berlin and Bayreuth, where Hitler told her that, 'In all my life I have never seen or heard an Isolde such as you.'

After the invasion of France she became a puppet in the direction of the Paris Opéra and sang as 'guest-artist' with visiting German companies. As so often, this appears to have been far more a matter of naïvety and time-serving than an active espousal of Nazi ideology, yet she was inevitably treated as a traitor after the Liberation, imprisoned, hounded, and broken: her son killed himself under the stress. 'Like Amfortas,' she told Lanfranco Rasponi at the end of her life, 'my wounds are destined to remain open . . . except for having eaten the flesh of children, there is nothing I was not accused of.' Whatever moral judgement one makes on her (and the evidence is by no means all on her side), the voice survives on record with a steely ringing quality—fiercer than Flagstad's, less emotional than Leider's—which has the exhilarating effect on a listener that we associate with Birgit Nilsson.

Lubin continued the direct line of succession when she coached Régine Crespin, the outstanding post-war French prima donna, in her assumption of the Wagner roles. Their encounters must have been interesting, for Crespin's highly idiosyncratic voice and style could never have found the underlying physical stability of Lubin's. Lubin's is a lighthouse of a voice, shining out unmistakably, whereas Crespin is a siren, alluring and elusive, who 'makes hungry where most she satisfies'. It is hardly surprising that her career has been so irregular, or that in a disarmingly frank autobiography she has revealed a life to complement it. Born in Marseilles in 1927, she was about to train as a pharmacist and only took up singing seriously when she failed her *baccalauréate*. From beginning to end she had a difficult relationship with the audiences and managements of the Paris Opéra, the house which should have gratefully nurtured her; and her most satisfying work was done in the French provinces, where she not only upheld all aspects of the French classical repertory (including Gluck's *Iphigénie en Tauride*, Berlioz's *Les Troyens*, and Fauré's *Pénélope*), but also sang Sieglinde, Tosca, and Desdemona. Internationally she kept the good name of French singing alive in an otherwise moribund period. She was a much-admired Kundry in *Parsifal* at Bayreuth and a knowing Marschallin at Glyndebourne, Covent Garden, and the Met, where she was coached by Lotte Lehmann. Later in the 1960s she was persuaded by Karajan to sing Brünnhilde in his *Ring* at Salzburg, but after nine performances she wisely renounced the role. By the early 1970s she had reached a crisis point. At the Opéra she was mercilessly booed by what she claimed to be an organized anti-Crespin cabal. Her control over her voice was failing, as was her marriage to a man whose sexual appetite exhausted and terrified her. A wretched love affair, divorce, and psychoanalysis were followed by a radical retraining of her voice under a German teacher. Crespin forgot about her top notes—which had been of a uniquely warm and gentle beauty—and focused herself on lower-lying roles. She reappeared as a histrionically low-key Carmen, which one critic described as reminiscent of a 'jaunty Paris matron' but which was generally acclaimed for its musicality. Then she suffered another unhappy involvement with the conductor

Henry Lewis, Marilyn Horne's ex-husband, and a bout of cancer, but again recovered from both.

In the last few years, after the timbre of her voice had become decidedly acrid and its volume diminished, she has limited herself mainly to comic or cameo roles. In particular she has given a grandly melodramatic performance as the dying Prioress in Poulenc's *Les Dialogues des Carmélites*, an opera in which she had taken a high lyric soprano role at its Paris première in 1957. One aspect of her technique has remained unimpaired throughout—her exemplary diction. Few singers use words so clearly and expressively as Crespin, for whom, as her champion André Tubeuf puts it, 'good singing is first of all good speaking'. Her art is perhaps best characterized as being one of superbly inflected declamation, on the models of Racine and Rameau, in which mere smoothness of line and roundness of tone are subordinated to the communication of emotion and meaning.

Crespin's singing is probably the nearest we can come to a definition of French style, although some would think in terms of something more sweetly girlish and a multitude of others of Edith Piaf, another singer whose power lay in rich forthright enunciation. It would, I think, be impossible to identify a French voice blind and it would certainly not be easy to make out any deep similarities between the singing of Calvé, Garden, Lubin, and Crespin. A much stronger archetype is presented by the Spanish prima donna. Here we can isolate definite characteristics: a pride of manner, vibrant, warm tone, and an unerring sense for the subtleties of rhythm, for instance. The stylistic character and demands of Spanish folk music is a deeply formative element in this. Robert Rushmore further believes that a Spanish singer can be detected by 'a sound like the tiniest of hiccups' in the attack on certain notes in the middle and lower parts of their ranges. For most of the world, however, it is *Carmen* which provides the most immediately memorable source of Spanish music. This is regrettable, since *Carmen*'s 'Spanish-ness' is little more than pastiche, with scarcely a trace of the melismatic orientalism that gives authentic Spanish music its hauntingly alien flavour.

Yet even *Carmen* can recover some of her ethnic roots with a Spanish interpreter. A French Carmen like Régine Crespin will turn her mind to Racine and compare the cigarette girl to the great heroines of Antiquity, but a Spaniard knows what a gypsy is and what a *habanera* really sounds like. With no one is this more striking than Conchita Supervia, the mezzo-soprano whose voice breathes an unschooled peasant directness and force which no other prima donna presents on record. Supervia was no drawing-room nightingale: her coloratura is not the disembodied carolling of a Marchesi pupil, but a dynamic emission of energy; her prominent vibrato (some say exaggerated by records) is not the result of tremulous over-refinement, but a sensual and robust buzz. Like many other of her compatriots, the smell of fertile sunburnt earth pervades her singing.

It would be pleasant to report that she was indeed a daughter of the soil, but in fact her origins are mysterious, and even her birth date is disputed, 1891, 1896, and 1899 being variously suggested. It is now widely thought that she was born in Barcelona in 1895, although this makes her first recorded appearances in Buenos Aires in 1910 and Rome in 1911 (as Octavian in *Rosenkavalier*) almost incredible. Her musical training is equally mysterious. Her only known teacher was one Alfredo Martino, and it is conceivable that such a firm and healthy voice never needed much moulding. Most of her singing years were spent in Spain, Argentina, and Italy, where in 1918 she bore a son to a lawyer who begged her to marry him and give up singing. But for Supervia singing must have been as necessary as breathing and she refused him, strongly influenced by her dominating mother. In the 1920s, inspired by the conductor Vittorio Gui, she first sang in the operas of Rossini, the composer to whose spirit she was perhaps best suited. At that time he was only remembered as the composer of *Il Barbiere di Siviglia*, but Gui and Supervia reminded Europe of *La Cenerentola* and *L'Italiana in Algeri* as well, leaving matchless recordings of some of the major scenes and arias. For Supervia at her most inimitably vivacious, listen to the quarrel duet 'Ai capricci della sorte' from *L'Italiana*, where her clarity, wit, and responsiveness are devastating. Should you at the same time be contemplating suicide, allow Supervia to sing you out of it with Cenerentola's rondo 'Non più mesta'. Its embracing kindliness and sheer cheerfulness, as well as its irresistible rhythmic impetus, could make anyone feel that life was worth living.

Such was her success in these Rossini roles that, along with Carmen, she sang little else in the opera house. In 1931, in an attempt to give her son George legitimacy and a proper home, she married an English timber-merchant, Ben Rubenstein, and moved to London. The arrangement did not turn out well for either Supervia or her son, but the English public was delighted with its catch. She became an enormous favourite in the concert hall, where she did much to popularize the Spanish folk- and art-song. Her regular accompanist in these years was Ivor Newton, who described her as 'intensely alert and possessed of an apparently inexhaustible vitality. Her gaiety, good temper, sympathy and charm cloaked a keen intelligence and adamantine will-power . . . She needed only to say "I would like so-and-so" and whomever she addressed immediately said "Of course".' But there were times when the wheels of gallantry did not turn so smoothly, and nothing illustrates Newton's characterization of the singer better than the story of her only Covent Garden appearance in 1934–5.

She was engaged to sing Carmen and Cenerentola, but found the roles difficult to perform at the same time, since their vocal requirements are so different; nor did she wish to sing Carmen *before* Cenerentola. When the fulfilment of these conditions proved impossible without a cut in the number of performances originally signed for, Supervia withdrew in a fury and threatened to sue for breach of contract. She went off to make a film of Beverley Nichols's novel *Evensong*, based loosely on the supposed rivalry between Melba and the young Toti dal Monte on their 1924 Australian tour. Eventually a compromise was reached: only *Cenerentola* would be performed, but Supervia's wishes would be met in the subsequent season. Sir Thomas Beecham, Covent Garden's musical director, had been thoroughly sceptical of the worth of Rossini's score and irritated by the instance of prima donna's privilege, but his resistance soon melted. When the ponies which draw Cenerentola's coach were unavailable during rehearsal, Supervia invited Beecham and the administrator Geoffrey Toye, who were sitting in the auditorium, to stand in. They gamely accepted and hopped around the stage dragging the coach behind them, while the triumphant prima donna whipped them on. The performance proved a wild success, and Supervia was so pleased with it all that she asked Ivor Newton to find her a graven image of Rossini somewhere in London: he came up with the frieze round the Albert Memorial, and together they went and laid a wreath of flowers at the master's feet—a snapshot exists of the little tribute.

Supervia then wrote to Toye suggesting the supporting casts that she would like for her forthcoming appearances: all her hints were taken. Opera historians have deplored this as unpardonable arrogance, but one must remember that it was Supervia who persuaded the management to take the risk on Rossini in the first place and that no one would have known more about who could sing his music than she did. And *L'Italiana in Algeri* emerged in London as happily as had *Cenerentola*, special delight being occasioned when Supervia made her entry carrying a small Pomeranian dog—a detail perfectly in accord with the character in question. Her Carmen followed, magnificently costumed by Lanvin: this divided opinion, some critics finding her too ingratiating. This is surprising, inasmuch as the recordings communicate a creature of fierce determination, amoral yet not unfeeling, with an appeal that is anything but sugary—'predatory' is the word aptly used by John Steane.

Supervia died suddenly in childbirth in 1936, having been warned by her doctor that pregnancy would be dangerous. Ironically for a singer whose art is so full of ordinary human happiness, she died sadly, unhappy with her husband's tight-knit family circle and her son's hatred of his new situation. She was buried in the Jewish cemetery in Golders Green, having converted to Judaism to please her husband; her money and property were fiercely contested in an atmosphere of much resentment and recrimination. Fortunately these tragic complications could not affect the priceless legacy of her singing.

If she is irreplaceable, the line of Spanish prima donnas has continued and flourished. Victoria de los Angeles—another native of Barcelona, born in 1923—has had something of the same ability to inspire love in her listeners, although her charm is a much more shy and modest thing than Supervia's wonderful swagger. Los Angeles is the most restful of singers and whatever she sings has a natural intimacy and grace. 'For sheer quality of sound, Victoria's [voice] affects me more than any other,' admitted her accompanist Gerald Moore. Her Madama Butterfly is miraculously pathetic and dignified without ever sinking into the morass of sentiment implied by libretto and score, just as her Carmen (which she very rarely sang on stage) avoids any sort of snarling or strutting.

Despite an important operatic career in the mainstream—she was particularly popular in the 1950s at the Met, where her virtues and repertory recalled memories of another great Spanish soprano of the inter-war years, Lucrezia Bori; and she had a range extending from Massenet's Manon to Elisabeth in *Tannhäuser*, which she sang at Bayreuth—it has been in the intimacy of the song recital that her most essential qualities were fulfilled. Here her infallible gift has been the realization of the heart of the song, of its emotional point: Schwarzkopf could get more colour and subtlety into a song's *meaning*, but she is rarely as simply moving as Los Angeles. Truly, she has been a singer with a Midas touch, turning gold in the tender and melancholy reaches of Spanish song as well as in the less florid areas of Purcell, Handel, and Monteverdi. Nobody has better communicated the desperate, breathless happiness of Schubert's 'Mein' or more sharply tossed off the humour in Brahms's 'Vergebliches Ständchen'. To everything, she grants an artless beauty, and if Supervia is the singer to save one from suicide, it is Los Angeles who could sing one to a peaceful and painless grave.

Another outstanding singer in the Supervia line is Teresa Berganza, a rich-voiced mezzo-soprano with a remarkable facility in coloratura. More straightfaced than her predecessor in Rossini and more austere as Carmen, she has been at her finest in Mozart, where Supervia's forthrightness might be considered *de trop*. Finally, there is Montserrat Caballé, without doubt one of the greatest singers since the war and a prima donna as people like to think of them.

Caballé's voice has all the vibrancy and her musicality the supple sense of rhythmic gravity that we associate with the Spanish. A less obvious comparison would be with Flagstad: both had the quality of a huge cathedral organ with a vast range of stops which cannot be hurried. André Tubeuf expressed this perfectly when he called Caballé's 'a slow voice . . . spreading out like a becalmed sea'. Her singing is on the grandest scale, moulding vaults of sound filled with exquisite detail. She could pull out a phrase to heavenly lengths, moving effortlessly from dreamy *pianissimo* to a thrillingly metallic top C. Fuller-voiced than Milanov, more individual than Tebaldi, more versatile than Leontyne Price, in the later 1960s and early 1970s she was regarded as a peerless singer of the Italian repertory who could do no wrong.

Again like Flagstad, she had a long apprenticeship before her talent coincided with her luck. Born in Barcelona in 1933, her parents were very poor and badly hit by the Civil War: at sixteen, she was working in a handkerchief factory in order to pay for an operation on her father. For seven years her musical ambitions (which had begun with training for the ballet) were sponsored by the wealthy Bertrand family, on the sole condition that she never neglected Barcelona's opera house, the Liceo. In 1956 she joined the Basle Opera, where at first she had to supplement her minute income by waitressing. Over the next few years she sang anything from Salome (her favourite role) to Mimi, and in one season alone her Aida was heard a total of twenty-six times! Her career and reputation slowly built up, but it was not until April 1965, almost ten years since her operatic début, that she broke through the invisible barrier, when she stepped at short notice into a concert performance of Donizetti's *Lucrezia Borgia* at Carnegie Hall in New York, and provoked a sensation. The great years followed, during which she was particularly in demand for the more dramatic Donizetti, Rossini, and early Verdi roles, which had long been awaiting such a voice.

Then she announced in *Opera News* that she would retire in 1973, explaining that she could no longer bear the periods of separation from her husband and daughter. For some reason, this never happened, but since that time Caballé's singing seems to have lost its moorings. She has given many ravishing and memorable performances and even on an off-night can produce *belles minutes* of a splendour that none of her contemporaries can match. Yet all regularity and reliability was lost. She cancelled a large number of engagements (Tubeuf reckoned twenty out of seventy; lately the proportion has risen), often flying back to Barcelona and causing considerable irritation to those left behind. She was observed to be smoking heavily; and there was scandalous chatter about the behaviour of her brother and manager, Carlos Caballé. The voice itself sometimes betrayed an unpleasantly brassy vibrato and a loss of her miraculous control. It was as though she knew perfectly what she wanted to do, but couldn't quite do it, and the undertaking of heavy roles such as Norma and Turandot cannot have contributed to its preservation. In particular, her singing at Covent Garden, where she first appeared in 1972, was consistently disappointing, and London only heard her at her best in concert, where she was probably happiest anyway. On stage she had an impressive presence but her bulk prevented much involvement in the action, and she rarely worked with any of the more imaginative producers. To opera's radical wing Caballé stands exposed as an archetype of the old-fashioned prima donna, who cares only for vocal accomplishment and nothing for dramatic credibility. Equally one could regard her loss of motivation—if that is the verdict reached on the evidence —as an indictment of the modern opera system, with its high-speed international turnover and pressurized working conditions. One thing is certain: without voices as sumptuous as Caballé's at its best, opera will wither. The arts of singing are not an excrescence or parasite on the tree of music drama, but its essential soil.

Are there any conclusive generalizations to be drawn from the notion that there is a distinctively 'French' or 'Spanish' prima donna? It could be said that the French prima donna is defined by the language that she sings and the way she will sing it, while the Spanish prima donna shows a more definite vocal character and sensibility, nurtured by a peculiarly rich tradition of folk-song. But to come full circle, we should beware of taking this too far. What matters is what is done to the raw elements, how they are trained, moulded, and sent out to work. Great voices arise without much reference to geography or heredity.

# 9

# *The Callas Revolution*

Once the struggle for national unification in Italy was won, Italian opera abandoned the heroic romanticism which Verdi's music had so gloriously embodied. Inevitably, the new political stability left the public less engaged by the issues of war and peace, rulers and subjects, power and the powerful. Instead it turned inward to dilemmas more personal and subjective, psychologically intense rather than socially extensive: something of this is evident even in the different orientations of Verdi's *Aida* (1871) and *Otello* (1887). '*Verismo*' is the term used to describe this trend, but like '*bel canto*' or 'Wagnerism', it has become a label of operatic history so indiscriminately applied as to be misleading.

The origins of *verismo* are in fact French. The naturalistic novels of Zola which depict industrial and working-class life in an analytic manner were the sensational modernism of their day, influential throughout the Italian *avant-garde*. The playwright Sardou's meaty melodramas like *Fedora* and *La Tosca*, both written for Sarah Bernhardt, also had obvious operatic potential—and *Tosca*, of course, contains its own prima donna. Italian composers were deeply impressed by the heart-on-the-sleeve idiom of Massenet's early operas, which trade on exotic and pathetic situations far more accessible to the average opera-goer than Wagner's complex mythologies. The moment at which all these elements decisively came together was the production in 1890 of a one-act opera called *Cavalleria Rusticana*, by the twenty-six-year-old Pietro Mascagni. This was, as it were, the musical version of a tough little play made very popular through Duse's performance as the betrayed Sicilian peasant Santuzza. Mascagni set the piece to boldly crude music and not only created a *furore* but set a new course for Italian opera. The concentration made possible by the single-act form was much imitated, as in the original version of Leoncavallo's *I Pagliacci* and

Massenet's 'answer' to *Cavalleria Rusticana, La Navarraise*. Physical violence in a low-life setting, sometimes contemporary, involving characters who have compromised themselves sexually became a standard format, and the fustian clichés of conventional operatic Italian—from *'padre, pietà'* to *'crudel fato'*—gave way to librettos closer to recognizably human speech.

All sorts of operas have been categorized as *verismo*, even if they really do not fit the above characterization. Ponchielli's *La Gioconda* appeared some fourteen years before *Cavalleria Rusticana* and is based, like *Rigoletto*, on a drama by Victor Hugo; Cilea's *Adriana Lecouvreur* is set in seventeenth-century Paris and deals with a noble-hearted actress of the Comédie-Française; Giordano's *Andrea Chénier* is a high-flown tale of the French Revolution—yet all are commonly thought of as *'verismo'*. The greatest Italian composer of the period, Giacomo Puccini (1858–1924), only wrote one opera, the one-act *Il Tabarro*, which can properly be called *verismo*, however unsavoury the flavour of *Butterfly* or *Tosca* might have been at the time they were written.

What more fully unites all these works are certain musical characteristics: not very good ones, it has to be said. Under the twice-removed example of Wagner, the harmony is glutinously chromatic; the orchestration tends to the thick and lurid, rarely rising to the complexity and imaginativeness of a Richard Strauss; and crashingly obvious *'leitmotivs'* blaze out repeatedly at crucial moments of looming doom and ultimate destruction. The vocal line depends heavily on overt rises and falls in pitch and dynamic indicative of emotional torture. To maximize the expressive potential, singers of the time resorted to a number of vocal tricks which had no place in the Italian training given by a Garcia or Marchesi: Michael Scott lists them as 'the sob and catch in the breath, the glottal attack, the aspirate and those sudden shifts from a *mezza voce* . . . to a *forte* in which the words are uttered with explosive force'. It is not unfair to say that the pitfalls of *verismo* opera led, with notable exceptions, to a general slovenliness of technique among Italian prima donnas which has only been reversed in the post-war period. It also brought about a considerably more energetic and uninhibited style of acting, which in turn all too often descended into fits of hysteria, throat-clutching, extended death-throes, and other clichés in the vocabulary of melodrama.

For the prima donna, *verismo* caused a crisis comparable to that presented by Wagner. The art of coloratura required by Donizetti or Meyerbeer was of no use to someone singing Santuzza, nor could the Verdian *spinto* who had mastered legato and purity of intonation always muster the dark colouring and throbbing heartache necessary for a Butterfly or Tosca. The result was a specialization in particular areas of the repertory that had not previously been so definite. Before the turn of the century, a sound coloratura with a facility in runs, trills, and other ornaments, had been part of the equipment of every prima donna, from Lilli Lehmann and Nordica to Melba and Calvé; now it became the extraordinary endowment of a few singers revered as freak vocal acrobats. A truly popular prima donna of the previous generation like Patti could sing trills and high notes without any problem, but the heart of her appeal lay in her ability to make something lovely out of something very simple which everyone crooned, be it 'Home, sweet home' or 'Comin' through the Rye'. The new breed of coloratura soprano won applause when she exploded into her top register, singing ever faster and higher without squeaking or blurring. Doing anything else, she could be pretty dull.

Luisa Tetrazzini, for instance, the biggest voice and most striking personality among the coloraturas, did not infallibly impress. When she made her New York début in *La Traviata* to wild public acclaim, the respected critic W. J. Henderson pointed out that however accurate and powerful her runs and high notes, there were some fundamental inadequacies underneath. Tetrazzini's was as indisputably a badly schooled and unbalanced voice as it was a phenomenally brilliant one. Her lower medium notes 'were all sung with a pinched glottis and with a color so pallid and a tremolo so pronounced that they were often not a bad imitation of the wailing of a cross infant ... her *cantabile* was uneven in tone quality, the breaks between her medium and her upper notes coming out most unpleasantly', while her ascending scales were 'sung in a manner which would not be tolerated by any reputable teacher in a pupil of a year's standing'. When asked for her opinion of the new prima donna, Melba replied with customary sharpness, 'Get her to sing me a slow scale,' justifiably confident of the firmness of her own grounds in such basic technical matters.

Tetrazzini herself candidly admitted in her autobiography that 'My actual training was probably the shortest of any prima donna that the world has produced.' Born in Florence in 1871, she had the initial advantage of coming from a musical family, in which her elder sister Eva, later married to the chief conductor of the Manhattan and Chicago Operas, Cleofonte Campanini, was also to become an operatic soprano of some repute. Luisa spent a few unfruitful months in a music conservatory before making her début in Florence in 1890. She then embarked on the provincial Italian opera circuit, where she was much in demand for her accomplishments in the 'old' pre-*verismo* repertory. It was in Florence some years later that E. M. Forster heard her as Lucia di Lammermoor. The comedy attached to her performance found its way into *Where Angels Fear to Tread* and provides a vivid picture of the theatrical conditions under which she performed.

> The climax was reached in the mad scene. Lucia, clad in white, as befitted her malady, suddenly gathered up her streaming hair and bowed her acknowledgments to the audience. Then from the back of the stage—she feigned not to see it—there advanced a kind of bamboo clothes-horse, stuck all over with bouquets ... With a scream of amazement and joy she embraced the animal, pulled out one or two practicable blossoms, pressed them to her lips, and flung them into her admirers. They flung them back with loud melodious cries, and a little boy in one of the stage-boxes snatched up his sister's carnations and offered them. '*Che carino!*' exclaimed the singer. She darted at the little boy and kissed him. Now the noise became tremendous. 'Silence! Silence!' shouted many old gentlemen behind. 'Let the divine creature continue!'

From 1892, Tetrazzini also toured in Central and South America, which had recently developed a vigorous operatic life, relying strongly on imported Italian singers. Tetrazzini is an example of a prima donna famous for years on the 'Latin' circuit, while remaining completely unknown in the 'Anglo-Saxon' centres of London and New York. It was not until 1907, when she was engaged for the quiet autumn season at Covent Garden, that she made the breakthrough. The manager Harry Higgins was not enthusiastic at first and even tried to renege on the contract, but Tetrazzini was determined to sing where her idol Patti had sung. She arrived in London in November to find the city enshrouded in one of the legendary 'pea-soupers', which was hardly propitious. No one expected anything of her at all. The opera house was half empty

—few ventured out to brave the fog which had even invaded the auditorium and rendered the stage half invisible. But when Tetrazzini started singing her first-act aria, Higgins was stunned. In the interval he rushed to telephone Fleet Street to send down some reporters to witness what was obviously going to be a sensation. Tetrazzini's status duly changed overnight, and *le tout Londres* came out to hear her. The greatest accolade came from no less a personage than Patti herself, who wrote an enthusiastic and generous letter.

> My dear Madame Tetrazzini, *Bravo! Bravo!* and again *Bravo!* I cannot tell you how much pleasure it gave me to hear you last night and what a joy it was to me to hear your beautiful Italian phrasing . . . I shall take the first opportunity of going to hear you again. I heartily rejoice in your well-deserved triumph. Yours sincerely, Adelina Patti-Cederström

Critics soon became rather more sceptical: 'Madame Tetrazzini's most striking characteristic as Violetta,' wrote one in 1908, 'is the unfailing good temper with which she puts up with the trying circumstances of that lady's career. Then comes the voice, that astonishing voice which is like some incredibly perfected mechanical toy. Her acting—but enough. Madame Tetrazzini knows that it is sufficient to be just herself.' That 'perfected mechanical toy' was enough to keep audiences happy, however, and for five subsequent seasons she dominated Covent Garden alongside Melba and Destinn. On one mind-boggling night, the Coronation Gala of 1911, the three of them appeared together: Destinn sang in the triumph scene from *Aida*, Melba the second act of *Roméo et Juliette*, and Tetrazzini the last act of *Il Barbiere di Siviglia*. The evening was capped with dancing from Karsavina and Nijinsky. Unfortunately the scent from the 100,000-odd roses decorating the auditorium was so overpowering that many of the audience (who had paid up to £1,000 for a box and £100 for a seat) fainted. Perhaps the whole occasion was a dismal anti-climax . . .

Tetrazzini repeated her London operatic success in New York and Chicago. At her Manhattan début Mary Garden was observed to applaud so loud that she split her gloves, and though the critics echoed their London colleagues' reservations, audiences remained frantic with approval. After the outbreak of the First World War, she abandoned the stage for the less taxing and more lucrative sphere of concert tours. These continued much, much too long, but Tetrazzini loved singing and loved her publics. She was not, like Patti, someone who immediately cancelled if she felt slightly off-colour. If people wanted to hear her sing, then she must sing. Part of her appeal was her simple but abundant warmth of manner: at the beginning of concerts, she would pass round the platform waving, shaking available hands and kissing available children. The ritual became increasingly painful, however, and by the early 1930s, when she was in her sixties, she only endured the agonies and indignities of touring because she was desperate for money. The record producer Fred Gaisberg remembers a provincial matinée concert in 1933. The hall was virtually empty and the stage could only be reached from the dressing-rooms via a narrow spiral staircase, up and down which the wretched Tetrazzini, covered in costume jewellery, extremely stout and in poor health, had to be firmly pushed. Gaisberg saw her kiss her rosary, tears trickling silently down her cheek.

Her life had ended in a mess, largely due to her invincible gullibility and extravagance. 'I am of a very buoyant nature and am a born optimist,' she claimed, and it was just as well that she was. She lost fantastic sums of money, throwing it away on schemes run by any plausible swindler. Her third husband, for instance, twenty years her junior, turned out to be a charlatan and she was forced to sue him for extortion. Previously she had bought an entire mountain on the unjustified assumption that it was 'made of gold'. Her paranoid superstition made her even more vulnerable, as well as exasperating. Despite her terror of travelling and a readiness to see imminent disaster signified by anything from hunchbacks to paper-knives, she was equally game to try anything. Once, in San Francisco in 1919, she went up in a bi-plane for charity with the stunt pilot Ormer Locklear:

Sailing over the bank of eucalyptus trees at the far side of the field, Locklear nearly lost control of the plane when Tetrazzini let loose an impromptu high C. Glancing round in terror, he was reassured by Madame's jolly cherubic face that the golden note had been thrown out on the breeze only as an expression of delight. He circled the field a couple of times and gave Tetrazzini an extra thrill by buzzing the grandstand twice before landing.

'Ah, it is so exquisite,' she told Locklear while getting out of her flying togs. 'So much more exciting than hitting high C when singing, and almost as momentous to me.' (*Opera News*, 10 October 1970)

She died in 1940 on *terra firma*, in some poverty and was buried in Milan at the expense of the Italian state.

Tetrazzini's voice is one that I have to admit that I simply do not like. At the risk of contradicting Patti, I find her phrasing perfunctory and inexpressive, something cruelly revealed by her leaden singing of Cherubino's 'Voi che sapete' and it is not surprising that rumour has it that she was unable to read music. Of course, the coloratura is extraordinary, but on record at least a display of energy is just not enough to make one want to listen again. Her 'Caro nome' from *Rigoletto* is jerkily articulated and the accelerations of tempo are ridiculously exaggerated, while the showpieces like La Sonnambula's 'Ah! non giunge' seem to me little more than the result of switching on that 'perfect mechanical toy'. And compared with Melba, another singer who can sound mechanical, there is neither the dazzling light in the timbre nor the warmth and evenness in the middle of the voice.

Far more *simpatico* is the singing of her 'successor', Amelita Galli-Curci (1882–1963), a coloratura soprano of much less power and firmness, but an unfailing simple charm, gentler in manner than Tetrazzini and possessed with what one imagines to be something of Patti's gift for making her art sound spontaneous. Galli-Curci is an easy singer to like: she sounds such an innocent little thing Uncle Matthew in Nancy Mitford's novel *The Pursuit of Love* could not get enough of her and woke the rest of his household up at five o'clock every morning with her dulcet tones emanating from recor invariably played at the wrong speed.

The fact that Galli-Curci's singing could penetrate the mu depths of upper-class English philistinism is tribute indeed, then few prima donnas have lent themselves so well to cl marketing. The voice was soft-grained enough to record th clearly and warmly, and she was assiduously exploited the recording companies. She had married into the Italian n lity. Her long, languid face and olive colouring was the stuff every chocolate-box Renaissance painting. An aura of romance as not hard to fabricate round her life and circumstances, once e had reached an initial point from which she could be exposed to the public.

That point was Chicago in 1916: before this her career had followed a standard pattern. Born in Milan into a musical home, she had begun as a pianist, but was encouraged by Mascagni to develop her voice. For ten-odd years she sang the 'old' repertory on the 'Latin' circuit, without making much of a stir. Her luck changed after the sinking of the *Lusitania*, when she was stranded in South America, with the Atlantic unsafe for the return passage to Europe. The obvious alternative was to go north, especially as with European sources effectively cut off, opera houses in America would be seeking out fresh blood. Gatti-Casazza at the Met turned her down because she sang flat, while in Chicago, the conductor Campanini (Tetrazzini's brother-in-law) unenthusiastically offered her two trial performances. Only at the dress rehearsal of *Rigoletto* did he realize her potential. She was immediately booked for the rest of the season at twice the fee for which she had originally signed, and after that the star-making machine took over. The début was sensational; every imaginable sort of offer followed. Her manager Charles Wagner mapped out the tactics:

> We had at least one condition greatly in our favour. The public just about to plunge into a frightening and horrible war was in the mood for a new thrill that would give them pleasure and take their minds from this tragic prospect . . . Dressing her in old-fashioned gowns added considerably to her early popularity. The Mona Lisa story was well-timed[1]—appearing just when the famous masterpiece had been stolen and was on all the front-pages. Then when a dear old lady in Columbus, Ohio, who had heard Jenny Lind, told me how much Galli-Curci reminded her of the Swedish Nightingale, I was inspired to give out the story of that celebrated singer of the past century. Papers were delighted to print it and the public gobbled it up.

one of this would have worked had the lady herself not delivered basic commodity. Henderson, a critic notoriously hard to satisfy, at first convinced that she did, calling hers 'a well-equalized vo', with a fine welding of registers . . . lending itself readily to

[1] Charles Wagner liked to claim that Galli-Curci had a strong facial resemblance to the subject of Leonardo's painting.

gradations of power, which its owner employs with the most delicate musical skill and admirable taste'.

A great majority of her records confirm this—the voice is physically a better balanced instrument than Tetrazzini's, and of a colour perfectly appropriate to the either sparkling or miserable heroines in which she specialized—Amina, Norina in *Don Pasquale*, Lucia, Rosina, Dinorah, etc. On the other hand, Galli-Curci never communicates any particular shade of meaning or any sense of drama, nor can she match Tetrazzini's sheer razzamatazz. She trips happily through the florid arias and wistfully spins out the ballads: more than this one must not ask.

After 1916 Galli-Curci's opera career was surprisingly circumscribed. She very rarely sang on stage outside the Chicago or Met companies, and instead spent an extraordinary amount of time in the recording studio, where she was more of a perfectionist than most of her contemporaries. When her charms as a 'live' performer began to fade—and fade they very speedily did—her records continued to sustain her reputation. The problems began in the mid 1920s, when she discovered that, as her ludicrous biographer puts it, 'the path of art is never entirely one of roses. Wasps in human form attack the flowers.' Critics of her performances had first become bored with her obvious limitations and then fastened on to her painful tendency to sing off the note. One of her most decisive humiliations was her first London concert in 1924, given to an Albert Hall packed with an audience keenly anticipating the Galli-Curci of the records. One of those most disappointed was Nancy Mitford's Uncle Matthew, whose 'disillusionment caused by her appearance was so great that the records remained ever after silent, and were replaced by the deepest bass voices that money could buy . . . These were, on the whole, welcomed by the family, as rather less piercing at early dawn.'

In 1929 she announced that she was giving up opera altogether, because of its 'essential absurdities' and henceforth would concentrate on world concert tours. By this time the flatness in her singing had become persistent and her control was generally in decline. Finally, a throat specialist risked operating on a goitre which had grown to the grotesque dimensions of four and a half by two inches. It was duly removed, and in 1936, presumably no longer inhibited by absurdity, she braved a return to Chicago and opera, in the undemanding role of Mimi in *La Bohème*. The trouble, however, must have lain deeper than her throat, because this too proved a complete failure and she was forced to move into teaching and thence into an idyllically happy Californian retirement, as memorably commemorated by her biographer C. F. Lemassena, whose silly and pretentious book, in which each chapter is named after a phase in an inexorable spiritual cycle, as though its subject was some sort of female Buddha, does disservice to a prima donna whose art was not a pretentious thing:

> Evenings were devoted to music, art, books, and conversation appertaining to some suggested mental trend, which, no matter whither it led, the hostess . . . could meet and carry on with erudite assurance, for she was a reader and a thinker, a scholar and a sage . . . Nothing gave her more delight than to scramble with a flock of gladsome children . . . they would inspect the cows and chicks and wind up in the dairy to sip sweet cream from earthen jugs, then lick their coated fingers clean mid laughter and enraptured merriment . . . No stray dog or cat or bird applied in vain at her open door for succour . . .

All the elevation of Galli-Curci's fragile accomplishment was substantially the work not of the press, so much as the technology of recording and broadcasting, and the fact that by the 1920s gramophones and wirelesses were no longer luxury items. Girls of that time, the Mitfords included, grew up with the processed voice of Galli-Curci, and if they wanted to sing, they wanted to sing like her. It would not be an exaggeration to say that Galli-Curci formed a new style of prima donna. In the opera house, her most distinguished successors were probably Toti dal Monte and Lily Pons, her most ill-fated imitator Marion Talley;[1] but her influence spread deep into the new entertainment media, and it was in the even more modest talents of such singing movie stars as Miliza Korjus, Deanna Durbin, and Jeanette MacDonald that the style and tone of voice lived on. Coloratura did not, as is often said, die out, only to be revived by Maria Callas: its fate was not temporary death, but temporary emasculation. It became decorative, dainty, and harmless, associated with a bodiless femininity as sexually inert as the Hays Censorship Code could wish. Had the cinema and wireless

---

1 See p. 197.

public been listening to Ponselle as Norma or Donna Anna, the received image might have been different.

Opposite this new brand of 'old-fashioned' prima donna was what for convenience we shall call the '*verismo*' prima donna, specializing in the post-*Cavalleria Rusticana* repertory of the modern Italian school. The single greatest influence on the formation of this type was the actress Eleonora Duse, whose performances in the new dramas of social realism had a power and emotional range which shattered theatrical convention and stereotype. We have already seen how deeply Emma Calvé was affected by Duse, but the first true *verismo* prima donna was Gemma Bellincioni (1864–1950), the first Santuzza in *Cavalleria Rusticana* and a Violetta whose originality and force were much admired by the elderly Verdi. Puccini's favoured sopranos—Cesira Ferrani (the first Manon Lescaut and Mimi), Rosina Storchio (the first Butterfly), and Hariclea Darclée (the first Tosca)—are other historically significant names, but the run of *verismo* prima donnas who survive on record sound excruciatingly over-blown. John Steane has listened to most of them and his verdict is clear-cut:

> If a well-produced voice should be a well-equalised one, without a sharp break between registers; if it should be steady, without wobble or obtrusive flutter-vibrato; if it should not be shrill at the top and white in the lower half of the range: then there was hardly a well-produced voice among them. If a good stylist should phrase broadly, keep a smooth line, show a respect for the score by following its instructions (and these seem to be not unreasonable conditions): then there was hardly a good stylist either.

The fallacy upon which these prima donnas operated was that authentic involvement in their roles precluded attention to these basic facts of singing life. Sobbing, screaming, gasping, rasping became more important to them and their audiences than accurate pitch and sustained breath control. The excitement of opera was no longer essentially musical: music simply intensified and exacerbated the histrionics, as the climaxes of *Tosca*, for example, all too plainly show.

Probably the best and certainly the most celebrated of the *verismo* prima donnas was the enigmatic Claudia Muzio. Charles Jahant remembers her acting as a mannered display of *grand guignol*, yet as a singer she expresses a purer form of tragedy. Like so many others of her generation, she cultivated the brown and purple colouring of her voice to excess, and her technique shows many real shortcomings when compared to that of a Melba or Calvé: but Muzio always *sang*, and never resorted to mere noise-making. In Lanfranco Rasponi's book of interviews with prima donnas, it is Muzio who wins the most extravagant tributes. Mafalda Favero went backstage after a performance and spontaneously dropped to her knees in front of her; on Eva Turner she made 'the most unforgettable impression of all'. Others spoke of 'the divine Muzio', 'Muzio, my idol', 'a case apart, you cannot classify her', or 'the only word to describe Muzio is sublime'. The ability she had to move her audiences seems to have been unique, and it is Muzio on whom the 'Duse of Song' label has most fairly stuck.

Her life seems to have been almost entirely unhappy—a fact which her voice, 'made of tears and sighs and restrained inner fire', as the tenor Giacomo Lauri-Volpi described it, does not allow one to forget. She was born illegitimate in 1889 as Claudina Versati, although her parents later married. Her mother was a chorus singer, her father a stage director at the Met and Covent Garden. An education at convents in Tottenham and Hammersmith bequeathed her the beautiful unaccented English audible on some of her song recordings, and Eva Turner remembers having a very English tea with her in Chicago years later at which she was plied with questions about those areas of London.

In 1906 she went back to Italy to study voice and made her début as Gilda in *Rigoletto* in Messina in 1910. After some success in Turin and La Scala, she returned to Covent Garden in 1914, singing among other roles Tosca and Mimi, opposite Caruso. Then in 1916 she was engaged by the Met to replace the indisposed Bori and the incarcerated Destinn. She stayed there until 1922 and created the role of the bargee's wife Giorgetta in Puccini's *Il Tabarro*, as well as introducing Tatyana in *Eugene Onegin* and Maddalena in *Andrea Chénier* to the house. Like Farrar, she was pushed out of New York by the arrival of the all-vanquishing Jeritza, and her career was thereafter concentrated in Chicago, Buenos Aires, and Rome. Her repertory was mostly later Verdi, Puccini, and *verismo*, but in South America she also sang the Marschallin in *Rosenkavalier*, Elsa in *Lohengrin*, and even Norma. In 1932 she opened the War Memorial Opera House in San Francisco as

Tosca; in 1934 she created the title-role in Refice's briefly sensational 'mystical' opera *Cecilia* and returned to the Met. In 1936 she died in a hotel in Rome.

This is an impressive catalogue of achievement. There were no crises, vocal or otherwise, no lapses of taste or disastrous errors of judgement, no publicity stunts. The critics were almost invariably favourable, the public appreciative: Muzio's problems began outside the opera house. She was known to be acutely self-conscious about her height (five foot nine or ten inches), despite a face of great beauty and a dress sense and deportment to match. Perhaps her apparently pathological shyness was exacerbated by her illegitimacy; perhaps it was just the hauteur which prima donnas commonly use as a self-protective wall. Whatever its cause, Muzio was not bubbling with fun. The jokiness and camaraderie around Caruso infuriated her: 'She came to the theatre, rehearsed, sang and left, exchanging barely a few sentences with fellow-singers, who remember her as a soprano "who never said anything", "who acted as if we were all devils".' Frida Leider shared a dressing-room with her in Chicago:

> Her Italian maid used to spend entire mornings arranging her costumes. When Claudia appeared for rehearsal, her maid would help her to change, for she had a kind of rehearsal uniform which consisted of a heavy black silk dress, a black jacket trimmed with ermine, and a little hat to match. Always the *grande dame*, she would stride majestically across the stage to the prompter's box, clasp her gloved hands, and simply mark her way through her entire role without moving an inch.

She shared her heyday in Chicago with Mary Garden, but more of a contrast cannot be imagined. Garden was a hard-boiled exotic who courted and flirted with publicity; no one could make anything of Muzio. In his memoir of the city in the 1920s Arthur Meeker claims that 'people who knew her painted a gruesome picture of rooms from which all daylight was excluded, full of jabbering relatives and cooking spaghetti, in the midst of which Claudia, wearing a gorgeous *robe de chambre*, with her hair down her back, lay prone and weeping over the machinations of her rivals, sentimental or professional.'

The key to it all seems to lie in her relationship with her mother. After her adored father had died, wrote Mary Jane Matz, 'her strange silent mother became her exclusive companion . . . fanatically religious, suspicious, possessive, she kept Muzio apart from those of her father's cronies whom the singer had known. The two women gradually became virtual recluses.' On tour in South America, Muzio and her mother 'sat in the corner of the hotel dining-room farthest from the rest of the company "never speaking, never even nodding to the rest of us".' She lived 'almost as the older woman's slave', without any other friend or confidante. Throughout all this, she was deceiving her mother with a series of lovers, and here the story becomes depressingly familiar. One of them, according to Leider, was an impresario who absconded with a lot of her money; then in 1929, after her mother's death, she married a man seventeen years younger than herself, with the predictable result. The cause of her death at the age of forty-seven has been variously reported as suicide, nephritis, cancer, tuberculosis, Bright's disease, or a heart condition.

Shortly before, she had embarked on her last recordings, an event also surrounded with various pathetic tales. Out of the sessions came a record of 'Addio del passato' from the last act of *Traviata* which immediately became a classic. Like all classics, it has suffered some knocks from latter-day critics, but it stands up to them. Everything about it illustrates the best of the *verismo* style. Muzio sang the role frequently (including in a modern-dress production in Rome in 1928), but the overwhelming impression the record gives is of emotional immediacy. There is a superb command of *parlando* effects: this Violetta reads the letter from Germont like a sick woman who has been turning the words over in her mind obsessively for days. Her cry of 'E tardi!' ('It is too late') is heavy with fate. In the aria itself Muzio exploits the use of short breaths—not sobs, so much as an effortful intake of air—until the memory of 'l'amor di Alfredo' brings out a full passionate grief for what has been lost. A constant seesaw between *crescendo* and *diminuendo*, within both single notes and full phrases, further intensifies the feverishness. At the end the little spasms of breath return inexorably, culminating in a perfectly pitched scream of agony, cut sharply off into silence. The singing is graphically descriptive of Violetta's mental and physical state (whether Muzio herself was also dying of consumption is another question) in a manner that a Violetta of the older school, like Melba, would have thought horribly vulgar.

An earlier series of recordings made in 1917–18 shows Muzio's

**44.** Amelita Galli-Curci.

**42.** *above left* The enigmatic Claudia Muzio as Berthe in Meyerbeer's *Le Prophète*, photographed by Mishkin. **43.** *top right* Luisa Tetrazzini with her third husband. One of the more pitiful prima donna marriages, it ended in the law courts, with Tetrazzini suing for extortion. **45.** *above* Maria Callas as Norma, Catania, 1951. This rare photograph provides interesting evidence that Callas was not, as is often assumed, chronically fat throughout the early years of her career.

**46.** One of the finest of all musical intellects at work on her score during a recording session: Elisabeth Schwarzkopf in 1962.
**47.** *left* Janet Baker as Penelope in the famous Glyndebourne production of Monteverdi's *Il Ritorno d'Ulisse.*

voice fresher in tone and freer in movement, the melancholy less pervasive than in the 1934–5 series. Some of her attempts at Verdi's most heroic arias may lack the last degree of power and expansiveness; her coloratura is sketchy; but in the music of Boito, Catalani, Puccini, Giordano, and their fellows, she is unforgettable and unsurpassed. All their music's temptations to mawkishness and morbidity is cast out by her burning light of conviction. The pathos in Muzio's art remains quiet and withdrawn, where others fling their self-respect to the gallery. Her sense of a phrase's gravity is unfailing, and she shares with the greatest singers the gift of surprising the listener by turning a single word or note into something unexpectedly telling. A final little surprise—Garbo smiles and Muzio laughs!—is her pert and cheerful rendition of a ditty by Delibes, 'Good morning, Sue', which also exemplifies the purity of her English.

Only by bearing in mind this major division between the 'Galli-Curci coloratura' and the 'Muzio *verismo*' sopranos can we properly appreciate the revolution in the years after the Second World War which went under the banner of Maria Callas (1923–77). So much journalistic copy has been expended on this singer (of prima donnas only Malibran provoked such a degree of prurient international interest) that history has become distorted. For many people, the idea of the prima donna still begins and ends with Callas. This is absurd. Callas was indeed a revolutionary, but not a revolutionary without a tradition to inherit or a band of comrades. And like many of the most successful revolutionaries, she was in many ways a restorer rather than an iconoclast.

The first important fact about Callas is that her principal teacher was Elvira de Hidalgo, a light coloratura soprano of the Galli-Curci type who had been popular on the 'Latin' circuit between about 1910 and 1925. Callas's natural vocal colour, as a Hellenophile friend of mine pointed out, can be heard on any Greek island when the peasant women start shouting at each other. Peremptory, black, strident but *vibrato*-less, it is a sound of tragic absolutes, quite different from the dark tints of Italian *morbidezza*, let alone the sweet warblings of a Galli-Curci. Normally a voice of Callas's type would have been groomed for Tosca, Gioconda, and a round of *verismo* heroines, but de Hidalgo seems to have been concerned with brightening and colouring her timbre and with passing on the discipline of old-fashioned flexibility. She thus left her pupil in the odd position of having a great dramatic voice trained to sing little-girl roles like de Hidalgo's own favourites, Rosina, Lucia, and Gilda. Callas did go on to sing those roles, but she gave them a radically new complexion; and beyond them she brought back more grandly scaled figures such as Donizetti's Anna Bolena and Cherubini's Medea.

In the immediate post-war period, however, when her career began in Italy, Callas sang in the accepted heavy dramatic repertory, parts such as Turandot, Gioconda, and Isolde, none of which exploited the facility de Hidalgo had given her. It was only when she met the great Italian conductor, Tullio Serafin, that her voice found its destiny. At the end of 1948 she sang her first Normas under his direction, and a few weeks later he inspired her to the unprecedented, almost lunatic feat of singing Brünnhilde in *Die Walküre* and Elvira in Bellini's *I Puritani* within days of each other. Serafin had a profound understanding of the great Italian tradition represented by the art of Pasta, Malibran, and Grisi, and the music Bellini and Donizetti had provided for them. It was above all he who led what became known as the '*bel canto* revival', meaning the revival of the *dramatic* potential of coloratura singing, as opposed to its evergreen 'nightingale' aspect. This revival started long before Callas. In the 1920s and 1930s many dramatic sopranos in Italy sang *Norma*, and some of the obscurer Donizetti and Rossini operas were also heard again after fifty or more years. In 1935, for instance, the centenary of Bellini's death, Gina Cigna sang his *La Straniera* at La Scala; in 1933 Vittorio Gui had conducted *I Puritani* and Donizetti's *Lucrezia Borgia* at Florence's Maggio Musicale. Supervia was singing superbly brazen Rossini coloratura from the mid 1920s all over Europe; there was also Ponselle, with whom Serafin had worked closely on *Norma* and Spontini's *La Vestale*. The war checked the impetus of the revival, but even without Callas it would surely have continued to gain ground in the 1950s. Yet Callas did provide a magic ingredient missing in the equipment of the fiery but technically ill-prepared sopranos of the previous generation— a true coloratura—and it was Serafin who appreciated the possibilities this presented. He taught her authority of phrasing and attack, the value of a pause, and the way to shape a recitative. In her own words, he 'showed me that there was a reason for everything, that even *fioriture* and trills ... have a reason [*sic*] in the composer's mind, that they are the expression of the *stato d'animo* of the character . . . He taught me exactly the depth of music . . . I really drank all I could from that man.'

Sadly, Serafin was on bad terms with the La Scala management and thus never conducted Callas in the opera house which offered her the highest standards of production and musical preparation, when her art was at its peak. Their partnership was however substantially preserved on record, thanks to the good sense of EMI's producer Walter Legge, one of Callas's most cogent critics and admirers.

Callas's La Scala years have become the core of her legend, but her triumphs there were not easily won and the stories of her skirmishes are well known. Every performance was a battle with hostile factions in the audience and backstage intrigue, doubtless exacerbated by the tough business negotiations of her husband and manager Giovanni Battista Meneghini, and her own highly explosive temperament. Nevertheless, she was surrounded there by colleagues whose artistic ideals were as high as hers and whom Callas could trust. She was not a prima donna who simply wanted to be attractively framed or delicately coddled. She wanted to work, and the capacity to work was intrinsic to her genius. 'I do not believe with Descartes: "I think, therefore I am,"' she said. 'With me, it is: "I work, therefore I am."' La Scala gave her the tools— the innovative repertory, the extensive rehearsals, conductors like Karajan, Bernstein, Giulini, producers like Visconti and Wallmann, baritones of the calibre of Gobbi, mezzos such as Stignani and Simionato, one of her closest friends, and the best of the Italian tenors.

One of Callas's major problems at La Scala was Renata Tebaldi (born 1922). Whatever their private feelings for each other and whatever the justice in their feud, there is no doubt that as singers Callas and Tebaldi were chalk and cheese to the public, and that the fierce admirer of one was likely to be antipathetic to the other. Callas was in the vanguard of a revolution, while Tebaldi stood tranquilly for what had now become the 'classical' *verismo* style, her voice as soft-grained and plangent as Muzio's, with whom she was frequently compared. Their repertories did not overlap to any great extent and Tebaldi had no pretensions to coloratura, although it is interesting to note that early in her career she too sang in revivals of rare Spontini, Rossini, and Handel operas. Callas never sang

Puccini with the ravishing intimacy and fluidity that Tebaldi could give to such arias as 'Signore, ascolta' from *Turandot* or 'Senza mamma' from *Suor Angelica*, and Tebaldi had little of Callas's fire and imagination in their mutual Verdi roles. It was mostly a matter of taste, and which singer one heard first; to anyone accustomed to Tebaldi's smoothness and steadiness, Callas would have sounded shockingly self-assertive, and Tebaldi was established at La Scala before Callas 'arrived' in 1950, replacing Tebaldi in *Aida* after she had fallen ill.

Professionally, a *modus vivendi* was reached. Tebaldi recorded for Decca, Callas for EMI–Angel; Tebaldi left La Scala in 1954 and sang at the Met for almost twenty years. Callas sang only a handful of performances at the Met, but stayed on at La Scala and sang regularly at Covent Garden, well out of Tebaldi's way. But as with the Faustina and Cuzzoni incident over two hundred years earlier, the press exploited the whole business *ad nauseam*, casting the two roles in starkest black and white. Tebaldi smiled sweetly ('She has dimples of iron,' remarked Rudolf Bing) and was presented as a homely body who consulted Cardinal Spellman on the advisability of taking the veil after her mother died in 1957; Callas snarled at the cameras and was reported in *Time* as having told her mother to 'jump out of the window' if she could not earn enough to support herself.

Tebaldi herself had other problems apart from Callas. She was always a stiff actress, physically inhibited by a childhood bout of polio. She needed to pray for her top Cs, and her otherwise beautiful timbre could become harsh under pressure. In 1963 she had a fiasco at the Met as Adriana Lecouvreur and retired for a year to retrain her voice, without ever quite recovering its earlier purity. Nothing, however, about her decline was anything but graceful, whereas Callas's failure—if that is the right word—was spectacular and controversial, her every vocal utterance mercilessly scrutinized.

None of the offered explanations for this are completely satisfactory, since great voices are not rational quantities. The weight-loss idea, for example, is absurd: muscular control, not bulk, is the key to healthy vocal production. Some of the causes for the failure are inherent in the fact that Callas had been schooled to push her voice beyond its natural limitations. John Ardoin, who knows Callas's art as well as anyone, writes in his book *The Callas Legacy* that 'There is no doubt that [she] demanded more from her voice than it could comfortably deliver. Yet a parallel conclusion is equally clear: had she put herself in less peril, had she taken fewer chances or remained within safer limits, she would never have been Callas.' He also notes from the recorded evidence that as early as 1950, she could be squally on top notes, heavy in style, uneven, over-forceful, and unable to sustain a *pianissimo*, but that as late as 1964 she could still be 'impressively secure'. Much of her difficulty stemmed from her psychology: what Walter Legge referred to as her 'superhuman inferiority complex' and her obsessive quest for self-improvement which must have started in her sad childhood efforts to win her mother's love. Something of this, as well as the cruel pace at which she was being worked,[1] is revealed by a letter she wrote from London to a close friend in New York early in 1957:

Dear Leo, It's been such a long time since I heard from you—Don't you love me any more? Some other soprano has taken your interest?

Last time I passed from New York—I didn't have time to see you and couldn't trace you even by telephone.

Everything since Chicago [where she had given a concert a few weeks earlier] has gone perfectly well—it's as though since the allergy I had in New York has cured me of something [*sic*] and I'm singing as I never did. Thank God!

My Norma here the other day [at Covent Garden] would have been the pride of all my admirers first of all you dear Leo! I'm so happy! They all say I've never done a performance like that before—tomorrow is my second and last. After that I'm recording the 'Barber' until the 14th and then on to the Scala for the 'Sonnambula' on the 23rd of February—on the 12th of April we have the 'Anna Bolena', just God [her début in the role], and then 'Iphigenie en Tauride', then Vienna with 'Traviata' on the 4th of July. On the 24th June opening of the Radio season with Lucia broadcast. And then around the first of July, Cologne, Germany, always with the Scala—Then some recordings of Turandot and Manon of Puccini, some rest and then Edinburgo with

1 How many of the performances listed here actually materialized may be checked in John Ardoin and Gerald Fitzgerald's authoritative *Callas* (1974).

'Sonnambula' [the series of performances from which she made one of her most notorious walk-outs]—San Francisco with Macbeth-Lucia [her failure to appear here led to her being sued], Scala opening with 'Moses' of Rossini and then 'Pirata' of Bellini and then finally New York—if I'm still alive by then. So dear Leo, please write all your news; and don't forget your favourite singer so quickly. Write about the 'Traviata' at the Met [which she was scheduled to sing in 1958]—also about the costume . . .

Perhaps the first decisive catastrophe was the infamous *Norma*, performed before the Italian President and other dignitaries in Rome in January 1958, when Callas abandoned the performance after a disastrous first act during which she had been heckled for her efforts to sing over bronchitis and tracheitis. The adverse publicity Callas received over this affair was savage enough to finish her career in Italy, since no opera house could afford the astronomically high insurance premium put on the possibility of her cancellation, quite apart from the bad feeling created. Later that year Bing dismissed her from the Met, after disagreements over repertory. Then in 1959 she left Meneghini, a dull husband who valued her artistic well-being, for Onassis, an exciting lover whose interest in her singing extended only as far as the glamour and status she had incurred. She was now in a position to fulfil what Zeffirelli described as her 'stupid ambition of becoming a great lady of café society', and by 1960 she was in semi-retirement: a very few stage appearances and occasional recordings or concerts made up her professional life for the next four years. This retreat was partly the effect of a failure of confidence too: Callas did not take criticism lightly. 'My biggest mistake,' she said, 'was trying to intellectualize my voice . . . the press was writing so frequently that I had lost my voice, I got to the point of believing it myself . . . I got complexes for the first time and lost my audacity.' With the encouragement of the record producer Michel Glotz, she managed a triumphant return to the stage in 1964–5 for *Tosca* and *Norma*, her tone harder and her control diminished, but her unique authority and intelligence still blazing. Yet she was again unable to sustain the pressure she put on herself, and the impetus fell away.

In an interview given to *Life* in October 1964, she brightly proclaimed, 'Now at last I am a happy normal woman of my age, even though I have to say that life for me really began at forty.' The truth was that she was about to plummet into a period of barren misery, without marriage to Onassis or a resuscitated career. At the end of the 1960s, she began a protracted search for something to fill the hiatus. Apart from a ceaseless flood of rumours and abortive announcements, there was a film of *Medea*, directed by Pasolini, vastly underrated but obviously not the beginning of a solution; a misguided attempt to become an opera producer: and negotiations over the possibility of becoming Artistic Director at the Met. From the historian's point of view, the most interesting of all these enterprises was the series of master classes that she gave at the Juilliard School in 1971-2, from which a set of tapes was made. Her manner as a teacher emerges as scrupulous, polite, and patient, and she showed an almost comic concern for the health of her students, but the actual teaching had none of the engagement, energy, and precision that Schwarzkopf, for example, infallibly provides at similar functions. The points Callas made were very largely general interpretive ones, often with reference to Serafin, and assertions of basic principles: 'feel what you're singing', 'lean on the words', 'legato legato, legato!' were continual insistences. As she must have realized, the subtleties of her art were not easily communicated or even articulated.

All the while she was teaching, she was herself back at rehearsal with a *répétiteur* and John Ardoin is surely justified in thinking that the master classes 'were simultaneously serving a greater and somewhat ulterior purpose—the rebuilding of Callas's confidence before an audience'. Buttressed by the ageing tenor Giuseppe di Stefano, she made her return to public singing in a world concert tour. To those who had heard her in her prime, this proved a terrible disappointment, but to a new generation—of which I was one—it was something. In November 1973, she returned to her 'caro public di London', as she addressed us, and the city which had given her the most steady and sympathetic support. The hope that the disembodied voice which had haunted my discovery of Italian opera on records would be made flesh before me was not realized, but what I heard was more than the rattling of bones. There was still a lot of volume—she had no difficulty in projecting through the difficult acoustics of the Festival Hall; the unmistakable grainy tone of the middle of the voice, more resonant with emotion than anything I have ever heard in music, was still alive; and above all, there was that ability to arch a phrase in such a way that its absolute rightness of expressive shape, as clear and pure as the line of a suspension bridge, was revealed. It was not, unfortunately, possible to ignore the shaky intonation, colourless *mezza voce*, and painfully raw top notes that ravaged her singing, but there was yet another dimension to Callas which seized one's attention. She involved her whole body in the dramatic import of the music and instinctively acted out its meaning. I felt this most in the duet from *Cavalleria Rusticana* as a desperate Santuzza, fighting back against the boorish Turiddu, clenching her fists on his chest, turning from him with scorn, watching him with hawk-eyed jealousy, emerged from Callas's elegant façade.

When the tour finished Callas's morale was no higher. 'Anything to survive, my dear. At my stage of the game, anything to survive,' she had told John Ardoin in 1968, and that was still the position in 1974. Everyone tried to help: Zeffirelli for instance, suggested *L'Incoronazione di Poppea* (and how magnificently Callas would have sung Monteverdi), while Covent Garden offered her a *Cavalleria Rusticana* with Domingo. When this latter plan fell through in 1976, she asked Covent Garden to send her a *répétiteur*, as she wanted to work towards a concert there. Jeffrey Tate was duly sent to her Paris apartment and found her even more nervous than he was. In rehearsal she proved pathetically inhibited, constantly muttering remarks like 'I don't think I can do this . . . Is this possible? . . . I am frightened.' A few months after the petering-out of this scheme, she died at the age of fifty-three in circumstances of some ambiguity. Meneghini for one suspected that she killed herself, and Jeffrey Tate's verdict is even bleaker: 'I think eventually she died of neglect. She just neglected herself as a person. She abandoned her life.'

As a victim of the images and prejudices that hedge a prima donna, Callas recalls none of her predecessors so much as Mrs Tofts, with whom this history began. Callas's life had an even harsher nemesis than that of the demented Mrs Tofts who retreated to her Venetian garden, and none of the popular treatments of the story detract from the waste and pain involved in either her professional collapse or her emotional difficulties. But it is important not to romanticize Callas. She was a martyr rather than a saint, and was fuelled by an overweening morality—'I am Victorian,' she told an interviewer—of discipline and self-restraint. Every failure was taken hard; she alone was responsible for her shortcomings. All this made her cold, withdrawn, and quintessentially egocentric.

One searches her biography in vain for any instances of spontaneous generosity or kindness. Instead one finds the persistent insecurity of the unloved child, the anxiety to find people she could depend upon, and a proud automatic mistrust of anyone not completely dedicated to her. 'We are all vulnerable,' she told *Life* in 1964. 'I am extremely so and have naturally tried not to show it for my own self-preservation. My shyness and insecurity have often made me seem arrogant—it's a form of self-protection for timid people.' Other prima donnas would not have defended themselves thus. A Melba or a Mary Garden were blessed with a canny Scots self-awareness and never lost sight of their own value, but Callas, as Montague Halbrecht put it, 'carried within her a sense of her unworthiness, almost ugliness'.

None of this made Callas lovable. Walter Legge judged her on occasion as 'vengeful, vindictive, and malicious', and when provoked the younger Callas was not afraid of physical violence. Meneghini tells the story of her reaction in 1951 to the administrator of the opera house in Rio when he told her that she had given a 'lousy' performance and was being replaced. 'On his desk was a large bronze inkstand and paper holder. It weighed over twenty pounds. Maria picked it up and, holding it in the air, said, "Repeat what you just said, if you have the nerve, and I'll smash your skull".' When the administrator threatened to have her arrested, she threw herself at him 'striking him in the stomach with her knee. It could have been a fatal blow. Maria at that time weighed more than two hundred pounds, was twenty-eight years old, and had the power of a young bull.' Her victim keeled over, and Meneghini rushed Callas back to their hotel: 'Maria, however, was now very calm. She walked about the room humming, totally pleased with what she had done. "Don't you think you overdid it?" I asked. "I only regret not having broken his head," she said with a smile.'

At the end of her life, an unremitting fatalism set in. 'Her view of the world was totally depressing,' said Jeffrey Tate. 'I had the terrible feeling that here was a woman who had gone beyond the edge of possibility.' The worst had indeed happened. Life did turn against her and she bore an immense burden of defeat. If one thinks back to the retirement of her great sister-in-art, Pasta, contentedly pottering about with her turkeys wearing an old coat, the cruelty of Callas's lot becomes all the more poignant.

Throughout her singing, as throughout her life, the tone of

tragedy sounds deeper and truer than any other. To wistful lyricism (her *Sonnambula* is too earnest) or tearful melancholy (for which we listen to Muzio), let alone comedy, she was less well suited. To misquote Dorothy Parker, she ran the whole gamut of the emotions from A to about S: inevitably, there were moods and shades that eluded her. John Steane, yet again, best expresses in what lay Callas's extraordinary stamp: 'She will seize the moment, say, of noble or tragic decision, summoning all the dramatic force of what has gone before, evoking our knowledge of what the consequences are to be, and focusing precisely upon the moment on which all depends.' Anger, grief, contempt, passion, madness, despair, and isolation were her points of emotional reference.

Next one must emphasize the musicality which she developed under Serafin's tutelage and which remained even when a rich, firm tone had deserted her. She always found the proportion, scale, and depth of phrase required for any musical episode, be it recitative, arioso, or pure melody, and her sense of a climax was infallible. The way she sustains and colours the span of Norma's 'Casta Diva' *scena* is an egregious instance of this. The same gift for timing clearly applied to her acting as well. Connoisseurs will tell you that the film made of Act II of *Tosca* shows but the shadow of its impact—yet how much remains! This Tosca is not just an outraged prima donna, but a tough and direct woman trapped in a situation that makes her panic. There is no strutting or false dignity, rather a last-ditch effort to keep control. She gulps down the wine for quick dutch courage, and then stands mesmerized by the sight of the knife, putting the glass down slowly as the thought of murder passes inexorably into her mind. Only at the last second does the animal release itself, the tension held in her hand clasped over the top of the glass. At the end of the scene she weeps with nervous exhaustion as she lurches blindly round the chamber,[1] grabbing at her stole, repelled at touching a dead body, unable to believe what she has just done, desperate not to forget anything vital or leave incriminating evidence. The complexity of movement and the telling use of details and props, all matched to the musical cues, proves how extensive the thought and rehearsal behind this explosion was, how carefully Callas and her collaborators Gobbi and

---

1 How she managed at all with her chronic myopia and without contact lenses is one of the minor mysteries of operatic history.

Zeffirelli had worked out the pace and shape it should follow.

Callas's art has been deeply influential on a whole generation of dramatic sopranos who have sought to imitate that very feeling for pace and shape, that intensity and command of the stage which the *Tosca* film allows us to glimpse. Just as Pasta was followed by the aptly-named Teresa Parodi,[1] so Callas has been followed by Elena Souliotis, Grace Bumbry, and Sylvia Sass, all at times exciting prima donnas, but all in varying degrees liable to lapse into what have become the 'Callas clichés' of scornful glances, rasping chest-notes, etc. Others have built on her example more creatively, and at this point it is important to repeat that Callas is not, as it were, the first and last note in the '*bel canto* revival'. In the period preceding her emergence, Ponselle and Supervia, to name but two, had sung what by any standards were superlative accounts of parts of the early nineteenth-century Italian repertory; and in the 1960s the remarkable work of Callas, Serafin, and her colleagues in revaluing the operas of Donizetti and Bellini in particular would be carried even further by singers whose techniques were in some respects superior to Callas's.

The name which comes most immediately to mind in this respect is that of the Australian Joan Sutherland (born 1926). Her ample and inexhaustibly brilliant top voice recalls that of Tetrazzini, although Sutherland has an altogether fuller middle range and sounder musicianship. Comparisons apart, Sutherland has made her own distinctive mark on operatic history, and whatever her shortcomings as an interpreter, she has had a long and distinguished career, steadily 'at the top' for as long as Patti or her compatriot Melba.

The history of Sutherland's voice and its development is an interesting and exemplary one, illustrating the importance of physiological endowment and the effects of teaching. Sutherland was blessed with a broad face, strong jaw, powerful vocal cords, and strapping physique—all of which gave her the muscular foundation for resonance, flexibility, breath control, and sheer endurance. From childhood, she also suffered from a variety of potentially

---

1 Of whom Chorley wrote: She 'presented a singular imitation of Madame Pasta's voice out of tune . . . all the more singular because she was obviously no mocking-bird, bent to mimic the song of somebody else, but a sincere and careful artist'.

crippling ailments: sinus trouble, bad teeth, back pain, and poor circulation have all been enemies against which she fought long tactical battles in the war to perfect her technique.

Sutherland's apprenticeship began with her mother, from whom she learnt by imitation. Muriel Sutherland had studied with a Marchesi pupil, and by all accounts had a superb mezzo-soprano voice 'as powerful as Stignani's', which she never used professionally, choosing instead the roles of wife and mother (how many great voices must have been hidden thus!). Joan grew up in Sydney as a mezzo and shorthand typist, chronically self-conscious about her height and ungainly deportment but aware that she had a gift. Others were aware of it too, and a doctor had wisely refused to remove her troublesome tonsils in case her vocal cords were damaged in the process. At the age of nineteen she won two years' free singing lessons with teachers who pushed her voice into its soprano range, leading Sutherland to decide that she would become a Wagnerian singer along the lines of Kirsten Flagstad. She duly cultivated a bright, steely edge to the voice and won enough competitions on the strength of it to finance the trip to London, as inevitable for an Australian singer as Paris had been for an American fifty years earlier.

Before her departure in 1951, she had been giving song recitals around the New South Wales music clubs, accompanied by Richard Bonynge, a teenage piano prodigy who was also about to set off for London and who was to become the decisive influence over her life and singing. Like Legge with Schwarzkopf or Serafin with Callas, Bonynge had a great master-plan for her voice which he was gradually and tenaciously to put into practice. His childhood love of Chopin had brought him to Bellini, and from there he had developed an antiquarian's passion for the obscurer reaches of that period of Italian opera. He also became fascinated by the possibility of reviving contemporary performing styles, especially the custom of ornamentation, which Callas and Serafin had only very chastely adopted.

In London, Sutherland studied with Clive Carey, a pupil of Jean de Reszke's, who 'fattened up', as she graphically puts it, the top of her voice. Bonynge came along to the lessons, accompanying her, making suggestions, and throwing out criticism; at home, he worked on the flexibility of her voice, putting her through endless scales, runs, and trills, and by cheating her into starting her exercises at a higher pitch than she thought she was singing at, further developed the all-important top notes. He also married her.

When she first joined the Covent Garden resident company in 1952, everyone except Bonynge thought of her as a potential *spinto* soprano—an Aida or a Tosca, perhaps even a Wagnerian. Over the next few years she had a fair degree of success in the mainline repertory, but it soon became clear from her execution of the coloratura passages written for Gilda in *Rigoletto* or Jenifer in Tippett's *The Midsummer Marriage* that another and rarer sort of voice was secretly coming to maturity. In 1957 she showed the full extent of her accomplishment in concert performances of forgotten Handel, Scarlatti, and Donizetti operas, and the Covent Garden management decided to mount a new production of *Lucia di Lammermoor* for her in 1959, to be produced by the young Zeffirelli and conducted by the great Serafin himself. Callas came to the dress rehearsal and sat next to Schwarzkopf, whispering conspiratorially. Afterwards, she expressed her approval of Sutherland's 'beautiful singing', but her private feelings must have been very mixed. She herself was about to bow out of the operatic arena for a life in Onassis's *haut monde*; her voice, although still passionately admired, was increasingly criticized for curdled top notes and thin tone. And here was a hefty and amiable Australian girl whose voice was in the pink of health, singing a role on which Callas had lavished all her unique tragic fervour, in a style which, in important ways, flew against everything Callas had restored to Donizetti's music. Sutherland and Bonynge appreciated Callas but they also appreciated Galli-Curci, and it was the latter model they followed in moulding a sweet, open, and girlish quality into the voice. Callas would also have heard naïvely perfect coloratura, replete with ornaments and used essentially as a vehicle of virtuosity rather than of emotion and meaning. Later Callas pointed the finger at Bonynge, accusing him of 'setting my work back a hundred years'.

It would have been futile for Sutherland to have emulated Callas. She had the sense to realize that she simply *was* a different sort of coloratura singer, and that she must present herself on her own terms. The public certainly accepted them ecstatically enough, and from her first Covent Garden Lucia Sutherland sustained a supreme position, in the wake of Callas's withdrawal. Strangely, Serafin thought that she ought to go on to sing the declamatory and mostly low-lying role of Verdi's Lady Macbeth, but apart from a glorious Donna Anna in a Giulini recording of *Don Giovanni* later in 1959, she preferred a softer-edged and more lyrical repertory.

From 1962 Bonynge began to conduct at his wife's performances, and the knives were drawn. The Sutherland-Bonynge 'circus' or 'package deal' was found to be a deplorable instance of prima donna's privilege, doubly so as Bonynge's conducting was considered noisy and amateurish (it has continued unpopular in some quarters, but singers invariably find him extraordinarily considerate of their needs). Sutherland herself came in for her share of criticism, as the bright, crisp, and open sound of her early recordings gave way to a drifting, mooning way with anything that was not perforce fast and glittering. Among the ranks of the *bien pensant*, she could soon do nothing right. 'Spot the consonant,' became a favourite opera buff's game every time a new Sutherland record came out, for her diction had been reduced to a series of vowels connected by the broadest and most generalized of *portamenti*. Victor Gollancz stormed out of a Sutherland evening at Covent Garden muttering the much-quoted remark, 'God, she's as dull as Melba,' while her Norma was compared to Callas's and found wanting in energy and temperament.

Sutherland had an immense support system, however, in the form of her husband (who by the mid 1960s was conducting virtually all her performances), a long-term recording contract, excellent management, and a band of regular colleagues. Her returns to Australia, first in Melba-style touring companies, later as prima donna of the new Australian Opera, were invariably triumphant; in Italy the gallery dubbed her 'La Stupenda', a label which delighted the press; and in America rumours that her fees were at least as high as any other singer's was in itself a potent recommendation. What is more important, Sutherland proved herself a real trouper, reliable, hard-working, and always ready to deliver the coloratura goods that her audiences were paying for. She is widely thought of as a sunny and extrovert Aussie, Antipodean to Callas in every way, but in conversation a more complex person emerges, wryly self-deprecating and also deeply determined. Occasionally her habitual good temper has snapped, but as in the incident in Genoa when an understudy was mercilessly booed and she walked out on the performance, the generosity of feeling has been all on her side.

In the 1970s her reputation among the critics began to swing up again, partly because of a marked improvement in her diction and partly because, although younger sopranos of her range might be more expressive and imaginative musicians, she remained indisputably the supreme technician. There were some surprises too, such as an opulent Turandot (on record), in which the *spinto* metal in her voice came to the fore again, and some Bonynge-inspired discoveries from nooks and crannies of the operatic archives. One may not want to hear Massenet's *Esclarmonde* or Bononcini's *Griselda* more than once, but without Sutherland and Bonynge one might never have heard them at all.

Sutherland can at times be a fussily correct singer, lacking in daring and vision; but, given the right music, she can also be a tremendously beautiful one. Few would, I think, claim that she could match the command of phrase, word, and inflection shown by Callas in Donizetti and Bellini or Janet Baker in Handel and Mozart. Yet, like Melba, her singing can still mesmerize, and for sheer brilliance it has only been rivalled by two singers of the last twenty-five years, Montserrat Caballé and Marilyn Horne.

Horne, an American mezzo-soprano born in 1929, represents some sort of ultimate triumph of technique, and the unique completeness of her vocal equipment opened up further paths for 'the *bel canto* revival'. After a bewildering start to her career, dubbing the voice of Dorothy Dandridge for the film of *Carmen Jones*, working with Stravinsky and Robert Craft, and a three years' stint as a lyric soprano in the German provinces, Horne encountered Sutherland at the latter's New York début in 1961. Their subsequent partnership has passed into history. Throughout the 1960s they sang together regularly, in *Norma* and *Semiramide* in particular, and became close friends, whiling away the dead hours of rehearsals, intervals, and recording sessions in elaborate needle-point projects. With the help of Bonynge and her own husband, the conductor Henry Lewis, Horne brought back much of the music in which 'Rossini' mezzos such as Pisaroni and Alboni had excelled, decorating it in authentic style and singing with a confidence and precision that no one could remember equalled. In the early 1970s she changed direction somewhat, breaking away from her image as 'Sutherland's mezzo' and embarking on a more mainstream repertory. She had success as Carmen, but was generally considered miscast in Verdi; plans to appear as the *Götterdämmerung* Brünnhilde never materialized. Latterly she appears to have turned decisively

319

back to the Rossini and Baroque music for which she is most celebrated.

Horne has frequently and quite seriously been called 'the world's greatest voice' or 'the greatest singer in the world'; she has even been compared to the most legendary of the castrati. At certain levels, her claims cannot be easily dismissed. Her technique *is* staggering: listening to her one might well think—this is the human limit of such things. At its best, the voice is more heroic than Sutherland's, more secure than Caballé's, with an evenness and richness from top to bottom that recalls Ponselle. The power of the chest register, the fluency of the runs, the control of dynamics, are all barely credible. Talking to Jerome Hines, she revealed her belief that singing was 'ninety per cent' the economical emission of breath and 'ninety-five per cent brains'. She advocated 'military-type posture' and for coloratura a tightening of the buttock muscles, remarking that she frequently finished a performance with stiff legs.

More revealing to the uninitiated public is Robert Jacobson's feeling that in personality Horne resembled 'the High School overachiever who always has her hand up first'. 'Overachievement' is a particularly apposite word, for Horne's singing sometimes recalls the proverbial hammer brought in to crack a nut. In everything she sings there is an assertive dignity and intelligence, but a lot of Rossini, for example, also demands a lightness and individuality of touch that she largely lacks. One wishes in something like *L'Italiana in Algeri* that she would expend less energy on singing with the determination of an imperturbable steamroller, and more on the delicacy, wit, and playful *rubato* which make Supervia so enchanting.

With Horne, the '*bel canto* revival' reached its peak and inevitably lost some of its impetus. There was not so much vitally important work to be done—the better of the operas were recorded and to some extent re-established and the prima donnas had shown spectacularly how they ought to be sung. In the last fifteen-odd years, there has been a rise in the *general* standard of coloratura singing unimaginable thirty years ago and Bellini, Donizetti, and Rossini are settling into their rightful places—not too low, not too high—in the repertory of the world's opera houses.

One other American singer calls for mention, not only on the grounds of her own merits but also because she represents the full circle of the revolution. Callas, Sutherland, and Horne had at least one quality in common—the enormous size of their voices. Beverly Sills, on the other hand, had the small, soubrettish voice typical of the pre-war coloratura which by dint of good old American determination she pushed into dramatic soprano territory.

Sills, born Belle Silverman in Brooklyn in 1929, suffered—or enjoyed—the full indignity of being a child star, making her début at the age of three on a radio commercial. Her mother, not surprisingly, was a Galli-Curci fan, the proud owner of eleven of her records, which like Uncle Matthew she played compulsively. 'She would play them even before she made coffee in the morning, and they would echo throughout the house all day long,' Sills remembered. 'Before I was seven I had memorized all twenty-two arias on the recordings and could sing them in phonetic Italian.' With this training, Sills became a regular feature on a number of radio shows of the 1930s, including *Uncle Bob's Rainbow House*, *Our Girl Sunday*, and *Major Bowes' Amateur Hour* (on which Callas in her girlhood had also appeared, probably under the name of Nina Foresti).

What saved Sills from an ordinary fate was being sent for lessons to Galli-Curci's erstwhile coach, Estelle Liebling, last of Marchesi's pupils, with whom she was to remain for thirty-four years. In Liebling's studio she encountered many of the great operatic names of the time, not least that of Maria Jeritza, who patronized her extravagantly. More significantly, Liebling managed to curb the Sills precocity with a regime of scales and arpeggios without crushing her ebullience. 'Singing was always so easy for me, so natural,' she later told an interviewer. 'Iron lungs, that's me, and I was never really taught to sing, just helped by discipline.' By the age of twenty, she claims to have known fifteen roles by heart, some of them, like Salome, learnt for love alone. After a gruelling initiation in touring opera—she once sang sixty-three consecutive Micaelas in *Carmen* —and a spell with Ponselle's company in Baltimore, she joined the New York City Opera in 1955. For the next ten years she was the useful house soprano, and it was not until 1966 that she won wider recognition, when City Opera eclipsed the new Met's opening production of Samuel Barber's *Antony and Cleopatra* with a revival, appropriately enough, of Handel's *Giulio Cesare*, in which she sang a sensational Cleopatra.

She stayed loyal to City Opera, but moved on to even more

ambitious undertakings, notably the queens in Donizetti's 'Tudor' operas, *Roberto Devereux*, *Anna Bolena*, and *Maria Stuarda*, to the demands of which her light, bright timbre was patently unsuited. But Sills gave them her all, and more—'*Devereux* shortened my career by three or four years,' she admitted—making a compelling impression by virtue of her vivid acting and eloquent musicianship. In vocally less taxing roles such as Lucia or Massenet's Manon she was even more satisfying.

Sills sang relatively little outside North America, mainly due to the needs of her two children, one deaf, the other mentally retarded, but the most difficult engagement to clinch was one only a hundred yards from home, at the Met. Rudolf Bing was well known for his dislike of purely American-grown singers, and was infuriated that the possibility of scheduling the 'Tudor' trilogy with Montserrat Caballé had been taken from him. He made Sills a couple of paltry offers, and created a little running scandal. Sills herself was not over-concerned: 'In an odd way, Mr Bing made my career by keeping me out of the Met for so long. Nothing infuriates the American public quite as much as the notion of a haughty, foreign-born aristocrat being mean to one of its native-born girls.' Unfortunately, when in 1975 she finally 'crossed the Plaza' her voice was beginning to shrink away and the size of the house was unkind to her. She wisely retired from the stage in 1979, and became directa of City Opera, with distinctly mixed results.

Not since the days of Geraldine Farrar had a serious prima donna projected so brilliantly as a personality. Farrar was from shopkeeping New England stock, whereas Sills was wisecracking Brooklyn Jewish, but they were both all-American girls with the right touch for the times. Sills's capacity to sustain exposure on the television and in the popular press made her the very first 'superstar' —otherwise the American translation of *diva*. She had infectious energy and enthusiasm, a broad and ready smile, a private tragedy in her children, and even a nauseating nickname, Bubbles. She performed consummately on innumerable chat shows including her own, and brought opera to millions, theoretically at least, by prancing about with puppets, muppets, and Carol Burnett. She was never high-falutin' about her considerable art and she never pulled the prima donna wool over her public's eyes. She was, as she put it, 'a communicator', and a natural theatre-bird. 'I found singing such a joyous experience that I couldn't wait to get on the stage . . . I was always the first person in the theater all the time. If it was an eight o'clock curtain, I was here at five-thirty, and it wasn't that I needed to vocalize, because I was all warmed up. I couldn't wait for it to begin.'

The traditions of Italian singing have not been altogether wrested from native Italians. The most impressive representative is Renata Scotto, a cherub-cheeked soprano who first came to notice when she replaced Callas in *La Sonnambula*, after her default from the Edinburgh Festival in 1957. As a teenager she had communicated at a *séance* with the spirit of Malibran who had urged her to carry on her good work. Scotto certainly went on to show something of her predecessor's tremendous dedication, and of all the Italian singers of the post-Callas era she is possibly the most intelligent and original. Her repertory has been enormous, embracing virtually all the most challenging roles in the nineteenth-century and *verismo* repertories. Some dramatic coloratura roles like Norma have plainly over-taxed her, but she is a worthy heir to Muzio and Tebaldi in Puccini, with a genuine *morbidezza* in her voice as well as a stern and adult emotional temper that has made her Violetta, Desdemona, and Manon Lescaut unusually moving. Her most famous part was Madama Butterfly, from whom, in her own phrase, she sheared the *bambolaggiamento*, the Japanese-doll kitsch which many lesser singers fall back on as a means to pathos.

Scotto has had a long and sometimes controversial contract with the Met: perhaps that house has been too large for a voice that is inclined to force itself, and a stage manner liable to over-emphatic projection. Her contemporary Mirella Freni has been more cautious and moved her range slowly up from delightful interpretations of Susanna in *Figaro* and Marguerite in *Faust* to selected Verdi and Puccini. Her voice has been aptly likened to a Sauvignon—the problem being that *spinto* roles should be sung by a red Burgundy. Tebaldi among others expressed doubts as to her suitability for *Aida* and *Don Carlos*, but Freni is never less than soundly and attractively musical. The younger Katia Ricciarelli has come under an even greater barrage of criticism on the score of 'over-parting' herself.

The combination of size, flexibility, and interpretive imagination which Callas offered will not be repeated. There will be no 'second Callas', and the wiser sopranos have not allowed themselves to be inhibited by the thought that there might be. Every generation should concentrate on being grateful for what it has, rather than eat itself up with what it has just missed. If the Callas revolution is over, we must look to the new order, not back to the lost glories of the old.

# The Future of
# the Prima Donna

Opera buffs are not happy people, and at least nine-tenths of what they see and hear in the opera house fills them with amused contempt. Should you dare to praise any young singer in a particular role, the response will be either the unanswerable, 'Thirty years ago she would not have been tolerated,' or 'Have I never played you my 1922 recording of X singing it, you sad, sad person?' A lot of such gambits are part of an overall conspiracy to intimidate candid outsiders, but they are also the result of a common tendency to feel that humankind is generally in decline: we feel nostalgia for what we have never experienced. I do not mean to imply that singing is now as good or even better than it has been, or that Mme X of 1922 might not be enthralling—only that people have been talking about the collapse of standards in operatic singing since the beginning of the eighteenth century without paying attention to the facts of *change*. Thus the pedagogue Tosi in 1723 lamented that only Faustina and Cuzzoni 'keep up the tottering profession from immediately falling into ruin'; in 1834 Mount Edgcumbe was unmoved by Pasta and Malibran and admitted, 'I never expect to hear again what I have done, or any new music, or new singers, that will make me amends for those which are gone'; in 1906 Henderson, worried by Wagnerism, reported that 'It is plain to every careful observer that the race of beautiful singers is diminishing with every year, and that in its place there is growing up a generation of harsh, unrefined, tuneless shouters'; while in 1982 Lanfranco Rasponi produced a book called *The Last Prima Donnas*, in which he interviewed the last 'members of an extinct race'. 'There are today some capable young singers,' he goes on, 'but none of them have that intangible magic that gave to the past ones a very marked personality and glamour.' All along, local standards of taste and style are assumed to be historical absolutes, and the great living body of laws, traditions, and controversies connected with good singing is reduced to the pedantry of Beckmesser's slate.

In the post-war period a new set of complaints has accumulated without any real acknowledgement of loss and gain, of a complexity of factors. If singers 'over-part' themselves and find it hard to cope with large opera house orchestras, do we therefore have to return to Verdi and Wagner played with reduced scoring? Do we tolerate the random cuts and transpositions which composers of the nineteenth century fought so hard to eliminate? If aeroplane travel is so bad for singers, was lurching across the Atlantic in a steamer any more comfortable? And how did Catalani, Pasta, or Malibran feel after a month-long coach tour of one-night engagements, driving along bumpy and dangerous roads in wind and rain? If some singers are now 'over-exposed', does anyone remember that many nineteenth-century prima donnas regularly performed four or five times a week? If producers today often make unreasonable demands and impose trivial concepts, do we therefore reject altogether the fertilization that a theatrical mind like Strehler's can bring to the musical egg, and listen instead to 'concerts in costume'? Is the producer's or conductor's prerogative any more or less desirable than that of the prima donna? None of these questions have simple answers.

There are still times when the prima donna appears at the centre of the scandal which has always been such a significant element in the sociology of opera. A recent egregious example of this is the *furore* created by Montserrat Caballé's withdrawal from performances at La Scala in 1982 of Donizetti's *Anna Bolena*. This was an important revival of Visconti's famous 1957 production for Callas, eagerly anticipated and completely sold out. A few minutes before the first performance was due to begin, an anonymous voice announced over a loudspeaker that Caballé had withdrawn owing to a 'gastric attack' and a near-unknown Ruth Falcon would take her place. The auditorium erupted in a storm of boos, whistles, and catcalls which became increasingly hysterical. The manager of the opera house withdrew from his box and the conductor withdrew from the podium, unable to start the opera. The uproar continued and scuffles broke out in the gallery. Eventually, the greatly respected Giulietta Simionato, who had sung with Callas in the original 1957 performances, agreed to step on to the stage and attempt to quell the noise. After she failed to command the audience's attention, a further announcement was made to the effect that the performance was cancelled and that monies would be refunded. This of course precipitated a further wave of fury.

Every newspaper contained a different version of Caballé's behaviour, and her ailments were variously reported. She claimed that she had informed the management the day before of her indisposition, but certainly no one at La Scala had made any effort to warn the public of the situation. Further performances of *Bolena* were cancelled as Falcon also fell ill, and when Caballé finally did return to fulfil one of her scheduled engagements, she was greeted with booing. She now left for her home in Barcelona, where her mother was said to be ill, and twenty-one-year-old Cecilia Gasdia, winner of a competition held in memory of Callas, took over to some acclaim.

But this was not all. The Russian mezzo-soprano Elena Obratzsova was also booed in the 'Simionato' role in *Bolena*, and withdrew from both it and the role of Cassandra in *Les Troyens*. This latter had proved another hornet's nest for La Scala, since Marilyn Horne had agreed to sing in *L'Italiana in Algeri*, on the understanding that, should *Les Troyens* be performed, she should be offered Cassandra as well. However, La Scala wanted Obratzsova to replace Agnes Baltsa, who had withdrawn from the Simionato role in *Bolena*, and as bait offered her the golden opportunity to sing both Dido and Cassandra in *Les Troyens*. Having read about this in the press, Horne, justifiably appalled at La Scala's behaviour, cancelled her appearances in *L'Italiana in Algeri*. La Scala then managed to get Lucia Valentini-Terrani for one performance of *L'Italiana*, but were forced to substitute *Cenerentola* with Julia Hamari for the others!

The intrigues of management are among the prima donna's oldest obstacles, and there are ways in which the dilemmas involved in the performance of opera seem unchanging. Singing itself, for instance, remains a dangerous activity involving sheerly physical risk to delicate and mysterious bodily organs. Every prima donna has to weigh up her own scale of priorities and calculate the likely sacrifices. Great singers such as Pasta, Viardot, Fremstad, and Callas have had to exert unnatural strain on their voices in order to encompass certain roles: had they been cautious, their audiences would have been the poorer. Others have made mistakes that have not been worth the price paid, but one cannot therefore argue that opera would be healthier if singers all played safe.

Other problems are new, and dominant among them are questions of the ethics of recording. The elaborate processing this now involves can give as misleading an idea of a voice as the crudest and earliest equipment did. If Mme. Y cannot naturally ride a loud orchestra climax, the balance can be technologically redressed to create a wholly artificial and more flattering acoustic situation. Audiences then come to the opera house with inflated expectations of a voice's stamina and dynamic range and miss the engineered smoothness of their recording. A more recent sophistication is the videotape on which, contrariwise, the quality of sound reproduction (at least at the time of writing) is so poor that the music somehow falls from prominence and becomes incidental to the ability of the singer to act credibly within the naturalistic conventions of television.

Certain sorts of singer have flourished in this soil, while others seem to have withered. There is a real shortage nowadays in the lowest vocal ranges, a phenomenon often blamed partly on the marked rise in standard orchestral pitch since the beginning of the century. The plummy sound of a contralto or a true bass has become ludicrous with unfamiliarity, and we now like the lower voices to have an upward gravitational pull, a slim and athletic character which eschews the once-prized 'flab' of *vibrato*. This has produced some superb bass-baritones and a remarkable generation of versatile dramatic mezzo-sopranos, among whom one could single out Baltsa, Brigitte Fassbaender, and the electrifying Tatiana Troyanos. At the top end of the range, voices which combine beauty, power, and security are as rare as contraltos or basses, and Wagner has suffered worst from the dearth of dramatic sopranos and heroic tenors. Mozart, however, has been well served by lyric singers of sensitivity and intelligence following in the line of Schwarzkopf, Jurinac, and Seefried: mezzos such as Frederica von Stade, also lovely in French music, Maria Ewing, and Ann Murray; sopranos such as Lucia Popp and the heartbreaking Ileana Cotrubas. The coloratura end of the lyric soprano's repertory has the Czech Edita Gruberova—who maintains the middle European traditions of Sembrich, Selma Kurz, and Maria Ivogün. The singing of Jessye Norman and Margaret Price embodies the highest ideals of *bel canto*: liquid tone, impeccable control of legato, and profound exploring musicianship. A generation which hears such singers cannot complain of the dearth of the grand style.

More distinctively modern in temperament are sopranos such as Anja Silja, Teresa Stratas, and Josephine Barstow, commonly known as 'the singing actresses'. Their voices rebel against the classical beauty of Price's and Norman's and on a bad night can break out in a rash of insecure intonation, raw top notes, wide *tremolo*, and violent breaks between registers. The compensations, as with their great precursor Mary Garden, are a strongly projected stage presence and the valuable ability to colour their voices to convey the nature and feelings of the characters they are portraying. All three have sung widely in nineteenth-century opera, but perhaps have been heard at their best in the early twentieth-century repertory—Berg, Janáček, Weill, Prokofiev, Strauss's *Salome*. Whether the flaws and ugliness—-the word is unavoidable—in their singing is necessary to their art is, I think, doubtful: the excitement they generate in the opera house is not in question.

The three prima donnas of the 1970s I am now going to discuss have not followed this path: Elisabeth Söderström, Janet Baker, and Kiri Te Kanawa all, in their different ways, prove the strengths of modern opera *singing*. Söderström and Baker have both been pioneers; Te Kanawa represents a more mainline lyric tradition.

Elisabeth Söderström, a Swede born in 1927, is a soprano who has miraculously avoided vocal compromises while still communicating the extremes of emotion demanded by the twentieth-century 'expressionist' operas. Her consistency and dedication throughout a very long career (she made her début in 1947 and has been a member of the Royal Opera in Stockholm since 1950) is matched to a constant desire to challenge herself. Few prima donnas since the war have been so flexible, so responsive, so ready to work in ensembles and smaller companies taking long rehearsal periods— hence her long association with Glyndebourne.

Söderström's repertory is a unique one, although she is a very careful singer who has never 'over-parted' herself and who has made a point of appearing regularly in smaller opera houses in which nuance can be more lucidly projected. She has sung Monteverdi, Mozart, and a lot of Russian music, as well as Berg, Henze, and Britten; Boulez conducted her in a memorable series of performances at Covent Garden as Debussy's Mélisande and in Stockholm she created an erotic role in Ligeti's glorious *Le Grand Macabre*.

One of her closest associations is with the Strauss *grande dame* roles, in which she won the blessing of no less than Schwarzkopf, who rehearsed her as the Marschallin and forthrightly expressed her admiration. Söderström does not have Schwarzkopf's mystique or aristocratic reserve: instead, everything she does has an evident sincerity and warmth. As Peter Hall noted while rehearsing her in *Fidelio*, this can teeter on 'a radiant sentimentality' which Strauss gives the prima donna plenty of opportunity to indulge. The operas of Janáček have a harsher emotional cut, and here, on stage and records, Söderström achieved very moving results. No opera composer has shown a more overwhelming sense of the pain in ordinary human life, and for the prima donna Janáček offers release from the stereotype of the pure-hearted maiden who lives only to sacrifice herself for love and a violent contrast to the sophisticated dilemmas of the Strauss heroines, cushioned by lush orchestration and substantial incomes. Janáček's women have the stature of the heroines of nineteenth-century fiction—the betrayal of Jenůfa, the frustration and vulnerability of Katya Kabanová, the desperate *ennui* of Elena Makropoulos, are the stuff of George Eliot and Tolstoy laid out naked in music. Underneath and beyond these distorted and deformed lives runs Janáček's tremendous affirmatory vision of the splendour of nature, of pity, hope, and continuity. Söderström's singing rises to this suppressed joy as well as the scalding anguish, without any evasion of the score's requirements. Janáček is tough on the vocal cords and the pace and concision of his music allows no respite. Many sopranos resort to *verismo* mannerisms—sobbing, shouting, *parlando*—to pile on the agonies and avoid the stress, but Söderström's musical honesty reaps the most profound rewards.

Honesty has been a corner-stone of the English mezzo-soprano Dame Janet Baker, although honesty alone cannot account for the full earnestness of her dedication to her art. At the beginning of her career, she remembers calling 'silently on the name of Jesus to help me. I was in this situation only because I honestly believed he had given me work to do as a singer.' Of all the prima donnas in this book only Fremstad can match Baker's religious depth of belief in herself as the bearer of a sacred flame, and anyone who doubted her commitment was given short shrift. A music critic of *The Times* once suggested casually that at a certain performance Dame Janet had perhaps not given her all: shortly afterwards a stinging retort appeared on the newspaper's letters page. 'He has absolutely no right to suggest that I in some way shortchanged the public by singing "as if marking her part, rehearsal-fashion". All my working life I have given my heart and soul to my audiences: last Thursday was no exception. To suggest I deliberately gave less than the best is to question my integrity ... my intention to serve the public to the utmost cannot be questioned.'

She was born in Yorkshire in 1933 into a family in which music was not particularly important. But the flame ignited early: taken as a child to hear the D'Oyly Carte in Gilbert and Sullivan, she recalled that she 'thought it was all very well, but it wasn't really music'. In her teens she benefited from the North Country traditions of choral singing; when she was twenty she came to London, working as a bank clerk while taking singing lessons. Most of her early operatic appearances were in Baroque pieces, and it could be said that, working with conductor-scholars like Charles Mackerras and Raymond Leppard, she realized their dramatic potential much as Callas and Serafin did Donizetti's and Bellini's. Gluck's *Orfeo*, Purcell's *Dido*, and the operas of Handel have been central to Baker's art throughout her career, and to all of them she brought a revolutionary energy and depth of expression which made the previous generation of interpreters sound both stolid and lightweight. A steady loss of inhibition and what Lord Harewood described as her 'rather English want not to wear your heart on your sleeve' led her to the performance which more than any other brought her sensational fame, that of Dido in Berlioz's *Les Troyens*, which she first sang in 1969 with Scottish Opera. She became a superb tragic actress, commanding a perfectly judged economy of movement and gesture and an extraordinary capacity to project pride, scorn, and isolation. In all this, as in the splendour of her declamation and recitative, her ability to colour words and tone, it is Callas to whom one compares her.

In 1970 at Glyndebourne she sang Diana in an unforgettable revival of the seventeenth-century Venetian composer Cavalli's *La Calisto* (in which she incidentally brought off a brilliantly witty impersonation of Jove-dressed-up-as-Diana) and two years later Penelope in Monteverdi's *Il Ritorno d'Ulisse*. This latter interpretation will be remembered for its stillness and rapt inner strength: when Penelope cried 'Non voglio amar' or 'Torna, deh, torna, Ulisse', the grief spilled out in the voice, but the body held back —just as in the final duet, where Penelope is reunited with her husband, it took her an eternity before she dared touch Ulisse and believe in his physical presence, so long denied her. Outside Glyndebourne, she gave Covent Garden a Vitellia in Mozart's *La Clemenza di Tito* where the vocal strains of the part became integral to the expression of the character's full vicious self-centredness; and a chilling portrait of the small-minded and suburban Kate in Britten's *Owen Wingrave*, in which she credibly allowed a chink of vulnerability to show through the girl's monstrous complacence.

One further performance should be singled out, that of Donizetti's Mary Stuart (as the English National Opera had it), which gave full rein to her impeccable technique and intensity of temperament, as well as transfiguring what can seem third-rate music. The mounting fury of her encounter with Elizabeth, and the last burst of fanatical self-justification, her body shaking with defiance as she ripped stunningly through the *cabaletta*: this must have been the art of Pasta and Malibran too. I remember, in fact, fatuously asking her at the stage door one night what she had thought when one critic had written that the first Mary, Malibran herself, could not have been better. 'How does he know?' was her typically blunt and proper answer.

Janet Baker never sang in opera houses abroad (except with the Royal Opera when they visited La Scala) for reasons of firm self-limitation, but she has travelled the world as a *lieder* singer. Schubert in particular brought out her gentler qualities and the full beauty of her voice, but many will say that, like a number of the finest *lieder* singers, all her mature knowledge of a song's detail and meaning has been mastered at the expense of spontaneity. In concert and oratorio, she has been a Bach singer of gravely devoted spirituality and has vividly realized the Italian cantatas of Handel and Haydn. So the catalogue continues . . .

In 1982, after a mountain of publicity which even Patti's or Melba's farewells cannot have equalled, she closed the door on opera. Her timing was just, for there were moments at which exhaustion was evident, and her irritation with *The Times* critic shows how impossible she found it to give less than everything. At her very last performance—a staged Prom in the Royal Albert Hall, where she took the title-role in Glyndebourne's production of Gluck's *Orfeo*—she left the stage with a striking image. Acknowledging the final applause, she held up above her head the lyre she had been using as Orfeo, as if to direct the audience's tribute back to the spirit of music itself. It was a gesture that signified the depths of her idealism and her somehow Victorian conception of the nobility of the singer's calling, with its exalted mission to communicate the essence of music—but it amused a certain section of the public. Her diary of her last year as an opera singer was published to patronizing sneers at her reflections on art and life; and a glossy magazine nicknamed her 'Dame Granite'. Peter Hall, who knew her well and produced that last *Orfeo*, saw it from another angle in his diary: 'My goodness, she seems to be together, that woman. She knows what she wants, and she knows the sacrifices she has to make in order to get it. She also treats her talent not as a meal ticket, but as a serious responsibility that's got to be used to the full. She's a very remarkable person.'

A very remarkable singer too, if in her case the two can be separated. Matthew Arnold once wrote of Aeschylus that his plays conveyed 'the most agitating matter under the conditions of severest form'—a statement that seems to suggest one of Janet Baker's fundamental qualities. She takes the most intense and essential human emotions to the very limit that physically perfect singing allows: one never, for instance, finds her obscuring her diction, fudging a high note, or breaking legato to make a cheap effect. Hers is lean, purposeful singing without frills, fakery, or rhetoric; impassioned, evangelistic, but not sensual. It is the singing of a born and bred Yorkshire Protestant, as much an expression of that landscape and culture as *Wuthering Heights*. Other mezzo-sopranos have had more volume and ample caressing warmth in their voices, and in that respect her Mahler or Brahms is not as satisfying as, say, that of Kathleen Ferrier to whom she was so frequently and inevitably compared. Ferrier was a mother-earth contralto whose art had great simplicity of feeling, while Baker is a dramatic mezzo of the post-Callas dispensation, *our* singer, as Pasta was Stendhal's and Chorley's.

Much more accessible to a public which wants glamour and entertainment is Kiri Te Kanawa (born 1944), a prima donna of irregular but exotic beauty and a gorgeous lyric soprano. Sexy, jokey, a keen golfer, with two adopted children and a nice husband, she has provided plenty of innocent copy for newspapers in search of a good-sport prima donna along the lines of Geraldine Farrar, acting up to the part without taking it too seriously. Kiri is marketable. She has appeared on *This is Your Life* and endless 'television specials', 'starred' in a very successful film by Joseph Losey of *Don Giovanni*, advertised Rolex watches, and, as some large percentage of the world knows, sang at the Royal Wedding in 1981.

Her life has a sweet and simple story-line. She comes of Maori ancestry and her first singing teacher in New Zealand was a nun, Sister Mary Leo. Like Sutherland, she collected a lot of prizes in Australia and came to London on the proceeds, joining the now defunct London Opera Centre. The first shock, appropriately enough, was a master class with Richard Bonynge, at which he told her that she was not a mezzo, as she had previously thought, but a soprano. For some time, she was utterly disoriented. 'At twenty, I was *dreadful*,' she claimed, 'always late, untidy, just totally useless.' She was not happy at the Centre, and word got around that she was not completely serious in her approach. At a number of Covent Garden auditions she was rejected on her personal reputation rather than her vocal merits, which were glaringly obvious to anyone who heard her. Fortunately she found Vera Rosza, a formidable Hungarian émigré, who took the girl and her singing in hand. Madame Rosza continues to be centrally important in Te Kanawa's career, and she is said to remain in mortal terror of her judgements. By 1971 she was ready to be cast in her first major role at Covent Garden, the Countess in *Le Nozze di Figaro*, since when she has been that opera house's nearest thing to a resident prima donna. Her popularity is also particularly high in Paris—which likes its prima donnas to have style, if not chic—and in New York, where in 1964 she first stood in at short notice as Desdemona in *Otello*, replacing a stricken Teresa Stratas. Schuyler Chapin, acting General Manager of the Met, remembers the self-assurance of his hot new property. 'She knew exactly what she would do and what she would not do, the repertoire she wanted to sing over the next several seasons, the directors she wished to work with, the conductors she would tolerate, the costumes she would wear and the attitude of the theater she wanted when working in it. She said all these things while sitting seductively on the couch, her knees tucked up, her long hair touching her shoulders, her deep-set brown eyes staring out of a *café-au-lait* face.' In other words, Te Kanawa had learnt how to cope, bargain, charm, and get her way. Peter Hall records an incident in Salzburg in 1979 when 'Kiri made a number of forays to the hotel's jewellery shop which seems to stay open all night. She kept reappearing every few minutes with a ring worth

£40,000 or a necklace worth £50,000. She tried them on, paraded them for a giggle. Perhaps that's how a *diva* should behave.'

Te Kanawa the singer is more difficult to place or assess. The voice itself is straightforward enough. Like her idol Leontyne Price, she has a 'juicy lyric' soprano, and within a certain repertory it makes some of the most sumptuous sounds to be heard in any opera house today. Her schooling is secure, she has a glistening top register and a generous sense of phrase. The little problems—in 1983, for instance, she suffered from a series of throat infections which marred an embarrassing number of her performances—cannot detract from an underlying glowing healthiness of tone. Trouble starts with the fact that she is not a skilled sight-reader or a fast learner. Her anxieties over German, in particular, are self-evident (I have never heard a singer so long and loudly prompted as she has been in Strauss's admittedly very wordy *Arabella*) and diction often gets swallowed up in tone. She has made some very puzzling mistakes—a singer sparing of her chest voice is not going to find Puccini easy, and her Manon Lescaut was sadly under-projected because of this. With Verdi, she is happier with the lighter roles of Desdemona and Amelia in *Simon Boccanegra* than with the complexities of *La Traviata*. In her Straussian incarnations she comes closer to Lisa della Casa's silvery shimmer than to Schwarzkopf's insistent subtlety, and at the time of writing her Marschallin and Arabella are attractive, but not deeply involving. Her Mozart, however, has grown magnificently over her years of fame, and a great Mozart singer rarely fails the Strauss challenges. In sum, she is still maturing: behind the solid patina of her glamour and popularity is a surprisingly tentative and hesitant artist who has refused the easy options and is working out the best alternatives.

Finally, I close this history with three younger sopranos who are still growing and learning. All three have immense talent, for which teachers, conductors, agents, critics, and managements bear a crucial responsibility: all three have tests ahead. One of these tests is coping with the stereotyped expectations of the prima donna.

Rosalind Plowright and June Anderson met in the summer of 1982 when they sang together in San Diego's revival of Verdi's early opera *Il Corsaro*. 'Two sopranos!' said Anderson. 'Everyone quaked, and thought that one or the other of us would end up flouncing off, with blood on her claws. Of course, we got on very well and everyone was a bit disappointed.' Not with their performances, however: *Opera*'s reviewer Martin Bernheimer was deeply excited by them both:

> Miss Plowright . . . could just be the Verdi *diva* we have been waiting for. Her voice is big, limpid at the top, rich at the bottom, warm in timbre, dusky in colour, and used with remarkable finesse. Here at last is a soprano who can meet the lyrical and dramatic aspects of this sort of challenge with equal authority . . . Miss Anderson . . . traced the ornate, ascending cantilena with a purity and ease worthy—and reminiscent—of a young Sutherland, singing with generous, even tone throughout the considerable range and never resorting to the chirps and/or lunges that have become the standard or lamentable procedures for others.

Both singers put great store by professional behaviour. June Anderson finds that the one really significant advantage of prima donna status is the power to insist on good working conditions, a proper schedule of rehearsals, and serious-minded colleagues. 'People think of America as the bastion of shoddy opera perform- ances, but I can assure you that plenty of European houses just fling it all together—and I've decided that I'm simply not going to put up with it.' The arrogance and lack of musicality among producers has also left her open-mouthed. Rosalind Plowright talks about conductors: 'Nothing can demoralize me quicker than conductors who don't give me moral support or recognize that I'm trying to do my best. I need to feel that they think I'm singing well, that they're on my side—but some of them just grunt, and I find that devastating. I hate to single people out, but both Sinopoli and Abbado were absolutely wonderful—and I think I did some of my best work for them.'

Plowright believes that it is very important to keep one's feelings back as a singer and to avoid explosive situations:

> I can honestly say that I've only had one tantrum so far, and it was perfectly justified. I arrived for my début at the Carnegie Hall to find that I hadn't been given a dressing-room, and no one was going to do anything about it. Otherwise I think it's imperative to keep calm and relaxed—singing's nerve-racking enough as it is. I must say that I never see other people having tantrums either. And I may be naïve, but I don't see any prima

336

**49.** Elisabeth Söderström as Janáček's Katya Kabanova, an unforgettable and deeply moving performance devoid of any false glamour or histrionics.

**48.** Two antipodean prima donnas: Kiri Te Kanawa and Joan Sutherland, during a recording of Gay's *The Beggar's Opera* in which they sang the rivals Polly Peachum and Lucy Lockit.

**50.** Shirley Verrett and Grace Bumbry happily acknowledge the reception of their Covent Garden concert in 1983.

51. Rosalind Plowright as Maddalena in Giordano's *Andrea Chénier*.

52. June Anderson, perhaps the outstanding Violetta of her generation, in the Welsh National Opera production of *La Traviata*.

53. Elise Ross as Marie in Berg's *Wozzeck*.

donna jealousy around: Kiri Te Kanawa and I are up for some of the same roles, but she's been terribly kind to me and I think she's great fun. June Anderson and I have formed a mutual admiration society! The reality of being a prima donna, I suppose, is the wall one puts around oneself. I see myself being very reserved and distant sometimes—which is strange, because I'm naturally quite out-going. But it's the only way to keep sane when you're constantly travelling, meeting and working with new people. You can't give everything away: that's something I have learnt over the last couple of years.

Plowright is one of the prima donnas, like Tetrazzini and Flagstad, who can point to one particular performance which pushed her forward. In September 1981 she sang Desdemona in a new production of Verdi's *Otello* at the London Coliseum. 'It was the last step in a long process,' she admits,

> and all the publicity was carefully prearranged. I had been building up to it for a couple of years since I won a big international competition in Sofia. Fortunately Desdemona is a lovely role, with nothing hair-raisingly difficult in it—I just try and sing it as beautifully as possible—and the whole thing was the success we'd all been hoping for. I even got on to the front page of *The Times*!

Plowright came from a musical family,

> ... at least on my father's side. He played double bass in an Oscar Peterson type trio, and my sisters are both singing in musicals at the moment. All my family gave me tremendous support throughout. I was born in Nottinghamshire, but we moved to the West Country and it was there when I was about fourteen that I heard my first opera—*The Mikado*, which I adored. When I left school I went to the Royal Northern College of Music and a marvellous teacher, Frederic Cox. My voice was a warm and plummy mezzo then, but Mr Cox brightened it up and brought the resonance forward. My top notes came and went, and I think Mr Cox nearly despaired, even though he always told me that my voice would not settle and mature until my mid-thirties. Anyway, things started off quite nicely and I sang soprano with most of the British provincial and touring companies. Then in 1978 there was a complete standstill. I didn't

337

know what to do, where or how to sing. I was reduced to singing at dinner dances and the whole business became so depressing that I was on the verge of giving up. Then out of the blue Peter Knapp, a baritone who had bravely organized his own small-scale touring opera company, asked me to sing Fiordiligi in *Così fan tutte.* Something quite extraordinary happened. We were in Sheffield, I remember, and in ten minutes flat Peter explained to me how to project those top notes. I can only say that my top Bs and Cs seem to come out of the crown of my head, a sort of fourth register, above the normal head voice. It was like a new toy and I used to play with it in the most inappropriate places out of sheer joy. Since then I've continued working on my technique with an Australian, Erich Vietheer ... I now know how to avoid strain, how to use my back and shoulders for support, and as Erich puts it, how to push down for top notes 'as though you're giving birth'!

After winning the competition in Sofia singing Leonora in *Il Trovatore*, Plowright's career began to take shape. Her portrayal of Miss Jessel in Britten's *Turn of the Screw* had already won her an award as 'outstanding operatic performer of 1979'; she now made her début at Covent Garden as a Valkyrie, and sang for a season in Berne, which gave her invaluable experience as a regular house soprano. Since the decisive outcome of her Desdemona, she has sung Queen Elizabeth opposite Janet Baker's Farewell Mary Stuart, Donna Anna opposite Kiri Te Kanawa's Donna Elvira in *Don Giovanni* at Covent Garden, and recorded *Il Trovatore* with Domingo and Giulini ('my idol—when I auditioned for him I was almost struck dumb with awe'). At La Scala she sang Puccini's Suor Angelica: 'That audience is petrifying, but I got through quite well'; Vienna is scheduled for 1986. She loves the enthusiasm of American audiences, and despite the dressing-room débâcle, fondly remembers the wild appreciation which greeted her 1983 New York début in Strauss's *Liebe der Danae.* She has sung quite a lot of Strauss, including Ariadne in San Francisco, but has decided to concentrate on the Italian repertory, at least for the next five years. In 1984 she was cast in two new productions in London: *Andrea Chénier* at Covent Garden, followed by *The Sicilian Vespers* at the Coliseum. Desdemona, Manon Lescaut, and Amelia in *Un Ballo in Maschera* are among her favourite roles, and she longs to sing Leonora in *La Forza del Destino*. There are plans to try out *Traviata*, Norma, and Butterfly in small American houses, and perhaps one day she will tackle Donizetti's Anna Bolena and Lucrezia Borgia.

Among the prima donnas of the past she especially admired Tebaldi (with whom she is often compared), and Callas fascinates her. 'But I suppose the singer who means most to me is Ponselle. In a lot of those early recordings, the expressiveness in the singing doesn't come through, but with her it does. I love the softness in her voice and that shimmer in her timbre.' Together we listened to a recording of Ponselle singing Aida's Nile Scene aria, which Plowright had never heard before. 'What can you say about singing like that? It leaves me speechless.' She did, however, ruefully note that the infamous top C which comes at the end of the aria was slightly flat and that Ponselle had had to take an extra breath to prepare for it.[1] Plowright herself finds the note terrifying:

> There's no support from the orchestra—nothing to come up there with you, as it does at the climax of Amelia's first aria in *Ballo*. That one passage has left me dreading Aida [which she has sung in Germany], although I find it physically exhausting anyway. The funny thing is that when I first learnt the role while I was at the English National Opera, I sang it *dolce* and *diminuendo* without any trouble at all, until someone told me how notorious it was, how Tebaldi had cracked on it, and so forth. Now I've developed this inhibition about it to the point at which I feel paralysed.

Plowright claims that she is 'no more nervous than any other singer', but everything about her suggests someone whose confidence is fragile. Conductors, other singers, her teachers, her agent Tony Kaye, her family: all clearly have to work hard to convince her that she is the prima donna she already is. This vulnerability gives an added dimension of personality to her singing. She is not, I think, a true dramatic soprano with the sheer power of other current white hopes, Ghena Dmitrova, Eva Marton, and Elizabeth Connell—the basic quality is gentler, more glowing and humane. Nerves can affect her voice at the beginning of the evening, and the tone takes on an edge, leaving her sounding tight and wiry at the top: but once

1 See pp. 201, 218.

she relaxes, the instrument reveals its dazzling richness of colour and that rare *spinto* fullness. Listening to her in *Chénier*, for instance, one was made aware of just what ambitious lyric sopranos like Freni and Ricciarelli lack in size and sweep. Her manner is very warm and sincere, and one senses in her a vein of romantic melancholy which comes across on stage. She has the added advantage of a strikingly attractive appearance, tall, dark, and slim. 'I've given up bending my knees when I'm with short tenors,' she laughs. 'They can start stretching for a change.'

June Anderson is an altogether different type, though no less engaging. She is charmingly definite, openly critical, highly articulate, and held together with the best sort of American grit. If there are any doubts, she is not going to tell an interviewer about them, but I am quite sure she has never bent her knees for anyone. Her singing is characterized by great intelligence and delicacy, but so far it is as a coloratura that she has, as it were, made headlines. Critics compare her to Sutherland, something which irritates her. 'Sutherland has been an enormously important singer for me, but, truly, our voices are different, even though our repertories may look similar at the moment.'

She was born in Connecticut and her parents forced her into singing lessons,

> . . . after my complete failure to turn into a baby ballerina. They weren't musical, but they pushed me hard, against my will. At seventeen, I was a finalist in the Met auditions—it was the year Jeanine Altmeyer won—and I was completely turned off by the competitiveness of it all. I then went to Yale, majored in French Literature, and tried to forget about a career in music. The trouble was that I soon had to realize that I wasn't going to set the academic world on fire—so it was back to singing.

She made her way to New York and found a young teacher who taught her 'the purest Garcia technique'. Even though she is now based in London, she still speaks to or sees Robert Leonard whenever she can. In her early thirties, she considers that her voice is still developing.

> After singing it for the film version of *Amadeus*, I've given up the Queen of the Night and those killing top Fs. Instead, I find that all sorts of wonderful things are happening in my lower register,

and from the repertory point of view, that's far more exciting to me than hitting the pipsqueaks.

Anyway, when I started off in New York in 1976, I still wasn't sure that singing was what I wanted to do, and strangely enough, it was only when I was down to my last fifty dollars that I started to burn to get somewhere. One of my first jobs was in Chicago, when I sang one of the nieces in *Peter Grimes* with Jon Vickers. He was very good to me, sat me down, and warned me that I might not be tough enough for the business. Now I'm scheduled to sing with him in Handel's *Samson*, and I'm wondering whether he'll remember.

In 1978 I joined the New York City Opera and stayed with them until 1982. What can I call it? A baptism of fire? It was certainly not a happy experience, but it may have been a necessary one, because I now feel that if I survived that, I can survive anything. I do not feel that I got a fair deal from Beverly Sills [who had a number of fine young sopranos such as Carol Vaness on her roster], and I spent most of my time covering or stepping in for one performance at the end of a run. I sang my first *Puritani*, for instance, without any stage or orchestral rehearsal, and I also did Gilda, Donna Elvira, Olympia in *Hoffmann*, the Queen in *Coq d'Or*, Queen of the Night, and what I suppose what was my first big public success, Cleopatra in *Giulio Cesare*. Despite the way I was used, I found myself with a wonderful little following who came to all my performances and cheered me up.

My big break was finding an Italian agent who was prepared to hawk my cassette around the Italian opera houses. Through that I got *Semiramide* in Rome and *Lucia* in Florence, both of which seemed to work very well. I left New York City Opera, and then found myself covering again—only this time it was Caballé, who was down for *Semiramide* at Carnegie Hall. Oh well, I thought, it's worth waiting around for. Then she appeared and did all the rehearsals, and I thought she'd sing it. She cancelled on the day of the performance and I took over. It made my name in New York. Now I'm planning to put my efforts into Europe for a few years. I care more about singing at Covent Garden than anywhere, and at the moment I'm just about signed up for a *Semiramide* there, with Marilyn Horne. They wanted me to do some Lucias after Sutherland's farewells to the role in 1985, but I think that's a bit cheap, and I don't think it's really fair on her or myself.

Anderson's repertory is carefully circumscribed: new roles are not undertaken lightly, and some of the most prestigious opera houses have been somewhat mortified at having their offers refused.

I find I get increasingly cautious about what I do and increasingly sure about what I don't want to do. I am not for instance a Mozartean although I can sing the notes perfectly well, and I am not going to be rushed into *Norma* or *Anna Bolena* before I'm ready. I enjoy singing Handel, but what really obsesses me at the moment are Rossini's early operas. I'm about to record *Maometto Secondo*, an early version of *Le Siège de Corinthe*, and I've already done *Mosè in Egitto*. Both of those, as well as *Semiramide* and some others, were written for Colbran, so I've naturally become fascinated by that woman and her voice [picking Stendhal's *Vie de Rossini* off her drawing-room table]. She had this very strong lower register which I seem to be developing too. Anyway, I *must* sing these operas—people don't realize yet what beautiful music they contain, not just in the arias but in the ensembles. They're also tremendously difficult to sing, I can tell you.

Anderson's technique is not one to be easily fazed, either. What she glaringly shares with Sutherland is the same strong jaw, and there is doubtless some good physiological connection between that and the ability to control the muscles which work hardest in coloratura. Her voice is radiantly secure and focused—how does she look after it?

Garcia exercises and I don't know what. Every morning when I wake up, I growl, and if that works OK, then I know I'm still in business. I vocalize through three octaves, and I start by humming them. On the day of a performance, I will sing through the role in half-voice. I have a dehydration problem and can't drink wine within days of a performance or major rehearsal. I gulp down about three litres of water a day; I have to be careful about salt. I also admit to being very superstitious, and my dressing-room is one long ritual. On the table I put pictures of my cat—I've had to leave her behind in New York while I'm in Europe—cameos of Bellini, Patti, and the rest, a Jenny Lind paperweight. I have to have a long nail on every finger, and just to keep the good fairies happy, I sing a snatch of music by all the composers in my repertory that I'm *not* singing that night.

Anderson and Plowright both embody the modern transformation of a standard centuries-old conception of the prima donna: high fees, jet travel, recording contracts, a repertory based in nineteenth-century Italian opera, and a schooling in classical technique. Elise Ross is something quite different from any other singer in this book. From the beginning of her life she has been off the ordinary treadmills of effort, goal, and achievement. The aura of the prima donna means nothing to her, and her voice will probably never build up the resources of Anderson's and Plowright's. Her existence is a proportioned one: married to the conductor Simon Rattle, she had just given birth to her first child when I spoke to her, and their small house in Islington was as full of the baby as it was of music. Neighbours bang on the window and drop in; two racing bicycles block the path through the hall.

Her father, a Polish Jew who emigrated to New York City, is a composer who studied with Milhaud, and in New York both he and his wife taught at the Dalcroze School of Eurhythmics, where Elise was grounded in '*solfège*, modern dance, and improvisation' rather than the standard curriculum. The Samuel Smiles-Horatio Alger morality of success which in some form impels so many prima donnas never came near her.

My childhood was saturated in twentieth-century music, and it has never sounded strange or incomprehensible to me. I started off determined to be a composer, and I studied composition at Northwestern University in Chicago and briefly at Yale, which I hated. Meeting Luciano Berio was the first turning-point. He came to teach at Northwestern, only he wasn't nearly as interested in the music I had written as in my singing. In 1972 he took me to Rome, where I sang The Woman in his music-theatre piece *Pasaggio*. For the next four years I was mostly in Italy with Berio, singing a lot of the music he had written for his first wife Cathy Berberian: *Laborintus*, *Circles*, the folk-song arrangements. All wonderful music and a wonderful time, but I was absurdly young for such a demanding schedule and I hated the 'second Cathy Berberian' type-casting. It was all contemporary music—not just Berio either. I toured with the London Sinfonietta, almost sang the title-role in Tavener's *Thérèse* at Covent Garden, and I did a lot with Sylvano Bussotti, like his *Phèdre* at Piccola Scala and his production of Schönberg's *Pierrot Lunaire*. Working in Italy was crazy, the whole thing was crazy, and it had to stop. For one thing I got very bored with having new scores flung at me which often simply weren't very good: you'd sweat blood learning them, sing them once, and then no one would ever want to hear them again. Secondly, I was forgetting how to sing. I could do *glissandi*, screams, howls, *sprechgesang*, I could sing standing on my head, but I felt I was picking up a vocabulary of gestures rather than a technique. I wanted to sing legato, I could sing legato, but there was never any to sing.

The next problem she faced was finding the right teacher.

Most of them just threw up their hands at the thought of new music, and I had no time for that sort of thing. I saw the mezzo Jennie Tourel whenever I could in New York, then Marjorie Thomas was a great help, now I'm with Kiri's teacher Vera Rosza, who has a razor-sharp mind, very open to new things, very exciting and fierce. I suppose the next turning-point for me was singing Marie in *Wozzeck* for Scottish Opera in 1980. It was a tremendous experience, and it made me realize how deeply I wanted to do more opera. I love working with producers who have radical ideas and I love the stage. Since *Wozzeck*, I've done a number of things but my general strategy is to move into the early twentieth-century repertory rather than try and become a Mozartean overnight. But I did tour England with a small company as Cherubino in *Figaro*, which was very rewarding. One of the reasons I don't like working in the US is the size of the halls and theatres you have to sing in, but here we were singing in conditions of complete intimacy and I never had to force. Some of the most surprising places like Preston had the most perfect acoustics, and the audiences were marvellous. I also do a lot of work with amateur orchestras—the amateur music network in England is astonishing—not because I need to fill up my diary with engagements, but because all those people are there for love of music alone, and it makes for an atmosphere that I prefer, really.

As for the future, I long to sing anything by Mozart and I'd go down on my knees for the opportunity to do some Janáček. *Lulu*, of course, but I don't think people realize that the reason that part is such a killer is not because of all the high stuff, but because of all the low passages which no one seems to notice. My dream, I'm sorry to say—it borders on the neurotic, I ought to see an analyst about it—is one of the Strauss trouser roles, the Composer in *Ariadne* or Octavian. I'm basically a lyric soprano and they're usually done by mezzos nowadays, but like Irmgard Seefried, whom I admire enormously, I'm sure I could manage them happily. I love *schmaltz*, you see, I love leaping about on stage, I love sex in music, and Strauss has them all.

Recently Ross has been singing a lot of Kurt Weill, and was full of praise for Teresa Stratas's record of some of the lesser known songs.

I first got to know my husband when we were working together on a cabaret evening of Weill in the rather stuffy Purcell Room. Well, we were determined not to be genteel or elegant about it and the critics were pretty poisonous, which didn't surprise anyone. But the audience went mad with excitement, and I knew afterwards that I could have become a star of art-song cabarets —except that it would be another type-casting trap. I also did a television film of the *Seven Deadly Sins* which was pretty strong stuff [it was updated to a punk Manhattan night-club ambience, and, for once, the decadence did not look cosmetic] and I'm getting ready for Jenny in the *Kleine Mahagonny* at the Coliseum and Ravel's *L'Enfant et les sortilèges* which Simon and I are doing in Los Angeles. I haven't sung for about five months, but Vera Rosza thinks that a baby does physical and psychological wonders for a singer. I feel on top of the world right now.

Ross's career—and it is still a very young one—prompts various thoughts. First, that she is a singer who, like the majority of prima donnas up until Jeritza and Garden, has concentrated on the music of her own time; and that like Garden in particular she has inevitably had a fair amount of dross foisted on her which only the inevitable processes of history can sift out. Second, that the singer of post-war music has regained a lot of the power over the score that she held in the Baroque era: what was then known as ornamentation now goes under the name of improvisation. A composer like Berio does not always notate his score precisely, demanding considerable creativity from the interpreter. Third, that contrary to the prophets

345

of despondency of which opera is so full, the twentieth century has been rich in great opera and great roles for a prima donna with imaginative musicianship and a willingness to extend her technique. Of course modern music is 'excruciatingly difficult to sing' (Henry Pleasants in the gloomy closing pages of his excellent history *The Great Singers*)—so is Handel, Rossini, and Wagner.

There are still some people, singers included, who claim that Marie in Alban Berg's *Wozzeck* and the title-role in *Lulu* involve nothing but screaming. This is philistinism, a straightforward failure to listen. *Lulu* in particular—left unfinished at the composer's death in 1935 and a staggering popular success in its recent completed state—contains music for Lulu herself that is difficult to sing, high-lying, complex, and exhausting. But so do *Norma* or *Elektra*, and *Lulu*, one of opera's most moving tragedies of love, is as powerful in its way as either of them.

For voices that lack the heroic vocal capacities that Lulu requires, plenty of composers since the Second World War have provided fine operas, conservative in idiom and full of lyrical substance. Stravinsky's *The Rake's Progress*, Poulenc's *Dialogues des Carmélites*, Britten's *The Turn of the Screw*, Tippett's *The Midsummer Marriage*, or Einem's *Der Besuch der Alten Dame* have all offered the prima donna vocal opportunities which she has eagerly taken up; while radicals such as Berio, Ligeti, Birtwistle, and Stockhausen have demanded extension of technique which singers such as Ross, Berberian, Phyllis Bryn-Julson, and Jane Manning have provided. They may well be the vanguard of the art of singing as Colbran was for Rossini or Lilli Lehmann for Wagner, and an immediate lack of large and appreciative audiences for their work is no proof of either their failure or the collapse of opera.

Other forms and levels of modern music may be more threatening. Beyond those educated in operatic conventions, the operatic soprano has come to sound pompous and affected in her upper reaches and tonal refinements. From Lind and Patti to Melba and Farrar, the soprano prima donna was the most popular and familiar of singers: fifty years after Galli-Curci, she is the most alien. Pop music, even in the more sophisticated areas of rock and soul, uses almost exclusively only the high baritone chesty mezzo-soprano range. A high note is a freak sound, a joke, and electronic amplification is now more natural-sounding than purely human projection. Placido Domingo may get away with singing with John Denver, but

346

it is hard to imagine what, say, Kiri Te Kanawa could do with Joan Armatrading.

The prima donna survives, but she needs defence. Another history might argue that in terms of widespread popular appeal, she has been superseded in this century by the tenor. The prevalent notions of her characteristic behaviour—her role—remain confused. The myths are still being fed, without much regard for the intelligence and hard work which play more part in a great singer's life than 'charisma', tantrums, or avarice. In the past, she has fought against the odds loaded against women, in a trade which functions in conditions of ruthless competition, but today the prima donna is no longer the awesome and menacing exception to the rule that she was in the days of Lilli Lehmann and Melba. Western society has learnt to accept the idea of dominating women, and there are now various celebrated prima donnas in politics, public service, medicine, law, academic life, business, even sport. The operatic prima donna is no longer lonely and no longer a revolutionary example. She has only one remaining responsibility, but it is still the most important one of all: the noble art of expressive and beautiful singing.

# ACKNOWLEDGMENTS

Among the many people who have helped me write this book, two (non-singing, as far as I know) prima donnas must take particular credit: Jill Black, my editor, whose patience and persistence have astonished and inspired me, and Caroline Dawnay of A. D. Peters, who has been a complete and dedicated ally throughout. My heartfelt thanks to them both. Among relations and friends, I must especially thank my mother and sister, Kay and Anna Christiansen, for their encouragement and support; Cassandra Jardine, who is no opera fan, but has nobly put up with it all; Robert Turnbull, who has kept a close musical ear on the proceedings and proved a marvellous sounding-board; and Gill Morgan, who did more for me than she knows. I have also benefited from the labours and favours of Francesca Franchi of the Royal Opera House Archive; Anthony Gasson, who generously allowed me to reproduce pictures from his unique collection; Tony Kaye; Robert Rattray; David Scrase; Joan Sutherland and Richard Bonynge; James Supervia; Robert Tuggle of the Metropolitan Opera Archive; and Alan Williams of Viking Penguin Inc., whose enthusiasm at a decisive moment fired me on; also in New York, Juliet Annan and Charles Jahant, who gave me some useful leads, and Victoria Pryor. Of the many libraries I have used, I must single out the extraordinary resources and atmosphere of the London Library, and the British Sound Archive. I would also like to acknowledge assistance I have received in the British Library; Westminster City Libraries; Bibliothèque de l'Opéra, Paris; Library of the Performing Arts, Lincoln Center, and the Pierpont Morgan Library, New York; the Museum of La Scala, Milan; and the State Library in Vienna.

*John Calder Ltd:* From Frida Leider, *Playing My Part* (tr. Osborne) and Stendhal, *Life of Rossini* (tr. Coe).

*Duckworth:* From *The Grand Tradition*, by J. D. Steane.

*Harper & Row Publishers, Inc., and Hamish Hamilton:* From *Peter Hall's Diaries*, edited by John Goodwin. Copyright © 1983 by Petard Productions Ltd.

*Alfred A. Knopf, Inc., and Faber and Faber Ltd:* From *On and Off the Record*, Elisabeth Schwarzkopf, ed.

*The Lantz Office and The Putnam Publishing Group:* From *Musical Chairs*, by Schuyler Chapin.

*The Society of Authors on behalf of the Shaw Estate:* From *Shaw's Music*, Bernard Shaw, Vols 1–3.

*Simon and Schuster Inc.:* From *Mary Garden's Story*, by Mary Garden and Louis Biancolli. Copyright © 1951 by Simon & Schuster, Inc. Copyright renewed © 1979 by Mary Garden and Louis Biancolli.

Thanks are also due to the following holders of copyright photographic material: The National Gallery of Victoria, Melbourne, plate 1; the Royal College of Music, plates 2 and 11; The Royal Opera House Archives, plates 6, 10, 14, 19, 24, 27, 29, 38; Bibliothèque Nationale, Paris, plates 8 and 33; Roger Viollet, Paris, plate 9; the Performing Arts Center, New York Public Library, plates 13, 18, 23, 25, 28, 30, 40; *Opera News*, Metropolitan Opera Guild, New York, plates 17, 22, 37, 42; Culver Pictures, New York, plate 20; Bayreuth Festspielhaus, plate 21; Austrian National Library, plate 35; G. Macdomnic, plate 46; Clive Barda, plates 48 and 50; Julian Sheppard, plate 49; The Trustees of the British Museum, plate 31; Fritz Curzon, plate 51; Zoe Dominic, plate 52; Glyndebourne Festival Opera, plate 47; the Gasson Collection, plates 3, 4, 5, 7, 12, 15, 16, 26, 32, 34, 36, 39, 41, 43, 44, 45.

# SELECT BIBLIOGRAPHY

I have confined this to books and journals that should be available through public libraries with good music collections. For fuller bibliographies, see *Grove's Dictionary of Music and Musicians* (1980). *The Concise Oxford Dictionary of Opera*, ed. Harold Rosenthal and John Warrack (2nd edn., 1979) is full and generally reliable. Alfred Lowenberg's *Annals of Opera* (2nd edn., 1955) is invaluable for the amount of information it gives about dates and places of operatic performance. D. J. Grout's *A Short History of Opera* (1947), 2 vols., is still the best of its kind. For individual prima donna discographies, see *Le Grandi Voci*, ed. Celletti (1964).

*Chapter One*
On the period and its singers generally, see Charles Burney, *A General History of Music* (repr. 1935), 2 vols.; George Hogarth, *Memoirs of the Opera* (repr. 1969); Richard Mount Edgcumbe, *Reminiscences* (repr. 1973); Henry Pleasants, *The Great Singers* (2nd edn., 1981), esp. chs. 1–7; and H. Sutherland Edwards, *The Prima Donna* (repr. 1978), 2 vols.; Eric Walter White, *A History of English Opera* (1983). For scholarly accounts of opera's beginnings see Robert Donnington's *The Rise of Opera* (1981) and S. T. Worsthorne, *Venetian Opera in the Seventeenth Century* (1954); and for a translation from Marcello's *Teatro alla Moda*, see Oliver Strunk, *Source Readings in Music History* (1950).

**Mrs Tofts**: Mollie Sands, 'Mrs Tofts', *Theatre Notebook* (Spring 1966).
**Faustina and Cuzzoni**: P. H. Lang, *George Frideric Handel* (1967), esp. chs. VII–X; Pier Tosi, *Observations on the Florid Song*, trans. Galliard (repr. 1926).
**The Castrati**: Angus Heriot, *The Castrati in Opera* (2nd edn., 1974); Vernon Lee, *Studies of Italy in the Eighteenth Century*, (1880); Dennis Arundell, *The Critic at the Opera* (1957), Part II, which also gives a fascinating account of popular taste in opera in eighteenth-century London.
**Banti**: Lorenzo da Ponte, *Memoirs*, tr. Abbott (1929).

**Mara**: Alan Yorke-Long, *Music at Court* (1954)—excellent essays on an interesting subject.

**Mrs Billington**: Michael Kelly's entertaining *Reminiscences* (repr. 1975).

On Mozart's operas, see Alfred Einstein, *Mozart* (1946); R. B. Moberly, *Three Mozart Operas* (1967); and the highly provocative Brigid Brophy, *Mozart the Dramatist* (1964). *The Letters of Mozart and his Family*, tr. Anderson (1938), 3 vols., are also well worth reading, and contain passages pertaining to Mara and Cavalieri.

*Chapter Two*
The finest book of the period is undoubtedly Stendhal's *Life of Rossini*, tr. Coe (1956), which contains witty and idiosyncratic thoughts about every aspect of early nineteenth-century opera, including his views of Colbran and Pasta. See also his *Memoirs of an Egoist*, tr. Ellis (1975); and *Rome, Naples, Florence*, tr. Coe (1959). For more soberly factual reading, Herbert Weinstock, *Rossini* (1968) and *Bellini* (1972); William Ashbrook, *Donizetti and his Operas* (1982); and the outstanding Julian Budden, *The Operas of Verdi*, vol. 1 (1973). Henry Chorley's *Thrity Years' Musical Recollections* (repr. 1926) is a classic, and J. E. Cox's *Musical Recollections* (1872) 2 vols., usefully supplements it. See also Luigi Arditi, *My Reminiscences* (repr. 1976); Ellen C. Clayton, *Queens of Song* (repr. 1972), 2 vols.; John Ebers, *Seven Years of the King's Theatre* (repr. 1969); Benjamin Lumley, *Reminiscences of the Opera* (repr. 1976); J. H. Mapleson, *The Mapleson Memoirs* (repr. 1966); Harold Rosenthal, *Two Centuries of Opera at Covent Garden* (1958). Also Hogarth, Mount Edgcumbe, Pleasants, Edwards, op. cit.

**Pasta**: M. Ferranti-Giulini, *Giuditta Pasta e suoi tempi* (1935); *Opera News*, 13 February 1982; John Rosselli, *The Opera Industry in Italy from Cimarosa to Verdi* (1984) has much interesting material on the business and financial side of opera during Pasta's career.

**Malibran**: Howard Bushnell, *Maria Malibran* (1979) is a model piece of scholarship with an excellent bibliography.

**Viardot**: April FitzLyon, *The Price of Genius* (1964); Hector Berlioz, *Memoirs*, tr. Cairns (1968); George Sand, *Correspondance* (1964). For French Grand Opera, see the book of that name by W. Crosten (1948), a pioneering study.

Grisi: G. Pearse and F. Hird, *The Romance of a Great Singer* (repr. 1977) and Elizabeth Forbes, 'Mario', *Opera*, December 1983–January 1984.

*Chapter Three*
General pictures of various phases of the Victorian opera scene are provided by Arditi, Chorley, Cox, Lumley, Mapleson, Rosenthal, op. cit. Also Hermann Klein, *Thirty Years of Musical Life in London* (1903) and for the last years of the century, the incomparable G. B. Shaw, *Shaw's Music* (1981), 3 vols., and Clara Leiser, *Jean de Reszke* (repr. 1970). See Michael J. Baker, *The Rise of the Victorian Actor* (1978) for analysis of the status of the theatre in the nineteenth century and much interesting information about conditions of employment. *Opera News*, August 1980, devoted an issue to 'Opera and the Phonograph'.

Sontag: Chorley's remains the best essay on Sontag in English; otherwise the German E. Pirchan, *Henrietta Sontag* (1946) and Bushnell, op. cit.
Lind: a vast number of books have been written about the Jenny Lind phenomenon, but the best is probably Joan Bulman, *Jenny Lind* (1956), particularly strong on her early years. For the Bunn Affair, see Lumley, op. cit.; and for the American tour Phineas T. Barnum, *Struggles and Triumphs* (repr. 1981), usefully complemented by the meticulous P. Ware and T. Lockard, *P. T. Barnum presents Jenny Lind* (1980). The letter quoted on p. 110 is housed in the Pierpont Morgan Library, New York.
Patti: lacks a good modern English biography. Hermann Klein, *The Reign of Patti* (repr. 1977) is reliable and comprehensive, but obviously biased; equally Clara Louise Kellogg, *Memoirs of an American Prima Donna* (repr. 1978) and Mapleson op. cit. have obvious axes to grind, entertaining as they are. For an interesting assessment of Patti in the 1860s, see Eduard Hanslick, 'Adelina Patti' in *Vienna's Golden Years of Music*, tr. Pleasants (1950). The letter quoted on p. 119 is housed in the Library of the Performing Arts, Lincoln Centre, New York.
Melba: John Hetherington, *Melba* (1965) is an adequate modern biography; her own autobiography *Melodies and Memories* (repr. 1980) makes painful reading. Sir Thomas Beecham makes some

illuminating comments on her in *A Mingled Chime* (repr. 1976); John T. Cone, *The Manhattan Opera* (1966) gives a superb account of Oscar Hammerstein's dealings with Melba and many extracts from contemporary reviews of her performances. Also Blanche Marchesi, *A Singer's Pilgrimage* (repr. 1977) and Mathilde Marchesi, *Marchesi and Music* (repr. 1978); Ivor Newton, *At the Piano* (1974).

*Chapter Four*

Ernest Newman's *The Life of Richard Wagner* (repr. 1976), 4 vols. is one of the great biographies of the century and also contains what amounts to a history of nineteenth-century German opera. Geoffrey Skelton's *Wagner at Bayreuth* (1965) deals with the history of performance in the Festspielhaus and Robert Hartford has collected reactions to and comments on the first festivals in *Bayreuth: The Early Years* (1980). For Wagner in his own words, see *My Life*, tr. Gray and Whittall (1983); *Wagner on Music and Drama*, ed. Goldman and Sprinchorn and tr. Ellis (1970); and *Cosima Wagner's Diaries*, tr. Skelton (1978–80), 2 vols. See also Hanslick and Shaw op. cit., Newman, *Wagner Nights* (repr. 1977); and for a modern reinterpretation see Curt von Westernhagen, *Wagner*, tr. Whittall (1978) 2 vols.

On the singing of Wagner on record see J. B. Steane, *The Grand Tradition* (1972) and Michael Scott, *The Record of Singing* (1977–9), 2 vols.

For a picture of modern attitudes to Wagner production see Skelton's *Wieland Wagner* (1971) which also contains an interesting account of Anja **Silja's** early years; and Pierre Boulez, Patrice Chéreau, *et al*, *Histoire d'un 'Ring'* (1980).

**Schröder-Devrient**: see Newman's *Life of Wagner* and Chorley op. cit.

**Lilli Lehmann**: *My Path through Life* (repr. 1977) and *How to Sing* (repr. 1949); also Hanslick op. cit., *Opera News*, 20 February 1965; and Geraldine Farrar, *Such Sweet Compulsion* (repr. 1970).

**Leider**: *Playing my Part*, tr. Osborne (1966) and Vincent Sheean, *First and Last Love* (1957). Leider was interviewed a few years before her death in *Opera News*, 28 January 1967.

**Flagstad**: Louis Biancolli, *The Flagstad Manuscript* (1953); and

Edwin MacArthur, *Flagstad: A Personal Memoir* (1965). For her post-war return to the USA, see Rudolf Bing, *5,000 Nights at the Opera* (1972) and for her last years, John Culshaw, *Ring Resounding* (1967). Also Newton, op. cit.

**Nilsson**: *My Memoirs in Pictures* (1981), which is delightfully unpretentious; the interesting essay in Winthrop Sargeant, *Divas* (1973); and the interviews in *Opera News*, 15 February 1975 and 9 February 1980.


*Chapter Five*
The Met has been rich in historians: one can safely recommend Quaintance Eaton, *The Miracle of the Met* (1968) for its wit and narrative flair; Irving Kolodin, *The Metropolitan Opera* (4th edn., 1966) for its comprehensiveness; and Martin Mayer, *The Met* (1983) for both its lavish illustration and lightly-worn scholarship. W. H. Seltsam's *Metropolitan Opera Annals* (1947; supplts. 1957, 1968) is the Met's encyclopedia. On opera in New York in this period *c*. 1880–1950, see variously W. J. Henderson, *The Art of Singing* (repr. 1978); O. Thompson, *The American Singer* (repr. 1969); Frances Alda's acid *Men, Women and Tenors* (repr. 1970) and Giulio Gatti-Casazza's disappointingly bland *Memories of the Opera* (repr. 1980).

**Nordica**: Ira Glackens, *Yankee Diva* (1963) is outstanding. See also Thompson, Henderson, Shaw, op. cit. and Mary Lawton, *Schumann-Heink: Last of the Titans* (repr. 1977).

**Schumann-Heink**: Lawton op. cit. is couched in the women's magazine idiom of the day, but is still revealing. See also *Opera*, November 1967 and *Opera News*, 4 December 1965 and 24 January 1977.

**Fremstad**: Much about Fremstad remains a mystery but Mary W. Cushing, *The Rainbow Bridge* (repr. 1977) tells much, with humour and compassion, about her years of fame. See also Carl Van Vechten, *Interpreters* (repr. 1977) and Cushing's analysis of Fremstad's scores in *Opera News*, 14 March 1956. Letter quoted on p. 189 from the Metropolitan Opera Archives.

**Farrar**: *Such Sweet Compulsion*, op. cit.; Thompson, Vechten, op. cit. Harvey Sachs, *Toscanini* (1978) gives brief glimpses of the relations between singer and conductor. Many articles in *Opera News*: see esp. 12 January 1953, 25 February 1957, 29 January 1966, and 15 April 1967.

**Cavalieri**: Scott, op. cit., vol. 1.

**Moore**: Charles O'Connell, *The Other Side of the Record* (repr. 1970); her autobiography, *You're Only Human Once* (1947) is not edifying.

**Ponselle**: her posthumous autobiography, written with James A. Drake, *Ponselle: A Singer's Life* (1983) tells much about operatic life in the inter-war period and contains Ponselle's frank views on the state of singing today. See also Walter Legge's essay in *On and Off the Record*, ed. Schwarzkopf (1982); John Ardoin's 'A Note on Ponselle's *Norma*', *Opera*, March 1976—a discussion of her musical practices, in particular her habits of transposition; and *Opera News*, 12 March 1977. For a challenging negative appraisal of her art, see Scott, op. cit., vol. 2. Letter quoted on p. 202, from Archives of the Royal Opera House, Covent Garden.

**Traubel**: her autobiography is *St Louis Woman* (repr. 1977). See also O'Connell, Bing, op. cit. and *Opera News*, September 1972.

**Foster Jenkins**: *Opera News*, 16 March 1963.

On opera singers on film, see entries in *The Oxford Companion to Film*, ed. Bawden (1976) and *Opera News*, 19 December 1964. There is no substantial work on the interesting subject of caricatures of prima donnas. On fees, see Michael Scott's exposé in *Opera*, July 1977.

*Chapter Six*
On vocal technique, see Robert Rushmore's witty and readable *The Singing Voice* (1971), with its excellent bibliography. Also Scott, vol. I, op. cit. and Jerome Hines, *Great Singers on Great Singing* (1983), which includes interviews with Crespin, Horne, Milanov, Nilsson, Ponselle, Sill, Sutherland and Verrett. On Verdi, see Julian Budden, *The Operas of Verdi*, 3 vols. (1973–81) and Frank Walker, *The Man Verdi* (1962), both of which contain valuable material on **Strepponi** and **Stolz**. Gabriele Baldini's *The Story of Giuseppe Verdi*, tr. Parker (1980), although unfinished, is radical in its views and enthralling.

**Falcon**: Charles Bouvet, *Cornélie Falcon* (1927).

**Tietjens**: Arditi, Klein, *Thirty Years*, op. cit. and *Great Women Singers* (1931); Lumley, Shaw, and Sutherland Edwards, op. cit.

**Destinn**: Victor Gollancz, *Journey into Music* (1964), a delightful account of half a century of opera-going in England and Europe; A. Rektorys and J. Dennis in *Record Collector*, July 1971; Desmond Shawe-Taylor, *Opera*, September 1955.

**Turner**: Lanfranco Rasponi, *The Last Prima Donnas* (1983); J. B. Richards in *Record Collector*, February–March 1957.

**Milanov**: Rasponi, op. cit.; *Opera News*, 1 May 1968 and April 1977.

**Price**: Sargeant, op. cit.; *Opera News*, 12 February 1972 and 6 March 1976; interview with Alan Blyth in *The Gramophone*, August 1971.

**Verrett**: *Opera News*, 17 January 1976.

**Bumbry**: *Opera News*, 16 December 1967 and October 1981.

*Chapter Seven*
A generously illustrated and richly gossipy history is provided by Marcel Prawy, *The Vienna Opera* (1970). For Mahler and the Vienna Opera, see *Gustav Mahler in Vienna*, ed. Wiesmann, tr. Shelley (1976); and for a sane and modest critical biography of Strauss, see Michael Kennedy, *Richard Strauss* (1976). Detailed analyses of the operas are contained in William Mann's *Richard Strauss: a Critical Study of the Operas* (1966). Strauss's correspondence with Hofmannsthal, published as *The Correspondence between Richard Strauss and Hugo von Hofmannsthal*, tr. Hammelmann and Osers (1980), gives great insight into their compositional methods; Lotte Lehmann's *Singing with Richard Strauss* (1964) deals with both the facts of the collaboration and her own views of the roles she sang. See also Bruno Walter's autobiography, *Theme and Variations*, tr. Galston (repr. 1981).

**Jeritza**: *Sunlight and Song* (repr. 1977); Prawy and Strauss/ Hofmannsthal op. cit.; *Opera News*, 18 March 1957 and 18 February 1961. I myself profited enormously from Nigel Douglas's radio programme on Jeritza, first broadcast by the BBC in March 1984.

**Lotte Lehmann**: see her autobiography *Wings of Song*—in USA, *Midway in my Song*—(1938); Prawy, Sheean, op. cit.; Walter Legge's essay in *On and Off the Record*, op. cit.; Marcia Davenport, *Too Strong for Fantasy* (1968); and *Opera News*, 22 December 1962. Also *Opera 66*, ed. Osborne (1966).

On music in the Third Reich, see Richard Grunberger, *A Social History of the Third Reich* (1974) and Henry Bair's articles on opera in Berlin 1933–9, *Opera*, January–February 1984.

**Ursuleac**: see the fascinating interview she gave Lanfranco Rasponi, op. cit.

**Schumann**: see the articles by A. Mathis in *Opera*, August, September, November 1973 and January 1974 and in *Record Collector* 1952; also Peter Heyworth, *Otto Klemperer*, vol. I (1983).

**Schwarzkopf**: see *On and Off the Record*, op. cit. and her frank interviews with Edward Greenfield in *The Gramophone*, October–November 1976. André Tubeuf's *Le chant retrouvé* (1979) devoted to modern prima donnas (also including essays on Jurinac and Rysanek) cannot be recommended too highly. See also Gerald Moore on accompanying Schwarzkopf in *Am I too Loud?* (1962) and his assessment of Legge in *Furthermore* (1983). *L'Avant Scène: Opéra* devoted a special issue to Schwarzkopf in Autumn 1983.

J. B. Steane op. cit. treats the recordings of Lehmann, Schumann, and Schwarzkopf with particular sensitivity and wisdom.

**Popp**: *Opera*, February 1982.


*Chapter Eight*

On 'national style' in singing, see Rushmore op. cit. Steane and Scott, vols. 1 and 2, op. cit. also have interesting ideas on the subject. For French opera in this period, see Martin Cooper, *French Music from the Death of Berlioz* (repr. 1969).

**Calvé**: in *Emma Calvé* (1983) Georges Girard has edited and filled in the gaps in Calvé's autobiographical volumes, the first of which was tr. Gilder as *My Life* (repr. 1977). See also Shaw, Henderson, op. cit.

**Garden**: see Mary Garden and Louis Biancolli, *Mary Garden's Story* (1952); R. L. Davis, *Opera in Chicago* (1966); also Sheean, Vechten, op. cit. A modern full-length biography is badly needed.

**Lubin**: N. Casanova, *Isolde 39* (1974). Her interview with Rasponi, op. cit. is poignant and revealing.

**Crespin**: see her autobiography, *La vie et l'amour d'une femme*

(1982); Tubeuf, op. cit.; *Opera News*, 13 December 1975 and 13 January 1979.

**Supervia**: Newton, op. cit. gives an affectionate account, elaborated in *Recorded Sound*, 52 (1973)—although his facts are not reliable. See also H. M. Barnes and V. Girard, in *Record Collector*, March 1951 and Desmond Shawe-Taylor in *Opera*, January 1960; for the story of her Covent Garden appearances, Rosenthal, op. cit.

**Los Angeles**: Peter Roberts, *Victoria de los Angeles* (1982); Moore, *Am I too Loud?*, op. cit.

**Caballé**: Tubeuf, op. cit., *Opera News*, 9 March 1974.


*Chapter Nine*
I do not know of a book in English that can be confidently recommended on late nineteenth-century Italian opera, although William Weaver, *The Golden Century of Italian Opera* (1980) is excellent as far as it goes. See also Julian Budden's article, 'Puccini, Massenet, and *verismo*', *Opera*, May 1983.


**Tetrazzini**: her autobiography *My Life of Song* (repr. 1977). Also Cone, Henderson, Newton, op. cit. Charles Gattey's *Queens of Song* (1979) contains a plethora of Tetrazzini stories.

**Galli-Curci**: C. E. Lemassena, *Galli-Curci's Life of Song* (repr. 1978); Rasponi, op. cit.; *Opera News*, 22 February 1964.

**Muzio**: Charles Jahant's definitive article is in the *Saturday Review of Literature*, 30 November 1957. See also *Opera News*, 16 April 1960.

**Callas**: the leader in the field is still John Ardoin and Gerald Fitzgerald, *Callas* (1974), supplemented by Ardoin's review of Callas's singing on record, *The Callas Legacy* (1977). Arianna Stassinopoulos's *Maria* (1981) is romanticized and hardly a profound picture of the artist, but none the less full of interest and containing a useful bibliography. G. B. Meneghini's *My Wife, Maria Callas* (1982), though much criticized, is probably the most accurate account we have of Callas in the 1950s. See also Legge, op. cit.; *Opera*, September–October 1970; Montague Halbrecht, *The Quiet Showman* (1975); and Jeffrey Tate, interviewed by Patrick O'Connor in *Harpers and Queen*, December 1983. Letter quoted on p. 309 is lodged in the Library of the Peforming Arts, Lincoln Center, New York.

**Tebaldi**: Kenn Harris, *Renata Tebaldi* (1975) is almost absurdly adulatory. See *Opera News*, 30 January 1965 and Rasponi, op. cit.

**Sutherland**: Brian Adams, *La Stupenda* (1981) and Edward Greenfield, *Joan Sutherland* (1973); Sargeant and Tubeuf, op. cit.; *Opera News*, 4 December 1982.

**Horne**: her autobiography, with Jane Scovell, *My Life* (1983) is well worth reading; see also *Opera*, December 1967; *Opera News*, 10 March 1973 and 14 February–14 March 1981.

**Sills**: her autobiography, *Bubbles* (1976); Sargeant, op. cit.; *Opera News*, 19 April 1975, 14 February 1976, and October 1980.

**Scotto**: *Opera News*, 17 December 1977.


*Chapter Ten*
On the decline of the modern prima donna, compare Rasponi with the more balanced views of Steane, op. cit. and John Stratton 'Operatic Singing Style', *Recorded Sound*, XXII, 3 (1966). On twentieth-century opera, see H. H. Stückenschmidt, *Twentieth-century Music* (1969), and *The New Oxford History of Music x, 1890–1960* (1974). For sensitive, informed, and considered opinions of the singing of many modern prima donnas see Andrew Porter, *Music of Three Seasons* (1978) and *Music of Three More Seasons* (1981).


**Söderström**: has written a modest volume of essays, translated into English as *In My Own Key* (1979). See also *Opera News*, September 1981, for a report on rehearsals with Schwarzkopf for *Rosenkavalier; Opera*, January 1969.

**Baker**: *Full Circle* (1982), the diary of her last year of opera; Alan Blyth, *Janet Baker* (1973); Moore, *Farewell Recital*, op. cit.; and *Opera News*, July 1977.

**Te Kanawa**: David Fingleton, *Kiri* (1982); *Opera News*, 26 February 1983.

# INDEX

Author's Note: In respect of individual operas and prima donnas
I have referred the reader only to substantial or informative
passages in the text and omitted passing references. Major
entries are in bold type, and italicisation of page numbers
denotes reference to a photograph of the subject.

# INDEX